GODS & HEROES

PANTHEON FAIRY TALE AND FOLKLORE LIBRARY

GUSTAV SCHWAB

GODS & HEROES

Myths and Epics of Ancient Greece

Introduction
by Werner Jaeger

PANTHEON BOOKS, NEW YORK

Pantheon Fairy Tale and Folklore Library

Library of Congress Catalog Card Number: 47-873
ISBN: 0-394-41834-4
0-394-73402-5 pbk.

Manufactured in the United States of America
98

TRANSLATED FROM THE GERMAN TEXT
AND ITS GREEK SOURCES BY
OLGA MARX AND ERNST MORWITZ
INTRODUCTION BY WERNER JAEGER

The publishers wish to express their special gratitude to Mr. James E. Walsh of the Institute for Classical Studies at Harvard University for his valuable help and advice with this book in general and for establishing the index, and to Dr. Hans Nachod for his assistance in assembling the illustrative material.

CONTENTS

CONTENTS

CONTENTS

CONTENTS

PART II

CONTENTS

CONTENTS

INTRODUCTION

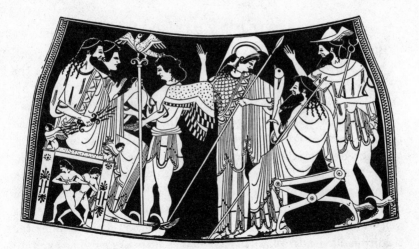

INTRODUCTION

OFTEN have I told my youngest daughter the legends of ancient
Greece, and have found myself wishing that I could give her a
book that would show her more of that magic world which was the
delight of my own youth, and to which I love to return, now that I
am older. But I have wished in vain. Then a while ago I heard of the
plan of a publisher who had had a similar experience with his son,
and I hailed his project. He had had the happy thought of preparing an English edition of Gustav Schwab's *Die Sagen des Klassischen
Altertums*, and at once I declared I was eager to help him realize
this plan. Of course there are other books of this kind in English,
but most of them, at any rate, fill a different need from the one I felt.
They are intended to appeal primarily to children, though no one
would deny that they are entitled to their share of these wonderful
old tales. The Greeks themselves thought so. Plato wanted the future
citizens of his ideal republic to begin their literary education with
the telling of myths rather than with mere facts or rational teachings. This plan of the great philosopher of education mirrors the
life of Greece as it then was, for there too the education of man—
the *paideia*—began with the telling of myths, just as later, in the
Christian era, Bible stories and legends of the lives of the saints
were the basis of all education.

But in the life of a Greek of the classical age myths never ceased to be a subject of deep interest. In early childhood they were the first food for his spirit, which he sucked in, as it were, with his mother's milk. And as he grew older, he returned to them again on a higher plane when he was introduced to the masterpieces of the Greek poets. Now it is true that even today millions of people learn the ancient Greek myths through reading Homer in modern translations; but at that time the mythical tradition reached Greek youth through hundreds of other channels, beside the stories of the Trojan cycle which survive in the *Iliad* and the *Odyssey*, for the poetry as well as the art of Greece was chiefly concerned with shaping the traditional legends. What the boy had eagerly absorbed as exciting stories, the youth found brought in its most perfect form in the art and poetry of his people. And later, when he grew to manhood, Homer's characters passed before his eyes on the stage of the Greek theater, in the tragedies of Aeschylus, Sophocles, and Euripides, where their destinies no longer seemed a tale of long ago, but of immediate, dramatic interest. The audience which filled the benches at these performances regarded the events and sufferings they beheld as the most profound expression of the meaning of all human life.

Thus the entire humanistic education of the Greeks was welded into unity through the majesty and spiritual force which myths exerted on all stages of the inner development of the individual. And this continued to be so, even when—in the course of time—other branches of human knowledge and more and more applied arts were added to the traditional education. Ancient legends continued to be the source of all poetry and art for the nation, and the basic element of the literary education of the individual. They were also the point of departure for all philosophical thought, for the entire development of the Greek intellect. The fact that the Greek people was destined to be the nation of philosophers and the creator of western culture was certainly connected with its wealth of heroic legends and the overwhelming amount of its mythical speculation about the world, gods, and men. This tradition has been an inexhaustible mine of treasure for the poetry and philosophy of the Greeks themselves and of later centuries. Our completely rational civilization can boast of nothing comparable to this. Rome took over the legends of the Greeks because she had none of her own. And even in the

Middle Ages, when new peoples came into the foreground of history, peoples who had national legends of their own, the Greek gods and heroes held their place and were no less popular than the new heroes of new nations. Thanks to their deep human significance which remains valid for all men, the Greek myths were universally recognized, and their characters live on to this day, either in simple tales or in the poetry of all the peoples in the cycle of western civilization. This survival of the myth—and it is by no means the only heritage we have taken over from the Greeks—reminds us that our so-called Christian civilization does not spring from Jewish-Christian sources alone, but is deeply rooted also in classical Greek and Roman tradition. The world of Greek myths is a constantly visible and effective symbol of this truth.

Realizing this fact, we want to reveal this world not only to the enraptured eyes of children but also to the more deeply searching vision of the young student, who is driven to probe for the universal significance of these tales beneath their poetic beauty. This was what Gustav Schwab had in mind when he went about retelling the legends of classical antiquity, simply but movingly. His book has delighted many generations, and no similar work has surpassed it. It owes its freshness and color to the wise restraint the author imposed on himself. He was neither the philosopher who expounds the meaning of myths, nor the scholar who investigates their source and ultimate significance and tries to restore them to their original form. Since this was not the author's aim, his book is of little interest to the learned mythologists of our own day and age. He wrote for the average reader and wanted to convey the legends in the form they have come down to us from the classical period of antiquity. He was enchanted by the great art with which Greek and Roman poets —from the epics of Homer to the *Heroides* and *Metamorphoses* of Ovid—shaped and reshaped these myths; and whoever knows the texts he drew from, feels in every line of his book the profound effect they had on his imagination. Because of his naïveté and complete lack of scholarly ambition, the poetic power with which the poets of antiquity told these tales is preserved in Schwab's retelling—often to an astonishing degree. He is, so to speak, the last of the mythographers of ancient times who retold the myths they found in the works of poets in their own language and style, and thus made them accessible to a wide circle of readers.

His close adherence to the models of the individual stories resulted in something the critical reader is sure to observe, in a change of tone from one tale to the next. To give a few examples chosen at random, the tale of Prometheus, which opens the book, is based mainly on Hesiod, the didactic Boeotian poet who probably lived in the eighth century B.C. To him mythical tradition was the source of all wisdom and all knowledge of the past. To him it provided the answer to all the enigmas of life. Prometheus, his favorite character, appears both in his *Theogony*, an epic on the dynasties of the gods and their origin, and in his *Works and Days*, a didactic poem full of wise sayings designed for all the days and all the exigencies of peasant life. In each of these works the poet is concerned with the problem of the origin of the evil from which the world suffers. The story of Prometheus provided him with an explanation for the otherwise incomprehensible fact that the life of man is full of sickness and need. The race of man shares in atoning for the guilt which Prometheus, the mythical helper of man, took on himself when he stole the fire from Olympus and brought it to helpless mortals. Hesiod's attitude toward this myth is sober and devout reflection. He accepts it as an instrument for his own meditations on the origin of toil and suffering on earth, the "social problem" as we should call it. Obviously, Hesiod welded together a number of legends which were originally independent into a long drawn-out, carefully constructed story. The tale of the theft of fire and the fact that Prometheus was punished for this deed, which many people must have regarded as meritorious, had to be motivated by some previous fault which had called forth the anger of the gods and determined Zeus to withhold fire from man. Hesiod found the cause of this anger in the myth of the bone-sacrifice in Mecone, a tale which originally had nothing whatsoever to do with the theft of fire but merely served to explain an old religious rite. A certain type of myth, called *aition*, was devised to give explanations of this kind. The seams in Hesiod's fabric are quite visible to the practiced eye: his style is not very smooth. His attempt to weave his scattered sources closely together and his superimposed theological interpretation of events are quite apparent.

The next story in our book is that of Phaethon, the son of the sun-god, who begged his father to let him drive the chariot of the sun for one whole day, and plunged headlong from the heights of heaven because he did not know how to manage the immortal horses. This tale is vivid and colorful, and told with brilliant technique, but with a tendency to rhetorical effect and a touch of the didactic. Here Schwab follows Ovid, who tells the story in his *Metamorphoses*, and we cannot fail to admire the sophisticated artistry of this Roman poet who wrote in the reigns of Augustus and Tiberius, even though it is far removed from the naïveté and the gravity and devoutness of Hesiod. Ovid deals with the myth to suit himself; now he uses it merely as a means to exhibit his masterly style, now he is swept away by the charm of the story itself and succeeds in sweeping away his readers. The scholar cannot deal with the tales of Hesiod and Ovid on the same plane. In Hesiod's telling, one still feels the living breath of an era which reshaped and expanded myths, an age in which myths possessed deep meaning; while in Ovid one sees only mythology. But aside from the fact that nowhere else can we find the Phaethon episode told as fully as in Ovid, no one else could have told it so fascinatingly; and so Schwab accepted what each poet had to say for the story in it.

Thus the author goes back to the most various antique sources. Many of the myths are taken from the dramas of the three great Athenian masters of tragedy: Aeschylus, Sophocles, and Euripides (fifth century B.C.). Others are borrowed from later, post-classical writers of the Hellenistic age—the legend of the Argonauts, for instance, which is told according to the epic of Apollonius of Rhodes (third century B.C.). But Schwab has treated his material with the greatest freedom. Frequently he introduces episodes taken from various poets of antiquity into a story whose main outlines he took from another source. In other words, he does just what his predecessors of old did—mythographers such as Apollodorus, for example. An instance of this is the story of Prometheus. While it follows Hesiod in the main, the description of the hero is enriched by borrowings from other sources. Plato relates that Prometheus secretly stole fire from the smithy of Hephaestus; Aeschylus also has Prometheus steal it from Hephaestus and bring it to earth in a hollow fennel stalk. But Sappho knew another version of this incident. According to her, Prometheus brought fire from heaven to earth after lighting a torch at one of the fiery wheels of the sun chariot, and this is the version Schwab blended into Hesiod's story. The concept of Prometheus, as not only the faithful aide but also the creator of man, he took from Aeschylus. This version of the role of Prometheus can also be found in other literary sources and in Greek vase painting. Schwab follows Aeschylus in making Hesiod's story of the fire-thief symbolize the beginning of civilization. The author practiced the same eclecticism in the telling of other legends. For instance, the story of the Argonauts, as we already know, is based on the epic of Apollonius of Rhodes, but for the Medea episode the author drew largely on Euripides' play *Medea*. We do not intend to enumerate all the sources Schwab used for one reason or another, but only to suggest to the reader that the many different themes his ear will catch in the development of the tales are all part of the rich symphony of the poets of antiquity.

We have already indicated that in classical antiquity myths were a part of poetry, and poetry was closely connected with myth. In later centuries this relation came to mean little more than a law of style. From the period of Greek enlightenment on, that is, from the fifth century B.C., the Greeks took myth to mean everything which was legendary and miraculous, everything which could not be proven as a fact or demonstrated through reason. And the word retained this meaning forever after. "Mythical" came to mean "unreal," and with this the world of poetry became an imaginary world. That is why the poetry of the ancients, their gods, and their heroes, were tolerated by Christianity: to them they had merely aesthetic significance; they were not true. But this devaluation of the myth had begun long before the Christian era. It was initiated by the Greeks themselves as soon as they replaced mythical tradition by their own experience, and imagination by reasoning. The earlier ages accepted the myth as something true and actual. Then the word *mythoi*—if it was used at all—did not mean fables but merely tales, because these stories were transmitted by telling, by word of mouth. Other words for them were *phemé*, which indicates rumor, and *kleos*, which means glory. These names suggest the true nature of legend itself, for the legends of heroes, as well as those which dealt with the gods, were a message from the dark long ago. They preserved the memory of glorious deeds.

Even centuries before Homer there must have been singers such as Homer describes in his epics, who appeared at the courts of princes or in the market places of cities and celebrated in song the heroes of the past. This oldest poetry was known as "Praise of the

Deeds of Gods and Men." Homer himself tells us this in the verses of the *Odyssey* which deal with the calling of the singer and his place in his environment. Thus it was the "myth," as it was later called, which originally constituted the essential content of epic song. The poet proclaimed the fame of heroic *areté*, that is of those powers and virtues of man which enabled him to attain to the highest achievements. This vocation of the poet's made him the true carrier of tradition and the expounder of legend. These primitive songs in praise of heroes, then, were the precursors of Homer's epics, which aimed at a more comprehensive vision of human life; but even later developments of Greek poetry still show the unchanged close relationship of the poet to mythical tradition. Not only was the glorification of the heroes of the past a fitting tribute due from the present generation, but it also provided a glowing example for imitation. The Greeks believed that the poet or singer whose words stirred the heart with a desire for glory was the true educator of men. Examples drawn from myths, especially when used as arguments in the speeches of the characters in the Homeric epic, clearly prove that this purpose of presenting noble models for emulation was inherent in mythical tradition from the beginning. In early Greece the myth had the value of factual truth and was accepted as the norm. By idealized pictures of heroes and their deeds and destinies the poetry of ancient times bodied forth those truths which later philosophical ages expressed as general ideas and precepts. That is why the poets of Greece were able to present all the problems of human life in the form of mythical happenings and characters. The memory of legend and the thought and feeling of each new generation were always indissolubly joined.

It is understandable that this dual character of the myth has given rise to extreme and one-sided interpretations of its essence. Either it was denied historical verity altogether and declared mere poetic fiction, or it was claimed to be history and nothing else. The truth of the matter is that the mythical tradition which we find in Greek poetry is a complicated structure made up of very different elements. It is easy to see that the heroic myth has in it much of the fairy tale, and that a portion of it is of a purely imaginary character. This also holds for another aspect of legend, the legends concerning the gods. These constituted a part of religion and sprang from the speculation on nature and the origin of the gods. But even these legends of the gods contain a germ of empirical reality, for they are connected with cosmic phenomena, such as the sky, the stars, earth, and sea, or they take for their point of departure religious rites and institutions and relate a mythical story to explain their origins. But the part of the myth of greatest interest to us here is that which is concerned with heroes. Many of the most famous legends of this kind are based on historical fact and go back to civilizations earlier than the Greek itself. It has often been stated that the body of Greek legend includes different legend cycles bound up with different localities. The legends which were rooted in the pre-Greek civilizations of Troy, Mycenae, Argos, Tiryns, and Thebes, throve in greatest abundance. Excavations in these places have brought to light pre-Homeric settlements and palaces of powerful kings. These discoveries prove the historical reality of certain legends, such as those which tell of the destruction of Troy by the Achaeans, coming overseas from Argos, or those of the campaign of the "Seven against Thebes," which also started from Argos. Attic legend has preserved the memory of Minos, of Crete's supremacy over the sea, and of the dynasts whose palaces Evans excavated in Knossos on Crete. In the course of centuries legendary happenings crystallized around such memories, and poetic fancy came to adorn the historical fact.

This process of poetic adornment began in the very earliest phase, when the wonder tales of the days of old lived only in the hearts of the people. The so-called historical core of the legend probably never existed pure of any alloy of imaginative interpretation, and whether one person or many were concerned in this process of admixture hardly matters. Legend remains legend whether individual singers or entire guilds of rhapsodists transmit it in the form of epic song. The only prerequisite is that this process through which "memory" is constantly being shaped and reshaped into poetry springs from the life of the people. Considered from this point of view, the poems of Homer and of the Greek tragic poets are genuine myths even when they alter the mythical tradition with the help of creative imagination and introduce into it new characters and motifs. But very early a tendency to compile and set down legends as a body of knowledge appeared alongside of this impulse toward molding legends through fancy, for they were, after all, regarded as true reports of the past. Taking over Homer's style, certain poets wrote lengthy epics on those bodies of legend which had not yet been worked into poems. With these works, the so-called "cyclic poems," they filled the gaps in the account of events before and after the Trojan War, or supplemented the picture Homer gave of the war since he only covered the last period of the struggle for Troy. Thus the epic and the legend along with it were made historical. Other post-Homeric poets invented genealogies for their mythical heroes, which they traced back to a divine ancestor or ancestress and on to a noble house with living scions. In this way they tried to bridge the chasm between the age of legend and the present. From this kind of poetry it was only a small step to converting these epics, which were more or less genealogies and catalogues, into prose books that form the transition to the beginnings of historiography. It is due to this scholarly preoccupation with myths that so many contradictory variants concerning the father or mother of famous heroes appear in Greek mythical tradition. These prose redactions of myths, which count among their best-known authors such writers as Pherecydes, Acusilaus, and Hecataeus (fifth century B.C.), do not exist except in a few fragments, which is true also of the cyclic poems which followed Homer's work. But both served as sources for later mythographers of antiquity, such as Apollodorus, whose works have survived. It is evident that what these later books of legend took over from such genealogical works was not all true legend, but was partly based on the artificial and arbitrary constructions of these older pseudo-historians. In other words, it was, to some extent, a product of the rational thinking of the early redactors whose logic ironed out the incredible element of the tradition.

It is amazing proof of the inexhaustible vitality of legend that subsequent to, and side by side with this development whose external symptom was the decline of epic production, a great new form of poetry sprang up in Attica toward the end of the sixth century B.C., which woke the myth to new life. This new form was the tragedy. The powerful dramatic impulse which now leaped into being was born of the increased intensity of the spiritual struggle with the problems of actual life. But this life projected its reality into the world of ancient legend, just as at an earlier stage Homer's era had projected itself into the epic. For the generation of Aeschylus and Sophocles this world of ancient legend became the ideal mirror of their own concept of man, the gods, and the world. Thus legend, dramatized in tragedy, experienced a radiant rebirth and proved its indestructible power to survive. The vase painting and choral songs of the sixth century were the first symptoms of the people's new and increased interest in the old myths which formed the content of the epic. The manner in which the writers of Attic tragedy used these myths gave the characters of legend their final form. What constituted the tragic in tragedy? The passionate awareness of destiny, the sense of how freedom and limitation are mixed in life, and the way in which man reaches heroic stature under the impact of his appointed fate. The great masters of Greek tragedy found the outlines of this basically "tragic" attitude toward life clearly limned in the myths of their people. And so the tragedians gave the old vocation of the singer as a carrier of the tradition a new and deeper significance. Homer himself presented the poet as far more than a man who glorifies the deeds of heroes. To him he was an interpreter of human destiny, and this idea he embodied in his treatment of Achilles and Odysseus. Plato was, therefore, quite right in calling Homer the father of tragedy. This aspect of legend was brought to the peak of perfection only by the tragic poetry of the Greeks of the fifth century.

This development from legend to tragedy brings to light still another force latent in Greek myth, the inimitable plastic vigor of the characters of legend, which were shaped into living and acting persons by the tragedians. For the dramatist the characters of legend were a most fruitful subject. The heroes in Greek legends are not majestic but insubstantial apparitions, such as we sometimes find in the legends of other peoples. They are amazingly real, individual, and convincing. That was why, in his famous epistle on poetry, Horace advised the younger generation of poets in Rome to give up the ambition of inventing their own dramatic characters, for these so often lacked all individual life and were nothing but shadows. It would be better, he said, for them to utilize the characters in Greek legend, who were indestructibly actual. And no one can fail to agree with this Roman critic, at least in his evaluation of the myth as potential poetry, for even after so many centuries the heroes and heroines of Greek legend are still as clear, as three-dimensional to us, as though we had met them in the flesh: Achilles and Patroclus, Odysseus and Penelope, Oedipus and Antigone, Prometheus, Agamemnon, Clytaemnestra, Orestes, Iphigenia,

Electra, Ajax, Medea, Jason, and many more. It is true, of course, that these figures are, in part, the creations of great poets; for us it is hardly possible to distinguish between their share in the formation of these characters and that of the mythical tradition. Still, though the myths do not give the fully developed features of these characters, they contain the seeds which flower later in tragedy.

The myth also contained another important trait of the characters of Greek tragedy: their universality. For not one of them is merely individual. They are convincing because they represent the coincidence of individuality and type. The Greek mind had the capacity of detecting the basic law, not only in all human beings, but in all things. They called this "idea" inherent in every thing and every human creature the "form of its being." Aeschylus saw Prometheus as a creative genius, inspired by warm love for suffering humanity, always ready to help the weak but defiant toward the higher powers and egregiously self-confident. Antigone is the idealist who readily sacrifices herself to the claims of divine law. Full of tender love for her dead brother to whom his fellow-citizens deny the rites of burial because they regard him as a traitor, she is fanatically inflexible in her opposition to the laws of worldly power which claim her as their victim. Achilles, a character of heroic greatness, is essentially noble, and just because of this, he loves honor and is given to sudden anger against everyone who offends this sense of honor. Oedipus has an agile and penetrating brain and solves every riddle with the greatest ease; but he is nevertheless blind to his own share in the disaster he unwittingly brings upon his city and his people. Bellerophon is a great hero in his fight against all external dangers and resists every temptation devised by feminine shrewdness and desire. But a strain of melancholy in his blood separates him from his fellow men and finally drives him, the radiant hero, to go his lonely way sick and bewildered, like one who is hated by all the gods, and finally to destroy himself to no purpose. Thus the philosophic mind of the Greek people shaped the characters of legend into a series of ideal types which serve as significant examples for the understanding of human nature.

The great poetry of the classical period of Greek literature clung to the primitive myth because it was intimately related to it. The myth was its soul as well as its body. But the increasingly rational criticism which the fifth century directed against all tradition likewise affected the myth, not only its gods and the picture it gave of the world, but also its heroes and its tragic concept of life. In the plays of Euripides, the last of these three great writers of tragedies, the rational doubting spirit invades even the shaping of the myth itself. His characters were modernized and in this process became less profound. These so-called "heroes" are unashamedly loquacious and discussed the everyday problems of the burghers of the poet's own day and age. Under such circumstances it was difficult for them to maintain their heroic poise. It became merely a pose, and their words degenerated to empty declamation. The next step on this path was necessarily the abandonment of the myth. Drama became a mirror of modern middle-class life, and comedy with its happy ending carried the day against heroic tragedy. There were, to be sure, still some poets who in a highly artificial style wrote dramas based on myths, but they were ineffective. The only successful use of the tradition was the parodying of mythical content and characters which we find in the comedies of the time. Not until the post-classical period of Greek literature did serious poetry turn to the myth again to produce romantic and sentimental epics and elegies on mythical themes. But this poetry was academic, and the living myth had been converted into "mythology." That was all the myth was to the Romans and to Roman poets.

It remained for the Romantic Movement of the nineteenth century to rediscover the true greatness of the mythical tradition. Since Romanticism was fundamentally opposed to the exaggerated rationalism of the preceding epoch, it tended to regard myths as a sort of primordial wisdom of mankind, a form of wisdom which modern man had impiously sacrificed in his arrogant pride of reason. It was in this spirit that a large part of modern research in the field of mythology was dedicated to the attempt to penetrate to the roots of mythical thinking and reveal its true meaning.

I have already pointed out that the book we have here is untouched by this speculative and symbolical conception of myths. The investigator of myths along the lines laid down by the Romantic School will think that the naïve teller of these tales has often ignored profundities. But this book is meant not only for children but also for the childlike spirit of the young and old alike. It conveys a breath of the imperishable strength of youth in Greek genius, which is perhaps most alive and beautiful in the myth. The Greeks felt this themselves. Plato called the mythical period of Greek poetry the flowering time of his people. In a certain sense this strength has never left the Greeks. "You Greeks are always children; there is no such thing as an old Greek," said an Egyptian priest, the representative of an age-old civilization, to Solon, the sage of Athens, who came to Egypt by ship to see the wonders of the land of the Nile. These words of Plato's are quoted from the *Timaeus*, the work of his old age, and Plato himself bears surpassing witness to the inexhaustible impulse of the Greeks to create myths in an era (the fourth century B.C.) in which the mythical tradition seemed to be dying off everywhere else. In his dialogues he invented a new kind of myth which blends old mythical elements of symbolic force with new philosophical ideas. Even Aristotle, Plato's greatest pupil, the master of pure reason, once said: "The friend of wisdom (*philosophos*) is also a friend of the myth (*philomythos*)." That is how the most profound spirits among the Greeks thought at the zenith of their civilization. In a letter to an intimate friend this same Aristotle made a more personal confession. He wrote: "The lonelier I am, the more of a recluse I become, the greater is my love for myths."

WERNER JAEGER

Cambridge, Massachusetts
Harvard University
Summer 1946

I wish to express my gratitude to Miss Aileen Ward, of Radcliffe College, for her generous assistance in the revision of the English version of the text of my introduction.

W. J.

PART I

PROMETHEUS

HEAVEN and earth had been created. The sea ebbed and flowed between its shores, and fish frolicked in the waters; in the air sang winged birds, and the earth swarmed with animals. But as yet there was no creature in whose body the spirit could house and from there govern the world around it. Then down to earth came Prometheus, "Forethought," a descendant of the ancient race of gods which Zeus had dethroned, a son of Iapetus, whom Gaea had borne to Uranus. Now Prometheus was crafty and nimble-witted. He knew that the seed of heaven lay sleeping in the earth, so he scooped up some clay, moistened it with water from a river, kneaded it this way and that, and shaped it to the image of the gods, the lords of the world. To give life to his earth-formed figure he took both good and evil from the core of many animals and locked them in man's breast. He had a friend among the immortals, Athene, the goddess of wisdom, who marvelled at what this son of the Titans had created, and she breathed the spirit, the divine breath, into his creature which, as yet, was only half alive.

In this way the first men were made, and soon they filled the far reaches of the earth. But for a long time they did not know what to do with their noble limbs or the divine spirit which had been breathed into them. They saw, yet they did not see; they heard, yet they did not hear. Aimlessly they moved about, like figures in a dream, and were ignorant of how to profit from creation. They did not know the art of quarrying and cutting stone, of burning bricks from clay, of carving out beams from the trees they hewed in the forest, or of building houses with all these materials. Like scurrying ants they thronged in sunless caves beneath the surface of the earth. They did not discern the sure signs of winter, of spring decked with flowers, of summer rich in fruits. There was no plan in anything they did. Then Prometheus came to their aid. He taught them to watch the rising and setting of the stars, discovered to them the art of counting and of communicating by means of written symbols. He showed them how to yoke animals and make them share in man's labor. He broke horses to the rein and wagon and invented ships and sails for journeying over the sea. And he concerned himself with all the other affairs of human life also. Formerly, a man who fell ill knew nothing of herbs, of what to eat or not to eat, what to drink or not to drink, nor did he have salves to ease his pain. For lack of physic men had perished wretchedly. But now Prometheus showed them how to compound mild remedies that would dispel every kind of disease. Then he taught them to foretell the future and interpreted dreams and signs for them, the flight of birds and the omens of offerings. He guided them to explore underground, so that they might find ore, iron, silver, and gold. In short, he introduced them to all the arts and comforts of living.

Now the gods in heaven, and among them Zeus, who had but lately deposed his father Cronus and established his own supremacy, began to notice this new creation, man. They were willing enough to protect him, but—in return—demanded that he pay them homage. In Mecone, in Greece, mortals and immortals met on a set day, to determine the rights and duties of man. At this assembly Prometheus appeared as man's counsel, to see to it that the gods—in their capacity of protectors—did not impose too burdensome levies upon men.

On this occasion his cunning prompted him to trick the gods. In behalf of his creatures, he slaughtered a mighty bull and bade the immortals take whatever parts of it they pleased. Now when he had cut up the animal, he made two heaps of the pieces. On one side he put the flesh, the entrails, and the fat, covered these over with the hide, and placed the paunch on top; on the other, he put the bare bones cleverly concealed in the suet of the victim. And this heap was bigger! All-knowing Zeus saw through his trickery and said: "Son of Iapetus, illustrious king, my very good friend, how unequally you have divided the portions!" At this Prometheus was sure that he had deceived him, smiled to himself, and answered: "Illustrious Zeus, you, who are supreme among the immortal gods, take what your heart bids you choose." And Zeus was vexed and felt his anger swell within him, but he deliberately took the white suet in both his hands. When he had pried it apart and saw the picked bones, he pretended only then to have discovered the trick and said dourly: "I know very well, my friend, O son of Iapetus, that you have not yet forgotten the art of deception!"

To punish Prometheus for his knavery, Zeus denied mortals the last thing they needed to perfect their civilization: fire. But the shrewd son of Iapetus improvised a way to provide even this lack. He broke a stalk of pithy fennel, approached the chariot of the sun as it spun through the heavens, and held the stalk to its blaze until it smouldered. With this tinder he descended to earth, and soon the first pile of brushwood was flaming to the sky. Pain pierced the soul of Zeus the Thunderer when he saw fire rising among men and casting its radiance far and wide.

To offset the advantages of fire, which could not be taken from men, now that they had it, he instantly devised a new evil for them. He ordered Hephaestus, the fire-god, famed for his skill, to fashion an image in the shape of a beautiful young woman. Athene herself, who had grown envious of Prometheus and withdrawn her favor from him, clothed the image in a robe of shimmering white, placed over her face a flowing veil, which the girl held, parting it with her hands, garlanded her head with fresh flowers, and bound it with a fillet of gold. This was also the work of Hephaestus, who—to please his father—had wrought it with great art and adorned it exquisitely with the many-colored shapes

of various animals. Hermes, the messenger of the gods, bestowed
language on the lovely mischief, and Aphrodite tricked her out
with all possible charms. Thus, under the guise of something most
desirable, Zeus had contrived a dazzling misfortune. He named
the girl Pandora, which means, "she who has gifts from all," for
each of the immortal gods had given her some baleful gift for
man. Then he led the girl down to earth, where gods and mortals
were walking about and taking their pleasure. And they were
all filled with wonder at this incomparable creature, for never yet
had men laid eyes on a woman. She, in the meantime, went up to
Epimetheus, "Afterthought," the brother of Prometheus, and
less wily than he.

In vain had Prometheus warned his brother never to accept a
gift from the ruler of Olympus, lest men take harm from it, but
to return it without delay. Epimetheus forgot this warning; he
received the beautiful young woman with the utmost delight and
failed to recognize evil until it was upon him. For up to this time
—thanks to Prometheus' counsel!—men had been free from misfortune and had lived without excessive toil or the long sufferings
of disease. But this woman came bearing a gift in her hands, a
large box tightly closed. Hardly had she reached Epimetheus
when she flung back its lid, and out fluttered a host of calamities
that spread over the earth with the speed of lightning. Yet one
single good thing lay hidden at the very bottom of the box: hope!
But on the advice of the father of the gods, Pandora shut the lid
before it could fly forth, and closed her box forever. And now
misery in countless forms filled the earth, the air, and the sea.
By day and by night sicknesses prowled among men, secretly and
silently, for Zeus had not given them a voice. A flock of fevers be-
leaguered the earth, and Death, who had been coming to mortals
on slow, reluctant feet, now walked with winged steps.

When this had been accomplished, Zeus turned to the matter
of taking revenge on Prometheus himself. He handed the culprit
over to Hephaestus and his servants Cratos and Bia. Force and
Violence. These he bade drag him to the wastes of Scythia and
there—above a sinister chasm—forge him to a steep cliff of the
Caucasus with stout, unyielding chains. Hephaestus carried out
his father's commands unwillingly, for he loved the son of the
Titans because he was his kin, his peer, the child of gods, a

descendant of Uranus, his great-grandfather. He was compelled to have the cruel order executed, but he spoke words of compassion, at which his more brutal henchmen frowned. So Prometheus was forced to hang from the cliff, upright and sleepless, and never could he bend his tired knees. "You will utter many plaints and sighs, and they will all be in vain," said Hephaestus. "For the purpose of Zeus is unshakable; hard of heart are those who have but lately wrested power from others and taken it to themselves."

The torments of the captive were intended to endure forever, or for thirty thousand years at the very least. He moaned aloud and called on the winds and the rivers, on the zodiac, from which nothing is hidden, and on Earth, the mother of all, to witness his agony, but his spirit remained steadfast. "Whoever has learned to accept the unshakable power of necessity," he said, "must suffer what Destiny decrees." Nor could the threats of Zeus induce him to explain his dark prophecy that new wedlock would bring ruin and destruction to the king of the gods. Zeus was true to his word. Every day he sent an eagle to feed on his captive's liver, which, however much it was devoured, always grew back again. This torture was to last until one came who, of his own free will, would consent to suffer in Prometheus' stead.

This came about earlier than the son of the Titans might have supposed, considering the sentence Zeus had pronounced upon him. When he had been hanging from his cliff for many a bitter year, along came Heracles, bound on his quest for the golden apples of the Hesperides. He saw the descendant of the gods shackled to the Caucasus and was about to ask him for advice on how to prosper in his search, when he was overwhelmed with pity at his fate, for he observed the eagle perched on the knees of the luckless Prometheus. Heracles laid his club and his lion's skin on the ground behind him, bent his bow, launched the arrow, and shot the cruel bird from the liver of its anguished host. Then he loosed the chains, delivered Prometheus, and led him away. But to satisfy the conditions stipulated by Zeus, he brought Chiron, the centaur, as a substitute, for even though Chiron had claim to immortality, he offered to die in the Titan's stead. And to fulfill the judgment of Zeus, son of Cronus, in every point, Prometheus, who had been sentenced to the cliff for a far longer time, had always to wear an iron ring, set with a chip from the stony wall of the Caucasus, so that Zeus could boast that his enemy was still forged to the mountain.

THE AGES OF MAN

THE first men the gods created were the race of the Men of Gold. As long as Cronus (Saturn) ruled the heavens, they lived free of care and untouched by toil or sorrow, almost like the gods themselves. Nor did they ever grow old. Their hands and feet retained their young strength. Lithe of limb, unvexed by ills, they rejoiced in feasting and gaiety, and the immortals loved them and gave them plentiful harvests and stately herds. When their time came to die, they slipped into untroubled sleep, but while they lived they had many desirable things. Earth yielded them her fruits of her own accord and in great abundance. Rich in all they had need of, they lived out their days in calm serenity. When Destiny decreed that they pass from the earth, they became benevolent patron deities, who pace the length and breadth of the land garmented in cloud, grant gifts, uphold justice, and avenge wrongs.

Then the gods created a second race, the race of the Men of Silver. These were very different from the first, both in appearance and spirit. Their sons remained boys for a full hundred years, immature in their ways, tended and indulged by their mothers. And when such a child at last grew to young manhood, only a brief span of life was left him. Reckless actions plunged these new men into disaster, for they could not check their passions. They were savage and proud, sinned against one another, and no longer paid homage to the gods by bringing fitting sacrifice to their altars. Zeus was so displeased at this lack of reverence for the immortals that he removed this race from the earth. But even the silver race was not so devoid of all virtues that certain honors were not accorded them, for when they had ceased to live as human beings, they were permitted to roam the earth as demons.

And now Father Zeus created a third race, the race of the Men of Bronze. These, in turn, were utterly unlike the silver, cruel and violent, concerned only with wars, and always eager to hurt one another. They disdained the fruits of the field and fed on the flesh of animals. Their stubborn will was hard as the diamond. From their enormous shoulders grew massive arms which none ventured to brave. They wore armor of bronze, dwelt in houses of bronze, and worked with brazen tools, for at that time there was no iron. But though they were mighty of build and terrible and fought one another incessantly, they were powerless against death. And when they left the clear and radiant atmosphere of earth, they descended into the murky night of the underworld.

When this race too had died out, Zeus, the son of Cronus, produced a fourth race, to live on the nourishing earth. These new men were nobler and more just than those before them. They were the heroes whom Antiquity calls "demigods." But in the end they too fell in feuds and wars, some before the seven gates of Thebes, where they were fighting for the realm of King Oedipus, others on the field of Troy, where they had come in ships for the sake of beautiful Helen. When their existence on earth had ended in battle and disaster, Zeus assigned them a region at the very rim of the universe, on the Islands of the Blest gleaming in the dark sea. Here they lead a tranquil and happy life after death, and three times a year the rich earth grants them a harvest of honey-sweet fruits.

The old poet Hesiod, who tells the legend of the ages of man, ends with a sigh of regret: "Ah, if only I did not belong to the fifth age of men which is now come. Had I but died earlier, or come into the world later! For this is the iron age. These men are utterly corrupt. By day and by night they labor and fret, and the gods send them more and more gnawing cares. But they bring their greatest trouble upon themselves. The father does not love his son, nor the son his father. Guest hates host, and friend hates friend. Even brothers do not cherish each other with a whole heart, as in times gone by, and the grey hair of parents commands no reverence. The aged must listen to shameful language and suffer blows. O ruthless men! Have you forgotten the judgment the gods will pass, that you deny your old parents thanks for the care they had of you? Everywhere the right of might prevails, and city destroys its neighbor city. Whoever is true to his oath and is good and just finds no favor, while the evildoer and the hardhearted blasphemer are heaped with honors. Fairness and moderation are no longer esteemed. The wicked are allowed to harm the noble, to lie, and to swear false oaths. And that is why these men are so unhappy. Discordant and malicious envies pursue them and cast gloom upon their brows. The goddesses of virtue and awe, who until now have frequented the earth, sadly veil their lovely limbs in robes of white and flee from men, back to the gathering of the eternal gods. Nothing but misery is left to mortals, and no end of this mournful state is yet in sight."

PYRRHA AND DEUCALION

I n the age of the Men of Bronze, when Zeus, the ruler of the
world, heard evil things about those who dwelt in it, he decided
to walk the earth in mortal shape. But wherever he went, he
found that rumor had fallen far short of the truth.

One evening, as twilight deepened into night, he came to the
halls of inhospitable Lycaon, king of Arcadia, who was known
for his savagery. By miraculous signs and tokens Zeus made
evident his divine origin, and the people knelt and worshipped
him. But Lycaon scoffed at their devout prayers. "Let us see,"
he said, "whether this guest of ours is a god or a mortal!" And
in his heart he resolved to destroy him at midnight, when his
sleep would be soundest.

But first he killed a poor hostage the people of Molossia had
sent him, cast part of the body, still warm, into boiling water,
roasted part over the fire, and served this dish to the stranger
for his evening meal. Zeus, who had seen through both what was
done and what was intended, started up from the board and
launched avenging flames upon the palace of this impious king.
Shaken with terror he fled into the open. But the very first sound
of distress he uttered turned into a howl. His skin roughened
to a shaggy pelt, his arms became legs. He had been changed
into a bloodthirsty wolf.

Then Zeus returned to Olympus, sat in council with the gods,
and determined to wipe out the whole infamous race of man. He
was just about to do this by scourging all the earth with lightning, when he held back for fear the sky might catch fire and
burn the axis of the world. So he laid aside the thunderbolts the
Cyclopes had forged for him and resolved to send torrents of rain
down upon the earth and drown mortals in a vast flood. Instantly
the north wind and all the other winds that clear the skies were
locked into the cave of Aeolus, and only the south wind was allowed to issue forth. Down to earth he flew with dripping wings,
shrouded in darkness as black as pitch. Tides flowed from his

white hair, fogs covered his forehead, and water oozed from his breast. He reached up to the sky, swept the clouds into his mighty grip, and began to squeeze them out. Thunder rumbled, and masses of rain beat down from the heavens. The violence of the storm bent the harvest and shattered the farmer's hopes. The long labors of the seasons had been in vain.

Poseidon, the brother of Zeus, also helped in this orgy of destruction. He called together the rivers, saying: "Let loose your currents! Engulf the houses and wreck the dams!" And they carried out his commands, while he himself struck the earth with his trident and shook the ground to make way for the waters. The rivers rolled over the open meadows, deluged the fields, and tore down the saplings, temples, and homes. If a few palaces still loomed here and there, the great tide rose to their roofs in no time at all, and the tallest towers were caught up in a whirlpool. Soon no one could distinguish between water and land. Everything was sea, shoreless sea.

Men tried to save themselves as best they could. One climbed a high mountain, another took to his boat and rowed over the roof of his submerged house, or over his vineyards, where the vine-sprays brushed against the keel. Fish struggled in the boughs of trees, while the fleeing stag and boar were at the mercy of the tide. Whole peoples were swept away, and those who were spared died of hunger on hills where nothing grew but barren heather and ferns.

In the land of Phocis there was still one mountain which lifted its peaks above the waste of water. It was Mount Parnassus. Deucalion, whose father Prometheus had warned him of the coming flood, and built him a boat, floated up to this mountain with Pyrrha his wife. No man and no woman created ever surpassed these two in goodness and fear of the gods. When Zeus, looking down from the sky, saw only endless swamp where the earth had been, and only two people left of thousands upon thousands, both guiltless and devout worshippers of his deity, he sent the north wind to drive away the black clouds and scatter the fogs. Once more he showed heaven to earth and earth to heaven, while Poseidon, sovereign over the sea, laid down his trident and smoothed the waves. The sea had shores again; the rivers returned to their beds. The tops of trees, smeared with mud, began to rise from the depths. Next came the hills, and at last the level plain spread clear and dry. Earth was restored.

Deucalion looked around. The land lay ravaged and silent as the tomb. At the sight, tears ran down his cheeks, and he said to Pyrrha: "My only and beloved companion, in all directions, as far as eye can reach, I see no living thing. We two are the only humans left on earth; all the rest have been drowned in the flood. And we, indeed, are not yet sure of our life. I tremble at every cloud. And even if all danger were past, what should two lonely people do on the abandoned earth? Oh, how I wish my father Prometheus had taught me the art of creating men and breathing spirit into shapes of clay!"

So he spoke, and in their solitude both he and his wife began to weep. Then they fell on their knees before a half-ruined altar of Themis and pleaded with the immortal goddess. "Tell us, goddess, how we may recreate the vanished race of man. Oh, help the world to live again!"

"Go from my altar," said a voice. "Veil your heads, loosen the garments from your limbs, and cast the bones of your mother behind you."

Long they pondered over these mysterious words. Pyrrha was the first to break the silence. "Forgive me, great goddess," she said, "if I shudder and do not obey you, for I hesitate to offend my mother's shade by scattering abroad her bones."

But Deucalion's mind was suddenly illumined as by a flash of light. He calmed his wife with soothing words. "Unless I am much mistaken," he said, "the command of the gods never bids us do wrong. The earth is our mother, and her bones are the stones. It is the stones, Pyrrha, that we are to cast behind us!"

Nonetheless both were very doubtful about this explanation of the command of Themis. Yet—so they thought—there is no harm in trying. So they went to one side, veiled their heads, loosened the clasps of their garments as they had been told, and flung stones backward over their shoulders. And a miracle happened: the stones no longer remained hard and brittle. They became supple, and grew, and took on shape. Human forms stood out, not very distinctly at first, but rather like the first rough outline an artist hews from marble. Whatever was earthen and moist about the stones changed to flesh, and what was firm and hard was transformed to bones, while the veins turned into human veins. So, in a very short time, with the help of the gods, the stones cast by the man became men, those by the woman, women.

The human race does not deny its origin. It is a sturdy race, well-fitted for a life of toil, and it never forgets the stuff from which it was made.

ZEUS AND IO

INACHUS, king of the Pelasgians, the hereditary monarch of an age-old dynasty, had a beautiful daughter called Io. Zeus, the lord of Olympus, once happened to see her as she was tending her father's flocks in the meadows of Lerna, and love for her leaped up in the god like a flame. Disguised as a mortal, he came to tempt her with sweet, seductive words.

"How happy will he be who one day calls you his own! Yet there is no mortal worthy of you, you who are fit to be the bride of the ruler of the gods. I am he! I am Zeus! No, do not run away! See, it is burning noon. Come with me to that shady grove, over there to the left, which invites us with its coolness. Why should you toil in the midday heat? You need not be afraid to enter the dim forest where beasts crouch in the dusky ravines, for am I not here to protect you, I, who weigh in my hand the scepter of the sky and flash jagged lightning over the earth?"

But the girl sped from her tempter, and fear winged her feet, so that she would surely have escaped him, had he not abused his power and plunged the entire region into darkness. She was muffled in mists and slowed her steps in alarm lest she stumble against a rock or lose her footing and slip into a river. And so unhappy Io fell into the snares of Zeus.

Hera, the mother of the gods, had long since grown accustomed to her husband's faithlessness, for he frequently turned from her to lavish love on the daughters of demigods and mortals. Yet she had never learned to curb her anger and jealousy, but watched every move of Zeus on earth with unflagging distrust. Now too her gaze rested upon that very region where her husband was disporting himself without her knowledge, and she saw with amazement that in one particular spot the clear day was blurred with heavy mists which rose neither from the river nor the ground, nor were they due to any other natural cause. Her suspicions were instantly aroused. She looked for Zeus over all Olympus, but he was not there. "If I am not mistaken," she said sullenly to herself, "my husband is doing me a grave wrong."

And forthwith she left the high air of heaven, floated down to earth in a cloud, and bade the mists which walled in the seducer and his quarry break apart. Zeus had divined her coming, and to save his beloved from her vengeance, he changed the lovely daughter of Inachus into a snow-white heifer. Even so, the girl was still fair to look upon. Hera, seeing at once through her husband's ruse, praised the stately animal and guilefully asked to whom it belonged, what breed it was, and where it had come from. In his embarrassment and desire to put an end to her questions, Zeus lyingly told her that the heifer was a mere creature of earth and nothing more. Hera pretended to be satisfied with his answer, but begged him to make her a present of the fine beast. What was the cheated cheat to do? If he granted her request he would lose his beloved; if he refused, her smoldering suspicions would burst into flame and she would surely destroy the unfortunate girl. For the time being, then, he decided to do without her and gave his wife the shimmering creature, whose secret he thought well-hidden.

Hera seemed charmed with the gift. She knotted a ribbon about the neck of the beautiful heifer, whose heart beat under the animal pelt in mortal despair, and led her off in triumph. But the goddess herself had misgivings about her action and knew she would not be at ease until she had given her rival into very safe keeping. She went in search of Argus, the son of Arestor, who seemed well suited for the task she had in mind. For Argus was a monster with a hundred eyes, of which he closed only one pair at a time, while the rest, glittering like stars over the front and back of his head, remained open and faithful to their duties. It was to Argus that Hera entrusted Io, so that Zeus would be unable to regain the mistress she had deprived him of. Fixed by those hundred eyes, the heifer was allowed to graze on slopes, green with luxuriant grass, the livelong day, but wherever she went, never was she out of sight of Argus, even when she moved behind him. At nightfall he locked her up and weighed her neck with heavy chains. She dined on bitter herbs and leathery leaves, lay on the hard bare ground, and drank from turbid pools. Often Io forgot that she was no longer human. She wanted to lift her hands in supplication, only to remember that she had no hands. She wanted to plead with Argus in sweet, compelling words, but when she opened her mouth she shrank from the lows she uttered. Argus did not keep her in one place, for Hera had bidden him pasture her far and wide, so that it would be difficult for Zeus to discover her. Thus it was that she and her guard roamed the countryside, until one day she found herself in her native land, on the bank of the river where she had so often played as a child. Now for the first time she saw herself in her altered shape, and when the head of a horned beast stared back at her from the bright mirror of the waters, she fled from her own image in shuddering alarm. Driven by longing, she turned toward her sisters and her father, but they did not recognize her. Inachus did, indeed, stroke her shimmering flank and proffer her leaves plucked from a bush growing near by. But when the heifer licked his hand in gratitude, and covered it with kisses and human tears, the old man still did not guess whom he had caressed, nor who had returned his caresses. At last the poor girl, whose mind had suffered no change along with her form, had a happy thought. With her hoof she began to trace written symbols in the sand, and soon her father, whose attention had been attracted to this curious behavior, deciphered the news that his own child stood before him.

"What misery!" exclaimed the old man, as he clung to the horns and neck of his moaning daughter. "Must I find you like this, you whom I have looked for the world over! Alas, I grieved less when I was seeking you than now that I have found you. You are silent? Can you give me no word of comfort, but only low? Fool that I was! All my thoughts were bent upon choosing a son-in-law worthy of you, and now you are like those who run in a herd . . ." Inachus could not finish his lament, for Argus, the cruel watchman, snatched Io from her father and dragged her far away to a solitary pasture. Then he himself climbed to the peak of a mountain and performed his office by peering to the four corners of the world with his hundred wary eyes.

And now Zeus could no longer endure the sorrows of Io. He summoned his dear son Hermes and commanded him to trick hated Argus into closing his eyes. Hermes bound his winged sandals to his feet, grasped in his strong hand the staff which scatters sleep, and put on his travelling cap. In this raiment he left his father's house and sped down to earth. There he laid aside his cap and wings and kept only his staff, so that he looked like a shepherd with his crook. He coaxed a flock of wild goats to follow him and went to the lonely meadow where Io was nibbling the young blades under the stare of the ever-watchful Argus. Then Hermes drew forth a shepherd's pipe, called a syrinx, and began to sound notes more full and sweet than mortal herdsmen play.

Hera's servant, pleased with the unexpected music, rose from his lofty seat and called down: "Whoever you may be, most welcome piper, come and rest on this rock with me. You will find no thicker or greener grass for your beasts, and that clump of close-growing trees offers pleasant shade to the herd."

Hermes thanked Argus and clambered up beside him. He began to speak, and his talk was so lively and beguiling that the hours passed unnoticed. Those hundred lids grew heavy, and now Hermes fingered his reed and thought to put Argus to sleep with his playing. But Io's guard feared the anger of his mistress, should he slacken his watchfulness, and fought his desire for sleep to the extent of keeping at least part of his eyes open. With a great effort he marshalled his drowsy wits and, since the reed pipe was something new, asked his companion its origin.

"I shall be glad to tell you," said Hermes, "if you have the patience to listen at this late hour. In the snow-covered hills of Arcadia lived a famous hamadryad called Syrinx. The woodland gods and satyrs were charmed with her loveliness and wooed her ardently, but again and again she eluded their pursuit, for she feared the yoke of marriage. Like Artemis with her girdle, Artemis, lover of the chase, she was loath to give up her maidenhood. Finally the great god Pan saw the nymph as he was roaming the forest and began to court her insistently, though with the proud bearing the knowledge of his own majesty gave him. But him too she spurned and fled through pathless wilderness until she came to the sandy river Ladon, whose waters were just deep enough to block her crossing. She hesitated on the bank and implored her sisters, the nymphs, to take pity upon her and change her form before the god overtook her. Just then he came and clasped her in his arms, but to his great astonishment he found himself holding a reed instead of a maiden. His deep sighs entered the reed, were multiplied in passage, and echoed their own sound in mournful murmurs. The magic of these notes soothed the bereft god's anguish. 'So be it, O Loveliness transformed,' he cried in pain and delight. 'Even so we shall be united and nothing can ever part us.' Then he cut himself reeds of various lengths, joined them with wax, and named his flute for the fair hamadryad. Ever since that time we have called the shepherd's pipe syrinx . . ."

This was the tale of the messenger of the gods, and never did he turn his gaze from Argus in the telling. Before the end he saw one eye after another veiled beneath its lid, until at last heavy sleep had put out all the hundred lights. Now Hermes checked the ripple of his voice and with his magic staff touched each of those closed eyes to deepen their oblivion. Then he swiftly drew forth the sickle-shaped sword he had concealed under his shepherd's smock, cut through the bowed neck of Argus where it was closest to the head, and both head and trunk plunged down from the peak and stained the stones with jets of blood.

Now Io was free, and though she was still in the shape of a heifer, she sped away in unshackled liberty. But the sharp eyes of Hera detected all that had happened below. She cast about for some instrument to inflict exquisite torment upon her rival, and chanced upon the gadfly. This insect almost crazed Io with its sting and drove her from her own country and over all the earth: to the Scythians, to the Caucasus, to the tribe of the Amazons, the Cimmerian Isthmus, the sea of Maeotis, and thence into Asia. After long and difficult wanderings she came to Egypt. Here, on the shores of the Nile, she sank down upon her forefeet, bent back her head and gazed upward to Zeus in heaven in mute accusation. So stricken with pity was he at sight of her, that he hastened to Hera, embraced her, implored her mercy for the poor girl, who had done nothing to provoke his faithlessness, and swore by the waters of the underworld (on which the gods take their oaths) that he would give up his fondness for her. While he was still beseeching her, Hera heard the low of the heifer which rose through the clear air, even up to Olympus. Her heart softened, and she gave her husband leave to return Io to her own true shape.

Zeus hurried to earth and swept on to the Nile. He passed his hand over the heifer's back, and a curious change ensued: the shag vanished from her body, the horns dwindled, her eyes narrowed, the muzzle curved to lips, shoulders and hands appeared, and the hooves were suddenly gone. Nothing of the heifer remained but her fair white color. Io rose from the ground and stood erect, and beauty breathed about her. There, on the bank of the Nile, she bore Zeus a son, Epaphus, and because the people venerated her, who had been so miraculously saved, as though she were a goddess, she ruled over that country for many years. But even so, she was never quite safe from the wrath of Hera, who incited the savage Curetes to steal young Epaphus. So again Io wandered up and down the earth, this time in a futile search for her son. At last—after Zeus had struck the Curetes with lightning—she found Epaphus on the border of Ethiopia, took him back to Egypt, and shared the throne with him. He married Memphis, who bore him Libya, for whom the land of Libya is named. When mother and son died, the peoples of the Nile built temples for them and worshipped them as gods, her as Isis, and him as Apis.

PHAETHON

Borne by luminous pillars, the palace of the sun-god rose lustrous with gold and flame-red rubies. The cornice was of dazzling ivory, and carved in relief on the wide silver doors were legends and miracle tales. To this beautiful place came Phaethon, son of Phoebus, and asked for his father, the sun-god. He dared not approach too closely, but stopped at a little distance, because he could not endure that glittering, burning nearness.

Phoebus, robed in crimson, was seated on his throne adorned with matchless emeralds. To the right and the left of him stood his retinue ranged in appointed order: the Day, the Month, the Year, the Centuries, and the Seasons: young Spring with his fillet of flowers, Summer garlanded with sheaves of yellow grain, wine-stained Autumn, and Winter, whose locks were white as hail. The all-seeing eyes of Phoebus, in the midst of these, soon noticed the youth, who was gazing at the glory about him in silent amazement. "Why did you undertake this journey?" he asked him. "What brings you to the palace of your father, my son?"

"O father," answered Phaethon, "it is because on earth men are making mock of me and slandering my mother Clymene. They say that I only pretend to be of heavenly origin, and that, in reality, I am the son of a quite ordinary, unknown man. So I have come to beg of you some token which will prove to the world that I am indeed your son."

He paused, and Phoebus laid aside the beams which circled his head and bade him come close. Then he embraced him tenderly, flinging his arms around him, and said: "Clymene, your mother, told you the truth, my son, and I shall never disown you in the face of the world. But to dispel your doubts forever, ask a gift of me. I swear by the Styx, that river in the underworld upon which all gods take their oath, that your wish shall be granted, no matter what it may be."

Phaethon barely waited for his father to finish. "Then make my wildest dream come true!" he cried. "For one whole day let me guide the winged chariot of the sun!"

Fear and sorrow shadowed the god's shining face. Three—four times he shook his radiant head. At last he said: "O son, you beguiled me into speaking rash words. If only I could retract my promise! For you have asked something which is beyond your strength. You are young, you are mortal, but what you crave is granted only to the gods—and not to all of them, for only I am permitted to do what you are so eager to try. Only I can stand on the glowing axle which showers sparks as it moves through the air. My chariot must travel a steep path. It is a difficult climb for the horses even when they are fresh, at dawn. The middle of the course lies at the zenith of the sky. I tell you that I myself am often shaken with dread when, at such a height, I stand upright in my chariot. My head spins when I look down on the lands and seas so far beneath me. And the last stretch of the way descends sharply and requires a sure hand on the reins. Even Thetis, goddess of the sea, who waits to receive me in her smooth waters, is full of alarm lest I be hurled from the sky. And there is still another peril to consider, for you must remember that heaven turns incessantly and that the driving is against the sweep of its vast rotations. Even if I gave you my chariot, how could you overcome such obstacles? No, dear son, do not insist that I keep my word to you, but mend your wish while there is still time. You can read my concern from my face. Could you but look through my eyes into my heart, heavy with a father's anxiety! Choose anything that earth and heaven have to offer, and by the Styx I swear it shall be yours!—You fling your arms around me? Alas, that it is to ask this dangerous thing!"

The youth pleaded and pleaded, and Phoebus Apollo had, after all, sworn a most sacred oath. So he took his son by the hand and led him to the sun-chariot, the work of Hephaestus. Pole, axle, and the rims of the wheels were of gold, the spokes of silver, and the yoke glittered with chrysolite and other precious stones. While Phaethon was still marvelling at this perfect craftsmanship, Dawn wakened in the east and flung wide the doors to her rosy chamber. The stars faded, last of all the morning star, which lingers longest at his post in the heavens, and the horns of the crescent moon paled on the brightening horizon. Now Phoebus ordered the winged Hours to yoke the horses, and they did as he bade, bringing the shining-flanked animals, sated with ambrosia, out of their splendid stalls, and putting them into the gleaming harness. Then the father salved the face of his son with a magic ointment to enable him to withstand the heat of the flames. He crowned his head with sun-rays, sighing all the while, and said warningly: "Child, spare the goad and use the reins, for the horses will run of themselves, and your labor will lie in slowing their flight. The course slants in a wide and shallow curve. Keep away from both the South and the North poles. You will find the road by the tracks the wheels have left. Do not drive too slow, lest the earth catch fire, nor too high, lest you burn up the sky. So go now, if you must! Darkness is passing. Take the reins in your hands, or—dear son, there is still time to give up this folly! Leave the chariot to me, and let me shed the light on the world. Be content to watch!"

The boy scarcely heard what his father said. One spring, and he was up in the chariot, exultant at having the reins in his own hands. He only nodded and smiled his thanks to unhappy Phoebus. The four winged horses neighed, and the air kindled with their burning breath. In the meantime Thetis, knowing nothing of her grandchild's venture, opened wide her portals; the vast spaces of the world lay before Phaethon's eyes, and the horses bounded up the course and broke through the mists of morning.

But soon they felt that their burden was lighter than usual, and like ships which toss on the ocean when the hold is not heavy with cargo, the chariot reeled and floundered through the air and swerved aimlessly, as though it were empty. When the horses became aware of this, they wheeled from the beaten paths of the sky and jostled each other in savage haste. Phaethon began to tremble. He did not know which way to pull the reins, he did not know where he was, nor could he curb the animals straining from him with headlong speed. When he looked down from the arch of the heavens and saw the land spread out so far below, his cheeks grew pale and his knees shook with terror. He glanced back over his shoulder, and much of the sky lay in his wake; he turned forward, and more loomed ahead. In his mind he measured the vast reaches before and behind, and not knowing what to do he stared into space. His helpless hands neither slackened nor tightened the reins. He wanted to call to the horses but did not know their names. He saw the many constellations strewing the heavens, and his heart numbed with horror at their strange shapes, like those of monsters. Chill with despair he dropped the reins, and instantly the horses shied from their course, leaping sidewise into unfamiliar regions of air. Now they sprang forward, now they plunged down. Now they rushed against the fixed stars, and now they slanted toward earth. They grazed against drifts of cloud, which kindled and began to smoulder. Lower and lower hurtled the chariot until the wheels touched the tall mountains. The earth panted and cracked with heat, the saps were dried out of growing things, and suddenly everything began to flicker. The heather yellowed and drooped. The leaves of the forest trees shrivelled and burst into flame. The fire sped on to the plains and scorched the harvests. Entire cities went up in smoke, and whole countries with all their peoples burned to cinders. Hills were consumed, and woods, and mountains. They say that it was then the skin of the Ethiopians turned black. Rivers ran dry or streamed backwards to regain their sources. The sea itself shrank and narrowed so that what its waters had only lately covered was now nothing but dry sand.

The world was afire, and Phaethon began to suffer from the intolerable heat. Every breath he drew seemed to come from a seething furnace, and the chariot seared the soles of his feet. He was tortured with fumes and blasts of ashes cast up by the burning earth. Smoke black as pitch surged around him, while the horses jounced and tossed him hither and thither. And then his hair caught fire. He fell from the chariot and whirled through space like a shooting star, such as sometimes trails its brightness through the clear sky. Far from his home the broad river Eridanus received him and closed over his throbbing limbs.

His father, the sun-god, who had witnessed this sight of destruction, veiled his radiant head and brooded in sorrow. It is said that this day brought no light to the world. Only the great conflagration shone far and wide.

EUROPA

IN the land of Tyre and Sidon, Europa, daughter of King
Agenor, was reared in the seclusion of her father's palace.
Once, at midnight, when mortals are visited by fanciful dreams
which have a clear core of truth, Heaven sent her a curious vision.
It seemed to her that two continents—Asia and that which lies
opposite—in the guise of women, were fighting to possess her.
One of the women had a foreign air. The other—and this was
Asia—looked and acted like one of Europa's own countrywomen,
and claimed her warmly and vehemently, saying that it was she
who had borne and nurtured this lovely child. But the strange
woman clasped her in her strong arms like a stolen treasure and
drew her away with her. The oddest part of the dream was that
Europa did not resist her with any real force or purpose.

"Come with me, little love," said the stranger. "I shall bring
you to Zeus, the Aegis-Bearer, for Destiny has appointed you
his beloved!"

Europa awoke. The blood pulsed madly in her temples, and
she started up from her couch, for the vision of night had been
as bright and distinct as the reality of day. For a long time she
sat upright and motionless, staring into space with wide-open
eyes, and still seeing the two women before her. At last her lips
moved, and she asked herself in alarm: "What god has sent me
this vision? What curious dream has beguiled me while I slept,
safe in the house of my father? Who was the strange woman?
What new yearning quickened my heart at sight of her? How
lovingly she approached me, and even when she snatched me
away she looked at me with a mother's tender gaze! May the gods
let my dream be for the best!"

Morning had come, and the fair light of day dispelled the
darkness of her visions from Europa's spirit. She rose to busy
herself with her usual girlish tasks and pleasures. Friends and
companions of her own age gathered about her, the daughters of
noble houses, who attended her on her walks, at choral dances,

and the rites of offering. They came to conduct their young mistress to a meadow strewn with many flowers, close by the sea where the girls of that region assembled to delight in the mass of blooms and the sound of the surf lapping the shore. All the girls carried baskets, and Europa herself had one of gold, carved with shining scenes from the lives of the gods. It was the work of Hephaestus, and Poseidon, the Earth-Shaker, had given it to Libya in those long-ago days when he was courting her. It had passed from hand to hand until Agenor received it as an heirloom. Swinging this basket, which was more like a bride's finery than an article for everyday use, lovely Europa ran before her playmates, on to the shoreland meadows bright with color. The girls scattered with merry words and gay laughter, each to pluck those flowers that pleased her fancy. One broke the glistening narcissus, another the fragrant hyacinth; a third chose the fainter-scented violet. Some preferred the spicy thyme, others the yellow crocus. So they ran here and there over the meadow, but Europa soon found what she was seeking. Taller than they, like the foam-born goddess of love among the Graces, she stood among her friends, and held high in her hands a great bunch of glowing roses.

When they had gathered all they wanted, the girls flung themselves down in the soft grass and began to plait wreaths, which later they would hang on green boughs as thank-offerings to the nymphs of that place. But their pleasure in their dainty work was doomed to be short-lived, for—of a sudden—Fate broke in upon Europa's carefree maidenhood, the fate the dream of the past night had shadowed forth.

Zeus, son of Cronus, struck by the arrow of Aphrodite, who alone among the immortals could overcome the unconquerable father of the gods, was stirred by the beauty of young Europa. But because he feared the anger of jealous Hera and could hardly hope to tempt the girl's innocent spirit if he came in his own form, the god contrived a ruse. He assumed the shape of a bull. But no ordinary bull! Not like one that paces the common field, bends to the yoke, and draws the loaded wagon! He was great and splendid, with swelling neck and massive shoulders. His horns were slight and graceful as though a hand had wrought them, and more transparent than flawless jewels.

Yellow-gold in color was his body, but in the very middle of his forehead shimmered a silvery mark shaped like the crescent moon. Rolling restlessly in their sockets, his blue-black eyes smoldered with desire. Before transforming himself, Zeus had summoned Hermes to Olympus and—without a word about his purpose— had directed him to do him a certain service. "Hasten, dear son, loyal executor of my commands," he said. "Do you see that land below us, to the left? It is Phoenicia. Go there and drive the herds of King Agenor, which you will find grazing on the mountain slopes, down to the shore of the sea." Instantly the winged god, obedient to his father's words, flew to the Sidonian pastures and drove the king's cattle, among which Zeus—unbeknown to Hermes—had mingled himself in his new shape, down to those very meadows in which Agenor's daughter, surrounded by her Tyrian maidens, was lightheartedly toying with garlands. The herd dispersed and began cropping the grass at a distance from the girls. Only the beautiful bull that housed a god approached the green mound on which Europa and her playmates were seated. He moved with perfect grace. His forehead did not threaten, and his flashing eyes begot no fears. He seemed gentleness itself. Europa and her maidens admired the noble proportions of the animal and his peaceful manner. They wanted to see him more closely and stroke his shimmering back. The bull seemed to be aware of this, for he drew nearer and nearer and finally came to a stand right in front of Europa. At first she was startled and shrank back, but the bull did not move. He appeared to be quite tame, so she took courage, went up to him, and held the roses to his foam-flecked lips, which breathed out the scent of ambrosia. Caressingly he licked the proffered flowers and the delicate hand which wiped the foam from his mouth and began to stroke him with tenderness and love. More and ever more enchanting did the glorious creature seem to the girl. She even ventured to kiss his silken forehead. At that he bellowed joyfully, but it was not the bellow of a common bull, but like the sound of a Lydian flute echoing through a gorge between high mountains. Then he crouched at her feet, looked at her full of longing, and turned his head as if to point his broad back to her.

And now Europa called to her maidens. "Come closer," she cried. "Let us climb on the back of this beautiful bull and ride him. I think there is room for four of us at a time. See how tame he is, how gentle! Not in the least like other bulls! I do believe he has the power of reason, just like human beings, and all that he lacks is speech!" While she was speaking, she took the wreaths from the hands of her playmates and hung them one after another on the lowered horns of the bull. Then she sprang lightly to his back, while the other girls hung back, hesitating and afraid.

When the bull had thus got what he wanted, he bounded up from the ground. First he walked slowly, yet so that Europa's companions could not quite keep pace with him. But when the meadow lay behind and the empty strand stretched ahead, he doubled his speed and seemed a flying steed rather than a trotting bull. Before the girl knew what was happening, he had leaped into the sea and was swimming away with his quarry. With her right hand she clung to one of his horns, with her left she steadied herself on his back. The wind billowed out her gown as though it were a sail. In terror she looked back at the receding shore and called to her comrades—but in vain. The waters lapped against the sides of the bull, and shying from the wet she drew up her little heels. The bull floated on like a ship. Soon the land vanished from sight, the sun set, and in the vague shimmer of night, the girl saw nothing but waves and stars. All the next day the bull swam through vast reaches of sea, but he parted the water so adroitly that not a drop touched his rider. At last, toward evening, they reached a far-off land. The bull swung himself ashore and let the girl slip from his back under the arching boughs of a tree. Then he vanished, and in his place stood a man, beautiful as the gods, who told her he was the ruler of the island to which she had come, the island of Crete, and that he would protect her if she consented to be his. In her sadness and desolation, Europa gave him her hand in token of agreement. Zeus had accomplished his desire.

Europa woke from the numbness of long sleep when the sun stood high in the heavens. She was alone and looked about her, helpless and bewildered, as though she expected to find herself at home. "Father, father!" she cried in distress. Then she remembered and said: "How dare I even utter the word 'father,' I who have had no care for my maidenhood! What madness made me forget a child's love and devotion?" Again she looked around, and slowly everything came back to her. "From where, and to what place have I come?" she said. "Death would be a penalty too light for my failing. But am I really awake? Am I mourning an actual disgrace? Perhaps only a misty dream, which will dissolve when I close my lids again, is troubling my spirit. It is impossible to think that I chose to climb on a monster's back, that I swam the seas, rather than pluck fresh blooms in sweet security!"

Even as she spoke, she passed her palm across her eyes as if to banish a nightmare. But when she opened them, she saw the same alien scene: unfamiliar trees and rocks, and the white churn of the tide, dashing against looming cliffs and rushing on to a shore she had never seen. "Oh, if someone would only deliver that bull up to me now!" she cried in anger. "I should rend his flesh and break his horns. Idle wish! I have left my home thoughtlessly and without shame, so what is there for me but to die! If all the gods have forsaken me, let them at least send a lion or a tiger. Perhaps my beauty will tempt their appetites, and I need not wait for hunger to fade the bloom on my cheeks."

But no savage beast appeared. Smiling and tranquil the unfamiliar landscape spread before her, and the sun shone from a cloudless sky. As though pursued by the Furies, the girl sprang to her feet. "Miserable Europa," she cried, "do you not hear your father's voice? He is far away, but still he will curse you unless you put an end to your shameful life. Do you not see him pointing to that ash tree, on which you can hang yourself by your girdle, or that steep cliff, from which you can plunge to an unquiet grave in the stormy sea? Or do you prefer to be the concubine of a barbarian lord and slave for him day after day, spinning your wool, you, the daughter of a great and powerful king?"

In this way she tormented herself with the thought of death without finding the courage to die. Suddenly, she heard a low mocking whisper, and fearing an eavesdropper, looked over her shoulder in alarm. There, bright with unearthly radiance, stood Aphrodite and beside her Eros, her son, with lowered bow. A smile lingered on the lips of the goddess. "Calm your anger and rebel no longer," she said. "The bull you loathe will come and hold out his horns so that you may break them. It is I who sent you the dream you had in your father's house. Be comforted, Europa! You were carried off by a god. You are destined to be the mortal wife of Zeus, the Unconquerable. And your name shall be immortal, for from this time on the continent which received you shall be called Europe!"

CADMUS

Cadmus was Europa's brother, a son of Agenor, king of Phoenicia. When Zeus, in the shape of a bull, had carried off Europa, Agenor sent Cadmus and his brothers in search of her, telling them not to come back until they had accomplished their quest. For a long time Cadmus wandered through the world in vain, unable to find her whom the wiles of Zeus had spirited away. He feared his father's anger at his failure, and so—not wishing to return to his own country—he consulted the oracle of Phoebus Apollo and asked what land he should dwell in the rest of his life. And the sun-god replied: "In a lonely meadow you will find a heifer who has never borne the yoke. Follow her, and where she lies down to rest in the grass, in that place you shall build a city and call it Thebes."

Scarcely had Cadmus left the Castalian Fountain, the site of Apollo's oracle, when he came to a green pasture, and in it grazed a heifer whose neck bore no marks of the yoke. With a silent prayer to Phoebus, he slowly followed in the creature's tracks. She waded the ford of Cephisus and had just crossed a wide tract of land when she stopped, pointed her horns at the sky, and filled the air with her lowing. Then she glanced back at Cadmus and his retinue and finally lay down in the thick-growing tender grass.

Full of gratitude, Cadmus prostrated himself and kissed the alien earth. Then he prepared to offer sacrifice to Zeus and sent his servants in search of a living spring to provide water for the libation. In that place, there was an age-old wood which had never been thinned by the axe. In the very heart of it rocks, joined with a network of bush and underbrush, formed a low vault over a gorge running with clear water. Hidden in this cavern was a wicked dragon. His scarlet crest shone from afar; his eyes flashed flame; his body was swollen with venom, and three tongues flickered from his mouth which was armed with a triple row of teeth. The Phoenicians had only just entered the grove and let their pitcher down into the water, when the dragon darted his azure head out of the cavern and uttered a fearful hiss. The urns slipped from their hands, and the blood froze in their veins. The dragon, meanwhile, had coiled himself into scaly folds, drew back for the thrust, and, reared to half his height, looked down upon the wood. Then he lunged forward at the Phoenicians, killed some with his fangs, strangled others in his coils, and destroyed the rest by his poisonous spittle or the mere fetid breath from his mouth.

Cadmus could not imagine what was keeping his servants. At last he went in search of them. His tunic was a pelt he had torn from a lion, his weapons were a lance and javelin and—stronger and better than these—his brave heart. Upon entering the grove he saw a mass of bodies, his lifeless servants, and triumphing above them the enemy, his body distended, his tongue lapping the blood of his victims.

"My poor friends," cried Cadmus, "I shall either avenge you or share your death!" And he picked up a boulder and hurled it at the dragon. The block was so huge that walls and towers would have shaken at its impact, but the dragon remained unmoved. His thick black hide and stiff scales protected him like a coat of mail. Now Cadmus threw his javelin, and with this he fared better, for the iron point bit deep into the entrails of the monster. Raging with pain, he turned his head and crushed the shaft of the javelin, but the top stuck fast in his body. A sword-stroke goaded him to fury, his throat swelled out, and white foam gushed from his poisonous jaws. Straight as an arrow the monster rushed forth, and his breast struck against the trunks of the trees. Agenor's son dodged the onslaught, drew his lion's skin close about him, and let the dragon's teeth spend their force on the point of his lance. At last the blood began to stream from the throat of the beast and stained the green grass around him.

But the wound was light, and the dragon evaded every further thrust. Finally Cadmus buried his sword in his neck. It came out on the other side and pierced an oak tree so that the dragon was nailed to its trunk. The tree was bowed by the weight and mcaned as it felt the tip of the monster's tail lashing its bark.

For a long time Cadmus gazed at the slain dragon. When he took his eyes from it and looked around, he saw Pallas Athene, who had descended from heaven and now commanded him to turn up the earth and sow the dragon's teeth, the seed for a future race. He obeyed the goddess, ploughed a broad and long furrow, and scattered the dragon's teeth in the groove. Of a sudden there was a stir in the clods, and out came, first the point of a lance, then a helmet with a crest of variegated plumes, then shoulders, breast, limbs, and finally a warrior, fully armed, sprang from the earth. This happened in many places at once, so that a whole crop of armed men grew up before the very eyes of the Phoenician.

He was greatly alarmed and prepared to fight a fresh foe. But one of the earthborn men called out to him: "Do not lift your hand against us. Do not interfere in this war between brothers!" Even as he spoke he raised his sword against one of the other warriors and was, at the same instant, struck by a flying javelin. Its thrower, in turn, was wounded and gave up the breath of life he had only just received. And now the entire host fought one another in bitter battle, and soon almost all lay on the ground, writhing in the throes of death, while Mother Earth drank the blood of the sons she had borne for so brief a span. Only five were left. One of these—who later was called Echion— was the first to throw down his arms at Athene's bidding, and offer peace. The others followed his example.

With these five earthborn warriors, Cadmus, the stranger from Phoenicia, built the city as Apollo had bidden, and—in accordance with the god's command—he called it Thebes.

PENTHEUS

IN Thebes, Bacchus or Dionysus, grandson of Cadmus, the son of Zeus and Semele, was born in a miraculous manner. This god of fruitfulness, the discoverer of the grape, was reared in India, but soon left the nymphs who had sheltered and cherished him and voyaged from land to land to spread his new teachings, to instruct people how to grow the vine which gladdens the heart, and bid them found shrines in his honor. Great was the measure of kindness he lavished upon his friends, and just as great the harshness he dealt those who refused to recognize his divinity. His fame had already reached Greece and penetrated to the city of his birth.

Thebes at that time was ruled by Pentheus, to whom Cadmus had given his kingdom. Pentheus was the son of earthborn Echion and Agave, the sister of the wine-god's mother. This king of Thebes scorned the gods and most of all his kinsman Dionysus. And so when he approached with his retinue of exultant Bacchantes to reveal himself as a god, Pentheus ignored the warning of Tiresias, the blind and aged seer, and when he heard that Theban men and women and girls were flocking to adore the new god, he began to rage against them.

"What madness has come upon you?" he asked. "You Thebans, who are descended from the dragon, you who have never retreated from the trumpet that summons to battle, or from the death-bringing sword, will you now surrender to a mob of soft-handed fools and women? And you people of Phoenicia, who came from beyond the sea and founded a city in honor of your old gods, have you forgotten the race of heroes who begot you? Will you suffer an unarmed boy to conquer Thebes, a weakling whose locks drip with myrrh, who wreathes his tender brow with vine-leaves, who goes robed in purple and gold rather than in mail, who cannot master a horse, and is indifferent to wars and feuds? If only you will come to your senses, I shall soon force him to own he is mortal just like myself, who am his cousin; that Zeus is not his father, and that all these rites and mummeries are the invention of a pretender." And he turned to his servants and commanded them to seize the author of this new madness, wherever they might come upon him, and bring him to the city in chains.

The friends and kinsmen of Pentheus were aghast at his insolent words. His grandfather Cadmus who was still alive though very old, shook his white head in disapproval. But counsel and dissent only served to swell the king's rage, which leaped over all the stumbling-stones set in his path as an angry river breaks through a dam.

In the meantime his servants returned, and their faces were stained with blood. "Where is Dionysus?" Pentheus shouted to them.

"We could not find him anywhere," they replied. "But we have brought you one of his followers. He has not been with him very long, it seems."

Pentheus studied his captive with furious eyes and cried: "You are doomed! You must die on the instant, as a warning example to the rest. What is your name? Who are your parents? Where did you come from? And tell me also why you perform these silly, newfangled rites?"

The prisoner answered, and his voice was calm and without fear. "My name is Acoetes, Maeonia is my country, and my parents are of the common people. Neither fields nor flocks did my father leave me. All he taught me was how to fish with the rod, for this skill was the sole treasure he possessed. Soon I also learned how to manage a ship and to recognize the stars and the constellations, to know the winds, and what harbors are good. I became a seaman. Once, on a voyage to Delos, I came to an unknown coast where we cast anchor. I jumped from the ship, landed on the wet sand, and spent the night ashore without my comrades. The next morning I rose at early dawn and climbed a hill to find out what the winds held in store. In the meantime my comrades had also left the ship and, on my way back, I met them dragging with them a youth they had seized on the empty strand. The boy had a girlish beauty. He was dazed with wine and drowsy, and walked with faltering steps. When I looked at him more closely it seemed to me that his face, and the way he moved and bore himself, betrayed one more than mortal. 'I do not know what god it is who is hidden within this youth.' I called to the

crew. 'But I am wholly certain that it *is* a god.' Then I turned
to the boy. 'Whoever you may be,' I said, 'I implore you to give
us your favor and speed our work. Forgive these who carried
you off!'

"'What foolishness is this!' cried one of the men. 'Leave off
praying to him.' And the others laughed. Blinded by their greed
for profit, they took hold of the boy and started dragging him
on to the ship. It was in vain that I resisted. The youngest and
sturdiest in the mob, a fugitive from a Tyrrhenian city where he
had committed murder, took me by the throat and cast me overboard. Had I not caught my foot in the rigging, I would surely
have drowned. All this time the boy lay on deck as though in a
deep sleep. Suddenly, wakened perhaps by the noise, he started
up, sobered, and went up to the sailors. 'What is all this?' he
cried. 'Tell me what destiny has brought me here and where you
are taking me?'

"'Do not be afraid, boy,' said one of the men, falsely reassuring him. 'Just tell us the port you wish to go to, and we will set you ashore wherever you say.'

" 'Then steer your course to the island of Naxos,' the youth replied, 'for that is my home.'

"They swore by all the gods to do as he bade them, and told me to set the sails. Naxos lay to our right, but when I shortened the sails accordingly, they signed to me and whispered: 'What are you up to, you fool! Are you mad? Go left!'

"I was amazed and incredulous. 'Let another take over and steer the ship,' I said, and stepped aside.

" 'As if our welfare on this voyage depended upon you!' a coarse fellow called to me derisively, and proceeded to set the sails in my stead. And he turned the ship away from Naxos and steered an opposite course. The young god stood at the stern and gazed out upon the sea. His lips curved to a scornful smile as though he had only just discovered the sailor's crude deceit. At last he spoke, pretending to weep. 'Alas! These are not the promised shores. This is not the land I asked to go to! Do you think that grown men ought to trick a child?' But the impious crew made mock of his tears and mine and plied their oars with swift and lusty strokes. But suddenly the ship stood still in the ocean, as motionless as if it were beached. In vain did they strike the waves with their poles, spread all the sails, and strive on with redoubled effort. The oars were twined with ivy, and vines clung about the mast with delicate tendrils and, growing upward in wide curve, hung the sails with rich clusters of fruit. Dionysus himself—for it was he!—stood upright in divine splendor. A fillet of leaves bound his forehead, and in his hand was the thyrsus garlanded with vine. Around him, in unsubstantial vision, tigers, lynxes, and panthers crouched on the deck, and a stream of scented wine flowed through the ship. The crew recoiled from him in terror and madness. One was about to scream, but found his lips and nose grown to a fish's mouth, and before the rest could give voice to their horror at the sight, the same thing happened to them. Their bodies dwindled, and the skin hardened to bluish scales. Their spines arched, their arms shrank to fins, their feet fused to a tail. All had turned into fish, leaped into the sea, and bobbed up and down with the waves. Of twenty men I was the only one left, and I trembled in every limb, thinking that on the very next instant I too should lose my human shape. But Dionysus spoke to me kindly, for I had done him no harm. 'Do not be alarmed,' he said. 'Take me to Naxos.' And when we reached the island, he initiated me into the mysteries of his service at his holy altar."

"We have been listening to your chatter far too long," cried King Pentheus. "Seize him!" he commanded his men. "Rend him with a thousand tortures and dispatch him to the underworld!" His henchmen obeyed. They shackled the seaman and cast him into a deep dungeon, but an invisible hand set him free.

This incident marked the beginning of the persecution visited upon the followers of Dionysus. Agave, mother of Pentheus, and her sisters had taken part in the wild rites of the god. The king sent for them and had all the Bacchantes thrown into the city prison. But they too slipped from their bonds without mortal aid. The gates of their jail flew open, and they rushed out into the woods, their veins hot with Bacchic frenzy. As for the servant who had been sent to capture the god himself with the aid of an armed force—he returned in utter bewilderment, for Dionysus had held out his hands for the shackles with a smile. And now he stood bound before the king, who could not help wondering at his radiant young beauty. Yet Pentheus obstinately held to his error and persisted in treating him as a vagabond, an adventurer who feigned to be a god. He had the captive weighed with chains and thrust into a dark cell at the back of the palace, where the horses had their mangers. But at a word from the god the earth shook, the walls crumbled, and his bonds dissolved. Unharmed and in even greater loveliness he appeared among his worshippers.

Messenger after messenger came to King Pentheus and brought him tidings of the miracles the bands of frenzied women, led by his mother and sisters, were working in the wood. They had only to strike the rock with their wands, and clear water or fragrant wine bubbled and gushed from the barren stone. Beneath the touch of the thyrsus, streams turned to milk, and hollow trees dripped with pale honey. "And had you, yourself, been there, O king," said one of the messengers, "and seen the god against whom you rail, you would have thrown yourself on the earth at his feet, and your lips would have uttered prayers."

All this only served to make the hatred of Pentheus more bitter. He ordered his riders and armed troops, heavy and light, to pursue the host of women. At this Dionysus returned of his own accord and came before the king as his own emissary. He promised Pentheus to bring back the Maenads, if the king would don woman's raiment, lest seeing him—a man, and uninitiate— they tear him to pieces. Reluctantly and full of suspicion Pentheus accepted this proposal. In the end he followed the god out of the city, already stricken with the madness Dionysus had sent upon him. He seemed to see two suns, a twofold Thebes, and each of the city gates doubled. Dionysus looked like a bull to him, a beast with great horns on his head. Against his will he fell under the Bacchic spell. He begged for a thyrsus and, when it was given him, stormed away in frenzy and exultation.

In this fashion they came to a deep valley, rich in springs and shaded with pines, where the priestesses of Bacchus were assembled, some singing hymns to their god, others twining their staffs with fresh ivy. But either Pentheus was stricken with blindness, or his guide had succeeded in leading him by such roundabout ways that he did not observe the throngs of women. And now the god lifted his hand and—a marvel having come to pass —it reached to the top of a tall pine, which he curved as one twists a willow withe. Then he perched Pentheus in the topmost boughs and gradually, and with due care, allowed the tree to return to its upright position. Oddly enough, the king did not fall and suddenly appeared in full sight, high up in the pine where the Bacchantes could see him without being seen themselves. And now Dionysus called down into the valley, and his voice rang loud and clear: "Behold him who made mock of our holiest rites! Behold and punish him!"

The air was still. No leaf quivered on its stem, no creature made a sound. The Maenads lifted their heads. Their eyes were glazed with wild light as they listened to the voice which came a second time. When they knew it for their master's, they sped swifter than doves. In divine madness they forded the rivers which had overflowed their banks, and thorny thickets parted to let them pass. At last they were close enough to recognize their king and persecutor clinging to the topmost boughs of the pine. First they hurled stones, boughs torn from trees, and their wands, but they could not reach the height where he hung precariously among the green needles. Then they took the hard wood of oak and dug around the pine until the roots were laid bare, and Pentheus, groaning aloud, fell with the falling trunk. His mother Agave, on whose lids the god had laid a spell so that she did not recognize her son, signed for the slaughter to begin. Terror had restored the king to his senses. "Not you, Mother! Let it not be you who punishes the sins of her own child!" he cried, throwing his arms about her neck. "Do you not know your own son, your son Pentheus, whom you bore in Echion's house?" But the frantic priestess of Bacchus foamed at the mouth and stared at him with wide-open eyes. And what she saw was not her son but a mountain lion, and gripping his right shoulder she tore out his arm. Her sisters wrested out his left, and then the whole raging band closed upon him, each seizing some part of his body until he was wrenched limb from limb. Agave herself clutched his head in her bloodstained hands, fastened it upon her thyrsus, still believing it to be the head of a lion, and carried it triumphantly through the woods of Cithaeron.

Thus did the god Dionysus take revenge on one who had scoffed at his sacred rites.

PERSEUS

An oracle had informed King Acrisius of Argos that his grandson would deprive him of his throne and his life. Because of this he had his daughter Danae and Perseus, her child by Zeus, shut in a chest and cast into the sea. Through wave and wind Zeus guided the course of the chest, and the tide at last beached it on the island of Seriphus, over which two brothers ruled: Dictys and Polydectes. Dictys was fishing when the chest hove out of the water, and he dragged it ashore. Both he and his brother lavished affection on Danae and her child. Polydectes took her to wife and had Perseus, the son of Zeus, carefully reared.

When he was fully grown, his stepfather urged him to go in search of adventure and undertake some quest that would bring him glory. The youth was willing enough, and soon they agreed that he was to find the Medusa, strike off her terrible head, and bring it to the king in Seriphus.

Perseus set out on his quest, and the gods guided him to a far-off region where Phorcys, father of many monsters, made his home. There Perseus came upon his three daughters, the Graeae. These were gray-haired from birth and had between them only one eye and one tooth, which they took turns in using. Perseus robbed them of both, and when they pleaded with him to return their priceless property, he consented on one condition: that they show him the way to the nymphs.

These nymphs were magical beings with certain prized possessions: a pair of winged shoes, a wallet, and a helmet of doghide. Whoever wore these things could fly wherever he wished and see whom he would without being seen himself. The daughters of Phorcys pointed out the road which led to the home of the nymphs, and so recovered their eye and tooth. From the nymphs Perseus found out what he wanted and seized the wallet, throwing it over his shoulder, the winged sandals, which he bound to his feet, and the helmet, which he set on his head. Hermes lent him a brazen shield, and furnished with all these aids he flew toward the ocean where the Gorgons, the three other daughters of Phorcys, lived. Only the third, who was called the Medusa, was mortal, and that was why Perseus had been sent to cut off her head. He found the Gorgons asleep. Instead of skin, they had dragon-scales, instead of hair, snakes twined their brows. Their teeth were like the tusks of a boar, and they had hands of metal and golden wings which could cleave the air. Perseus knew that anyone who looked at them would instantly be turned to stone, so he stood with his back to the sleepers, caught their triple image in his shining shield, and singled out the Medusa. Athene guided his hand, and he cut off the monster's head without mishap.

Scarcely had he done this, when a winged horse, Pegasus, sprang from her trunk, and after it the giant Chrysaor, both of them the children of Poseidon. Perseus hid the Medusa's head in his wallet and moved off again, walking backwards in the same manner as he had approached. But now the sisters of the Medusa awoke and left their couch. Their glance fell on the body of their slain sister, and instantly they rose into the air in pursuit of the slayer. The helmet of the nymphs, however, made Perseus invisible, and they could not discover him. As he flew above the earth the winds tossed him hither and thither like a rain cloud and shook his wallet, so that the Medusa's head oozed drops of blood which fell upon the sandy waste of Libya and changed to many-colored serpents. Ever since, Libya has been infested with poisonous vipers and adders. Then Perseus flew westward and floated down to earth in the realm of King Atlas to rest.

This king had a grove of trees bearing golden fruits, over which he had set a mighty dragon as guard. In vain did the conqueror of the Gorgon ask shelter for the night. Atlas feared for his treasure and drove him from the palace. This angered Perseus, and he said: "Since you refuse to grant me what I ask, it is I who shall grant you a gift!" And with that he drew the Medusa's head from his wallet, turned aside, and held it out to the king, who was at once turned to stone, or rather—because of his gigantic stature—to a mountain. His beard and hair became spreading forests. His shoulders, hands, and bones stiffened to rocky ledges, and his head changed into a peak which loomed into the clouds. And now again Perseus bound the winged sandals to his feet. He strapped the wallet to his side, put the helmet on his head, and leaped into the air.

On his travels he came to the coast of Ethiopia, where King Cepheus held sway. Here he saw a girl chained to a cliff which jutted into the sea. Had her hair not blown in the wind and the tears trembled in her eyes, he would have taken her for a statue carved of marble. In his delight at her loveliness he almost forgot to move his wings. "Tell me," he implored her, "why you, who should be decked out in shimmering jewels, are bound with chains? Tell me the name of your country. Tell me your own name."

At first she was silent and shy, afraid to speak to a stranger. Had she been able to move, she would have covered her face with her hands. But so the youth might not believe she had some guilt to conceal, she answered at last. "I am Andromeda, the daughter of Cepheus, king of Ethiopia. My mother boasted to the sea nymphs, who are the daughters of Nereus, that she was more beautiful than they. This made the Nereids angry, and their friend, the sea-god, churned up a flood which swept across the land. With it came a monster, devouring whatever crossed his path. An oracle promised liberation from this plague provided I, the king's daughter, were thrown to the beast for food. My father's people pressed him to save them, and in despair he had me fettered to this cliff."

She had hardly finished when the waves parted with a rushing noise, and from the depths of the ocean rose a monster whose broad breast stretched over the surface of the waters. The girl screamed with terror, and her parents hastened toward her, frantic with grief, her mother's sorrow doubled by her sense of guilt. They embraced their daughter but could think of nothing to do but weep and lament.

Then Perseus spoke: "There is always time enough for tears, but the hour to act passes swiftly. I am Perseus, son of Zeus and Danae. Magic wings carry me through the air, and the Medusa fell by my sword. Even if this girl were free and had her choice among many suitors, I should make no mean husband for her. Yet I woo her now, as she is, and offer to save her." Who could have hesitated under such circumstances? The happy parents promised him not only their daughter but their own kingdom as her dowry.

While they were still intent on questioning each other, the monster approached like a ship with the wind full in her sails, and was soon only a stone's throw from the cliff. Then the youth took off from land, thrusting against it with his foot, and bounded into the upper air. The beast saw his shadow on the sea and made for it with furious speed, scenting an enemy who threatened to cheat it of its prey. Perseus darted from the sky like an eagle, landed on the animal's back, and plunged the weapon with which he had killed the Medusa into its body just below the neck, up to the very hilt. Hardly had he drawn forth the blade, when the scaly thing now leaped high into the air, now dived deep into the tide, and there raged in all directions like a boar pursued by the pack. Perseus struck at it again and again until the black blood gushed from its throat. But his wings were dripping, and he no longer dared trust to his water-logged plumage. Fortunately he espied a reef whose highest point projected from the waves. With his left hand he supported himself on this slender pinnacle, while his right drove the blade twice, three, four times, into the monster's bowels. The current carried the vast body away, and soon it vanished from the face of the deep. Perseus had sprung ashore. He climbed the cliff and loosed the bonds of the girl, who welcomed him with a look of gratitude and love. He brought her to her rejoicing parents, and the golden palace flung its gates wide for the bridegroom.

The wedding feast was still steaming on the board, and the hours sped nimbly by in carefree happiness, when the courts suddenly filled with a muttering throng. Phineus, the brother of King Cepheus, who had wooed his niece Andromeda but abandoned her in her need, had come to renew his claims, supported by a host of armed men. Brandishing his spear, he entered the wedding-hall and cried out to Perseus, who listened in amazement: "I have come to avenge the theft of my promised bride. Neither your wings nor Zeus, your father, will help you escape me!" And even as he spoke he aimed his spear.

Then Cepheus rose and called to his brother. "You are mad!" he said. "What is driving you to this evil deed? It was not Perseus who robbed you of your beloved. You gave her up when we were forced to consent to her death, and you stood by while she was being bound and failed to offer aid either as her uncle or her lover. Why did you not carry off the prize from the cliff yourself? The least you can do now is leave her to him who has won her fairly and comforted my old age by preserving my daughter for me!"

Phineus did not deign to reply. He shot angry glances, now

at his brother, now at his rival, as if weighing in his mind which of the two should be his first victim. After that instant of hesitation, however, he hurled his spear at Perseus with a force doubled by rage. But he missed, and the weapon buried its point in a cushion on one of the couches. And now Perseus leaped up and flung his javelin toward the door through which Phineus had entered, and it would have pierced his breast had he not saved himself by darting behind the altar. As it was, the weapon struck the forehead of one of his companions, and now his entire retinue pressed forward and engaged in a hand-to-hand fight with the wedding guests, so rudely startled from the banquet. They strove hard and long, but the intruders outstripped the guests in numbers, and at last Perseus found himself surrounded by Phineus and his warriors. Arrows whirred through the air like hailstones in a storm. Perseus covered his back by standing up against a column and from this point of vantage turned upon his foes, checked their forward surge, and slew one after another. But there were too many of them, and only when he realized that valor alone would not avail him here did he resort to the last sure means at his disposal. "Since you force me to it," he cried, "my old enemy shall help me! Let whatever friend I have here turn his head away!" With this he drew the Medusa's head from the wallet he always wore slung across his shoulder and held it up to the nearest assailant. The man cast a rapid glance at the object before him and laughed in derision. "Go, find someone else to impress with your miracles," he shouted. But even as he lifted his hand to throw the javelin, he turned to stone, his hand still raised in mid-air. And the same thing happened to one after another. When only two hundred were left, Perseus held the head of the Medusa so high that all could see it at once, and the whole two hundred stopped in their tracks and became rock. Not until then did Phineus feel a qualm at his unrighteous warfare. Right and left he saw nothing but statues, and when he called to his friends, no one answered. He touched the flesh of those nearest him with unbelieving fingers, but it had turned to marble! Then at last he succumbed to terror, and his defiance changed to confusion. "Only leave me my life," he pleaded. "The bride and the realm shall be yours!" But in his sadness at the death of his new friends, Perseus was implacable. "Traitor," he replied, "I shall found an enduring monument to you in the house of my parents-in-law," and though Phineus tried to evade it, he was forced to look upon that awful head. The tears in his eyes stiffened to stone, and there he stood with cowardly mien, arms hanging at his sides, in the humble attitude of a servant.

And now Perseus could take home his beloved Andromeda. Long, radiant days lay in store for him, and he even found his mother Danae again. But he could not escape being the tool which brought disaster to his grandfather Acrisius, who, for fear of the oracle, had fled to an alien land, to the king of the Pelasgians. Here he was attending athletic contests, held on a certain festival day, when Perseus, bound on a voyage to Argos, arrived on the scene. He took part in the games and by unlucky chance struck Acrisius with the discus. When he knew what he had done, and who it was he had killed, he deeply mourned the dead, buried his grandfather beyond the confines of the city, and bartered the kingdom he had inherited. And now envious Fate stopped persecuting him. Andromeda bore him many beautiful sons, and in them their father's glory lived on.

CREUSA AND ION

ERECHTHEUS, king of Athens, had a beautiful daughter named Creusa. Without her parents' knowledge she had become the bride of Apollo and borne him a son whom, for fear of her father's wrath, she hid in a basket and placed in the grotto where she and the sun-god had so often met secretly. Her hope was that the immortals would have pity on the child. In order that the newborn boy might not be without some token of his identity, she put upon him a necklace linked of small golden dragons, which she had worn as a girl. Apollo, whose divine insight revealed to him the birth of his son, did not want to betray his beloved nor fail to help the boy, so he turned to his brother Hermes, the messenger of the gods, for—since he was a go-between familiar to both heaven and earth—he could walk among men without attracting undue attention.

"Dear brother," said Phoebus, "a mortal, the daughter of the king of Athens, has borne me a child and, for fear of her father, has hidden it in a grotto. Help me rescue my son! Take him to my oracle at Delphi in the basket in which you will find him, and with the linen in which he is wrapped, and lay him down on the threshold of the temple. The rest you may leave to me, for he is my own child, and I shall see to him."

And Hermes, the winged god, sped to Athens, found the boy in the hiding-place Apollo had described, and carried him to Delphi in the basket woven of willow withes. There he set it down at the gates of the temple and raised the lid a little, so that the child might be seen easily. This he did by night. The next morning at sunrise, when the Delphic priestess moved toward the temple, her eyes fell on the infant asleep in the basket. She took it for the child of some ne'er-do-well and was about to thrust it away from the sacred threshold when the god filled her spirit with compassion for his son. So she lifted him tenderly and reared him herself, and the boy played about his father's altar and knew nothing of his parents. He grew tall and handsome, and the inhabitants of Delphi, who had become accustomed to seeing in him a little guardian of the temple, now put him in charge of the precious offerings made to the god. He lived an honorable and dedicate life in the precincts of Phoebus Apollo.

In all these years Creusa had heard nothing from her divine husband and could not help thinking he had forgotten both her and her son. About this time the Athenians began to wage a fierce war with the people of the neighboring island of Euboea, and in the end the Euboeans were defeated, largely because a certain stranger from Achaea brought particularly effective aid to the Athenians. It was Xuthus, a son of Aeolus, who was himself a son of Zeus. In return for his assistance he asked, and was granted, Creusa's hand in marriage. But it seemed as though the sun-god took revenge on his beloved for marrying another, for she did not conceive, but lived childless. After a number of years it occurred to her to go to the oracle of Delphi and pray for the fertility of her womb. This was just what Apollo wanted.

The princess and her husband, accompanied by a small retinue of servants, set out for Delphi. At the very moment they reached the temple, the son of Apollo crossed the threshold to sweep the court with laurel twigs, according to the custom. His glance rested on the woman of noble bearing who came toward the temple, weeping at sight of the sanctuary. Struck by her air of majesty, he ventured to ask the cause of her sorrow.

"I do not wonder," she answered with a sigh, "that my sadness drew your attention to me. For the fate I mourn may well be visible in my face."

"It is not my wish to intrude upon your grief," said the boy. "But—if you will—tell me who you are and from whence you have come."

"I am Creusa," the princess replied. "My father's name is Erechtheus, and Athens is my native land."

In eager excitement the boy cried out: "What a glorious land! How famous the family from which you are descended! Is it true—what we have seen pictured—that your father's grandfather Erichthonius came up out of the earth like a young tree? That the goddess Athene placed the earth-born child in a chest, with two dragons to guard it, and brought it for safekeeping to the daughters of Cecrops? And that these could not check their curiosity, opened the chest and—beholding the boy—were stricken with madness, so that they hurled themselves to their death from the rocks of the citadel?"

Creusa nodded silently, for the story of her ancestors had reminded her of the fate of her lost son. But he, standing before her, continued his guileless questioning. "And tell me, noble princess," he asked, "is it also true that in obedience to an oracle your father Erechtheus sacrificed his daughters, your sisters, with their full consent, in order to overcome his foes? And if so, how is it that you alone escaped death?"

"I was only just born," said Creusa. "I lay in my mother's arms."

"And did the earth split and devour your father Erechtheus?" persisted the boy. "Did Poseidon really destroy him with his trident, and is his grave near a grotto dear to Pythian Apollo, whom I serve?"

"O stranger, speak not of that grotto!" Creusa interrupted him with mournful agitation. "It was the scene of a breach of faith and a great wrong." For a while she was silent; then she collected herself and told the youth, in whom she saw only the guard of the temple, that she was the wife of Prince Xuthus and had come to Delphi with him to implore the god to grant her sons. "Phoebus Apollo," she said with a sigh, "knows the cause of my childlessness. He alone can help me."

"So you have no children?" the youth asked her sadly.

"None," said Creusa. "And I envy your mother so fair a son."

"I know nothing of my mother, nor of my father," the boy answered dejectedly. "I never lay at my mother's breast, nor do I know how I came here. All that my foster-mother, the priestess of this temple, told me is that she took pity upon me once and brought me up. As far back as I can remember, the house of the god has been my dwelling. I am his servant."

As she listened the princess grew thoughtful, but her thoughts were vague and did not take definite shape. "I know a woman whose fate is very like your mother's," she said. "It is for her sake I have come to consult the oracle. And I shall confide her secret to you, who are the god's servant, before her husband arrives. He accompanied her upon this journey but stopped on the way to hear the oracle of Trophonius. This woman claims that she was the wife of Phoebus Apollo before she married the man who is now her husband, and that she bore the god a child. This son she exposed in a certain place, and ever since that time she has not known whether he is alive or dead. On this my friend's behalf I have come to ask whether her son yet lives or is long since dead."

"How long ago was all this?" asked the youth.

"If the child lived," said Creusa, "he would be of your age."

"Oh, how like my own is the destiny of your friend!" cried the youth sorrowfully. "She is looking for her son, and I seek my mother. But what happened to her took place in a far-off land, and we are strangers to each other. Do not hope, however, that the god will give you the answer you desire. For in your friend's name you have come to accuse him of faithlessness, and he will not wish to pronounce judgment upon himself."

"Stop!" said Creusa. "There comes the husband of the woman I was speaking of. Try to forget what I have told you—perhaps too readily and openly."

Xuthus advanced joyfully toward his wife. "Creusa!" he

called out to her, "Trophonius has given me happy tidings. I shall not leave this place without a child! But who is this with you? Who is this youthful priest?"

The boy modestly approached the prince and told him that he was only Apollo's servant, that the noblest among the men of Delphi, chosen by lot, were in the innermost sanctuary, seated around the tripod from which the priestess was preparing to issue the oracle. When the prince heard this, he bade Creusa adorn herself with the sprays which suppliants must carry, and implore a favorable answer from Apollo at the god's altar, which stood in the open under the sky and was wreathed about with branches of laurel. He himself hastened to the shrine within, while the boy remained on guard in the outer court. Before long he heard the doors open and close with a sound like thunder. Then he saw Xuthus hurrying forth with an air of happy bewilderment. Impetuously he flung his arms about the boy, called him "son" over and over, and begged him to clasp him in return and kiss him with filial devotion, until the young servant of Apollo thought the old man must be out of his mind and thrust him aside with youthful strength. But Xuthus would not accept such denial. "The god himself revealed this to me," he insisted. "The oracle issued to me was that the first person I met outside should be my son—a gift of the immortals. How this can be I do not know, for my wife has never borne me a child. But I trust in the god. If and when he will, let him lay bare the secret."

And now the boy too gave up his reserve and yielded himself up to happiness. But not utterly, for even as he kissed and embraced his father he sighed: "O darling mother, where are you? When may I look on your dear face?" He was, moreover, in grave doubt as to what the childless wife of Xuthus, whom— so he thought—he had never seen, would say to this unexpected stepson, and how the city of Athens would receive one who was not his father's legitimate heir. But Xuthus bade him be of good courage, promising to present him to his wife and to his people, not as his son, but as a stranger. He then gave him the name of Ion, the Pacer, because he had clasped him to his breast as his son while the boy paced the court of the temple.

Creusa, in the meantime, had not stirred from Apollo's altar, at which she had prostrated herself in prayer. But her earnest supplication was interrupted by her servants, who came to her lamenting loudly. "Unhappy mistress!" they called out to her, "your husband rejoices, but you will never hold a child in your arms or suckle it at your breast. Apollo has granted him a son, a son full-grown, who was probably borne to him years ago by heaven knows what concubine. He came to meet Xuthus, as he was coming from the temple. And now the father will delight in the son he has recovered while you will live in your empty house like a widow."

The poor princess, whose spirit the gods must have struck with blindness, since she did not solve so transparent a secret, brooded over her sad fate in silence. After a little she inquired after the name and person of this stepson she seemed to have acquired.

"He is the young guard of the temple, the one you spoke with," her servants replied. "His father has named him Ion. We do not know who his mother is. And now your husband has gone to the altar of Dionysus to make secret sacrifice for his son. Later there will be a solemn banquet. He threatened us with death if we told you these things, and only the love we bear you compels us to disobey him. But do not betray us to him!"

And now an old servant, who was completely loyal to the house of Erechtheus and loved his mistress with deep devotion, separated himself from the rest and began to rail against Prince Xuthus, calling him a faithless adulterer. In his passionate zeal he even offered to do away with this bastard son, who would otherwise unlawfully acquire the heritage of the Erechthides. Creusa thought herself deserted both by her husband and her lover of long ago. Confused with sorrow and hopelessness she agreed to the evil plans of the old man and, in return, confided to him her relationship to the god.

When Xuthus left the temple with Ion, he took him to the double peak of Mount Parnassus, where the people of Delphi used to worship Dionysus, whom they held no less sacred than Apollo himself and celebrated with wild orgies. After the prince had poured a libation in gratitude for his son, the boy—with the help of the servants who had accompanied him—set up a large and magnificent tent under the open sky and covered it with tapestries finely woven, which he had bidden them bring from the temple of Apollo. Long tables were placed within, and on them silver platters heaped with rich and dainty foods, and golden cups of fragrant wine. Then Xuthus sent his herald down to the city of Delphi and invited all its inhabitants to share in his joy. Soon the great tent was filled with guests whose heads were garlanded with wreaths. They dined in gaiety and splendor, and when the dessert was served, an aged man, whose curious gestures amused the guests, came out into their midst and took upon himself the office of cup-bearer. Xuthus recognized him as Creusa's old servant, praised his industry and faithfulness, and, for the rest, let him do as he pleased. So he went to the board which held the wines and saw to the cups and the needs of the guests. Toward the end of the banquet, when the flutes were beginning to play, he bade the serving-boys take the small cups from the festal board and set large vessels of gold and silver before the guests. He himself took the most beautiful of all and filled it to the brim with the noblest wine, as if to honor his new young lord, but secretly he added a deadly poison. As he approached Ion and poured a few drops on the ground as a libation, a servant who stood close by inadvertently uttered a curse. Ion, who had grown up among the sacred rites of the temple, knew this for an evil omen, emptied all the wine, and asked for a fresh draught from another cup, from which he himself solemnly poured the libation. All the guests followed his example. Just then a flock of holy doves, bred and fed in the temple of Apollo, under the god's protection, fluttered into the tent, and when they saw the streams of wine flowing on all sides, greedily alighted and began to sip with thrust-out bills. And none was harmed save one which settled where Ion had emptied his first cup. Hardly had she wetted her bill when she began to beat her wings and reel about, until at last she died in spasms of pain, while the guests looked on in amazement.

At this Ion rose from his seat, angrily shook his arms free of his robe, clenched his fists, and cried: "Who is it that wanted to kill me? Speak, old man, for it was you who lent your aid. You blended the draught and handed me the cup!" And he gripped the servant's shoulder and would not release him. Taken off his guard and alarmed, he confessed his crime but shifted all the blame to Creusa. Then Ion, whom Apollo's oracle had declared son of Xuthus, left the tent, and all crowded after him in wild confusion. Under the open sky, within a circle of the noblest Delphians, he lifted his hands and said: "Holy Earth, you are witness that this alien woman of the line of the Erechthides wanted to kill me with poison!"

"Stone her, stone her!" clamored the people as if with a single voice, and they followed Ion in search of Creusa. Xuthus himself was swept away with the rest, hardly aware of what he was about, for the dreadful discovery had dulled his reason.

Creusa was awaiting the outcome of her desperate attempt at Apollo's altar. But it was quite other from what she expected. A gust of sound from far off roused her from her lonely brooding, and as it swelled and came nearer, one of her husband's serving-men, who was loyal to her above all others, ran in the van of the surging mob to tell her that her plot had been discovered and that the people of Delphi were resolved to kill her. "Hold fast to the altar," her women counseled, pressing about her, "and if this holy place does not save you from your murderers, they will, at least, incur blood guilt which no penance can atone for."

In the meantime the furious Delphians, led by Ion, came closer and closer, and even before they reached the temple, the boy's angry words were carried to her by the wind. "The gods have favored me!" he cried. "For this crime, which was never accomplished, was intended to free me of a hostile stepmother. Where is she? Where is that viper with poisonous fangs, that she-dragon with eyes flashing flames of death? Let us hurl the murderess from the highest cliff!" And the throngs around him howled their applause.

They reached the altar, and Ion seized the woman who was his mother, but who seemed to him his deadly foe, and tried to drag her from the sanctuary whose holiness she had invoked to save herself. But Apollo did not wish the son to murder his mother. His divine will carried the news of Creusa's attempted crime and of the punishment to be meted out to her to the ears of his priestess and illumined her spirit, so that she suddenly grasped the meaning in all that had happened and knew that her foster child Ion was not the son of Xuthus, as she herself had declared in ambiguous prophecy, but of Apollo and Creusa.

She left her tripod and fetched forth the basket in which the newborn babe, together with certain tokens she had carefully preserved, had once been found at the gates of the temple at Delphi. With these in her hands, she hastened to the altar where Creusa was struggling with Ion for her very life. When Ion saw the priestess, he at once loosened his hold and advanced toward her reverently. "Welcome, dear mother," he said, "for so I must call you, although you did not give birth to me. Have you heard what wicked designs I have just escaped? Scarcely had I found a father, when my evil stepmother planned my destruction! Now tell me what to do, and I will obey your command."

The priestess lifted a warning finger and said: "Ion, start for Athens with unstained hands, and under favorable auspices."

Ion thought for a moment and then countered: "Is he not stainless who kills his foes?"

"Do not kill until you have heard me," said the priestess in majesty. "Do you see this basket in my hands? And the fresh garlands I have twined around the old withes? In this you were once exposed; from this I took you and reared you."

Ion looked at her in astonishment. "You never told me anything of this, mother," he said. "Why have you kept this secret so long?"

"Because the god wanted you to serve him all these years," she answered. "Now that he has given you a father, he has freed you to go to Athens."

"But how is this basket to help me?" asked Ion.

"It contains the linen in which you were wrapped, dear son," said the priestess.

"Linen?" exclaimed Ion. "Why, that is a token which may lead me to my rightful mother!"

The priestess held out the basket to him, and he eagerly thrust his hand into it and drew out the folded linen. While his eyes, dim with tears, rested on this treasured keepsake, Creusa had gradually regained her composure. A glance at the basket discovered the whole truth to her. She rushed from the altar, and with a single jubilant word, "Son!" clasped Ion in her arms.

With renewed suspicion he tried to free himself from her embraces, thinking that this was only another ruse. But Creusa herself released him and stepping back said: "This linen shall testify to the truth of my words. Do not hesitate to undo the folds. You will find the tokens I shall describe to you. The embroidery which adorns them I myself stitched long ago, when I was a girl. In the middle of the stuff you will see the Gorgon's head, ringed with serpents, as it appears on the shield of Athene."

Dubiously Ion unfolded the linen, but suddenly he cried out joyfully: "O mighty Zeus, here is the Medusa, and these are the serpents!"

"It is not enough," said Creusa. "There must be a necklace of small dragons, wrought of gold, in memory of the dragons in the chest of Erichthonius."

Ion searched the basket and, smiling in delight, drew out the necklace.

"And the last token," said Creusa, "is a wreath of unfading olive leaves which I set on the head of my newborn son. They come from the first olive tree planted in Athens."

Ion put his hand into the bottom of the basket and lifted out a fresh green olive wreath. "Mother, mother!" he cried in a voice broken with sobs, flung his arms around Creusa, and covered her face with kisses. At last he tore himself away and asked about Xuthus, his father. Then Creusa told him the secret of his birth, that he was the son of the god in whose temple he had served so long and faithfully. Now he understood the mystery of those early events and Creusa's mistake and was glad to pardon her designs upon one she did not know. Xuthus embraced Ion, whom he accepted as a stepson and a cherished gift of the gods, and all three went into the temple to give thanks to Apollo. Seated at her tripod, the priestess prophesied that Ion would be the father of a glorious race, to be named Ionians, in honor of him. And to Xuthus she prophesied that Creusa would bear him a son, Dorus, who would father the Dorians, famed throughout the world. Rejoicing in fulfilment and hope, Xuthus and Creusa set out for Athens with the son who had been restored to her, and all the people of Delphi came to speed them on their way.

DAEDALUS AND ICARUS

DAEDALUS of Athens, son of Metion and great-grandson of Erechtheus, also belonged to the family of the Erechthides. He was an architect and a sculptor—the greatest artist of his age. His works were admired in all quarters of the world, and those who beheld his statues said that they lived and moved and saw; that they were not mere likenesses, but animate beings. For while the masters of earlier times had made images with closed eyes and hands hanging slackly down and joined to the sides of the body, he was the first to give his marbles open eyes, hands that reached out, and feet that seemed to walk. But this perfect craftsman was as envious and conceited as he was gifted, and these flaws in his nature tempted him to wrongdoing and drove him into misery.

Talus, his sister's son, whom he instructed in his art, was more talented than his teacher. When he was little more than a boy, he had contrived the potter's wheel, and he became the much-acclaimed inventor of the saw by copying a tool which Nature herself put into his hands; for once, when he had killed a snake, he found he could use its jawbone to cut through a thin strip of wood. Immediately he set about notching a metal bar with a series of zigzag teeth and so made a sturdier replica of the serpent's jaw. He also built the first turning lathe by joining two metal arms, one of which turned while the other stood still. He devised other ingenious implements, all without his uncle's help, and acquired such fame that Daedalus began to fear that the name of his pupil would outshine his own. Overcome with envy he killed the boy in secret, hurling him down from the Acropolis in Athens. But someone saw him digging the grave for his victim and, although he pretended to have been burying a serpent, he was accused of murder and pronounced guilty by the court of the Areopagus.

He escaped and wandered through Attica as a fugitive. Later he fled to Crete, where King Minos afforded him shelter and honored him both as a distinguished artist and as his personal friend. He commissioned Daedalus to build an abode for the Minotaur, a monster of evil origin, whose head and shoulders were those of a bull while the lower part of his body resembled that of a man. The artist drew upon the rich resources of his mind and built the labyrinth, a structure full of intricate windings which bewildered the eyes and the feet of anyone who entered it. The countless corridors twined like the serpentine flow of the Phrygian river Maeander, which seems to turn back upon its course and meet its own waves. When the building was completed and Daedalus went over it, he, its builder, could scarcely find his way back to the threshold of the maze he had constructed. At its very center dwelt the Minotaur, who every ninth year devoured seven youths and seven girls, whom, according to an old agreement, Athens sent as a tribute to the king of Crete.

Notwithstanding the praise and friendship accorded him, Daedalus grew oppressed by his long exile from his beloved country, and the thought of spending the rest of his life on an island encircled by the sea and with a ruler who distrusted even his friends, became more and more tormenting. He pondered a way out. After long reflection he exclaimed exultantly: "Let Minos block my escape on land and sea, but I shall still have the air! Be he ever so great and powerful, there he is helpless, and through the air I shall depart!"

It was no sooner said than done. Daedalus yoked Nature by the vigor of his imagination. He began to arrange the feathers of birds in a certain order, putting the shortest first, and then the longer, so that it looked as if they had grown of themselves in increasing length. In the middle he bound them together with linen threads, and the ends he fastened with wax. Then he bent them to a curve so shallow and so gradual that they appeared to be wings.

Daedalus had a son by the name of Icarus. The boy watched his father's labors, and his childish hands joined eagerly in the work. Now he reached out for the feathers whose down stirred at a breath of wind; now he kneaded the yellow wax between thumb and forefinger. And Daedalus let him be and smiled at the child's awkward efforts. When all was made perfect, he fitted the wings to his body, balanced himself for an instant, and then floated up into the sky, light as any bird. After he had lowered himself to earth, he instructed his young son Icarus, for whom he had fashioned a smaller pair of wings. "Always fly the middle course, dear child," he said. "If you sink too low, your wings will touch the sea, grow waterlogged, and pull you down into the waves. But if you rise too high into the upper regions of the air, your plumage will approach the sun and catch fire. So fly between sea and sun, and stay close behind me." While he warned him, Daedalus bound the wings to his son's shoulders, but the old man's fingers trembled, and an anxious tear fell on his hand. Then he took the boy in his arms and kissed him—for the last time.

And now the two rose upon their wings. The father flew ahead like a bird who guides her tender brood on their first flight from the nest. He beat his wings artfully and with care, so that his son might do likewise, and from time to time glanced back to see how he was succeeding. At first all went well. They passed the island of Samos on their left, then skimmed by Delos and Paros. They saw still other coasts recede and fade, when Icarus, emboldened by the ease of the flight, darted out of his father's track and steered to higher zones with boyish daring. But the threatened punishment came swift and sure. The powerful rays of the sun melted the wax which held the feathers in place, and before Icarus was even aware of it, his wings dissolved and fell from his shoulders. The unhappy boy tried to fly with his bare arms, but these could not hold the air, and suddenly he plunged headlong through the sky. He wanted to call to his father for help, but before he could open his lips, the blue sea had closed above him. It all happened very quickly. And now Daedalus, looking back, as he did from time to time, no longer saw his son. "Icarus, Icarus," he called through the empty space. "Where shall I look for you in the regions of air?" At last his troubled, searching eyes glanced downward, and he saw feathers floating on the water. Descending, he laid aside his wings and paced the coast disconsolately, until the waves cast the boy's body on the sand. And now murdered Talus was avenged. Frantic with sorrow, Daedalus journeyed on to Sicily. The ruler of this great island was King Cocalus, who received Daedalus just as hospitably as Minos of Crete had once done. The work of the artist astonished and delighted the people. For many years one of the sights of that country was an artificial lake he had made, from which a broad river poured into the nearby ocean. On a rocky plateau where there was space for only a few trees and which was so steep that it could never be stormed, he built a city and constructed so narrow and winding a path leading up to it that three or four men sufficed to defend the fortress. King Cocalus chose this invincible stronghold to house his treasures. The third work which Daedalus completed on the island of Sicily was a deep cave. Here he caught the steam of subterranean fires by skillful devices, so that the grotto, usually cold and dank, was as pleasant as a moderately heated room, and the body gradually broke into beneficent sweat without suffering unduly from excessive warmth. He also enlarged Aphrodite's temple on the promontory of Eryx and dedicated to the goddess a golden honeycomb so artfully wrought that it looked as though the bees themselves had modelled the six-sided cells.

But now King Minos, from whom Daedalus had secretly fled, learned that he had taken refuge in Sicily and resolved to pursue him with a host of his men. He equipped a vast fleet and travelled from Crete to Agrigentum. Here he landed his troops and sent a messenger to King Cocalus, asking him to return the fugitive. But Cocalus was galled by the demand of this foreign tyrant and brooded how he might destroy him. He pretended to agree to his request, promised to do as he wished, and to this end invited him to a meeting. Minos came and was received with elaborate hospitality. A warm bath was prepared to rest him from the fatigue of his journey, but when he was in the tub,

Cocalus had it heated until his guest died in the boiling water. The king of Sicily delivered the body to the Cretans, explaining that the king had slipped in the bath and fallen into the hot water. His men, thereupon, buried Minos near Agrigentum with great pomp and splendor and erected a temple to Aphrodite near his grave.

Daedalus remained in Sicily and enjoyed the unwavering favor of his host. He attracted many famous masters to him and became the founder of a school of sculptors there. But he himself had felt no happiness since the death of his son Icarus, and while he made the land which had given him refuge serene and radiant by the work of his hands, he passed into a troubled and mournful old age. He died in Sicily, and there he was buried.

THE STORY OF THE ARGONAUTS

JASON AND PELIAS

JASON was the child of Aeson, son of Cretheus. Now Cretheus had founded the city and the kingdom of Iolcus on a bay in the land of Thessaly, and he left it to his son Aeson. But his younger son Pelias usurped the throne, Aeson died, and Jason, his child, was hurried away to Chiron, the centaur, who had reared many boys to greatness. Chiron gave Jason a training befitting a hero. When Pelias was quite old, he was disturbed by a strange oracle which warned him of one who wore but a single shoe. Pelias had been vainly trying to unravel the meaning of these words, when Jason, who had been in Chiron's care for twenty years, secretly set out for his native land of Iolcus to assert his family right to the throne against Pelias.

In the manner of the heroes of old, he carried two spears, one for throwing, the other for thrusting. The hide of a panther he had strangled covered his travelling garb, and his uncut hair hung loose over his shoulders. On his journey he came to a broad river and there he saw an old woman who begged him to help her

across. It was Hera, the queen of the gods, and the foe of King
Pelias. Jason did not recognize her in this disguise, but full of
pity lifted her and waded the river with her in his arms. Midway
one of his shoes stuck in the mud. Notwithstanding he went on
and arrived in the market place of Iolcus just as his uncle Pelias,
surrounded by the populace, was making a solemn offering to
the sea-god Poseidon. The people marvelled at Jason's tall
beauty and thought that Apollo or Ares had suddenly appeared
among them. Then the king, who was offering the sacrifice, also
noticed the stranger and saw with horror that only one of his
feet was shod. When the holy rites had been performed, he went
up to the youth and, hiding his deep concern, asked him his
name and his country.

Jason answered with dauntless bearing but in a gentle voice
that he was the son of King Aeson, that he had been reared in
Chiron's cave, and had now come to visit his father's house.
Crafty Pelias listened affably and concealed his alarm. He had
his nephew guided through the palace, and with yearning eyes
Jason looked on the halls and chambers which had housed him
in early childhood. For five days he celebrated his return in joyful feasting with friends and kinsmen. On the sixth, they left
the tents which had been put up for the guests and came before
King Pelias. Modestly and with due decorum Jason said to his
uncle: "You know, O king, that I am the son of the rightful king,
and that everything you possess is mine. Yet I shall leave you all
the herds of cattle and sheep and all the fields you took from
my parents. I shall ask nothing of you but the scepter and the
throne which was once my father's."

Pelias bethought himself swiftly. His answer was cordial. "I
am willing to fulfill your demands," he said, "but in return, you
must grant me a request and perform a deed in my stead, which
well becomes your youth, but which I am too old to accomplish.
For a long time, the shade of Phrixus has been haunting my
dreams, and what he asks is that I bring peace to his soul by
journeying to Colchis, to King Aeetes, and fetching back the
fleece of the golden ram. The glory of this quest shall be yours,
and when you return with your magnificent prize, you shall have
the kingdom and the scepter."

THE CAUSE AND THE OUTSET OF
THE VOYAGE OF THE ARGONAUTS

Now the story of the golden fleece was this: Phrixus, the son of
Athamas, king of Boeotia, was ill-treated by his stepmother Ino,
his father's concubine. To save him from her plots, his own
mother, Nephele, abducted him with the help of Helle, his sister.
She set both her children on the back of a winged ram, whose
fleece was of pure gold, a gift she had received from the god
Hermes. On this magical creature brother and sister rode the
air over lands and seas. But the girl became giddy and plunged
to her death in the sea, which ever after was called the Sea of
Helle, or Hellespont. Phrixus arrived safely in the land of Colchis, on the coast of the Black Sea. Here King Aeetes received
him hospitably and married him to one of his daughters. Phrixus
sacrificed the ram to Zeus, who had furthered his flight, and
presented the fleece to the king. Aeetes, in turn, consecrated it
to Ares, nailed it to a tree in a grove sacred to this god, and
put it in the care of a monstrous dragon, for an oracle had told
him that his very life depended on the possession of the ram's
golden pelt.

All over the world the fleece was regarded as a priceless treasure, and rumor had long since brought word of it to Greece.
Many a hero and prince longed to own it, and so Pelias had not
erred when he thought to stir his nephew Jason with the dream
of this wonderful prize. And Jason was, indeed, very willing to
go. He did not see through his uncle's plan to let him perish on
this venture, but gave his solemn word to accomplish the quest.

The most famous heroes of Greece were asked to share in this
bold undertaking. At the foot of Mount Pelion, under Athene's
direction, the best shipbuilder in Greece constructed a splendid
ship of a kind of wood that does not rot in seawater. It had space
for fifty oars and was named Argo after its builder Argus, the
son of Arestor. It was the first long ship in which the Greeks
dared steer out into the open sea. Built into the prow was a piece
of wood from the prophetic oak tree of Dodona, a gift from the
goddess Athene. The sides of the vessel were adorned with rich

carving, yet the ship was so light that the heroes could carry it upon their shoulders for twelve days in succession.

When the whole was completed and the Argonauts gathered around the ship, they cast lots for the places they were to occupy in it. Jason was to command the entire expedition. Tiphys was the helmsman, Lynceus, the keen-eyed, pilot. In the bow of the ship sat glorious Heracles, in the stern Peleus, the father of Achilles, and Telamon, the father of Ajax the Great. Among the rest of the crew were Castor and Polydeuces, the sons of Zeus, Neleus, the father of Nestor, Admetus, the husband of devout Alcestis, Meleager, who had slain the Calydonian Boar, Orpheus, the sweet singer, Menoetius, the father of Patroclus, Theseus, who later became king of Athens, and his friend Pirithous, Hylas, the younger friend of Heracles, Poseidon's son Euphemus, and Oileus, the father of Ajax the Less. Jason had consecrated his ship to Poseidon, and before leaving all the heroes made solemn offering and prayer to him and the other gods of the sea.

When all had taken their places they weighed anchor. The fifty rowers began to ply their oars, which dipped in and out of the sea with a regular rhythm. A favorable wind swelled the sails, and soon the harbor of Iolcus was left behind. Orpheus stirred the courage of the Argonauts with the notes he struck on his lyre and by the compelling sweetness of his voice. Blithely they sped by promontories and islands. But on the second day a storm arose and drove them into the harbor of the island of Lemnos.

THE ARGONAUTS AT LEMNOS

On this island, the women, only a year ago, had killed their husbands and, indeed, all the men in the land, because they had brought concubines from Thrace and Aphrodite had roused their wives to jealousy and rage. Hypsipyle had saved only her father, King Thoas, and hidden him in a chest which she entrusted to the sea. Ever since, the women of Lemnos had been in constant fear of an attack from the Thracians, the kinsmen of their rivals, and often turned their frightened eyes toward the open sea. So now when they saw the Argo nearing the coast, they armed themselves from head to foot and rushed out of the gates and down to the shore like a host of Amazons. The heroes were greatly surprised when they saw the strand swarming with armed women and not a single man. In a small boat they dispatched a herald to this curious gathering, and when the women had taken him to their unwedded queen, Hypsipyle, he conveyed in courteous words the Argonauts' request for hospitable shelter. The queen assembled her women about her in the market place of the city and seated herself on her father's marble throne. Next to her, leaning on a cane, was her aged nurse, and on each side sat four golden-haired girls of delicate loveliness. After she had informed the gathering of the peaceful intent of the Argonauts, she rose and said: "Dear sisters, we have committed a great crime, and in our madness deprived ourselves of our men. We ought not reject those who would be our friends. On the other hand, we must see to it that they learn nothing of what we have done. Therefore my counsel is that we send food and wine and all else the strangers may need down to their ship, and with this courtesy keep them from our walls."

The queen seated herself again, and now the old nurse with much effort raised her nodding head and said: "Send the strangers gifts, by all means. That is well done. But do not forget what awaits you when the Thracians come. And even should a merciful god hold them off, does this mean that you are safe from all ills? Old women like myself have no cause for concern. We shall die before need becomes pressing, before our supplies are exhausted. But how do you younger ones propose to live? Will the oxen place themselves under the yoke unbidden and draw the plough through the fields? Will they harvest the ripened grain in your stead, when summer is over? For you yourselves will not wish to perform these and other galling labors! I advise you not to spurn the protection that offers itself, and which you need. Trust your lands and possessions to these noble-born strangers and let them govern your beautiful city."

This counsel found favor with all the women of Lemnos. The queen sent one of the girls seated near her to accompany the herald to the ship and inform the Argonauts of the decision reached by the assembly, and the heroes were pleased with this message. They had no doubt at all that Hypsipyle, after her father's death, had peacefully succeeded to his throne. Jason slung his crimson mantle, a gift from Athene, over his shoulder and strode toward the city, radiant as a star. When he entered the gates, the women streamed out to meet him in clamorous greeting and were glad of their guest. He, however, kept his eyes upon the ground both from modesty and good breeding and hastened toward the palace. Handmaids flung wide the tall portals for him, and the young woman who had gone to the ship conducted him to her mistress's chamber. Here he seated himself opposite her in a sumptuous chair. Hypsipyle lowered her smooth white lids, and her virgin cheeks were rose-red with blushes. Shyly she addressed him with flattering words: "Stranger, why did you hesitate to enter our gates? In this city there are no men for you to fear. Our husbands broke faith with us. With Thracian women, whom they captured in wars, they moved into the country of their concubines and took with them their sons and serving-men, while we remained behind—helpless! And so, if it please you, come and be one of our people, and, if you will, rule over your men and over us in my father Thoas' stead. This country will find favor in your eyes; it is by far the most fruitful island in these seas. You, who have come on ahead, go tell your companions of my offer."

These were her words, but what she did not say was that the men had been murdered. Jason replied: "O queen, with thankful hearts we accept the help you are willing to give us, who are in need. As soon as I have told my companions of your offer I shall return to your city, but do you yourself retain your scepter and your island! It is not that I spurn them, but danger and conflicts await me in a far country."

He gave the queen his hand in parting and hurried back to the shore. The women soon followed him there in swift chariots laden with many gifts. It was easy for them to persuade the heroes, who had already heard Jason's report, to enter the city and lodge in their houses. Jason lived in the palace itself, the others here and there. Only Heracles, who despised life among women, remained behind in the ship with a few chosen companions. And now the gaiety of feast and dance surged through the city. The fragrant smoke of offerings floated to the sky, as both the dwellers in the city and their guests paid honor to Hephaestus, the patron god of the island, and to his wife Aphrodite.

Departure was put off from day to day, and the heroes would have loitered on indefinitely with their lovely hostesses, had not Heracles come from the ship and gathered them about him without the women's knowledge.

"You are a wretched lot!" he told them. "Were there not enough women for you in your own country? Did you have to come here for want of wives? Do you wish to plough the fields of Lemnos like peasants? Why, of course! A god will fetch the fleece for us and lay it at our feet! It would be better if each of us returned to his own country. Let Jason marry Hypsipyle, populate the island of Lemnos with his sons, and ever after listen to the tale of heroic feats performed by others."

No one dared raise his eyes to the hero or contradict him. They left the gathering and made ready to depart. But the women of Lemnos, who guessed their intention, beset them like buzzing bees with pleading and lament. At last, however, they submitted to the men's decision. Hypsipyle, her eyes full of tears, went apart from the rest, took Jason by the hand and said: "Go, and may the gods grant you and your companions the golden fleece you desire! Should you ever wish to return to us, this island and my father's scepter await you. But I know very well that you do not plan to come back. Think of me, at least, when you are far away."

Jason left the queen filled with admiration for her goodness and poise. He was the first to board the ship, and the others came after him. They loosed the ropes which moored the vessel to the shore, the rowers pulled at their oars, and in a short time the Hellespont was left behind.

THE ARGONAUTS IN THE LAND OF THE DOLIONES

Winds from Thrace swept the ship toward the coast of Phrygia, where earthborn giants, untamed savages, lived side by side with the peaceful Doliones on the island of Cyzicus. These giants had six arms, one springing from each massive shoulder, and two on each side. The Doliones were descended from the sea-god, who protected them even against their monstrous neighbors. Their king was devout Cyzicus. When news of the ship and its company of men reached the island, he and his entire people went to meet the Argonauts, received them hospitably, and urged them to anchor their ship in the harbor of their city. For an oracle given long ago bade the king greet the band of divine heroes with kindly words and above all to refrain from fighting them. And so he supplied them with an abundance of wine and slaughtered beasts. He was still a youth, and his beard was just beginning to grow. His young wife, whom he had taken from her father's house not long before, was awaiting him in the palace, but obedient to the oracle, he stayed to share the strangers' meal. Then they told him of the aim and the purpose of their quest, and he instructed them what path to take.

The next morning they climbed a high mountain, so that they might see for themselves where the island lay in the ocean. In the meantime the giants had rushed forth from the other side and closed off the harbor with tremendous blocks of stone. But in the harbor lay the Argo, guarded by Heracles, who had again refused to leave the ship. When he saw the huge fellows begin working their mischief, he shot many of them to death with his arrows. And now the other heroes returned and wrought such havoc among the giants with their spears and arrows that they were utterly beaten and lay in the narrow harbor like a forest of hewn trees, some with head and breast in the sea and their feet on the sandy shore, others with their limbs in the water and head and breast on the strand, but all of them destined to be the prey of fishes and the food of birds.

When the heroes had thus successfully emerged from the battle, they weighed anchor and sailed out to sea. But in the night the wind changed, and a storm drove in upon them from the opposite side, so that they were forced to cast anchor near land. This land was again the island of the hospitable Doliones, but the Argonauts thought they were on the coast of Phrygia. Nor did their erstwhile hosts, whom the noise of the landing had roused from sleep, recognize the friends with whom they had caroused so merrily only the day before; they reached for their arms, and an ill-starred battle ensued. Jason himself thrust his spear into the heart of the king, and neither did the slayer know his victim nor the victim the slayer. Finally the Doliones were put to flight and shut themselves up in their city. The next morning both sides saw their mistake.

Jason, the leader of the Argonauts, and all his men were filled with bitter grief when they beheld good king Cyzicus lying in his own blood. For three days, the heroes and the Doliones together mourned their dead. They tore their hair and arranged bouts and funeral feasts in honor of the slain. Then the Argonauts set out on their way. But Clite, the wife of the fallen king, strangled herself with a rope, for she could not bear to go on living now that her husband was no more.

HERACLES LEFT BEHIND

After a stormy voyage, the heroes landed in the bay of Bithynia where the city of Cius lies. The Mysians, who lived here, received them kindly, heaped dry faggots for a fire to warm them, piled green leaves to make soft beds, and, even though night had fallen, served them with an abundance of wine and food.

Heracles, who scorned all comforts, left his companions seated at their feast and went off into the woods to carve himself a better oar for the work of the coming morning. He soon found a pine which seemed just what he wanted, not too thick with boughs, and in length and breadth somewhat like a slender poplar. He laid his bow and quiver aside, threw off his lion's skin, put his club down next to it, gripped the trunk with both hands, and pulled the tree out by the roots—the earth still clinging to them —so that it looked as if a tempest had torn it from the ground.

Now his young friend Hylas had also left the banquet board. He had risen and taken a bronze pitcher to draw water for his master and friend, in order to prepare for his return. On an expedition against the Dryopes, Heracles had killed the boy's father in a dispute, but had taken Hylas himself with him and reared him as his servant and friend. When the beautiful boy reached the well, the moon was full and radiant. As he leaned over the water, pitcher in hand, the nymph of the well saw him, and was so charmed by his beauty that she twined her left arm around him, while with her right hand she clutched his elbow and drew him down into the depths. One of the heroes, Polyphemus by name, who was awaiting Heracles not far from the well, heard the boy cry out for help. But he could not find him. Just then he saw Heracles coming from the woods. "Must I be the first to tell you the sad news?" Polyphemus called to him. "Your Hylas went to the well and did not return. Robbers must have seized him, or perhaps wild animals. I myself heard him cry out in distress." When Heracles heard this, the sweat broke out on his forehead, and the blood beat painfully in his veins. Angrily he threw down the pine and, as a bull stung by the gadfly leaves the herd and the herdsman, he ran through the thickets to the well, uttering cries of grief.

The morning star stood over the mountain peak, and a favorable wind arose. The helmsman urged the heroes to make the most of it and come aboard. They were gliding along gaily in the faint flush of dawn, when too late they remembered that two of their number, Polyphemus and Heracles, had been left behind. A stormy quarrel broke out over whether or not they should sail on without their valiant friends. Jason said nothing. He sat in silence, and sorrow gnawed at his heart. But Telamon was overcome with wrath. "How can you sit there so quietly?" he called to their leader. "I suppose you are afraid that Heracles might put your own prowess to shame! But why do I waste words! Even if all our companions agree with you, I alone should turn back to the man we have deserted."

And with this he gripped Tiphys, the helmsman, by the breast, and would have compelled him to put about for the land of the Mysians, had not Zetes and Calais, the two sons of Boreas, seized his arm and held him back with angry words. But while they were still contending with one another, Glaucus, a god of the sea, rose out of the foamy tide, grasped the stern of the ship with his strong hand, and called to the voyagers: "Do not quarrel, O heroes! You shall not take fearless Heracles with you to the land of Aeetes, against the will of Zeus! Destiny has decreed other labors for him. A love-struck nymph stole Hylas, and Heracles has remained behind because of his yearning for him."

After he had revealed these things, Glaucus sank back into the sea, and the dark waters swirled over him. Telamon was ashamed. He went up to Jason, laid his hand in his, and said: "Do not bear me a grudge, Jason. Sorrow led me astray and I

spoke rash words. Let my fault be gone with the winds, and may
we wish each other well as before."

Jason was glad to make peace, and they journeyed over the
waves with a fresh and fair breeze. Polyphemus made his home
with the Mysians and built them a city. But Heracles went on
where the will of Zeus called him.

POLYDEUCES AND THE KING OF THE BEBRYCIANS

The next morning, at sunrise, they cast anchor near a peninsula stretching far into the sea. Here Amycus, king of the wild
Bebrycians, had his stables and country house. This sovereign
had imposed an irksome rule upon all strangers: that no one
was to leave his territory without first having boxed with him.
In this way he had already done away with a great number of
his neighbors. On this occasion also he approached the ship which
had just arrived and challenged the oarsmen with mocking
words. "Listen, you rovers of the sea," he called to them, "there
is one thing you must know: that is that no stranger may quit
my country without having boxed with me. So choose the best
man among you and send him to me, or your doom will be sealed."

Now it happened that one of the Argonauts was the best boxer
in Greece, Polydeuces, the son of Leda. Stung by the challenge,
he said to the king: "Do not wrangle with us. We are ready to
obey your rules, and I am your man."

The king of the Bebrycians looked at the bold hero, and his
eyes rolled in their sockets like those of a wounded mountain
lion glaring at its assailant. But young Polydeuces was serene
as a star in the heavens and swung his hands about in the air to
see if, what with the long hours of rowing, they had lost their
suppleness.

When the heroes left the ship, the two boxers took up their
positions opposite each other. One of the king's slaves threw
two pairs of boxing thongs on the ground between them. "Choose
whichever pair you like," said Amycus. "I do not want to go to
the trouble of selecting them by lot. You will soon be able to tell
from your own experience that I am an excellent tanner and
can darken cheeks with blood."

Polydeuces smiled quietly, took the thongs which lay nearest him, and had his friends strap them to his hands. The king of the Bebrycians did the same, and now the boxing began. Like a breaker which rushes upon a ship and whose force the skillful helmsman counters only with great difficulty, the king hurled himself against the Greek and allowed him no breathing-spell. Yet lithe Polydeuces always succeeded in dodging the onslaught and suffered no wounds. Soon he found out his adversary's weak side and dealt him many an unparried thrust. But the king too took his advantage where he saw it, and so jaws rang with the sound of blows, and teeth rattled with thwack after thwack, nor did they stop until they both were panting, and had to step to one side to rest and dry the sweat streaming from every pore. Hardly had they resumed the bout when Amycus missed his opponent's head and struck only his shoulder, while Polydeuces hit him near the ear, so that the bones in his head cracked and he dropped to his knees in great pain.

The Argonauts shouted with joy, but the Bebrycians came to the aid of their king and attacked Polydeuces with their clubs and hunting spears. His companions whipped out their swords and threw themselves into the struggle. In the end the Bebrycians were put to flight and sought refuge in the interior of their country. The heroes then entered their stables and seized the herds, so that they had rich spoils. They spent the night ashore, bound up their wounds, and made offerings to the gods, nor did sleep weigh upon their lids as they passed the brimming cup. From the laurel to which the ship was bound with ropes they broke sprays to wreathe their brows, and sang a hymn of praise while Orpheus plucked the strings of his lyre. The very shore seemed to listen in silent delight while they sang of Polydeuces, victorious son of Zeus.

PHINEUS AND THE HARPIES

Dawn put an end to their feasting, and they continued on their way. After more adventures they cast anchor opposite the land of Bithynia, in which Phineus, son of the hero Agenor, now dwelt. This Phineus had been afflicted with great misfortune. Because

he had abused the gift of prophecy Apollo had granted him, he had, in his old age, become blind, and those evil witch-like birds, the harpies, would not allow him to eat his food in peace. They snatched whatever they could, and whatever food remained they polluted so intolerably that no one could touch it. Phineus had only one consolation, an oracle of Zeus to the effect that he would eat unmolested when the sons of Boreas came with the Greek oarsmen. And so, when the old man heard of the arrival of the Argo, he left his chamber, starved to a very skeleton, a mere shadow. His limbs trembled with weakness, he supported his tottering steps with a staff, and when he reached the Argonauts, he sank to the ground in exhaustion. They surrounded the unhappy old man, appalled at his appearance. When he heard them about him and had collected his strength, he spoke to them pleadingly. "O noble heroes, if you are really those foretold by the oracle, help me! For the goddesses of vengeance have not only taken my eyesight but have also sent upon me these horrid birds to deprive me of my food. You will not be giving your aid to a stranger, for I am a Greek—Phineus, the son of Agenor. Once I was king of Thrace, and the sons of Boreas, who must be partners in your quest and are destined to save me, are the younger brothers of Cleopatra, who was my wife in that land."

At these words, Zetes, the son of Boreas, threw himself into the arms of the king and promised that, with the help of his brother, he would free him from those preying birds. Then they prepared a meal for him, but scarcely had the king touched the food when the harpies headed down from the clouds like a gale and greedily perched on the platters. The heroes shouted and cried out, but the birds were undisturbed and stayed until they had devoured the last crumb. Then they flew into the air, leaving a horrible stench behind. Zetes and Calais, the sons of Boreas, pursued them with drawn swords, and Zeus lent them wings and untiring strength, which they had need of, indeed, for the harpies sped faster than the swift western wind. But the sons of Boreas were close on their trail and at times could almost lay hands on the monsters. At last they were so near that they would certainly have slain them, had not Iris, the messenger of Zeus, suddenly appeared and addressed the two heroes. "Sons of Boreas," she said, "the harpies sent by Zeus must not be slain by the sword. But I swear to you by the Styx, on which the gods take their oath, that these birds shall no longer trouble the son of Agenor." At that Zetes and Calais gave up the pursuit and returned to the ship.

In the meantime the Greek heroes busied themselves about the aged Phineus and prepared a sacrificial feast, to which they invited the starving old man. Avidly he ate of the clean and abundant food, though he seemed to be satisfying his hunger as if in a dream. Night came, and while they were awaiting the return of the sons of Boreas, King Phineus made them a prophecy in gratitude for what they had done for him.

"First," he said, "you will come to the Symplegades in the narrows of the Euxine Sea. These are two steep, rocky islands, which have no roots in the bottom of the ocean but are afloat in the water. Often the current drives them toward each other, and then the tide between them swells with turbulent force. If you do not want to be ground to splinters, along with all you possess, row through them as swiftly as a dove flies. After that you will come to the land of the Mariandyni, which boasts the entrance to the underworld. You will pass many other promontories, rivers, and coasts, the women's state of the Amazons, and the land of the Chalybes, who dig iron out of the earth by the sweat of their brows. Finally you will come to the coast of Colchis, where the river Phasis pours its broad stream into the sea. You will see the towered stronghold of King Aeetes, and there the sleepless dragon guards the golden fleece, which is spread over the topmost boughs of an oak-tree."

As the heroes listened to the old man, they could not suppress a shudder, and were just about to question him further when the sons of Boreas flew down into their midst and gladdened the king with the message of lovely Iris.

THE SYMPLEGADES

Full of gratitude and moved in heart, Phineus took leave of his liberators, who sailed on to new adventures. For forty days a wind blew from the northwest and halted their voyage until offerings and prayers to all the twelve gods once more speeded them on their way. They were sailing along smoothly and swiftly when a thunderous crash struck upon their ears. This was the roar of the Symplegades striking together and recoiling, mixed with the vast echoes from the shore and the hiss of the frothing sea. Tiphys, the helmsman, stood watchfully at the tiller. Young Euphemus rose in his place, holding a dove in the palm of his right hand, for Phineus had said that if a dove flew fearlessly between the rocks, they too might venture the passage. Euphemus let fly the bird, and all heads were raised in tense expectancy. It sped through, but already the rocks were approaching each other, and the water foamed and churned in the narrow strait. Air and sea were loud with clamor, and now the cliffs met and clipped off the tail feathers of the dove. Yet it had come through unharmed, so Tiphys encouraged the oarsmen in a loud voice. The rocks fell apart, and the current streaming between drew the ship in its wake. Destruction beset them on all sides. A tall breaker surged forward, and the sight was so menacing that they shrank back in terror. Then Tiphys bade them stop rowing. The foaming wave rushed under the keel and lifted the ship high above the rocks closing in on each other. The men strained at the oars until the blades almost seemed to bend. Now the whirl bore them down between the rocks again, and they would surely have been crushed had not Athene, the patron goddess of the Argonauts, thrust the ship forward—though she was invisible to them—until it escaped, with only the tip of the stern shattered.

When the heroes saw the sun and the open sea again, they shed their fears and drew their breath freely, feeling as though they had come up from the underworld. "This did not come about through our own strength," cried Tiphys. "Behind me I felt the divine hand of Athene, pushing the ship strongly through the cleft. Now we have nothing more to fear, for Phineus said that after this danger was passed, all our other labors would seem light."

But Jason shook his head sadly and said: "My good Tiphys, I have tried the gods by allowing Pelias to impose this task upon me. Rather should I have let him destroy me. Now I must spend my days and nights in sighs and distress, not for myself, but for your lives and welfare, and in pondering how I may save you from peril and return you unharmed to your native land." And Jason said all this only to test his comrades, but they acclaimed him lustily and wanted nothing better than to follow their beloved leader forever.

FURTHER ADVENTURES

The heroes continued on their quest. Tiphys, their faithful helmsman, fell ill and died, and they had to bury him on an alien shore. In his stead they chose one of their number versed in the art of steering, Ancaeus, but for a long time he refused to take over this difficult office. Finally Hera inspired him with courage and confidence, and he took his place at the tiller and guided the ship as well as Tiphys had done. Under his direction, on the twelfth day, they made for the open sea and soon, with all sails spread, came to the mouth of the river Callichorus.

There, on a mound near the shore of the sea, they saw the tomb of the hero Sthenelus, who had gone forth against the Amazons with Heracles, and, struck by an arrow, had died in this place. They were about to continue their voyage, when the sorrowful shade of Sthenelus, whom Persephone had given leave to ascend from the underworld, appeared to them and gazed at his kinsmen with longing eyes. He stood on the very top of the mound, looking just as he did when he went forth to battle, with a crest of four scarlet feathers streaming from his helmet. But he was visible for only a few brief moments, and then sank back into the cheerless depths of the earth. The heroes rested on their oars, appalled at the apparition, and no one but Mopsus, the seer, understood what it was the departed spirit wanted. He counselled his companions to offer a libation for the peace of the slain man's soul. Quickly they lowered the sails, made fast the ship, and ranged themselves around the grave. They sprinkled it with libations and slaughtered sheep and burned them.

Then they proceeded on their journey and, after a time, came to the mouth of the river Thermodon, which was like no other in all the world. For it rose from a spring far up in the mountains, but soon after leaving its source separated into a great number of branches and rushed toward the ocean in so many streams that, indeed, it lacked only four to make up a hundred. They swarmed into the open sea like writhing snakes.

At the widest of the outlets dwelt the Amazons. This nation of women was descended from the god Ares and loved the trade of war. Had the Argonauts landed here, they would doubtless have become embroiled in bloody battle with these women, whose courage equalled that of the bravest men. They did not all live in one city but were scattered over the countryside in separate tribes. A propitious wind from the west drove the Argonauts far from these strange beings.

After a day and a night, just as Phineus had foretold, they came to the land of the Chalybes. Its people did not plough the earth. They planted no fruit trees, nor did they pasture herds on dewy meadows. Their sole occupation was to dig in the hard earth for ore and iron and exchange these for food. No dawn ever saw them making merry. Every day they labored in pits as black as night and in the heavy murk of smoke.

The Argonauts passed many other peoples. Once, when they were near an island called Aretia, or the island of Ares, a bird, native to that country, flew toward them moving his wings with powerful strokes. When he was immediately above the ship, he shook his pinions and dropped a pointed plume. It pierced the

shoulder of Oileus, and the pain was so great that he let the oars
slip from his fingers. His companions looked at the winged missile in astonishment, and the one nearest him drew out the feather
and bound up the wound. Soon a second bird appeared. Clytius,
who had been holding his bow in readiness, shot him in flight,
and he fell into the ship.

"The island is nearby," said Amphidamas who was an experienced voyager. "Beware of those birds. There are probably so
many of them that, if we landed, we should not have enough
arrows to destroy them. So let us think of some way to drive
these creatures away. Let us all put on our helmets with their
tall, flowing crests and take turns at rowing, while the rest deck
out the ship with shining lances and shields. Then we will raise
our voices in terrifying cries, and when the birds hear us and see
the waving plumes, the sharp lances and the glittering shields,
they will take fright and fly away."

This plan pleased the heroes, and they carried it out in every
detail. Not a living creature did they see as they approached
the island. But when they had come close and rattled their spears,
countless birds flew up from the shore and stormed over the ship.
But just as one closes the shutters of a house to keep out the
hail, so the heroes covered themselves with their shields, and the
sharp quills fell without harming them. The birds themselves,
the terrible Stymphalides, fled far across the sea to the opposite
coast, while the Argonauts followed the advice of King Phineus,
the seer, and landed on the island.

Here they found unexpected friends and companions. For
scarcely had they taken a few steps along the shore, when they
met four youths in tattered clothing and appearing to be in sad
need of everything. One of them came toward them. "Whoever
you may be," he cried, "help the poor shipwrecked! Give us
clothing! Give us food to quench our hunger!"

Jason promised them aid and asked them their names and
descent. "You must have heard of Phrixus, the son of Athamas,"
the youth replied. "He, who brought the golden fleece to Colchis!
King Aeetes gave him his eldest daughter in marriage. We are
his sons, and my name is Argus. Our father Phrixus died a short
time ago, and in obedience to his dying wish we embarked to
fetch the treasures he left in the city of Orchomenus."

The heroes were overjoyed, and Jason greeted the youths as his kinsmen, for his grandfather Cretheus had been the brother of Athamas. The boys went on to tell how their ship had been wrecked in a storm and how a plank had carried them to this inhospitable island. But when the heroes told them of their plan and asked them to share their venture, they did not conceal their horror. "Our grandfather Aeetes," they explained, "is a cruel man. He is said to be a son of Apollo, and this accounts for his superhuman strength. Countless tribes in Colchis are under his sway, and a dreadful dragon guards the fleece."

Some of the heroes paled at this report. But Peleus rose and said: "Do not think that we must necessarily be defeated by the king of Colchis, for we too are the sons of gods! If he refuses to give us the golden fleece of his own accord, we shall wrest it from him in defiance of his power and his men."

During the banquet which followed, they spoke further with one another of this matter. The next morning the sons of Phrixus, clothed and revived, went aboard the ship, and the Argo continued on her voyage. After they had rowed a day and a night, they saw the peaks of the Caucasus mountains looming above the surface of the sea. When twilight fell, they heard a rushing sound over their heads. It was the eagle flying to Prometheus, to feed on his liver. He soared high above the ship, but the beat of his wings was so strong that the sails bellied out as in a high wind. Soon after, they heard Prometheus groan as the giant bird hacked at his entrails. Then the sound died away, and they saw the eagle returning through the lofty regions of the sky.

That very same night they reached their destination, the mouth of the river Phasis. Nimbly they climbed the masts and took down the rigging. Then they rowed up the broad river, whose waters seemed to retreat before the massive hull of their ship. To their left was the lofty Caucasus and Cyta, the capital of Colchis, to the right a far-flung meadow and the sacred grove of Ares, where a dragon with keen, unblinking eyes guarded the golden fleece where it hung in the leafy boughs of a tall oak. And now Jason stepped to the edge of the ship, lifted high in his hand a golden cup brimming with wine, and offered a libation to the river, to Mother Earth, to the gods of that country, and to the heroes who had died on the journey. He begged them all to give him loving help, and to watch over the cables of the ship, which they were about to make fast.

"So now we have reached Colchis safely," said the helmsman. "And the time has come to decide whether we are going to approach King Aeetes in a friendly manner or carry out our intentions in some other way."

"Tomorrow!" cried the tired heroes. Jason bade them cast anchor in a shady bay of the river. They lay down and sank into a sweet sleep, but their rest was brief, for the dawn soon woke them.

JASON IN THE PALACE OF AEETES

In the early morning, the heroes took counsel with one another, and Jason rose and said: "If you, my noble companions, will take my advice, you will remain quietly aboard, but with weapons in your hands, while I, the sons of Phrixus, and two of your number, make our way to the palace of King Aeetes. First I shall try the expedient of courtesy and ask him in seemly words to give us the golden fleece. But I do not doubt that, confident of his strength, he will reject my request. In this way, however, we shall learn from his own lips what it is we must do. And who can be entirely certain but that our words may, after all, strike him favorably? For, on another occasion, did not words induce him to give hospitality and protection to innocent Phrixus, who was fleeing from his stepmother?"

The young heroes approved Jason's scheme, and so he took in his hand the staff of peace and left the ship with the sons of Phrixus and his comrades Telamon and Augeas. They entered a field overgrown with willows, known as the Circean Field. Here, to their horror, they saw many dead bodies hanging in chains. But these were neither criminals nor murdered strangers. The custom in Colchis was to wrap dead men in rawhide, hang them on trees at a distance from the city, and let the air dry the flesh on their bones. To burn or bury them was considered blasphemous, but so that earth might yet have her due, they buried their women.

Colchis had many inhabitants, and in order to protect Jason and his companions from them and from the suspicions of King

Aeetes, Hera, the patroness of the Argonauts, shrouded the city in a thick blanket of mist while they were on their way and did not disperse it until they had reached the palace. They stopped in the court and marvelled at the massive walls of the king's house, at the high gates, and the great pillars. The entire building was circled by a jutting rampart of stone, slit with a series of triangular openings. Silently they crossed the threshold of the forecourt and found spacious arbors covered with grapevines and four ever-flowing fountains. The first bubbled with jets of milk, the second streamed wine, the third fragrant oil, and the fourth water, which was warm in winter and in summer cold as ice. These Hephaestus had artfully contrived, and he had also made for the king bulls of bronze from whose throats blew a fiery breath, and a plough of solid iron. All this he had done out of gratitude to the father of Aeetes, to the sun-god, who had once rescued Hephaestus in the battle with the giants by snatching him away in his chariot.

From this outer court they came to the colonnade of the middle court, which stretched to the left and to the right and opened up vistas of entrance-ways and chambers. Directly opposite were the two main wings of the palace, one the dwelling of King Aeetes himself, the other of his son Absyrtus. The remaining rooms were occupied by the servants and the daughters of the king, Chalciope and Medea. Medea was the younger daughter and rarely seen about, for almost all her time was spent in the temple of Hecate, whose priestess she was. But on this morning Hera, the patron goddess of the Greeks, had put in her heart a desire to stay in the palace. She had just left her chamber to go to her sister, when she suddenly beheld the Greek heroes. At sight of them she uttered a loud cry, whereupon Chalciope hastened forth with all her tirewomen. She too broke into joyful cries and lifted her hands to heaven in thanks, for in the four young heroes she recognized her own sons, the children of Phrixus. They clasped their mother close, and for a long time these five wept and rejoiced at finding one another again.

MEDEA AND AEETES

Finally Aeetes too appeared with Idyia, his wife, for the sounds of jubilation and tears had aroused their curiosity. In a moment the entire forecourt was swarming with excitement. Here slaves were slaughtering a splendid bullock for the new guests; there others were splitting wood for the fire, while still others heated water in great cauldrons. There was not one who was not occupied with something in the service of the king. But unseen by them all, Eros floated high in the air. He drew a pain-bringing arrow from his quiver, dropped down to earth, and, crouching behind Jason, made taut his bow and launched the dart at Medea. No one saw it fly, not even she herself, but it burned under her breast like flame. From time to time she took a deep panting breath, like one in the grip of some malady, and then again she cast sidelong glances at Jason in the radiance of his heroic youth. Her mind was empty of everything else. Sweet sorrow filled her spirit, and she paled and reddened in turn.

In all that joyful confusion, no one had observed what was going on within her. Servants came bearing platters of food, and the Argonauts, who had bathed themselves after the toil of their rowing, sat down at the board to refresh themselves with rich and dainty fare and drink. In the course of the feast the grandsons of King Aeetes told him of the fate that had overtaken them, and then, in a low voice, he inquired about the strangers.

"I shall not conceal it from you, grandfather," whispered Argus. "These men have come to ask you for the golden fleece of Phrixus, our father. A king who is anxious to cheat them of their possessions and drive them from their country sent them on this dangerous quest, in the hope that they would not escape the anger of Zeus and the revenge of Phrixus. Pallas Athene herself helped them build their ship, which is not of the sort used in Colchis. We, your own grandchildren, let me tell you, had a very poor one, for at the very first blast of wind it fell to pieces. But these strangers have a ship so firmly joined, so stout, that it defies the wildest storms, and they themselves ply the oars unceasingly. The bravest heroes of all Greece have gathered on this vessel." And he told Aeetes the names of the noblest of them, and also the line from which Jason was descended.

When the king heard this, he was afraid and grew very angry at his grandsons, for he thought that it was through them the strangers had come to his court. His eyes burned under their bushy brows, and he said aloud: "Out of my sight, blasphemers and plotters that you are! You have not come to fetch the fleece, but to snatch from me my scepter and my throne. Were you not guests at my board, I should have your tongues torn out and your hands hacked off, and leave you only your feet to go away with."

When Telamon, the son of Aeacus, who sat nearest the king, heard this talk, his spirit seethed with rage and drove him to leap from his place and retort to Aeetes in words more violent than his own. But Jason held him back and himself gave answer in a gentle voice: "Contain yourself, Aeetes. We have not come to your city and into your palace to rob you. Who would undertake so long a journey over a perilous sea for the purpose of acquiring another's possessions? My resolve was prompted by Destiny and the command of an evil king. Grant our request! Give us the golden fleece, and all Greece will acclaim you! We are ready, moreover, to pay our debt of thanks at once. If there is a war anywhere about, or if you desire to subdue a neighboring people, take us for your allies, and we shall fight for you."

Thus Jason spoke to propitiate Aeetes, but the king was

undecided whether to have them slain immediately or first to prove their strength. After some reflection the latter course seemed the wiser to him, and he answered with more composure: "Why these timid overtures, stranger? If you are, indeed, the sons of gods or, at any rate, no less wellborn than I, and desire another's possessions, then take the golden fleece away with you. I begrudge nothing to brave men. But first you must perform a labor I usually do myself, since it involves great danger. I have two bulls which graze in the field of Ares. They have brazen feet and from their nostrils leap tongues of flame. With them I plough the rough field, and when I have turned over the clods, I do not sow Demeter's yellow kernels in the furrows, but the teeth of a horrid dragon. From these spring a crop of men who press in upon me from all sides, but I slay them with my lance. At early dawn I yoke the bulls, and in the late evening I rest from the harvest. When you have done the same, on that very day, O leader, you may take the golden fleece away with you to your king. But not before, since it is only just that the less valiant man should give way to the better."

Jason sat in his place, silent and undecided, for he did not venture to promise offhand to perform so fearful a labor. But he marshalled his wits and replied: "The task is heavy, O king, but I shall do it, though I perish in the doing. After all, a man cannot meet with worse than death. I shall obey the destiny which sent me here."

"Very well," said the king. "Go to your men now. But consider! Unless you intend to carry out the feats I have described, leave the work to me and shun my country."

THE COUNSEL OF ARGUS

Jason and the two heroes he had brought with him rose from their seats. Only one of the sons of Phrixus followed him, Argus, who had signed to his brothers to remain behind. But those others left the palace. About Jason hung a glow of beauty and grace. Medea's glances strayed toward him through her veil and dreamily followed his every move.

When she was alone in her chamber again, the tears welled

from under her lashes. "Why do I allow sorrow to beset my heart?" she asked herself. "How does this hero concern me? Whether he be the foremost or the least of all the demigods—let him die, if such be his lot. And yet—if only he could escape destruction! O Hecate, revered goddess, let him return home! But if it is decreed that the bulls overpower him, let him know before he goes to meet them that I, at least, do not rejoice in his awful fate."

While Medea was thus tormenting herself, the heroes were on their way to the ship, and Argus said to Jason: "Perhaps you will spurn my advice, but still I must give it. I know a girl who understands the brewing of magic potions, an art which Hecate, the goddess of the underworld, has taught her. If we could win her over to our side, I am certain you would be victorious in this task. If you agree, I shall go and try to enlist her favor in our behalf."

"Go if you like," said Jason. "I shall not prevent you. But we are in a sad way if our homeward voyage depends on women!"

While they were talking, they had reached the Argo and their companions. Jason told them of the task which had been set him and of his promise to the king. For a little his friends sat, exchanging mute glances. Finally Peleus rose and said: "If you believe that you are able to do what you have pledged, prepare yourself. But if you are not wholly confident of the outcome, stay away, nor look to any of these men to help you, for what could be in store for them but death?"

At these words Telamon and four other youths sprang up full of eager joy at the thought of a perilous venture. But Argus quieted them and said: "I know one who is versed in magic. She is my mother's sister. Let me go to my mother and persuade her to win the girl over to our plans. Not until then is there any use in discussing the task Jason has promised to perform."

He had scarcely finished speaking when Heaven granted them a sign. A dove, who was being pursued by a hawk, took refuge in Jason's lap, while the bird of prey, darting close behind, fell to the deck in the stern of the ship. Now one of the heroes remembered that old Phineus had prophesied, among other things, that Aphrodite would aid them in returning home. So all agreed with Argus except Idas, the son of Aphareus, who rose testily from his seat and said: "By the gods, have we come here as women's minions? Shall we invoke Aphrodite instead of turning to Ares? Is the sight of hawks and doves to keep us from battle? Very well then, forget about war and win glory by deceiving weak maidens." Thus he spoke in anger, and many of the heroes agreed with him and murmured their disapproval of Jason's plan. But he decided in favor of Argus. The ship was moored to the shore, and the heroes awaited the return of their messenger.

Meantime Aeetes had called a gathering of the Colchians outside the palace. He told his people of the arrival of the strangers, their demand, and the end he had in mind for them. As soon as the leader was killed by the bulls, he would have a whole forest of trees hewn and burn the ship with all her crew. And he would devise a terrible punishment for his grandsons, who had guided these adventurers to his country. While this was going on, Argus had sought out his mother and pleaded with her to enlist the aid of her sister Medea. Chalciope herself was filled with pity for the strangers, but had not dared face her father's rankling displeasure. And so her son's request was welcome to her, and she promised to assist him.

Medea lay on her couch in restless slumber, haunted by anxious dreams. She seemed to see Jason make ready to fight the bulls, only that he had not assumed this labor for the sake of the golden fleece, but to take her home to his own country as his wife. In her dream it was she herself who got the better of the bulls, but her parents refused to keep their word and give Jason the promised prize, because not she, but he, should have yoked the beasts. Her father and the strangers began to quarrel bitterly on this point, and both sides chose her as arbiter. And in her dream she gave judgment in favor of the stranger! Her parents cried out in resentment and grief—and Medea awoke.

The mood begot by her dream drove her to her sister's apartment, but for a long time she dallied in the forecourt, ashamed and undecided. Three times she went forward, three times she turned back, and at last she threw herself weeping on her own couch again. One of her trusted young handmaidens found her there, distraught and tearful, and, filled with sympathy for her mistress, reported what she had seen to Chalciope. When the message reached her, she was sitting among her sons and discussing how they might win over Medea. She hastened to her sister and found her with her palms pressed to her cheeks and her breast shaken with sobs. "What has happened to you, dear sister?" she asked in deep concern. "What sorrow is torturing your soul? Has a god afflicted you with some malady? Has our father slandered me and my sons to you? Oh, that I were far from the house of my parents, in a country where the name of Colchis is never uttered!"

MEDEA PROMISES TO HELP THE ARGONAUTS

Medea reddened at her sister's questions, and shyness kept her silent. Now the words were on the tip of her tongue, now they retreated to the very core of her being. But love, at last, emboldened her, and craftily she said: "Chalciope, my heart grieves for your sons. I fear that our father may kill them together with the strangers. An anxious dream has given me these forebodings, but I pray that a god may prevent them from coming true."

These words filled Chalciope with great alarm. "I have come to you about this very matter," she said. "And I implore you to support me against our father. Should you refuse, my murdered sons and I will pursue you even from the underworld and haunt you like Furies." She clasped Medea's knees with both hands and buried her head in her lap. And the sisters mingled their tears.

Then Medea said: "Why speak of Furies, sister? I swear to you by heaven and earth that whatever I can do to save your sons, that I will gladly do."

"Well then," Chalciope countered, "for the sake of my sons, consent to furnish the stranger with some device whereby he can survive the terrible ordeal with the bulls. For he has sent my son Argus to beg your help."

Medea's heart danced with joy, her lovely face flushed, and for a moment giddiness clouded her shining eyes. Then she said impetuously: "Chalciope, may the dawn never again gladden my sight if I do not hold your life and that of your sons more dear than my own! For did not you—so my mother often told me— suckle me together with them when I was a tiny child? Therefore

I love you not only with a sister's but a daughter's love. Early tomorrow morning, I shall go to the temple of Hecate and there fetch for the stranger the magic which shall tame the bulls." Chalciope left her sister's chamber and told her sons the welcome news.

All night Medea struggled with herself. "Have I not pledged too much?" she said. "May I do all this for a stranger? See him and touch him with no one near—for this is necessary if the ruse is to succeed? Yes, I shall save his life! Let him go where he will. But on the day of his victory, I shall die. A rope or poison will serve to free me from an existence I loathe. But will not vicious rumors pursue me over all the land of Colchis? Will they not whisper that I have disgraced my house by dying for love of a stranger?" With these tangled thoughts in her head, she went to fetch a small box which contained those herbs that cure and those that kill. She set it on her knees and had already opened it to taste of deadly poison, when she remembered all the vexing sweetness of life, all its delights, all her playmates. The sun seemed fairer to her than before, and she shivered with unconquerable fear of death and put the casket down on the floor. Hera, Jason's patron goddess, had changed her heart. She could hardly wait for the dawn to brew the promised magic and bring it to the hero whom she had come to love.

JASON AND MEDEA

Argus hurried to the ship with his joyful message, and when Dawn had only just streaked the sky with light, Medea leaped from her couch, combed and bound her blond locks, which in her grief had hung matted about her cheeks, washed the traces of tears from her face, and anointed herself with precious oils. She put on a splendid robe, fastened with curved golden clasps, and threw a white veil over her radiant head. All sadness was forgotten. She ran through the halls on nimble feet and bade her handmaids, twelve in number, yoke the mules to the chariot which was to take her to the temple of Hecate. While this was being done, Medea took from her box an ointment called Prometheus' oil. Whoever salved his body with it, after offering a prayer to the goddess of the underworld, could not on that day be either wounded by a blade or scorched by fire, but would, indeed, be able to defeat any opponent. The ointment was prepared from the black sap of a root nourished by the blood oozing down to the grassy slopes of the Caucasus from the gashed liver of Prometheus. Medea herself had caught the sap of that plant in a shell and hoarded it as a rare and potent remedy.

The chariot was ready. Two of her handmaids mounted it with their mistress, who herself held the reins and the goad and drove through the city, while the others accompanied her on foot. And all along their course, the people reverently stepped aside to let the king's daughter pass. When she had crossed the open field and reached the temple, Medea sprang lightly from the chariot and spoke to her maidens with wily deceit.

"I think I have done a great wrong in not keeping away from the strangers who came to our country. And now, on top of this, my sister and her son Argus have requested me to accept gifts from their leader and make him invulnerable by magic charms. I pretended to assent and asked him to come to this temple, where I can see him alone. When he arrives, I shall take the gifts, which we shall later divide among ourselves, but offer him a potion which will hasten his destruction. Now go, lest he suspect a plot, for I told him that I would receive him alone."

The girls were well pleased with her plan. While they dispersed within the temple, Argus and his friend Jason set out on their way, and Mopsus, the soothsayer, went with them. No mortal, not even a child of the gods, had ever been as beautiful as Hera on this day made Jason! She endowed him with all the gifts of the Graces. Whenever his two companions glanced sidewise they wondered at his radiance—as if a star had taken on human form! Medea, meanwhile, waited in the temple with her maidens, and although they tried to shorten the time with singing, their mistress was intent upon such very different matters that no song pleased her for long. Her eyes did not dwell upon her handmaids but roved longingly through the temple gate and across the road. At every passing step, at every rustle of wind, she eagerly raised her head.

It was not long before Jason entered the temple, tall and fair as Sirius rising from the sea. It seemed to Medea that her heart fluttered out of her breast. The world turned black before her eyes, and the hot blood surged into her cheeks. Her handmaids had left her. For a long time the hero and the king's daughter faced each other in silence. They were like two slender oaks which stand close to each other, deep-rooted in the hills, with the air windless around them. But suddenly a storm comes, and all the leaves tremble and move and toss on their stems. So these two, touched by love, exchanged words quick with emotion.

Jason was the first to break the silence. "Why do you fear me, now that I am alone with you?" he asked. "I am not boastful like other men, and never was, even at home! Do not hesitate to ask and to say whatever your heart bids you. But remember that we are in a holy place, where a lie would be blasphemy. Therefore, do not deceive me with vain words. I come as a suppliant to beg you for the charm you promised your sister to give me. Harsh necessity compels me to seek your help. Ask what you like in return, and know that the aid you give will dispel the dark cares of my companions' mothers and wives, who are perhaps already mourning us on the shores of our country, and that undying glory will be yours in all of Greece."

The girl allowed him to finish. She lowered her lids, and a faint smile touched her mouth. Her heart rejoiced in his praise. She looked up at him, and words crowded to her lips. She would have liked to say everything at once, but love numbed her tongue. So she only drew the small box from its perfumed wrappings. He took it from her hands in glad haste, but she would willingly have given him her very soul had he asked it, for Eros was kindling flames of sweet desire from Jason's golden locks, and she caught their light and fragrance. Her spirit warmed as the dew on roses begins to glow in the beams of the morning sun. Both looked down and then at each other again, and yearning glances sped from under their lashes. It was only after a long time and with great effort that Medea spoke.

"Listen, and I shall tell you what you must do. After my father has given you the terrible dragon's teeth for sowing, bathe alone in the waters of the river, put on black garments, and dig a circular pit. Within this heap a pyre, slaughter a ewe lamb, and burn it to ash. Then offer a libation of honey to Hecate, dripping it from your cup, and leave the pyre. Do not turn around for any step you may hear, or for the bark of a dog, otherwise the sacrifice will be in vain. The following morning salve yourself with this magic ointment. It bestows great power and incredible strength. You will feel equal not only to men, but even to immortals. You must also anoint your lance, your sword, and your shield, and then no metal directed by human hands and no flame launched by the magic bulls will be able to harm you or withstand you. This will last only for that one day, but I shall give you still other aid. When you have yoked those enormous bulls and ploughed the field, when the dragon's seed has borne harvest, throw a great stone among the earthborn men. They will fight for it as dogs for a crust of bread, and while they are so engaged, you can rush upon them and kill them. Then you may take the golden fleece away from Colchis unhindered, and go—yes, go wherever you please."

She spoke, and furtive tears trickled down her cheeks as she thought of this noble hero sailing far over the sea. She continued mournfully and took him by the hand, for her pain made her forget what she was doing. "When you reach home, do not forget the name of Medea. I too will think of you when you are gone. And now tell me the name of that land to which you will return on your beautiful ship."

While the girl was talking, Jason was overcome with irresistible love for her, and broke out impetuously: "Noble princess, should I escape death, not a day will pass, not an hour, in which I fail to remember you. My home is Iolcus in Haemonia, where Deucalion, the son of Prometheus, founded many cities and built many temples. In that place not even the name of your country is known."

"So you live in Greece," said the girl. "Perhaps men are more hospitable there than here. Do not tell them how you were received in Colchis, and remember me when you are alone. As for me—I shall think of you when everyone else here has forgotten. But if you should forget— Oh, that a wind would carry to me a bird from Iolcus, through which I could remind you that you escaped by my help. Oh, that I myself were in your house then and could remind you in person!" And she burst into tears.

"Let winds blow and birds fly," answered Jason. "This is idle talk. But if you yourself came to Greece and to my home, how both women and men would honor you, even worship you as a goddess, because through you their sons and brothers and husbands escaped death and returned to their native land safe and sound! And you—you would belong to me, and to me only, and nothing but death could end our love."

Her soul melted at his words, but at the same time she was dimly aware of how terrible it is to leave one's country. Yet she was drawn toward Greece with compelling force, for Hera had set this yearning in her heart. The goddess wanted Medea to leave Colchis and go to Iolcus, to bring destruction to Pelias.

In the meantime the maidens waited for their mistress and were silent and sad, since the time for her return was long past. She herself would have forgotten to go home for very delight in their exchange of heartfelt words, had not Jason, who was more cautious, reminded her: but even he did not think of it until late. "The time for parting has come," he said at last, "lest the sun set, and we be still here, and the others suspect some plot. Let us meet again in this place."

JASON DOES THE BIDDING OF AEETES

In this manner they parted. Jason returned to the ship and his comrades, his spirit filled with joy. The girl went to join her handmaids, who hurried toward her. But she did not notice their solicitude, for her soul was soaring in the clouds. With light feet she mounted the wagon, urged on the mules, who ran homeward of themselves, and re-entered the palace. Chalciope had been waiting for her long since, full of anxiety for her sons. She was sitting on a stool, with her head bowed. Her eyes were moist beneath her lowered lids, for she was thinking of the evil web in which she was entangled.

Jason meanwhile told his friends how the girl had given him a wonderful magic ointment, and as he spoke he held it out to them. All rejoiced with him except Idas, who sat apart and ground his teeth in rage. The next morning they dispatched two men to King Aeetes to fetch the dragon's teeth. They came from the very same dragon Cadmus had slain at Thebes, and Aeetes gave them quite confidently, for he believed Jason could not possibly survive the battle, even if he succeeded in yoking the bulls. In the night which followed upon this day, Jason bathed and made an offering to Hecate, as Medea had bidden. The goddess herself heard his prayer and emerged from the depths of her cave, her awful head twined with writhing vipers and fiery sprays of oak. At her heels ran the hounds of the underworld and barked around her. The field trembled beneath her steps, and the nymphs of the river Phasis moaned in fear. Horror smote even Jason as he prepared to return to the ship, but he obeyed his beloved and did not look back. And the shimmering Dawn stained the snow-covered peaks of the Caucasus with rosy light.

Then Aeetes put on his cuirass, the one Ares had taken from the giant Mimas on the field of Phlegra. On his head he placed his four-crested helmet of gold, and in his hand he took the shield covered with four layers of oxhide, which none besides him could have lifted, save Heracles alone. His son held the swift horses harnessed to the chariot. He mounted it, took the reins, and flew through the city followed by throngs of people. Even though he was to be a mere spectator, he wished to appear fully armed, as if he himself were going to do battle.

Jason, obedient to Medea's directions, had salved his lance, his shield, and his sword with the magic ointment. His companions formed a ring around him, and each tried his weapon on the lance, but it did not give and would not even bend ever so slightly. It was like stone in his steady hand. This vexed Idas, the son of Aphareus, and he aimed his blow at the shaft under the point. But his sword sprang back like the hammer from the anvil, and the youths exulted in the happy prospect of victory. Not until then did Jason anoint his body. Miraculous strength flowed through his limbs; the veins in his hands swelled with power, and he craved battle. As a war-horse neighs and paws the earth before the fray and then lifts high its head and points its ears, so the son of Aeson stretched in readiness to fight, tapped the ground with restless feet, and swung shield and lance in his hands.

The heroes rowed their leader to the field of Ares, where they found Aeetes and the Colchians waiting for them. The king sat on the bank, and his people were scattered about the jutting ledges of the Caucasus. When the ship was made fast, Jason leaped ashore with his lance and shield and immediately received a shining helmet full of pointed teeth. He strapped his sword to his shoulder and came forward, radiant as Ares or Apollo. Looking about the field, he soon discovered the yokes lying on the ground, and near them plough and ploughshare, all of hammered iron. When he had studied these implements carefully, he fastened the iron point to the sturdy shaft of his lance and laid down the helmet. Then, covered by his shield, he went forward, searching for the tracks of the bulls. But these animals suddenly rushed at him from another side, coming from a subterranean cave, where they were stabled. Both of them breathed flame, and thick clouds of smoke rolled about them. Jason's friends shook with fear at sight of these monsters, but he himself stood with his legs well apart, holding his shield before him, and awaited their onslaught like a rock pounded by the sea. And when they came at him, tossing their horns, their impact could not budge him from his position. As in a smithy, when the bellows roar and the fires now leap in a shower of sparks, now hold their mighty breath, so the bulls roared and redoubled their thrusts, spewing flame all the while, and the fitful glow played about the hero like lightning. But the magic kept him unharmed, and finally he took the bull at his right by the outer horn and tugged at him with all his might until he had dragged him over to the iron yoke. Here he kicked the brazen feet and forced the beast to the earth with bent knees. In the same way he subdued the second, who was charging toward him. He flung aside his broad shield and, though the flames licked about him, held down the kneeling bulls with both his hands. Aeetes himself was forced to admire the stupendous strength of the man. Then, as they had agreed upon before, Castor and Polydeuces handed him the yokes, and he fastened them to the necks of the animals with sure and deft hands. Last he picked up the iron shaft and fitted it into the ring of the yoke. And now the twin brothers lost no time in leaving that place, for they were not immune to fire like Jason. He took his shield again and threw it across his shoulder, so that it dangled over his back by the strap. Then he reached for the helmet with the dragon's teeth, gripped his lance, and using it as a goad, forced the angry bulls to draw the plough. Their strength and that of the mighty ploughman tore deep gashes in the earth, and the huge clods crashed in the furrows. Jason walked with a firm step and sowed the turned earth with the teeth, cautiously looking back to see if the harvest of dragon men was already up and having at him. And the bulls plodded on with their brazen hooves.

When only two thirds of the day had passed, in the bright afternoon, the whole field was ploughed, though it measured more than four acres. And now he unharnessed the bulls and threatened them with his weapons, so that they fled in fear. The hero himself returned to the ship, for the furrows still showed no sign of life.

His comrades surrounded him with loud acclaim, but he said nothing, only filled his helmet with water from the river and quenched his burning thirst. Then he felt the joints of his legs and his heart filled with fresh joy of combat, even as a raging boar grinds his teeth in readiness for the huntsmen. For all along the field the harvest was up. The entire grove of Ares bristled with shields and sharp lances and glittered so brightly with helmets that the gleam flashed up to the sky. Then Jason remembered the words of wily Medea. He picked up a great round stone. Four strong men could not have lifted it from the ground, but he took it effortlessly in his hand and tossed it far among the warriors who had sprung up from the earth. Bold yet cautious, he crouched down on one knee and covered himself with his shield. The Colchians shouted aloud as the waves roar when they break on jagged rock, and Aeetes stared at that astonishing throw in undisguised wonder. But the earthborn men fell upon one another like snarling dogs, and each killed the other with dull cries of rage. Stricken down by their spears, they fell to Mother Earth like pines or oaks uprooted by a whirlwind. When the fight was hottest, Jason rushed among them like a shooting star which falls through the dark air of night and seems an omen sent by the gods. He unsheathed his sword, pierced now this one, now that, struck down some who were already up, mowed down like grass others who had grown out only to their shoulders, and cleft the heads of still others running to join in the battle. The furrows streamed with blood. Dead and wounded fell on all sides, and many sank into the earth almost as deep as they had been sown.

Anger gnawed at the soul of King Aeetes. Without a word he

left the shore and returned to the city, brooding only on how he could rid himself of Jason and inflict some grim hurt upon him to boot. These events had taken up the day. It was dusk. Jason rested from his labors, and around him his friends rejoiced.

MEDEA TAKES THE GOLDEN FLEECE

All night long with the elders among his people King Aeetes held council in the palace, how the Argonauts might be outwitted, for he was well aware that all that had happened the past day could not have taken place without the help of his daughters. Hera, queen of the gods, saw the danger threatening Jason and filled Medea's heart with misgivings, until she trembled as a deer in the depths of the forest at the bay of the hounds. She at once divined that her father had guessed the truth, and she also feared that her handmaids might well know of the matter. Tears burned under her lids, and there was a rushing in her ears. She let her hair hang dishevelled, as though in mourning, and if Fate had not willed otherwise, she would have taken poison and so put an end to her misery that very hour. Her hand already held the brimming cup, when Hera revived her courage and turned her purpose, so that she poured the poison back into the flask. She regained command of herself and resolved to flee, covered her couch and the doorposts with kisses, touched the walls of her room one last time, sheared a lock from her head, and put it on her bed for her mother to remember her by.

"Farewell, dear mother," she said with a voice full of tears. "Farewell, Chalciope, and all the house! O stranger, it would have been better had you drowned in the sea before coming to Colchis!"

And she left her cherished home as a captive flees the harsh prison where he has been enslaved. The palace gates flew open at her murmured spells. On bare feet she ran along narrow paths, drawing the veil over her cheeks with her left hand, while her right raised the hem of her garment to keep it from the ground. The watchmen did not recognize her, and soon she had passed beyond the confines of the city and was hastening to the temple by a little-known road, for in gathering roots and herbs for her po-

tions and poisonous brews she had come to know all the trails
through field and wood. Selene, goddess of the moon, saw her and
said smilingly to herself, as she shed her radiance upon the earth:
"So others too are tormented by love, as I for my beautiful
Endymion! Often have you driven me from the sky with your
magic. Now you, yourself, are suffering agonies for Jason. Well,
go if you must, but do not think that your craftiness will avail
to escape the bitterest sorrow of all."

So said Selene to herself, but Medea went her way on swift
feet. And now she turned toward the shore, where the great fire,
which the Argonauts had lit and tended all night in Jason's
honor, served to guide her. When she was opposite the ship, she
called Phrontis, her sister's youngest son, and he, along with
Jason, recognized her voice and replied three times to her triple
call. The heroes, who had heard and seen, were astonished at first,
but then they rowed to meet her. Before the ship was moored,
Jason leaped ashore, and Phrontis and Argus followed him.

"Save me," cried the girl, clasping their knees. "Save yourselves and me from my father! All is betrayed, and there is no
help. Let us flee on the ship before he can mount his swift horse.
I will get you the golden fleece by putting the dragon to sleep.
But you, O stranger, swear by your gods and in the presence of
your friends, that you will not disgrace me when I am alone, an
alien in your land."

She said this sadly, but Jason rejoiced in his heart. Gently he
raised her from her knees, embraced her and said: "Beloved, let
Zeus and Hera, the patron goddess of marriage, be my witnesses
that I shall take you into my house as my rightful wife as soon as
we are back in Greece." This he swore and laid his hand in hers.
Then Medea bade the heroes row to the sacred grove to take the
golden fleece that very night. The ship flew on with arrowy speed.
Jason and the girl left it before dawn and took the path across
the meadow. In the grove they found the tall oak on which the
golden fleece hung, shining through the night like a morning
cloud suffused with the first beams of the sun. But facing it was
the sleepless dragon, whose sharp eyes pierced the distance. He
stretched his long neck toward the comers and hissed so fiercely
that the margin of the river and the whole forest echoed the
sound. As flames roll through a burning wood, so the monster

with his glittering scales wound his way, loop upon loop. But the girl went toward him boldly and made a sweet-voiced prayer to Sleep, the most powerful of the gods, to lull the dragon to rest. And she begged the great queen of the underworld to bless her doing. Jason followed her fearfully, but already the dragon was growing drowsy at the girl's magical song. He lowered the arch of his back and stretched out the coils of his vast body. Only the horrid head was still upright and threatened to devour them both with its open jaws. But now, with a sprig of juniper, Medea sprinkled magic dew into his eyes while she conjured him with certain words. Drowsiness flowed over him at the fragrance of the liquid: he closed his jaws, spread his scaly length through the wood, and slept.

At her word, Jason pulled the fleece from the oak, while she kept sprinkling the dragon's head with her magic tincture. Then they hurried from the dense grove, and from afar Jason held up the broad ram's fleece, which shed a gleam over his forehead and his blond hair and lit up the dark path. He carried the shimmering treasure over his left shoulder, and it hung from his neck to his ankles. But then he rolled it up for fear that if man or god encountered him, he might rob him of his precious burden. At dawn they boarded the vessel, and the Argonauts surrounded their leader and marvelled at the fleece, which glittered like the lightning of Zeus. Each wanted to touch it with his hands, but Jason would not allow this and hid it under a cloak. He seated the girl in the stern of the ship and said to his friends: "Now let us travel quickly to our native land. This girl's counsel has helped us accomplish what we undertook. In return I shall take her into my house as my lawful wife. And you must help me protect her, for she is the rescuer of all Greece. Besides, I have no doubt that soon Aeetes will come with his people and try to prevent us from leaving the river for the open sea. So let half of us row, while the other half hold our great shields of oxhide toward the foe and so cover our retreat. For our return to our own people and the honor or shame of Greece are in our hands."

With these words he cut the ropes that held the ship, armed himself, and took his place near the girl beside Ancaeus, the helmsman. The swift oars smote the waves, and the ship glided down to the mouth of the river.

THE ARGONAUTS ARE PURSUED AND ESCAPE WITH MEDEA

In the meantime Aeetes and all the Colchians had learned of Medea's infatuation, of her actions, and her flight. They met in the market place, fully armed, and soon after marched to the riverbank with a rattling of arms like the sound of thunder. Aeetes rode in a well-joined chariot drawn by the horses the sun-god had given him. In his left hand he carried a round shield, in his right a long pitch torch. At his side leaned his tall and heavy lance. His son Absyrtus held the reins. But when they reached the mouth of the river, the ship, driven on by its tireless rowers, had already gained the open sea. Torch and shield dropped from the king's fingers. He raised his hands to heaven, called on Zeus and Apollo to witness the wrong done to him, and sullenly declared to his subjects that unless they seized his daughter on land or on sea and brought her to him so that he could revenge himself to his heart's desire, they should all lose their heads. The terrified Colchians put out to sea that very day, hoisted sail, and sped in pursuit of Medea. Their fleet, under the command of Absyrtus, the son of Aeetes, looked like an endless flock of birds which darken the air as they trail over the waters.

A favorable wind bellied out the sails of the Argonauts, and on the morning of the third day they entered the river Halys and moored their ship to the shore of Paphlagonia. Here, at Medea's request, they made offering to the goddess Hecate, who had saved them. Then their leader, and some of the others as well, remembered that Phineus, the aged prophet, had bidden them return by another route. None of them knew these regions, but Argus, son of Phrixus, came to the rescue, for from the writings of priests he had learned that they were to steer for the river Ister, which rises from springs in the Rhipaean Mountains and divides into many branches, so that the wealth of its waters pours into both the Ionian and the Sicilian Sea. When Argus had advised them thus, the sky was suddenly cleft by a broad rainbow in the quarter toward which they were supposed to sail. A fair wind blew and blew, and the sign in the heavens shone on and on, until they were safe in that mouth of the river Ister which empties into the Ionian Sea.

But the Colchians had not ceased in their pursuit and, since they had lighter ships and could sail more swiftly, they arrived at the mouth of the Ister before the Argonauts and scattered among the various bays and islands. There they lay in wait for the heroes and blocked their passage to the sea after they had cast anchor in the delta of the river. The Argonauts, who were alarmed at the great numbers of the enemy, went ashore and occupied one of the islands. The Colchians followed them, and it seemed that battle must ensue. Then the harried Greeks began to negotiate, and both sides finally agreed that the Argonauts were, at all events, to carry off the golden fleece which the king had promised Jason for his labors. But Medea, the king's daughter, was to be left on another island, in the temple of Artemis, until a neighboring king, noted for his justice, should decide whether she was to return to her father or follow the heroes to Greece. When the girl heard this, she grew frantic with fear, took her beloved aside to a place where his companions could not hear her, and pleaded with him tearfully. "Jason, what are you going to do with me? Has your good fortune made you forgetful of everything you solemnly swore to me when you were in terrible need? How thoughtless I was to stake my hopes upon you, hold cheap my honor, and leave my fatherland, my house, my parents, and all I loved best! It is because of what I did for you that I am now borne far over the open sea. My foolhardiness got you the golden fleece. For you I yielded up my maidenhood and am following you to Greece as yours, as your wife. But now, because of all this, you must protect me. Do not leave me here alone! Nor let kings pronounce judgment upon me! If I am allotted to my father I am lost. And how could you, then, rejoice in your return? How could Hera, the wife of Zeus, whom you boast as your protectress, approve such a course? If you abandon me, the time will come when, deep in disaster, you will think of Medea, when the golden fleece will slip from you like a dream. Then vengeful spirits shall drive you from your native land, just as I, through your trickery, was driven from mine!"

So she spoke, maddened with passion, and would gladly have set fire to the ship, burned up everything, and cast herself into the flames. Jason looked at her and grew uncertain. His conscience smote him, and he said propitiatingly: "Compose your-

self! I was not serious in closing this agreement. It is only for
your sake that we are trying to delay the battle, because our foes
are thick as locusts in summer. All who live here are friends of
the Colchians and would help your brother Absyrtus capture you
and take you back to your father. Besides, if we fought now,
we should all perish miserably, and your lot would be still more
hopeless, for with us dead, you would fall a prey to the foe. This
agreement, I tell you, is only a ruse through which we hope to
destroy Absyrtus. And once their leader is no more, the neighbors
of the Colchians will not wish to give them aid."

This he said to placate her, and now Medea gave him grim
counsel. "I have strayed from my duties once," she said. "Blinded
by emotion I have done an evil thing. I cannot go back, and so I
must go forward in crime. I will coax my brother until he gives
himself into your hands. Have a lavish banquet prepared for
him. I shall try to induce the heralds to leave him alone with me
—and then you can kill him and vanquish the leaderless Colchians."

So these two planned to trap Absyrtus. They sent him many
gifts, including a sumptuous robe which the queen of Lemnos had
once given to Jason. The Graces had woven it for Dionysus with
their own hands, and in the fine mesh of the purple stuff clung
the perfumes of heaven, for the god himself, drowsy with nectar,
had slumbered in its folds. Medea slyly urged the heralds to
bring Absyrtus to the other island, to the temple of Artemis, at
dead of night, and pretended that she would devise a way for him
to seize the golden fleece and take it back to King Aeetes. For she
herself—so she lied—had been forcibly given over to the strangers by the sons of Phrixus. After she had thus deceived these
messengers of peace, she sprinkled the wind with so much of her
magic brew that the scent would have been enough to lure the
wildest beast from the highest mountain. And what she hoped
for took place. At midnight Absyrtus, deceived by solemn
pledges, rowed to the holy island. Alone with his sister, he tried
to probe her guileful mind and to discover whether she was, indeed, setting a snare for the strangers. But it was as if a boy
were trying to wade a swollen mountain stream which a grown
man cannot cross unimperilled, for when they were deep in talk,
and his sister seemed ready to do all he asked, Jason suddenly

rushed out of ambush, brandishing his naked sword. And the girl turned away and hid her eyes in her veil, so that she might not see her brother done to death. Like a victim at the altar, the king's son fell under the blow of Jason's blade, and Medea's gown was splashed with her brother's blood. But the goddess of vengeance, from whom nothing is hidden, looked forth from her secret dwelling with angry eyes and beheld the terrible deed committed here.

After Jason had cleansed himself of the blood and buried the body, Medea signalled to the Argonauts with a torch, for so it had been agreed. These drew up their ship beside the vessel in which Absyrtus had come to the island of Artemis and fell on his leaderless companions like hawks on flocks of doves, or lions on sheep. Not a single man escaped death. Jason, who came to aid his friends, was not needed. The battle was already decided.

THE ARGONAUTS ON THEIR HOMEWARD JOURNEY

On the advice of Peleus, the heroes left the mouth of the river and
sped swiftly away before the remaining Colchians had realized
what had happened. When they saw what had been done, they
set out to pursue their foes, but Hera deterred them by kindling
a flash of lightning in the sky. They feared her warning, and
since they also feared the anger of their king if they returned
without either his daughter or his son, they remained on the isles
of Artemis in the mouth of the river and settled there.

But the Argonauts continued on their way and passed many
coasts and islands, among them that on which Queen Calypso, the
daughter of Atlas, had her dwelling place. Already they thought
they discerned the tallest peaks of their homeland rising in the
distance, when Hera, fearing the plots of Zeus, stirred up a
mighty storm, which drove their ship to the inhospitable Amber
Islands. And now the wood from the oak of Dodona, which Athene
had set in the timbers of the prow, began to speak, and the
listeners shook with dread. "You will not evade the wrath of
Zeus, and you will wander over the sea," said the oak, "until
Circe, the sorceress, purifies you of the cruel murder of Absyrtus.
Let Castor and Polydeuces pray to the gods to point you the
paths which lead to Circe, the daughter of the sun-god and
Perse."

So said the prow of the Argo at the hour of dusk. The heroes
shuddered when they heard such misfortune foretold and sat
motionless at their oars. Only Castor and Polydeuces leaped from
their bench and ventured to beg the immortal gods for their protection. But the ship dashed on to the inner reaches of the Eridanus where Phaethon, burned by the chariot of the sun, had
once fallen into the water. And even now, from the bottom of the
river, his searing wounds still poured forth fire and smoke. There
is no ship which can sail lightly across these waters, for the flames
suck it into their midst. Along the shores Phaethon's sisters, the
Heliades, who were changed into poplars, sigh in the wind and
drip bright tears of amber on the earth, which the sun dries and
the river draws into its tide. Thanks to their stout ship, the

Argonauts overcame this peril, but they lost all desire for food or drink. By day they were harassed by the intolerable stench of scorching flesh; by night they heard the Heliades lament, their gold-colored tears oozing into the sea like drops of rich oil. They rowed along the shores of the Eridanus, came to the mouth of the Rhodanus, and would have entered there and met their death had not Hera suddenly appeared on a crag and warned them away with her clear-ringing divine voice. She shrouded the ship in black fogs, and so they journeyed for endless days and nights and passed many places where Celtic families had settled, until they saw the Tyrrhenian Sea and soon after rode safely into the harbor of Circe's island.

They found the sorceress on the shore, leaning over the sea and washing her face in the waves. She had dreamed that her chamber, that her entire house was running with blood, that a flame had devoured all the magic herbs and brews with which she used to bewitch strangers, and that she was cupping the blood in the hollow of her hand and trying to quench the fire. This nightmare had startled her from sleep at dawn and driven her to the shore. Here she washed her garments and her locks, as though they were really stained with blood. Great beasts came after her in flocks, as cattle follow the shepherd from the stalls, and they were unlike any known animals, being formed of the limbs of one kind of creature and the head or body of another. The heroes stood aghast, for they had only to look at Circe to know that she was the sister of cruel Aeetes. When the goddess had cleansed herself of the terrors of the night, she turned homeward, called to the beasts, and stroked them as one fondles dogs.

Jason had his entire crew remain aboard. Only he and Medea went ashore, and, once on the beach, he drew the reluctant girl on to the palace of Circe. The sorceress did not know what the strangers had come for. She bade them be seated in sumptuous chairs, but quietly and mournfully they sat down by the hearth. Medea bowed her head in her hands, and Jason thrust the sword with which he had murdered Absyrtus into the ground, laid his palm upon it, and supported his chin on the hilt, without raising his eyes. Then Circe knew that those before her were suppliants, brought to her by the need for expiation and by the bitterness of exile. In honor of Zeus, the protector of suppliants, she made the necessary offering by slaughtering a young pig whose mother was still alive and calling upon Zeus who grants purification. Her servants, the Naiads, were told to collect all the means of atonement that were in the house. She herself went to the hearth and burned sacrificial cakes, praying all the while to pacify the Furies and beg the gods to forgive those who had stained their hands with murder. When all was done she first seated the strangers on splendid chairs and sat down opposite them. Then she asked them about their journey, from where they had come, why they had landed on her island, and how it was they had begged her protection; for she recalled her dream with its streams of blood. Now when Medea raised her head to reply and looked into her face, Circe was struck by the girl's eyes, for Medea as well as she was descended from the sun-god, and all his descendants had eyes glinted with gold. When she noticed this, Circe asked the fugitives to speak in their native tongue, and—in the language used in Colchis—the girl began to tell her all that had happened between Aeetes and the heroes, quite truthfully, only that she suppressed the murder of her brother Absyrtus. But the sorceress knew even that which remained unspoken. She pitied her niece and said: "Poor girl, you have fled from home, leaving a dishonored name behind, and you have committed a grave wrong. Surely your father will come to Greece to take vengeance upon you for the murder of his son. I shall do you no harm, for you are a suppliant and my kinswoman to boot, but you must leave with this stranger, whoever he may be, for I cannot commend either your plans or your shameful flight." At these words the girl was filled with aching grief. She covered her head with her veil and cried bitterly, until Jason took her by the hand. With faltering steps she followed him out of Circe's palace.

But Hera took pity on those she had chosen to protect. Down the many-colored path of the rainbow she sent Iris, her messenger, to summon Thetis, the goddess of the sea, and when she had come, entrusted the ship and the heroes to her care. As soon as Jason and Medea went aboard, gentle winds began to blow. With lighter heart, the heroes weighed anchor and hoisted sail. The Argo sped on in a fresh breeze, and soon they saw a beautiful island, green and flower-laden, the habitation of the beguiling sirens, who lure passers-by with their singing, but only to destroy them. Half bird and half maiden, they always lay in wait for new quarry, and no one who came near could escape them. Now they sang their sweetest airs to the Argonauts, who were just about to cast their rope ashore and make fast the ship, when Orpheus, the singer from Thrace, rose in his seat and began to strike such rich and ringing chords on the strings of his divine lyre that he drowned out the voices decoying his friends to death. At the same time the gods sent a swift and sounding wind to the stern of the ship, so that the song of the sirens soon died away in its wake. Only one of the heroes, Butes, the son of Teleon, had been unable to resist the silvery strains. He sprang from his rowing bench, dived into the sea, and swam toward the enchanting sounds. And he would have perished, had it not been for Aphrodite, who ruled over Mount Eryx in Sicily. She snatched him from the whirlpool and cast him ashore on a promontory of the island, where he lived from that time on. The Argonauts mourned him as one dead, and went on to other adventures.

They came to a strait, flanked on the one side by Scylla, a steep rock which jutted out into the sea and seemed as if it would dash the Argo to pieces, on the other by Charybdis, the whirlpool, sucking the waters down and threatening to swallow the ship. The waters between these two were full of floating rocks, torn from the depths. There Hephaestus had once had his smithy, but now only smoke rose through the water and darkened the air. As the heroes approached, suddenly from all sides sea nymphs, the daughters of Nereus, came to meet them, and Thetis, their queen, put her own hand on the rudder. They all swam around the ship, and whenever it neared the floating rocks, one nymph flicked it to another, like girls playing ball. Now it flew up to the clouds on the crest of a wave, now it sank into deep troughs. From the top of a crag Hephaestus, his hammer slung over his shoulder, watched the game, and Hera, the wife of Zeus, saw it from the star-spangled sky. But she clutched Athene's hand, for she could not look on without giddiness. At last they were safe from danger and sailed on over the open sea until they came to the island of the Phaeacians and their good king Alcinous.

THE COLCHIANS CONTINUE THEIR PURSUIT

He received them hospitably, and they were taking their ease when a great Colchian fleet, which had come by another route, suddenly appeared and landed a host of warriors. These demanded Medea, the daughter of their king, whom they wished to take back to her father. If she were withheld, they threatened the Greeks with battle that very instant, with worse to come when Aeetes arrived with a still greater army. They were, indeed, just about to begin fighting when wise King Alcinous succeeded in restraining them, saying that he wished to settle the quarrel without spilling blood.

Medea clasped the knees of Arete, his wife. "I beseech you," she said, "do not let them return me to my father! You too belong to the race of mortals, that race which errs so easily and plunges into sudden disaster. I acted without thinking. It was not lightly, however, that I fled with this man, but only for fear of my father. Jason is taking me to his country. So have pity on me, and may the gods give you long life, and many children, and grace your city with everlasting splendor."

She also threw herself at the feet of one hero after another, and each one bade her be of good courage, shook his lance, brandished his sword, and promised to help her if Alcinous attempted to give her up to her enemies.

In the night the king and his wife took counsel concerning the girl from Colchis. Arete pleaded for her and told him that Jason intended making her his lawful wife. Alcinous was a kindly man, and his heart softened still more when he heard this. "For the girl's sake," he answered his wife, "I should be glad to drive the Colchians away at the point of the sword, but I am reluctant to violate Zeus' law of hospitality; besides, it is unwise to annoy Aeetes, who is a powerful king, for even though he lives far away, he is quite able to bring war upon all of Greece. So this is what I have resolved: if the girl is a virgin, she must be returned to her father. If she were Jason's wife, I should not take her from her husband, for then she would belong to him more than to her father."

Arete was alarmed when she heard the king's decision. That very night she sent a messenger to Jason to tell him of it and advise him to marry Medea before daybreak. When Jason put this unexpected proposal before the heroes, they were well pleased, and in a sacred grotto, to the music of Orpheus, Medea became Jason's wife.

In the morning, when the shores of the island and the dewy fields glittered in the early beams of the sun, the Phaeacians were astir in the streets of their city, and at the other end of the island stood the Colchians fully armed. According to his promise Alcinous came from his palace, holding his golden scepter, to pronounce judgment on the girl. The noblest among his subjects formed his retinue. The women too had come to marvel at the Greek heroes, and much country folk had assembled, for Zeus had spread the tidings far and wide. All was in readiness before the walls of the city, and smoke from the offerings rose toward heaven. The heroes had been waiting for a long time. When the king had seated himself on his throne, Jason came forward and declared, swearing to the truth of his words, that Medea, the daughter of King Aeetes, was his lawful wife. When Alcinous heard this and had questioned those who had witnessed the ceremony, he took a solemn oath that Medea should not be delivered up and that he would protect his guests. It was in vain that the Colchians objected. The king bade them either remain in his country as peaceful settlers or leave in their ships. Since they were afraid to return to their king without Medea, they chose the former alternative. On the seventh day, the Argonauts took leave of Alcinous, who parted with them regretfully and gave them lavish gifts. They boarded the ship and continued on their journey.

THE LAST ADVENTURES OF THE ARGONAUTS

Again they passed the shores of many lands and many islands, and in the distance had just caught sight of their native coast, the land of Pelops, when a cruel storm, blowing from the north, descended upon their ship and for nine whole days and nights drove it on uncharted ways through the Libyan Sea. At the end of that time, they drifted toward the wastes of Africa and ran into one of the bays of Syrtis, whose waters, covered with thick weed and sluggish foam, form a menacing marsh. Round about there was nothing but sand—no beast, no bird. The ship edged so close to the shore that the keel stuck in a sandbank. In great alarm the heroes disembarked and saw with horror that the broad land spread limitlessly in all directions, vast and empty as air. There was no spring, no path, no shelter. A dead silence hung over everything.

"Woe to us," they lamented. "What is the name of this country? Whither has the tempest driven our ship? It would have been better had we crashed into the floating rocks! Had we only done something against the will of Zeus, and perished in one glorious attempt!"

"Yes," said the helmsman. "The tide has left us high and dry and will not come for us again. All hopes of voyage and home-coming are cut off. Let anyone steer who can and will!" And with that, he took his hand from the rudder, sat down in the ship, and wept. As men in a pest-stricken city loiter in ghostly grief and wait for death, so the heroes sorrowed, and slunk along the barren shore. When evening came, each took the others' hand in farewell, lay down on the sand without food or drink, wrapped himself in his cloak, and waited for death through the long sleepless night. A little apart from them the Phaeacian handmaids Alcinous had given Medea as a gift huddled around their mistress and sighed like dying swans which breathe their last song into the air. And surely all, men and women alike, would have perished, unmourned, had not the three demigoddesses who ruled over Libya taken pity upon them.

At burning noon they came, covered with goatskin from neck to ankles, gently took hold of the mantle which Jason had thrown over his head, and drew it from his temples. He leaped up in alarm and reverently turned his eyes from the goddesses. "Luckless man," they said, "we know all your troubles. But grieve no longer. When the sea-goddess has unharnessed the horses from Poseidon's chariot, give thanks to your mother, who bore you so long in her womb. After that you shall return to the happy and radiant land of Greece."

The goddesses vanished, and Jason told his companions the comforting, if puzzling utterance. While they were still wondering about it, a second and equally strange miracle appeared to them. A mighty stallion, with golden mane streaming to both sides of his neck, rushed up from the sea, shook the foam from his flanks, and stormed away, as if shod with the wind. Then Peleus cried joyfully: "The first part of the mystery is solved. The sea-goddess has unharnessed her chariot, which was drawn by this steed. And the mother, who has carried us so long in her womb—that is our ship! We are to give her the thanks which are her due. Let us lift the Argo and bear her on our shoulders over the sand, in the tracks of the sea-stallion. For he will not disappear in the earth but show us the way to some launching-site."

No sooner was it said than done. The heroes took the ship upon their shoulders and groaned under her weight for twelve days and nights. On and on they plodded over waterless wastes, and had not a god given them strength, all would have perished on the first day. But as it was, they reached the bay of Tritonis with vigor unimpaired. Here they let their load slide from their shoulders and, frantic with thirst, looked for a spring, running hither and thither like mad dogs. In this search, Orpheus, the singer, came upon the Hesperides, the sweet-throated nymphs who dwell in the holy field where the dragon Ladon guards the golden apples. Orpheus implored them to lead him to a well, and the nymphs were moved to compassion. Aegle, the stateliest among them, told him of a curious matter.

"The bold robber who appeared here yesterday," she said, "who slew the dragon and took our golden apples, must have come to bring help to you. He was a savage man, and his eyes flashed under brows beetling with anger. A lion's skin hung over his shoulder; in his hands he carried a club of olive wood and the arrows with which he killed the monster. He too was thirsty after walking through these wastes. When he failed to find water, he kicked the rock with his heel and the stone gushed water, as though from a magic touch. The mighty man flung himself to the ground, cupped his hands against the rock, and drank to his heart's content until, like a bull whose thirst is stilled, he lay down on the earth."

So spoke Aegle and pointed out to them a spring spurting from the rock. The heroes crowded about it, and when they had quenched their thirst they grew merry again.

"Truly," said one, cooling his hot lips with one last draught, "even though he was not with us, Heracles saved the life of his comrades. If we only could meet him somewhere on our further journey!" And at that they set out to look for him, some here and some there. When they assembled again, no one had seen him save sharp-eyed Lynceus, who claimed to have glimpsed him from afar, but only like a farmer, who thinks he has caught sight of the new moon behind driving clouds, and he assured the rest that it would be impossible to catch up with him.

Unfortunate accidents killed two of the Argonauts. After their comrades had given them fitting burial, they again boarded the ship. For a long time they tried to leave the bay for the open sea, but the wind was against them, and the Argo crossed and re-crossed the harbor like a serpent which vainly seeks to leave its hiding-place and darts its head hither and thither with glassy eyes and hissing tongue. At the advice of Orpheus, they went ashore and dedicated to the gods of that place the largest tripod they had in the ship. On the way back they met Triton, the sea-god, who had assumed the form of a youth. He lifted a clod from the ground and handed it to Euphemus in token of hospitality, and the hero hid it in his bosom.

"My father sent me to watch over the waters of these regions," said the sea-god. "Look! Do you see that patch, where the bay is dark and deep and motionless? Row over there, and you will find a narrow passage from the bay to the open sea. I shall send you a fair wind and you will soon reach the Peloponnesus." They boarded the Argo full of joy. Triton lifted the tripod to his shoulder and vanished in the waters.

After a few days, they came to the rocky coast of Carpathus, and from there they intended crossing to the lovely island of Crete. But it was guarded by the terrible giant Talos. He alone was left of the generation of the Men of Bronze who had once sprung from beeches, and Zeus had made him doorkeeper to Europe and bidden him make the rounds of the island on his brazen feet three times a day. His body was of bronze, and he was invulnerable. Only one little place on one ankle was of flesh, with sinews and a vein with coursing blood. Whoever knew of this spot and hit it could be sure of slaying him, for he was not immortal. When the heroes approached the island, he was keeping watch on a cliff at the edge of the sea. As soon as he saw them, he began breaking off blocks of stone and hurling them at the ship. In great alarm the Argonauts rowed backwards and would have given up their plan of landing on Crete, though they were again tormented with thirst, had not Medea risen and told them to take heart.

"Listen," she said. "I know how to subdue this monster. All you need do is to keep the ship out of throwing distance." Then she held high the folds of her crimson gown and walked along the ship, Jason guiding her. In a low voice she pronounced a weird spell, calling three times upon the Fates who cut the thread of life, and the swift hounds of the underworld that race through air and hunt the living. With her charms she caused the lids of Talos to close and sent black dreams to haunt his soul. Dazed with sleep, he bent to pick up a stone for the defence of the harbor, but he hit his vulnerable ankle against a pointed crag, and the blood welled from the wound, thick as molten lead. Like a pine, half-hewn by the woodcutter, which the first gust of wind tumbles crashing to the ground, so Talos swayed on his feet and then plunged into the sea with a roar like thunder.

Now the Argonauts could safely land, and they rested on that beautiful island until morning. Hardly had they left Crete, however, when a new and fearful adventure confronted them. Moonless night fell, and not a single star lit the sky. The air was black as though all the darkness in the world had gathered there, and they did not know whether they were sailing the sea or the tides of Tartarus. With lifted hands, Jason implored Phoebus Apollo to set them free from this spectral darkness. Tears of terror coursed down his cheeks, and he promised the god to dedicate priceless offerings to him. And the sun-god heard. He descended from Olympus, leaped upon a cliff, and taking his golden bow in his hand, shot silver arrows over that region. In the sudden light they saw a small island toward which they steered. There they cast anchor and waited for the dawn. When they were riding the high seas in the broad light of the sun, Euphemus remembered a dream he had had that night. The clod of earth which Triton had given him and which he carried against his breast, seemed to suck itself full of milk, stir with life, and grow into a lovely maiden who said: "I am the daughter of Triton and of Libya. Give me to the daughter of Nereus, so that I may live in the sea close to Anaphe. Thereafter I shall again come out into the sun, for I am destined to provide for your grandsons."

Euphemus recalled all this because the name of the island where they had waited for morning had been Anaphe. Jason, to whom he told his dream, at once knew what it signified. He advised his friend to cast the clod he carried in his bosom into the waves. And when this was done, lo! before the eyes of the heroes a fertile island sweet with flowers and fruits rose up out of the sea. They called it Calliste, which means the fairest of all, and in after years Euphemus peopled it with his children.

This was the last adventure of the Argonauts. They soon reached the island of Aegina and from there steered toward their native land and ran into the harbor of Iolcus. In the strait of Corinth, Jason consecrated the ship to Poseidon. When it had crumbled to dust, the gods set it in the heavens, and it glittered in the southern firmament as a shining constellation.

JASON'S END

Jason did not succeed to the throne of Iolcus, for whose sake he had gone on his dangerous quest, taken Medea from her father, and wickedly murdered her brother Absyrtus. He had to leave the realm to Acastus, the son of Pelias, and flee to Corinth with his young wife. Here he lived with her for ten years, during which time she bore him three sons. The two eldest were twins, and their names were Thessalus and Alcimenes; the third, Tisander, was much younger. During these years, Jason had loved and honored Medea, not only for her beauty but for her quick wits and resourceful mind as well. But later, when time lessened the charms of her person, he fell deeply in love with a beautiful young girl, Glauce, the daughter of Creon, king of Corinth. He wooed her without his wife's knowledge, and only after her father had agreed to the union and appointed a day for the wedding did Jason tell Medea and urge her to consent to dissolve their marriage. Not that he had wearied of her, he protested, but it would be of advantage to their children if he were kin to the ruling house. Medea received his demand with bitter resentment and angrily called the gods to testify to the oaths he had sworn her. But Jason ignored her fury and insisted on wedding the king's daughter.

In despair Medea wandered through her husband's palace. "Woe is me," she cried. "Would that a flash from heaven might strike me down! Why should I live any longer? If only Death would take pity upon me! O father! O country I left in disgrace! O my brother, whom I murdered, and whose blood is now coming upon me! But it was not Jason, my husband, who should have punished me! It was for him that I sinned! O goddess of justice, I call upon you to destroy him and his young concubine!"

Creon, Jason's father-in-law, came upon her in the palace as she raged through room and court. "You with your scowling eyes," he said, "you who are smoldering with fury at your husband, take your sons by the hand and leave my country this very instant. I shall not return home until I have driven you from my borders."

Medea suppressed her anger and answered him composedly. "Why fear evil from me, Creon? You have done me no wrong; you owed me nothing. You gave your daughter to a man who met with your approval. How did I concern you? I hate only my husband, who owed me everything! But what is done is done. Let them live together as man and wife. Oh, let me continue to dwell in your country, for though I have been greatly wronged, I shall be silent and submit to those mightier than I."

But Creon saw the rage in her eyes and did not trust her, even when she clasped his knees and implored him by the name of his own daughter Glauce, her hated rival. "Go," he said, "and free me of care." But when she begged him to put off her exile for one short day, so that she might find a refuge for her sons, he replied: "I am not harsh of spirit. Many times I have foolishly yielded, beguiled by misplaced pity. Now too I feel that I am not acting wisely. Nonetheless—have your way in this."

As soon as Medea had gained the respite she desired, madness came over her, and she prepared to carry out a deed she had vaguely planned, yet never really considered doing. First, however, she made one last attempt to convince her husband of his disloyalty and injustice. "You have betrayed me," she cried.

"You took another wife, notwithstanding the fact that I have given you sons. If you were childless, I could forgive you; you would have an excuse. As it is, you have none at all. Do you think the gods who ruled the world when you swore faith to me are no more, or that men are living by new laws, that you dare break your word? Tell me—I shall ask you as though you were my friend—where do you advise me to go? Will you send me back to my father, whom I deceived, whose son I killed for love of you? Or what other refuge would you suggest for me? It will, indeed, add glory to the new-wed pair if your first wife and your own sons roam through the world as beggars!"

But Jason was deaf to her reproaches. He promised to supply her and the children with gold and send messages to friends who might offer her hospitality, but she rejected such help. "Go, marry," she said. "You will celebrate a bridal which will end in sorrow."

When Jason had left her, she regretted these last words, not because her purpose had changed, but because she feared he might keep watch on her and prevent her from putting her evil plan into execution. And so she sent for him again, put on a more gentle manner, and chose wistful words. "Jason, forgive me for what I said. I was blinded with rage. Now I see very well that all you have done is for the best. We came here as poor fugitives. By this new marriage of yours, you expect to provide for yourself, for your children, and even for me. When they have been away from you for a little, you will recall your sons and let them share in the fortune of their sisters and brothers. Come, my children, and cast out your bitterness against your father, just as I have cast out mine."

Jason really believed that she had put from her the grudge she had borne him. He rejoiced at this and made many promises to her and the children. And Medea set out to make him still more certain of her good faith. She begged him to keep the children and let her go alone. To gain consent for this from Glauce and her father, she had precious robes of gold fetched from her stores and gave them to Jason for the king's daughter. At first he hesitated, but finally she convinced him, and he had a servant take the gifts to the bride. But those beautiful robes were made of stuffs which had been drenched with poison. When Medea had bidden her husband a falsely sweet farewell, she waited from hour to hour for the messenger who was to report to her how her presents had been received. At last he came and called from afar: "Board your ship, Medea, and flee! Your foe and her father are both dead. When your sons entered the palace at their father's side, we servants rejoiced that the feud was healed. The young princess received your husband with smiling lips, but when she saw the children, she veiled her eyes and turned away her face as if she loathed their presence. Jason tried to placate her, spoke kindly words in their behalf, and spread out the gifts before her. The sight of the magnificent robes gladdened her heart. She softened and promised the bridegroom to agree to everything he wished. When your husband and sons had left her, she reached eagerly for the marvellous raiment, cast the golden mantle about her shoulders, twined the gold wreath in her hair, and joyfully looked at the image shining out at her from the clear mirror. Then she trailed through her apartments, childishly proud of her new apparel. But soon her feelings changed. She paled, her limbs shook. Her feet faltered, and before she could reach a seat, she fell. The color ebbed from her face, she turned up her eyes so that only the whites showed, and foam gathered on her lips. The palace rang with cries. Some of the servants hurried to her father, others to her husband. In the meantime the magic wreath on her head had burst into flame. Poison and fire contended for her flesh, and when her father rushed in to her with loud lament, he found only the dead disfigured body of his daughter. In his despair, he threw himself upon her, and the poison in the murderous robe worked on him also, so that he too lost his life. I know nothing of Jason."

Instead of cooling Medea's rage, the recital of these horrors only served to fan it to hotter flame. Like an avenging Fury she ran out to deal the fatal blow to her husband and herself. Night had fallen, and she hurried to the room where her sons lay asleep. "Steel yourself, my heart," she muttered on the way. "Why do you shudder from doing the awful, the needful deed? Forget that these are your children, that you have borne them. Forget it for this one hour only, and then mourn them all your days. You are doing them a welcome service. If you do not kill them, they will die at the hands of their foes."

When Jason hastened toward his house to find the murderess
of his young bride and take vengeance on her, he heard the
screams of his children. Running through the open door of their
chamber he found them bleeding from deadly wounds, slain like
victims at the altar. Medea was nowhere to be seen. When he left
his house, he heard a rushing sound overhead. Looking up, he
beheld her in a dragon-drawn chariot, which her magic art had
conjured, riding the wind away from the scene of her revenge.
Jason had no hope of punishing her for her crime. Despair en-
gulfed him. His soul remembered the murder of Absyrtus. He
rushed upon his sword and died on the threshold of his house.

MELEAGER AND THE BOAR

Oeneus, king of Calydon, brought the first fruits of a lavish harvest season as an offering to the gods: grain to Demeter, wine to Dionysus, oil to Athene, and so to each deity the proper gift. Only Artemis was forgotten, and no fumes of incense rose at her altar. This angered the goddess, and she resolved to take revenge on him who had neglected her. She set a great boar on the king's domains. His red eyes darted fire, his neck bristled. Lightning seemed to dart from his foaming jaws, and his tusks were like those of an elephant. This huge beast trampled the meadows and fields, so that barns and lofts gaped empty of the promised crops. He devoured the grapevines, clusters, and leaves, and ate the branches along with the olives. Neither shepherds nor their dogs were able to defend the flocks against the monster, nor the most savage bulls their herds.

At last the king's son, fair Meleager, assembled hunters and hounds to slay the wild boar. The most famous heroes of all Greece were invited to join in the chase, and with them Atalanta of Arcadia, the warlike daughter of Iasus. She had been abandoned in a forest and suckled by a bear. Later, huntsmen had found her and reared her. She had grown into a beautiful maiden, but she despised men and spent her days hunting in the forest. Not only had she rejected all men who approached her, but she even shot two centaurs who persisted in their suit. Now it was love of the chase that lured her into the company of these heroes. Her hair was caught in a simple knot, her ivory quiver slung across her shoulder, and in her left hand she carried her bow. Her face looked girlish for a boy, and boyish for a girl. When Meleager saw how fair she was, he said to himself: "Happy the man she will consider worthy to be her husband!" But he had not time to pursue this train of thought, for the dangerous hunt allowed no delay.

The group of hunters walked toward a wood of ancient trees, which covered the level countryside and the slope of the mountain.

When they arrived, some went about setting snares, while others unleashed the hounds and still others followed the tracks of the quarry. Presently they came to a steep and narrow valley, carved out by swollen streams. This gorge, thick with reeds, swamp grass, and osiers, was the boar's hiding place. Now that the hounds had roused him, he broke through the wood like lightning speeding from a cloud and charged into the very midst of his foes. The youths cried aloud and pointed their spears, but the boar evaded them and crashed through the pack. Missile after missile flew at him, only to graze his hide and increase his fury. With flashing eyes and heaving breast he turned, made for the right flank of the hunters like a stone shot from the sling, and bore three of them to the ground, killing them instantly. A fourth —Nestor, destined to become a great hero in times to come— saved himself by climbing into the branches of an oak tree, on whose trunk the boar sharpened his terrible tusks. And here the twin brothers, Castor and Polydeuces, charging on snow-white horses, would have pierced him with their spears, had he not fled into impenetrable thickets. Then Atalanta fitted an arrow to her string and shot at the monster through the bushes. It struck him under the ear, and now at last his bristles were stained with blood. Meleager was the first to see the wound, and jubilantly he pointed it out to his comrades. "Atalanta," he cried, "it is you who deserve the prize of valor!" At this the men felt ashamed to think that a woman was cheating them of victory, and all threw their spears at once. But the very shower of their missiles prevented a single one from reaching the animal.

Now Ancaeus, the Arcadian, proudly raised his two-edged battle-axe in both hands and made ready to deal the blow. But before it fell, the boar drove his tusks into the hero's side and laid bare his entrails, so that he died in a pool of blood. Then Jason cast his spear, but it missed the mark and glanced sidewise and into the body of Celadon. Finally Meleager hurled two spears, one after the other. The first fell to the ground, but the second pierced the boar in the middle of the back. The beast began to rage and run in circles. Blood and foam spurted from his mouth. Meleager dealt him a fresh blow on the neck, and now lances struck him from all sides. The dying boar lay stretched on the earth and writhed in the blood pouring from his wounds.

Meleager pressed his foot against his head, and with his sword ripped the rough hide from the beast and presented it to brave Atalanta along with the head and the gleaming tusks. "Take these trophies," he said. "They are mine by right, but you shall share in my glory."

But the hunters were angry that such honor should be accorded a woman, and a murmur ran through their ranks. The brothers of Meleager's mother, the sons of Thestius, clenched their fists, shook them at Atalanta, and threatened her with loud words. "Put down those trophies at once, woman," they cried. "Do not think you can trick us of what is ours. Your beauty will aid you just as little as Meleager, that love-sick waster of these gifts!" With that they took the head and hide from her, disputing Meleager's right to dispose of them. At this he was overcome with rage, ground his teeth, and roared: "You who would rob the deserts of another, let me teach you how threat differs from deed!" And before his uncles knew what he was about, he had plunged his sword first into one and then the other.

Althaea, Meleager's mother, was on her way to the temple of the gods to offer thanks for her son's victory when the bodies of her brothers were carried by. She beat her breast in anguish, hastened back to the palace, changed her golden robes of rejoicing for the black of mourning, and filled the city with lament. But when she heard that the murderer was her own son Meleager, she dried her tears. Her sorrow changed to the lust to kill, and she suddenly remembered something she had long since forgotten.

When Meleager had been but a few days old, the Fates had appeared at his mother's bedside. "Your son will become a brave hero," the first foretold. "Your son will be a great man," prophesied the second. "Your son," concluded the third, "will live until that brand on the hearth is consumed by fire." Hardly had the Fates vanished when Althaea took the brand from the hearth, quenched it in water, and, full of solicitude for the life of her son, hid it in a secret chamber.

Now, in her vengeful anger, she thought of the brand and hurried to the place where she had locked it away. She had kindling and wood brought, and when the flames leapt high, seized the brand she had taken from its hiding-place. But in her heart, the mother struggled with the sister. Her face grew pale and then flushed. Four times she reached forward to place the brand in the fire, and four times she drew back her hand. In the end her sisterly love overcame her.

"Turn your eyes upon me," she said. "Look at me, goddesses of vengeance, look at this offering to the Furies! And you, spirits of my brothers, so recently fled from the body, know what I am doing for your sake! Accept the hapless fruit of my own body as your burial gift—ah! so dearly bought! My heart is breaking with motherlove, and soon I shall follow him whose life I am taking for your sake!" So she spoke and, turning away her gaze, threw the brand into the fire with shaking fingers.

Meleager, in the meantime, had returned to the city, brooding with mingled emotions on his triumph, his love, and his crime. Suddenly he felt his innermost being burn with fever, and he threw himself on his couch in an agony of pain. He bore it like a hero but grieved to die an inglorious death far from the battle-field, and envied his comrades who had perished from the thrusts of the boar. Moaning he called for his brother, his sisters, his aged father, and his mother, who was still standing at the hearth, watching with stony gaze while the fire consumed the brand. Her son's pains waxed with the flames, but when they waned and nothing was left but pale ash, his suffering grew less, and at the last spark he breathed his last, and the spirit left his body. His father, his sisters, and all Calydon mourned at his bier. But his mother was absent. They found her strangled in a noose, stretched at the very hearth which held the brittle cinders.

TANTALUS

TANTALUS, son of Zeus, ruled over Sipylus in Lydia. He was very rich in worldly goods and famed for his wealth in both Asia and Greece. If ever the Olympian gods paid honor to a mortal, it was to him. Because of his divine origin, they cherished him as a friend, and at last he was even permitted to dine at the board of Zeus and listen to the words which passed between the immortals. But his vain human spirit could not bear the exquisite burden of unearthly bliss, and he began to sin against the gods in a number of ways: he betrayed their secrets; he filched nectar and ambrosia from their board and distributed it among his companions in the world below; he hid the image of a dog, wrought of precious gold, which another had stolen from Zeus' temple in Crete, and when the king of the gods demanded it back, he swore he had never seen it. Finally, in his matchless arrogance, he invited the gods to his palace as a return for their hospitality, and in order to test whether they really knew all things, he had his own son Pelops slain and prepared for their meal. Only Demeter ate of the gruesome dish—one shoulder-blade. The other gods recognized what had been put before them and threw the torn limbs of the boy into a cauldron, from which Clotho, one of the Fates, drew him forth in fresh beauty. But one shoulder was of ivory!

With this, Tantalus had exceeded all bounds of iniquity, and the gods thrust him down to Hades, where he was punished with cruel torments. He had to stand in the middle of a lake whose waters came to his chin, yet he suffered burning thirst, for he could not reach the draught so close to his lips. Whenever he bent down to quench his thirst, the water receded, and at his feet lay the dark dry earth. At the same time he had to endure the pangs of hunger. Behind him, on the margin of the lake, grew beautiful fruit trees which arched their boughs over his head. Looking up, he saw juicy pears, red-cheeked apples, glowing pomegranates, plump figs, and green olives. But the moment he reached to pluck them, a strong wind whipped the branches up into the clouds. His last and most terrible torment was the incessant fear of death. A great block of stone hung in the air over his head and constantly threatened to crush him. So impious Tantalus, who scorned the gods, was destined to threefold, perpetual suffering in the underworld.

PELOPS

TANTALUS had done the gods great wrong; his son Pelops honored them devoutly. After his father had been thrust into Hades, a war with his neighbor, the king of Troy, drove Pelops from his own country of Lydia, and he journeyed to Greece. The chin of the youth was only just touched with the first dark down, but his heart had already chosen a wife. It was Hippodamia, the daughter of king Oenomaus of Elis, and she was a prize not easily won. For an oracle had foretold that the king would die when his daughter married, and so he did all he could to keep her suitors at a distance. Throughout the land he issued a proclamation that he who would wed his daughter must first defeat her father in a chariot race. If, however, the king were victorious, the contestant was to forfeit his life. The race was to begin at Pisa and end at Poseidon's altar on the isthmus of Corinth, and the start Oenomaus arranged as follows: he would first sacrifice a ram to Zeus, taking his time about it, while the suitor set off in his four-horse chariot. Only when the rites of offering were duly fulfilled would he begin the race and pursue the other, spear in hand, in the chariot guided by Myrtilus, his charioteer. If he caught up with him, he should have the right to pierce him to the heart.

When the many youths who wooed Hippodamia for her beauty heard these conditions, they were of good courage, for they regarded the king as a feeble old man who knew very well that he could not race with the young, and gave them so great a start in order to explain his probable defeat by this act of generosity. One after another came to Elis and asked the king for his daughter. He received each in a most friendly manner, gave him a splendid four-horse chariot, and went to sacrifice a ram to Zeus without the slightest show of haste. Only then did he mount his light chariot, drawn by his two mares Phylla and Harpinna, who ran swifter than the north wind. And every time the charioteer caught up with the suitor long before the goal was reached, and the cruel king pierced him with his spear. In this fashion he had already slain more than twelve youths.

On the way to his beloved, Pelops had landed on the peninsula which was one day to bear his name. He soon heard all that was happening in Elis. At nightfall he went to the shore and called upon his patron god, Poseidon, swinger of the mighty trident, and the waves parted and he surged up through the sea. "O Poseidon," cried Pelops, "if the gifts of Aphrodite are welcome to you, turn the sharp spear of Oenomaus from me. Send me to Elis in the swiftest chariot, and lead me to victory. Already he has destroyed thirteen wooers, and he is still putting off marriage for his daughter. Great danger calls for a brave spirit. I am determined to try my luck. I must die someday, so why sit in gloom, awaiting inglorious old age, and share in no brilliant conquests? I want to undertake this race. Give me the success I pray for!"

And Pelops did not plead in vain. For again the waves surged and parted, and a chariot of shimmering gold with four winged horses swift as arrows rose from the depths. On this Pelops sped to Elis, guiding the sea-god's horses at will and outrunning the wind. When Oenomaus saw him coming he quailed, for he recognized Poseidon's chariot at a glance. But he did not refuse to race with the stranger on the usual conditions. After Pelops' horses had rested from their journey along the isthmus, he started them off on the race track. He was close to the goal when the king, who had sacrificed the ram according to his custom, suddenly caught up with him, brandishing his spear to deal the bold suitor the fatal blow. But Poseidon, the protector of Pelops, loosened the wheels of the king's chariot while it was going at full speed, so that it crashed to earth. Oenomaus fell and was killed instantly. At that very moment, Pelops reached the goal. When he looked back, he saw the king's palace in flames. A flash of lightning had set it afire and destroyed it until only a single pillar was left standing. But Pelops sped toward the burning house in his winged chariot and fetched his bride out of the ruins.

NIOBE

NIOBE, queen of Thebes, had much to be proud of. The Muses had given her husband Amphion a lyre whose strings breathed sounds of such persuasive sweetness that once at his playing the very stones had joined themselves to rear the palace of Thebes. Her father was Tantalus, the guest of the immortals. She herself ruled over a mighty realm and was famed for her noble spirit, for her beauty, and for her stateliness. But nothing made her heart beat higher than the thought of her fourteen children, seven sons and seven daughters. Niobe was known as the happiest of all mothers, and this she would, indeed, have been, had she not vaunted her happiness too exultantly. As it was, her awareness of it proved her destruction.

One day the seeress Manto, daughter of Tiresias, was moved to cry out in the streets, exhorting the women of Thebes to do

honor to Leto and her twin children Apollo and Artemis. She
bade them wreathe their brows with laurel, make fervent prayer,
and offer sacrifice. While the women of Thebes gathered to listen,
Niobe suddenly appeared amid a throng of her followers. She
wore a gown worked with golden thread. Radiant in her beauty,
except where anger clouded her countenance, tossing her lovely
head with its lustrous hair rippling down over her shoulders, she
stood among the women who were preparing the sacrifice under
the open sky. Her haughty glances swept over the assembly, and
she said:

"Are you mad that you honor the gods, who are no more than
idle tales among you, while beings more favored by heaven actually dwell in your midst? You set up altars to Leto! Why does not
incense rise to my divine name? Is not my father Tantalus the
only mortal who ever ate at the board of Zeus? My mother Dione
is sister to the Pleiades, who shine as a brilliant constellation in
the skies. One of my ancestors, Atlas, was so strong that he carried the broad heavens on his shoulders. My father's father is
Zeus himself. Even the peoples of Phrygia obey me. The city of
Cadmus, the walls that rose to the playing of Amphion, are subject to me and my husband. Every chamber in my palace is filled
with marvellous treasures. Add to this that I have a face worthy
of a goddess, and children such as no other mother can boast of:
seven flower-like daughters and seven sturdy sons, and soon I
shall have an equal number of sons- and daughters-in-law! But
you have the boldness to prefer to me Leto, the unknown daughter
of Titans, whom the wide earth once grudged even a little space
wherein to bear children to Zeus, until the floating island of
Delos took pity on her and granted her a temporary refuge!
And there the poor creature bore her two children—a mere
seventh part of my joy-bringing harvest. Who will deny that I
am happy? Who will doubt that I shall remain so? The Fates
would have much to do if they set about harming my possessions.
Even if they took one or the other of my brood, how could their
number ever sink to a mere two, such as Leto's children? So away
with your offerings! Snatch the wreaths from your heads! Disperse and go home, and never again let me find you engaged in
such foolishness."

The women were afraid. They tore the laurel from their brows, left the sacrifice unfinished and crept home, honoring the offended goddess with silent prayers.

On the peak of Mount Cynthus in Delos stood Leto with her twin children, gazing with divine eyes upon what was happening in far-off Thebes. "Behold, my children," she said, "I, your mother, who am so proud to have borne you, I who give place to no goddess but Hera, must suffer the disdain of insolent mortals! Unless you aid me, I shall be thrust away from my ancient holy altars. Yes, and Niobe is slandering you also by placing you second to her own brood." She was complaining thus when Phoebus interrupted her.

"Leave off lamenting, mother," he said. "You are only delaying punishment." And his sister seconded him. Both veiled themselves in cloud and sped through the air to the city of Cadmus. Before its walls was a spacious field, not intended for sowing and reaping, but for races and practice with horses and chariots. There the seven sons of Amphion were engaged in gay sport. Ismenus, the eldest, was just driving his mount in a circle at a trot, reining him in with a sure hand close to the bit in his foam-flecked mouth, when he suddenly groaned, "Alas!" and the rein slipped from his powerless fingers. Struck to the heart by an arrow, he slowly sank to earth at the horse's right flank. His brother Sipylus, who was nearest him, had heard a quiver rattling in the air and fled at full gallop, like a helmsman who catches the lightest wind in his sails to make the harbor before the storm. And yet an arrow whirring down from the sky pierced him in the nape of the neck, and its iron point jutted from his throat. Over the mane of his speeding horse he slid to the ground and spattered the earth with his blood. Two others, Tantalus, named after his grandfather, and Phaedimus were wrestling with each other, locked breast to breast. Once more the bowstring twanged, and an arrow stabbed both at once. They moaned, writhed on the earth, their limbs contorted with pain, their eyes dimmed, and they died in the dust at the selfsame moment. A fifth son, Alphenor, saw them fall. Beating his breast, he ran toward them and tried to warm the cold bodies of his brothers in his embrace, but while he was performing this office of love, Apollo launched a deadly dart at him, and when he drew it forth from his heart, his blood and breath flowed from him. Damasichthon, the sixth, a charming youth with long locks, was struck in the hollow of the knee, and when he bent backward to pull out the missile, a second arrow entered his open mouth up to the feathering, and his blood spurted out like a fountain. Ilioneus, a mere boy, the last and youngest son, who had watched his brothers perish one after another, fell on his knees, spread wide his arms, and began to plead: "O gods, all ye gods, spare me!" Even the grim archer was moved to compassion, but it was too late. The arrow could not be recalled. The boy fell, but he died of a painless wound, for the point barely grazed his heart.

Rumor of the disaster soon spread through the city. When Amphion heard the awful tidings, he pierced his own breast with his sword. Presently the loud laments of the servants and the people reached the women's chambers. For a long time Niobe could not grasp her misfortune. She did not want to believe that the immortals had so much power, that they dared, that they had succeeded! But soon she could no longer doubt the truth. Ah, how different was this Niobe from her who had just driven the people away from the altars of the mighty goddess and paced through the city, her head held high! Then she had seemed enviable to her dearest friends, but now she evoked the pity even of her foes. She rushed out to the field and threw herself on the cold bodies of her sons, kissing now this one, now that. Then she lifted her weary arms to the sky and cried: "Gloat over my misery! Sate your angry heart, cruel Leto! The death of these seven will cast me into the grave! Triumph over me, yours is the victory!"

Now her seven daughters, already garbed in mourning and with loosened locks, came and stood beside their fallen brothers. At sight of them a gleam of malice flickered over Niobe's pale face. She forgot herself, shot a mocking glance at the sky, and said: "Victory? No! Even in my wretchedness I have more than you in your triumph! Though all these are dead, I am still the richer!"

Hardly had the words left her lips, when through the air came a sound as of a sinew tightened on the bow. Everyone trembled, all but Niobe, whom disaster had dulled. Suddenly one of the sisters put her hand to her heart and drew out an arrow. She fainted, and as she fell turned her dying gaze upon the dead body of the brother lying nearest her. Another of the girls hastened

to her mother, to give her words of comfort, but her mouth was forever closed by an unseen dart. A third fell as she turned to flee, and still others faltered while they bowed over their dead sisters. Only the youngest was left. She fled to her mother, hid her face against her knees and clung to her, covering herself with the folds of her robe.

"Leave me this one!" Niobe cried out to heaven in pain. "Only this youngest of so many!" But even as she uttered her plea, the child loosened her hold on her, and now Niobe sat alone among the bodies of her sons and daughters. She grew rigid with sorrow. Not a hair on her head stirred in the wind. The color ebbed from her cheeks. Her eyes stared motionless in her ravaged face. The blood stopped running in her veins. Her pulse fluttered and died. Her neck, her arms, her feet were utterly still. Even her heart had turned to stone. She was lifeless save for the tears flowing unceasingly from her stark eyes. And now a tempest swept her through the air and across the sea to her old home in Lydia and set her down among the cliffs of Sipylus. Here, on the peak of the mountain, she still stands, a block of marble, which even now is washed with her tears.

SALMONEUS

SALMONEUS, ruler over Elis, was a wealthy and unjust prince with an arrogant heart. He had founded a beautiful city and called it Salmonea, and he grew so overbearing in his pride that he commanded his subjects to give him the honors and offerings due to a god. He wanted to be taken for Zeus himself, and he traversed his country and other parts of Greece in a chariot meant to resemble that of the Thunderer. To accomplish this, he tried to imitate lightning with torches launched through the air, and thunder with the hoofbeats of champing horses which he drove over a brazen bridge. He even had people killed and then pretended that his lightning had struck them down. From the heights of Olympus Zeus noted his folly. He reached into the thick of the clouds, drew forth a real thunderbolt, and hurled it at this mortal, raging in madness and insolence below. The bolt shattered the king and destroyed the city he had built with all those who dwelt in it.

HERACLES

THE INFANT HERACLES

HERACLES was the son of Zeus and Alcmene, the grand-daughter of Perseus. His stepfather, Amphitryon, was also a grandson of Perseus. He was king of Tiryns, but had left that city to take up his dwelling in Thebes. Hera, the wife of Zeus, hated her rival Alcmene and begrudged her the son for whom Zeus himself had predicted a glorious future. And so when Alcmene had borne Heracles, she did not think that he would be safe in the palace, and fearing the jealousy of the mother of the gods, exposed him in a field, which even in later times was still called the Field of Heracles. Here the child would surely have perished, had not curious chance brought Athene and Hera, his enemy, along the very path where he lay. Athene looked at the beautifully formed child with wonder, had pity on him, and induced her companion to nurse him at her divine breast. There he sucked far more lustily than his tender age warranted, and he hurt Hera, who put the boy ungently back on the ground. But Athene lifted him up, carried him to the nearby city, brought him to Queen Alcmene as a poor foundling, and asked her to rear him. Thus while his real mother, for fear of Hera, had suppressed her love and had been willing to let the child perish, his stepmother, filled with hatred for him, had unwittingly saved her rival's child from death. And she had done even more for him! Heracles had sucked at her breast only an instant, but those few drops of the goddess' milk had made him immortal.

Alcmene had recognized the child at first glance, and joyfully she laid him in the cradle. But Hera too became aware who the child was that had lain at her breast and how carelessly she had let the moment for revenge slip by. Immediately she sent two horrible serpents, which crawled through the open doors of Alcmene's bedchamber and, before the sleeping mother and her handmaids knew what was happening, writhed into the cradle

and wound their coils around the boy's throat. He woke screaming and lifted his head. The unaccustomed necklace was irksome
to him. It was then he first proved his superhuman powers. With
each hand he seized a serpent by the neck and strangled them
both with a single clenching of his fists. His nurses had only just
seen the serpents, but they were too frightened to go to the child's
aid. Alcmene had wakened at his scream. She leaped from her
bed and ran toward him, calling for help, but found the serpents
already dead in the boy's hands. Startled by her cries, the lords
of Thebes armed themselves and hastened to the bedchamber, and
King Amphitryon, who loved his stepson and regarded him as a
gift from Zeus, came brandishing his naked sword. When he saw
and heard what had happened, he shuddered with terror and
delight at the miraculous strength of his newborn son. This deed
seemed to him a portent, and so he summoned Tiresias, whom
Zeus had lent the gift of prophecy. The seer forecast the boy's
future to the king and queen and all those present: how he would
slay many monsters on earth and in the sea; how he would strive
with giants and defeat them; and how, when his toils in the world
were over, he would share in the everlasting life of the gods and
be given Hebe, the goddess of eternal youth, in marriage.

THE REARING OF HERACLES

When Amphitryon heard of the noble destiny in store for the
boy, he resolved to give him an education worthy of a hero and
called upon great men from many lands to teach young Heracles
all he should know. Amphitryon himself instructed him in the art
of driving the chariot; Eurytus showed him how to bend the bow
and aim his arrows. Harpalycus trained him in wrestling and
boxing; Castor, one of the twin sons of Zeus, in fighting, fully
armed, in field formation. And Linus, the aged son of Apollo,
taught him to sing and pluck the strings of the lyre with sureness and grace. Heracles was an apt pupil, but he could not endure harshness, and old Linus was a fault-finding teacher. Once,
when he struck the boy—unjustly it seemed to him—Heracles
snatched up his instrument, flung it at his teacher's head, and
killed him on the instant, an act which filled him with remorse. He

was summoned to court for murder. But the just and famous judge Rhadamanthys acquitted him and made a new law to the effect that if death occurred as a result of self-defense, blood-vengeance should not be sought.

But now Amphitryon feared that this over-strong son of his might become guilty of other similar offenses, and so he sent him to the country to tend his cattle. Here Heracles grew up, surpassing all men in strength and size. This offspring of Zeus was marvellous to behold. He was four ells tall, and fire flashed from his eyes. He never missed the mark, whether he shot with arrows or threw the javelin. At eighteen he was the handsomest and strongest man in Greece, and now the time had come when it was to be seen whether he would use his gifts for good or for evil.

HERACLES AT THE CROSSROADS

Heracles left the shepherds and their beasts and went to a solitary region to consider what his course in life should be. Once, as he sat pondering, he saw two women of tall stature coming toward him. One was beautiful and noble, with modest mien, and her robe fell about her in folds of stainless white. The other was full-bosomed and seductive, and the whiteness of her skin was stressed by powder and tinctures. She carried herself so arrogantly that she seemed taller than she was, and her gown revealed as much of her charms as possible. Now she complacently regarded her own person with bright, vacant eyes, then again she looked around to see if others were watching her, and often she gazed admiringly at her own shadow. As they approached, the first did not quicken her step, but the other crowded past her and ran toward the youth, whom she at once addressed.

"Heracles, I see that you are undecided what course to take in life. If you choose me for your friend, I shall guide you along a path most smooth and easy. There is no pleasure you will not taste, no discomfort you shall not avoid! You will not be concerned with war or other hardship. You shall think of nothing but the enjoyment of exquisite foods and wines, of indulging your eyes, your ears, and your whole body with pleasant sensations, of sleeping on a soft couch—and all these joys will be yours without labor or effort. Should you ever run short of the means for leading this manner of life, do not fear I might urge you to bodily or mental toil. Quite the contrary! You will reap the fruits of another's labors and refuse nothing that could bring you profit. For I accord my friends the right to use everyone and everything to their own advantage."

When Heracles heard these seductive promises, he asked in astonishment: "What is your name?" Whereupon she replied: "My friends call me Happiness, but my foes, to humiliate me, have given me the name of Idle Pleasure."

In the meantime the other woman had approached. "I too have come to you," she said. "I know your parents, your gifts, and your upbringing. All this leads me to hope that, if you choose the path I show you, you will become a master in all that is good and great. But I have no slothful joys to bribe you with. I shall tell you the will of the gods for those on earth. Know then that the immortals grant nothing to men without effort and toil. If you would have the gods look upon you kindly, you must honor them. If you would have your friends love you, you must aid them. If you would be held in esteem by a city, you must render it services. Would you have all Greece admire you for your virtue, you must become the benefactor of all Greece. If you would harvest, you must sow, if you would wage war and win, you must learn the art of warfare. If you would have control of your body, you must work and sweat to harden it."

Here Pleasure interrupted her. "Now you see, dear Heracles," she said, "what a long and hard way to satisfaction this woman proposes, while I will guide you to happiness by the shortest and easiest of paths."

"Miserable creature!" said Virtue to her. "You have nothing that is really good. How could you? You do not know true pleasures, for you are sated before you even approach them. You eat before you are hungry and drink before you thirst. To prick your desire for food, you seek out resourceful cooks; to sharpen your urge to drink, you purchase costly wines. In summer your whim is for snow. No bed is soft enough for you. You let your friends spend the night in carousing and the day in sleep. That is why in youth they go adorned on nimble carefree feet, but drag themselves through a sordid and painful old age, ashamed of what they have done and faltering under the load of what they have still to do. And you yourself, though you are immortal, are an outcast among gods and an object of derision among good men. You have never heard what sounds sweetest to the ear: true praise! You have never seen what gladdens the eyes more than all else: good works of your own! I, however, am welcome among the gods and all virtuous men. Artists hail me as their helper, fathers as a faithful watch, servingmen as kindly aid. I am an honest sharer in the pursuits of peace, a faithful ally in war, and a loyal companion in friendship. Food and drink and sleep have more savor for my friends than for idlers. The young are glad when the old commend them, the old when they are honored by the young. To recall what they have done is sweet, and they rejoice in what they are doing. Because of me, the gods cherish them, their friends love them, and their country respects them. And when the end has come, they do not fade into oblivion; their glory lives after them in the world, in the memory of times to come. Resolve, O Heracles, to choose this life, and yours will be a blessed lot."

THE FIRST ADVENTURES OF HERACLES

The apparitions vanished, and Heracles was alone. He determined to walk in the path of Virtue, and soon found an opportunity to do a good deed. At that time Greece was still covered with forests and swamps inhabited by savage lions, raging boars, and other dangerous beasts. To clear the country of these monsters and to free it from the robbers who lay in wait for the traveller in lonely places was one of the great goals of the heroes of old. Heracles was destined to continue this work.

When he returned to his people, he learned that a fierce lion had his lair on Mount Cithaeron, at whose foot the herds of King Amphitryon were pastured. The young hero—Virtue's words still ringing in his ears—made a quick decision. He armed himself, scaled the wild wooded mountain, overcame the lion, flung the skin over his shoulder, and set the gaping jaws on his head as a helmet.

As he was returning from this quest, he met the herald of Erginus, king of the Minyans, who had come for the shameful and unjust yearly tribute exacted from the Thebans. Heracles, who now regarded himself as the champion of all the oppressed, made short work of the messengers, who were already guilty of many abuses, and sent them back to their king mutilated and with ropes around their necks. Erginus demanded that the culprit be delivered up to him, and Creon, king of Thebes, was inclined to obey for fear of his great power. But Heracles persuaded a number of brave youths to go against the enemy with him. In no dwelling, however, were arms to be found, for the Minyans had removed all weapons, lest the Thebans revolt. Then Athene summoned Heracles to her temple and fitted him out with armor of her own, while the youths took from the temples the weapons their fathers had won in conquest and dedicated to the gods. Thus equipped, the hero and his little group of men marched toward the Minyans until they reached a narrow pass, where the vast army of the foe was of no avail. Erginus himself fell in the fight, and his entire host was beaten and dispersed. But in the fray, valiant Amphitryon, the stepfather of Heracles, died of a fatal wound. After the battle was over, Heracles swiftly advanced toward Orchomenus, the capital of the Minyans, forced his way through the gates, burned the king's palace, and destroyed the city.

All Greece admired his extraordinary courage, and Creon, king of Thebes, rewarded him by giving him his daughter Megara to wife, who later bore him three sons. His mother Alcmene

married again, taking for her second husband the judge Rhadamanthys. Even the immortals showered gifts upon the victorious demigod: Hermes gave him a sword, Apollo arrows,
Hephaestus a golden quiver, and Athene a brazen cuirass.

HERACLES FIGHTS THE GIANTS

The hero soon had an opportunity to make the gods generous
return for the precious gifts they had given him. The giants,
creatures with frightful faces, long hair and beards, and scaly
dragon tails instead of feet, were monsters whom Gaea, the Earth,
had borne Uranus, the sky-god. Now their mother stirred them
up against Zeus, the new ruler of the world, because he had ban-

ished her elder sons, the Titans, to Tartarus. And so they rushed forth from Erebus, the underworld, to the broad fields of Phlegra, in Thessaly. The very stars paled at sight of them, and Phoebus Apollo turned his sun-chariot in the other direction.

"Go and avenge me and the children of the older gods," said Mother Earth. "An eagle is tearing at Prometheus, a vulture at Tityus; Atlas is sentenced to carry the sky, and the Titans languish in chains. Avenge them! Come to their rescue! Use my own limbs, the mountains, for rungs and weapons! Ascend to those starry halls! You, Typhoeus, snatch scepter and thunderbolt from the hands of Zeus. Enceladus, you shall conquer the sea and drive Poseidon from his stronghold. Rhoetus shall tear the reins from the hands of the sun-god, and Porphyrion take over the oracle of Delphi."

At her words the giants burst into deafening applause, as though they had already won the victory and were leading Poseidon or Ares in the triumphal procession, or dragging Apollo away by his beautiful locks. One spoke as though Aphrodite were even now his wife, another planned to woo Artemis, a third Athene. Confident and rejoicing they went toward the mountains of Thessaly, from whence they intended to storm Olympus.

In the meantime, Iris, the messenger of the gods, called together all those in high heaven and those who dwell in rivers and springs. She even summoned the Fates from the underworld. Persephone left her realm of shadowy shapes, and her husband, the king of the silent dead, yoked his steeds that shun the light and drove them up to shining Olympus. As in a besieged city whose dwellers stream from all sides to defend the citadel, so the throng of immortals assembled at their father's hearth.

"You, who have come together here," so Zeus addressed them, "see how Gaea is conspiring against us with that new brood of hers. On with you, and see to it that for every one of her sons she sends against us, you send her back a dead body."

When the father of the gods had ended, a great clap of thunder rang out from the sky, and Gaea answered with a mighty earthquake from below. Nature lapsed into chaos, and all things were as confused as when they were first created. For the giants tore one mountain after another out by the roots. They piled Ossa and Pelion, Oeta and Athos one on top of the other, plucked out

Rhodope with half the source of the Hebrus, and when they had climbed this ponderous ladder to the very seat of the gods, they set out to storm Olympus with huge boulders and whole oaks for fire-brands.

An oracle had told the gods that they would not slay a single giant unless a mortal fought on their side. Gaea knew this, and so she cast about for a way to make her sons invulnerable to mortal men. And there was an herb which could have accomplished this, but Zeus stole a march on her. He forbade the dawn, the moon, and the sun to shine, and while Gaea groped about in darkness, he himself quickly cut the herbs and had Athene summon his son Heracles to take part in the fight.

On Olympus, the gods were already in the midst of the struggle. Ares had guided his war-chariot with its snorting steeds into the very thick of the onrushing foe. His golden shield burned brighter than flame, and the crest on his helmet streamed in the wind. He slew the giant Pelorus, whose feet were live serpents, and drove his wheels over the writhing limbs of his fallen adversary. But not until he beheld mortal Heracles, who had just mounted the last step to Olympus, did the monster yield up his three souls. Heracles glanced about the field and selected a mark for his bow. His arrow felled Alcyoneus, who plunged down from that great height but rose with fresh vigor the moment he touched the ground. At Athene's advice, Heracles too descended and lifted the giant from the earth which had borne him. The instant he was suspended in an alien element he breathed his last.

Now the giant Porphyrion took a threatening step toward Heracles and Hera at once, in order to fight them one by one. But swiftly Zeus roused his desire to look upon the divine face of the goddess, and while he was still tugging at the veil with which she had covered herself, the father of the gods struck him with a thunderbolt, and Heracles finished the work with one of his arrows. Soon after this, the giant Ephialtes stepped out from the ranks of his brothers and looked ahead with enormous flashing eyes.

"What glittering goals for our arrows!" said Heracles to Phoebus Apollo, who was fighting at his side, and shot the right eye from the giant's head, while the sun-god struck the left. Dionysus felled Eurytus with his thyrsus. A hailstorm of glowing iron from the hand of Hephaestus threw Clytius to the ground. Pallas Athene hurled the island of Sicily upon fleeing Enceladus. The giant Polybotes, whom Poseidon pursued across the sea, fled to Cos, but the sea-god tore off a piece of the island and covered him with it. Hermes, who wore Pluto's helmet on his head, slew Hippolytus, and the Fates destroyed two others with their brazen clubs. The rest Zeus mowed down with lightning or Heracles shot with his arrows.

For these deeds, the immortals held the demigod in high favor. Those among the gods who had helped in the fight Zeus called Olympians, a term meant to distinguish the brave from the cowards. Two of his sons born of mortal women were also considered worthy to bear this name of honor: Dionysus and Heracles.

HERACLES AND EURYSTHEUS

Before Heracles was born, Zeus had once declared in the council of the gods that the first grandson of Perseus should rule over all of Perseus' other descendants. This distinction he intended for his and Alcmene's son. But Hera, who begrudged the son of her rival this honor, had recourse to trickery and saw to it that Eurystheus, who was likewise a grandson of Perseus, was born sooner, although he was supposed to come into the world after Heracles. This made Eurystheus king of Mycenae in the land of the Argives, and the later-born Heracles his subject. With growing concern the ruler watched his young kinsman's rise to fame and summoned him, as a king summons his subject, to impose various labors upon him. Since Heracles would not obey, Zeus himself, who did not wish to oppose his own decree, commanded his son to serve the king of the Argives. And still the demigod was reluctant to become the servant of a mortal. He went to Delphi to consult the oracle, which gave answer that the gods would make amends for the supremacy Eurystheus had got through Hera's wiles: that Heracles would, indeed, have to perform twelve labors the king imposed upon him, but that thereafter he would become immortal.

This reply weighed on Heracles. To serve one beneath him-

self offended his pride and wounded his dignity, but he felt that
it was unwise and not even possible to disobey Zeus, his father.
Hera, who still hated Heracles in spite of the aid he had given the
gods, took advantage of this moment and changed his sullen-
ness to savage frenzy. He became so utterly mad that he tried to
murder his cherished nephew Iolaus, and when the boy managed
to escape, shot the children Megara had borne him, imagining
that he was aiming his arrows at the giants. It was a long time
before his madness left him. But when he realized his terrible mistake, he was bowed down with grief, locked himself into his house,
and refused to have anything to do with his fellow men. When
time at last lessened his sorrow, he resolved to accept the labors
of Eurystheus, and went to him at Tiryns, which was part of
his kingdom.

THE FIRST THREE LABORS OF HERACLES

The first labor the king imposed on him was that Heracles should
bring him the skin of the Nemean lion, who lived on the Peloponnesus, in the region of Argolis, in the forests between Cleonae
and Nemea. This lion could not be harmed by the weapons of men.
Some said he was the son of the giant Typhon and the serpent
Echidna, others that he had dropped down to earth from the
moon. Against this lion Heracles now set out, his quiver on his
back, his bow in one hand, in the other a club made of the trunk
of a wild olive tree he had found on Helicon and torn out by the
roots. When he entered the woods of Nemea, Heracles looked
sharply on all sides to discover the beast before it caught sight of
him. It was noon, and nowhere could he find a trace of the lion
nor ask the path leading to his lair, for he met no one, either with
the herds in the fields or felling trees in the forest. All had fled
to their houses, far from the haunts of the lion, and locked themselves in for fear.

Throughout the afternoon Heracles roved through the thickets, determined to prove his strength the instant he saw the lion.
But it was evening before the beast came loping down a woodland trail, returning from the hunt to rest in a ravine. He had
sated himself with flesh. His head, his mane, and his breast

dripped with blood, and with his tongue he licked up the drops oozing from his jaws. Heracles, who saw him from afar, took refuge behind a wall of dense bushes, waited until he approached, and aimed an arrow at his flank between the ribs and the haunch. His dart did not pierce the flesh but rebounded, as though from a stone, and fell on the moss-covered ground. The animal raised his bloodstained head, turned his eyes questioningly in all directions, and bared his terrible teeth. And now he was facing toward the demigod, who launched a second arrow at his breast, at the very seat of his life breath. This time too the missile did not even prick the skin, but glanced off and fell at the lion's feet. Heracles was just about to fit a third shaft to his string when the monster saw him. He drew his long tail forward to the hollows of his legs. His neck swelled with rage. His mane bristled, a roar rumbled in his throat, and his back arched like a bow. Intent on the kill he sprang at his enemy. Heracles let the arrows drop from his hand, cast off his lion's skin, and with his right hand swung his club over the head of the beast and struck his neck so that he crashed to earth, his leap arrested in mid-air, and then rose on unsteady feet, his head rolling from the shock. Before he could catch his breath, Heracles rushed at him. But this time he flung aside his bow and his quiver to have his hands free, approached the lion from behind, wound his arms around his neck, and choked him to death, so that his hideous soul sped back to Hades. For a long time Heracles tried to skin his victim, but the hide resisted both iron and stone. Finally he hit on a method of skinning the beast with its own claws, and this proved successful. Later he made himself a cuirass out of the magnificent skin and used the jaws for a new helmet. But for the time being, he gathered up the hide and the arms with which he had come, slung the skin of the Nemean lion over his shoulder, and started back to Tiryns. When King Eurystheus saw him coming with the hide of the dreadful beast, he was so terrified at the divine strength of Heracles that he crawled into a brazen cauldron. From this time on he refused to see Heracles and had Copreus, a son of Pelops, communicate his commands to the demigod beyond the walls of the city.

The second labor of Heracles was to slay the Hydra, who was also a child of Typhon and Echidna. She had grown up in Argolis, in the swamps of Lerna, and it was her custom to crawl ashore to tear the cattle limb from limb and lay waste the fields. She was not only fierce, but vast in size, a water snake with nine heads, eight of which were mortal, while the ninth, the middle one, was deathless. For this venture, too, Heracles prepared with high courage. He mounted a chariot, took with him as charioteer Iolaus, his inseparable companion, the son of his half brother Iphicles, and flew over the ground to Lerna until they caught sight of the Hydra on a hill near the springs of Amymone. Here Iolaus stopped the horses. Heracles leaped from the chariot and with arrows routed the snake from her hiding-place. Hissing she lashed out and reared her nine heads, which swayed like the boughs of a tree in a storm. Heracles went up to her unafraid, seized her in his mighty grip, and held her fast. But she twined herself around one of his feet, without attempting to battle him more directly. Now he began to smash her heads with his club, but this was of no avail, for whenever he crushed one head, two new ones grew out in its stead. Besides, the Hydra had an ally, a giant crab, which hurt Heracles by clawing at his feet. He killed it with his club and then called to Iolaus for help. The boy was holding a torch in readiness. He set part of the nearby wood afire, and with the brands seared the new heads the instant they budded forth, so that they were thus prevented from attaining their full size. This freed the hero of these constant fresh menaces, and now he cut off the Hydra's deathless head, buried it by the wayside, and rolled a heavy stone upon the grave. He split the trunk of the snake in two and dipped his arrows in her blood, which was full of venom. Ever thereafter he dealt wounds which would not heal.

The third labor imposed on him by Eurystheus was to take alive the hind of Mount Cerynea. This was a beautiful creature with golden horns and brazen hooves, who dwelt on one of the hills of Arcadia. She was one of the five hinds through which Artemis had first proved her skill in hunting, and the only one she had allowed to run free in the woods again, since Fate had decreed that one day Heracles should weary in the chase of her. For a whole year he pursued her, and in his wanderings came to the Hyperborei and to the source of the Ister. At last he caught up with the hind on the bank of the river Ladon, not far

from the city of Oenoe, near the mountain of Artemis. But the
only way he could capture the animal was to lame her with a
shaft and carry her through Arcadia on his shoulders. Here he
met the goddess Artemis with Apollo, her brother. She upbraided
him for planning to kill a creature sacred to her and even prepared to rob him of his quarry.

"Great goddess," said Heracles to justify himself to her, "it
was not idle sport which prompted me to do this, but sheer necessity. For how else could I fulfill the wish of Eurystheus?" These
words calmed her anger, and he brought the hind alive to
Mycenae.

THE FOURTH, FIFTH, AND SIXTH LABORS OF HERACLES

Almost immediately he undertook his fourth quest. It consisted
of delivering unharmed to the king a creature also sacred to
Artemis, the Erymanthian Boar, who laid waste the region of
the Erymanthus Mountains. On his journey to those mountains,
he stopped with Pholus, the son of Silenus. He, like all centaurs
half man and half horse, received his guest hospitably and set
before him roast meat, while he ate his own share of it raw. But
when Heracles asked for a good draught to accompany this
tasty fare, Pholus said: "Dear guest, there is, indeed, a jar in
my cellar, but it belongs to all of my people in common, and I
hesitate to have it opened, since I know how little regard centaurs
have for strangers."

"Open it without misgivings," Heracles answered. "I promise
to defend you against any attack. I am thirsty."

Now Dionysus, the god of wine, had himself given this jar to
a centaur and ordered him not to open it until, after four generations had passed, Heracles should visit this region. Pholus
then went into the cellar, but hardly had he opened the jar when
the centaurs caught the fragrance of that strong old wine. They
gathered and thronged around the cave of Pholus, armed with
boulders and trunks of pine. The first who dared enter Heracles
thrust back with firebrands. The rest he pursued with arrows
even to the promontory of Malea, where his old friend Chiron
lived. Chiron's brother centaurs took refuge with him. Heracles

aimed his bow at them and launched a shaft which grazed the
arm of one of his foes, but unluckily it sped on and into Chiron's
knee, where it stuck fast. Only now did Heracles recognize one
who had befriended him in his childhood. He ran to him in grave
concern, drew out the arrow, and applied those remedies which
Chiron, well versed in the art of medicine, had once given him.
But the wound was drenched with the Hydra's venom and could
not be healed. So the centaur had them carry him to his cave
where he wanted to die in the arms of his friend. Alas! how vain
a wish! Poor Chiron had forgotten that he was immortal and
that his agony would last forever. Heracles bade him farewell
with many tears and promised to send Death, the liberator, to
him, no matter at what cost. From the story of Prometheus we
know that he kept his word. When Heracles returned to Pholus,
he found his gentle host dead in his cave. He had drawn an arrow
from the body of one of his brothers, and as he weighed it in his
hand, marvelling that so small a thing could fell such mighty
creatures, the poisoned dart had slipped from him, grazed his
foot, and killed him on the instant. Sorrowfully Heracles gave
him an honorable burial. He laid him under the mountain which
from that time on was called Pholoe.

Then the hero continued on his way to the boar. With ringing
shouts he drove him out of the thick underbrush, followed him
up the snowy slopes, caught the weary animal with a noose, and
brought it to Mycenae alive, as he had been bidden.

After this King Eurystheus sent him off to his fifth labor, which was, indeed, unworthy of a hero. He was to clean the stables of Augeas in a single day. Augeas was king of Elis and had countless herds of cattle. According to the custom of the ancients, he kept his beasts in a great enclosure in front of the palace. Three thousand cattle had been living there for a long time, and so, in the course of years, great piles of dung had accumulated. These Heracles was to clean out in a single day, a task which was humiliating for one thing, and almost impossible for another.

When the demigod stood in the presence of Augeas and offered to perform this service, without however mentioning that it was at the command of Eurystheus, the king measured this stalwart youth in his lion's skin and could hardly suppress laughter at the thought that so noble a warrior could wish to do the task of a common servant. But he said to himself that the love of gain had already tempted many a brave man and that perhaps this one wanted to enrich himself at the king's expense; that, moreover, it would not hurt to promise him a substantial reward for cleaning the stables in a day, since there was no doubt whatsoever that he could not accomplish this feat. Therefore he said confidently:

"Stranger, if you can, indeed, clear out all this dung in a day, I shall give you a tenth of all my cattle."

Heracles accepted the conditions, and the king thought he would at once begin to ply the shovel. But after the hero had called Phyleus, the son of Augeas, to witness the agreement, he trenched the ground of the cattle yard on one side, and let the streams Alpheus and Peneus, which flowed close by, run in through a canal and out through another opening, bearing away with them the entire mass of filth. In this way he carried out a disgraceful order without degrading himself to a service which would have been unworthy of an immortal. When Augeas learned that Heracles had done this thing at the command of Eurystheus, he not only refused to pay the reward but denied ever having promised it. However, he agreed to let a court decide the matter. When the judges were assembled, Phyleus appeared at Heracles' demand, bore witness against his own father, and declared that it was true he had promised Heracles a reward. Augeas did not wait to hear judgment. In high dudgeon he bade both the stranger and his son leave his kingdom on the instant.

After other adventures, Heracles returned to Eurystheus, who declared that the labor he had just performed did not count, because he had asked for payment. The king at once sent him forth on a sixth quest: to drive away the Stymphalian birds. These were birds of prey as large as cranes and armed with iron wings, beaks, and claws. They nested around Lake Stymphalus in Arcadia, and had the power of launching their feathers like shafts and piercing even a brazen cuirass with their beaks. Throughout that region they had destroyed countless men and beasts. It was they that had troubled the heroes on the Argo. After a short journey, Heracles reached the lake, which lay in the shadow of tall trees. A large flock of the birds had just fled to these woods for fear of becoming the prey of wolves. Heracles stood there helplessly, wondering how he could master a foe which appeared in such vast numbers, when suddenly he felt a light tap on his shoulder, and turning, saw the majestic form of Pallas Athene. She gave him two enormous rattles of bronze which Hephaestus had made for her, instructed him to use them against the Stymphalian birds, and vanished from his sight. Heracles climbed a hill near the lake and frightened the birds by shaking the giant rattles. Not for long could they endure the strident noise. Stricken with terror they flew out from the shelter of the trees, and Heracles gripped his bow and shot one after another in flight. The rest left that region, never to return.

THE SEVENTH, EIGHTH, AND NINTH LABORS OF HERACLES

Minos of Crete had promised Poseidon to sacrifice to him whatever first emerged from the depths of the sea, for the king had claimed that no creature in his possession was worthy to offer so great a deity. The god caused a beautiful bull to rise up through the waters. But the king was so enchanted by the splendid animal that he secretly mingled it with his herds and substituted another bull for the offering. This angered the sea-god, and as a penalty he afflicted the beast with madness, so that he wrought confusion and destruction on the island of Crete. Heracles' seventh labor was to tame him and bring him to Eurystheus.

He travelled to Crete, and when he told Minos of his purpose the king was greatly pleased at the prospect of ridding his country of so dangerous a creature, and he even helped Heracles catch him. The demigod then tamed the raging bull so well that he was able to ride him to the shore, whence he was to depart for the Peloponnesus, and his gait was as easy as a ship sailing a smooth sea.

Eurystheus was satisfied with this achievement, but after he had looked over the captured animal with delight, set it free again. The moment the bull no longer felt the restraining hand of Heracles, his madness returned. He roamed through all of Laconia and Arcadia, crossed the isthmus to Marathon in Attica, and here laid waste the region, just as he had once ravaged Crete. It was not until much later that Theseus succeeded in mastering him.

Heracles' eighth labor was to bring to Mycenae the mares of Diomedes of Thrace. Diomedes was the son of Ares and king of the warlike people of the Bistones. His mares were so strong and so savage that they had to be shackled to their brazen troughs with chains of iron. And they did not feed on oats! Any strangers who were so unfortunate as to seek out the city of Diomedes were cast into their mangers, that the mares might eat their flesh. When Heracles came, his first act was to capture the cruel king, overpower the guards in the stables, and serve Diomedes up to his own mares. After this meal the creatures grew gentle, and he drove them down to the shore of the sea. But the Bistones armed and pursued him, so that he had to turn back and fight them. He put the mares in charge of his dearest friend and constant companion, Abderus, the son of Hermes, but with Heracles gone, they were again seized with the lust for human flesh, and when he returned, after putting the Bistones to flight, he found that they had torn Abderus limb from limb. Heracles mourned his death deeply and in his honor founded the city of Abdera. Then he again tamed the mares and brought them safely to Eurystheus, who dedicated the horses to Hera. They bore young, and their race multiplied through the years. It is even said that Alexander of Macedon rode one of their descendants. When Heracles had accomplished this labor, he joined Jason and the Argonauts

in their quest for the golden fleece. But the tale of this expedition to Colchis has already been told.

After long wanderings, the hero set out against the Amazons, in order to achieve his ninth labor: to bring the girdle of Hippolyte, their queen, to Eurystheus. The Amazons lived in the region around the river Thermodon in Pontus. They were a nation of women who plied the trades of men and reared only those of their children who were girls. Often they marched to wars with all their forces. In token of her majesty, their queen Hippolyte wore the girdle Ares himself had given her.

Heracles asked for volunteers to aid him in this quest and assembled them on a ship. After many adventures he entered the Black Sea, came to the mouth of the Thermodon, and rowed into the harbor of Themiscyra, the city of the Amazons. Hippolyte met the strangers and was struck by the strength and beauty of the demigod. When she learned the cause of his coming, she promised to give him her girdle. But Hera, who persisted in her hatred of Heracles, assumed the shape of an Amazon, mingled with the others, and spread the rumor that an alien and savage man was about to abduct their queen. Instantly all mounted their horses and attacked Heracles outside the city, where he had pitched camp. The common Amazons fought his men, but the noblest confronted the hero himself. The first to fight him was Aella, the tempest, so named because she could run with the speed of a gale. But Heracles was swifter of foot than she. Aella was forced to retreat, and though she raced like the wind, he overtook and slew her. A second Amazon fell at the first stroke, and after her a third, Prothoë, who seven times had won in single combat. After her, he brought down eight others, three of whom were chosen companions in the chase of Artemis and had always cast their spears straight at the mark. But this time they missed and though they tried to take cover under their shields the darts of Heracles found them out. Alcippe, who had sworn to remain unwed all her days, also fell. Her oath was indeed kept, but her days were cut short. When Melanippe, the dauntless leader of the Amazons, was taken captive, the rest fled wildly in all directions, and Hippolyte surrendered the girdle she had promised even before there was any thought of battle. Heracles accepted it as a ransom for Melanippe, to whom he gave back her liberty.

On the homeward journey a new adventure awaited him on the coast of Troy, for here he found Hesione, the daughter of Laomedon, fettered to a rock, waiting in speechless terror for the monster which was to devour her. Poseidon had built the walls of Troy for her father, but the king had withheld the reward he had pledged. In revenge the god sent a sea-monster which ravaged the region of Troy, until Laomedon, in despair, agreed to offer up his own daughter to save his land. As Heracles was passing, the unhappy father called to him and asked his help, promising to give him in return for his daughter's rescue the splendid horses Zeus had given his father. Heracles made fast his ship and waited for the monster. When it came with jaws gaping to consume the maiden, he leaped down its throat, slashed its entrails, and clambered forth as though he were coming up from the pit of death. But again Laomedon broke his word. He did not give Heracles the horses, and the hero went on his way uttering furious threats.

THE LAST THREE LABORS OF HERACLES

When the hero laid Queen Hippolyte's girdle at the feet of Eurystheus, the king did not yet allow him to rest from his toils but sent him immediately to fetch the oxen of Geryon. This was a giant who dwelt on the island of Erythia, in the gulf of Gadeira. He owned a herd of fine chestnut-colored cattle, which a fellow giant guarded for him with the help of a two-headed dog. Geryon himself was unimaginably huge and had three bodies, three heads, six arms, and six feet. No man of mortal birth had ever dared brave him, and Heracles realized very well what careful preparations would be necessary for this difficult undertaking. All the world knew that Chrysaor, Geryon's father, who had been given the name of Goldsword because of his great riches, was king of all Iberia and that, in addition to Geryon, he had three other valiant sons of vast size who fought for him, and that each of these three commanded a host of strong and warlike followers. It was for this very reason that Eurystheus had enjoined this task upon Heracles. He hoped that on such an expedition and in such a country the demigod would at last lose the life so hateful to his taskmaster. But Heracles was no more afraid of these new perils in store for him than of all the dangers of his earlier quests. He assembled his armies on the island of Crete, which he had freed from wild beasts, set sail, and chose Libya for his first landing. Here he wrestled with the giant Antaeus, whose strength was renewed whenever he touched the earth, his mother. Heracles, observing this, held him up in the empty air, where he was helpless, and strangled him in his grip. Then he cleared Libya of beasts of prey, for he hated savage animals and wicked people, because these reminded him of the unjust ruler he was compelled to serve for so many years.

After a long journey through desert regions, he came to a fertile valley watered by broad rivers. Here he founded a city of great size and called it Hecatompylos, the city of the hundred gates. At length he found himself opposite Gadeira, on the Atlantic Ocean, and set up two pillars, known and famed as the Pillars of Heracles. The sun burned down upon him with intolerable heat, until he could endure it no longer. Lifting his eyes to heaven and pointing his bow upward, he threatened to shoot down the god of the sun. Apollo admired his intrepid courage and aided him on his way by lending him the golden bowl in which he himself journeyed by night, from the setting to the rising of the sun. In this Heracles floated to Iberia, his fleet sailing along beside him. Here he found the three sons of Chrysaor, with three vast armies, camped close to one another. But Heracles did not have to fight the hosts. He challenged the leaders to single combat, killed them one and all, and conquered their country.

After this he went to Erythia, where Geryon dwelt with his herds. As soon as the two-headed dog scented the new arrival he rushed at him, but Heracles gripped his club more firmly and crushed him. When he had also killed the giant herdsmen who came to the aid of the dog, he hurried off with the oxen. Geryon however overtook him, and a grim battle followed. Hera herself came to the giant's aid, but Heracles wounded her breast with a shaft, so that the goddess was forced to flee. A second dart pierced the giant in the region of his stomach where his three bodies joined, and he fell dead.

Heracles' homeward course through Iberia and Italy—for he took the land route, driving the cattle before him—was beset with glorious adventures. Near Rhegium, in lower Italy, one of the oxen got away, swam the strait, and so escaped to Sicily. Heracles at once drove the other oxen into the water and swam across to Sicily, holding one of them by the horn. After many other exploits, the hero left Italy and returned to Greece and the isthmus over Illyria and Thrace.

Now he had completed ten labors, but because Eurystheus refused to hold two of them valid, he had to do two others in their place.

Very long ago, at the wedding of Zeus and Hera, when all the gods came with gifts for the bridal pair, Gaea too did not want to be remiss in generosity. On the western shore of the ocean she brought forth a tree with many boughs, all laden down with golden apples. Four virgins, the Hesperides, daughters of Night, were set to watch the sacred garden in which the tree grew, and they were aided in their task by Ladon, the hundred-headed dragon, who had sprung from Phorcys, the father of all manner of monsters, and Ceto, a daughter of Gaea. The dragon never slept, and a deafening chorus of hisses betrayed his presence, for each of his hundred throats uttered a different sound. And it was from this monster—so ran the orders of Eurystheus—that Heracles was to snatch the golden apples.

The demigod set out on his long and arduous journey. He chose the road haphazardly, for he did not know where the Hesperides were to be found. First he came to Thessaly, the land of the giant Termerus, who killed all the travellers he met by running at them with his forehead, which was hard as rock. But when the giant's head touched the brow of divine Heracles it was dashed to pieces. Farther on, near the river Echedorus, the

hero met with another monster, Cycnus, son of Ares and Pyrene.
When Heracles asked him the way to the Garden of the Hesperides, he refused him a civil answer and challenged him to single
combat. But he was slain by the demigod. At that Ares himself
appeared to avenge the death of his son, and Heracles was compelled to fight him. Since Zeus, however, did not wish his sons to
spill each other's blood, he hurled a bolt of lightning to separate
them. After this Heracles wandered through Illyria, crossed the
Eridanus, and came to the nymphs, the daughters of Zeus and
Themis, who dwelt on the banks of this river. Of these too he inquired the way to the Hesperides. "Go to Nereus, the old river-
god," they replied. "He is a seer and knows all things. Overwhelm him in his sleep and bind him, and then he will be forced to
point you the right direction." Heracles followed this counsel
and mastered Nereus, even though he changed himself into many
and various shapes according to his custom. But the son of Zeus
and Alcmene did not loose his hold on him until he had learned
in what part of the world he would find the golden apples. Then
he went on through Libya and Egypt.

Busiris, the son of Poseidon and Lysianassa, was the king of
that country. After nine years, during which the land had been
afflicted with barrenness and drought, a soothsayer from Cyprus
had issued the cruel oracle that the earth would grow fertile if a
stranger were sacrificed to Zeus every year. Busiris showed his
gratitude for this utterance by offering up the soothsayer himself first of all. Gradually the barbarous king developed so great
a liking for the yearly tribute that he took to slaying all strangers who came to Egypt. Heracles too was seized and dragged
to the altar of Zeus. But he rent his fetters and killed Busiris,
along with his son and the priest who had acted as a herald for
the king.

In the course of his further journey, Heracles freed Prometheus from his bondage in the Caucasus and, following the directions the liberated Titan gave him, came to that part of the
world where Atlas stood, bearing the broad sky on his shoulders.
Near him the tree with the golden apples spread its boughs under the watchful eyes of the Hesperides. Prometheus had counselled the demigod not to attempt the theft of the apples in his
own person, but to send Atlas on this mission. Heracles offered

to assume his burden while he was gone, and bore the weight of the sky on his mighty shoulders. In the meantime, Atlas entered the garden, lulled to sleep the dragon who encircled the tree with his coils, slew him, outwitted the watchful maids, and returned safely with the three apples he had plucked for Heracles. But he had tasted freedom! "My shoulders have felt what it is to have nothing resting upon them," he said. "I shall not strain them again!" And with this he tossed the apples on the grass at the feet of Heracles and left him bearing the intolerable load. But quickly the hero thought of a ruse to rid himself of it.

"Just let me twist a coil of rope around my head," he said to the bearer of the sky, "otherwise the weight will crush me." Atlas considered this a fair request and assumed the burden for what he thought was a few moments. But if he was waiting for Heracles to relieve him, he would have to wait through all eternity, for the cheat had been cheated. The demigod picked up the apples and went his way. He carried them to Eurystheus, who, since Heracles had not lost his life in the getting of them, as he had hoped, gave them back to him as a gift. Heracles, in turn, placed them on the altar of Athene, but the goddess, who knew that these divine fruits must not be kept elsewhere, took them back to the Garden of the Hesperides.

Instead of destroying his hated rival, Eurystheus had up to this time only succeeded in helping Heracles to greater glory in the course decreed for him by Fate. His mastery of the labors enjoined on him had made him appear the true champion of mortals, the avenger of all inhumanity on earth. But his final quest—so the crafty king planned—was to take place in a region where heroic strength would be of no avail. He was to battle with the sinister powers of the underworld, to bring out of Hades Cerberus, the watchdog of Hell. This monster had three dog-heads with gaping jaws always slobbering venom, his body ended in a dragon's tail, and the hairs on his heads and his back were writhing snakes.

To prepare himself for this terrible quest, Heracles went to the city of Eleusis in Attica, where wise priests headed a secret cult concerning divine matters both in the upper and in the underworld. In this holy place the priest Eumolpus initiated him into mystic teachings, after he had first purified him of the murder of the centaurs. Thus girded with the knowledge of secret things and prepared to face the terrors of the lower world, he journeyed to the Peloponnesus, to the city of Taenarum in Laconia, where there was an entrance to Hades. Hermes, shadowy conductor of souls, accompanied him down the deep cleft in the earth, and they came to the city of King Pluto. The shades who were hovering joylessly about the gates—for in the underworld life is not merry as it is in the light of the sun—took flight when they beheld men of flesh and blood. Only the spirit of Meleager and the Gorgon Medusa remained steadfast in the face of life. Heracles brandished his sword and made as if to slay the Gorgon, but Hermes held him by the arm and explained that the spirits of the dead are nothing but empty shadows, which cannot be harmed by the sharpest blade. But with the soul of Meleager Heracles conversed tenderly and promised to carry his greetings to his sister Deianira on earth.

When he was close to the gates of Hades, he saw Pirithous, who had come to the underworld accompanied by Theseus in order to woo Persephone. Pluto, angered by this insolent design, had fettered both to the stone on which they had sat down to rest. When they caught sight of the demigod who was their friend, they stretched imploring hands toward him and trembled with the hope of regaining the golden light of day. And Heracles did indeed take Theseus by the hand and cut his bonds, but when he tried to free Pirithous as well he failed, for the earth began to quake under his feet. Going forward, Heracles recognized Ascalaphus, who had once betrayed Persephone by telling that she had eaten of the pomegranates of Hades, and this hindered her return to earth. He rolled from him the stone with which Demeter, in despair at the loss of her daughter, had all but crushed him. Then he fell upon Pluto's herds and slaughtered one of the oxen, in order to quench the thirst of the souls of the dead with blood. But Menoetius, the herdsman, would not allow this and challenged the hero to a wrestling match. Heracles at once gripped him around the body and broke his ribs, nor would he have released him had not Persephone herself come between them. At the gates of the city of the dead stood King Pluto and blocked the entrance. But the arrow of Heracles pierced the god's shoulder and he endured the agonies of mortals, so that when Heracles modestly asked his permission to take with him the hound of hell, he no longer refused, but imposed the condition that the demigod master the dog without using the weapons he carried with him. So the hero stripped himself of everything but his breastplate and lion's skin and went to look for the monster. He found him crouched at the mouth of the Acheron, and ignoring his triple bark, which sounded like dull thunder multiplied a hundredfold, he clamped the heads between his legs, twined his arms around the necks, and did not loosen his hold, though the creature's tail—in itself a dragon—lashed out at him and bit him in the flank with its teeth. He held fast and choked the monster's throats until he had gained the upper hand. Then he lifted up the dog and, issuing from Hades through another entrance near Troezen in Argolis, returned safely to the upper world. When the hellhound Cerberus saw the light of day, he grew mad with fear and began to spew venom on all sides. This caused the poisonous aconite, a plant which still abounds in that region, to spring from the ground. Heracles at once went to Tiryns and showed the shackled monster to Eurystheus, who could scarcely believe his eyes. And now the king despaired of ever ridding himself of this powerful son of Zeus. He resigned himself to his fate and discharged the hero, who took the dog back to his owner in the underworld.

HERACLES AND EURYTUS

After all his toil and effort, Heracles was at last free from the service of Eurystheus and returned to Thebes. He could not remain with Megara, his wife, whose children he had killed in a fit of madness, and so with her own consent he gave her to his beloved nephew Iolaus and began to look for a new wife for himself. His fancy turned to lovely Iole, the daughter of Eurytus, King of Oechalia in Euboea, who, when Heracles was a boy, had instructed him in the art of shooting with the bow. This king had promised his daughter to that man who, in a contest with the arrows, could outdo him and his sons. When this was proclaimed Heracles hastened to Oechalia, mingled with the throng of contestants, and soon proved that he was a not unworthy pupil of old Eurytus, for he carried off the victory. The king gave his guest due honors, but in his heart he was sorry that Heracles had won, for he remembered Megara's lot and feared his daughter might suffer a like fate. Because of this he put off Heracles day after day and said he needed time to consider this marriage. In the meantime, Iphitus, the eldest son of Eurytus, who was of the same age as Heracles and admired his strength and courage generously, without envy, had become the hero's friend, and he used every trick of persuasion to influence his father in favor of the noble stranger. But Eurytus persisted in his refusal.

Deeply offended, Heracles left the palace and was for a long time a wanderer in foreign lands. While he was away, a messenger came to Eurytus to report that a robber had stolen cattle from the royal herds. The culprit was knavish Autolycus, whose thieving was known far and wide. But in his vexation the king said: "No one but Heracles has done this thing! This is his ignoble revenge because I refused to give my daughter to him, the murderer of his own children!" Iphitus defended his friend with warmth and eloquence and offered to seek out the hero, so that with his aid he might find the stolen cattle. Heracles received the king's son hospitably and was willing to join him in his search. But they were unsuccessful, and when they had climbed the walls of Tiryns to try to discover the herd from this lofty lookout, Heracles was again overcome by his madness, for angry Hera darkened his mind. Taking his faithful friend Iphitus for one of Eurytus' conspiring allies, he hurled him down from the ramparts of Tiryns.

HERACLES AND ADMETUS

After Heracles had sullenly left the palace of the king of Oechalia and wandered far and wide, a curious thing happened. In the city of Pherae, in Thessaly, lived King Admetus with his young and beautiful wife Alcestis. These two had several beautiful children and were surrounded by the affection and loyalty of happy subjects. Long ago, when Apollo had slain the Cyclopes and had fled Olympus and been compelled to serve a mortal, Admetus, the son of Pheres, had welcomed him kindly and made him shepherd over his flocks. After Zeus had restored the sun-god to favor, he became the king's patron, and ever since had bestowed his favors upon him. When the span of Admetus' life was drawing to a close, Apollo, being a god, knew of this and wrung from the Fates a promise that the king should escape Hades, even now threatening him, provided another mortal consented to die and go down to the underworld in his stead. Apollo, therefore, left Olympus and sought out his former host to warn him of his approaching death and at the same time to reveal the secret of the means whereby he might evade it. Admetus was an honest man, but he loved life. And not only he, but all his family and his subjects were greatly alarmed to learn that the pillar of the royal house, the husband and father, the kind ruler of his people, was to be taken from them. So the king went about and looked for a friend who would die for him. But there was not a single one who was willing to do this. Although they all had broken into loud lament when they heard of the loss they were to suffer so soon, they grew silent and cold when they were told of the condition by which the king's life could be prolonged. Even his old father Pheres and his aged mother, both of whom knew they must die at any moment, did not want to give up the few hours of life left to them, to save their son. Only Alcestis, in the fullness of her bloom, only his wife, the mother of his children,

in the lovely spring of her life, was moved by such pure and un-
selfish love for her husband that she declared she would give up
the light of the sun for his sake. Scarcely had the words left her
lips when Thanatos, the dark god of death, approached the
palace to claim his victim and lead her down to the realm of
shades. For he knew exactly the day and the hour the Fates had
decreed for the death of Admetus. When Apollo saw Death
coming, he swiftly left the king's house, lest he, a god of life, be
defiled by that sinister presence.

When devout Alcestis felt that her time was come, she purified
herself in flowing water, as befitted an offering to Death, took
festive raiment and strings of jewels out of a chest carved of
cedar, and went thus adorned to the household shrine to pray to
the goddess of the underworld. Then she clasped her husband and
her children in her arms. Day by day she wasted more and more,
until at last, at the appointed hour, she entered the chamber
where she was to receive the messenger from the lower world.
Her family and servingwomen accompanied her. She bade them
a solemn farewell. "Let me tell you what is in my heart," she
said to her husband. "Because your life is dearer to me than my
own, I am about to die for you before death was decreed for me,
even though I could have taken a second husband, a noble from
Thessaly, and had a long and perhaps even happy life. But I
did not want to live without you and look upon my orphaned children. Your father and mother have failed you, though it would
have been better for them to die, for then you would not have to
be lonely and bring up children without their mother. But since
the gods have willed it so, I only beg you to remember what I
have done, and not to give these little ones, whom you love as
I, another mother who out of envy might be cruel to them." With
many tears her husband swore that just as she had been his in
life, so in death too only she and none other should be his wife.
Then Alcestis led the crying little ones toward him and fell fainting to the ground.

It chanced that while they were preparing for the burial,
Heracles in his wanderings reached Pherae and came to the
palace gates. The servants admitted him, and while he was talking to them Admetus himself appeared. Hiding his sorrow he
extended a warm welcome to him. And when Heracles, struck by

his robe of mourning, questioned him, he did not want to sadden or perhaps even drive him away, and answered so vaguely that his guest was given the impression that a distant relative had died in the course of a visit to the palace. So Heracles' merry mood was unmarred, and he had one of the slaves conduct him to the guestchamber and serve him with wine. When he noticed the man's downcast air, he reproached him with it. "Why do you look so serious and solemn?" he asked. "It is a servant's duty to be obliging to strangers. And if some alien woman died in this house—what of it? Dying is, after all, the common lot of mortals. The gloomy-hearted have a sad time of life. Go, set a wreath on your brows, as I have done, and drink with me. I know very well that a brimming cup will soon smooth the lines from your forehead."

But the slave turned away in distress. "We have suffered a blow," he replied, "which drives away all thought of laughter and feasting. The son of Pheres is, indeed, most hospitable, perhaps too hospitable, to admit a lighthearted stranger to his house of mourning."

"Why should I not be light of heart?" asked Heracles. "Because an unknown woman has died?"

"Unknown woman!" cried the servant in amazement. "She may have been unknown to you, but not to us!"

"Then Admetus did not tell me the whole truth about this matter," Heracles observed thoughtfully.

And the servant said: "Be as merry as your soul desires. The ruler's bereavement concerns only his friends and those who serve him."

But now Heracles gave him no peace until he had found out what had happened. "Is it possible!" he cried. "Admetus lost his fair and noble wife and yet received a stranger with such perfect hospitality! I felt some secret reluctance about entering these gates, and now I have wreathed my head in a house of mourning and drunk and made merry! Tell me, where is Alcestis buried?"

"If you take the road that leads to Larissa," answered the slave, "you will see a splendid monument which has already been put up on her grave." And as he uttered these words he began to weep and left the room.

When Heracles found himself alone, he did not break into lamentation but made a quick resolve. "I must save this woman who has died," he said to himself. "I must bring her back to her husband. In no other way can I repay his courtesy. I shall go to her grave and wait for Thanatos, the ruler of the dead. I shall see him coming to drink the sacrificial blood, poured for him over the monument. Then I shall leap out of hiding and catch hold of him. No power on earth shall wrest him from me until he agrees to give up his prey." And having made his decision, he left the palace secretly and silently.

Admetus had returned to his solitary house and lonely children. He mourned his wife deeply, and no faithful servant could comfort him in his despair. But suddenly Heracles crossed his threshold, holding a veiled woman by the hand. "It was not well done, O king, to conceal from me the death of your wife," he said. "You received me as though you were mourning a mere stranger. And so, unknowingly, I did great wrong, and made libations in a house bereaved of its mistress. But I shall not disturb you any longer in your sorrow. I only returned for one thing: this girl I have here is mine, a reward I received for victory in a contest. Now I am going to win fresh combats, and while I am away, you shall have her for your handmaid. Guard her as the possession of a friend."

Admetus was appalled at Heracles' words. "I did not conceal my wife's death from you because I scorned or underestimated a friend," he said, "but only because I did not wish to add to my sorrow by having you leave and go to another's house. As for this woman, I beg you to give her to some other man in Pherae, not to me, who have borne so much. You must have many friends in the city! How could I look upon this girl in my house without weeping? Besides, she cannot live in the men's quarters, and neither can I install her in the rooms of my dead wife! Far be it from me! I should fear the gossip of the people of Pherae and the reproaches of her who is gone."

But although the king had rejected her, a curious longing drew his eyes to the veiled shape before him. "Whoever you may be," he said to her, "you strangely resemble my Alcestis in stature. By the gods, Heracles, I implore you to take this woman away, and not add to the torment of one who is already suffering too greatly. Whenever I saw her, I should feel as though I were seeing my wife. I should burst into tears, and my sorrow would be renewed again and again."

Heracles hid his true thoughts and answered sadly: "O that Zeus had given me the strength to rescue your noble wife from the realm of shades, to lead her back to the light, and so repay you for your great kindness!"

"I know you would do it if you could," replied Admetus. "But when has one dead ever returned from the underworld?"

"Well," Heracles continued in a livelier manner, "since this, indeed, cannot be, let time ease your sorrow. For the dead take no pleasure in the grief of the living. Do not entirely close your mind to the hope that a second wife may some day bring cheer into your life. And finally, for my sake, receive this girl I have brought you into your house. At least try it! The moment you find that she annoys you, she shall leave again."

So Heracles pressed Admetus, who did not wish to offend his guest. Reluctantly he commanded a servant to conduct her to the inner apartments, but Heracles would not hear of this. "Do not entrust this priceless gem of mine to the hands of slaves," he said. "You yourself, if it so pleases you, my friend, shall lead her in."

"No," said Admetus. "I shall not lay a finger on her. Even the lightest touch would seem to me a violation of the pledge I gave her who is dead."

But Heracles gave him no peace until he took the veiled woman by the hand. "And now cherish her," he said. "And look at her closely to make sure that she really resembles your wife, and end your grieving." With this he parted her veils, and the king, incredulous and amazed, beheld his own wife! Almost fainting with emotion, he held her, who had returned to life, and feasted his eyes on her in gladness and fear, while the demigod described his encounter with Thanatos: how he had seized him at the burial mound and wrestled with him for his prize. When the king knew, at last, that it was really Alcestis, he clasped her in his arms, but she remained silent and could not reply to his loving words. "You will not hear her voice," explained Heracles, "until the dawn of the third day, when the bonds of death will be severed. But do not hesitate to take her into your chamber and rejoice in her possession. She is yours in return for your noble hospitality to strangers. And now you must let me go where Fate calls me."

"Go in peace, then, Heracles!" Admetus called after him. "You have guided me back to a better life, for now I am not only happy, but thankfully aware of my bliss. All my people shall celebrate with choruses and dances. The fragrant smoke of sacrifice will rise from the altars. And in all this, we shall think of you, O mighty son of Zeus, with gratitude and love."

HERACLES IN THE SERVICE OF OMPHALE

Although Heracles had been mad when he killed Iphitus, the murder weighed upon his spirit. He wandered from one priest-king to another in search of purification; first to Neleus of Pylos, then to Hippocoon, king of Sparta, both of whom refused to do him the service he asked. But the third, Deiphobus, king of Amyclae, consented to purify him of his crime. Nonetheless the gods punished him by afflicting him with a grave illness. The hero, used to lusty health and splendid strength, could not endure the wasting disease they sent upon him. He went to Delphi in the hope that the Pythian oracle might heal him. But the priestess withheld her utterance from the murderer; this angered him so that he stole her tripod, carried it out into the field, and set up his own oracle. Infuriated by this bold infringement of his rights, Apollo appeared and challenged the hero to single combat. But this time, too, Zeus did not want brother to shed brother's blood, and he put an end to the bout by flinging a bolt of thunder between them. And now, at last, Heracles was told that he would be freed from affliction if he were sold into slavery for a period of three years, and, in atonement for his crime, gave the price he brought to the father whose son he had slain. Heracles was so weak from his illness that he had to submit to this harsh decree. With a number of his friends he sailed to Asia, and there one of them, with his consent, sold him to Omphale, daughter of Iardanus, the queen of a country which at that time was known as Maeonia, and later as Lydia. In obedience to the oracle, the seller sent the price he had received for Heracles to Eurytus, and when he refused it, gave it to the children of slain Iphitus. Immediately Heracles was healed.

In the first flush of recovered strength, he began to act the hero, even though he was Omphale's slave, and resumed his role of benefactor of mankind. He punished all the robbers who were troubling the domains of his mistress and her neighbors. He slew part of the Cercopes, who lived in the region around Ephesus and did great damage by plundering the countryside, and some he brought to Omphale in chains. King Syleus in Aulis, a son of Poseidon, who captured travellers and forced them to work in his vineyards, he struck down with a spade and dug out his vines by the roots. He razed to the ground the city of the Itones, who time after time had invaded Omphale's territories, and enslaved all the inhabitants. In Phrygia, Lityerses, a natural son of Midas, was playing malicious pranks. He was a man of great possessions and courteously invited all strangers who passed through his estates to be his guests. After the evening meal, he compelled them to work at his harvest and, if they failed to surpass him, cut off their heads. Heracles killed this evildoer and flung him into the river Maeander.

On one of his expeditions, he came to the island Doliche and saw a lifeless form that had been washed ashore by the waves. It was the body of Icarus who, on his flight from the labyrinth of Crete, had come too close to the sun with the wings his father had made for him and had fallen into the sea. Filled with compassion, Heracles buried the boy and, in his honor, named the island Icaria. In return for this, the artist Daedalus, father of Icarus, erected a statue of Heracles, a marvellous likeness, in Pisa. Once, when the hero arrived there at nightfall, the statue seemed alive to him in the dim light. His own heroic pose looked to him like the threatening gesture of a foe. He picked up a stone and shattered the beautiful monument which his friend had reared to commemorate his kindness. The chase of the Calydonian Boar also took place during the time Heracles was Omphale's slave.

The queen admired the valor of her servant and divined that she had in her household a hero of world-wide fame. After she had learned that he was Heracles, the son of Zeus, she not only restored his liberty, in recognition of his merit, but made him her husband. In the sumptuous life of the Orient, Heracles forgot the teachings Virtue had once given him at the crossroads. He became voluptuous and effeminate, and Omphale took delight in humiliating him. She draped herself in his lion's skin, but had him robed in the soft garments the women of Lydia wear, and so great was his blind passion for her that he obeyed when she bade him sit at her feet and spin wool. The neck which had once supported the burden of Atlas and found it light, now bore a woman's necklace of gold; bracelets set with jewels clasped his sinewy arms. His uncut locks flowed over his shoulders from under a Lydian headdress, and long and dainty folds veiled his splendid limbs. He sat among the Ionian maids with the distaff before him, spinning the frail thread with his lean and muscular fingers, and feared the reproof of his mistress when he failed to finish the work set for the day. But when she was in good humor, this man in woman's attire had to tell her and her handmaids the exploits of his glorious youth: how he had strangled serpents with his childish hands; how, as a stripling, he had slain the giant Geryon and struck off the deathless head of the Hydra, and how he had wrested the hound of hell from the very depths of the underworld. The women delighted in the tale of his deeds, as children take pleasure in the stories their nurses tell them.

When his years of service to Omphale were over at last, Heracles awoke from his infatuation. Full of disgust, he stripped himself of women's gear, and it cost him only a brief effort to be himself again, the strong son of Zeus, filled with heroic resolves. In his new freedom he decided to take revenge on his enemies.

SUBSEQUENT EXPLOITS OF HERACLES

Before all else, he set out to punish King Laomedon, the insolent
and willful ruler who had built the walls of Troy. For when on
his way back from battling with the Amazons Heracles had freed
Hesione, Laomedon's daughter, from the dragon which was
threatening her, the king had not only broken his word and withheld the swift horses of Zeus he had promised the hero in reward,
but dismissed him with scornful words. Now Heracles took with
him six ships and only a small number of warriors, but among
them the foremost heroes of Greece: Peleus, Oileus, and Telamon. Heracles, clad in his lion's skin, had come to Telamon
while he was seated at his board. Telamon had risen, made welcome his guest, and offered him wine in a golden cup. Heracles,
joyfully moved by this warm hospitality, had lifted his hands to
heaven and prayed: "Father Zeus, if ever you have listened
graciously to my pleas, hear me now: I implore you to give childless Telamon a bold son, an heir, who shall be as invulnerable
as I in this lion's skin of mine. Let him always be quickened with
noble courage!"

Hardly had Heracles ceased speaking, when the god caused an
eagle, the king of birds, to fly over his head. At this the hero
exulted in his heart, and he began to speak like a soothsayer, in
a voice resonant with power and ecstasy. "Yes, Telamon, you
shall have the son you desire, and he will be as majestic as this
imperial bird. Ajax shall be his name, and he will be great in
the service of the god of war."

When he had said this, he seated himself at the board. A short
time after, he and Telamon, together with the other heroes, set
out for the war against Troy.

When they had landed, Heracles made Oileus watchman over
their ships, while he with the others advanced toward the city.
Laomedon hastily marshalled his forces, fell upon the ships,
and slew Oileus in combat. But when he went to return, he found
himself encircled by Heracles' companions. In the meantime the
heroes besieged Troy. Telamon broke through the wall and was
the first to invade the city. Heracles came after him. It was the

first time in his life that the demigod had been second to anyone.
Black envy clouded his soul, and an evil design swelled in his
heart. He raised his sword and was about to strike down his
friend, who strode on before, when Telamon looked back and
guessed his intention by his gesture. With great presence of
mind he began to collect the stones lying nearest him, and when
his rival asked what he was doing, replied: "I am building an
altar to Heracles, the victor!" At these words envy and anger
melted away. Again the two fought side by side, and Heracles
killed Laomedon and all his sons but one with his arrows. When
the city was conquered, he gave Hesione, King Laomedon's
daughter, to his friend Telamon, as the prize of victory. But he
permitted her to select one captive whom she wished liberated.
She chose Podarces, her brother. "It is well," said Heracles. "He
shall be yours, but first he must suffer disgrace and be another's
servant. Then you may have him for the price you offer." When
the boy was sold as a slave, Hesione snatched the diadem from
her head and gave it to ransom her brother, who ever after was
called Priam: he who was sold.

Hera begrudged the demigod his triumph. On his homeward
journey she beset him with savage winds, but Zeus was angered
and soon put an end to her plotting. After various adventures,
Heracles decided that the second victim of his revenge should
be King Augeas, who had also failed to give him a promised reward. He invaded his country and slew him and his sons. The
kingdom of Elis he gave to Phyleus, who had been driven into
exile for the friendship he bore Heracles.

After this victory, Heracles restored the Olympic games and
dedicated an altar to Pelops, who had initiated them, and six
altars to the twelve gods, one for every two. It is said that at that
time Zeus assumed the guise of a mortal, wrestled with Heracles,
suffered defeat, and wished his son happiness in his divine
strength. Then Heracles set out against Pylos and King Neleus,
who had once refused to purify him of his crime. He fell on his
city and slew him and ten of his sons. Only young Nestor was
spared, since he was far away in the land of the Gerenians, where
he was being educated. In this battle, Heracles wounded even
Hades, the god of the underworld, who had come to the aid of
the Pylians.

The only one left to punish was Hippocoon of Sparta, the other king who had refused to purify Heracles of the murder of Iphitus. Hippocoon's sons, moreover, had added fuel to the flame of the demigod's hatred, for when he had come to Sparta with Oeonus, his uncle and friend, a large Molossian shepherd dog attacked his kinsman while he was looking at the palace. Oeonus threw a stone at the animal, whereupon the sons of the king rushed toward the stranger and killed him with cudgels. So now, to avenge his friend's death along with his own grievance, Heracles assembled a host to go against Sparta. When they were marching through Arcadia, he invited King Cepheus and his twenty sons to join the expedition, but at first he refused, for he feared an invasion from his neighbors, the Argives. Now Athene had given Heracles a lock of the Medusa's hair, enclosed in a brazen urn. This he gave to Sterope, the daughter of King Cepheus, saying to her: "When the Argive armies approach, all you need to do is raise this lock three times above the walls of the city, without looking at it yourself, and your enemies will take to flight." When Cepheus heard this, he let himself be persuaded to take part in the campaign, but though the Argives were indeed forced to flee, he himself suffered disaster after disaster, and was finally slain with all his sons. Iphicles, the brother of Heracles, also fell, but Heracles himself conquered Sparta, killed Hippocoon and his sons, brought Tyndareus, the father of Castor and Polydeuces, back to that city, and reinstated him as king. But he retained the right to have his own descendants inherit the realm he had handed over to Tyndareus.

HERACLES AND DEIANIRA

After the hero had done many bold deeds in the Peloponnesus, he came to Calydon, in Aetolia, to King Oeneus, who had a beautiful daughter, Deianira. She, more than any other woman in Aetolia, was much annoyed by the attentions of a most unwelcome suitor. Before coming to Calydon, she had lived in Pleuron, another city in her father's realm, and there a river, called Achelous, had come to woo her in three different shapes. First he appeared in the form of a bull, then as a dragon with glittering coils, and lastly in human form, but with the head of a bull, from whose shaggy jowls fresh streams broke forth. Deianira could not but look upon this strange suitor with great distress! And she prayed the gods that she might die. For a long time she persisted in her rejection of him, but he grew more and more wild and insistent, and her father did not seem disinclined to marry her to the deity of the river, who was descended from an ancient line of gods.

But now, though late, a second wooer arrived upon the scene, and fortunately he was still in time. It was Heracles, to whom his friend Meleager had described the loveliness of the king's daughter. The hero had divined that this fair girl would not be lightly won, and he had come equipped for battle. As he walked toward the palace, the wind fluttered the lion's skin on his back, his quiver clanged with arrows, and he swung his club in the air. When the river-god saw him coming, the veins swelled in his bull's head, and he tried out his horns for the thrust. King Oeneus saw these two, in their great strength and lust for battle, and not wishing to offend either of them, promised his daughter to the one who would overcome the other in combat.

The furious contest began, with the king, the queen, and their daughter as spectators. Heracles' fists dealt sounding blows, arrows whirred from his bow, but through it all the huge bull's head of the river-god emerged again and again and sought out its opponent with deadly lunging horns. In the end the combat turned into a wrestling match. Arm was locked in arm, foot twined with foot. The brows and limbs of the wrestlers glistened with sweat, and both groaned aloud while they strove with panting breath. Then the son of Zeus gained the upper hand and hurled the strong god to earth. He at once changed himself into a serpent. Heracles, however, was well versed in the handling of snakes and would have crushed him had not Achelous suddenly assumed the shape of a bull. But even this did not find Heracles at a loss. He gripped the monster by the horn and forced him down with such might that one horn broke off in his hand. The river-god declared himself defeated, and Deianira became the victor's prize. As for Achelous' horn: long ago the nymph Amalthea had given him a horn of plenty, spilling over with fruits of every kind, with pomegranates and grapes. Now he gave this horn to Heracles in exchange for his own.

The marriage of Heracles changed nothing in his way of life. Just as before he roamed from quest to quest. Once when he returned to the palace of Oeneus, he had the misfortune to kill a boy about to hand him a bowl of water to wash his hands at the board, and again he was forced to flee. His young wife and Hyllus, the son she had borne him, accompanied him on his wanderings.

HERACLES AND NESSUS

Their journey took them from Calydon to his friend Ceyx in Trachis. It was the most perilous Heracles had ever undertaken, for when he reached the river Euenus, he came upon Nessus, the centaur, who for a stated fee carried travellers across on his shoulders. He claimed that the gods themselves had assigned this post to him in recognition of his honesty. Now Heracles himself had no need of such a service, for he could stride through the swirling waters with great and powerful steps. But Deianira he left to Nessus, who took her upon his shoulder and bore her sturdily through the river. Midway across, however, he was so beguiled by her delicate beauty that he began to embrace her. Heracles, on the opposite shore, heard her cry for help and quickly turned to go back. When he saw her in the power of this shaggy half-man, he did not stop to consider but snatched a winged arrow from his quiver and shot Nessus, just coming ashore, in the back, and the dart came out through his breast. Deianira had escaped from the arms of the centaur and was about to run to her husband when Nessus, burning for revenge even on the threshold of death, called her back, and tricked her with lying words.

"Hear me, daughter of Oeneus! Since you are the last to be carried on my back, you shall have some profit from my service, provided you do as I say. Collect the fresh blood which flows from the wound of which I am dying. At the very spot where the arrow, poisoned with the venom of the Lernean Hydra, entered my body, you will find it clotted and easy to take up. Use it as magic to yoke the fancy of your husband. If you dye his tunic with it, he will never love any woman more than yourself." As soon as he had uttered this treacherous counsel, he died of the poisoned wound. And Deianira, though she had no doubt of her husband's love for her, did as she was told, collected the clotted blood in a vial she carried with her, and preserved it without the knowledge of Heracles, who was too far away to see what she was doing. After other adventures, they reached Trachis and made their home with the king, and with them were the men from Arcadia, who followed Heracles wherever he went.

HERACLES, IOLE, AND DEIANIRA. HIS END

The last venture which Heracles undertook was an expedition against Eurytus, king of Oechalia, for whom he cherished an ancient grudge for having refused him his daughter Iole. He assembled a mighty host of Greeks and marched to Euboea to besiege Eurytus and his sons in their city. And he was victorious. The lofty palace was shattered and lay in the dust, the king and his three sons slain, and the entire city destroyed. Iole, who was still young and fair, was the captive of Heracles.

Deianira had anxiously been awaiting news of her husband. At last a joyful clamor broke out in the palace. A messenger had come at full speed and gave his news to eager listeners. "Your husband lives, O princess," he cried. "He will return in all the glory of conquest, and even now is bringing the first fruits of the battle to his native gods. His servant Lichas, whom he sent to follow me, is proclaiming the victory to the people out on the open plain. He himself delayed only because he is making offerings of thanks to Zeus on the promontory of Cenaeum in Euboea."

Soon after, Lichas, the attendant of Heracles, arrived, and with him the captives. "Hail to you, wife of my lord," he addressed Deianira. "The immortals abhor wrongdoing. They have prospered the just cause of Heracles. They who lived sumptuously and boasted with an evil tongue have all been speeded to Hades. But these prisoners whom we have brought with us your husband commends to your mercy, above all this unhappy girl, who has thrown herself at your feet."

Deianira gazed compassionately on the lovely young creature, radiant with beauty, raised her from the ground, and said: "I have always ached with pity whenever I saw luckless people who had lost their homes dragged through alien lands, and the free-born suffering the lot of slaves. O Zeus, O conqueror, may you never lift your arm to inflict such sorrow upon my house! But who are you, poor girl? You are still a virgin, it seems, and the child of a noble house. Tell me, Lichas, who are her parents?"

"How should I know? Why do you ask?" he replied evasively, but his face betrayed that he was harboring a secret. After a brief pause he continued: "She certainly does not come from one of the humble homes in Oechalia."

Since the girl herself only sighed and kept silence, Deianira refrained from further questioning and had her taken into the house and treated with courtesy and kindness. While Lichas carried out her commands, the messenger who had been first to arrive approached his mistress, and when he thought himself unobserved, whispered: "Do not trust the man your husband sent, Deianira. He is concealing the truth from you. I, in the middle of the market place of Trachis, in the presence of countless witnesses, heard him say that your husband Heracles destroyed the lofty palace of Oechalia solely because of this girl. She whom you have welcomed into your house is Iole, the daughter of Eurytus, Iole, for whom Heracles burned with love before he ever knew you. Now she is come, not as your slave, but as your rival and his concubine."

When Deianira heard this she broke into loud lament, but quickly composed herself and sent for Lichas, her husband's servant. At first he swore by Zeus, the king of all the gods, that he had told her the truth, that he did not know who the girl's parents were. For a long time he obstinately clung to his lie. But —by that same Zeus—Deianira implored him not to mock her any longer. "Even if it were possible for me to resent my husband's faithlessness," she told him tearfully, "I am not so ignoble as to cherish hatred for this girl, who has never done me any harm. For her I have nothing but compassion, for her beauty has not only wrought havoc with her own happiness but has even caused her country to become enslaved."

When Lichas heard her express such kindly feelings, he confessed everything. Deianira dismissed him with no hint of reproach and only told him to wait until she had prepared a gift for her husband as a gracious return for the train of captives he had sent her.

Far from any ray of light, in strict obedience to the centaur's directions, Deianira had hidden the clotted blood she had collected from around his poisonous wound. Now for the first time since she had so carefully concealed it in a secret place did the princess, in her torment of jealousy, think of the magic ointment. Ignorant of the snare spun by the vengeful Nessus, she thought it a mere love-charm that would effect nothing but the regaining of her husband's heart. She must act at once! Softly she crept to that chamber and with a tuft of white lamb's wool, which she had dipped in the salve, she secretly dyed a gorgeous tunic to be sent to Heracles. While she busied herself with this work she scrupulously shielded from the sun both the wool and the stuff she was dying, laid the crimson garment in fair folds, and locked it in a box. When all was done, she threw the tuft of wool, which was of no further use, on the floor, summoned Lichas, and put in his hands the gift for Heracles. "Take this to my husband," she said. "It is a garment I wove with my own hands. None shall wear it but he; nor shall he expose the stuff to fire or the light of the sun before the day of offerings, when he shall solemnly adorn himself in it for the gods. For I made a vow that all this should be so, if he returned to me a victor. And that this is really my wish and message, he shall see by this signet which I entrust to you."

Lichas promised to do as his mistress had bidden him. Not an instant longer did he remain in the palace, but he hurried to Euboea, so that his lord, who was performing the rites of offering, might receive the greetings from home as soon as possible. A few days passed, and Hyllus, the eldest son of Heracles and Deianira, went to join his father, to describe to him his mother's impatience, and urge him to hasten his return. In the meantime Deianira happened to enter the chamber where she had dyed the tunic with the magic ointment. She found the tuft she had carelessly tossed aside lying on the floor in the full light of the sun and warmed by its beams. But she recoiled at the sight of it, for the wool had crumbled to dusty fragments, and from these brittle shreds a poisonous foam bubbled forth with a hissing sound. Weighed down by a dim premonition of what she had done, the wretched woman wandered through the rooms of her palace in an agony of unrest.

At last Hyllus returned, but he came alone. "O mother," he called to her, and his voice was harsh with hatred, "I wish you had never lived, that you were not my mother, or that the gods had imbued you with another spirit!" The queen, who was already troubled by vague forebodings, started at the words of her son. "What is there so hateful about me, child?" she asked.

"I come from the promontory of Cenaeum, mother," her son answered and paused because he was shaken with sobs. "It is you who have robbed me of my father!"

Deianira grew pale as death, but she collected her strength sufficiently to ask: "And who tells you this, my son? Who dares accuse me of so terrible a crime?"

"No one," said her son. "No one told me. There was no need, for with my own eyes I saw my father's pitiful end. I reached him on Cenaeum just as he was about to rear an altar to conquering Zeus and slaughter victims for thank-offerings. Then Lichas, his attendant, came bearing your gift, the death-bringing tunic. Obedient to your wish, my father at once put it on, and thus adorned, began the sacrifice of twelve stately bullocks. At first, pleased with the beautiful garment you sent, he prayed joyfully and serenely. But when the flames at the altars leaped heavenward, he broke into sweat. The tunic seemed welded to his body as though by a smith, and tremors shook him from head to foot. As if an adder were feeding on his flesh, he called aloud for Lichas, the guiltless bearer of the poisoned tunic. He came, and innocently repeated what you had bidden him say. My father seized him by the foot, dashed him to death on the cliffs near the sea, and hurled his shattered limbs into the beating waves. All the people were horror-stricken at this mad deed, but no one dared approach raving Heracles. Now he rolled on the ground, now he sprang up, screaming with pain, and the rocks and wooded mountains echoed his cries. He cursed you and the marriage which was now to end in his death. Finally he turned to me and said: 'My son, if you feel pity for your father, carry me aboard at once, so that I need not die on alien soil.' Thereupon we bore him into the ship and now, writhing with pain, he has reached his own land. Soon you will see him—perhaps alive, perhaps dead. And all this is your work, mother! You have shamefully done to death the most glorious hero of all time."

Deianira made no reply to his bitter charge. She did not try to clear herself but left her son Hyllus in silent despair. Then some of the house servants, to whom she had once confided the secret of how the magic ointment given her by Nessus would insure her husband's faithfulness, told the boy that his rage toward his mother was unjust. He ran after her, but he came too late. She lay in her chamber, stretched dead on her husband's bed, a double-edged sword in her breast. Hyllus threw his arms about her and flung himself across the bed, regretting his impetuous words. His father's coming interrupted his self-reproaches. "Son," he cried, "where are you? Unsheathe your sword; use it against your father! Sever my neck from my body and heal the frenzy with which your godless mother has stricken me. Do not delay! Have pity on me, a hero crying like a girl!" Then he turned to those around him, stretched out his arms in agony, and moaned: "Do you still recognize these, though the strength has been taken from them? They are the same that slew the terror of shepherds, the Nemean Lion, that strangled the Lernean Hydra, that helped put an end to the Erymanthian Boar, and carried Cerberus out of Hades. No spear, no wild beast of the forest, no host of giants could overwhelm me; but now I am destroyed by a woman's hand. My son, kill me, and punish your mother."

But when Hyllus told his father—swearing to the truth of his words—that his mother had never intended disaster for her husband, and that she had atoned for her thoughtless act by inflicting death upon herself, the wrath of Heracles ebbed and turned to sorrow. He betrothed his son Hyllus to Iole, his captive, whom he himself had once loved, and since an oracle had been issued from Delphi that he was to end his life on Mount Oeta, in the region of Trachis, he had himself carried up to the peak, in spite of the intensity of his pain. At his command, his people heaped a funeral pyre on which he had himself laid. And now he bade them light the woodpile from below, but no one was willing to obey him. Desperate with pain, the hero urged his request until his friend Philoctetes agreed to do what he asked. In gratitude, Heracles handed him his ever-victorious bow and the arrows which no one could withstand. The instant the pyre was lit, lightning flashed from heaven and quickened the flames. Then a cloud floated down, encircled the pyre, and bore the immortal hero to Olympus, while the air shook with thunder. When the pyre had burned to the ground, Iolaus and other friends approached to gather the remains of the hero out of the ashes, but they found not a single bone. No longer could they doubt that, true to the decree of the gods, Heracles had been taken from the bounds of earth and set among the immortals. They prepared the sacrifice and tendered him the honors due to a god. All of Greece worshipped him as a deity.

In heaven, Athene received the immortal hero and led him into the circle of the gods. Now that his earthly course was run, even Hera became reconciled with him. She gave him her daughter Hebe to wife, the goddess of everlasting youth, who on the shining peak of Olympus bore him children, beautiful and deathless.

BELLEROPHON

SISYPHUS, the son of Aeolus, craftiest of all mortals, built and governed the beautiful city of Corinth on the narrow isthmus between two seas and two countries. Because of the many deceitful deeds he had done, his punishment in the underworld was to roll a great block of marble from the plain up a hill, straining against its weight with hand and foot. Whenever he thought that now surely he had reached the top, his load escaped from him, and the knavish stone plunged back down the hill. And so this evildoer had to labor uphill with his burden again and again, until he doubled over in anguish and the sweat flowed from his limbs in streams.

His grandson was Bellerophon, the son of Glaucus, king of Corinth. Because of a murder committed by chance, the youth had been compelled to flee and took refuge in Tiryns, where Proetus ruled. The king received him with kindness and purified him of his crime. Now the immortals had given Bellerophon beauty of form and all manly virtues, and Anteia, the wife of Proetus, conceived a guilty passion for him and tried to tempt him to evil. But Bellerophon met her seductions with coldness, and her love turned to hate. She cast about for a lie that would bring about his ruin, appeared before her husband, and said: "Slay Bellerophon, if you yourself would escape an inglorious death! Your guest has confessed that he loves me, and tried to make me break faith with you."

When the king heard this, he seethed with blind fury. But because he had loved this grave and eager youth, he put from him the thought of slaying him and pondered some other means to destroy him. He sent his guiltless guest to Iobates, his father-in-law, king of Lycia, and gave Bellerophon a sealed tablet he was to present as an introduction on his arrival. But in reality the tablet contained a command to slay the bearer. Unsuspectingly Bellerophon started on his journey, but the all-powerful gods accorded him their protection.

When he had crossed the sea over to Asia and reached Xanthus, the golden river, he sought out Iobates in Lycia. This kind and hospitable king, following an ancient rule of courtesy, received the stranger without asking who he was or whence he came. His form, his fair face, and his noble bearing were enough to convince him that he was dealing with no common guest. He conferred all possible honors upon the youth, arranged fresh feasts for him day after day, and sacrificed a bullock to the gods every morning. In this way nine days passed, and not until the tenth morning streaked the sky with rose did Iobates ask his guest his name and his purpose in coming. Bellerophon told him that Proetus, Iobates' son-in-law, had sent him, and handed over his tablet as a token of the truth of his words. When Iobates had read the contents, calling for murder, he was filled with horror, for he had come to love this youth. Yet he could not believe that his son-in-law had condemned him without weighty cause, and so was forced to conclude that Bellerophon had committed a crime deserving death. But he could not decide to kill in cold blood one who had been his guest for so long and whose poise and grace had won his affection.

To escape this unwelcome predicament he resolved to send him on quests that would necessarily result in his death. The first of these was to slay the Chimaera, which was bringing ruin upon Lycia. This monster was of divine origin, begotten by awful Typhon and borne by the giant snake Echidna. Its forepart was a lion, its hindpart a dragon, and the middle a goat. The jaws breathed fire and blasts of searing heat. Even the gods themselves had pity on the innocent youth, launched on so dangerous a mission, and sent him as aid the winged horse Pegasus, sprung from the union of Poseidon and Medusa. But how could Pegasus be of help? This deathless horse had never borne mortal rider on his back. He could neither be caught nor tamed. Exhausted by his vain efforts, Bellerophon fell asleep near the well of Pirene, where he had found the horse. And there in a dream he saw Athene, his patron goddess. She stood before him, holding in her hands a beautiful bridle buckled with gold, and said: "Why do you sleep, O descendant of Aeolus? Take this; it will serve you well. Offer a fine bullock up to Poseidon, and then use the bridle." So the goddess spoke in his dream, and when she had ended, she

shook her dark aegis and vanished. He awoke from his sleep and
started up. He reached out, and lo! the bridle given him in his
dream was really there, though he was fully awake!

Bellerophon now went to the seer Polyidus and told him his
dream and the miracle that had come to pass, whereupon the
soothsayer bade him do Athene's command without delay,
slaughter a bullock for Poseidon, and rear an altar to his patron
goddess. When all was done, Bellerophon tamed the winged horse
with the greatest ease, slipped the golden bridle over his head,
and mounted him in his armor. Then, while Pegasus climbed the
wind, he shot at the Chimaera, and his arrows, soaring through
the air, killed the monster.

After this, Iobates sent him forth against the Solymi, a warlike nation who lived near the borders of Lycia, and when, counter
to all expectations, he prevailed in combat with them, the king
ordered him off to the Amazons. From this adventure also he
returned an unwounded conqueror. And now the king thought
it was time to do what his son-in-law had asked of him, and so he
laid an ambush for Bellerophon. For this he had chosen the
bravest and strongest men in the land, but not one of them returned, for Bellerophon destroyed those who had fallen upon
him, to the last man. This proved to the king that the youth
could not be an evildoer but must rather be the darling of the
gods. Far from persisting in his persecutions, he kept Bellerophon in his realm, shared the throne with him, and gave him his
lovely daughter Philonoë in marriage. The Lycians made him
gifts of their most fertile lands and most fruitful orchards. His
wife bore him three children, two sons and a daughter.

But this was the end of Bellerophon's good fortune. His eldest
son Isander did, indeed, become a mighty hero, but fell in battle
with the Solymi. His daughter Laodamia bore Zeus a son, Sarpedon, but died of an arrow shot by Artemis. Only his younger
son, Hippolochus, lived to glorious old age and sent a noble son to
take part in the war against Troy—Glaucus, who, accompanied
by his cousin Sarpedon, came to the aid of the Trojans with a
host of valiant men from Lycia.

Bellerophon himself grew insolent and proud because he possessed the winged horse, and he tried to ride it up to Olympus,
for though he was mortal, he wanted to mingle in the assemblage

of the gods. But the divine horse rebelled against this bold ambition, reared in the air, and threw his human rider down to earth. Bellerophon recovered from his fall, but from that time on the immortals hated him. Shunning his kind, he wandered lonely through many lands, avoiding the abodes of men, and his old age was inglorious and bleak with cares.

THESEUS

HIS BIRTH AND HIS YOUTH

THESEUS, king of Athens, was the son of Aegeus and of Aethra, daughter of King Pittheus of Troezen. On his father's side he was descended from King Erechtheus and those Athenians who, according to the legend of that country, had sprung directly from the earth itself. His maternal ancestor was Pelops, whose many sons had made him the mightiest king on the Peloponnesus.

Aegeus, the childless king of Athens, who reigned about twenty years before Jason's journey on the Argo, was once visiting one of these sons, Pittheus, founder of the city of Troezen, because he was bound to him by ties of hospitality. Aegeus was very much afraid of the fifty sons of his brother Pallas, for they were hostile to him and held him in contempt because he had no children of his own. And so he conceived the idea of marrying again, secretly, without the knowledge of his wife, in the hope thus to beget a son who would be the comfort of his old age and the heir to his kingdom. He confided his plan to Pittheus, his host, and, as luck would have it, the king of Troezen had just received an oracle foretelling that his daughter would not make a splendid marriage in the eyes of the world but would bear a son whose name would become famous. This swayed Pittheus to marry his daughter Aethra, in a secret ceremony, to a man who already had a wife. Aegeus remained in Troezen for only a few days after this and then journeyed back to Athens. When he bade his new-wedded wife farewell at the seashore, he laid his sword and sandals under a block of stone, saying: "If the gods favor our marriage, into which I have not entered lightly, but in order to raise up an heir for my house and my realm, if they grant you a son, rear him in secret and tell no one the name of his father. When he is old enough and strong enough to roll away this rock, lead him to this place, let him fetch out the sword and shoes, travel to Athens, and bring them to me."

And Aethra had a son. She named him Theseus and put him in the care of her father Pittheus. In obedience to her husband's wish, she never told who the child's true father was, and his grandfather spread the rumor that he was a son of Poseidon, for the sea-god was the patron of that city. The people of Troezen paid him honor by offering the first fruits of their fields to him, and the trident was the emblem of Troezen. In that country, therefore, it was anything but a disgrace that the king's daughter had been found worthy to bear this god a child. When the boy had become not only strong and beautiful but brave and steadfast, and showed an inborn knowledge of things, his mother took him to the block of stone, on the seashore, revealed his true origin, and bade him fetch forth the objects which would serve to identify him to his father, and travel to Athens. Theseus pressed his weight against the stone and pushed it aside without difficulty. The sandals he bound to his feet and the sword he strapped to his side.

He refused to go by way of the sea, although his grandfather and his mother pleaded with him to do so, since the land route to Athens was in those days beset with robbers and other evildoers. For that age produced men who, though powerful in body and strong of arm, did not use their strength to do deeds helpful to man but only to abuse and destroy whatever came their way and to revel in mischief and crime. Some of these Heracles had slain on his quests. At this time he was the slave of Queen Omphale in Lydia, but while he was ridding that country of lawlessness, violence broke out afresh in Greece, because there was no one to curb it That was why journeying to Athens by land was a perilous undertaking, and the young man's grandfather gave him vivid accounts of every one of these robbers and murderers and the particular cruelties they were reputed to inflict upon strangers.

But Theseus had long ago taken Heracles as his model. When he was only seven years old, this hero had visited his grandfather, and while he sat at the king's board and ate the feast prepared for him, little Theseus, among other boys of Troezen, had been allowed to watch him. At the banquet, Heracles had laid aside his lion's skin. When the other boys saw it, they ran away, but Theseus went fearlessly forward, snatched an axe from the hands of one of the servants, and brandishing it ran at the skin, which he took for a real lion. Ever since this visit of Heracles, Theseus had been so full of admiration for him that he had dreamed of him by night, and by day thought only of how he would perform feats like his in years to come. Besides, Heracles was his kinsman, for their mothers were cousins. So now sixteen-year-old Theseus could not endure the thought that while Heracles was seeking out evildoers and putting an end to their wickedness, he himself should avoid any conflicts he might chance upon. "What would the god they call my father think of a cowardly journey over the safe expanse of his waters?" he asked fretfully. "What would my real father think if as tokens I brought him sandals that were not grayed with dust and a sword unstained with blood?" These words pleased his grandfather, who had himself been a brave hero. His mother gave her blessing, and Theseus set out on his way.

HIS JOURNEY TO HIS FATHER

The first person he met was the robber Periphetes, who went armed with an iron club, to which he owed his name of Club-Bearer. With this he dashed to the ground all who came his way.

When Theseus reached the region of Epidaurus, this ruthless and savage man rushed at him out of the dark woods and blocked his path. But the youth called to him in a ringing voice: "Miserable rogue, you come in the very nick of time! Your club will be just the thing for one who intends to become a second Heracles in a world of rascals!" With these words he hurled himself upon the robber and, after brief combat, slew him. Then he took the club from the dead man and bore it away as a trophy and weapon.

On the isthmus of Corinth he came upon another evildoer, Sinnis, the Pine-Bender, so called because when anyone crossed his path he bent down the tops of two pines with his mighty hands, bound his captive to them, and then released the trees, so that his victim was torn in two. Theseus broke in his club by slaying that monster of cruelty. Sinnis had a lithe and lovely daughter, Perigune. Theseus had seen her flee into the forest when he was killing her father, and now he looked for her everywhere. The girl had hidden in a grove thick with shrubs, and in her childish innocence, pleaded with the bushes, as though they could understand, that never, never would she harm them or burn them if only they would conceal and rescue her. When Theseus called her back and assured her that he not only intended no harm but would take care of her, she came out of hiding and, from that time on, was under his protection. Later he married her to Deioneus, the son of Eurytus, king of Oechalia, and all her descendants kept her promise and never burned a single plant of the species which had given shelter to their ancestress.

But Theseus did not merely clear the road he travelled of destructive men. Always mindful of Heracles, he considered it his duty to wage war upon harmful animals as well. Among other brave deeds, he approached Megara and met with Sciron, a third notorious robber, who had chosen his abode on a high cliff between Megara and Attica. This insolent ne'er-do-well had the habit of thrusting his feet out at strangers and commanding them to wash his soles. While they did what he asked, he would give them a kick that plunged them into the sea. Now Theseus punished him with the same death he had inflicted on others. When he was already in Attica, near the city of Eleusis, he met Cercyon, who was in the habit of waylaying all who crossed his path, to challenge them to a wrestling match, and kill them after he had won the victory. Theseus accepted his challenge, was himself the winner, and rid the world of this plague. When he had gone a little farther, he came to the last and most cruel of the highway robbers, Damastes, who was better known by his nickname Procrustes, the Stretcher. This scoundrel had two beds, one very short and one very long. If a stranger who was small of stature came his way, he conducted him to the long bed, saying: "You can well see that my bed is much too big for you; let me arrange a better fit!" And with this he would stretch him on the rack until the man breathed his last. But if he had a tall guest for the night, he took him to the short bed, saying: "I am sorry, friend, but this bed was never made for you. It is much too small, but we can do something about that!" And with this he would lop off his feet and that part of his legs which protruded from the bed. Since Procrustes was a large man, Theseus forced him to lie in his own short bed and hacked him into shape until he died a miserable death. Thus Theseus made the punishment of most of these evildoers fit their crimes.

Up to this point, our hero had not come across anything of a pleasant nature on his journey. But now, when he reached the river Cephissus, he found men from the race of the Phytalides, who received him hospitably. At his request, they first purified him of the blood he had shed, with the rites proper to this service, and then set food and drink before him. After he had refreshed himself in their house and given them thanks in warm and courteous words, he turned in the direction of his father's home.

THESEUS IN ATHENS

In Athens, the young hero did not find the peace and happiness he had expected. The city was in confusion, the citizens were at civil war among themselves, and conditions in the house of his father Aegeus were not of a kind to favor his coming. Medea, who had left Corinth and unhappy Jason on her dragon-drawn chariot and taken refuge in Athens, had tricked old Aegeus into receiving her, by a promise to restore his strength and youth with one of her magic charms. The king and she were living in wedlock. Because she was a sorceress, she knew that Theseus had arrived in Athens before the news of his coming reached the palace. She persuaded Aegeus, whom the party strife in his city had made suspicious of every newcomer, that the stranger, whom he did not recognize as his son, was a dangerous spy and that it would be wise to treat him as a welcome guest and then do away with him by means of poison.

Theseus came to the morning meal without having revealed his identity, glad in the thought that his father would discover for himself who it was he had before him. The cup with the poisoned potion was at his place, and Medea waited impatiently for the new arrival, who she feared would drive her from the palace, to take the first sip, for she had seen to it that even a few drops would be enough to close his young and watchful eyes forever. But Theseus, who longed to feel his father's arms about him more than to drink of the cup, drew his sword, the one that had been left under the stone for him, seemingly to cut his meat, but actually that Aegeus might see it and know that this was his son. No sooner had the king laid eyes on the weapon, which he instantly recognized, than he dashed the cup to the ground. A few questions convinced him that this youth was, indeed, the son he had begged of Destiny, and he clasped him to his heart. Theseus was made known to the assembled populace, whom he told of the adventures he had met with on his journey. Joyful acclaim welcomed the youth, who had proved his hardihood so early and so often. But treacherous Medea was driven out of the land, for King Aegeus now felt only loathing for this cruel sorceress, who had almost succeeded in depriving him of his newfound happiness.

THESEUS AND MINOS

The first deed Theseus performed as prince and heir to the throne of Attica was to kill the fifty sons of his uncle Pallas. These young men had always hoped to succeed to the kingship if Aegeus died childless, and they were now enraged at the thought that not only was Aegeus an adopted son of Pandion, king of Athens, but that in the future this recently arrived vagabond and adventurer would hold sway over them and the entire land. So they armed

themselves and lay in ambush for him. But the herald they had
with them was not native to Attica and disclosed their plan to
Theseus, who fell upon them in their hiding-place and killed all
fifty of them. In order not to antagonize the people by the
slaughter he had been forced to commit in self-preservation, he
set out on a quest for the good of all: he overcame the bull of
Marathon, which had ravaged four provinces of Attica and har-
rassed the inhabitants, drove him through the streets of Athens
as a spectacle for the crowd, and finally sacrificed him at the altar
of Apollo.

At just about this time, King Minos of Crete sent messengers
to call for the tribute due him every ninth year. Now the reason
was this: it was said that Androgeos, the son of Minos, had been
treacherously murdered in Attica. In revenge, his father had
waged war against the people of that country, and the gods themselves had laid waste the land with drought and plagues. Then
the oracle of Apollo proclaimed that the anger of the gods and
the sufferings of the people of Athens would cease if they succeeded in placating Minos and obtaining his forgiveness. Hereupon the Athenians had pleaded with him and secured peace on
condition that every nine years they send a tribute of seven
youths and seven maidens to Crete. Rumor had it that Minos
locked these into his famous labyrinth, where they died of hunger
and thirst or were killed by the Minotaur, a terrible monster, part
man and part bull. So now, when the time for the third tribute
had come and those fathers who had unmarried sons and
daughters again faced the possibility of having to sacrifice them
to so terrible a fate, the citizens began to murmur against Aegeus.
He who was the cause of this disaster, they said, was the only
one who did not have to bear the burden of the consequences;
having made an adventurer, a bastard son, heir to his throne, he
was indifferent to their despair at having their legitimate children torn from them.

Theseus, who had come to regard the lot of his fellow citizens
as his own, was pained by their grief. He rose in the assembly and
declared that he himself would go, without being chosen by lot.
All the people were full of admiration for his noble selflessness,
and he clung to his purpose in the face of his father's fervent en-
treaty not to rob him, who had only just gained a son and heir,

of his new happiness. Theseus was steadfast in his resolve, but quieted his father by assuring him with proud self-confidence that he neither intended to perish nor to leave the other youths and maidens to their fate, but to overcome the Minotaur. Up to this time, the ship which took the unhappy victims to Crete had been rigged with a black sail, as a sign of their hopelessness. But now that Aegeus heard his son speak with such dauntless faith, he did, indeed, have the ship equipped in the old accustomed way, but he also gave the helmsman another sail of white stuff, which he was to hoist if Theseus returned safely. If not, he was to leave up the black sail, which would announce disaster from afar.

When the lots had been drawn, Theseus took the boys and girls on whom they had fallen to the temple of Apollo and, in their behalf, proffered the god the olive branch, twined about with white wool, the gift of those who crave protection. When the solemn prayer had been said, he and the thirteen with him went down to the seashore, accompanied by all the people, and they boarded the ship of mourning.

The oracle of Delphi had advised him to choose the goddess of love as his guide and implore her patronage. Theseus did not understand this counsel, but he made sacrifice to Aphrodite notwithstanding. Later the meaning grew plain to him. For when he landed in Crete and was brought before King Minos, his beauty as he stood there in the bloom of heroic youth attracted the gaze of the lovely princess Ariadne. Meeting him secretly, she confessed her love and handed him a ball of thread, one end of which he was to fasten to the entrance of the labyrinth and then unroll the ball as he went forward through the bewildering

maze to meet the Minotaur. She also gave him a magic sword
with which to kill the monster. Minos had all his victims taken to
the labyrinth. But Theseus guided them to the Minotaur, slew
him with the sword Ariadne had given him, and then, retracing
his steps by following the thread, led them through the maze of
passages. Once safely out, they fled with the help of Ariadne,
who accompanied them: she was the lovely and unexpected prize
Theseus had won for his feat. At her advice, he gashed the keels
of the Cretan ships so that her father could not pursue them in
their flight. He thought himself secure with his fair booty and
stopped at the island of Dia, which later was called Naxos.
There Dionysus appeared to him in a dream, declared that Ariadne was his own bride whom Fate had decreed for him, and that
he would afflict Theseus with evil fortune unless he renounced his
beloved. His grandfather had reared him in the fear of the gods,
so now he deferred to angry Dionysus and left the sorrowing
princess behind on that lonely island. But in the night, Ariadne's
true bridegroom came and spirited her away to Mount Drios.
There he vanished, and soon after Ariadne too became invisible.

Theseus and his friends were so saddened at the loss of Ariadne
that they forgot the ship was still riding under the black sail
which had been hoisted on the coast of Attica. They did not fetch
out the white, and so their vessel sped homeward under the color
of mourning. Aegeus was at the shore when the ship hove into
sight, for he was watching the open sea from a high lookout.
When he saw the black sail, he concluded that his son must be
dead. Filled with unbearable grief and weary of his life, he
threw himself into the waters below. In memory of him, they
called those waters the Aegean Sea.

In the meantime Theseus had landed. Before leaving the
harbor, he had made the gods those offerings he had pledged at
the time of his departure and dispatched a herald to bring the
news of his rescue and that of his companions to the city. This
messenger did not know what to make of the reception he met
with. While some welcomed him full of joy and placed a wreath
on his head as the bringer of good news, others were so sunk in
mourning that they did not even listen to his words. He did not
find an answer to the riddle until he learned of the death of King
Aegeus, which gradually became known throughout the city.

When he heard of it, he continued to accept the wreaths accorded him, but instead of adorning himself, he only twined them around his herald's staff and returned to the shore. Here he found that Theseus was still busy with the sacrifice, and so he remained standing at the entrance to the temple, in order not to disturb the sacred rites by a message of grief. As soon as the ashes of the victims had been strewn on the earth, he announced the end of King Aegeus. Struck with sorrow, Theseus flung himself on the ground, and when he rose again, all hastened to the city, not jubilantly, as they had planned, but with weeping and laments for the dead.

KING THESEUS

After Theseus had buried his father with tears and mourning, he kept his promise to Apollo and dedicated to him the ship in which the Attic youths and maidens had set out on so sad a voyage and come back unharmed. It was a vessel with room for thirty oarsmen, and since the Athenians wanted it to keep alive forever the memory of this miraculous return, they preserved it by replacing those planks which rotted away. That was why it was still possible to show this venerable relic even many years after the time of Alexander the Great.

Theseus was crowned king, and soon he proved that he was not only a hero in wars and quests but an able organizer of the state and one who could make happy a nation which was at peace. In this he excelled even Heracles, after whose example he had modelled his life. For he launched upon a great and admirable enterprise. When he came to power, most of the inhabitants of Attica lived in isolated farmsteads and small settlements scattered around the acropolis and little city of Athens. It was, therefore, difficult to assemble them to discuss matters of public interest and concern, and sometimes petty wars were waged about insignificant feuds between one neighbor and another. It was Theseus who united all the citizens of Attica and welded scattered communities into one common state. And he did not accomplish this great work by force, in the manner of a tyrant, but travelled from one community and one family to another, seeking

to obtain their voluntary agreement to his plan. Those who were
poor and of humble birth did not require much urging, for they
had everything to gain from association with the wealthy. To win
over the rich and the mighty, he promised that the power of the
king, which up to this time had been unlimited, should be cur-
tailed, and that he would give them a constitution which pledged
liberty. "I myself," said he, "will be your leader in wars, and at
all times the protector of laws, but beyond this all my fellow
citizens shall have equal rights with me." Many of the nobles
recognized the advantages this implied; others, who were less
eager for change in matters of state, feared his popularity among
the people, his great power, and his notorious courage, and these
therefore preferred to yield to the persuasion of one who could
compel them if he wished.

And so he abolished the semi-independent powers of the separate townships and concentrated those powers at Athens. He
also instituted a holiday for all Attic citizens and called it the
Panathenaea: the feast for all Athenians. Only now did Athens
grow into a true city. Before it had been little more than a palace,
called by its founder the "Palace of Cecrops," with a few houses
grouped around it. In order to enlarge his city still more, Theseus
invited people from many different regions to make their home
there and promised them the rights of citizens, for he wanted to
make Athens a city of many peoples. Lest this mass of persons
streaming into the city cause disorder in the newly founded state,
he divided the inhabitants into nobles, farmers, and craftsmen,
and assigned to each class its peculiar rights and duties. The
nobles were valued for their rank and their service to the state,
the farmers for their usefulness, and the craftsmen had the advantage of numbers. Theseus limited his own kingly powers, as
he had promised, and made them dependent upon the counsel of
the nobles and the assembly of the people.

THE WAR WITH THE AMAZONS

When Theseus had organized his state, he set about making it
secure and permanent by nurturing the fear of the gods. To
this end he introduced the worship of Athene as the patron goddess of the land, and as a mark of reverence for Poseidon, whose
special charge he was and who had long been taken for his father,
he initiated or at least revived the sacred contests on the isthmus
of Corinth, just as Heracles had once done in the case of the
Olympic games in honor of Zeus. While he was so occupied,
Athens was threatened with a curious and unexpected war.

In the course of a quest which Theseus had undertaken at an
earlier time, he had landed on the coast of the country of the
Amazons, and these warlike women, who were not in the least
afraid of men, not only did not flee from this splendid young
hero but sent him the gifts a host bestows upon his guest. Theseus
was pleased with the gifts but still more with the bringer, a lovely
Amazon by the name of Hippolyte. He invited her to visit him on
his ship and, when she came aboard, set sail and carried her off.
When they reached Athens he married her. Hippolyte was not
at all averse to being the wife of a hero, one who was a powerful
king to boot. But the belligerent Amazons, indignant at the bold
abduction, brooded on revenge long after the whole incident

seemed forgotten. They availed themselves of a time when Athens was unguarded, landed with a fleet of ships, occupied the land, surrounded the city, and invaded it, rushing in like a storm. They even pitched camp in the middle of the city, and the frightened inhabitants took refuge on the acropolis. Both sides hesitated to launch the attack, but Theseus finally began, after making offerings to the goddesses of vengeance, as an oracle had bidden him. At first the men of Athens were forced to retreat before the onslaught of these women fighters, and they were pressed back to the temple of the Eumenides. But then the battle was resumed from another direction, and the right wing of the Amazons were driven back to their camp and many slain. It is said that in this conflict Queen Hippolyte, unmindful of her origin, fought on her husband's side, but a spear struck her as she aided Theseus, and she fell dead. Later a column was reared to her memory. The war ended with a treaty of peace, which stipulated that the Amazons leave Athens and return to their own country.

THESEUS AND PIRITHOUS

Theseus was famed for extraordinary strength and courage. Pirithous, one of the most noted heroes of antiquity, a son of Ixion, was eager to put his valor to the test and to this end stole from Marathon cattle belonging to the king of Athens. Soon he heard that Theseus had armed and was coming in hot pursuit. At this he was greatly pleased and, far from taking flight, turned to meet his opponent. When the two heroes were near enough for one to measure the other, each was so moved with admiration for his adversary's beauty and boldness, that they both threw down their weapons as though at a given signal and hastened toward each other. Pirithous stretched his right hand out to Theseus and begged him to be judge concerning the theft of the herds, saying that he would willingly submit to whatever satisfaction Theseus thought fit. "The only satisfaction I ask," answered Theseus with shining eyes, "is that one who is my enemy and seeks to harm me, become my friend and comrade-in-arms." And now the two heroes embraced and swore everlasting friendship.

Soon after this Pirithous courted Hippodamia, a Thessalian

princess from the race of the Lapithae, and invited Theseus to
the wedding. The Lapithae, in whose country the feast was held,
were a well-known people of Thessaly, mountain-folk, resembling animals rather than men, the first mortals to succeed in
taming horses. But the bride, who was descended from this line,
had nothing in common with them. She was lovely of form, and
her face had such delicate charm that the guests thought Pirithous fortunate to have won her. All the princes of Thessaly had
come to the banquet, and the kinsmen of Pirithous also appeared.
They were centaurs, creatures half man and half beast, who
were descended from the monster borne by the cloud that Ixion,
father of Pirithous, had clasped, thinking it Hera. This was why
they were often called the "sons of cloud." These and the
Lapithae were enemies of long standing, but this time the fact
that the centaurs were kinsmen to the bridegroom had made them
forget their old grudge and lured them to the joyful ceremony.
The palace of Pirithous was gaily decorated and swarming with
guests and servingmen. Songs were sung for the bride, and the
halls were warm and fragrant with the steam and scent of food
and wines. They could not hold all who had come, so the Lapithae
and centaurs mingled with one another at tables spread in the
shadow of leafy groves.

For a long time the feast went on in lighthearted merriment.
But an overabundance of wine had maddened the heart of Eurytion, the wildest among the centaurs, and when he looked at lovely
Hippodamia, he conceived the bold plan of carrying off the bride.
No one knew how it happened, no one had noticed how it began,
but suddenly the guests saw Eurytion dragging Hippodamia,
who resisted and screamed for help, across the floor by her long
shining locks. The centaurs, heated and fuddled with wine, took
this as a signal, and before the Lapithae and their guests could
even rise from their places, each centaur had seized one of the
Thessalian girls who served at the king's court and clutched her
as his prize. Palace and gardens resembled a conquered city. The
cries of women shrilled through the wide halls. Quickly the
friends and kinsmen of the bride leaped from their seats. "What
folly is this, Eurytion?" cried Theseus. "Are you mad to insult
Pirithous while I am alive, and thus offend two heroes by provoking one?" With these words he snatched the girl from his

rough hands. Eurytion said nothing at all, for he could not defend his action, but he raised his arm and struck the king of Athens a blow in the chest. Theseus had no weapon at hand, but he reached for a bronze pitcher which happened to be standing near and dashed it in the face of his assailant so that he fell badly wounded.

"To arms!" The call rang out from the centaurs still seated at the board. First cups and jars and bowls hurtled through the air; then one impious fellow robbed the nearby temples and holy altars of the precious vessels dedicated to the gods, while another tore from the wall the metal rings which held the torches lighting the banquet, and yet another fought with the antlers which hung in the grotto both as adornments and votive offerings.

The Lapithae were slaughtered mercilessly. Rhoetus, second in fierceness only to Eurytion, snatched a brand from the altar and thrust it into the gaping wound of an opponent, so that the blood hissed like iron in the foundry. But Dryas, the bravest of the Lapithae, countered by casting a burning post between the shoulders and neck of Rhoetus. His fall halted the orgy of murder to which his comrades had given themselves up, and Dryas took advantage of the pause by killing five of them in succession. And now Pirithous flung his spear and pierced a giant centaur, Petraeus, who was just dragging an oak out of the earth to use as a weapon. While he was still gripping the tree, the missile pinned his heaving breast to the gnarled trunk. Dictys, another centaur, gave way before the Greek hero and in falling snapped a mighty ash. A third wanted to avenge him, but Theseus crushed him with a heavy oaken stave.

The youngest and fairest among the centaurs was Cyllarus. His long locks, the color of gold, floated about his face; his neck and shoulders, his hands and breast were as if moulded by an artist. The lower part of his body, which was that of a horse, was also flawless—broad-backed, the chest arched, black of hue save for his light-colored legs and tail. He had come to the wedding with his beloved, beautiful Hylonome, who had leaned against him tenderly while he feasted and now fought staunchly at his side. An unknown hand pierced him to the heart, and wounded unto death he sank into her arms. Hylonome clasped his dying form, kissed him, and tried in vain to keep the sweet breath in his body. When she saw he was dead, she drew the spear from his heart and threw herself upon it.

The battle went on and on, gaining in fury, until the Lapithae had utterly overwhelmed the centaurs. It ended only when flight and darkness saved them from further slaughter. Pirithous now had undisputed possession of his bride, and the next morning Theseus bade farewell to his friend. The fight in a common cause had strengthened the brotherly tie between them to a bond that could never be broken.

THESEUS AND PHAEDRA

Theseus had reached the peak and the turning point of his fortunes. It was his attempt to found his happiness solidly at his own hearth, rather than seek it in bold and passing quests, that plunged him into stress and pain. When, in the flower of youth, he had stolen Ariadne of Crete from her father, King Minos, her little sister Phaedra had accompanied her. After Dionysus carried off Ariadne, Phaedra, not daring to return to her tyrannical father, had gone to Athens with Theseus. Not until Minos was dead did she return to her home in Crete, and there, in the palace of her brother Deucalion, the eldest son of King Minos, who now ruled the island, she grew into a girl both beautiful and wise. Theseus, who had not remarried after the death of his wife Hippolyte, heard Phaedra's charms praised on all sides and hoped to find her as charming as his first love, her sister Ariadne. Deucalion, the new king of Crete, favored the hero, and when he returned from the wedding of his Thessalian friend, Pirithous, at which the blood had flowed so freely, the two kings formed a protective alliance. Theseus then asked Phaedra in marriage and was not refused. Soon after, he voyaged home with this girl from Crete, who was, indeed, so like her sister in face and in manner that it seemed to Theseus that the hopes of his youth were being fulfilled in his late manhood.

To fill the cup of his happiness, Phaedra bore him two sons in the first years of their marriage, Acamas and Demophoon. But she was not as virtuous and true-hearted as she was beautiful! Hippolytus, the king's young son, who was of her own age, pleased her better than his aging father. He was the son of Theseus by Hippolyte, the Amazon he had once abducted. The child Hippolytus had been sent to Troezen to be reared by the brothers of his father's mother Aethra. When he was grown, this chaste and beautiful youth, who had resolved to dedicate his life to Artemis, the virgin goddess, and who had never looked at a woman with desire, came to Athens and Eleusis, where he was to take part in the celebration of the mysteries. It was here that

Phaedra first saw him. As she looked at Hippolytus, it seemed as though she had before her Theseus as he must have been in his youth. The boy's fair body and innocent spirit kindled her heart, and she desired him; but she locked her passion in her breast and was silent. When the youth left, she had a temple built on the acropolis at Athens and consecrated it to the goddess of love. Standing within it one could look toward Troezen, so that later it was called The Temple of Aphrodite Who Gazes Afar. Here she went day after day, looking out to sea. When at long last Theseus journeyed to Troezen to visit his kinsmen and his son, she accompanied him and remained there for a long time. At first she fought the fires of love, fled into solitude, and wept out her sorrow under a myrtle. But in the end she confided her trouble to her old nurse, a shrewd but foolish woman who adored her mistress with blind, unreasoning faithfulness and undertook to inform the youth of his stepmother's passion for him. When Hippolytus received her message, he was filled with repugnance, which turned to loathing the moment undutiful Phaedra suggested that he thrust his father from the throne and share the rule with her. In the intensity of his disgust, he cursed all women, and it seemed to him that he was defiled by the mere hearing of so guilty a proposal. Since Theseus was, at the moment, absent from Troezen—an occasion his faithless wife had availed herself of—Hippolytus declared that not for another instant would he remain under the same roof with her. After he had given the nurse his answer, he ran into the open to hunt in the service of his divine mistress Artemis, to live in the forest, far from the palace, until his father should return and he could pour out to him his troubled soul.

Phaedra found it impossible to endure the rejection of her love and her scheme. Awareness of her fault and unbearable desire warred within her, but hatred born of wounded pride gained the upper hand.

When Theseus returned, he found she had hanged herself. Clasped in her right hand was a letter she had written before her death. It read: "Hippolytus had designs upon my honor. There was only one way to escape his pursuing. I die rather than become faithless to my husband."

For a long time Theseus stood rooted to the earth in horror

and revulsion. At last, his numbness leaving him, he lifted his hands to heaven and prayed! "Poseidon, father, you who have always loved me as though I were, indeed, your son, once you gave me three wishes which you promised to fulfill. Now I remind you of your pledge. I have only one wish for which I crave fulfillment: Let the sun not set for my son this day!" Hardly had he uttered this curse when Hippolytus, returned from the hunt and learning of his father's arrival, entered the palace. He followed the sounds of lament and came into the presence of his father and the body of his stepmother. Gently and calmly he replied to Theseus' accusations. "My conscience is clear," he said. "I know myself guiltless of crime." But Theseus held out to him his stepmother's letter and sentenced him to exile, unheard. Hippolytus could only call upon Artemis, his patron goddess, to witness his innocence, and with sighs and tears bid farewell to Troezen, his adopted country.

On the evening of the same day a messenger came to the palace and, when he was admitted to the king's presence, said: "O master and ruler, your son Hippolytus no longer sees the light of day!"

Theseus received this news coldly and said with a bitter smile: "Was he slain by an enemy whose wife he dishonored, just as he wished to do violence to his father's bed?"

But the messenger replied: "No, lord! His own chariot and the curse your lips pronounced have destroyed him."

Then Theseus raised his hands to heaven in thanks. "O Poseidon," he said, "today you have dealt with me as a true father and heard my prayer. But tell me, messenger, how did my son meet his death? How did the club of reprisal strike this ravisher?"

The messenger told his tale. "We were currying the horses of our young master Hippolytus, down by the shore of the sea, when we heard of his exile, and soon he himself came accompanied by a group of his childhood friends, all weeping and lamenting, and told us to make ready the chariot for a journey. When all was done he lifted his hands to heaven and prayed: 'Destroy me, Zeus, if I have been an evildoer! And, whether I be dead or alive, let my father discover that he has dishonored me without cause.' Then he took up his goad, leaped into the chariot, seized the reins, and drove toward Argos and Epidaurus, and we accompanied him on his way. We reached the barren coast; to our right lay the sea, to the left great boulders jutted from the hillside. Suddenly we heard a deep rumble like subterranean thunder. The horses took fright and pointed their ears, while we looked around full of alarm to see where the sound was coming from. When our glance fell on the sea, we beheld a terrible thing: a wave which towered up to the sky and blotted out the view of the further shore and the isthmus. White with surf and loud with clamor, this mountain of water made for the very path the horses were travelling. And as it broke it spewed forth a monster, a gigantic bull, whose roars echoed and re-echoed from the rocks. At sight of him the horses went wild with terror. Our master, who was skilled in driving, pulled the reins taut with both hands and used them as an experienced helmsman uses his rudder. But the horses had become unmanageable. They champed at the bit and strained away from their driver. Just as they were racing down the level road, the sea monster blocked their course, and when they turned toward the boulders, it crowded them by rushing close to the wheels. This finally forced the chariot onto the rocks. Your unfortunate son plunged headlong, and the horses stormed on in unguided flight, dragging him and the capsized chariot over sand and stones. It all happened so quickly that we could not come to our master's aid. Although he was bruised and half crushed he still called to his horses, which had always obeyed him, and cried out to the winds his grief at his father's curse. He vanished from our sight around a curve in the path. The sea monster was gone, as if the earth had swallowed it up. While the other servants breathlessly ran in search of the chariot, I hastened here to tell you of your son's fate."

Theseus was silent and stared at the floor. After a time he spoke, and he seemed sad and in doubt. "I do not rejoice at his misfortune and I do not bewail it," he said. "But I wish I could have him here alive to question him and talk to him about what he has done." His words were cut short by the screams of an old woman, who rushed through the rows of servants, her garment torn, her gray hair dishevelled, and threw herself at the king's feet. It was Queen Phaedra's old nurse, whose conscience had begun to prick her at the rumor of the death of Hippolytus, so that now she could no longer keep silence but with sobs and cries revealed to the king the innocence of his son and the guilt of her mistress. Before the unhappy father could gather his wits, Hippolytus was carried into the palace on a bier and brought before him, shattered, but still breathing. Penitent and despairing, Theseus threw himself over his dying son, who summoned the last shreds of his strength to ask: "Has my innocence been proved?" A nod from one nearby answered his question and gave him comfort. "My father, you were deceived," murmured the youth, and the breath fled from his body.

Theseus had him buried under the same myrtle where Phaedra had once striven with her love. Often her fingers, restless with passion, had pulled at its branches and crumpled the glossy green leaves. Since this had been her favorite place, she too was buried there and allowed to remain, for the king did not wish to dishonor his wife in death.

THESEUS AND HELEN

His friendship with young Pirithous stirred up in Theseus, who was lonely and aging, a desire for bold and even wanton adventure. Pirithous had lost his wife Hippodamia after a very short time, and since Theseus too was single again, the two set out to get themselves women by carrying them off by force. At that time Helen, daughter of Zeus and Leda, later to be so famous, was still almost a child, growing up in the palace of her stepfather Tyndareus, king of Sparta. But she was already the most beautiful girl of her time, and her loveliness was being talked about in all of Greece. When, in the course of their predatory expedition, Theseus and Pirithous came to Sparta, they saw her dance in the temple of Artemis. Both were inflamed with love. With insolent daring they stole the princess from the sanctuary and took her to Tegea in Arcadia. Here they cast lots for her, and each promised the other that he would help the loser steal some other fair maiden. Theseus was the winner. He took his prize to Aphidna, in Attica, and put her in the care of his mother

Aethra, and under the protection of a friend. After this he joined his comrade-in-arms again, and both began to plan a deed worthy of Heracles. For Pirithous had resolved to solace himself for the loss of Helen by abducting Persephone, the wife of Pluto, from the underworld.

You have already heard that the two friends failed in this attempt, that Pluto condemned them to remain in Hades forever, and that Heracles, who wanted to liberate both, succeeded only in freeing Theseus. Now while Theseus was away on this unfortunate expedition and held a prisoner in Hades, Helen's brothers, Castor and Polydeuces, went to Attica to recapture their sister. At first they did not commit any hostile act, but went to Athens on a peaceful mission to ask the return of Helen. But when the people in that city replied that the young princess was not there, nor did they know where Theseus had left her, the brothers grew angry and prepared to wage war with the help of the followers they had brought with them. This alarmed the Athenians, and one among them, Academus, who had discovered the king's secret in some way or other, told the brothers that Helen was kept hidden in Aphidna. Castor and Polydeuces besieged that place, won in battle, and took the city by storm.

In the meantime something else, unfavorable to Theseus, had happened in Athens. Menestheus, son of Peteus, a great-grandson of Erechtheus, had set himself up as the people's leader. He wanted the vacant throne, and to this end he flattered the rabble and incited the nobles to rebellion with the argument that by incorporating their country estates in the city, the king had made subjects and slaves of them. To the people at large he demonstrated that for an empty dream of freedom they had left their rural sanctuaries and gods, and that instead of being the dependents of many good and gracious lords of their own, they were serving a single master, an alien and a despot. When word came that the Tyndaridae had taken Aphidna, Athens was filled with terror, and Menestheus took full advantage of the confusion and dissatisfaction among the citizens. He persuaded them to open the gates of the city to the sons of Tyndareus, who were waging only a personal war against Theseus for stealing their sister. And Menestheus had really told the truth, for although Castor and Polydeuces entered Athens through gates flung wide and could have taken the city, they did no harm to anyone. Rather did they request that, like other wellborn Athenians and kinsmen of Heracles, they be initiated into the secret rites of the Eleusinian Mysteries. When this had been granted they left the city, escorted by the citizens who had come to love and honor them, and journeyed homeward with Helen.

THE END OF THESEUS

In the meantime Theseus had been freed by Heracles and returned from the underworld. But even now he was not to have peace on his throne. For hardly had he resumed his place at the helm of the state, when revolts broke out against him. Menestheus was always at the head of these, and he was backed by the nobles, who still called themselves Pallantides in honor of Pallas, the uncle of Theseus, and his sons, who had been vanquished and slain. Those who had hated their king before gradually lost their fear of him, and the common people had been so indulged by

Menestheus that they refused to obey and craved only more and more potent flattery. In the beginning Theseus tried to establish order by force, but when lawlessness and open rebellion set all his efforts at naught, the unhappy king decided to leave his insubordinate city of his own free will, having previously smuggled out his sons Acamas and Demophoon, whom he sent to Elephenor in Euboea. In a place in Attica called Gargettus he uttered a solemn imprecation against the Athenians, and for many years after that the field where he had stood to curse his people was remembered and shown. Then he shook the dust from his feet and sailed to Scyros, where he owned large estates left to him by his father. He regarded the inhabitants of that island as his particular friends.

At that time Lycomedes was king of Scyros. Theseus went to him, asking for his property, for there he intended to take up his abode. But Fate had led him a perilous way. Perhaps Lycomedes feared the fame of Theseus, perhaps he had a secret understanding with Menestheus. At any rate he cast about for some means to destroy this guest who had put himself in his hands. And so he took him to the highest peak on the island, a cliff which jutted out into the sea, claiming that he wished to give Theseus a good view of the estates his father had owned on Scyros. When Theseus gained the summit, he joyfully looked down over the fruitful fields spread out before him. Then the treacherous king pushed him from behind, and his body hurtled over the cliff and plunged into the sea.

The ungrateful people of Athens soon forgot him, and Menestheus ruled as though the throne had come to him as his rightful heritage from a long line of ancestors. The sons of Theseus followed the hero Elephenor and fought in the Trojan war as common soldiers. Not until Menestheus had fallen did they return to Athens and take the scepter into their own hands.

After many centuries the Athenians began to honor Theseus as a hero. And this is how it came about: When they were fighting the Persians on the plain of Marathon, the long-dead king rose from his grave fully armed and led his people in battle against the barbarians. Thereupon the oracle at Delphi bade the Athenians fetch the bones of Theseus and give them honorable burial. But how were they to set about finding them? For even if his grave on the island of Scyros were discovered, how to win his remains from brutal and savage barbarians? At about this time Cimon of Athens, the son of Miltiades, conquered the island on one of those expeditions which won him fame and glory. While he was eagerly looking for the grave of his nation's hero, he saw an eagle soaring above a hill. He hastened to that place, and the bird dropped from the sky and began to claw the earth of a burial mound. Cimon took this as a sign from heaven. He had his men dig down, and deep in the earth they found the coffin of a tall man, and beside it a lance and a sword of bronze. Neither he nor those with him had any doubt that they had discovered the remains of Theseus. Cimon had these sacred relics carried to Athens in a splendid trireme, and the Athenians received them with joyful acclaim, gorgeous processions, and solemn offerings. It was as though Theseus himself had returned to his city. Thus, after centuries, the descendants of his people paid the giver of their liberty and their constitution the debt of thanks and the honor his blind contemporaries had denied him.

THE STORY OF KING OEDIPUS

THE BIRTH OF OEDIPUS, HIS YOUTH, HIS FLIGHT, AND THE MURDER OF HIS FATHER

Laius, son of Labdacus, of the line of Cadmus, was king of Thebes. For many years he had been married to Jocasta, daughter of Menoeceus, a noble of that city, yet she had borne him no children. Because he longed so deeply for an heir, he questioned the oracle of Apollo at Delphi and was given this answer: "Laius, son of Labdacus, you desire a child. Well then, you shall have a son. But Fate has decreed that you shall lose your life at his hands. This is the will of Zeus, son of Cronus, who heard the curse of Pelops, whom you once robbed of his son." Laius had committed this wrong in his youth, when he had been forced to flee from his own country, had taken refuge with King Pelops, and then repaid the kindness of his host with rank ingratitude. For at the Nemean games he had carried off Chrysippus, Pelops' beautiful son.

Since Laius was well aware of what he had done, he believed the oracle and lived apart from his wife for a long time. But the great love they had for each other drove them into each other's arms again in spite of the warning they had received, and in due time Jocasta bore her husband a son. When the child was before their eyes, they remembered the utterance of the oracle, and in an effort to escape the decree of Fate, decided to expose the new-born infant in the mountainous region of Cithaeron, his ankles pierced and bound with a thong. But the shepherd who had been chosen to carry out this cruel command had pity on the innocent boy and handed him over to a fellow herdsman who, on the slopes of those same mountains, pastured the sheep of Polybus, king of Corinth. Then he went home and pretended to have done as he had been told. The king and his wife Jocasta were certain the child must have died of hunger and thirst or been torn to pieces by wild beasts, and that the oracle, therefore, could not possibly be fulfilled. They eased their conscience with the thought that, by sacrificing the child, they had saved him from murdering his father, and resumed the course of their days with lighter hearts.

In the meantime the shepherd of Polybus loosed the bonds of the child he had accepted, not knowing who he was or whence he came, and because his ankles showed wounds, he called the boy Oedipus, or Swollen-Foot. Then he took him to his master, the king of Corinth, who had compassion on the foundling and bade his wife Merope rear him as if he were her own son, and the court and the entire country did, indeed, regard him as such. He grew into young manhood as a prince, never doubting that he was the son and heir of King Polybus, who had no other children. But chance shattered his joyful self-assurance. Once at a banquet, a citizen of Corinth who bore him a grudge from sheer envy, grew heated with wine and called to Oedipus, who was reclining on the couch opposite him, that he was not the king's true son. The youth was so deeply disturbed by this taunt that he could hardly wait for the end of the feast. All that day he kept his doubts to himself, but the next morning he confronted the king and queen and asked for the truth. Polybus and his wife were indignant at the miscreant who had allowed such words to slip from him, and tried to quiet the youth with evasive replies. He was calmed by the love which shone through all they said, but from that time on suspicion gnawed at his heart, for the words of his enemy had made a deep impression on him. He resolved to leave the palace secretly, and without the knowledge of his foster parents he set out for the oracle of Delphi, hoping to hear the sun-god give the lie to what he had been told. Phoebus Apollo did not deign to reply to his question. Instead he revealed a new and far more terrible misfortune than the one Oedipus feared. "You will slay your father," said the oracle. "You will wed your own mother and leave loathsome descendants behind in the world." When Oedipus heard this, he was struck with horror, and since he still regarded Polybus and Merope as his father and mother, he did not dare return home, for fear that Fate might guide his hand against the king, and the gods afflict him with madness so wild that he would wickedly wed his mother.

He left the oracle and took the road to Boeotia. While he was still between Delphi and the city of Daulia he came to a cross-roads and saw a chariot rolling toward him. In it sat an old man he had never seen, and with him were a herald, a charioteer, and two servants. The charioteer and the old man impatiently crowded the wayfarer from the narrow path. Oedipus, who was quick to anger, lunged out at the charioteer, and at that the old man brandished his goad at the insolent youth and brought it down on his head. This roused Oedipus to senseless rage. For the first time he used the great strength the gods had given him, lifted the staff he carried on his journey, and struck the old man so that he toppled backwards from the chariot. A fight ensued, and the youth had to defend his life against three assailants. But he was younger and stronger than they. Two he killed. One escaped and ran away, and Oedipus continued on his journey.

He did not dream that he had done anything but take revenge on some common Phocian or Boeotian who had tried to harm him. For there had been nothing about the old man to show that he was a dignitary or of noble birth. In reality he was Laius, king of Thebes, his father, who had been bound on a journey to the Pythian oracle. And so Fate fulfilled the prophecy given to both father and son, the prophecy both had so zealously sought to evade. Damasistratus, a man from Plataea, found the bodies lying on the ground, was moved to pity, and buried them. Hundreds of years later, travellers could still see the monument: a heap of stones, lying in the fork of the road.

OEDIPUS IN THEBES

Not long after this, a fearful monster appeared before the gates of Thebes, a winged sphinx, whose forepart was that of a maiden while the hindpart had the shape of a lion. She was one of the daughters of Typhon and Echidna, the serpent-nymph whose fruitful womb had borne so many monsters, and a sister to Cerberus, the hound of Hades, to the Lernean Hydra, and the fire-spewing Chimaera. This sphinx settled on a cliff and asked the people of Thebes all sorts of riddles the Muses had taught her. If a man could not hit upon the answer, she tore him to pieces and devoured him. This affliction came upon the city just as the people were mourning their king, who had been slain on a journey—no one knew by whom. Creon, Queen Jocasta's brother, had become ruler in his stead, and the sphinx grew so bold that she consumed his own son, to whom she had posed a riddle he could not solve. This last blow decided King Creon to proclaim that whoever freed the city of the monster should receive the realm in reward and his sister Jocasta to wife. At the very moment the crier was calling out these words, Oedipus entered the city of Thebes. Both the danger and the prize challenged him, and besides he did not place too high a value upon a life so shadowed by gloomy prophecy. He climbed the cliff where the sphinx had taken up her abode and offered to solve a riddle. The monster was determined to confront this bold stranger with one she considered quite impossible to guess. She said: "In the morning it goes on four feet, at noon on two, and in the evening on three. Of all creatures living, it is the only one that changes the number of its feet, yet just when it walks on the most feet, its speed and strength are at their lowest ebb."

Oedipus smiled when he heard this riddle, which did not seem at all difficult to him. "It is Man," he replied. "In the morning of his life, when he is a weak and helpless child, he crawls on his two hands and two feet. At the noon of his life he has grown strong and walks on his two feet, but when he is old and the evening of his life is come, he needs support and takes a staff for a third foot." This was the correct answer, and the sphinx was so ashamed of her defeat and so enraged that she threw herself from the cliff and died on the instant. Creon kept his promise. He gave Oedipus the kingdom of Thebes and married him to Jocasta, who was his mother. Through the years she bore him four children: first the twin boys Eteocles and Polynices, and then two daughters, the elder of whom was Antigone, and the younger Ismene. But these four were not only his children but also his sisters and brothers.

THE DISCOVERY

For many years the dreadful secret remained hidden, and Oedipus, who was a good and just king, though he had his faults, ruled Thebes together with Jocasta and was loved and honored by his subjects. But in due time the gods sent a plague upon the land which wrought havoc among the people and against which no remedy could prevail. The Thebans regarded this pestilence as a punishment and sought protection from their king who, they believed, was a favorite of the immortals. Men and women, the aged and the children, came to the palace in a long procession led by priests with olive branches in their hands, seated themselves all about and on the steps of the altar standing before the palace, and waited for their king to appear. When Oedipus heard their clamor, he came out and asked its cause, and why the entire city fumed with the smoke of offerings and resounded with lament. The eldest among the priests answered in behalf of all: "You can see for yourself, O master," he said, "what wretchedness we are forced to endure. The hills and the fields are burned with drought and heat; the plague is raging in our homes. The city cannot lift its head through the waves of blood and destruction. And so we have come to take refuge with you, our beloved king. Once before you freed us from the tyranny of the Asker of Riddles. Surely this did not come to pass without the help of the gods. And so we put our trust in you, believing that either through gods or men you will find help for us again."

"My poor children," Oedipus replied, "I know the cause of your prayers. I know that you are wasting with disease. But my heart is sadder than yours, for I do not mourn this one or that one, but the entire city. To me your coming is no sudden awakening, as though I had slept! I have brooded over your distress and cast about for some cure, and I think I have found it at last. For I have sent my own brother-in-law Creon to Delphi, to the oracle of Apollo, to ask by what deed or what other means the city can be set free!"

Even as Oedipus spoke, Creon appeared in the throng and reported the oracle to the king before all the people. But it was not very consoling. "The god bade us thrust out an evil the land is harboring," said Creon, "and not to cherish that for which no purification can atone. The murder of King Laius weighs as bloodguilt upon the land." Oedipus, who did not guess that the old man he had killed was the very one for whose sake the wrath of the gods was visited upon his subjects, had them tell the story of the murder, but still his spirit was blind to the truth. He declared that he regarded it as his duty to deal with this matter himself, and dismissed the assembled people. Then he had proclaimed throughout the land that anyone who knew of the murderer of King Laius should report all he had learned; that if one dwelling in another land knew anything, the city of Thebes would give him thanks and reward for his information; but that he who kept silence to shield a friend, or to hide his complicity, should be excluded from all religious services, from the sacrificial feast, and even from intercourse with his fellow citizens. As for the murderer himself, he cursed him with awful imprecations and called down on him misery and need for all the days of his life, and in the end utter destruction. He was not to escape disaster, even if he were hiding in the palace itself. In addition to all this, Oedipus dispatched two messengers to the blind seer Tiresias, who almost matched Apollo in his power to probe the unknown and behold the unseen. Soon after, the aged seer came before the king and the assembly of the people. A boy led him by the hand. Oedipus told him of the misfortune which had fallen on the country and begged him to use his gift of prophecy to help find the murderer of King Laius.

But Tiresias broke into lament and, stretching his hands out toward the king as if to ward off some terrible thing, he exclaimed: "Awful is the knowledge that brings sadness to him who knows! Let me go home! O king, bear your burden and let me bear mine!" These veiled words only made Oedipus more and more insistent, and the people themselves fell on their knees to beg the seer to speak. When he refused to make his meaning clear, Oedipus grew angry and taunted Tiresias with being the confidant or perhaps even the helper of the murderer, saying that only the old man's blindness kept him from thinking that he himself had committed the crime. This accusation loosened the prophet's tongue. "Oedipus," he cried, "obey the orders you yourself proclaimed! Do not speak to me, do not speak to anyone of your people. It is you who are the evil that taints the city! Yes, it is you who murdered the king and live in guilty union with those dear to you!"

And still the mind of Oedipus was closed to the truth. He called the soothsayer a knave and a trickster and accused both him and Creon of plotting against the throne, of weaving a network of lies in order to drive him, who had liberated the city, from power. But Tiresias replied by calling him—unambiguously now—the slayer of his father and the husband of his mother, and then groped for his little guide's hand and went away in anger. Meantime Creon had heard of the accusation launched against him and hastened to confront Oedipus. A violent quarrel broke out between them, and Jocasta's attempts to calm them were of no avail. They parted unreconciled and rankling with bitterness and hatred.

Jocasta herself was blinder than the king himself; hardly had she heard that Tiresias had pointed him out as the slayer of Laius, when she protested against the seer and his vaunted powers. "It just goes to show," she said scornfully, "how little these prophets know! Take an example: An oracle once told my first husband Laius that he would die at the hands of his son. But actually he was killed by robbers, at a forking of the road, and our only son was tied by the feet and exposed in a waste mountain region when he was only three days old. That is how oracles are fulfilled!"

The queen laughed mockingly, but her words had a very different effect from that she had intended. "At a crossroads?" Oedipus asked, his heart shaken with fear. "Did you say that Laius fell at a crossroads? How old was he then? How did he look?"

Jocasta answered readily, unaware of her husband's agitation. "He was tall, and his hair was just turning white. He was not unlike you."

And now Oedipus was seized with real terror. It was as if a flash of lightning had split the darkness of his mind. "It is not Tiresias who is blind!" he cried. "He sees, he knows!" And though in his soul he recognized the truth, he asked question after question, hoping for answers which would prove his discovery a mistake. But the replies only established it more firmly, and at last he learned that a servant had escaped, come home, and told of the murder; that when Oedipus ascended the throne, this man had begged to be set as far as possible from the city, to the farthest pastures of the king. Now he was summoned, but just as he arrived, a messenger from Corinth entered the palace to announce to Oedipus the death of Polybus, his father, and to call him to the vacant throne.

When she heard this, the queen said triumphantly: "O divine oracle, where are the truths you utter! The father Oedipus was supposed to slay has just died peacefully of old age." But King Oedipus, who had greater reverence for the gods, thought otherwise. He wanted to believe that Polybus was his father, yet could not bring himself to think that an oracle might be false. And he hesitated to go to Corinth for still another reason. There was the second part of the oracle to consider! Merope, his mother, was living, and Fate might drive him into marriage with her. What doubts he still had were soon dispelled by the messenger, the very herdsman who, many years ago on Mount Cithaeron, had accepted the infant from a servant of Laius and loosed the thongs which bound his pierced feet. It was an easy matter for him to prove that Oedipus, though heir to the throne of Corinth, had been only the foster son of Polybus. And when the king of Thebes now asked for the servant who had delivered him to the herdsman, he discovered that it was he who had escaped death when King Laius was murdered and had been tending the king's cattle at the borders of the realm.

When Jocasta heard this, she left her husband and the assembled people with loud wails of despair. Oedipus, who still was trying to evade the inevitable, explained her going in this way: "She is afraid," he said to the people. "She is a proud woman and fears that I may turn out to be of humble birth. As for me, I regard myself as the son of Good Fortune, and I am not ashamed of a family tree such as that." And now the herdsman was brought, and the messenger from Corinth at once recognized him as the servant who had put the child into his hands. The old man paled with terror and stammered denials, but when Oedipus had him fettered and threatened him, he told the truth: that Oedipus was the son of Laius and Jocasta, that the oracle predicting he would slay his father had caused them to expose the child, but that he, out of pity, had saved his life.

JOCASTA AND OEDIPUS
INFLICT PUNISHMENT UPON THEMSELVES

And now everything was revealed in awful clarity. Oedipus fled from the great hall and ran through the palace asking for a sword to strike from the face of the earth the monster who was both his mother and his wife. But there was no one to answer him, for all scattered before this apparition of madness and rage. At last he reached his bedchamber, smashed the locked door, and broke into the room. He was halted by the sight which met his eyes. High above the bed hung Jocasta, her hair framing her face in tangled strands, a rope tightened about her throat. For a long time Oedipus stared at the corpse, and grief rendered him speechless. But then he cried aloud and lowered the rope until the body touched the floor. From her robe he tore the golden clasps, clutched them in his hand, raised them high, and bidding his eyes never more see what he did or suffered, pierced the balls until a stream of blood gushed from the sockets. He asked the servants to open the gates and lead him out to the people of Thebes, that they might see the slayer of his father, the husband of his mother, a monster on earth, one hated by the gods. They did his bidding, but his subjects, who had loved and revered their ruler for so long, felt only compassion for him. Even Creon, whom he had accused unjustly, did not make mock of him or rejoice in his misfortune. He hurried to remove from the sight of the populace this man laden with the curse of the gods, and put him in the care of his children. Oedipus was moved by so much kindness. He made his brother-in-law keeper of the throne for his young sons, requested that his ill-omened mother be buried, and put his orphaned daughters under the protection of the new ruler. For himself he demanded exile from the country he had tainted with his twofold crime. He wanted to live or die, according to the will of the gods, on Mount Cithaeron, where his parents had exposed him so long ago. Then he called for his daughters, whose voices he yearned to hear one last time, and laid his hand on their heads. He blessed Creon for all the undeserved love he had shown him, and fervently prayed that—under their new king —the people of Thebes would enjoy the favor of the gods he himself had been denied.

Creon led him back into the palace, and now Oedipus, whom many thousands had obeyed, whose glory as the liberator of Thebes had spread over the world, this man who had solved the most difficult of riddles and found the key to his own life's enigma all too late, prepared to go through the gates of his city like a blind beggar, and set out on the journey to the very borders of his realm.

OEDIPUS AND ANTIGONE

In that first hour, when Oedipus had discovered the truth about himself, the swiftest death would have been welcome. Had the people risen against their king and stoned him, he would have exulted. Since the boon of death had been denied him, he had begged to be exiled and accepted his banishment as a welcome gift. But when he sat in his room in utter darkness, when his frenzy abated, he began to conjure up the terrors of wandering through alien regions, blind and poor. The love of home stirred in his heart, and with it the feeling that, by the loss of his wife and his sight, he had already atoned for wrongs committed unknowingly; nor did he hesitate to voice his wish to remain in Thebes to Creon and to his sons Eteocles and Polynices. But now it appeared that Creon's kindness had been prompted by a very passing impulse, and that the two boys were selfish and hard of heart. Creon compelled his ill-starred kinsman to keep to his first decision, and the sons, whose foremost duty should have been to assist their father, refused him their aid. There was barely an exchange of words.

They thrust a beggar's staff into his hand and forced him to leave the palace.

Only his daughters had pity on him. Ismene, the younger, stayed behind in her brothers' house in order to further her father's cause. The elder, Antigone, shared his exile and guided the steps of the blind old man. She accompanied him on a journey full of hardships. On bare feet she walked, and she, so delicately reared, suffered hunger, the heat of the sun, the lash of the rain, and was content, if only her father had enough to eat. At first he planned to court wretchedness or find death in the barren region of Cithaeron. But because he loved the immortals, and did not want to take this step without knowing their will, he made a pilgrimage to the oracle of Pythian Apollo. And here he was given a small measure of comfort. The gods knew that Oedipus had sinned against the laws of nature and the most sacred laws of human society without his own knowledge or wish. So grave a fault had to be atoned for, even though it was done in ignorance, but the punishment was not to last forever. After a long time, so the oracle foretold, he was to be absolved, and this was to be when he reached the land appointed by Fate, the land where the stern Eumenides would grant him a refuge. Now the name of Eumenides, or Well-Wishers, was one which mortals had given to the Erinyes, or Furies, the goddesses of vengeance, in order to honor and placate them. Thus the oracle was obscure and strange. The Furies were to give Oedipus peace and absolution for his sins against nature! But Oedipus trusted the gods and, leaving to Fate the fulfillment of that peculiar prophecy, he wandered through Greece. His daughter led and tended him, and he lived on the alms of the compassionate. He always asked only little and received only little, but it sufficed him, for his long exile, his sorrow, and his noble spirit had taught him to do without all but the barest necessities.

OEDIPUS AT COLONUS

After long wanderings through lands inhabited and waste, one evening Oedipus and Antigone came to a pleasant village set in a grove of tall trees. Nightingales flitted through the boughs, and the air stirred with their song. The blooms of the vine breathed fragrance, and the rough gray rocks which strewed the region were half hidden by the foliage of olive and laurel. Even though Oedipus was blind, his other senses conveyed to him the loveliness of the scene, and from his daughter's description he concluded that they must be in some holy place. The towers of a city were visible on the horizon, and Antigone, upon asking, had learned that these belonged to Athens. Weary of the day's journey, Oedipus seated himself on a stone. But a villager, passing by, bade him rise, since this was sacred earth, not to be profaned by mortal foot. Then he told the travellers that they were in Colonus and had come to the grove of the all-seeing Eumenides, a name by which the Athenians honored the Furies. And now Oedipus knew that he had reached the goal of his wanderings and that his tangled destinies would soon unravel themselves. His bearing gave the villager pause, and he decided not to drive the stranger from his resting-place until he had told his king of the incident.

"Who is the ruler of your country?" Oedipus asked him, for he had been on the road so long that he no longer knew what went on in the world.

"Have you not heard of Theseus, our noble and mighty king?" the villager asked in return. "Why, his fame has spread through all the land!"

"If your ruler has, indeed, so noble a spirit," Oedipus replied, "then be my messenger and beg him to come to this place. Tell him that for so small a favor I pledge him a very great reward!"

"What has a blind man to offer a king?" said the peasant and smiled at the stranger half in pity, half in scorn. "And yet," he added thoughtfully, "were you not blind, the stateliness of your form and the majesty in your face would compel me to give you honor. And so I shall do as you say and bear your request to the king and my fellow citizens. Remain here, until I have done my errand. Then let the others decide if you may stay or must go on."

When Oedipus was once more alone with Antigone, he rose, threw himself on the ground, and poured his heart out in fervent prayer to the Eumenides, the dread daughters of darkness and Mother Earth, who had chosen this quiet place for their habitation. "You who inspire terror and yet are merciful too," he prayed, "fulfill the words of Apollo! Show me the course my life is to take, and tell me whether I must suffer still more misery than I have already endured. Have pity upon me, O Children of Night! O city of Athens, have pity on the shadow of King Oedipus which stands before you, for he himself is dead, even though he still breathes."

They were not alone for long. The news of a blind man of noble bearing who had sat down to rest in the grove of the Eumenides, where no mortal is allowed to set foot, had alarmed the village elders, and they came and gathered about him to hinder him from further desecration of holy ground. They were still more perturbed when it became plain that the blind man was pursued by Fate, for they feared that the wrath of the gods would descend on them as well if they permitted one whom the immortals had branded with their displeasure to remain in this sacred place. They told him to leave on the instant. Oedipus implored them not to banish him from the goal of all his wanderings, which the voice of a god had foretold, and Antigone too beset them with pleas. "If you have no compassion upon my father's gray hair," she said, "accept him for my sake, for the sake of one who is forsaken without any guilt on her part. Grant us what we have almost ceased to hope for, grant us your favor!"

The villagers were still hesitating between pity for the strangers and fear of the Erinyes, when Antigone saw a girl coming toward them. She was seated on a small horse and her face was shaded by a hat, such as travellers wear. A servant rode behind her. "It is my sister Ismene!" she cried in surprise and happiness. "She is bringing us news from home!" And it was, indeed, the youngest child of King Oedipus who dismounted and stood before them. She had left Thebes with one servant of proved loyalty and had come to tell her father of conditions in the realm he once had ruled. It seemed that his sons were on the verge of a disaster which had been brought upon themselves. At first they had intended leaving the kingdom to Creon, their uncle, for the curse on their family loomed threateningly before them. But as the memory of their father faded, they regretted their earlier impulse and burned with the lust for power and a king's glory and magnificence. Envy rose up between them. Polynices, invoking the rights of the eldest, took his turn at kingship first, but Eteocles, the younger, not content to alternate with him as he had suggested, goaded the people to insurrection and dethroned and banished his brother. Polynices had fled to Argos, in the Peloponnesus, so rumor had it in Thebes. There he had married the daughter of King Adrastus, won friends and allies, and was now threatening his native city with conquest and revenge. In the meantime, a new oracle had been proclaimed: that the sons of King Oedipus could do nothing without their father; that if they had their welfare at heart they must look for him and find him, living or dead.

This was the news Ismene brought her father. The people of Colonus listened in amazement, and Oedipus rose to his full height. "So that is how it is!" he said, and his blind face was radiant with kingly majesty. "They are asking help of an exile, of a beggar! Now, that I am nothing, I am the one they desire!"

"Yes," said Ismene and continued her tale. "Because of this oracle, our uncle Creon will be here soon. I was in great haste to get here before him. For he is out to talk you over, or to capture you and take you to the border of Thebes so that your presence may fulfill the oracle in favor of himself and Eteocles, and yet not profane the city."

"Who told you this?" asked her father.

"Pilgrims, on the way to Delphi."

"And if I die near Thebes, will they bury me in Theban earth?"

"No," answered the girl. "Your bloodguilt will deter them."

"Then they shall never have me!" the old king declared in bitter resentment. "If my sons lust for power more than they love me, may the immortals keep alive their fatal enmity. And if the judging of their feud rests with me, then he who now has the scepter in his hands shall not remain on the throne, nor shall he who is exiled ever see his native land again. Only my daughters are my true children. Let my guilt not be visited upon them! For them I implore the blessings of the gods, for them I ask your protection! Give them and me your help, and your city shall have gain and glory!"

OEDIPUS AND THESEUS

The people of Colonus were filled with deep reverence for blind
Oedipus, whose kingliness clung about him through poverty and
exile, and counselled him to pour a libation to atone for desecrat-
ing the sacred grove. Not until then did the village elders learn
the name and the inadvertent crimes of the king, and who knows
but that their horror at his deed might not have hardened their
hearts again, had not Theseus, whom the message had called from
the city, now joined their circle. He approached the blind
stranger with courtesy and awe and spoke to him compassionately. "Unhappy Oedipus, I know of your fate, and those eyes
which you yourself put out would be enough to tell me whom I
am addressing. Your misfortunes move my soul. And now tell me
why you have sought out my city and why you had me summoned.
Whatever you ask would have to be terrible, indeed, for me to
refuse you. I have not forgotten that, like you, I also grew up in
alien lands and suffered hardship and danger."

"In these few words you have spoken," said Oedipus, "I recognize a noble soul. I have come to you with a request which is also
a gift. I give you my weary self, an insignificant and yet precious
possession. You shall bury me and harvest a rich reward for your
kindness and charity."

"The favor you ask is slight," said Theseus in amazement.
"Ask something more, something better, and it shall be yours."

"The favor is not as slight as you believe," Oedipus continued.
"You will have to wage a war for this wretched old body of mine."
And now he told the story of his exile and his kinsmen's subse-

quent attempts to recover him for selfish reasons of their own. Then he implored Theseus to give him a hero's aid.

Theseus listened attentively. "If only because my house is open to every guest," he said solemnly, "I would not cast you out. How then could I deny hospitality to one whom the gods have guided to my hearth, who promises blessings for me and for my country?" Then he gave Oedipus the choice of accompanying him to Athens or remaining in Colonus as his guest. Oedipus chose to stay, since Fate had decreed that he should conquer his foes in the place where he was at the moment, and there live his life to an honorable and glorious end. The King of Athens pledged him ample protection and returned to the city.

OEDIPUS AND CREON

Soon after this Creon, king of Thebes, invaded Colonus with armed followers and hastened to Oedipus. "You are astonished that I have come to Attica," he said to the assembled villagers. "But there is no cause for excitement or anger. I am not young enough to enter lightly into battle with the strongest city in all Greece. I am old and have come only because my fellow citizens have dispatched me to urge this man to come back to Thebes." Then he turned to Oedipus and in carefully chosen words expressed false sympathy with the sad lot he and his daughter had suffered.

But Oedipus raised his staff and held it out before him as a sign that Creon was not to approach more closely. "Shameless traitor!" he cried. "If you took me away with you, this would be the drop to brim the cup of my sorrows! Give up all hope that through me you will ward punishment from your city, for that punishment will surely come. I shall not go with you; in my stead I shall send the demon of vengeance. And my two unfilial sons shall have only so much of Theban earth as they need for their graves!"

Now Creon tried to take the blind king by force, but the citizens of Colonus resisted and, citing Theseus as their authority, would not let Creon carry out his purpose. He, the while, had signed to his men, who now snatched Ismene and Antigone from their father and dragged them off in spite of the protest of the villagers. Then Creon said mockingly: "At least I have taken your staves from you. Now try your luck, blind old man, and wander on!" And emboldened by success he went up to Oedipus once more and was about to lay hands on him when Theseus, who had received word of the armed invasion of Colonus, appeared on the scene. As soon as he saw and heard what had happened, he sent servants on foot and on horseback up the road the Thebans had gone with the two girls. Then he declared to Creon that he would not release him until he had given Oedipus back his daughters.

"Son of Aegeus," Creon answered with feigned humility, "truly I have not come to make war on you and your city. I did not know that your people were so zealously devoted to that blind kinsman of mine, whom I meant to do a kindness, or that they prefer to shelter one who murdered his father and married his mother, rather than return him to his native land!"

But Theseus bade him be silent and instantly tell him where the girls were concealed. After a little, Antigone and Ismene were reunited with their father. Creon and his men had left.

OEDIPUS AND POLYNICES

Even so Oedipus was to have no rest. From his brief journey in pursuit of the daughters of his guest, Theseus brought word that one who was close kin to Oedipus, though he had not come from Thebes, had set foot on Colonus and prostrated himself as a suppliant before the altar in Poseidon's temple where Theseus had only just made offering.

"That is my son Polynices," Oedipus said angrily, "my son who merits nothing but my hatred. It would be intolerable to me even to talk to him!" But Antigone, who loved this brother because he was the gentler and kinder of the two, succeeded in soothing her father's wrath and gained his consent at least to hear his unhappy son. First Oedipus begged his protector to be ready to aid him in case an attempt were made to lead him away by force. Then he had his son summoned before him.

From the very outset, Polynices bore himself very differently from his uncle Creon, and Antigone did not fail to draw her father's attention to this. "I see someone approaching," she cried. "He comes alone. Tears are streaming from his eyes." Oedipus only turned his head away, asking, "Is it he?" "Yes, dear father," she answered. "Your son Polynices stands before you."

Polynices threw himself at his father's feet and clasped his knees. He looked up at him, and grief ate at his heart when he saw his beggar's dress, his empty eyes, and his gray hair blowing unkempt in the wind. "Too late I see all this!" he moaned. "I confess—I accuse myself—I forgot my father. What would have become of him, had my sister not given him care! Father, I have wronged you! Can you forgive me? You are silent? O speak, and do not turn from me in such relentless anger! Help me, my sisters, to unclose those bitter lips!"

"First tell us what brought you here," said Antigone gently. "Perhaps your own words will cause him to break his silence." And Polynices told how his brother had driven him from Thebes, how Adrastus, king of Argos, had received him and given him his daughter to wife, and that there he had won seven princes with their forces as his allies in a just cause; that these had already encircled the region of Thebes. Then he begged his father to go with him, promising that once his malicious brother had been dethroned, he, Polynices himself, would put the crown in his father's hands.

But his son's penitence could not soften a spirit so deeply offended. "Infamous wretch!" Oedipus cried and made no move to raise the suppliant from the ground. "When the throne and the scepter were yours, you drove your father from the land. You yourself put on him this beggar's cloak which moves you to pity, now that you have had to endure like hardships. You and your brother are not my true children. Had it depended on you, I should have been dead long since. But the vengeance of the gods awaits you. You will fall in your own blood and your brother in his. This is the reply you may take to those princes who have declared themselves your allies."

Antigone hastened over to her brother, who had risen from his knees in horror and recoiled from his father. "Obey my most fervent wish, Polynices," she besought him. "Return to Argos with your host! Do not make war on your native city."

"That is impossible," he answered after a moment's hesitation. "Flight would mean disgrace for me—more than disgrace—destruction. Though both of us be doomed to perish, we brothers still cannot be friends." And he freed himself from his sister's embrace and left with a troubled spirit.

Thus Oedipus resisted the tempting promises held out to him by both factions of his kinsmen and yielded them up to the gods of vengeance. And now the arcs of his destiny closed to their full circle. Crash after crash of thunder sounded from above, and the old man understood this voice from heaven and called for Theseus with urgency and longing. The darkness of impending storm crept over the land, and the blind king trembled with the fear that he might die or his reason be impaired before he could utter to his host his gratitude for all the kindness he had received at his hands. But Theseus came, and Oedipus gave his solemn blessing to the city of Athens. Then he asked its king to obey the call of the gods and conduct him to where he could die, untouched by the hands of any mortal, and beheld only by the eyes of Theseus. To no one should he point out the place where Oedipus had left the earth. Never should the grave which held him be revealed, for in this way it would defend Athens against her foes more than spear or shield or the strength of many allies. His daughters and the people of Colonus were permitted to accompany him part of the way, and the train wound into the shadow of the grove of the Erinyes. No one was allowed to touch Oedipus, and he, the blind man, who had been guided thus far, seemed of a sudden to see. He walked erect and strong in the van of the procession and led the way to the goal Fate had appointed for him.

In the middle of the grove of the Erinyes the earth gaped, and the opening was rimmed with a threshold of bronze, the mouth of many winding paths. Legend, taking shape from various ancient tales, had it that this cave was an entrance to the underworld. Oedipus chose one of the twisting ways, but he did not let his retinue accompany him to the grotto itself. Under a hollow tree he halted, sat down on a stone, and undid the belt of his stained beggar's dress. Then he called for water from a flowing stream, cleansed himself of the dust of his long wanderings, and donned a festive robe which his daughters brought him. When he rose refreshed and renewed, thunder rumbled up from the bowels of the earth. Tremulously Antigone and Ismene clung in his arms. He kissed them and said: "Farewell, my children. From this day on you will be orphaned." But while he was still clasping them close, a voice like a clapper striking on bronze vibrated, none knew whether from heaven or the heart of earth, saying: "Why do you loiter, Oedipus? Why do you delay?"

The blind king heard and knew that the god was demanding his own. He loosed the fingers of his children and laid them in the hand of Theseus to show that he put them in his care for the rest of their lives. Then he bade all turn their backs on him and leave. Only Theseus was permitted to approach the threshold of the opening. His retinue and his daughters obeyed him and did not look back until they had gone a long way. When they did, a miracle had come to pass. There was no longer any sign of King Oedipus. No flash of lightning split the sky, no thunder crashed, no stormwind swept the grove. The air was quiet and serene. The dark doors of the underworld had opened noiselessly, and the old man, purified and free from pain and regret, had descended into the depths, as though borne on the wings of gentle spirits. Theseus stood alone, shading his eyes with his hand, as if a vision too awesome and divine had dazzled his sight. They saw him lift his arms to Olympus and then throw himself on the earth, making supplication both to the immortals in heaven and to the gods of the underworld. After this brief prayer, the king returned to the daughters of King Oedipus and assured them of his protection. In unbroken silence, his spirit filled with holy divinings, he went back to Athens.

THE SEVEN AGAINST THEBES

POLYNICES AND TYDEUS
AS THE GUESTS OF ADRASTUS

ADRASTUS, son of Talaus, king of Argos, had five children, of which two, Argia and Deipyle, were daughters. Concerning these a singular oracle had been issued: their father, so it was said, would wed one of them to a lion, the other to a boar. In vain the king pondered over the meaning of this strange prophecy, and when the girls were grown, thought only of finding them husbands as quickly as possible, so that nothing might come of the terrible prediction. But the gods see to it that their words are fulfilled.

From two different directions fugitives came to the gates of Argos, one from Thebes: Polynices, who had been driven from the city by his brother Eteocles; the other, Tydeus, son of Oeneus, from Calydon, from which he had fled after unintentionally slaying a kinsman in the course of a hunt. The two met in Argos, in front of the palace. Night had fallen, and in the darkness they took each other for enemies and began to fight. Adrastus heard the clash below, descended with a torch, and separated them. As they stood to the right and left of him, two stalwart heroes, the king started as though he had seen a specter, for on the shield of Polynices was a lion's head, while the head of a boar stared at him from that of Tydeus. Polynices had chosen the lion for his emblem in honor of Heracles, while Tydeus had taken the boar in memory of Meleager and his hunt for the Calydonian Boar. Now Adrastus understood the meaning of the oracle. The fugitives became his sons-in-law. The elder daughter, Argia, was wedded to Polynices, the younger, Deipyle, to Tydeus. And Adrastus pledged both princes to reinstate them on the thrones of the countries from which they had been exiled.

Thebes was chosen as the goal of the first expedition, and Adrastus summoned the heroes of the land, seven princes, includ-

ing himself, with their seven hosts. Their names were Adrastus,
Polynices, Tydeus, Amphiaraus, the husband of Adrastus' sister,
Capaneus, his nephew, and finally Hippomedon and Parthenopaeus, brothers of the king of Argos. But Amphiaraus, the king's
brother-in-law, who had been his enemy for many years, was a
soothsayer and foretold a disastrous end to the whole campaign.
First he tried to shake Adrastus and the other heroes in their
resolve, but when he saw that his efforts were in vain, he went
to a hiding-place which no one knew save Eriphyle, his wife and
sister to the king, and there concealed himself from all men. For
a long time they searched for him, since Adrastus did not want
to go without him whom he called the eye of his hosts.

Now when Polynices had been compelled to leave Thebes, he
had taken with him a necklace and veil, which Aphrodite had once
given Harmonia at her marriage to Cadmus, founder of Thebes.
But both the necklace and veil were fraught with death for the
wearer and had already caused the destruction of Harmonia,
Semele, the mother of Dionysus, and Jocasta. The last to own
them was Argia, wife of Polynices, who was also to drain the cup
of sorrow, and now her husband decided to bribe Eriphyle with
the necklace and thus get her to reveal the whereabouts of her

husband. Eriphyle had long envied her niece the magnificent
jewels the stranger had brought her, and so when she saw the
glittering gems linked with gold, she could not resist, but told
Polynices to follow her and led him to the refuge of Amphiaraus.
The seer could not now well evade joining his fellows, all the less
because when he and Adrastus had called a truce to their feud,
and the king had given him his sister to wife, he had promised to
let Eriphyle be the judge of any future disagreement which
might come up between her brother and her husband. So Amphiaraus girt on his armor and assembled his warriors. But before
he set out, he called his son Alcmaeon and had him swear a solemn
oath that the moment he heard of his father's death, he would
take vengeance on the wife who had betrayed him.

THE HEROES SET OUT
HYPSIPYLE AND OPHELTES

The other heroes had also completed their preparations, and soon
Adrastus stood ringed by a mighty host, which set out in seven
divisions, commanded by seven heroes. They left the city of
Argos, their hearts high with hope and assurance, and the fan-
fares of trumpets and shrilling of flutes speeded them on their
way. But long before they arrived at their destination, misfortune overtook them. They had reached the woods of Nemea.
Every spring and river and lake had run dry, and they were
tormented with heat and burning thirst. Their armor weighed
upon their limbs; the shields were heavy in their hands, and the
fine dust their feet whirled up in the road settled on their dry
lips and gritted in their mouths. The very foam flecks dried on
the jowls of their horses; they distended their nostrils and
champed at the bit, their tongues swollen with thirst.

While Adrastus with some others was searching the woods for
a spring or a well, they came upon a mourning woman of singular
beauty. She was seated in the shadow of a tree, a boy-child at her
breast, and though her dress was mean, her floating locks and
proud bearing gave her the appearance of a queen. The king
was overwhelmed with astonishment, and thinking that this must
surely be the nymph of these forests, he fell on his knees before

her and implored her aid for himself and his men who were perishing of thirst. But the woman cast down her eyes and answered him humbly. "I am no goddess, stranger. And if you see about me something which is more than mortal, it must have been stamped on my features by greater suffering than others bear. I am Hypsipyle, daughter of Thoas. Once I was queen among the women of Lemnos. But I was seized by pirates and then, after unutterable misery, sold as a slave to King Lycurgus of Nemea. The boy I am nursing is not my own. He is Opheltes, the son of my lord, and I have been chosen to tend him. As for you, I shall gladly help you procure what you need. A single spring still gushes in this desolate waste, and no one but myself knows of the secret approach to it. There will be enough water to refresh all your host. Follow me!" And the woman rose, laid the child tenderly in the soft grass, and lulled him with a little song.

Adrastus and his men called the others, and soon the entire host crowded the narrow woodland path after Hypsipyle. Winding through the thick underbrush, they reached a rock-hewn gorge. Over it hovered cool spray. It blew into the hot faces of those who had outstripped the queen walking with their leader and slaked their skin with moisture. The sound of water, falling over stone in a torrent, grew louder and louder. "Water!" they cried exultingly, leaped down into the ravine, and stood on the wet boulders, catching the jets in their helmets. "Water, water!" echoed the host. Their voices rang above the surge of the cascade, and the cliffs echoed the shout. They threw themselves along the green margin of the brimming brook which issued from the ravine, and gulped the sweet cool water in long satisfying draughts. They found a wider passage for the chariots. The charioteers did not stop to unharness the horses but drove straight into the swirling tide, where the brook broadened to a river, and let their beasts cool their sweating flanks and dip their weary heads.

When every man and every creature was refreshed, Hypsipyle guided Adrastus and his followers back to the road, telling them of the deeds and sufferings of the women of Lemnos, while the host followed at a respectful distance. Before they reached the place where they had first seen Hypsipyle under the arched branches of a tree, her ear, sharpened by watchfulness for her nursling, plainly caught the frightened wail of the child, which the rest scarcely heard. She herself had been the mother of children, left behind in Lemnos when the pirates took her away from those she loved, and now all her love was lavished on little Opheltes. Her pulse beat faster with foreboding. Swiftly she ran to the place where she had held the child to her bosom. He was gone, and she no longer heard even his voice. But as her eyes swiftly searched about the tree, she suddenly realized the terrible fate which had befallen her charge while she was doing a kindness to the Argive host. For not far from the trunk lay a hideous serpent coiled in idle repose, heavy with the meal it just had made. Her very hair stood up in horror, and her cries of agony trembled on the wind and were carried to the heroes, who hurried to aid her. The first to see the serpent was Hippomedon. Without an instant's reflection he tore a rock from the ground and hurled it at the creature, but the stone rebounded from the scaly body, and crumbled as if it had been a handful of earth. Then Hippomedon lunged at the monster with his spear. It sped into the gaping jaws, spattered the grass with the serpent's brains, and the point came out at the crest. The body turned like a top on the long projecting spear, and the hissing breath came in slower and slower gasps until the creature lay dead.

And now the poor foster mother dared follow the traces of the child. The earth was red with his blood, and at last, far from the trunk of the tree, she found a pile of little bones picked bare. She knelt, gathered them in her lap, and gave them to Adrastus. He buried the boy who had lost his life because of them and arranged a solemn funeral feast for him. In his honor they founded the Nemean games and worshipped him as a demigod under the name of Archemorus, the Early-Perfect.

Hypsipyle did not escape the rage which the child's death kindled in Eurydice, wife of Lycurgus. She had her slave imprisoned and vowed she should die the cruelest of deaths. But by the grace of Chance, Hypsipyle's eldest sons were already on the trail of their mother, and soon after these happenings they reached Nemea and freed her from captivity.

THE HEROES ARRIVE IN THEBES

"This is an omen of how this expedition will end!" Amphiaraus, the seer, had said gloomily when they discovered the bones of Opheltes. But the others were more concerned with the killing of the serpent and claimed that this was a sign of good fortune. And because the host had fully recovered from the hardship of thirst, they were all in excellent spirits and paid no attention to the sighs of this prophet of evil. A few days more, and the Argives were before the walls of Thebes.

Eteocles and his uncle Creon were prepared to defend the city long and stubbornly, and now the son of Oedipus addressed his people: "Remember, fellow citizens, what you owe the city which was a gentle mother to you in childhood and reared you to stalwart warriors. All of you, from the youth who has not yet grown into manhood, to the man whose hair is graying, I call on you all to defend the altars of your native gods, your fathers, wives, and children, the free earth on which you stand. He who reads omens from the flight of birds has told me that during the coming night the Argives will concentrate their host and make an attack upon Thebes. On to the gates! To the walls! To arms! Occupy the ramparts! Man the towers! Guard every entrance and do not fear the numbers of the enemy. My spies are all about and will discover the tactics of the foe. I shall make my plans according to the message they bring."

While Eteocles was thus spurring his men to action, Antigone stood on the highest parapet of the palace, and with her was an old man, the armor-bearer of her grandfather Laius. Soon after her father's death she and her sister Ismene had left the protection of King Theseus out of a great longing for their own country. They came with the vague hope of assisting their brother Polynices, even though they did not approve of the siege he contemplated, and with the determination to share the fate of the beloved city of their birth. Creon and Eteocles had received Antigone with open arms, for they regarded her as a voluntary hostage and a welcome go-between.

On this day she had climbed the old palace stair, built of sweet-smelling cedar, and stood on the platform listening to the old man as he explained the position of the enemy. The great host was encamped on all the fields surrounding the city, along the banks of the Ismenus, and around the fountain of Dirce, famed since the days of old. There was motion among the men. They were dividing off into troops, and the entire region shone with the glint of metal, like the sea in the sun. Masses of foot-soldiers and riders churned around the gates of the besieged city. The girl was terror-stricken at the sight, but the old man comforted her. "Our walls are high and solid," he said. "And our oaken gates have heavy bolts of iron. The city lies secure within and is defended by many brave warriors who do not fear the grimmest battle." Then, in response to her questions, he pointed out to her the various leaders. "That one over there, whose helmet glitters in the light, who swings his great polished shield as though it were weightless and goes in the van of his men, is Prince Hippomedon, who lives in Mycene, near the waters of Lerna. He is tall of stature, like the giants who once sprang from the earth! More to the right, do you see? That one who is just jumping the waters of Dirce on his horse, who wears armor resembling that of barbarians—that is Tydeus, son of Oeneus, the brother of your brother's wife. He and his Aetolians carry heavy shields and are known for their skill in the use of the lance. I recognize him by his emblem, for I have visited the enemy's camp as a messenger."

"And who is that young hero?" the girl asked. "Young and yet with a man's beard, who looks about with such savage glances? He is just passing a burial mound, and his men are following him slowly."

"That is Parthenopaeus," the old man told her. "He is the son of Atalanta, friend of Artemis. But do you see those two over there, near the grave of the daughters of Niobe? The elder is Adrastus, who heads the entire expedition, and the younger— does he look familiar to you?"

"I can see only his shoulders and the outline of his body," said Antigone with painful emotion. "And yet I recognize my brother Polynices. Could I but fly like the clouds, float down to him, and clasp my arms around his neck! How he gleams in his golden armor—like the morning sun! But who is that charioteer who holds the reins in so firm a hand, drives a white chariot, and uses his goad with such calm deliberation?"

"That is Amphiaraus, the seer."

"And the one who is pacing along the walls, measuring them, and looking for the best places to attack?"

"That is arrogant Capaneus, who has scoffed at our city and threatened to take you and your sister to Mycenae, by the waters of Lerna—as slaves."

Antigone paled and asked to be taken back. The old man gave her his hand and helped her down the stair and to her chamber.

MENOECEUS

In the meantime Creon and Eteocles had been holding a council of war and resolved to send one leader to each of the seven gates of Thebes; thus seven Theban princes would oppose Polynices and his six allies. But before the battle broke out, they desired an omen, such as can be read from the flight of birds, to give them an inkling of the outcome. Now among the Thebans lived the seer Tiresias, son of Eueres and the nymph Chariclo. Once, in the days of his youth, he had surprised Athene visiting with his mother and had seen what he should not. For this the goddess had afflicted him with blindness. Chariclo had implored her friend to restore her son's sight, but this was beyond Athene's power. Out of pity for him she laid a spell on his ears and, of a sudden, he understood the language of birds. From that time on he had been soothsayer for the city.

Creon sent his young son Menoeceus to guide the old seer to the palace, and soon after Tiresias appeared before the king, standing with trembling knees between his daughter Manto and the boy. When he was pressed to tell what the birds boded for the city, he was silent for a long time. At last he spoke, and his words were sad. "The sons of Oedipus are guilty of a grave sin against their father. They will bring bitterness and sorrow to the land of Thebes. Argives and Cadmeans will slaughter one another, and brother will die at the hand of brother. I know of only one way to save the city, but that is too terrible to face even for the sake of rescue. My lips refuse to utter it. Farewell!" He turned to go, but Creon pleaded with him stormily, and at last Tiresias yielded to his importunity. "You insist on hearing it?" he asked, and his tone was stern. "Then speak I must. But first tell me where your son Menoeceus is who brought me here."

"He stands beside you," said Creon.

"Then let him flee as far as his feet will take him, before I utter the will of the gods!"

"But why?" asked Creon. "Menoeceus is his father's true child. He can keep silence if it is better so, and it will be a glad thing for him to know the means which may save us all."

"Then hear what I have learned from the birds," said Tiresias. "Fortune will again visit you, but the threshold she must cross will be mournful. The youngest of the race sprung from the dragon seed must perish. Only through his fall can you issue victorious from this encounter."

"Alas!" cried Creon. "What is the meaning of your words, old man?"

"That the youngest descendant of Cadmus must die if the city is to be saved."

"You demand the death of my darling child, of my son Menoeceus?" Creon drew himself up haughtily. "Away with you! Out of my city! I can dispense with your gloomy prophecies."

"Is the truth invalid because it brings sorrow to your heart?" Tiresias asked gravely. And now Creon cast himself at his feet, clasped his knees, and implored the prophet by his gray locks to retract what he had said. But the seer was firm. "The offering cannot be evaded," he said. "At the fountain of Dirce, where the dragon once rested his coils, the boy's blood must flow. Earth will be your friend only when in return for the human blood she once infused in Cadmus through the teeth of the dragon, she receives the blood of a kinsman of Cadmus. If Menoeceus consents to sacrifice himself for his city, he will, in death, be its liberator, and the homecoming of Adrastus and his host will be unblest. There are two ways before you, Creon. Now choose which it shall be."

When Tiresias had spoken, he left the hall with his daughter. Creon sank into a deep silence. At last he called out in anguish: "How gladly would I myself die for my country! But to offer up you, my child . . . Go, my son, as far as your feet will carry you. Leave this accursed land, too evil to contain your innocence. Go by way of Delphi, Aetolia, and Thesprotia to the oracle of Dodona, and there take refuge in the sanctuary."

"Yes," said Menoeceus, and his eyes shone. "Give me whatever I shall need for the journey, and you may be sure I shall find the way." But when Creon, calmed by his son's tractability, had hurried to his post, the boy threw himself upon the earth and made fervent prayer to the gods. "Forgive me, immortals, if I have lied; if by false words I freed my father from fears unworthy of him! It is not dishonorable for him, an old man, to be afraid. But what cowardice it would be if I betrayed the land to which I owe life! Hear my oath, O gods, and accept it graciously. For through my death I shall save my country. Flight would be too shameful! I shall mount the rampart and throw myself into the deep, dark gorge of the dragon, for in this way the prophet said I could save the land of Thebes."

And the boy rose and hastened to the highest point of the palace wall, measured the ranks of his enemies with one brief glance, and cursed them with solemn imprecation. Then he drew out the dagger he had hidden in the folds of his tunic, plunged it into his throat, and fell from that steep rampart. His shattered body came to rest on the margin of the fountain of Dirce.

THE ATTACK UPON THEBES

The oracle had been fulfilled. Creon bridled his sense of utter despair, while Eteocles assigned seven bands of men to the seven guardians of the gates, dispatched rider after rider to replace them, and set up light infantry behind the shield-bearers, so that every site where attack was probable might be fully protected. And now the Argive army moved across the plain, and the storming of the walls began. The air shook with ringing song, and trumpets blared, both from the ramparts of Thebes and the ranks of the enemy.

First Parthenopaeus, son of Atalanta, the huntress, led his battalions, shield crowded against shield, toward one of the gates. Embossed on his own shield was the image of his mother slaying the Aetolian Boar with her swift arrow. Amphiaraus, the sooth-sayer, moved toward a second gate, and in his chariot were sacri-ficial animals to offer the gods. His weapons were unadorned, and his shield shining and empty. Hippomedon advanced toward the third gate. His emblem was hundred-eyed Argus, watching Io, whom Hera had changed into a heifer. Tydeus guided his men toward the fourth gate. A shaggy lion's skin was pictured on his shield, and in his right hand he brandished a torch, swinging it angrily from side to side. King Polynices, exiled from his coun-try, led the attack against the fifth gate, and his coat of arms was a team of horses rearing in rage. The sixth gate was the goal of Capaneus, who boasted of being the equal of Ares, the war-god. Carved on the metal surface of his shield was a giant who had lifted a whole city from its foundations and was carrying it on his shoulders; this was meant to symbolize the fate Capaneus had in mind for Thebes. Toward the seventh and last gate came Adrastus, king of the Argives, and his escutcheon showed a hun-dred dragons bearing off in their jaws the children of Thebes.

When the seven leaders were close to the gates, they opened battle with slings, bows, and spears. But the Thebans fended off this first attack so fiercely that the Argives were forced to with-draw. Then Tydeus and Polynices bethought themselves quickly and cried: "Comrades, why wait until we fall beneath their mis-siles? Now, this very instant, let us storm the gates with our foot soldiers, riders, and charioteers—all together with one mass charge!" His words spread through the host like flame, and the Argives took heart again. They surged forward with concerted strength, but the outcome was no happier than before. With bashed heads the attackers sank at the feet of the defenders. Whole battalions died beneath the walls, and the dry earth was turned into rivers of blood. At that, Parthenopaeus hurled him-self at the gate like a tempest and called for fire and axes to demolish and burn it to the ground. Periclymenus, a Theban hero whose post was on the rampart nearby, watched his efforts and, at the given moment, tore loose from the wall a mass of stone large enough to fill a wagon, and it fell, crushing the blond head of the besieger and grinding his bones to dust. When Eteocles saw that this gate was safe, he flew to the others. At the fourth he came upon Tydeus raging like a dragon. He jerked his head under his helmet with its streaming plumes, and the shield he was holding over it shrilled with the clang of the metal discs fastened around the rim. High toward the wall he hurled his lance, and the band of shield-bearers around him launched a hail of spears at the top of the rampart, so that the Thebans had to retreat from the edge.

At this moment Eteocles appeared on the scene. He reassembled them as a huntsman gathers the pack which has scattered, and led them back to the wall. Then he hastened on from gate to gate. He met Capaneus, who was carrying a tall ladder and boasting that Zeus himself should not keep him from razing the conquered city to the ground. With these insolent words he set the ladder against the wall and, in a pelting storm of stones, climbed the slippery rungs under cover of his shield. But it was not the Thebans who punished him for his impious vaunt. Zeus himself lay in wait for the offender and slew him with a thunderbolt, just as he was leaping from ladder to wall. The blow was so mighty that the whole earth quaked. His limbs were strewn around the ladder, his hair flamed up to the sky, and his blood spattered the rungs. Like wheels, his hands and feet rolled in a circle, and his trunk burned on the ground.

King Adrastus took this for a sign that the father of gods was hostile to his undertaking. He guided his men away from the city moat and gave orders to retreat. And when the Thebans saw the happy omen given them by Zeus, they rushed from their city on foot and in chariots and wrought confusion among the Argive hosts. Chariot clashed against chariot and bodies struck the earth. The Thebans were victorious, but not until they had driven the enemy far from their walls did they return to their city.

BROTHERS IN SINGLE COMBAT

This was the end of the attack on the city of Thebes. But when Creon and Eteocles were back in the shelter of their own ramparts, the beaten Argive host gathered again and was soon ready to attack once more. The Thebans, quickly aware of this, had small hope of resisting a second time, since their numbers had been thinned and their strength weakened by the first attack. And

then King Eteocles came to a bold resolve. He sent his herald to
the Argives, who had again approached and were camped near
the city moat. He had him call for silence, and then he himself,
standing on the highest tower of his palace, cried to his own men
within and to the Argives without the walls. "Danai and Argives," he said in ringing tones, "all of you who have come to
beset this city, and you, the people of Thebes: do not sacrifice
so many lives for me and Polynices! Rather let me bear the brunt
of this feud and fight with my brother in single combat. If I slay
him, let me rule the land. But should I fall by his hand, the
scepter shall be his, and my foes shall lower their weapons and
return home without wasting more blood."

Then from the ranks of the Argives sprang Polynices, declaring his willingness to accept these conditions. Both sides were
already more than tired of a war which could benefit only one
of two, and so the opposing hosts applauded Eteocles' proposal.
An agreement was drawn up, and both leaders confirmed it with
solemn oath. And now the sons of Oedipus armed themselves from
head to foot. The noblest of the Thebans accoutred their king,
and the most powerful among the Argives fitted out Polynices,
the exile from his realm. They confronted each other sheathed in
bronze, and brother measured brother with strong and steadfast
gaze. "Remember," the friends of Polynices called to him, "remember that Zeus expects you to rear him a monument in Argos,
in gratitude for the victory he is about to grant you!" And the
Thebans urged on Prince Eteocles. "You are fighting for your
city and your throne," they said. "Let the thought of this double
prize spur you on to win!"

Before the combat began, the soothsayers from both sides
came together and made sacrifice, to discover from the shapes of
the flames what the outcome would be. But the signs were un-

certain; they could be read as victory or defeat for the one side or the other. When the offerings had been made and the brothers stood ready, Polynices lifted his hands in supplication, turned his head toward the land of the Argives, and prayed: "Hera, sovereign over Argos, from your country I chose my wife, in your country I live. Let me, your citizen, win, and dye my right hand in the blood of my foe!"

Eteocles, the while, looked toward Athene's temple in Thebes. "O daughter of Zeus," he pleaded, "guide my lance straight to its mark, to the breast of him who came to destroy my fatherland!" As the last word left his lips, a fanfare of trumpets proclaimed the beginning of the combat, and the two brothers ran forward and hurled themselves upon each other like savage boars who have whetted their tusks for the fight. Their lances crossed in mid-air and rebounded from the shields. And now they aimed their spears at each other's faces and eyes, but again the shields caught the thrusts. As for the spectators, the sweat broke out over their bodies in great drops at the sight of so grim a struggle. And now Eteocles put out his right foot to push aside a stone lying in his way and incautiously allowed his left to protrude from under his shield. At once Polynices reached forward with his spear and pierced his shin, while the entire Argive host shouted with joy as if this one wound had decided the victory. But even when Eteocles felt the point enter his flesh, he did not allow his senses to blur with the pain and, keeping a sharp lookout, saw his opponent's shoulder exposed. He launched his spear and it struck, but not deeply, so that only the point broke off, and the Thebans exclaimed only a little in halfhearted joy. Eteocles recoiled, picked up a fragment of marble, and casting it, split his brother's lance in half. And now they were even again since each had lost one of his weapons. They took a firm grip on their swords and fought breast to breast. Shield rang on shield, and the air quivered with the clash of battle. Then Eteocles remembered a trick he had learned in Thessaly. He suddenly shifted his position, drew backward, throwing his weight on his left foot, covered the lower part of his body with great care, and then leaped forward with his right foot and pierced his brother, who was unprepared for so sudden a change in position, through the stomach, just above the hips. Polynices leaned to one side and then sank to the ground in a pool of blood. Eteocles, sure of victory, cast aside his sword and bent over his dying brother to take his arms from him, but this was his undoing. For, in his fall, Polynices had not loosed his grasp on his sword, and now, though his breath came in feeble gasps, he still had strength enough to thrust the blade into the very liver of Eteocles, bending above him. Dying, he fell beside his dying brother.

And now the gates of Thebes were flung wide, and the women and slaves poured out to lament their dead ruler. But Antigone leaned over her brother Polynices whom she loved, to catch a last word from his lips. Eteocles had died almost immediately. A single long rattling sigh, and he was no more. But Polynices still breathed. He turned his dimming eyes toward his sister and said: "How I mourn your lot, my sister, and that of my dead brother, who was once my friend and became my foe! Only now that I am dying do I know how much I loved him! As for you, I beg you to bury me in the earth of my native land. Do not let the city of Thebes deny me this. And now close my eyes with your hand, for already the shadow of death lies cold upon my forehead."

He died in his sister's arms, and at once both sides began to wrangle aloud in bitter disagreement. The Thebans credited Eteocles, their lord, with the victory, while the Argives claimed it for Polynices. The friends of the fallen were also at cross purposes. "Polynices was the first to strike with the lance!" cried some. "But he was also the first to fall!" countered others. So heated grew the quarrel that they took to arms. Fortunately for the Thebans, they were ranged for battle, since they had flocked forth fully armed both during and after the combat between the brothers, while the Argives had laid aside their weapons, too certain of victory to observe caution. And so when the Thebans suddenly threw themselves upon their foes, giving them no time to gird on their armor, they met with no resistance. The unarmed Argives scattered over the plain in disorderly flight, and Theban lances slew them by the hundreds.

This was the occasion on which Periclymenus of Thebes pursued Amphiaraus, the soothsayer, to the shore of the river Ismenus. Amphiaraus was fleeing in a chariot, and the horses balked at the swirling waters. With the Theban at his heels, however, he had no choice but bid his charioteer ford the stream.

Before the horses even wetted their hooves, however, his enemy had reached the bank, and his spear almost touched the neck of the seer. But Zeus did not wish one whom he had lent the gift of prophecy to perish ingloriously. He cracked open the earth with a thunderbolt. It yawned like a black cave and swallowed up both chariot and soothsayer.

Soon the enemies of Thebes were swept from the surrounding countryside. From all sides swarmed the Thebans, bringing the shields of the foes they had slain and spoils from the fugitives they had overtaken. Laden with plunder, they made a triumphant entry into their city.

CREON'S RESOLVE

After the first outburst of jubilation was over, they thought about burying their dead. Since both the sons of Oedipus had fallen, Creon, their uncle, became king of Thebes, and as such it was his duty to see to the burial of his nephews. He at once arranged a solemn funeral for Eteocles, the defender of the city, and had him borne to his grave with the honors due to a king. All the citizens of Thebes walked in the funeral procession, but the body of Polynices lay unburied and abandoned. Creon had a herald proclaim throughout Thebes that the enemy of his country, who had come to destroy the city with fire, to sate himself with the blood of his people, to drive the gods from the land, and enslave all those who had not been slain, was not to be mourned; that he was to be denied a grave; that his body should be left for the birds and beasts to devour. He also commanded the citizens to have a care that his wishes were obeyed, and set special guards near the corpse, so that none might steal or bury it. The penalty for attempting either was death, death by stoning in a public place of the city.

Antigone heard these orders, which seemed so cruel to her, and remembered the promise she had given her dying brother. With a heavy heart she went to her sister Ismene and tried to persuade her to help remove the body of Polynices. But Ismene was all soft and delicate, with no drop of heroic blood in her veins. "Sister," she answered, and her eyes swam in tears, "have you forgotten the terrible death of our father and mother? Has the memory of our brothers' destruction already faded from your mind, that you want to drag us, who are left, to a like end?"

Coldly Antigone turned from her timid sister. "I do not want your help," she said. "I shall bury my brother unaided, and when this is done I shall gladly die and lie beside him whom I loved in life."

Soon after, one of the guards approached King Creon with hesitant step and troubled face. "The body you had us watch has been buried," he cried. "We do not know who did this, and whoever it was has escaped. We cannot understand how it was possible! When the guard on day duty told us what had happened, we were stunned at the thought. Only a thin layer of dust covered the body, only just enough to be accepted as burial by the gods of the underworld. There was no sign that a shovel had been plied, no trace of wagon wheels. We began to quarrel about it, each accusing the other of the deed, and finally it came to blows. But in the end we decided it would be best, O king, to tell you what had occurred, and the lot of being messenger fell upon me!"

Creon's anger was great. He threatened to have all the guards hanged unless they delivered the evildoer into his hands without delay. At his command, they removed the earth from the body and resumed their vigil. From early morning until noon they sat in the hot sun. Then, of a sudden, a storm blew up and filled the air with dust. The guards were still pondering the meaning of this sign, when they saw a girl approach, lamenting softly, like a bird who finds the nest empty. In one hand she carried a bronze pitcher. Quickly she stooped and filled it with dust and then cautiously drew near the body. She did not see the men, who were on a mound at some distance, since the stench of the body, unburied so long, sickened them at closer quarters. When she reached Polynices, she poured dust upon him three times, in lieu of burial. And at that the guards hurried to the spot, seized her, and dragged the doer, caught in the very act, to their king.

ANTIGONE AND CREON

Creon instantly saw that it was his niece Antigone. "Foolish girl!" he cried. "Now you stand with bowed head! Will you confess, or do you deny having done what they accuse you of?"

"I confess!" said the girl and lifted her head proudly.

"And did you know the orders?" the king continued questioning her. "And knowing them, dared transgress them so boldly?"

"I knew them," Antigone answered calmly and firmly. "But those orders did not come from one of the immortal gods. And I know other commands that are not of today nor of yesterday, but hold for all eternity, and none can say from whence they were given. No mortal may transgress these without incurring the wrath of the gods, and it was such a command that forbade me leave the dead son of my mother unburied. If this action of mine seems foolish to you, then he is a fool who accuses me of folly."

"And do you think your stubborn spirit cannot be broken?" asked Creon, angered still more by the girl's defiance. "The most inflexible blade is the first to crack. Whoever is in another's power ought not to show insolence!"

"You can do no more than kill me," Antigone answered. "Why delay? My name will not become inglorious through death. I know, moreover, that only the fear of you is keeping my fellow citizens silent. In their hearts they all approve of what I have done, for a sister's first and foremost duty is to cherish her brother."

Whereupon Creon cried: "Well, then—if cherish him you must—cherish him in Hades!" And he was about to bid the servants seize her, when Ismene, who had heard of her sister's capture, stormed into the hall. She seemed to have shaken off her weakness and timidity. Bravely she went up to her uncle, declared she had known of the burial, and demanded to die together with Antigone. But she reminded Creon that Antigone was not merely his sister's daughter, but the betrothed of his own son Haemon as well, so that by killing her he was depriving the heir to the throne of marriage with the one he loved. Creon did not deign to answer but had his servants take both the sisters to the inner chambers of the palace.

HAEMON AND ANTIGONE

When Creon saw his son hurrying toward him, he was certain that he had heard of the judgment passed on Antigone, and had come to rebel against his father. But with filial obedience Haemon replied to his wary questions, and only after he had convinced his father of his devotion did he venture to ask mercy for his beloved. "You do not know what the people are saying, father," he said. "You do not hear them demur, because your imperious eyes keep them from saying to your face anything that is unwelcome to your ears. But I know what is going on! And I can tell you that the whole city is bewailing the fate of Antigone, that every citizen considers her action worthy of eternal glory, that no one believes that a sister who refuses to let dogs gnaw her brother's bones or birds hack at his flesh is deserving of death. And so, dear father, yield to the voice of the people! Do as the trees along the swollen forest stream; they bend to the force of waters and stand unharmed, but those which resist are uprooted by the current."

"Does this boy propose to teach me?" Creon said contemptuously. "It seems you are fighting on the side of a woman."

"Yes, if you are a woman!" the boy countered swiftly and eagerly. "For I said all I did only to help you."

"I can well see," his father replied indignantly, "that blind love for an evildoer holds your spirit in bondage. But you shall not woo her alive. For this is my resolve: far away, where no man passes, she shall be imprisoned in a rock grave, and only so much food will be given her as is necessary to save the city from the taint outright murder might bring it. There she may plead for freedom with the gods of the underworld. She will learn too late that it is wiser to obey the living than the dead." And Creon turned from his son and ordered everything prepared to carry out his verdict. Publicly, before all the people of Thebes, Antigone was conducted to the tomb destined for her. Unafraid, and calling upon the immortals and her loved ones with whom she hoped to be reunited, she entered the cave which was to be her grave.

In the meantime the body of Polynices, falling into decay, still lay unburied, and the dogs and birds fed on him and fouled the city by carrying to this place and that the shreds of his rotting flesh. Then Tiresias, the aged soothsayer, who had once sought out King Oedipus, appeared before Creon and from the smoke of sacrifice and the voices of birds prophesied disaster. He had heard the croak of evil hungry throats, and the victim on the altar had charred in acrid smoke. "It is clear that the gods are angry with us," he ended. "Angry because of the treatment given the slain son of Oedipus. And so, O king, do not hold to your command. Yield to the dead and desist from murder. What glory is there in slaying the slain? Leave off, I say! I counsel you for your own good!"

But just as Oedipus once had done, so Creon now rejected the advice of the seer, accusing him of lies and greed for money. At that the old man smouldered with rage and mercilessly snatched the veil from the future before the very eyes of the king. "Know then," he solemnly said, "that the sun will not set until you, from your own blood, give one body for two that are dead. You are committing a twofold crime, by withholding from the underworld its due, and by keeping from the upper world the living who should dwell in the light of day. Quick, boy, lead me away from here. Let us give this man up to the fate in store for him." Leaning on his staff, he left at the hand of his guide.

CREON'S PUNISHMENT

The king followed the sullen seer with his gaze, and he trembled. He called together the city elders and took counsel with them as to what was to be done. "Release Antigone from her rock grave and bury the body of Polynices," they decided unanimously. It was not easy for Creon to bend his stubborn spirit to consent, but the heart had gone out of him. He agreed to do as Tiresias had said, since this seemed the only way to avert destruction from his house. First he himself, in the van of his retinue, went to the field where Polynices lay, and then to the tomb in which Antigone was kept imprisoned. His wife Eurydice remained behind in the palace alone.

Soon she heard the sound of lament rising from the streets,

and as the clamor grew louder and louder, she left her chamber and went into the forecourt. There she found a messenger, the very man who had guided her husband to the spot where the mangled body of his nephew lay exposed. "We prayed to the gods of the underworld," he said. "When the dead body had been washed in the sacred bath, we burned those pitiful remains and heaped a burial mound out of clods of his native earth. Then we went to the stone vault the girl had entered to suffer the death of starvation. A servant who had gone before heard from afar cries of agony and grief coming from that terrible place. He hurried back to tell his king of the voice which issued from the tomb, but Creon already knew, though hearing it but dimly, that it was that of his son. He bade us run and peer through a crack in the stone. And what did we see? In the back of the cave hung Antigone, strangled in a noose she had knotted of her veil, and at her feet, clasping her knees, lay your son Haemon, mourning his beloved and cursing the father who had robbed him of his bride. And now Creon reached the rock grave and entered through the opening. 'Unhappy boy,' he called to Haemon, 'what is your purpose? What does the madness of your gaze forebode? Come to me! On my knees I beseech you!' But the son only stared at him numb with despair. He gave no answer at all but snatched his two-edged sword from the scabbard. His father escaped the thrust by darting from the cave. And then Haemon leaned on the point and let it drive through his side. As he fell he threw his arm around Antigone, drawing her close, and now, in their last embrace, they both lie dead in the tomb!"

Eurydice listened in silence. He had ended, but still she was speechless. Then she hastened from the room. When the king returned to the palace, accompanied by his servants carrying his only son on a bier, he was told that Eurydice had stabbed herself with a sword and was lying within, in a pool of her own blood.

THE BURIAL OF THE HEROES OF THEBES

Of the family of Oedipus only two sons of the fallen brothers remained, and Ismene, Antigone's sister. Legend is silent concerning her. She died childless, unwed, and her death closed the tale of that unblest family. Of the seven heroes who had gone forth against Thebes, only Adrastus escaped the assault and slaughter of that last encounter. His immortal horse Arion, begotten by Demeter and Poseidon. bore him away in winged flight. He reached Athens safely and there took refuge in the sanctuary of a temple, holding to the altar as a suppliant. Stretching out a twig of olive, he begged the Athenians to help him obtain honorable burial for the men who had fallen before the walls of Thebes. The people of Athens granted his plea and accompanied him back to this city under the leadership of Theseus. And so the Thebans were forced to consent to the burial. For the bodies of the fallen heroes, Adrastus heaped seven pyres and held funeral games near the river Asopus in honor of Apollo. When the pyre of Capaneus burst into flame, Evadne, his wife, daughter of Iphis, threw herself into the fire. The body of Amphiaraus, whom the earth had swallowed up, could not be found, and the king sorrowed because he could not do honor to his friend. "I miss the eye of my army," he said. "I miss him who was both the greatest seer and the most valiant fighter in battle."

When the burial rites had been performed, Adrastus had a beautiful temple erected before the walls of Thebes and dedicated it to Nemesis, or Retribution. Then, with his allies from Athens, he left the country.

THE EPIGONI

TEN years later, the sons of the heroes who had fallen in the war against Thebes resolved on a fresh campaign to avenge the death of their fathers. There were eight descendants, and they were called Epigoni: Alcmaeon and Amphilochus, sons of Amphiaraus; Aegialeus, son of Adrastus; Diomedes, son of Tydeus; Promachus, son of Parthenopaeus; Sthenelus, son of Capaneus; Thersander, son of Polynices, and Euryalus, son of Mecisteus. The aged king, Adrastus, sole survivor of that first host which had fought against Thebes, joined the expedition but

would not assume command, for he wanted one who was young
and strong to hold so important a post. So the sons of the heroes
asked the oracle of Apollo whom to choose for their leader. The
answer was that it should be Alcmaeon, son of Amphiaraus. But
when they offered him the command, he was uncertain whether
to accept this honor before avenging his father. He too asked
the oracle what his course should be, and the god answered that
he was to do both.

Up to this time his mother Eriphyle had not only kept the
necklace destined to bring calamity upon its owner but had also
managed to lay hold of the veil, the second gift of Aphrodite.
Thersander, son of Polynices, who fell heir to this veil, had given
it to her for the same reason his father had once bestowed the
necklace: as a bribe, for he wanted her to persuade her son
Alcmaeon to take part in the campaign against Thebes. In
obedience to the oracle, Alcmaeon assumed command and postponed his act of vengeance until his return. He headed a con-
siderable host, for not only had he assembled the men of Argos;
many warriors who craved a chance to show their daring joined
him, and so it was a great army which advanced to the gates of
Thebes. And here the sons renewed the stubborn siege their
fathers had fought ten years before. But the new generation
were more favored by fortune, and Alcmaeon won a decisive
victory. Only one of the Epigoni fell in battle: Aegialeus, son
of King Adrastus, for Laodamas, son of Eteocles, slew him with
his own hand, but was killed by Alcmaeon, commander of the
Epigoni. When the Thebans had thus lost their leader and many
of their men besides, they left the battlefield and took refuge
behind their walls. There they consulted Tiresias, the blind seer,
who was still alive, although he was over a hundred years old.
He advised them to take the only way still open to them: to leave
the city, while they sent a herald bearing offers of peace to the
Argives. They acted on his words, dispatched a herald to their
enemies, and while he was negotiating with them, loaded their
women and children on wagons and fled from Thebes. In the
darkness of night they came to Tilphusium, a city in Boeotia.
Blind Tiresias, who had shared their flight, took a deep draught
from a cold spring flowing outside the city and died. But even
in the underworld the wise soothsayer kept aloof from the rest,

for not like the other shades did he rove about aimlessly with blank and idle mind. He retained the power of thinking great thoughts and of seeing beyond what is given mortals to know. His daughter Manto had not gone with him. She stayed behind and fell into the hands of the conquerors who occupied the abandoned city of Thebes. But these had made a vow to dedicate to Apollo the best of what they found in the city, and they now decided that no spoils could be more welcome to the god than Manto, who had inherited the divine gift of her father. And so the Epigoni took her to Delphi and consecrated her as a priestess of the sun-god. Here she grew more and more perfect in the art of soothsaying, her wisdom deepened, and she became the most noted seeress of her time. People often saw an old man come and go in the temple where she presided. She taught him verses full of vigor and sweetness and glory, which soon resounded through all the land of Greece. He was a singer from Maeonia—Homer.

ALCMAEON AND THE NECKLACE

WHEN Alcmaeon returned from Thebes, he decided to fulfill the second part of the oracle, the bidding to avenge his father. His bitterness toward his mother increased when he discovered that she had accepted bribes not only to betray her husband, but to play her son false as well. He overrode his scruples and slew her with his sword. Then he took the necklace and the veil and left the house of his parents, for which he had come to feel nothing but loathing. Now though the oracle had bidden him avenge his father, the murder of his mother was against the laws of nature, and so the gods could not allow it to go unpunished. They sent the Furies to pursue him, and afflicted him with madness. Bereaved of his senses he came to King Oicleus in Arcadia, but the goddesses of vengeance left him no peace, and he was forced to continue his wanderings. At last he found a refuge in another city of Arcadia, in Psophis, where Phegeus was king. He purified Alcmaeon and gave him his daughter Arsinoë in marriage, and now it was she who became the possessor of the fatal necklace and veil. Alcmaeon had been healed of his madness, but all the curse was not taken from him, for the land which had received him grew barren because of his presence. He questioned an oracle but was given small comfort: he would find peace when he came to a country which had not been on the face of the earth at the time he had killed his mother. Without hope, Alcmaeon left his wife and his little son Clytius and set out into the wide world. After long wanderings he found what the oracle had predicted. Coming to the river Achelous, he discovered an island which had emerged from the waters only a short time since. On this he settled, and the curse dropped from him.

But his release and his happiness only served to make him insolent and overbearing. He forgot Arsinoë and his small son and married lovely Callirrhoë, daughter of the river-god Achelous, and by her had two sons, Acarnan and Amphoterus. Now since rumor had spread the tale of the priceless treasures

Alcmaeon carried with him, his wife soon asked to see the shimmering necklace and the filmy veil. But these Alcmaeon had left with his first wife when he went from her in secret. He did not wish Callirrhoë to know of this former marriage, and so he invented some faraway place where he claimed to have stored his treasures, and offered to fetch them. In this way he returned to Psophis and his first wife, and in excuse for his long absence told her and her father that a residue of madness had driven him from them, and was still not wholly dispelled. "There is only one way to rid me utterly of this curse," he said craftily. "I have been told that if I take the necklace and veil I once gave you to Delphi, as a votive offering, all will be well at last." And Phegeus and his daughter believed his deceitful words and gave him what he asked. With a glad heart Alcmaeon left with his loot, not dreaming that those treasures were bound to bring destruction upon him as they had upon others. But one of his servants, who knew his secret, told King Phegeus of his second wife and that he had taken the necklace and veil only to bring them to her. And now the brothers of deserted Arsinoë followed in his tracks, lurked for him in ambush, and slew him as he went his way unsuspectingly. They took the treasures from him and brought them back to their sister, boasting that they had avenged her. But Arsinoë loved Alcmaeon, even when she learned of his perfidy, and cursed her brothers for having killed him. And now the fatal gifts were to prove their strength upon Arsinoë herself. Her resentful brothers thought no punishment too harsh for their sister's ingratitude. They seized her, locked her in a chest, bore her away to Tegea, to King Agapenor, to whom they were bound by ties of hospitality, and accused her of having murdered Alcmaeon. And so she died a most wretched death.

In the meantime Callirrhoë had learned of her husband's sad end, and her sorrow was tinged with the desire for swift revenge. She threw herself on her face and implored Zeus to work a miracle, to let her little sons Acarnan and Amphoterus grow suddenly into manhood, that they might punish the slayers of their father. Because Callirrhoë was guiltless and devout, Zeus heard her prayers. Her sons, who had gone to bed as children, awoke as men full of vigor and the lust for vengeance. They left on their mission and first went to Tegea. There they arrived at the very moment the sons of Phegeus reached the city with their unhappy sister Arsinoë and were about to depart for Delphi in order to dedicate those fatal gifts of Aphrodite to the oracle of Apollo. When the youths fell upon them to avenge the murder of their father, Agenor and Pronous did not know who their attackers were, and before they could even discover the reason for the onslaught, they died by the sword. The sons of Alcmaeon then justified their action to Agapenor and told him the true story of what had happened. Next they travelled to Psophis in Arcadia, entered the palace, and killed both King Phegeus and his queen. Escaping pursuit they reached their island in safety and brought their mother the news of vengeance taken. At the advice of their grandfather Achelous, they journeyed to Delphi and gave both necklace and veil to the oracle of Apollo. When this was accomplished, the curse which had hung over the family of Amphiaraus was at last dispelled, and his grandchildren, the sons of Alcmaeon and Callirrhoë, recruited settlers in Epirus and founded Acarnania. After the murder of his father, Clytius, son of Alcmaeon and Arsinoë, left his kinsmen on his mother's side with loathing and found a refuge in Elis.

THE HERACLIDAE

THE HERACLIDAE COME TO ATHENS

WHEN Heracles had been received in heaven and his cousin Eurystheus, king of Argos, had nothing more to fear from him, he turned on the children of the demigod. Most of these lived in Mycenae, the capital of Argos, with Alcmene, the hero's mother. When they became aware of the persecutions menacing them, they fled and put themselves under the protection of Ceyx, king of Trachis. But when Eurystheus asked this petty monarch to give them up and threatened to make war on him if he refused, they doubted the safety of their refuge and fled from

Trachis. Iolaus, the distinguished kinsman and friend of Heracles, cared for them like a father. As a boy he had shared all the adventures and hardships of Heracles, and now that he was aging and gray-haired, he took the orphaned brood of his friend under his wing and roamed through the world with them. They set out to occupy the Peloponnesus, which was their father's by conquest.

In the course of their journey, constantly pursued by Eurystheus, they came to Athens, which was ruled by the son of Theseus, Demophoon, who had just driven Menestheus from the throne he had usurped. On their arrival in Athens, the Heraclidae went straight to the market place, prostrated themselves before the altar of Zeus, and implored the protection of the people of Athens. They had been there but a short time when a herald, sent by King Eurystheus, appeared, faced Iolaus defiantly, and said to him in contemptuous tones: "You seem to think that this is a safe refuge for you and that you have come to a city which will act as your ally! Foolish Iolaus! Do you think that anyone at all would consider exchanging a mighty ally like Eurystheus for a weak one such as yourself? Away with you and all your charges! Away to Argos, where you will be fairly judged—and stoned to death!"

Iolaus answered him calmly. "Far be it from me to do as you say. For I know that this altar is a refuge which will protect me not only from an insignificant nobody like you but even from the hosts of your master. The land to which we have come is a land of freedom!"

"Then be advised," continued Copreus, for that was the name of the herald, "that I am not here alone. Enough men come behind me to snatch your charges from the refuge of this city which you seem to think safe for you!"

When the Heraclidae heard these words, they broke into lamentation, but Iolaus addressed the Athenians in a loud voice. "Citizens of Athens," he said, "do not allow the wards of Zeus to be led off by force, nor the wreaths we wear as suppliants to be soiled, lest your gods be dishonored and your city disgraced!"

At this call for help, the Athenians thronged together from all sides, and only now did they see the little group of fugitives huddled around the altar. "Who is that noble old man? And those beautiful youths with flying locks?" questioned a hundred lips. And when they learned that those seeking their protection were sons of Heracles, they were not only filled with compassion but with awe as well. They bade the herald who was about to lay hand on the boys to let them be, and to state his demands to the king of the land in proper fashion.

"Who is the king of this country?" asked Copreus, a little abashed by the firm and proud bearing of the Athenians.

"He is a man to whose judgment you well may bow," they answered. "Demophoon, the son of immortal Theseus, is our king."

DEMOPHOON

Before long the news of fugitives in the market place, of a foreign host, and a herald who asked that the suppliants be delivered up to him, reached the king in his palace. He himself went to the market place and heard from the herald's own lips the demand of Eurystheus. "I am an Argive," Copreus told him. "The persons I wish to take with me are also Argives and therefore under the jurisdiction of my king. You will not be so unreasonable, O son of Theseus, as to be the one and only man in all of Greece to take pity on these fugitives and for their sakes to engage in battle with Eurystheus and his many and powerful allies."

Demophoon was wise and contained. To the violent speech of the herald, he merely answered: "How can I hope to see this matter right, or decide in favor of one or another, before hearing both sides? Old man, you who are in charge of these youths, say what you can for yourself."

Iolaus, to whom Demophoon had spoken, rose from the altar steps, bowed reverently before the king, and replied: "Now I know, indeed, that I am in a free city, for here a man is permitted to speak for himself and finds a hearing. In all other places, they drove away my charges and me before I could open my mouth to speak in their behalf. The truth of our plight is this: Eurystheus was the cause of our leaving Argos. We dared not remain in his country for another hour. How can he call us his subjects and claim that we, as Argives, must bow to his decrees, when he has robbed us of all the rights of a subject? If there were truth in what he said, then he who fled Argos would have to avoid all of Greece as well! But—heaven be thanked!—not Athens! Those who dwell in this glorious city will not drive the sons of Heracles from their land. You, O king, will not permit a suppliant to be snatched from the very altar. My children, be calm! You are in a free country, and what is more, you are with your kinsman. For know, O king, that you are not sheltering strangers. Both Theseus, your father, and Heracles, the father of these boys, were great-grandsons of Pelops. And they were bound by a tie stronger than kinship: they were comrades-in-arms. Heracles liberated your father from the underworld!"

While Iolaus was speaking, he had clasped the king's knees, taken his hand, and touched his chin. The king raised him from the ground and said: "There are three reasons why I should grant your plea. First, Zeus and this holy altar; secondly, the kinship between me and your charges; and thirdly, the benefits I owe to Heracles' efforts in my father's behalf. If I allowed you to be taken from this sacred place, this land would no longer be a land of freedom, a land where virtue is practiced and the gods given their due." Then he turned to Copreus. "Herald," he commanded, "return to Mycenae and tell this to your king."

"I go," said Copreus, and brandished his herald's staff threateningly. "But I shall come again—and with the Argive host behind me. Ten thousand shield-bearers only wait for my king to give them the sign. And he himself will lead them. He is, indeed, already at your borders."

"Hades awaits you!" said Demophoon contemptuously. "I fear neither you nor all of Argos!"

The herald withdrew, and now the sons of Heracles, a band of strong youths and fair boys, joyously sprang up from the altar steps, put their hands into those of their kinsman, the king of Athens, and hailed him as their rescuer. Iolaus once more spoke for them and thanked Demophoon and the Athenians with words full of grateful emotion. "Should we ever return to our home," he said, "should the children of Heracles ever be reinstated in the house of their father, they will not forget their friends, their liberators. Never will they make war on this hospitable city, but always regard her as a dear ally with a claim on their utmost loyalty."

And now King Demophoon prepared for the attack of his new enemies. He assembled his seers and bade them make solemn sacrifice. Iolaus and his charges were, he said, to be his guests in the palace, but the old man declared that he did not wish to leave the altar of Zeus and would remain to pray for the welfare of the city. "Not until—with the help of the gods—victory is yours," he said, "will we rest our weary limbs under the roof of our host."

In the meantime the king had ascended the highest tower of his palace and, looking down, gauged the strength of the approaching army. Then he gathered his men, gave orders for the defense of the city, and took counsel with the soothsayers. Iolaus and his charges were fervently supplicating the gods, when Demophoon came toward them with swift steps, his face agitated and full of sorrow. "What am I to do, my friends?" he called to them with troubled countenance. "It is true that my army is ready for the Argives, but all my seers insist that I can defeat them only on one condition, and this I cannot fulfill! Hear what the oracle has said: 'You shall slaughter neither calf nor bullock, but a maiden of noble birth. Only then can you and your city hope for victory!' But how can this be? I myself have a daughter, young and lovely as a flower. But who can expect a father to make such a sacrifice? And what other noble citizen of Athens, having a daughter, would deliver her up to me, even if I ventured to ask her of him? Were I to do such a thing, I should have civil war to cope with at the very time I am fighting an alien foe."

The sons of Heracles listened to the doubts and fears of their protector, and their hearts sank. "Woe to us!" cried Iolaus. "We are like shipwrecked mariners who thought they had reached the shore but are swept out to sea again by the ruthless storm. Why did we deceive ourselves with idle hopes and dreams? We are lost! Demophoon will yield us up, and how could we reproach him?" But suddenly a ray of hope shone in his eyes. "Do you know, O king, what the spirit prompts me? What can save us all? If you will only help me accomplish it! Instead of the sons of Heracles, give me up to Eurystheus! It would give him pleasure to force me, the constant companion of a great hero, to die a shameful death. But I am old and would gladly sacrifice my very soul for these youths."

"You have made a noble offer," Demophoon said sadly, "but

it will not avail us. Do you think Eurystheus would be content
to kill an old man? No, what he wants is to destroy the young
and blooming sons of Heracles, to put an end to his line. If you
know other counsel, speak. But what you have proposed would
be useless."

MACARIA

At that so loud a clamor and cry of woe issued not only from
the Heraclidae but from the citizens assembled in the market
place, that the sound carried up to the palace. Soon after the
fugitives had come, Alcmene, Heracles' mother, bowed with age
and grief, and Macaria, the lovely daughter Deianira had borne
him, had been taken there to hide them from curious eyes, and
now they waited for what was to come. Alcmene was very old,
and her thoughts were turned within, so that she knew nothing
of what was going on in the world about her. But her grandchild
listened to the sounds of lament rising from the heart of the city,
and so great was her anxiety for her brothers that she forgot she
was a girl who had been reared in deep seclusion, forgot she was
unaccompanied, and hurried to the market place, into the very
midst of the throng. Not only Demophoon and the Athenians
but Iolaus and his charges as well were struck with amazement
when they saw her.

For a while she slipped in and out among the people and in this
way learned of the danger threatening Athens and the Heraclidae
and of the sinister oracle which seemed to block the path to a
happy issue. Now she came before the king, and her step was
firm. "Regard me as a victim," she said, "a victim which will
pledge you victory and whose death will save my poor brothers
from the rage of a tyrant. You were told to kill a virgin of noble
birth. Had you forgotten that the virgin daughter of the noblest
mortal, of Heracles, dwells in your midst? I offer myself as a
sacrifice, which must be all the more pleasing to the gods since it
is made of my own free will. If this city is generous enough to
engage in war for the sake of the Heraclidae, and to give up its
own sons by the hundreds, why should not one of Heracles' own
descendants be ready to give her life in order to insure victory

to such noble men? We should not be worth protecting and saving if one of us did not think in this way. So take me to the place where my body is to be offered up. Wreathe me, as you would wreathe a ewe or a hind. Brandish the blade, for my soul will rejoice to go."

For a long time after the girl had spoken the last impassioned word, Iolaus and those with him were silent. At last the leader of the Heraclidae said: "Macaria, you have proved yourself worthy of your father. I exult in your courage, even while I mourn your fate. Yet it seems to me that all the daughters of the line of Heracles should come together and decide by lot which is to die for her brothers."

"I do not want to die by lot," said Macaria. "Do not hesitate too long, or the enemy will fall upon you and the oracle be in vain. Bid the women of the city come with me, lest I die seen by the eyes of men."

And with a retinue of the noblest women of Athens, Macaria, steadfast and joyful, went forth to die the death she herself had willed.

THE BATTLE

The king and the citizens of Athens looked after her reverently, while Iolaus and her brothers, the Heraclidae, lowered their gaze in sorrow and pain. But Fate did not allow either side to dwell on their thoughts and emotions, for hardly had Macaria disappeared when a messenger came running toward the altar, his face bright with good tidings, his voice loud with joy. "Greetings, O sons of Heracles," he cried. "Tell me where I can find Iolaus. I have a message for him which will give him happiness." Iolaus rose from the altar, but he could not at once banish the lines of grief and care from his forehead, and the messenger asked him the cause of his gloom.

"I am troubled for those I love," said the old man. "Do not question me further, but rather tell me your joyful news."

"Do you not recognize me?" asked the messenger. "Do you not know the old servant of Hyllus, son of Heracles and Deianira? You will recall that my master separated from you in the course of your wanderings, in order to enlist allies for your cause and his. Now, at just the right moment, he has come with a mighty host and is camped opposite the army of King Eurystheus."

A stir of happy excitement ran through the group around the altar and spread to the citizens. The good news brought even old Alcmene from the women's apartments of the palace, and gray-haired Iolaus had them bring him weapons and gird on his armor. He commended the younger children of Heracles and their great-grandmother to the care of the elders of Athens who remained behind in the city. Then he himself went out with the youths and King Demophoon to join the host of Hyllus.

Now when the allies were drawn up in battle array and the field glittered with armor as far as eye could reach, when only a stone's throw away stood the army of King Eurystheus, who had placed himself at the head of countless rows of armed men, Hyllus, son of Heracles, descended from his war-chariot, and standing in the narrow space between the hosts, called to the Argive king: "King Eurystheus! Before we shed blood, before two great armies begin to fight for the sake of a handful of people and threaten each other with destruction, hear what I propose! Let us two decide this quarrel in single combat. If I fall at your hands, take with you my brothers, the sons of Heracles, and do with them as you wish. But if I defeat you, then let the sovereignty of my father, his house, and his rule in the Peloponnesus, be assured to me and mine."

The allied hosts expressed their approval of this plan in loud applause, and the Argives muttered their consent. But Eurystheus, who had long ago proved himself a coward and who was again deeply concerned for his life, flatly rejected the proposal and would not leave his column of men. So Hyllus too returned to his host, the seers made sacrifice, and soon the battle cry was sounded.

"Fellow citizens!" Demophoon called to his men. "Remember that you are fighting for house and hearth, for the city that gave you birth, that feeds and protects you!"

On the other side Eurystheus begged his men not to disgrace Argos and Mycenae, but to add to the glory of their mighty state. And now the Tyrrhenian trumpets blared, shield thudded on shield, wheels rattled, spears rang, swords clashed, and the groans of the fallen sounded between. For one awful instant the allies of the Heraclidae recoiled from the thrusts of Argive lances, which threatened to break their ranks. The next moment they not only hurled back the enemy but surged forward themselves. For a long time the outcome was uncertain. At last the Argives fell back in confusion, and armored men and chariots all turned to flee. At that, old Iolaus suddenly felt a craving to make glorious his age by one last bold deed. As the chariot of Hyllus rolled past him to strike at the fleeing host of the enemy from the rear, the old man stretched his right hand up to the stalwart hero and begged to mount the chariot in his stead. Hyllus reverently made way for his father's friend, for the protector of his brothers, and yielded his place to him.

It was not an easy task for those old hands to master four horses, champing the bit, but he drove forward and had just reached the temple of Pallas Athene when he saw the chariot of Eurystheus whirling up the dust ahead of him. Then he drew himself up and prayed to Hebe, the goddess of youth, to lend him the strength of youth for a single day, so that he might take vengeance on the foe of Heracles. And a miracle came to pass: two stars sank slowly out of heaven and came to rest on the horses' harness, and a moment later a cloud of impenetrable mist enveloped the entire chariot. But the next instant mist and stars alike had vanished. Standing erect in the chariot was Iolaus, young and sound. His brown locks blew in the wind, his neck was straight and strong. He had sinewy arms and gripped the reins of the four horses with a firm hand. Storming ahead, he caught up with Eurystheus who had already passed the Scironian Rocks and was about to enter the valley in which the Argives thought to find safety. Eurystheus did not recognize his pursuer and fought back. But by dint of the youthful power the gods had lent him, Iolaus was victorious, forced his old enemy from his chariot, tied him fast in his own, and drove him toward the allied host as the first fruits of victory. The battle was won, for the leaderless host of the Argives scattered in frantic flight. All the sons of Eurystheus and countless other warriors were slain, and soon not a single enemy was left on the soil of Attica.

EURYSTHEUS AND ALCMENE

The victors had entered Athens, and Iolaus, who had again become an old man, brought before the mother of Heracles the humbled pursuer of a race of heroes, bound hand and foot.

"Is it you, hateful Eurystheus?" the old woman cried exultantly. "Have the gods brought justice upon you at last? Do not bow your head to the ground but look your foe full in the eyes. So this is you, you who for many years heaped labors and disgrace upon my son, sent him forth to strangle fierce serpents and savage lions, hoping that he might die in the doing. It was you who drove him down to the darkness of Hades, certain that he would have to remain in the underworld. And then, with every device, with all the power at your beck, you hunted me, his mother, hunted his children from land to land, trying to drive us from all of Greece, and snatching us from the altars that offered asylum. But you came up against men who were not afraid of you. You came to a free city. And now you must die, and may think yourself fortunate if you suffer only instant death, for the crimes you have committed deserve torture and death many times over."

Eurystheus did not want to show fear before a woman. He collected himself and spoke with feigned coolness and calm. "You shall hear no word from my lips that might even seem to plead. I do not rebel against dying. But let me say this in justice to myself: it was not I, of my own free will, who faced Heracles as a foe. It was Hera, the goddess, who bade me work against him all my days. But once I had made an enemy of this mighty man, of this demigod—though it was counter to my wish—did I not have to do all I could to save myself from his anger? Even after his death, was I not compelled to persecute his sons, growing up as my foes, as the avengers of their father? Now do with me what you will. I do not long for death, but neither does it distress me to give up my life."

So said Eurystheus and appeared composed in the face of destiny. Hyllus himself spoke in defense of the prisoner, and the citizens of Athens invoked their city's gentle custom of showing mercy to a defeated foe. But Alcmene was implacable, for she could not forget the sufferings her immortal son had been forced to endure as the servant of this cruel king. She remembered the death of her beloved granddaughter, who had accompanied her to Athens and died of her own free will in order to snatch the victory from Eurystheus and his overwhelming numbers. Vividly she pictured the fate she and all her grandsons would have suffered were Eurystheus standing before her as a victor instead of a captive. "No, let him die!" she cried. "No mortal man shall save this evildoer from my revenge."

Then Eurystheus turned to the Athenians and said: "My death will not bring misfortune upon you, who have pleaded so kindly in my behalf. If you give me worthy burial and dig my grave near the temple of Pallas Athene, where defeat overtook me, I will guard your land as a guest who means well by his host, and no enemy shall ever cross your borders. For you must know that the descendants of these youths and children you are protecting will one day fall upon you with weapons and ill repay the kindness you have shown their fathers. Then I, who am the sworn foe of the line of Heracles, will be your liberator." With these words he went to his death unafraid, and died more nobly than he had lived.

HYLLUS AND HIS DESCENDANTS

The sons of Heracles vowed eternal gratitude to Demophoon and left Athens under the guidance of Hyllus, their brother, and Iolaus, their friend. Now they found allies in all quarters and journeyed to the Peloponnesus, the land which had been their father's. For a whole year they fought from town to town until all had surrendered save Argos. During this time, a terrible plague raged throughout the peninsula and would not abate. At last an oracle revealed to the Heraclidae that they themselves were the cause of this affliction, since they had returned before the appointed time. So they left the Peloponnesus, which they had already occupied with their forces, and journeyed back to Attica. Here they settled on the plain of Marathon. Hyllus, meantime, had fulfilled his father's wish by marrying lovely Iole, whom Heracles himself had once wooed, and pondered without ceasing how he might gain possession of his heritage. Finally he again consulted the oracle of Delphi and received this reply: "When the third harvest has been reaped, you will succeed in returning." Hyllus took this to mean quite simply that he was to await the third year of gathering the fruits of the field. So, when the third summer had passed, he once more invaded the Peloponnesus.

After the death of Eurystheus, Atreus, grandson of Tantalus and son of Pelops, had become king of Mycenae. When he learned of the approach of Hyllus, he joined forces with the city of Tegea and other neighboring towns and went forth to meet the sons of Heracles. On the isthmus of Corinth the armies came face to face. But Hyllus, who was always intent on saving the land of Greece from the ravages of war, again offered to decide the issue by single combat. He challenged any one in the host of the enemy who was minded to fight with him and, certain that he had fulfilled the oracle and thus gained the approval of the gods for his undertaking, set the condition that, should he win, the realm Eurystheus had governed should go to the sons of Heracles, but that if he were defeated, the descendants of Heracles should not set foot on the Peloponnesus for fifty years to come.

When his words became known in the enemy's camp, Echemus, king of Tegea, a warrior in the very prime of life, accepted the challenge. Both combatants fought with boldness and skill, but Hyllus was defeated. Even in death, his forehead was furrowed and his mouth bitter with brooding on the ambiguous oracle which had led him into battle. The Heraclidae kept to their agreement, desisted from further fighting, returned to Attica, and again settled near Marathon. The years passed and the sons of Heracles never thought of breaking their word. They made no new attempt to win back their heritage. In the meantime Cleodaeus, son of Hyllus, had passed his fiftieth year. Since the period for the truce had elapsed and his hands were no longer tied by a promise, he and the other grandsons of Heracles attacked the Peloponnesus at a time when the Trojan War was already thirty years past. But he too was luckless as his father before him; he perished in this campaign, and all his men with him. Twenty years later his son Aristomachus, grandson of Hyllus and great-grandson of Heracles, made another attempt. This was at the time when Tisamenus, a son of Orestes, ruled the Peloponnesus. Aristomachus too was led astray by the enigmatic words of an oracle: "The gods will grant you victory by the narrow passage." He invaded the Peloponnesus by way of the isthmus, was beaten back, and lost his life like his father and grandfather before him.

Thirty years passed, and for eighty years Troy had lain in ashes. And now the sons of Aristomachus, Temenus, Cresphontes, and Aristodemus, the grandsons of Cleodaeus, fared forth on their line's ancestral quest. Despite the seeming trickery of the oracles, they staunchly held to their faith in the gods, went to Delphi, and asked the priestess concerning the outcome of their enterprise. But the two answers she gave were word for word the same their forebears had received: "When the third harvest has been reaped, you will succeed in returning," and "The gods will grant you victory by the narrow passage."

Then Temenus, eldest of the three brothers, said mournfully: "My father, my grandfather, and my great-grandfather obeyed these utterances, and all met with destruction!" And at last the god took pity on these three and, through the priestess, disclosed to them the oracle's true meaning.

"Your forbears themselves were to blame for their misfortune," she said. "They could not interpret the wise words of the god. What the immortals meant was not the third harvest of the fruits of the earth, but the third harvest from the seed of your race. The first was Cleodaeus, the second Aristomachus, and the third harvest, that to which victory is promised, is that of you three brothers. As for the 'narrow passage'—there again those luckless ones, now dead, misunderstood what was implied. The gods were not speaking of the isthmus, but of a different passage: of the straits of Corinth. Now that you know the meaning of the oracle, do what you have set out to do, and embark upon your enterprise with the good fortune attending gods."

When Temenus heard this explanation, it was as though scales had dropped from his eyes. Together with his brothers he rapidly equipped a great host and had ships built in Locris, at a place which, to commemorate this, was later called Naupactus, which means shipyard. But even this expedition, launched under such happy auspices, was beset with difficulties for the descendants of Heracles and cost them grave concern and many tears. When the host was assembled, Aristodemus, the youngest of the brothers, was struck by lightning. His wife Argia, the great-granddaughter of Polynices, thus became a widow and his twin sons, Eurysthenes and Procles, were left fatherless. When Aristodemus had been buried and the squadron of ships was to leave Locris, a soothsayer appeared, one who was inspired by the gods and issued oracles. But the descendants of Heracles took him for a sorcerer or a spy sent by the Peloponnesians to destroy their host. They persecuted him with suspicion and harshness, and finally Hippotes, son of Phylas and great-grandson of Heracles, hurled his lance at the old man, who was killed on the instant. This roused the anger of the gods against the Heraclidae. A tempest shattered their ships and sank them to the bottom of the sea. Their landtroops suffered long famine, and soon the entire host dissolved.

Concerning this disaster also, Temenus sought the advice of the oracle. "Because of the seer you have killed," so ran the answer, "all this has overtaken you. For ten years you shall banish the murderer from the land, and put the three-eyed in command of the host." The first part of the oracle was quickly carried out. Hippotes was removed from the army and compelled to go into exile. But the second part drove the Heraclidae to the verge of despair. For how and where were they to find anyone with three eyes? Yet they looked for such a man untiringly, so great was their trust in the gods! At last they happened to find Oxylus, of the line of the kings of Aetolia, son of Haemon and descendant of Oeneus. At the very time the Heraclidae invaded the Peloponnesus, Oxylus had committed murder and been forced

to flee from his native Aetolia to the little land of Elis in the
Peloponnesus. Now that a year had gone by, he was on his way
back to his country and met the descendants of Heracles as he
was riding his donkey. This Oxylus had only one eye, for as a
child he had put out the other with an arrow. So his donkey had
to help him see, and man and beast together had three eyes.
The Heraclidae realized that the singular oracle had been fulfilled and chose Oxylus for their leader. In this way the conditions set by Fate were satisfied. They attacked their enemies with
fresh troops and a new squadron of ships and slew Tisamenus, the
leader of the Peloponnesian host.

THE HERACLIDAE DIVIDE UP THE PELOPONNESUS

When the Heraclidae had, in this way, conquered the entire Peloponnesus, they erected three altars to Zeus, their ancestor on their father's side, and made offerings. Then they began to distribute the cities by lot. The first city they were to cast for was Argos, the second Lacedaemon, and the third Messene. They agreed to drop their lots into an urn filled with water, and that each was to mark his own lot with his name. Thereupon Temenus, and Eurysthenes and Procles, the twin sons of Aristodemus, cast two marked stones into the water, but crafty Cresphontes, who wanted Messene most of all, threw in a lump of earth, which dissolved almost immediately. Now they decided that he whose stone was taken from the urn first was to have Argos, and it was the stone of Temenus. Then they cast lots for Lacedaemon, and the stone of the twin sons of Aristodemus was the one to be drawn. This made it superfluous to cast lots for the third city, and Cresphontes received Messene.

Hereupon they and their followers went to the three altars and made sacrifice to the gods, who accorded them certain strange signs. For each found an animal on his altar, and the animals were different. Those who had been allotted Argos found a toad; those who had got Lacedaemon, a serpent; and those who were to have Messene, a fox. They pondered these signs and finally asked a seer, a native of that land, to interpret them. "Those who were given a toad," he said, "had best remain at home in their city, for the toad is vulnerable and has nothing to protect its goings. Those on whose altar the serpent is coiled will be great aggressors and need have no fear in crossing the borders of their country. And those who saw the fox shall avoid both passiveness and force; their safeguard shall be shrewdness."

These animals later became the emblems on the shields of the Argives, Spartans, and Messenians. And now the Heraclidae remembered Oxylus, their one-eyed guide, and granted him the kingdom of Elis in reward for the help he had given them. In all the Peloponnesus, the mountainous land of Arcadia was the sole region left unconquered by the descendants of Heracles.

Sparta was the only one of the three realms they founded on the peninsula that endured for any length of time. In Argos, Temenus married his favorite daughter Hyrnetho to Deiphontes, another great-great-grandson of Heracles, and consulted his son-in-law on all matters of importance. At last rumor had it that he was planning to turn over the rule to him and Hyrnetho. This embittered his sons. They conspired against their father and slew him. The Argives did, indeed, recognize the eldest son as their king, but because they loved liberty and equality above all, they limited the king's power so much that he and his descendants had nothing left of the kingship but the mere title.

MEROPE AND AEPYTUS

Cresphontes, king of Messene, was no more fortunate than his brother Temenus. He had married Merope, daughter of King Cypselus of Arcadia, and she had borne her husband many children. The youngest of these was Aepytus. Cresphontes had a stately palace built for himself and his children. But he was not to enjoy his sumptuous halls for long. Since he was a friend of the common people, he favored them wherever and whenever he could. This angered the rich in his realm, and they killed him together with his sons—all but the youngest, Aepytus, whom his mother managed to hide from the murderers and had taken to Arcadia, to her father Cypselus. In the meantime Polyphontes, also a descendant of Heracles, seized the throne of Messene and compelled the widow of the murdered king to become his wife. When he heard it whispered that one of the rightful heirs to the throne was still alive, he set a great price upon his head. But there was no one who wanted to gain it—or even could, had he wanted to—for there was no certainty to go by, only vague rumors, and no one knew where the boy really was.

When Aepytus had grown into a youth he secretly left his grandfather's palace and, telling no one of his purpose, set out for Messene. There he heard of the price set on his head. He whipped up his courage, went to the court of King Polyphontes, where no one recognized him, not even his mother, and said in the presence of Queen Merope: "I have come, O king, to tell you that I intend to win the reward you have offered for the son of Cresphontes, who is a constant danger to your throne. I know him as well as I know my own self and shall deliver him into your hands."

When his mother heard these words, the color left her face. Quickly she sent for an old and trusted servant, who had helped her save little Aepytus, and who, for fear of the new king, was now living at a distance from the palace and the court. Him she secretly dispatched to Arcadia to guard her son from possible plots, or perhaps fetch him to Messene to lead the citizens in revolt against Polyphontes, hated for his tyrannical rule, and ascend the throne of his father.

When the old servant arrived in Arcadia he found King Cypselus and the entire palace in confusion and sorrow, for Aepytus had vanished and no one knew what had become of him. Anxiously the servant hastened back to Messene and told the queen what had happened. And now both had only one thought: that the stranger who had appeared before the king and offered to win the reward must have murdered Aepytus in Arcadia and brought his body to Messene. They did not waste time in mournful reflection. Polyphontes had given the stranger a lodging in the palace, and that very night the old servant and the queen, armed with an axe, went into his room with the purpose of killing the sleeper. The youth did not waken at her coming. A moonbeam fell on his face, quiet in gentle slumber. They leaned above him and Merope lifted her axe, preparing to strike, when the old servant, who stood closer to the couch and saw the boy's features more distinctly, suddenly gripped the queen's arm with a cry of amazement. "Stop! It is your son Aepytus you are about to kill!" Merope's arm fell to her side. She put down the axe and threw herself over her son, whom she woke with her sobs. When they had clasped each other lovingly and long, her son told her that he had not come to deliver himself up to those plotting against him, but rather to punish them, to free her from a husband she despised, and, with the help of the citizens whom he hoped to win over to his cause, to assume his father's sceptre.

After this, the three discussed the best means of taking revenge on wicked Polyphontes. Merope donned mourning robes, went to the king, and told him she had just received the sad news that her only remaining son was dead; that from now on she was willing to live at peace with her husband and to forget the unhappy past. The tyrant walked into the snare. He grew light of heart, since the heavy burden which had weighed upon him had been miraculously removed, and declared he would make thank offerings to the gods because now he had no more enemies in all the world. He summoned the citizens to attend these rites in the market place, but they came reluctantly and with downcast eyes, for the common people had loved good Cresphontes and now mourned his son, whom they had regarded as their last hope. When the city was assembled, Aepytus himself fell on the king as he was making sacrifice and stabbed him to the heart. Merope and her old servant swiftly proclaimed to the Messenians that the youth they had thought a stranger was, in reality, the rightful heir to the throne. At this they broke into deafening shouts of jubilation, and that very day Aepytus occupied the throne of his father. Conducted by his mother, he entered the palace as king of Messene. His first action was to punish the murderers of his father and brothers as well as all others implicated in the crime. But when the dead had been avenged, he proved so generous and so benevolent a ruler that he won over the nobles as well as the people of Messene. He was held in such esteem that his descendants were permitted to call themselves Aepytidae instead of Heraclidae.

PART II

TALES OF TROY

THE BUILDING OF TROY

Long, long ago two brothers, Jasion and Dardanus, sons of Zeus and an ocean-nymph, ruled over Samothrace, an island in the Aegean Sea. Jasion, well aware that he was descended from immortals, ventured to raise his eyes to a daughter of Olympus. Overcome with impetuous passion he wooed the goddess Demeter, whereupon his father punished him for his boldness by striking him dead with a thunderbolt. Dardanus grieved so sorely for the death of his brother that he left his realm and his country and journeyed to the mainland of Asia, to the coast of Mysia, where the rivers Simois and Scamander meet before they flow into the sea, and the lofty mountain range of Ida tapers off toward the shore and merges with the plain.

The king of this region was Teucer, whose ancestors came from Crete, and the people of his country, a people of shepherds, were called Teucri after him. This king received Dardanus hospitably, gave him his daughter to wife, and a strip of land of his own. This he called Dardania, and the Teucri who settled there were called Dardanians. His son Erichthonius succeeded to the throne and begot Tros; after him the country was called the Troad and its capital Troy. Both Teucri and Dardanians were now known as Trojans. Ilos, the eldest son of King Tros, succeeded his father.

Once, when he was visiting the neighboring country of Phrygia, the king of that country asked him to take part in contests which had recently been initiated there. Ilos won in wrestling, and his prize consisted of fifty youths and fifty maidens as well as a brindled cow which the king gave him, repeating an ancient oracle to the effect that wherever the cow lay down, he was to build a citadel. Ilos followed the cow, and since she lay down near the site which had been the capital of the country ever since the days of his father Tros, and was called Troy, he set about building on this hill the solid citadel of Ilios, or Ilium, which also went by the name of Pergamum, and from this time on the entire region was called Troy, or Ilium, or Pergamum. But before beginning the work, he begged Zeus, his divine forbear, to give him a sign if the plan were pleasing to him. On the very next day he found an image of Pallas Athene, called Palladium, which had fallen from heaven and was lying in front of his house. It was three cubits in height. The feet were placed close together. In her right hand the goddess held a spear, in her left a distaff and a spindle. Now the story of this image was as follows.

Legend had it that from the day of her birth the goddess was brought up by Triton, a sea-god, who had a daughter Pallas, of the same age as Athene. The two girls were inseparable companions. Once they decided to vie with each other in play to see who was stronger. Pallas, the child of the sea-god, was just aiming her spear at her friend when Zeus, who feared for his daughter, held before her a shield covered with goatskin, the aegis. Pallas was startled by this unlooked-for sight. She looked up timidly, and at that moment Athene dealt her a fatal wound. The goddess mourned her death deeply. In memory of her beloved friend she had an image made of her, furnished it with a breastplate of the same goatskin as the shield, set the image before the statue of Zeus, and held it in high honor. And from this time on she called herself Pallas Athene. With his daughter's consent, Zeus now cast this Palladium down from the sky into the region of Ilium, as a sign that both the stronghold and the city were to be under his and his daughter's protection.

The son of King Ilos and Eurydice was Laomedon, a self-willed and violent man who deceived not only his fellow men but the gods as well. It was he who thought of insuring the safety of Troy, which was not fortified like the citadel, by surrounding it with a wall and thus making it a real city. At that time Apollo and Poseidon, who had rebelled against the father of gods and been thrust out of heaven, were homeless wanderers in the world below. It was the will of Zeus that they help King Laomedon build the walls of Troy, so that this city which he and his daughter Athene cherished might be safe against aggressors. Fate brought the errant gods to the environs of Troy just as the building of the walls was begun. They offered the king their assistance, asked a certain wage which he promised them, and began their period of servitude. Poseidon helped with the building itself. Under his direction the wall rose broad and beautiful, a solid defense for the city. Phoebus Apollo, in the meantime, pastured the king's horned cattle in the winding valleys and ravines of the wooded mountains of Ida. The gods had pledged their service for the space of a year. When twelve months had passed and the wall stood complete in all its splendor, the treacherous king refused to pay them their due, and when they argued the matter and eloquent Apollo broke into bitter reproaches, he drove them off, threatening to bind the sun-god hand and foot and mutilate the ears of both. The gods left him in sullen anger and became implacably hostile to Laomedon and the entire Trojan people. Athene, too, withdrew her favor from the city which, up to this time, had been under her protection, so that, with the tacit consent of Zeus, Troy, which had just been safeguarded with a stately wall, Troy with her kings and her citizens, was abandoned to destruction by these immortals, who soon counted among their number Hera, who also turned against the city with burning hatred.

PRIAM, HECUBA, AND PARIS

What happened to King Laomedon and his daughter Hesione has already been related elsewhere. Priam, his son, whose second wife was Hecabe or Hecuba, daughter of Dymas, king of Phrygia, succeeded to the throne. Hecuba had one son, Hector. When she was carrying her second child she had a dream which filled her with dread. She saw herself giving birth to a flaming torch which set afire the entire city of Troy and burned it to ash. In great trepidation she told this to her husband, and Priam immediately summoned Aesacus, a son of his first marriage, for he was a soothsayer whom Merops, his grandfather on his mother's side, had taught the art of interpreting dreams. Aesacus declared that his stepmother Hecuba was about to give birth to a son who would cause disaster to his native city. He therefore counselled that the child be exposed upon birth. The queen bore a son, just as he had foretold, and regard for her country overcame her feeling of motherly love. She permitted Priam to put the newborn child into the hands of a slave, who was to take it up to Mount Ida and abandon it there. The name of the slave was Agelaus. He did as he was told, but a mother bear gave the child suck, and when, after five days, Agelaus returned to where he had left it, he found the baby lying in the moss sound and well-fed. He took him in his arms, reared him as his son on his own little strip of land, and gave the boy the name of Paris.

When, under the shepherd's care, the king's son had grown into a youth, he was noted both for the strength and the beauty of his body. He protected all the herdsmen of Mount Ida against the robbers roaming through those regions; for this they called him Alexander, the helper of men.

Now one day it came to pass that he found himself in a valley shaded by tall pines and broad oaks, far from his herd, which could not find the entrance to this green gorge among the mountains. As he was leaning against a tree with folded arms and gazing down at the palaces of Troy and the distant sea through a rift in the hills, he suddenly heard the footsteps of a god shaking the earth. Before he could collect himself he saw Hermes, the messenger of the gods, approaching on winged feet. In his hands he held the golden herald's staff. Yet, marvellous as he was to behold, he was only the forerunner of a still fairer vision, for now three goddesses from Olympus touched their light feet to the grass that had never been sheared or grazed upon. The youth shuddered with awe and the hair rose on his head, but the winged messenger of the gods called to him: "Do not be afraid! The goddesses have come to you so that you may judge them. They have chosen you to decide which of them is fairest. Zeus bids you accept the office to which they have elected you. He will not deny you his aid and protection."

So said Hermes and, rising on his wings, floated up from the narrow valley, and soon was lost from sight. But what Paris had heard gave him the courage to lift his shy gaze to the immortals who stood before him in divine majesty and loveliness, awaiting his decision. At first glance it seemed to him that each deserved to be called the most beautiful. But the longer he looked, the more he wavered, preferring now one and now the other. Gradually, however, the youngest, the most delicately fair, seemed to him more charming and desirable than the rest, and he felt as if her eyes caressed and caught him in a radiant snare.

And now the proudest of the three, she who was taller and statelier than the others, addressed the youth. "I am Hera, sister and wife of Zeus. If you accord me this golden apple which Eris, the goddess of discord, threw among the guests at the wedding feast of Peleus and Thetis, and on which are inscribed the words 'To the Most Beautiful,' you shall rule the richest realm on earth, even though once you were thrust from a palace and are now no more than a shepherd."

"I am Pallas Athene, the goddess of wisdom," said the second. Her forehead was broad and smooth, and the eyes in her grave and gracious face were of the deepest blue. "If you accord me the victory, you shall be famed as the wisest and most manly among men."

And now the third, who up to now had spoken only with her

eyes, looked at the shepherd still more earnestly and sweetly and said: "Paris, surely you will not allow yourself to be swayed by the promise of gifts which imply danger and are a most insecure pledge of success! I shall bestow on you something which cannot but bring you joy. What I shall give you, you need only love to become happy: I shall give you the most beautiful woman on earth to wife! I am Aphrodite, the goddess of love!"

When Aphrodite made this promise to Paris, the shepherd, she was wearing her girdle, which lent her irresistible loveliness. About her clung a shimmer of magic and hope before which the charms of the other goddesses paled. Dazzled by her radiance, Paris gave the goddess of love the golden apple he had received from Hera. Whereupon she and Athene angrily turned their backs and swore to revenge themselves for the wrong he had done them, upon Priam, his father, and upon Troy and all her people. From this moment on Hera, in particular, became the bitterest enemy of the Trojans. Aphrodite, however, solemnly repeated her promise and confirmed it with the oath of the gods. Then she took leave of the shepherd with a gesture both regal and tender and left him bewildered with happiness.

For some time after this, Paris continued to live on the slopes of Ida, an unknown herdsman, hoping for the fulfillment of Aphrodite's beguiling words. But when the wishes she had roused within him were not satisfied, he married Oenone, a girl bred in that region, who—so rumor had it—was the daughter of a river-god and a nymph. In her company he spent many joyful days in the solitude of the mountain, tending his herds far from the haunts of men. At last, however, he was lured down to the city he had never entered. It was on the occasion of funeral games which King Priam arranged after the burial of one of his kinsmen. There were to be contests, and the prize was a bullock, which the king ordered fetched from his herds on Ida. Now it happened that this very bullock was one Paris had chosen for his favorite, and since he could not very well withhold it from his master, the king, he decided he would at least take part in the contests and try to win the animal back. And he did, indeed, gain the victory, even over his brothers, even over Hector, the bravest and strongest of them all. One of the sons of King Priam, Deiphobus, was so overwhelmed with rage and shame at his defeat that he rushed forward to strike down this shepherd boy. But Paris fled to the altar of Zeus, and Priam's daughter Cassandra, on whom the gods had conferred the gift of prophecy, recognized him as her brother. In the joy of reunion his parents embraced him, forgot what the soothsayer had predicted at his birth, and accepted him as their son.

For the time being, Paris returned to his wife and his herds, but now he lived in a sumptuous house, as befitted his royal station. Soon, however, occasion arose to employ him on some of the king's business, and without knowing it he journeyed to the prize Aphrodite had promised him.

THE RAPE OF HELEN

We know that when King Priam was still a tender boy, his sister Hesione was carried off by Heracles, who had killed Laomedon, conquered Troy, and given her to his friend Telamon. Although Telamon had taken her for his lawful wife and made her queen over Salamis, neither Priam nor his house had ever become reconciled to this loss. Once, when the abduction of Hesione again came up in council, and Priam expressed deep longing for his distant sister, his son Paris rose and declared that were he but given a fleet and sent to Greece, he would, with the help of the gods, wrest his father's sister from their enemies and return victorious, crowned with glory. He founded these high hopes on the favor of Aphrodite and told his father and his brothers what had happened while he was pasturing his cattle on the slopes of Ida.

Priam no longer doubted that Paris was under the special protection of the gods, and Deiphobus too seemed confident that if his brother appeared in battle-array, the Argives would have to return Hesione. Among Priam's many sons was a soothsayer by the name of Helenus. He, of a sudden, broke into a flood of prophetic words, saying that if his brother Paris brought a woman home with him out of Greece, the Argives would come to Troy, raze the city to the ground, and slay the king and all his sons. This prediction caused a rift in the council. Troilus, Priam's youngest son, who was full of vigor and the lust for action, was impatient of his brother's forebodings, taunted him with a charge of cowardice, and exhorted the rest not to let his unfounded warnings keep them from battle. Some of the others, however, were doubtful. But Priam sided with Paris, for he was full of anxiety and longing for his sister.

The king called an assembly of the people and told them how in days gone by he had sent an embassy to Greece under the leadership of Antenor, to ask satisfaction for the rape of Hesione and bring her back to her kinsmen. Antenor's demand had been refused scornfully, but now—so said Priam—if the people were willing, he would send his own son Paris, with a formidable host, to accomplish by force what courtesy had failed to achieve. Antenor supported this proposal by rising and giving a vivid account of the insolence he, a peaceful emissary, had suffered in Greece, and described the Argives as arrogant in peace and timid in battle. His words kindled the people to fury and with noisy acclaim they called for war. But Priam, who was a wise king, did not wish this matter lightly concluded and invited anyone who had doubts about this enterprise to rise and have his say. Thereupon Panthous, one of the elders of Troy, rose in the assembly and related what he in his youth had been told by his father Othrys, who, in turn, had learned it from an oracle. It was that if ever a prince of the line of Laomedon brought home a wife from Greece, the Trojans would be faced with utter destruction. "And so," the elder concluded his speech, "let us not be tempted by the hope of martial glory, my friends. Let us live in peace and quiet rather than stake everything on the fortunes of war and perhaps lose everything, including our liberty." But the people muttered discontentedly, and begged Priam not to listen to the timid words of an old man, but to do what his heart had already resolved.

Then Priam had ships built on Mount Ida, equipped them for the voyage, and sent his son Hector into Phrygia, and Paris and Deiphobus into the neighboring country of Paeonia, to enlist allied peoples for the cause of Troy. All Trojans able to bear arms prepared for war, so that soon a vast host was assembled. The king put Paris in command of it and as aids assigned to him his brother Deiphobus, Polydamas, son of Pan-

thous, and Prince Aeneas. Then the great fleet put out to sea and
steered for Cythera, the Greek island where they expected to
make their first landing. On the way they met the ship of
Menelaus, king of Sparta, who was bound for Pylos on a visit
to wise Nestor. He was amazed at the long procession of stately
ships, and the Trojans, on their part, marvelled at the beautiful
vessel festively adorned, which apparently had aboard one of the
foremost princes of Greece. Neither side knew the other, but
each wondered where the other might be going, and thus the ships
passed, skimming over the waves. The Trojan fleet landed safely
on the island of Cythera. From there Paris was to go to Sparta
and treat with Castor and Polydeuces, twin sons of Zeus, for the
return of his father's sister. In the event the Argive heroes refused to give up Hesione, he was to take the fleet to Salamis and
carry off the princess by force.

Before embarking on this voyage to Sparta, Paris wished to
make offering in a temple sacred both to Aphrodite and Artemis.
In the meantime, the inhabitants of the island had reported the
arrival of this magnificent fleet to Sparta, where, in the absence
of Menelaus, her husband, Queen Helen was holding court alone.
This daughter of Zeus and Leda, the sister of Castor and Polydeuces, was the most beautiful woman of her time. She had been
abducted by Theseus when she was little more than a child, but
her brothers had gone in quest of her and brought her home
again. As she grew to maidenhood in the palace of her stepfather
Tyndareus, king of Sparta, her beauty attracted hosts of suitors,

but the king was afraid that if he chose any one of them for a son-in-law, he would make enemies of all the others. Then crafty Odysseus, king of Ithaca, gave him the wise counsel to demand from every suitor an oath that with his weapons he would defend the chosen bridegroom against anyone whose hostility the king might incur through his daughter's marriage. Tyndareus followed this shrewd piece of advice, had all the suitors swear the oath, and then chose Menelaus, king of the Argives, son of Atreus and brother of Agamemnon, gave him his daughter to wife, and made him the ruler of his realm. Helen bore her husband a daughter, Hermione, who was a mere infant when Paris reached Greece.

When lovely Helen, whose days were dull and joyless in the absence of her husband, heard that a foreign prince in gorgeous array had arrived on the island of Cythera, she was pricked with womanly curiosity to see this stranger and his martial retinue. To satisfy this desire, she arranged a solemn offering in the temple of Artemis, on Cythera, and entered the sanctuary at the very moment Paris was completing the rites of his own sacrifice. When he saw the queen, the hands he had lifted in prayer sank to his sides, and his spirit filled with wonder, for it seemed to him that he again beheld Aphrodite, the goddess who had appeared to him when he was a shepherd on Mount Ida. Word of Helen's beauty had come to him long ago and he had been eager to see her charms with his own eyes, but he had thought that the woman the goddess of love had promised him must be far fairer than the descriptions of Helen sounded to him. Besides, he had always had in mind a virgin, not the wife of another. But now that he beheld the queen of Sparta face to face and saw that her beauty rivalled that of Aphrodite, he suddenly knew with great clearness that this, and this only, could be the woman the goddess of love had promised him in reward for his judgment. The errand with which his father had entrusted him, the whole purpose of his journey, of his warlike array, vanished from his mind. He was convinced that he and those thousands of armed men had set out only to conquer Helen. While he stood silent, lost in the contemplation of her beauty, Helen too looked with undisguised pleasure at this handsome prince from Asia with his long curly locks and sumptuous robes of purple and gold. The image of her husband faded from her memory and in its place rose up the radiance and youth of this stranger.

But Helen tore herself away, returned to the palace in Sparta, tried to blot that fair image from her heart and rouse herself to long for Menelaus, who was still in Pylos. But soon Paris, with a select few in his train, appeared in the city of Sparta, and by stressing the importance of his mission gained entrance to the halls of the king, even though Menelaus himself was absent. The queen received him with the hospitality due to strangers and the distinction to which the sons of kings are entitled. And his skill on the lyre, the grace and sweetness of his words and his ardent love overwhelmed the unguarded heart of Helen. When Paris saw her falter in her faithfulness, he forgot the cause of his father, of his people, and, indeed, remembered nothing but Aphrodite's beguiling promise. He assembled the armed followers who had come to Sparta with him, and tempting them with the prospect of rich plunder, won their consent to help him in the plan he had conceived. Then he stormed the palace, seized the treasures of Menelaus, and carried off beautiful Helen who, to be sure, resisted—yet followed him to his fleet not altogether against her will.

While he was crossing the Aegean, the wind died down and the hurrying ships were becalmed on a quiet sea. The waves parted at the prow of the ship which bore Paris and Helen, and age-old Nereus lifted his head wreathed in waterweeds out of the salt foam, and the drops oozed from his hair and his curling beard. The ship stood as if nailed to the surface of the sea, and the sea seemed like a wall of bronze built about the ribs of the vessel. Then Nereus called out to them in terrible prophecy: "Birds of ill omen fly before you, accursed robber! The Achaeans will come with their armies; they will snatch you from your sinful union and shatter the ancient kingdom of Priam. Alas, how many horses I behold! How many men! How many dead bodies the descendants of Dardanus will owe to you! Already Pallas is donning her helmet, her shield, and the weapons of her anger. Much blood will flow; the struggle will last for many years, and only the wrath of a hero will delay the destruction of your city. But when the appointed time is come, the firebrands of the Argives will devour the homes of Troy."

So the old god foretold, then he sank back into the sea. Paris had listened in horror. But when a fair wind blew again and the white hand of Helen lay in his, he soon forgot the warning words he had heard. The fleet cast anchor in the harbor of the island of Cranae, and now Helen, faithless and light of heart, consented to be his. In the joy of being together, each forgot home and country. For a long time they lived royally on the treasure they had brought with them, and years passed before they set out on the voyage to Troy.

THE ARGIVES

Paris, as an emissary to Sparta, had been guilty of a grave breach of the laws governing a guest and his host and the rights of peoples. His action bore instant fruit. A line of kings, powerful among the heroes of Greece, was roused to raging fury. Menelaus, king of Sparta, and his elder brother Agamemnon, king of Mycenae, were descended from Tantalus. They were grandsons of Pelops, sons of Atreus, men of a noble house, whose history was rich in conquest. Besides Argos and Sparta, most of the states of the Peloponnesus were subject to these two brothers, and the rulers of the rest of Greece were their allies. So when Menelaus heard the news of the rape of Helen, he left his old friend Nestor and hastened from Pylos to Mycenae, where his brother Agamemnon and Clytaemnestra, Helen's stepsister, were king and queen. Agamemnon shared his brother's grief and anger, but spoke words of comfort to him and promised to remind Helen's former suitors of their oath. Then the brothers travelled over all of Greece and asked its princes to join in the war against Troy. The first to accept was Tlepolemus, famed ruler of Rhodes, a son of Heracles, who offered to furnish ninety ships for an expedition against the treacherous city of Troy. Then came Diomedes, son of Tydeus, who promised eighty ships with a crew of the most valiant men in Greece. After these two princes had conferred with the Atridae in Sparta, the Dioscuri, Castor and Polydeuces, sons of Zeus and brothers of Helen, were also invited to join. But they had already gone, for at the very first report that their sister had been carried off, they had sailed in pursuit of the robber and got as far as the island of Lesbos, close to the coast of Troy. There a storm struck their ship and it sank into the sea. The Dioscuri themselves disappeared. Legend, however, had it that they did not perish in the waves, but that Zeus, their father, set them in the heavens as a glorious constellation. And there, through the ages, they perform their office as protectors of ships that sail the seas and as patron gods of those aboard them.

And now almost all of Greece had risen to the call of the Atridae. Only two princes hung back. One was crafty Odysseus of Ithaca, Penelope's husband, who did not wish to leave his young wife and his infant son Telemachus for the sake of the faithless queen of Sparta. And so when Palamedes, son of Prince Nauplius of Euboea, the staunch friend of Menelaus, came to him with the king of Sparta, he pretended madness, yoked an ox and an ass to his harrow, ploughed his field with this ill-matched team, and scattered salt instead of seed in the furrows. He arranged for the two heroes to see him engaged in this strange occupation and hoped in this way to exclude himself from a campaign he did not favor. But wise Palamedes saw through the wiliest of all mortals. While Odysseus was guiding the harrow, he secretly went to the palace, took the child Telemachus from his cradle, and laid him in a part of the field where Odysseus was just about to turn up the earth. At that, the father carefully lifted the harrow across the boy, and the heroes shouted to him that he had proved he was quite sane. Now he could no longer refuse to take part in the expedition, and though in his heart he swore bitter enmity to Palamedes, he promised to put at the disposal of King Menelaus twelve ships from Ithaca and the neighboring islands, each with its crew complete.

The other prince who had not yet given his word to join and whose whereabouts were not even known, was Achilles, the young and splendid son of Peleus and Thetis, goddess of the sea. When he was newborn, his immortal mother wanted to make him immortal too. So when night came, unbeknown to Peleus, she laid the child in celestial fire, which was to purge him of whatever mortal parts he had inherited from his father. By day she healed his seared flesh with ambrosia. Night after night she did this, but once Peleus spied on her and cried aloud when he saw his son quiver in the flames. This hindered Thetis from perfecting her work. Sadly she abandoned her infant son, whom she had not succeeded in making wholly divine, nor did she return to the palace, but sped to the cool sea kingdom of the Nereids. Peleus, who thought that the boy bore dangerous wounds, lifted him up and carried him to Chiron, who was versed in the art of medicine. This wise centaur, the rearer of many heroes, took the boy tenderly and nourished him on the marrow of bears and the liver of lions and boars.

When Achilles was nine years old, Calchas, a Greek soothsayer, declared that Troy, the far-off city in Asia which was destined to destruction through the Argives, could not be conquered without the son of Peleus. Thetis, his mother, heard this prophecy in the depths of the sea, and because she knew that this campaign would bring death to her son, she rose through the waves, secretly entered her husband's palace, dressed the boy in girl's clothes, and in this disguise took him to King Lycomedes on the island of Scyros, who brought him up as a girl and had him perform the dainty tasks of a princess. But when the boy arrived at an age when the first down appeared on his lip, he discovered himself to Deidamia, the king's lovely daughter. A tender love sprang up between these two, and while the people on the island took Achilles for a kinswoman of their king, he was really Deidamia's husband.

Now that he was indispensable for the conquest of Troy, Calchas, the soothsayer, who knew his abode as well as what was destined for him, told the Atridae where he was to be found, and they at once dispatched Odysseus and Diomedes to enlist him in the war. When these heroes came to the island of Scyros, they were presented to the king, his daughter, her kinswoman, and handmaids. But the face of Achilles was still so delicately lovely that even though the two Achaean princes had watchful eyes, they could not detect him among the group of girls. Then Odysseus had recourse to ruse. He had a spear and shield carried into the room where the girls gathered, but so that it seemed by chance, and then bade one of his men sound the trumpet as if foes were approaching. At those martial notes every woman fled from the chamber, but Achilles remained and boldly seized the spear and the shield. When he realized that his disguise no longer availed him, he offered to join the army of the Achaeans with a fleet of fifty ships and promised that he himself would come at the head of his Myrmidons or Thessalians, accompanied by Phoenix, who had educated him, and Patroclus, his friend, who had been reared with him in the house of Peleus.

The leaders of the various peoples chose Agamemnon as their commander-in-chief, since he was the most active in furthering the enterprise, and he selected the port of Aulis in Boeotia, near the straits of Euboea, as the meeting place for all the Argive princes with their men and their ships. Besides those already mentioned there were many others. The noblest among these were mighty Ajax, son of Telamon of Salamis, and his half brother Teucer, the unerring archer; Ajax the Less from the land of Locris; Menestheus of Athens; Ascalaphus and Ialmenus, sons of Ares, and with them their people, the Minyans from Orchomenus; from Boeotia, Peneleus, Arcesilaus, Clonius, and Prothoenor; from Phocis, Schedius and Epistrophus; from Euboea, Elephenor with the Abantes; Diomedes, Sthenelus, son of Capaneus, and Euryalus, son of Mecisteus, with part of the Argives and other Peloponnesians; from Pylos, Nestor, the old man who had seen three generations grow up; from Arcadia, Agapenor, son of Ancaeus; from Elis and other cities, Amphimachus, Thalpius, Diores, and Polyxenus; from Dulichium and the Echinades, Meges, son of Phyleus; with the Aetolians came Thoas, son of

Andraemon; from Crete, Idomeneus and Meriones; from Rhodes, Tlepolemus, a descendant of Heracles; from Syme, Nireus, who in beauty exceeded all men in the Argive hosts; from the Calydnae, the Heraclidae Phidippus and Antiphus; from Phylace, Podarces, son of Iphicles; from Pherae in Thessaly, Eumelus, the son of Admetus and devout Alcestis; Methone, Thaumacia, and Meliboea sent Philoctetes; from Tricca, Ithome, and Oechalia came Podalirius and Machaon, both versed in the art of healing; from Ormenium, Eurypylus, the son of Euaemon; from Argissa, Polypoetes, the son of Pirithous, friend of Theseus; Guneus represented Cyphos, and Prothous, Magnesia.

Besides the Atridae, Odysseus, and Achilles, these were the princes and commanders of the Greeks who gathered in Aulis— and each came with a great fleet! In those days the Greeks were sometimes called Danai, a word derived from Danaus, an early king of Egypt, who had settled in Argos on the Peloponnesus, and sometimes Argives, after the most important region in Greece; Argolis or the land of the Argives. They also went by the name of Achaeans, because in olden times Greece had been called Achaea. It was not until later that they were called Greeks from Graicus, son of Thessalus, and Hellenes after Hellen, son of Deucalion and Pyrrha.

THE ARGIVES SEND PRIAM A MESSAGE

While the Achaeans were thus preparing for war against Troy, Agamemnon in an assembly of trusted friends and leaders of the people resolved first to try peaceful means: to send ambassadors to King Priam to protest the breach of laws and the rape of an Argive queen and demand the return of Helen and the treasures of Menelaus. The council elected Palamedes, Odysseus, and Menelaus to go on this mission, and though in his heart Odysseus was bitterly hostile to Palamedes, still, for the sake of the common good, he agreed to defer to the wisdom of this prince, famed throughout the hosts of Greece for his insight and experience, and did not dispute his right to speak for them all at the court of Priam.

The Trojans and their king were dumbfounded at the arrival of such messengers aboard ships so large and splendid. They were utterly ignorant of the cause of their coming, since Paris was still on the island of Cranae and had not been heard from in Troy. Priam and his people could not but believe that the Trojan warriors who had set out to support Paris in his demand for Hesione must have met with powerful resistance, that they had been destroyed, and that now the Argives, grown arrogant, had crossed the sea to attack the Trojans in their own country. And so the news that envoys from Greece were approaching the city made everyone taut with suspense. The gates, however, were flung wide, and the three princes were at once conducted to the palace of Priam and led before the king, who had summoned his numerous sons and the heads of the city to the council hall. Palamedes began to speak and in the name of all of Greece complained bitterly of the shameful breach of hospitality which Paris had committed by carrying off Helen. Then he pictured the dangers of war which this disgraceful action might bring on Priam and his people, enumerated the great princes of Greece who would come to Troy with countless warriors on more than a thousand ships, and demanded the return of their captured queen. "You do not know, O king," he concluded, "the kind of men your son has offended by what he has done. They are Danai who would die rather than suffer an insult on the part of a stranger to go unavenged. But in coming to avenge this wrong, they do not intend to die but to carry off the victory, for their number is as the sands of the sea; all have the courage of true heroes and burn to blot out the disgrace inflicted on their country by destroying the cause of it. That is why our commander-in-chief, Agamemnon, king of mighty Argos and foremost prince of all Greece, and with him all the other princes of the Danai, bids me say to you: 'Return the queen you have stolen from us, or all of you shall perish.' "

These words of defiance angered the king's sons and the elders of Troy. They drew their swords from the scabbard and struck blade against shield, full of the lust for battle. But King Priam ordered them to be quiet, rose from his seat, and said: "Strangers, you who have come in the name of your people and heaped such reproaches on me, first let me recover from my astonishment. For we know nothing of what you accuse us of; rather do we think that we are entitled to complain of just such an evil deed as you claim we have committed. It was your countryman Heracles who attacked us in the midst of peace. From our city he carried off Hesione, my innocent sister, and gave her as a slave to Telamon. And it is only due to the good will of that prince that he made her his lawful wife instead of keeping her as a servant or a concubine. But this is not enough to make up for dishonesty and rape. We have sent envoys to you before. Now my son Paris left for your country to demand the return of my sister, so that I might rejoice in her in my old age. How Paris has carried out my royal command, what he has done, and where he is—these things I do not know. But I am wholly certain that there is no Argive woman in my palace or in my city. And so, even if I wanted to, I could not give you the satisfaction you ask. Should my son Paris return to Troy safely, as his father ardently hopes, should he bring with him an Argive woman he has abducted, she shall be delivered up to you, unless she is a fugitive and, as such, implores our protection. But even then you shall have her only on one condition: that you bring back to me from Salamis my sister Hesione, so that I may clasp her in my arms."

The council of Trojans applauded the words of their king, but Palamedes spoke again, and his words were both angry and arrogant. "The granting of our request, O king, can depend on no condition whatsoever. We believe your words which assure us that the wife of Menelaus has not yet arrived within these walls. But she will! Do not doubt it! It is, unfortunately, only too true that your unworthy son has carried her off. As for us—we are not responsible for what Heracles did in our fathers' time. But we do demand satisfaction from you for a wrong perpetrated by one of your sons in our own day and age. Hesione went with Telamon of her own free will, and she herself is sending her son, Prince Ajax, to this war which is imminent unless you make amends. But Helen was carried off against her wish. Give thanks to the gods who have given you a respite through the tarrying abroad of that robber Paris, and come to a decision which will ward destruction from you and yours."

Priam and the Trojans were vexed almost beyond endurance by this insolent speech of Palamedes, but they observed the courtesy due to envoys. The assembly adjourned, and one of the elders of Troy, wise Antenor, son of Aesyetes and Cleomestra, escorted the foreign princes to shield them from the insults of the crowd, conducted them to his house, and lodged them there with perfect hospitality until the following morning. Then he accompanied them to the shore, where they boarded the shining ships which had taken them to Troy.

AGAMEMNON AND IPHIGENIA

While the fleet was assembling at Aulis, Prince Agamemnon whiled away the time with the chase. One day an exquisite hind, a creature sacred to Artemis, came within shooting distance. Overcome with eagerness, Agamemnon aimed at her and hit the mark, saying boastfully that Artemis herself could not have done better. Vexed by his impious act, the goddess stilled the wind and caused a deep calm to fall on the bay of Aulis, where the Argives had assembled with ships and horses and chariots. The fleet lay idly on the waters as the days crept by. In their trouble the Danai turned to Calchas, their seer, the son of Thestor, for he had already done good service to his people and had come to accompany them on their expedition as priest and prophet. "If

Agamemnon, the commander-in-chief of the Argives," so said Calchas, "sacrifices to Artemis Iphigenia, his cherished daughter, whom Clytaemnestra bore him, the goddess will be appeased. A fair wind will rise, and heaven will put no further obstacle in the way of the destruction of Troy."

When Agamemnon heard this, his courage sank. He sent for Talthybius of Sparta, the herald of the assembled Danai, and had him proclaim to all the peoples of Greece that Agamemnon was resigning his command over the Argive host because he did not wish to burden his conscience with the murder of his child. But when his resolve was announced to the Achaeans, they threatened revolt. Then Menelaus sought out his brother in his house and pictured to him the consequences of this decision and the disgrace which would cling to him, Menelaus, if his wife remained in the hands of the enemy. He marshalled so many arguments and presented them with such eloquence that Agamemnon at last consented to the monstrous deed.

He sent a message to his wife Clytaemnestra, in Mycenae, asking her to send Iphigenia to the army in Aulis, and gave as his reason for this odd request the pretext that before the fleet sailed for the coast of Troy the girl was to be betrothed to Peleus' young son Achilles, the glorious prince of Phthyotis, of whose secret marriage to Deidamia no one knew. Scarcely had the messenger been dispatched, however, before Agamemnon began to be tormented by qualms of conscience. In an agony of doubt and remorse at his ill-considered act, he called an old and trusted servant to him that very night and gave him a letter for Clytaemnestra. In it he had written that she should not send their daughter to Aulis, that he had changed his plan and wished to postpone the betrothal until the spring. The servant hurried off with the letter, but he never reached his destination, for before dawn, before he even rose from his bed, he was seized by Menelaus, who had observed his brother's indecision and kept a watchful eye on all he did.

When he had read the letter, he again went to his brother, the tablet in his hand. "Nothing in the world," he called out to him resentfully, "is worse than a wavering will! Nothing is more unjust and more untrue! Do you not recall, my brother, how eagerly you wanted the command, how you burned with ill-concealed desire to lead the army to Troy? You feigned the greatest humility toward all the Argive princes and graciously shook hands with each and every one. Your doors were never bolted. The very humblest among the people could enter, and all this show of friendliness was only for the purpose of obtaining an office you had set your heart on. But when you had it, things became quite different. Then you no longer were the friend of your old friends, as before. It was not easy to find you in your house, and you rarely showed yourself to the army. This was not the behavior of an honorable man, who should be most loyal to his friends at a time when they have the greatest need of him. But what did you do? When you had come to Aulis with the Greek host, when you waited in vain for a fair wind, when the gods turned from you, and our men began to grumble and finally cried aloud: 'Let us sail and not wait forever in Aulis,' how your glance roved about in dismay, how helpless you were! It was then that you turned to me to devise a way out, lest you lose that fine office you were so proud of. And when Calchas, the soothsayer, bade you offer up your daughter to Artemis, it needed small urging for you to agree. You sent a message to your wife Clytaemnestra, asking her to send Iphigenia—ostensibly that she might be betrothed to Achilles. And now you are again evading the issue. You sent another message, declaring that you cannot bear to be the murderer of your child. But why should I be astonished at such indecision! There have been thousands like you, eager to get the rudder into their hands, but slack when they discover that the privilege of guiding others entails personal sacrifice. But I say that no one is fit to lead armies or to administer a state who is not resourceful and wise and who cannot maintain these qualities in the face of all the toil and turmoil life brings with it."

Censure such as this, and from the lips of a brother, was not calculated to calm Agamemnon's troubled heart. "Why reproach me so violently?" he asked. "Your eyes are bloodshot with excitement. Who do you think is out to offend you? What are you so disturbed about? Your charming wife Helen? I cannot restore her to you. Why did you not guard what is yours with greater watchfulness? You seem to think it was foolish of me to try, in a saner moment, to correct a mistake made impetuously. But it seems to me that it is far greater folly to try to regain a faithless wife you are well rid of. No, I shall never commit a crime against my own flesh and blood! As for you—it were far better you meted out punishment to adulterous Helen!"

The brothers were still quarrelling when a messenger arrived to announce to King Agamemnon the coming of his daughter Iphigenia, of her mother, and his little son Orestes, who had left soon after her. Hardly had the messenger departed when Agamemnon gave himself up to such hopeless despair that Menelaus, who had been standing a little apart, approached his brother and reached for his hand. Agamemnon gave it to him while the hot tears gushed from his eyes. "There it is, brother," he said mournfully. "The victory is yours! I am destroyed!"

But now Menelaus swore to desist from his earlier demand. He even pleaded with him not to kill his child and declared that by no means would he injure and lose a beloved brother for the mere sake of Helen. "Do not wet your face with tears!" he cried. "If—through the oracle of the gods—I have a share in your daughter, I herewith reject it and cede it to you. Do not be astonished that my impulsive spirit has shifted from fury to brotherly love. For should not a man follow his better judgment when the waves of anger have ebbed from his heart?"

Agamemnon embraced his brother, but the destiny of his daughter was still uppermost in his mind. "I thank you," he said. "That your noble spirit would bring us together again was more than I could hope for. Nonetheless, my fate is sealed. Iphigenia must die. All of Greece demands it. Calchas and crafty Odysseus have come to an understanding with each other. They will have the people on their side, kill you and me, and then slaughter the girl. And believe me, even if we fled to Argos, they would come and drag us from within the walls and raze to the ground the old city of the Cyclopes. And so, dear brother, I beg you to do nothing except keep the truth from Clytaemnestra until our child has been offered up in obedience to the oracle."

And now the women approached. The brothers broke off their talk and Menelaus went away, deep in sorrowful thought.

The greeting between husband and wife was brief and, on Agamemnon's part, cold and constrained. But the young girl clasped her arms about her father and her voice was full of love and joy as she exclaimed: "O father, how I have missed you! How happy I am to see you again!" Looking at him more closely she continued: "But why are your eyes so somber and full of care? You were always so glad to see me!"

"Enough, child," Agamemnon answered, and his heart was full to bursting. "A king has many burdens and much to vex him."

"But now smooth those lines from your forehead and turn loving eyes upon your daughter!" said Iphigenia. "Oh, why are they wet with tears?"

"Because we must part for very long," her father replied.

"How happy I should be if I could be your companion on this journey!" the girl said wistfully.

"You too will go on a journey," Agamemnon said gravely. "But before that we must sacrifice—a sacrifice at which you shall be present, my daughter." As he uttered these words, he was almost choked by tears. Then he sent the girl, who suspected no harm, to the house where her handmaids were lodged. When she had gone, Agamemnon forced himself to spin out a tale of lies to his inquisitive wife, who was overflowing with questions about the family and the wealth of the bridegroom he had selected for their daughter. As soon as he had escaped the flood of her queries, he sought out Calchas, the soothsayer, to confer with him on the details of this sacrifice, which now seemed inevitable.

In the meantime, evil chance brought Clytaemnestra face to face with Achilles, who was on his way to Agamemnon because his men, his Myrmidons, were openly rebelling at the long delay. Since she regarded him as her future son-in-law, she did not hesitate to greet him with cordial words and make mention of the coming ceremony. But Achilles drew back in amazement. "What is this wedding you speak of?" he asked. "I, for my part, have never wooed your daughter, and Agamemnon has certainly never encouraged me to do so." At this Clytaemnestra realized that she had been deceived. She stood before Achilles doubtful and abashed. But he, with the ready warmth of youth, tried to comfort her in her dismay. "Do not be annoyed if some one has tried to play a trick on you," he said. "Let it rest lightly on your spirit and forgive me if I hurt you with my frank words." He was about to take leave of her reverently and go his way, when a servant, the trusted slave of Agamemnon and Clytaemnestra, the one Menelaus had waylaid with the letter, came toward the two from the house of the commander-in-chief.

"Listen!" he whispered breathlessly. "There is something you must know at once! Iphigenia's father intends to kill her with his own hands!" And now the mother, shaken with terror and grief, learned from the lips of the slave the secret so carefully guarded from her. She threw herself at the feet of Peleus' young son, clasped his knees like a suppliant, and moaned:

"It does not shame me to lie in the dust before you, I, a mortal, before you, the son of gods. A mother's love makes short work of pride. O son of a goddess, save me and my child from despair! It is to you I brought her wreathed, thinking she was to become your wife. And even now, though I know it is not true, I still think of you as her bridegroom. By all you hold sacred, by your divine mother, I beseech you to help me rescue my child. There is no altar here at which I could take refuge! My only altar is your knees. You have heard the cruel deed Agamemnon is about to commit. You see that I am defenseless, a woman in the midst of a host of violent men. But if you aid us, all will yet be well!"

Achilles raised the queen with deep reverence and said: "Be of good courage, O Clytaemnestra. I was reared in the house of a man both devout and kind. At Chiron's hearth I saw much simple goodness. I joyfully follow the sons of Atreus when they lead on to glory, but I obey no criminal commands! And so I shall protect you, as far as is within my power. Never shall your daughter, whose name has been coupled with mine, be given up to death. If she died as a result of the ruse which brought her here to a betrothal, I should hold myself guilty; I should consider myself a coward and the son of a rascal if I allowed my name to serve your husband as a pretext to murder his child."

"Is this, indeed, what is in your heart?" cried Clytaemnestra, beside herself with happy relief. "Shall my daughter clasp your knees as well as I? It would not be maidenly, but if it pleases you, she will come to you chaste and proud as befits a freeborn princess."

"No!" Achilles replied quickly. "Do not bring her to me, for that might give rise to rumors and evil gossip. A great army like this, with no cares and concerns of home to fill their minds,

is fond of idle talk. Only have faith in me. I have never stooped
to lies. May I myself perish if I do not save your child." With this
solemn assurance the son of Peleus left Clytaemnestra, who went
straight to Agamemnon, her husband. She faced him with undisguised loathing.

He, not knowing that she had discovered his secret, greeted
her with the ambiguous words: "Call your daughter from the
house, for flour and water and the victim which is to fall by the
sword before the wedding feast is begun—all these will soon be
in readiness."

"Indeed!" cried Clytaemnestra, and her eyes flashed omi-
nously. "Come, Iphigenia, for you are well aware of your father's
design. And bring your little brother Orestes with you." And
when the girl came she continued: "See, Agamemnon, here she
stands, obedient and at your mercy. But first let me ask you a
question: tell me without evasion or lies whether you have plotted
to kill your daughter and mine?"

For a long time the king stood silent. At last words broke from
him: "O Fate, why have you revealed my secret?"

"Now hear me to the end," said Clytaemnestra. "I shall pour
out to you all that is rankling in my heart. Our marriage began
with a crime. You carried me off by force, killed my first husband,
took the child I was suckling and slew it. My brothers Castor and
Polydeuces had already leaped on their horses and were pursuing
you with a host of armed men. But my old father Tyndareus
saved you when you implored his protection, and so you became
my husband. You will have to grant me that I was always true
to my marriage vows, a wife you could delight in at home and be
proud of before strangers. Three daughters I bore you, and one
son. And now you want to rob me of my eldest, and if you were
asked why, you would have to reply: 'So that Menelaus can recover that adultress of his.' By all the gods, I implore you not to
do this thing, lest I harden my heart against you. Do not harden
yours against me! You want to sacrifice your daughter? What
prayer will you utter as you slay her? What boon will you ask for
yourself as she dies? A return as unlucky as the outset of your
voyage? Or do you, perhaps, expect me to call blessings down
upon you? I could not well invoke the gods in behalf of a murderer! Why must it be your own child that falls as a victim? Why

do you not say to the Achaeans: 'If you wish the fleet to go to Troy, cast lots to decide on whose daughter is to die.' Why should I, your faithful wife, lose my child, while he in whose cause you are going to war, Menelaus, can freely rejoice in his daughter Hermione, while his faithless wife knows that her child is safe and well in Sparta? Tell me if I have said a single word that is untrue. But if you admit that I have spoken only what is true, then do not kill your daughter! Think! Listen to the counsel of your heart!"

And now Iphigenia knelt at her father's feet, and her voice faltered as she spoke. "Had I the magic voice of Orpheus, which could move stones, my father, I should speak eloquent words to rouse your compassion. But alas! I have no arts; I can only weep and embrace your knees with my arms instead of the olive spray. Do not let me die so young! The light of earth is sweet. Do not compel me to see what is hidden in darkness. Try to remember how you caressed me when I was still a child. I can so well recall everything you said: that you hoped to marry me to a man of noble lineage, to see me flower into womanhood and greet you joyfully whenever you returned from your quests. Have you forgotten it all? By my mother who bore me in pain, and who now suffers far greater pain at the thought of losing me, I beg you to give up your awful purpose. What have Helen and Paris to do with me? Why must I die because he came to Greece? Oh, look at me! Kiss me, that dying I may have a sign of love from you, since my words cannot move you. Behold your son, my brother! He utters no word and only pleads in silence. He is still a little boy. But I am nearly grown. Soften your heart and have pity on me. For mortals there is nothing fairer than life! To live in misery is better than to die the most glorious death."

But Agamemnon was firm in his resolve. Relentless as a rock he stood and said: "I feel compassion when it is lawful for me to do so. I love my children—only a madman would not! It is with a heavy heart that I carry out this sacrifice, but carry it out I must. You see the vast fleet under my command. You see the host of heroes who surround me. They will not find the way to Troy; they will not conquer the city unless I do what the oracle bids: unless I sacrifice my child. All those assembled here are determined to put an end to the rape of Argive women. They are firm in their resolve. If I refused to obey the order of the gods, they would kill me and then slay you as well. I have reached the bounds of my power. I am not yielding to Menelaus, my brother, but to all of Greece."

The king did not wait to hear their further pleas, but left the women to themselves. Suddenly, through their weeping, they heard the clash of weapons. "That is Achilles!" Clytaemnestra exclaimed joyfully. But Iphigenia was ill at ease and vainly tried to hide from the youth her father had falsely proclaimed as her bridegroom. Accompanied by a number of armed followers, the son of Peleus strode into the hall.

"Unhappy daughter of Leda," he called to the queen. "The camp is in open revolt. They ask the death of your child, and all but stoned me when I raised my voice in opposition to their insistent demands."

"And your Myrmidons?" Clytaemnestra asked, and her breath almost failed her.

"They were the first to rebel," Achilles replied. "And they called me a lovesick fool too ready with words. I come with these faithful few to protect you against Odysseus, who is on his way here. Let the daughter cling to her mother. I shall shield you with my body, and we shall see whether they dare attack the son of the goddess, the man on whose life the fate of Troy depends." These last words, quickened by a glimmer of hope, restored at least a degree of composure to Clytaemnestra.

But Iphigenia extricated herself from her mother's embrace, lifted her head and confronted the queen and the son of Peleus with courage and decision. "Listen to what I have to say," she said in a clear, unfaltering voice. "You are angry with my father, dear mother, but it is useless, for he cannot change what is appointed to be. The zeal of this stranger deserves all our gratitude and admiration, but he will live to repent it, and you will be slandered by evil tongues. I have thought this over and I am prepared to die. I shall banish all baser stirrings from my spirit. Every eye in the beautiful land of Greece looks to me. It is I who am responsible for the sailing of the fleet, for the fall of Troy, for the honor of Argive women. My name will be covered with glory, for they will call me the liberator of my country. Shall I, a mortal, oppose Artemis, the goddess, if it pleases her to ask my life for my fatherland? No, I shall give it up of my own free will. Sacrifice me, destroy Troy—this will be the monument in my memory, this will be my wedding feast."

As these proud, ecstatic words broke from Iphigenia's lips, she faced her mother and the son of Peleus, radiant as a goddess. And Achilles, the beautiful and the brave, dropped to his knee before her and cried: "Daughter of Agamemnon! The gods would, indeed, brim my cup of happiness, if they gave you to me as my bride. I envy Greece, to which you belong, and I envy you Greece, to which you are betrothed. Now that I have seen your loveliness and fearless spirit, I love you, I desire you. Think well! Death is a dreary thing. It is to life and to joy that I want to lead you."

Iphigenia answered him with a smile. "Through Helen, a woman's beauty has caused enough war and murder. You shall not die for me, nor kill for my sake. Let me come to the rescue of Greece if I can."

"Noble heart!" said the son of Peleus. "Do as you will, but I, with these weapons of mine, shall hasten to the altar to prevent your death. You shall not perish for your selflessness. Perhaps you will agree when the cold blade touches your throat." And he went in the van of the women. But Iphigenia told her mother to stop crying, took the hand of her little brother Orestes in hers, and went to her death in the exultant certainty of saving her country. Clytaemnestra threw herself on the ground and could not bring herself to follow her daughter.

In the meantime, the host of the Achaeans gathered outside the city of Aulis in a fragrant grove consecrated to Artemis. The altar was ready and beside it stood Calchas, priest and sooth-sayer. A cry of wonder and compassion surged through the ranks when the warriors saw Iphigenia and her faithful handmaids enter the grove and walk toward Agamemnon. He sighed deeply, turned away, and hid his tears in his robe. The girl came up to him and said: "Here I am, dear father. Before the altar of the goddess I do the bidding of the oracle and give my life for the Argive army and for the welfare of my country. I shall rejoice in your happiness, in your victory, and in your safe return. Let no one hold me. I will be quiet and brave and bare my throat to the blade."

A murmur of astonishment went through the throngs as they saw her matchless courage. And now the herald Talthybius, standing in the center of the circle, called for silence and prayer. Calchas, the seer, drew forth a sharp and shining blade and laid it down before the altar in a basket wrought of gold. In the midst of this solemn hush came Achilles, fully armed, and brandishing his sword. But when he saw the girl, his resolve was shaken. He cast his sword on the ground, sprinkled the altar with holy water, took in his hand the basket and paced around the altar like a priest, saying: "O Artemis, great goddess, accept this sacred voluntary offering, accept the pure blood of a virgin, which Agamemnon and all of Greece consecrates to you. Give our ships a fair voyage, and let our spears bring destruction to Troy." The Atridae and the entire host listened in silence and bowed their heads. Calchas gripped the blade, uttered a prayer, and fixed his eyes on the girl's throat. Distinctly all heard the sound of his blow. But a miracle came to pass, for at that very instant the human victim vanished before the eyes of the host, and in her place was a splendid hind, writhing before the altar and drenching it with blood. Artemis had taken pity on Iphigenia.

"Leaders of the united Argive host!" cried Calchas when he found his voice after his first gasp of amazement. "Here you behold the victim the goddess sent us, one more pleasing to her than the maiden whose noble blood she wished to spare. Artemis has restored us to her favor. She will give us a safe voyage and help us conquer Troy. Be of good courage, for on this very day you shall sail out of the bay of Aulis." So he spoke and watched the sacrificial hind burn in the flames. When the last spark had died, the still air was filled with a rushing sound. All eyes turned toward the harbor, and there they saw the ships rocking on the sea and the waters astir with wind. Shouting with joy the warriors left the sacred grove and made for the camp.

When Agamemnon entered his house, Clytaemnestra was no longer there. His trusted servant had preceded him and roused the fainting queen with the news of Iphigenia's rescue. A wave of thankfulness swept over her. She lifted her hands to heaven, but instead of speaking words of gratitude she cried aloud in bitter grief: "I am robbed of my child all the same! My husband has killed my happiness. Let us hasten, for I do not wish to see the slayer!" The servant quickly made ready the chariot and called her tirewomen to her. When Agamemnon returned from the sacrificial feast, his wife was far on her way to Mycenae.

THE ARGIVES SET OUT
PHILOCTETES IS ABANDONED

On that very day the Argive fleet set sail and a fair wind launched them swiftly on the high seas. After a brief journey they landed on the small island of Chryse to replenish their water supply. Here the son of Poeas, Philoctetes, Heracles' friend and comrade-in-arms and heir to his unerring arrows, discovered a crumbling altar which Jason, on his voyage with the Argonauts, had once dedicated to Pallas Athene, the goddess of that island. The hero rejoiced in his find and was about to make offering to the protectress of the Achaeans, when a poisonous adder, such as often guard the sanctuaries of gods, darted toward him and bit him in the foot. He was carried into the ship and the fleet sailed on. But the wound swelled and grew more and more painful. The son of Poeas was in torment, and his comrades could not endure the stench of his rotting flesh and of the poisonous discharge oozing from his foot. His screams of anguish and fear disturbed them in everything they undertook, even in the offerings made to the gods. Finally the sons of Atreus took counsel with crafty Odysseus, for the annoyance of those around the sick hero began to spread through the host. They feared that wounded Philoctetes would bring a plague upon them when they camped at Troy and embitter their days with his endless lamentations. And so these leaders of their people cruelly decided to abandon the brave hero on the barren and uninhabited coast of the island of Lemnos, which they were just passing. But they failed to consider that in losing the man they were also depriving themselves of his unconquerable arrows. Crafty Odysseus was chosen to execute the plan. He took the sleeping hero on his back, rowed him ashore in a small boat, and there laid him down in a cave, leaving with him enough food and clothing to enable him to live for a time. The ship had stopped near the island only long enough for the son of Poeas to be taken ashore. As soon as Odysseus returned, it continued on its course and quickly joined the rest of the fleet.

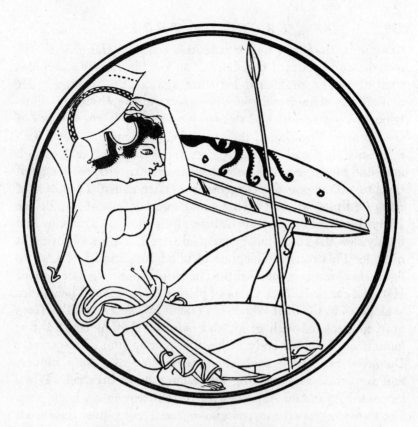

THE ARGIVES IN MYSIA. TELEPHUS

Safely the Argive fleet reached the coast of Asia Minor. But since the heroes were not familiar with this region, they let the fair wind drive them away from Troy, to Mysia, and there cast anchor. All along the shore they encountered armed guards, who in the name of their ruler forbade them to enter these domains before the king had been informed of their coming and told who they were. Now the king of Mysia was himself an Argive. It was Telephus, son of Heracles and Auge, who after curious adventures was reunited with his mother at the court of King Teuthras of Mysia. Later he married Argiope, daughter of Teuthras, and succeeded to the throne after her father's death.

Without asking who ruled the country they had come to, and without deigning to reply, the Achaeans took up their weapons and fell upon the coast guards. Only a few escaped, and these told King Telephus that unknown enemies had arrived by the thousands, that they had invaded his country, slaughtered the guards, and occupied the shore. The king hurriedly assembled what forces he could and led them against the strangers. He himself was strong and glorious, a son well worthy of his illustrious father, and he had trained his warriors in the manner of the Argives. The Danai, therefore, found themselves faced with resistance they had not looked for, and were soon involved in a long and bloody conflict, in which hero strove with hero. One of the bravest among the Argives was Thersander, grandson of King Oedipus, son of Polynices and comrade-in-arms of Prince Diomedes. Thersander raged through the host of Telephus and finally slew the king's most cherished friend, who was fighting at his side. This roused Telephus to blind fury, and he began to fight the grandson of Oedipus in single combat. The son of Heracles carried off the victory; pierced by his lance Thersander sank down in the dust. When his friend Diomedes saw this from afar, he groaned with grief, and before Telephus could throw himself on the dead body of his foe to strip him of his armor, Diomedes ran to the spot, slung the corpse over his shoulder, and carried it away, walking with a long, powerful stride. When he passed Ajax and Achilles with this burden on his back, they also were shaken with sorrow and anger. They rallied their men, divided them into two groups, and by a clever ruse turned the tide of the battle, so that the Argives were again at an advantage. Teuthrantius, the half brother of Telephus, fell, struck by a missile Ajax had launched. Telephus, who was just pursuing Odysseus, wanted to come to his aid, but stumbled over a vine, for the shrewd Achaeans had gradually lured the enemy into a vineyard where the terrain was more favorable to the Danai. Achilles seized the moment when Telephus was rising from his fall to pierce his left thigh with his spear. Nevertheless, Telephus rose, drew out the weapon, and, screened by some of his men, escaped death. The struggle, with its ups and downs for both sides, would have gone on indefinitely, had not night fallen and both armies retired from the field in sore need of rest. The Mysians returned to their city, the Argives to the shore where the ships were anchored. Brave men had died on both sides, and many were wounded.

On the following day, the Mysians and the Argives sent envoys to arrange for a truce, to give them time to find and bury the bodies of their dead. Only now did the Achaeans learn, to their utmost surprise, that the king who had defended his lands with such signal bravery was a man of their own people, a son of Heracles, their greatest demigod. And Telephus, in turn, realized that he had stained his hands with the blood of his countrymen. Now there were three princes in the Argive army, Tlepolemus, son of Heracles, and Phidippus and Antiphus, sons of King Thessalus and grandsons of Heracles; this made them kinsmen of Telephus. These three offered to accompany the envoys of Mysia to their brother and cousin and explain to him who the men that had landed on the coast of his country were and why they had come to Asia. King Telephus received his kinsmen with warm cordiality and could not hear enough of their story. He learned that Paris had offended the whole of Greece with his crime, and that Menelaus and his brother Agamemnon had set out with all their allies. "And so, dear brother," said Tlepolemus, who, being halfbrother to the king, spoke for the rest, "you who belong to our country, do not withdraw from your people, for whom our father Heracles always fought, even at the ends of the world, so that all of Greece is full of monuments testifying to his love for his country. Heal the wounds which you, an Argive, have dealt Argives, by joining your army to ours and going against the false Trojans as our ally."

Slowly and painfully Telephus half rose from his couch, for he was suffering from the wound inflicted on him by Achilles, and replied in a friendly manner: "My countrymen, your reproaches are unjust! It is your own fault that you are my enemies instead of friends and kinsmen in whose veins flows the same blood as mine. In asking you who you were and where you came from, the coast guards only did as I had ordered. They did not approach you like savage barbarians, but according to the laws governing Argive peoples. But you, thinking that anything at all was permissible in dealing with barbarians, leaped ashore without giving them the information they courteously asked, and killed my subjects without even listening to their words. And I too"—here he pointed to his thigh—"have received a memento which, I fear, will remind me of yesterday's encounter as long as I live. But I bear you no grudge for this and think no price too dear for the pleasure of entertaining kinsmen and fellow Argives in my country. As to your request that I join you in your campaign—do not expect me to fight against Priam! Astyoche, my second wife, is his daughter. Aside from this, he is a noble old man, and the rest of his sons are honest and steadfast and have no share in the escapades of frivolous Paris. See, this is my son Eurypylus! How could I grieve by giving aid to destroy his grandfather's realm? But though I do not wish to hurt Priam, neither do I want to harm my kinsmen. So accept from me the gifts of a host and take all the provisions you require. Then go and fight out your feud, which the gods must decide, for I cannot take the part of one or the other."

The three princes reported this kindly answer in the camp of the Argives and with great satisfaction told Agamemnon and the other leaders of the host that they had established bonds of friendship with Telephus. The war council immediately decided to send Ajax and Achilles to the king to confirm this cordial relationship and express sympathy for the pain he bore from the wound he had received. They found Telephus in great anguish, and Achilles wept and threw himself across his couch, lamenting that he had unwittingly struck the brave son of Heracles. But the king forgot the smart of his wound in joy at their coming, and only grieved that he had not known of their arrival in time to prepare a royal welcome for his noble guests. Then he solemnly invited the Atridae into the palace, served a lavish feast, and showered them with magnificent gifts. At the request of Achilles, Menelaus and Agamemnon had brought with them Podalirius and Machaon, physicians famed through all the world, to examine and heal the wound of Telephus. This, however, they could not do, for the spear of the son of Thetis was endowed with peculiar powers, and the wounds he struck defied cure. But they could at least alleviate the worst pain with soothing poultices, and the king, eased for the moment, gave the Achaeans much valuable counsel, furnished them with provisions for the entire fleet, and did not permit them to leave until the stormiest part of the winter, which had just begun when they landed, was over. He described to them the exact site of Troy, gave them directions how to go there, and told them that the only good landing place was in the mouth of the river Scamander.

PARIS RETURNS

Although the Trojans did not know that a great fleet had already reached their shores, the city had been in a turmoil ever since the Argive envoys had departed, for everyone feared war. Paris, the while, had returned with his beautiful prize and the ships with which he had set out. King Priam was ill pleased with this un-welcome daughter-in-law and at once summoned his numerous sons to a council of princes. But they were quickly beguiled by the gleam of the treasures their brother was so ready to share with them, and by the loveliness of the maidens Helen had brought in her train. These Paris was very willing to give in marriage to those who were still unwed. Besides, most of the brothers were young and all of them eager to fight, so the upshot of the discussion was that the stranger was to be taken into the palace and not handed over to the Achaeans. Matters were quite different among the common people! Fearing a siege of their city, they had not hailed the arrival of the prince and the fair woman he had carried off. Many a curse had speeded him on his way, and here and there even a stone was cast as he conducted his stolen bride to his father. But reverence for the old king and reluctance to cross his will restrained the Trojans from opposing this new resident of the palace more resolutely.

Now that the council called by Priam had decided not to drive Helen from the land, the king sent Hecuba to her to the women's chamber, in order to convince himself that the wife of Menelaus had really come to Troy of her own free will. Helen declared that her ancestry made her just as much kin to the Trojans as to the Danai, for Danaus and Agenor were her own forbears as well as those of the Trojan royal line; that she had, indeed, been carried off against her will, but that, having belonged to Paris for so long a time, she now loved this new husband of hers and wished to remain with him. Furthermore—so she said—she could hardly expect either her first husband or her people to pardon her, so that nothing but disgrace and death were in store for her should they yield her up to the Argives.

As she spoke her face was bathed in tears, and she threw herself at Hecuba's feet. The queen raised her tenderly and told her that the king and his sons had resolved to protect her from any attack that might threaten.

THE ARGIVES BEFORE TROY

For a while Helen lived at her ease at the court of the king of Troy and then moved with Paris to a palace of her own. The people grew to admire her loveliness and beauty, and when the alien fleet actually was sighted off the coast of Troy, the citizens were less intimidated than when they had feared some vague peril to come.

The leaders took stock of the inhabitants and of the allies who had promised to come to their aid and found that in numbers and equipment they equalled the Argives. And so, with the help of the immortals—for besides Aphrodite, several other gods, among them Ares, the war-god, Apollo, and even Zeus, the father of the gods, were on their side—they hoped to withstand the siege of their city and force the enemy to retreat after not too long a time.

King Priam himself was too old to fight, but he had fifty splendid sons of all ages, of whom Hecuba had borne him nineteen: some in the flower of youth, some at the peak of their strength—before all Hector, then Deiphobus, and the most distinguished after these, Helenus, the soothsayer, Pammon, Polites, Antiphus, Hipponous, and handsome Troilus. Four lovely daughters gathered round his throne: Creusa, Laodice, Cassandra, and Polyxena, who even in early childhood had been surpassingly beautiful. Chief of the host now preparing for battle was Hector, tall in his crested helmet. Next in power was Aeneas, King Priam's son-in-law, Creusa's husband, a son of Aphrodite and Anchises, the aged hero who was still the pride of the Trojans. Another battalion was led by Pandarus, son of Lycaon, whose bow had been given him by Apollo himself. Other battalions, some of which were made up of the allies of Troy, were headed by Adrastus, Amphius, Asius, Hippothous, Pylaeus, Acamas, Euphemus, Pyraechmes, Pylaemenes, Hodius, and Epistrophus. Chromius and Ennomus were the leaders of auxiliaries from Mysia; Phorcys and Ascanius of similar forces from Phrygia; Mesthles and Antiphus of Maeonians; Nastes and Amphimachus of Carians; and Sarpedon and Glaucus of a Lycian army.

In the meantime, the Argives had landed and settled along the shore between the two promontories of Sigeum and Rhoeteum. Their camp was so vast that it looked not unlike an entire city. They had beached their ships and placed them in rows, one behind the other, and, since the ground sloped up from the coast, the vessels stood in tiers. The sections of the fleet belonging to the various peoples who had joined in the expedition were ranged in the order in which they had landed. Each vessel was set on a base of stones, lest the keel rot from the moisture of the ground; in this way the air could pass around and beneath them. In the first row, seen from the land, were the ships of Ajax and Achilles. Both had built their huts facing toward Troy. That of Achilles was more like a comfortable house. Attached to it were barns and stables for supplies, chariot-horses, and cattle. And beside his ship there was room for races, burial rites and games, and other festivities. Next to the ship of Ajax came that of Protesilaus, then those of other Thessalians, then of the Cretans, Athenians, Phocians, Boeotians, and the last in the first row were those of Achilles and his Myrmidons. In the second row were the Locrians among others, the Dulichians, and the Epeans; in the third were the ships of less well-known peoples, but also those of Nestor with the Pylians, Eurypylus with the Ormenians, and finally Menelaus. In the fourth and last row along the coast and nearest to the sea were Diomedes, Odysseus, and Agamemnon: Odysseus in the middle, Agamemnon to the right, and Diomedes to the left.

Before the house of Odysseus was the *agora*, the open place where assemblies and councils were to be held and where altars had been reared to the gods. This open place ran through the third row also and divided it, so that Nestor was to the right and Eurypylus to the left. Toward the sea there was less space to begin with, and the *agora* took up so much room that the third and fourth rows numbered the least ships. The camp with its ships and huts was like a city cut by many streets and alleys, but the main thoroughfares ran lengthwise through all four rows.

From the land to the sea were cross streets which separated the ships of the various nations. The ships, in turn, were divided off from the huts of their crews by narrower spaces, and every nation was subdivided into several parts, according to cities or leaders. The huts were made of wood and earth and covered with reeds. Every leader had his quarters in the foremost row of his men, and every one of these lodgings was more or less elaborate according to the rank of its owner. The ships served to protect the camp as a whole. But in front of this bulwark of the fleet the Argives had heaped earth, which made way for a true wall with towers only during the last period of the siege. In front of this barricade of earth was a trench, and within it, a close-set palisade.

The king and the council of Troy had taken so long to confer on the best means of defense that the Argives had had ample opportunity to set up their camp in so careful a fashion and to complete all their arrangements. Each of the warriors had also to tend the ships. Bread was apportioned to everyone at public stations. For all other matters necessary for life, each was responsible for himself. The common soldiers had light weapons and fought on foot. Those of higher rank fought from chariots, and every one of these fighters had his own charioteer. The use of cavalry in wars was unknown to the peoples of that time. The chariots of the greatest among the heroes were intended for the front row, and always had to be the vanguard.

In the region between the Argive fleet and the city of Troy, the rivers Scamander and Simois, which joined near the camp of the Danai, enclosed the flowering meadows of the Scamander and the plains of Troy. This space was so large that it took four hours to cross it on foot. It was admirably suited for a battlefield. Behind it rose the stately city of Troy with high walls and ramparts and towers built by the hands of gods. It was situated on a height and could be seen from far off. Within, the city was hilly and cut by many thoroughfares. It was accessible—and even then only half accessible—from two sides only. On one of these stood the Scaean Gates, on the other the Dardanian Gates, both with towers. The other sides were on such uneven ground, and the undergrowth was so thick and tangled, that to enter through their gates and smaller entrances could not even be considered.

In the upper city or acropolis were the palaces of Priam and Paris, the temples of Hecate, Athene, and Apollo, and on the loftiest point the temple of Zeus. In front of the city, near the river Simois and to the left of the Argives, was the hill Callicolone; to the right, the road ran by the springs of the Scamander and then past the hill called Batieia, which lay outside the town and could be circumvented. Behind Troy was the Field of Ilium, which sloped gently upward and formed the lowest level of the wooded range of Ida, whose highest peak was Gargaron, and whose two topmost ridges to the right and left of the Argives constituted the promontories of Sigeum and Rhoeteum.

Before the battle between Danai and Trojans began, the Danai were privileged to receive an honored guest. King Telephus of Mysia, who had given them such generous aid, had been suffering from the wound dealt by Achilles' spear and the poultices prescribed by Podalirius and Machaon had long since ceased to be effective. In the throes of unbearable pain, he had consulted an oracle of Phoebus Apollo which was in his country and received the answer that only the spear which had given the wound could heal it. Though he was unable to fathom the meaning of these strange words, he had himself carried on a ship and followed the Argive fleet. When he reached the mouth of the Scamander, he ordered his men to take him to the house of Achilles. The moment the young hero saw the king in his suffering, his own pain at what he had done woke afresh. Sadly he took up his spear and laid it at the foot of the king's bed, for he did not know in what way it could serve to heal the festering wound. A number of heroes surrounded the king and all were helpless in this matter, until Odysseus thought of again consulting the two famed physicians who traveled with the host. Podalirius and Machaon obeyed the summons, and the instant they heard the oracle of Apollo, these wise and experienced sons of Asclepius understood what was meant. They filed a little of the rust from the spear of Achilles and spread it over the wound. And then all saw a miracle: as soon as the filings touched the swollen and infected wound, it began to close before the very eyes of the heroes; in a few hours, noble King Telephus was healed with the help of the spear which had pierced him, just as the oracle had predicted. Sound and joyful he boarded his ship and left his hosts as they had but recently left him: with gratitude and blessings. But he hastened back to his own country, since he did not wish to witness the forth-coming struggle between the guests he had cherished and the Trojan kinsmen he loved.

FIGHTING BEGINS. PROTESILAUS. CYCNUS

While the Argives were taking King Telephus and his retinue to his ship, the gates of Troy suddenly flew open and the Trojan army in full battle array poured across the plain of the Scamander. Under the leadership of Hector, they moved toward the fleet of the unsuspecting Danai without meeting resistance. Those of the Argives who were camped farthest from the shore seized their weapons and advanced in scattered groups, but they were quickly dispatched by the foe who far outnumbered them. But even this brief struggle detained the Trojans long enough for the other Argives to assemble and advance on the enemy in ordered battle formation. Now the fighting began, but the fortunes of war were very uneven; for wherever Hector appeared the Trojans gained the upper hand, but those Dardanian warriors who fought far from him were beaten and scattered by the Argives. Among the Achaean heroes slain by the sword of Aeneas was Protesilaus, son of Iphicles. He had left for Troy as a youth, as the betrothed of the fair daughter of Acastus, the Argonaut, and he had been first to leap ashore at the landing. Now he was first to die, and never would Laodamia hail the return of the bridegroom to whom she had bidden such a sorrowful farewell.

Achilles was still far from the battlefield. He had accompanied Telephus, the king of Mysia, first wounded and then healed by his spear, down to the sea, and with thoughtful eyes watched the ship as it sailed on and faded into the distance. Suddenly he felt a hand on his shoulder, and Patroclus, his friend and comrade-in-arms, cried: "Where have you been? The Argives need you! The fighting has begun! Hector, King Priam's eldest son, rages at the head of his troops like a lion whose den is surrounded by hunters. Aeneas, the king's son-in-law, has slain noble Protesilaus, your equal in youth and courage though not in strength. If you do not come, more of our heroes will be killed!"

Achilles started from his dream. He turned and saw his friend, and at the same moment he heard the distant clash of battle. Without answering he raced through the streets of the camp, making straight for his house. Once there, he found his tongue, called his Myrmidons to arms in ringing tones, and surged forward with them like stormwind and thunder. Even Hector could not withstand the force of his attack. The son of Peleus slew two sons of Priam, and from the walls the king mourned his children who had died at the hand of the Argive. Ajax fought close to Achilles. His tall form loomed above all the other Achaeans. From the strokes of these two heroes the Trojans fled like a herd of deer before a pack of hounds. They retreated to their city, and the gates of Troy closed behind them. But the Danai calmly returned to their ships and continued building their camp. Agamemnon appointed Achilles and Ajax to guard the ships, and they in turn had other heroes watch the various parts of the fleet.

Then they set about the burial of Protesilaus. They laid his body on a pyre, high-heaped and adorned, and under tall elms with far flung branches they buried his bones on the shore, where the land jutted out into the sea. Hardly had they finished performing the burial rites when a second attack surprised them in the midst of the funeral games.

Colonae, near Troy, was ruled by Cycnus. This king was a son of Poseidon, borne to the sea-god by a nymph, and reared by a swan on the island of Tenedos. For this reason he had been given the name of Cycnus, which means swan. He was an ally of Troy, and when he saw alien warriors landing, he considered himself duty-bound to come to the help of his old friend, even though King Priam had not summoned him. And so he assembled a sizable army, laid an ambush near the Argive camp, and had just settled in this hiding-place when the Danai returned as victors from their first encounter with the Trojans and began to pay the last honors to their dead. As they stood around the pyre, far from fully armed and intent only on the solemn rites they were performing, they found themselves suddenly surrounded by war chariots and warriors, and before they had time to wonder whether earth had spewed forth these fighters or where else they

had come from, King Cycnus and his men had begun their ruthless slaughter.

But only a part of the Argives had attended the burial of
Protesilaus. The others, who were near the ships or in their huts,
had their weapons close to hand and, headed by Achilles, swiftly
came to the aid of their fellows in full-armed serried ranks. Their
leader, the son of Peleus, stood in his chariot, striking terror into
all who beheld him, and with his death-bringing lance pierced
now one, now another of the Colonians until, penetrating the
enemy host, he discerned their commander-in-chief by the mighty
thrusts he dealt right and left, standing erect in his battle chariot.
Toward him Achilles drove his snow-white horses, and face to
face with Cycnus he swung his lance with sinewy arm, calling
out: "Whoever you may be, let this comfort you in death: that it
is Achilles, son of Thetis, who has struck you down!" His lance
followed close on his words, but though he had aimed straight
and sure the point only grazed the breast of Poseidon's son with
a faint thud. Achilles measured his opponent with wondering
eyes, for he seemed invulnerable.

"Do not be so amazed," Cycnus said to him smilingly. "It is not
my helmet, which you are regarding with such astonishment, and
not the hollow shield in my left hand which ward the strokes from
my body. I wear these merely for adornment, as Ares, the god
of war, sometimes dons weapons in jest, for he does not need
them to protect his immortal body. Even if I take off all my
armor, your spear will not so much as scratch my skin. For from
head to foot I am hard as iron. After all, you must realize that
it means something to be, not the son of a mere sea-nymph, but
the cherished son of him who rules over Nereus and all his
daughters and all the seas. You are face to face with the son
of Poseidon himself!"

With these words he cast his spear at Achilles. The point
pierced his shield and passed through the bronze and nine layers
of oxhide, but in the tenth it stuck. Achilles shook his shield until
the lance fell out and in return hurled his at Cycnus. But still he
was not harmed by it, and even the third lance Achilles flung at
him left him whole and sound. And now the son of Peleus grew
furious as a bull who runs at a red cloth held up to tantalize him
and thrusts his horns into empty air. Once more he aimed his

lance, carved of ash, at his opponent, smote his left shoulder, and shouted with joy to see blood on it. But he did not exult for long, for the blood was not that of Poseidon's son. It came from a wound Menoetes, fighting beside Cycnus, had received from another hand. Gnashing his teeth with rage, Achilles leaped from his chariot, made for his enemy, and lunged out at him with his sword. But even this powerful weapon rebounded from that iron flesh. Then in despair Achilles raised his shield with its ten layers of hide and brought the buckle down on the temple of his invulnerable foe, three, four times. And now Cycnus faltered. His vision blurred. He retreated a few steps and stumbled over a stone. Achilles gripped him by the nape of the neck and threw him flat on the ground. Then, keeping his foe prostrate by pressing his shield and his knees against his breast, he strangled him with the strap of his own helmet.

When they saw their leader fall, the Colonians lost courage and sped from the battlefield in frantic flight. All that was left was a welter of bodies—Argives and barbarians—scattered about the half-finished burial mound of Protesilaus. And now the Argives mourned their dead and set about digging their graves.

The aftermath of this encounter was that the Danai invaded the realm of King Cycnus and from its capital, the city of Mentora, carried off his children as spoils. Then they attacked the neighboring city of Cilla, conquered it also, though it was well fortified, and returned to their carefully guarded camp, laden with vast stores of priceless booty.

THE DEATH OF PALAMEDES

Palamedes was the wisest man in the Argive army. All knew him
to be tireless, just, steadfast, and thoughtful. He was of delicate build and versed in the art of singing and playing the lyre.
It was his eloquence that had swayed the greater part of the
princes of Greece in favor of the campaign against Troy, and
his shrewdness that had discovered the ruse of the wily son of
Laertes. But this had gained him an implacable foe, one who
pondered revenge day and night and who brooded the more sullenly the more wise Palamedes was honored by the other princes.
Now an oracle of Apollo informed the Argives that in the place
where his statue and his temple stood they were to sacrifice a
hecatomb to Apollo Smintheus—the name he was known by in
Troy—and that Palamedes had been chosen to take the victims
to their destination. Chryses, the priest of Apollo, was to receive
the stately animals and make the offering. The worship of the
sun-god in this region was of curious origin. In earlier times,
when King Teucer and his men had come from Crete and landed
on this part of the coast of Asia Minor, an oracle commanded
them to remain where their enemies would crawl out of the
ground. Now when they arrived in Hamaxitus, a city in that
region, mice, slipping out of holes in the earth, came at night
and gnawed at their shields. This they regarded as the fulfillment of the oracle and therefore they settled in that vicinity and
erected a statue to Apollo with a mouse at his feet. In the dialect
of Aeolia *sminthos* is the word for mouse.

So it was to Apollo Smintheus whose temple stood on a height
not far from Chryse that Chryses, the priest, offered the hundred sacred sheep brought there by Palamedes. The fact that
Apollo himself had chosen Palamedes for this and thus accorded
him special honor only hastened his destruction. For now Odysseus began to boil with envy and thought up a despicable plan to
put an end to his rival. With his own hands he concealed a sum
of money in the hut of the man he hated, going there in secrecy.
Then, in the name of Priam, he wrote a letter to Palamedes, in
which the king of Troy expressed thanks for his having betrayed

the secrets of the Argive host. This letter was allowed to fall into the hands of a captive from Phrygia, in whose possession Odysseus discovered it, apparently by chance. Immediately he ordered the innocent bearer killed. Then the son of Laertes showed the letter in an assembly of Argive princes. The indignant leaders summoned Palamedes to a council to which Agamemnon had appointed the foremost among the Achaeans and over which Odysseus had arranged to preside. At his suggestion, men were sent to dig in the accused man's hut, and, of course, they found the gold Odysseus himself had buried under Palamedes' couch. The judges, knowing nothing of the true state of affairs, unanimously condemned him to death. Palamedes did not deign to defend himself. He saw through the plot but had no hope of proving either his own innocence or the guilt of his enemy. When he heard that he was to die by stoning, he only cried out: "O Argives, you are about to kill a nightingale, most innocent, most wise, and rich in moving song." But the dull princes only laughed at this singular form of defense and led Palamedes, the noblest among them, away to an unmerciful death, which he suffered with gentleness and courage. After the first stones had struck him down, he called: "Rejoice, O Truth, for you have died before me!" When he said these words, a stone thrown by vengeful Odysseus struck his temple, his head drooped and he died. But Nemesis, the patroness of justice, gazed down from the ramparts of heaven and resolved to punish the Achaeans and Odysseus, who had tricked them into this crime, at the very goal of their desires.

ACHILLES AND AJAX

Legend has little to tell of the next few years of the war against Troy. The Argives were not idle, but since the Trojans husbanded their strength and seldom attacked, they turned their attention to the region surrounding Troy. In the course of time Achilles destroyed and looted twelve towns with his ships and conquered eleven on land. In a marauding expedition to Mysia he carried off Chryseis, the lovely daughter of Chryses, a priest of Apollo. When he invaded Lyrnessus he took the palace of

Briseus, the king and priest of the city, who hanged himself with
a rope. Briseis, his beautiful daughter, who was also called
Hippodamia, fell into the hands of Achilles and he took her with
him as his favorite among the captives. The island of Lesbos and
Thebe in Cilicia, a city founded at the foot of Mount Placus,
were also forced to yield to him.

The king of this city was Eetion, a son-in-law of Priam, since
his daughter Andromache had wedded Hector, the greatest
among the heroes of Troy. Seven sons, in the flower of youth,
were still in their father's palace. But Achilles stormed the high
gates and slew the king with all seven of them. When Eetion's
body lay upon its bier in forbidding majesty, young Achilles
was shaken with dread and dared not strip the dead king of his
arms and vaunt them as his spoils. He had the corpse burned,
clad in the full glory of armor artfully wrought of shining
metals, and heaped for Eetion a mighty burial mound which for
many years adorned the region. It loomed high under the shadow
of stately elms. But he carried off Eetion's wife as a slave. Later
he released her for a large ransom. She returned home, where an
arrow launched by Artemis killed her as she sat weaving at the
loom. Out of the king's stables Achilles took Pedasus, his slender-
ankled horse, which, though born and bred on earth, equalled
his own immortal steeds in strength and speed and vied with them
in running at the chariot. And from the armory of King Eetion
he carried off splendid spoils, among them an iron discus so huge
that it would have yielded enough metal to make all the field
implements a peasant needed for five years.

After Achilles, the tallest and bravest of the heroes was Ajax,
son of Telamon. He too did not waste his time in idle waiting but
took his ships toward the Thracian Chersonesus, where Polymnestor had his palace. To this king, Priam of Troy had sent his
youngest son Polydorus, whom Laothoë, a concubine, had borne
him, for he wanted him reared in Thrace, safe from war. He had
given gold and treasure to Polymnestor to pay for the care and
upbringing of the child. But when Ajax invaded his country and
besieged his citadel, the faithless barbarian used both the funds
and the boy entrusted to him to buy peace from the Argives. He
betrayed King Priam, heaped him with imprecations, and divided the money and grain he had received for the nurture of

Polydorus among the Achaean fighters. To Ajax himself he gave the gold and treasure of his ally and finally the boy as well.

Ajax did not immediately return to the Argive fleet with his spoils but made for the coast of Phrygia. There he attacked the realm of Teuthras, slew the king, who met him at the head of his warriors, and took captive his daughter, queenly Tecmessa. Her great beauty and noble spirit commanded his esteem and won his love. He honored her as his wife and would have married her, had Argive custom permitted him to wed a barbarian.

Returning from their successful marauding expeditions, the son of Peleus and the son of Telamon arrived at the camp before Troy at the same time, their ships laden with spoils. The Danai went to the shore to meet them and broke into loud cheers. Heroes thronged around Ajax and Achilles who stood in the midst of the gathering and received the prize of victory: the olive wreath, set on their heads with joyful acclaim. After this ceremony a council was held for the distribution of the spoils which were considered common property among the Achaeans. And now the captive women were shown and all marvelled at their beauty. Achilles was given the daughter of Briseus and Ajax was confirmed in the possession of queenly Tecmessa. The son of Peleus was, moreover, permitted to keep Diomedea, the playmate of his beloved, who had refused to be parted from the friend she had grown up with in the house of Briseus. When she was brought before the heroes, she threw herself at the feet of Achilles, imploring him with tears not to part her from her young mistress. Chryseis, the daughter of Chryses, the priest, was given to Agamemnon, the leader of the entire host, as a mark of honor to his kingship, and Achilles granted her willingly. The other spoils of war—captives and provisions—were divided equally among the warriors. At the request of Odysseus and Diomedes, Ajax had the treasure of King Polymnestor unloaded from his ships. Of this also Agamemnon was awarded an ample share of silver and gold.

POLYDORUS

And now the heroes took counsel about the most precious part of their spoils, the boy Polydorus, son of the king of Troy. After a brief discussion, they decided that Odysseus and Diomedes should be sent to Priam to offer him his young son in exchange for Helen. Menelaus, Helen's husband, was appointed a third envoy, and the three set out with young Polydorus. The Trojans admitted them to their city without demurring, for envoys were held sacred according to the laws which governed the intercourse between nations.

Priam and his sons, remote from the city in their palace on the acropolis, had not even heard what was happening below, when the envoys arrived in the market place of Troy. Surrounded by throngs of Trojans, Menelaus addressed his audience, complaining bitterly of the grave breach of hospitality Paris had committed by carrying off his most prized possession—Helen, his wife. He spoke so eloquently and with such ardor that the crowd, among them the elders and leaders of Troy, were moved by his words. They wept tears of pity for his plight and agreed that his claims were just. When Odysseus observed which way the wind was blowing, he too began to speak. "Elders and citizens of Troy," he said, "I think you should know that the Argives are not a people to embark lightly on any enterprise, and that it has always been their custom to look for glory in all they undertake. Even after the outrage we suffered when Paris, the son of your king, carried off Helen, an Argive princess, we sent peaceful envoys to you to settle this matter in friendly fashion before we prepared to take to arms. It was only when our embassy failed that war began, and it began with an attack of your men against ours! Even now that you have felt our strength, now that cities allied or subject to you lie in ruins and you yourselves have suffered the hardship long siege brings with it, a happy issue from our quarrel is still within your power. Give up to us what was taken from us, and we shall instantly break camp, board our ships, weigh anchor, and forever leave your coast with the fleet that has already done you so much harm. Nor do we make this offer empty-handed. We are bringing your king a treasure which should be far dearer to him than the stranger your city has been forced to shelter to his disadvantage and yours. We bring Polydorus, his youngest son, whom Ajax took from King Polymnestor, and who now stands bound before you, waiting your decision and that of the king. This very day give us Helen, and we shall loose the bonds of the boy and return him to his father's house. If you refuse, your city will be destroyed, and before that your king will have to look on what he would give his life not to see."

When Odysseus had ended, deep silence prevailed among the Trojans. At last Antenor, aged and wise, answered: "You Argives, who were once my dear guests! All that you say we know ourselves and in our hearts we agree with you. But though we have the will to mend this matter, we lack the power. We live in a state in which the king is all-powerful. The laws of our realm, the faith we have inherited from our fathers, and the conscience of our people deter us from revolt against his commands. Only if the king summons us to council are we permitted to speak on public affairs, and when we have spoken, he is still free to do as he wishes. But that you may know what the best among our people think concerning your claim, our elders will assemble and speak their mind in your presence. This is all we can do, and even the king cannot deny us this right."

And so it was done. Antenor called a council of the elders and the envoys attended it with him. One by one he asked the foremost among his people what they thought of high-handed Paris, and one by one they declared his action insolent and lawless. Only Antimachus, a man full of malice and eager for battle, defended the rape of the Argive princess. Paris had bribed him with many gifts so that he might take his part whenever occasion demanded and speak against the return of Helen to her people. Now too he worked toward this end and behind the backs of the elders he counselled the Trojans to kill the three brave and wise heroes whom the Achaeans had sent as envoys. When they refused he advised them to hold prisoner Odysseus, Diomedes, and Menelaus, at least until they had yielded up their captive, Polydorus, without ransom or any talk of exchange. This counsel was also rejected, and since Antimachus would not stop mocking at the Argive heroes, even in public assembly, his fellow citizens drove him from their midst with sharp words, to show the envoys that they disapproved of his advice and his unprincipled behavior.

Angrily Antimachus hastened to the acropolis and told the king what had taken place. And now Priam and his sons held council, and noble Panthous, his trusted friend, was with them. For a long time they argued the matter, some saying one thing, some another. At last Panthous turned to Hector, the bravest and the most just and virtuous of Priam's sons, and begged him to yield to the counsel of the best among the Trojans and surrender the cause of this war—Helen, who had brought nothing but disaster to her hosts. "Paris," he said, "has now had many years in which to enjoy the possession he acquired so unfairly, and also to suffer for his delight. The cities which were our allies are destroyed, and their fall forewarns us of our own fate. Add to this that the Argives have your little brother in their power and that we do not know what will become of him if we refuse to give them Helen!"

Hector reddened with shame and tears welled up in his eyes when he thought of the infamous act of Paris. Nevertheless he did not speak in favor of delivering up the stolen princess. "She is one who sought protection in our house," he answered Panthous. "We must not forget that. As such we received her. Had we thought otherwise, we should not have permitted her to cross the threshold of the palace. Not only did we let her enter, we even built her and Paris a palace of their own where they have lived in luxury and pleasure for many years, and none of you opened his mouth against it, though you knew that war was inevitable. Why should we drive her from us now?"

"I did speak out," Panthous replied. "My conscience is clear. I told you of my father's prophecy. I warned you. And I warn you again! Come what will, I shall faithfully help you defend the king and the city, even if you do not do as I say." And with these words he left the council of the princes.

At Hector's suggestion they at last came to the decision that they would not give up Helen, but would replace with gifts of equal value everything which had been carried off along with her. In her stead they would offer Menelaus one of the daughters of King Priam in wedlock—wise Cassandra or flower-like Polyxena, and with her a royal dowry. When the Argive envoys were brought before the king and faced with this proposal Menelaus grew very angry. "Things have, indeed, come to a pretty pass," he said, "if after years of doing without the woman of my choice I must let my enemies select a wife for me! Keep your barbarian daughters and return to me her whom I wedded when I was young."

Then up rose Aeneas, husband of Creusa and son-in-law of Priam, and harshly cried out to Prince Menelaus who had spoken with a scornful smile: "If it depended on me and on the word of all those who love Paris and hold high the honor of this ancient house of kings, you should have neither the one nor the other. The kingdom of Priam still has men who will protect it. And if the boy Polydorus, the son of his concubine, be lost to him, Priam has many other sons. Shall we encourage the Argives to carry off more women? But enough of talk! If you do not instantly leave with that fleet of yours, you shall feel the strength of the Trojans. We have countless young warriors thirsting to fight, and every day more and more great and powerful allies are joining us, even if those nearby weakened and were conquered."

These words of Aeneas were greeted with tumultuous applause on the part of the Trojan princes, and had it not been for Hector, the envoys would have suffered rough treatment at their hands. These, ill suppressing their rage, left with Polydorus, whom King Priam had seen only from afar, and returned to their ships. When the news spread of the reception they had met with in Troy, news of the malice of Antimachus and the arrogance of Aeneas and all the sons of Priam except Hector, the Argives gathered in a riotous mob and angrily called for revenge. Without even consulting the princes, a disorderly and confused assembly resolved to visit the wrongs of Priam and his sons on luckless Polydorus, and they at once set about carrying out their verdict. The boy was taken within range of the walls of Troy and the moment King Priam and his sons appeared on the walls, called out by the great throngs and the loud clamor, the first moan of pain broke from the child's lips. With their own eyes the Trojans were forced to witness the execution of the threat Odysseus had uttered. From all sides stones flew at the boy's bare head and unprotected body, until, struck down by countless missiles, he died a cruel and miserable death. The Argive princes gave permission for the shattered corpse to be returned to Priam for honorable burial; soon the king's servants, accompanied by Idaeus, a hero of Troy, came and with many tears laid the boy's body in the wagon which was to take him to his unhappy father.

CHRYSES, APOLLO, AND THE WRATH OF ACHILLES

It was early in the tenth year of the war. Ajax had returned from various expeditions along the coast, laden with spoils. The killing of Polydorus had fanned the hatred between the two nations to greater fury, and now the gods openly took part in the conflict. Hera, Athene, Hermes, Poseidon, and Hephaestus sided with the Argives, while Ares and Aphrodite helped the Trojans, so that of this tenth and last year of the siege of Troy ten times more has been told and sung than of the nine years which went before. For it is at this point that Homer, the prince of poets, begins his tale of the wrath of Achilles and the many misfortunes which the anger of this greatest among their heroes brought upon the Argives.

The cause of Achilles' anger was this. When their envoys returned from Troy, the Argives, mindful of the threats of the Trojans, set about preparing for decisive battle. While they were so engaged, Chryses, Apollo's priest, whose daughter Achilles had carried off and given to Agamemnon, came into the camp holding the golden staff of peace twined with the laurel sacred to his god, and offered rich ransom for the return of his child. He made this request to the Atridae and the entire host, saying: "Sons of Atreus, heroes and men of Greece, may the gods on Olympus grant you victory over Troy and a safe homeward journey, if you give honor to Apollo the Far-Darter, whose priest I am, by returning my beloved daughter to me for the ransom I bring you."

The host applauded his words and recommended that reverence be shown the priest and that the treasure he offered be accepted. But Agamemnon, unwilling to lose his fair prize, objected, saying: "Do not let me find you near the ships again, old man, either now or in the days to come. Your daughter is my servant and shall remain so. She will sit at the loom in my palace in Argos as long as she lives. Beware of provoking my wrath, and go while you can!"

Chryses was filled with fear and obeyed. Silently he hastened to the shore, but there he lifted his hands to the god he served and prayed to him: "Hear me, Apollo Smintheus, you who reign over Chryse, Cilla, and Tenedos! If ever I have adorned your altar to your liking and brought you offerings carefully chosen, avenge me on the Achaeans and loose your darts upon them!"

So he pleaded aloud, and Apollo heard his prayer. He slung across his shoulder his bow and quiver filled with clanging arrows and left Olympus. Sullen and threatening as night he sped toward the Argive ships and when he was near them, dart after dart whirred from his silver bow and the taut string twanged with an ominous sound. Whoever was struck by the invisible arrow died of the plague—a swift and sudden death. At first he shot only at the mules and dogs in the camp, but soon he aimed at the men as well, until one after another sank to the ground and the flames of many funeral pyres flared day and night unceasingly.

For nine days the plague raged among the Argive host. On the tenth, Achilles, whom Hera, the patron goddess of the Achaeans, had so counselled, called an assembly and advised the people to ask a priest, a soothsayer, or one who unravels the meaning of dreams, what sacrifice would avert the wrath of Phoebus Apollo and turn disaster from the camp.

Then the wisest seer in the host arose, Calchas, who prophesied from the flight of birds and declared that he was ready to expound the reasons for the anger of the immortal archer, provided Achilles would protect him. The son of Peleus bade him be of good courage and Calchas spoke: "The god is not offended because of a broken vow or neglect of sacrifice. He is angry because of Agamemnon's lack of respect for his priest, nor will he stay his hand from dealing us evil until the girl is returned to her father without ransom and sent back to Chryse with hundredfold offerings of atonement. This is the only way in which we can win back the favor of the god."

At these words Agamemnon's blood beat hotly in his veins.

His eyes blazed and he addressed the seer with beetling brows: "You prophet of ill omen, you who have never yet said anything that prospered me, now you arouse the people against me by claiming the Archer has sent us the plague because I refused ransom for the daughter of Chryses! It is true: I should like to keep her in my house, for she is dearer to me than Clytaemnestra, the wife of my youth, and her equal in beauty of body and loveliness of face, in wisdom and skill. But rather than see Argive warriors perish I shall send her back. If I do this, however, I demand a gift in return!"

When the king had ended, Achilles replied: "Great son of Atreus," he said, "I do not know what gift, in your greed, you demand of the Argives. We have no longer any great stores of treasure in common. The spoils we took from the cities we conquered were distributed among us long ago, and surely we cannot take from a man what has already been given him! Therefore, release the daughter of Chryses! If Zeus, in the days to come, accords us the conquest of Troy, we shall make up your loss to you three, no, four times over!"

"Son of Peleus," the king called to him, "do not think you can cheat me! Do you fancy I shall do as you say and give up my prize of war while you keep yours? No! If the Argives deny me recompense, I shall fetch myself what I want from one or another of you, a gift belonging to Ajax, or Odysseus, or perhaps to you, Achilles! It does not matter to me how angry you may be! But of that we shall speak another time. Now make ready a ship and a hecatomb. Put the fair-skinned daughter of Chryses aboard and let one of the princes, the son of Peleus for all I care, command the ship."

The eyes of Achilles grew dark with anger as he answered: "O shameless prince, you who think only of your own ease, how can the Danai obey one such as you? I, to whom the Trojans did no wrong, followed you to help you avenge Menelaus, your brother. But you forget this and try to take from me the prize I won by my own effort, the prize the Achaeans allotted to me. City after city I conquered and yet I never received a share like yours. I always bore the brunt of the struggle, but when it came to dividing the spoils, you carried off the best part while I returned to the ships weary of battle and content with the little

I had. But now I am going home to Phthia. No more shall I increase the toppling stores of your treasure."

"Very well, flee if you must," Agamemnon replied. "I have brave men enough without you, and besides you are one who is always ready to quarrel. But first I want you to know that I am, indeed, returning the daughter of Chryses to her father, but instead I shall take from your house lovely Briseis, to teach you that I am greater than you and to warn others not to defy me as you have done."

Achilles' heart swelled with fury and he hesitated whether to bare his sword on the instant and slay the son of Atreus, or to bridle his rage. But suddenly, invisible to all the rest, Athene stood behind him and revealed herself to him by catching at a lock of his brown hair. "Curb your anger," she whispered. "Do not draw your sword. But you may fume with words to your heart's content. If you obey me, I pledge you a threefold gift."

When Achilles heard her warning, he thrust the silver hilt of his sword back into the scabbard. But to his words he gave free rein. "Unworthy son of Atreus," he said, "never did your own heart teach you to lay an ambush with the noblest among the Argives or to fight in the foremost ranks in pitched battle! It is, of course, much easier to steal a prize from one who has dared to oppose you. But I swear to you by this staff that just as surely as it will not put forth green shoots as it did when it branched on a tree, so from this time on you shall not see the son of Peleus in battle. In vain will you look for aid when Hector, the killer of men, mows down the Argives row on row. In vain will bitterness gnaw at your soul for having denied due honors to the noblest among the Achaeans." So said Achilles, and he threw his staff on the ground and sat down. Aged Nestor tried to reconcile the opponents with calm and gentle words, but to no avail.

Finally Achilles rose from his seat in the assembly and called to the king: "Do what you will, only do not imagine that I shall obey you! Never shall I lift my arm against you or another for the sake of this girl. You gave her to me and you may take her her from me. But do not attempt to touch the very least of the other possessions in my house or my ships, for if you do, my lance will drip with your blood."

The assembly dispersed. Agamemnon had the daughter of Chryses and the hecatomb put aboard ship and bade Odysseus take it to its destination. Then the son of Atreus summoned Talthybius and Eurybates, the heralds, and commanded them to fetch him Briseis from the house of Achilles. Unwillingly they went, and only for fear of their king. When they reached the camp they found the son of Peleus sitting in front of his house, and he was not happy to see them. Reverence and timidity sealed their lips so that they did not tell him why they had come, but he had already guessed their purpose. "Do not be distressed," he said to them. "Approach, O heralds of Zeus and of mortals. The fault is not yours but Agamemnon's. Come, Patroclus, bring the girl and give her over to them. But they shall bear witness to me before gods and men that if, in the days to come, anyone requires my help and it is not given, not I shall have the blame but the son of Atreus!"

Patroclus, Achilles' friend, led out Briseis who followed the heralds reluctantly, for she had learned to love her gentle lord. As he sat weeping on the shore, he gazed down into the dark sea and begged Thetis, his mother, to help him. And from the depths of the waters he heard her voice. "Woe to me, my child, that ever I bore you. So brief is your life to be, and yet you must suffer such insult and sorrow! But I myself shall go to the Thunderer and implore him to give you aid. It cannot be at once, for only yesterday he departed for Oceanus to a feast of the devout Ethiopians, and he will not return for twelve days. But on that twelfth day I shall hasten to him and clasp my hands about his knees. Until then, stay near your ships." When Achilles had received this answer from his mother, he left the shore and seated himself in his house in sullen silence.

In the meantime, Odysseus had reached Chryses and given his daughter back to him. Filled with joyful surprise the priest raised his hands to heaven in thanksgiving and begged Phoebus Apollo to avert the plague he had sent upon the Argives. Instantly the plague began to abate, and when Odysseus returned to camp he found that it had ended.

And now the twelfth day dawned since Achilles had withdrawn to his house, and Thetis did not forget her promise. Through the mist of early morning she rose from the sea and went up to Olympus. Here, on the loftiest peak of the jagged mountain, aloof from the other gods, she found imperious Zeus. Clasping his knees with her left hand and touching his chin with her right in the manner of suppliants, she said to him: "Father, if ever I have served you well with words or with deeds, grant me my prayer. Honor my son, whom Fate has doomed to die so soon. Agamemnon has offended him and taken away the prize he himself won as the spoils of war. And so I beg of you, father of all gods, let the Trojans keep winning until the Argives pay my son the honor that is his due." For a long time Zeus was silent and made not the slightest motion. But Thetis clung closer to his knees and whispered: "Now grant my request or refuse it flatly, to show me that among all the gods you favor me least."

So with her wiles and coaxing ways she beset Zeus until he answered, but his voice betrayed displeasure. "It is not well that you beseech me to act counter to the wishes of Hera who is always against me as it is. Leave quickly before she observes your presence and let my nod pledge you that I shall do as you have asked." Even as he spoke Zeus gave a faint token of assent with his eyebrows only, yet the great mountain of Olympus shook at the sign. Thetis, well pleased, hastened back into the deep waters of the sea. But Hera, who had seen them talking together, went to Zeus and vexed him with reproaches. He, however, replied calmly: "Do not think that you can fathom my decisions. Be still and obey my commands." And Hera trembled at the words of her husband, the father of gods and men, and did not venture to gainsay him or further object to the resolve he had taken.

AGAMEMNON TRIES THE ARGIVES

Zeus remembered the nod he had given Thetis, goddess of the sea. He sent the god of dreams to the Argive camp and bade him enter the tent of sleeping Agamemnon. And the dream god, assuming the form of Nestor, whom of all the elders Agamemnon honored most, stood at the head of the king's couch and spoke to him. "Are you still asleep, son of Atreus?" he asked. "The man who decides the actions of a whole people should not sleep so long. Hear what I have to say, for I have come to you as a messenger from Zeus. He commands you to muster the Argive hosts, for the hour to conquer Troy has come. The gods have made their decision and destruction hovers over the city."

Agamemnon awoke and swiftly rose from his couch. He bound his sandals to his feet, donned his tunic, slung his sword over his shoulder, seized his scepter, and strode toward the ships through the early morning mists. At his command the heralds went from hut to hut to call the men, but the princes of the host were summoned to council on Nestor's ship. Agamemnon was first to speak. "Friends," he said, "a heaven-sent dream, visiting me in the form of Nestor, revealed to me that Zeus is set on ruining Troy. Let us see whether we can rouse our men who have grown slack and discontented because of the wrath of Achilles. First I shall tempt them with words, counselling them to board the ships and leave the Trojan coast. Then it will be your turn. Disperse through the camp, some here, some there, and urge them to stay."

When Agamemnon had ended, Nestor rose and addressed the princes. "Had another told us of such a dream," he said, "we should brand him a liar and turn from him full of contempt. But since he who has spoken is the foremost prince among the Danai, we cannot but believe him. So let us follow his plan."

Nestor left the council and all the princes followed him to the market place where the men had gathered like a swarm of bees.

Nine heralds marshalled them into groups and seated them in a great circle; gradually their talk died down to whispers until at last there was silence. Then Agamemnon, standing in the midst of the gathering, raised his scepter and began: "Brave warriors of the Argive people who have come together here, Zeus has deceived me with blindness of soul, for though he once so graciously promised that I should return to my home as the destroyer of Troy, now he, who has shattered so many cities and in his great might will shatter still more, is pleased to command me to go back to Argos ingloriously, so that all those who have fallen will have died in vain. It would, indeed, be a disgrace if future generations learned that the great people of the Danai continued losing battles against enemies who are so much weaker. For if we were at peace and could measure the number of the Trojans against our own, if we assigned one Trojan as cup-bearer to every table of ten Achaeans—then many tables, I believe, would have to do without the cup. To be sure, they have powerful allies from many cities who hinder me from burning Troy to the ground, as I should like to do. Be that as it may—nine years have passed. The timbers of our ships are cracking, the ropes rot; our women and children wait at home, full of yearning for us. And so it is, perhaps, best to submit to the bidding of Zeus, go to our ships, and return to the dear land of our fathers."

Agamemnon's words stirred the throng to motion as a wind swells and churns the waves of the sea. In a moment the entire host was afoot in wild confusion. They rushed to the shore so swiftly that the dust whirled up in clouds. Each spurred on the other to drag the ships into the water. Here they pulled the prop from under a keel, there they cleared the channels connecting the camp with the sea.

Even up on Olympus those who supported the Argives were alarmed to see how earnestly they were taking Agamemnon at his word, and Hera urged Athene to hasten down to earth and with sweet persuasive words halt the flight of the Danai. Pallas Athene consented, and down from the craggy heights of Olympus she flew to the Argive camp. Here she found Odysseus standing before his ship. He did not move or venture to lay his hand upon it, and grief ate at his heart. The goddess approached him, revealed herself, and said in a gentle voice: "And so you really want to flee? Will you let Priam triumph? You are willing to leave the Trojans Helen, because of whom so many Argives have given their lives far from their native land? Surely you will not allow this! Go quickly in and out among the host! Do not hold back now! Use all your shrewdness and eloquence! Reason with them, stop them!"

At Athene's words Odysseus threw off his mantle and hastened toward the people. Whenever he met a prince or a noble, he stopped him and spoke with kindness and insistence. "Is it right, my good and brave friend," he asked, "to give up the game like a coward? If you remained calm, you would calm the rest also. Remember that you do not know what the son of Atreus really thinks. Perhaps he was only trying the Argives!" But if he came upon a common man who was making a great noise and shouting, he struck him with his staff and threatened him in a loud voice: "Wretch! Stay where you are! Listen to what others say, you on whom no one can count either in battle or in the assembly! We Argives cannot all be kings. When many rule, no one prospers. To one alone Zeus gave the scepter, and him the rest shall obey."

In this way Odysseus sent his imperious voice ringing through the camp and at last induced the people to leave the ships and return to the place of assembly. Slowly they quieted down and waited for what was to come. Only one man could be heard in that hush. It was Thersites, who, as usual, was making shrill complaints against the princes and leaders of the people. He was the ugliest man who had come from Greece to Troy: cross-eyed, lame in one foot, hunchbacked, narrow in the chest, his head long and pointed, and sparsely covered with woolly hair.

This troublemaker was hateful to Odysseus and the son of Peleus even more than to the rest because he was constantly maligning them. But this time Thersites derided Agamemnon, the commander-in-chief. "What have you to complain of, son of Atreus?" he shrieked. "What is it that you need? Is not your house full of precious metals and lovely women? You are living in comfort and taking your ease! Why should we allow you to lead us into misery? We should do better to sail home in our ships, leave you alone before Troy, and let you gorge yourself with gifts." Then Thersites turned to his comrades. "He has done dishonor to mighty Achilles!" he shouted. "He has deprived him of his rightful prize of war. But the listless son of Peleus has no gall in his liver, or this tyrant would have done wrong for the last time!"

While Thersites was speaking, Odysseus had gone up to him. He measured him with a baleful look, then lifted his staff and gave him a great thump over the back with it, crying: "If ever again I find you shouting like a madman, then let my head not stand on my shoulders, nor may I be called the father of Telemachus if I do not tear the clothes off you, scourge you, and send you wailing back to the ships!" Thersites writhed under the blow, and a bloody weal rose up on his back. He cowered down and began to snivel, and a big tear rolled down his nose. But among the Achaeans, one man nudged the next, laughing merrily, and all were pleased that this noisy fellow had been given the punishment he so richly deserved.

And now Odysseus faced the people and beside him was Pallas Athene who had assumed the shape of a herald and bade the gathering be silent. He himself raised his staff to gain the attention of those about him, and said: "Son of Atreus! Truly, things have come to a sorry pass when the Argives are ready to disgrace you and break their promise not to leave until Troy is conquered. They wail for home like women and children and complain to one another of the hardships they must endure. But think how shameful it would be for us to go home empty-handed after waiting here for so long a time! O my friends, have patience a little longer! Remember the sign that was given us before our departure from Aulis, when standing around the spring gushing from the earth we offered hecatombs on sacred altars under a spreading maple. To me it seems only yesterday! A serpent with dark scaly body slipped from under the altar and wound its way up the maple. Swinging on one of the branches was a sparrow's nest, and in it were fledglings, eight of them huddled among the leaves, and the ninth bird was the brooding mother. With frightened twitters she hovered over her young until the serpent turned its head toward her and caught her by the wing. When it had devoured the mother and her little ones, Zeus, who had sent it, wrought a miracle and turned it to stone. And you Argives stood by and quaked with wonder. But Calchas, the seer, cried: 'Do you not see what Zeus is foretelling by way of this miracle? The nine sparrows are the nine years in which you will battle for Troy. In the tenth you shall conquer that glorious city.' So Calchas predicted, and now his words are about to be fulfilled. The nine years of fighting are at an end. The tenth has come and shall bring us victory. So let us wait together a little longer, O Danai! Stay until we destroy the citadel of King Priam!''

The Argives applauded the words of Odysseus, and wise Nestor made the most of the shift in the mood of the mob and counselled Agamemnon to let anyone who could not quell his longing go to his ship and set sail for home. But he advised that after this he should range his men according to family line and rank and let them fight. In this way, said Nestor, he would soon learn which of the warriors or leaders was brave and which was timid, and whether the will of the gods, or fear, or lack of skill in the trade of war was delaying the conquest of Troy.

Agamemnon rejoiced at this sage advice and answered: "Nestor, you, who are old, surpass all others in wisdom! If only I had ten more like you in the council of the Argives, Troy's lofty citadel would soon lie in the dust. As for me, I must admit that I acted foolishly when I quarrelled with Achilles for the sake of a girl. Zeus must have struck me with blindness of heart. But if we two become reconciled, the fall of Troy cannot be long in coming. And now let us prepare for the attack. Each man shall eat, make ready his shield and lance, give food and drink to his horses, examine the chariots, and think only of battle. But he who fears and remains with the ships—his body shall be the prey of dogs and vultures."

When Agamemnon had ended, so mighty a roar burst from the throats of the Argives that it sounded like the tide of the sea when the south wind lashes it shoreward and it breaks against towering cliffs. The men leaped up from their places. Each hurried to his ship, and soon the smoke rose from among the huts where the meal was being prepared. Agamemnon sacrificed a bullock to Zeus and called the noblest among the Achaeans to him. When all had eaten, he bade the heralds summon the Argives to battle, and they stormed to the meadow of the Scamander like flocks of cranes or swans which fly along a river. The leaders, foremost among them the son of Atreus, ordered the battalions,

and splendid to behold was Agamemnon, the king of kings: his
eyes and his brow were like those of the father of gods, his broad
breast like that of Poseidon, and his cuirass and lance and
shield like those of Ares himself.

PARIS AND MENELAUS

The host which at Nestor's advice had been ordered according
to family line stood ready for battle when at last they saw the
dust whirled up by the Trojans advancing from behind their
walls. The Argives too began to move forward. When the two
armies were close enough for the fight to begin, out from the
ranks of the Trojans came Paris, girt with the spotted panther's
skin, his bow over his shoulder, his sword at his side. Brandishing two bronze-tipped lances, he challenged the bravest among
the Danai to single combat. When Menelaus saw him spring forward from the mass of soldiers, he exulted as a hungry lion who
sees a buck or a stag crossing his path. Fully armed he leaped
down from his chariot, eager to punish the thief who had robbed
his house. But Paris shuddered at the sight of such an opponent.
As if he had seen an adder, he paled and drew back, mingling
with the throng. When Hector saw him recoil he called to him
angrily: "Brother, you are a hero only in stature. At heart you

are timid as a girl and nothing but a clever seducer. I wish you had died before wooing Helen! Do you not see that the Argives are laughing at you because you are not man enough to stand up against him whose wife you carried off? You deserve to discover what sort of man you have offended, and I, for my part, should have no pity on you if you lay on the earth, covered with wounds, and soiling your fair locks in the dust."

Paris replied: "Hector, you are hard of heart, and your courage is firm as the brazen axe with which the shipbuilder cuts his timber, but you reproach me unjustly. Do not mock my beauty, for beauty too is a gift of the immortals. If you desire to see me fight, bid the Trojans and Danai rest their arms. Then for Helen and all her treasure I will venture single combat with Menelaus, the hero, in the sight of all the people. The victor shall carry her home with him. This shall be sealed by a treaty, and soon you shall plough the earth of Troy in peace, and those others will sail for Argos."

At his brother's words, Hector was filled with glad surprise. He advanced from the ranks and, holding up his spear, stemmed the onrush of the Trojan troops. When the Argives saw him, they vied in aiming at him with darts and arrows and stones. But Agamemnon called to them: "Stop! Do not cast your weapons at him! Hector of the crested helmet desires to speak." At that the Argives paused and waited. Then Hector, in ringing tones, proclaimed to both hosts the resolve of his brother Paris. His words were followed by a long silence. At last Menelaus spoke.

"Hear me!" he cried. "Hear me, on whose spirit the burden we bear in common weighs most heavily! At last I dare to hope that you, Trojans and Argives alike, who have suffered so greatly in the war kindled by Paris, will part from one another reconciled. One of us two, whichever Fate chooses, will die. But the rest of you shall go in peace. Let us make offerings and take the oath, and then the combat shall begin."

All rejoiced at these words, for they yearned for the end of this war. On both sides the charioteers reined in their horses, the heroes dismounted from the chariots, took off their armor, and laid it on the ground. In great haste Hector sent two heralds to Troy to bring lambs for the offering and to summon King

Priam to the battlefield. King Agamemnon also sent a herald, Talthybius, to the fleet to fetch the victims. And Iris, the messenger of the gods, hastened to Troy in the form of Laodice, Priam's daughter, to tell Helen what had happened. She found her seated at the loom, working a sumptuous robe with scenes of the battle, her eyes lowered and fixed on her weaving. "Come, dear and lovely one!" Iris called to her. "You shall see a curious thing. The Trojans and Argives who only a short time ago confronted one another with rage in their hearts are now silent and calm. Their spears are thrust into the ground, and they are leaning on their shields. War has ended. Only Paris and Menelaus are to fight, and the winner will carry you off as his wife."

So spoke the goddess, and Helen's heart was filled with longing for the husband of her youth, for her home and her friends. Quickly she covered herself with a silver-white veil with which she hid the tears shining on her lashes, and hastened toward the Scaean Gates followed by two of her handmaids, Aethra and Clymene. There, on the rampart, was King Priam with the oldest and wisest among the Trojans: Panthous, Thymoetes, Lampus, Clytius, Hicetaon, Antenor, and Ucalegon. The two last were the sagest citizens of Troy. Their great age kept them from going to war, but in the council their words were the shrewdest. When from their high outlook they saw Helen coming, they marvelled at her grace, and one whispered softly to the other: "No one, indeed, should blame the Trojans and Argives for their willingness to suffer years of misery for such a woman! Is she not as fair and radiant as an immortal goddess? Still, with all that loveliness of hers, let her return to her home with the Argive fleet so that we and our sons may have no further harm from her."

But Priam called Helen fondly to him. "Come, sweet daughter," he said. "Come, sit here beside me and I will show you your first husband, your friends, and your kinsmen. I do not hold you responsible for this wretched war. The gods have sent it on us. And now tell me, who is that man who shines out among the Danai in stature and majesty? Here and there among the ranks of his army are men taller than he, but not one is like him in kingliness and splendor."

Helen answered the king, and her voice was reverent. "My honored father-in-law, when I approach you I am timid and shy.

Far better I had died a most bitter death than left my home, my daughter and my friends, and followed your son here. I could weep rivers of tears that I did this! But you asked me a question. Well then: he whose name you wish to know is Agamemnon, the best of kings and a valiant warrior. And he, alas! was once my brother-in-law."

"O happy son of Atreus!" exclaimed Priam, gazing at the hero. "O favorite of Fortune, to whose scepter countless Argives bow! I too once headed a great host. Then I was young. It was the time we were fending off hordes of Amazons from Phrygia. But my army did not equal yours in numbers." Then he turned to Helen again. "And now, sweet daughter," he asked, "tell me the name of that one over there. He is not as tall as the son of Atreus, but his breast is broader, his shoulders more massive. His arms are lying on the ground. He prowls down the rows of men like a ram around sheep."

"That is the son of Laertes," Helen replied. "It is crafty Odysseus. The rocky island of Ithaca is his home."

Here old Antenor joined in their conversation. "You are right, princess," he said. "I know him well, him and Menelaus, for once they came to my house as envoys. When they stood up, Menelaus was taller than Odysseus, but when they were seated, Odysseus seemed the more majestic. Menelaus spoke little, but every word, though uttered ever so casually, was full of meaning. When Odysseus was about to speak, he fixed his eyes on the ground and held his staff motionless in his hand, so that he looked like one ill at ease, and it was difficult to guess whether he was malicious or stupid. But when once he began, when his mighty voice rang out, his words crowded one another like snowflakes in winter, and no mortal could compare with him in eloquence."

In the meantime, Priam had been looking farther afield. "Who is that giant over there?" he cried. "That tall and powerful man who stands out among the rest?"

"That is Ajax," Helen answered. "He is a pillar of strength to the Argives. And nearby, standing among his Cretans like a god, is Idomeneus. I know him well. Menelaus often was host to him in our palace. And now I recognize one after the other the lusty warriors of my country. Had we the time, I could tell you all their names. The only ones I miss are Castor and Polydeuces, my own brothers, my own flesh and blood. Have they not come, or are they reluctant to appear in battle because they are ashamed of their sister?" And as she thought about this, Helen fell silent. She did not know that her brothers had died long ago.

While they were talking, the heralds carried through the city offerings of two lambs and, for the libation, a goatskin full of wine grown in that country. Idaeus, a third herald, followed with a gleaming bowl and a golden cup. When they passed through the Scaean Gates, Idaeus approached King Priam and said to him: "Rise, O king! Both the Trojan and Argive princes summon you to the battlefield to take an oath on a solemn agreement. Paris, your son, and Menelaus are resolved to fight for Helen in single combat. He who wins is to carry her off with all her treasure. And after that the Achaeans will return to their country."

The king was amazed but commanded that his horses be harnessed. Then he mounted the chariot and Antenor with him. Priam seized the reins, and the horses flew through the gates and out to the field. When the king had reached the two armies, he and his companion dismounted and stood between them. Agamemnon and Odysseus hurried toward him. The heralds led the victims to these four, mixed the wine in the bowl, and sprinkled the two kings with sacred water. The son of Atreus drew the sacrificial knife he always had with him, hanging beside the great scabbard of his sword, cut the hair from the foreheads of the lambs as the rite of sacrifice demanded, and called upon Zeus to witness the covenant. Then he slit the throats of the animals and laid them in the dust. The heralds prayed and poured the wine out of the golden cup, and all the people of Troy and of Greece made loud supplication: "O Zeus and all the deathless gods! Let the brains of the first to break this solemn oath be poured over the earth like this wine, theirs and those of their children!"

And now Priam said: "I shall return to my citadel in Ilium, for I cannot bear to see my son fight with King Menelaus in mortal combat, of which Zeus alone knows the outcome." So the old man mounted the chariot with his companion and guided the horses back to Troy.

Hector and Odysseus now measured the space for the combat and in a brazen helmet shuffled two lots to decide who was to be first to cast the lance at his opponent. Hector shook the helmet, and out fell the lot of Paris. Then both heroes girt on their armor and strode out between the Argive and Trojan hosts, wearing breastplate and helmet, tall lance in hand. Their eyes were bright with angry challenge, and both peoples marvelled at them as they passed. When they confronted each other in the space which had been measured, they raised their spears defiantly. Since it had been so decided by lot, Paris hurled his first. It hit the shield of Menelaus, but the point of the lance bent as it struck the bronze.

Then Menelaus lifted high his spear and prayed aloud: "Zeus, let me punish him who offended me first, so that on through the generations our descendants shall fear to wrong their hosts." With this he flung his weapon. It pierced the shield of Paris, penetrated his breastplate, and cut his tunic at the thigh. And now the son of Atreus snatched his sword from the scabbard and aimed it at the helmet of his opponent. But the blade splintered with a shrill sound. "Cruel Zeus, why do you grudge me victory?" cried Menelaus, and he rushed at his foe, took him by the helmet, and, turning, drew him toward the Argive host. He would have dragged Paris along the ground and strangled him in his chin strap, had not Aphrodite seen his agony and broken the strap, so that Menelaus was left holding the empty helmet. This he hurled toward the Argives and prepared to rush at his enemy afresh.

But Aphrodite had veiled Paris in sheltering mist and taken him back to Troy. Here she set him down in a fragrant chamber, and then, in the guise of an old Spartan woman, she went to Helen who was sitting up in a tower, among other Trojan women. The goddess caught at her robe and said: "Come, Paris is asking for you. He waits in the chamber robed as for a feast. To look at him you would think he were ready for the dance rather than having just come from single combat."

When Helen looked up, she saw the goddess vanish in all her divine loveliness. Unnoticed by the other women, she stole from the room and hastened to her palace. There she found her husband, adorned by Aphrodite. He was flung on a couch at his ease. She seated herself opposite him, turned her eyes from his carefree comfort, and upbraided him: "Back from the battle?

Rather would I see you dead by the hand of that mighty hero, my first husband! Only a short while ago you boasted that you could subdue him with your arm and spear. Go then, and challenge him once more! No, wait—stay here! It might go worse with you a second time!"

"Do not vex me with mocking words," Paris replied. "If Menelaus vanquished me it was with Athene's help. Another time I shall vanquish him, for the gods have never yet forsaken me." Then Aphrodite moved the heart of Helen. She looked at her husband with tenderness and held up her lips for his kiss.

On the battlefield Menelaus was still storming through the host in search of Paris. But neither Trojan nor Argive could show him where he was, and surely they would not have concealed him, for they hated him more than death. At last Agamemnon raised his voice and said: "Listen to my words, Dardanians and Danai! It is clear that Menelaus is the victor. So give us Helen and her treasure and pay us tribute for all time to come." The Argives greeted this proposal with shouts of approval. The Trojans were silent.

PANDARUS

The gods had gathered in a great assembly on Olympus. Hebe went in and out among the tables, pouring nectar, and the immortals drank to one another from golden cups and looked down on Troy. It was then that Zeus and Hera resolved to destroy the city. The father of all gods turned to his daughter Athene and told her to hasten to the battlefield and incite the Trojans to break the treaty they had agreed to, by insulting the Argives who were celebrating their victory.

So Pallas Athene assumed the form of Laodocus, son of Antenor, and mingled with the Trojans. She sought out the son of Lycaon, haughty Pandarus, whom she regarded as well suited to perform what her father had ordered. Pandarus was an ally of Troy and had come from Lycia, bringing with him many warriors.

The goddess soon found him standing among his men, and she touched him lightly on the shoulder and said: "Listen to me, wise Pandarus! Now is the time to do a deed which will win you the gratitude and praise of all the Trojans, above all of Paris, who will doubtlessly reward you with priceless gifts. Do you see Menelaus over there, so arrogant, so proud of his victory? Why not launch an arrow at him—if you dare!" So said the goddess in her disguise, and the foolish heart of Pandarus was stirred by her words. Swiftly he took his bow, lifted the lid of his quiver, selected a feathered shaft and fitted it to the string which twanged as the arrow was released. But Athene guided it to Menelaus' belt, so that, though it pierced the leather and the armor, it only scratched the skin. Even so, blood oozed from the wound, and a shudder shook Menelaus.

Agamemnon and his friends surrounded him in consternation. "Dear brother," cried the king, "we have made a treaty that brings death to you, for our tricky foes have disregarded it! They shall atone for this, and I know the day will come when Troy and Priam with all his people will fall. But your wound fills me with bitter grief. If I return without you, if your bones moulder in Trojan earth and the work we set out to do is not accomplished, what disgrace awaits me in my native land! For without you I am not destined to vanquish Troy and carry off Helen. And the Trojans will trample on your grave and speak of you and me with contempt. If only the earth would open to devour me!"

But Menelaus comforted his brother. "Calm yourself," he said. "My wound is not fatal. My belt has protected me."

"If only it be so!" sighed Agamemnon and quickly dispatched a herald to summon Machaon, versed in the art of healing. He came, drew out the arrow, unclasped the belt, opened the armor, and examined the wound. Then he sucked the blood welling from it with his own lips and applied a soothing salve.

While the physician and the heroes busied themselves about Menelaus, the Trojan troops were already advancing. The Argives too girt on their armor again, and Agamemnon entrusted his horses and chariot to Eurymedon with orders to bring them to him should he see him grow weary from striding through the ranks on foot. Then he went among the rows of his warriors and spurred them to battle, praising the bold and admonishing those who hung back. In this way he came to the Cretans, grouped around their leader Idomeneus who stood among them, raging to fight like an angry boar. When Agamemnon saw this brave array, his heart grew light. "You are one of the very best, Idomeneus," he called to him. "You excel in everything, in war and at the banquet, when the sparkling wine is blended in great pitchers. While the rest drink their modest measure, your cup is always as full as mine. But now you shall go with me to the fight, as you so often swore you would."

"I shall, indeed, be a faithful comrade-in-arms to you!" answered Idomeneus. "Go, and drive others on! I have no need of that. May death and destruction overtake those breakers of treaties, the Trojans!"

And now Agamemnon had come up with the two Ajaces, in whose wake seethed a tide of foot soldiers. The king called to them as he hurried by: "If only courage such as yours quickened the spirits of all the Argives, Priam's fortress would soon fall!" Going on farther he saw Nestor engaged in drawing up his men. In the van he placed the warriors with horses and chariots, in the rear many and brave men on foot, and wedged between these two bulwarks, the cowards. And while he was drawing them up in this way, he exhorted them with wise words: "Let no one venture forward too far with his chariot, and let no one retreat. If chariot strikes on chariot, hold out the lance."

When Agamemnon heard him counselling his men thus, he cried: "Old man, may your knees obey you, and may the vigor of your body match the courage which still beats in your breast! If only another could take from you the burden of age, if only you were young again!"

"How I should like to be as I once was!" Nestor replied. "But the gods do not give a man all things at all times. So now the young shall hurl the spear, while I do my part with the words of wise counsel age can give."

Agamemnon went on and found Menestheus, son of Peteus. Around him the Athenians clustered, and beside him were the Cephalonians under the command of Odysseus. Both battalions were waiting to let others storm on before. This vexed the king and he said to them gruffly: "Why do you huddle together, waiting for others to bear the brunt of danger? When we dine on roast meat and drink wine, you are always first, but now it would not displease you to see ten other Argive troops precede you into battle!"

Odysseus scowled at him and said: "What is this you say, son of Atreus? You call us loiterers? Just wait until we break forth and you will see with what a vengeance we press the fury of the fight against the Trojans, and how I shall go ahead of all. So do not be so quick with ill-considered words!"

When Agamemnon saw the hero roused against him, he answered smilingly: "Well I know, noble son of Laertes, that you need neither reproof nor counsel. And at heart you are as gentle as I, so let us not speak harsh words to one another." And he left him and hastened on.

Next he encountered the son of Tydeus, proud Diomedes, standing in his magnificent chariot next to Sthenelus, son of Capaneus, his friend and charioteer. To him too he expressed displeasure in order to test him. "It seems," he said, "that the son of Tydeus is looking about in dismay. How different your father was when he fought against Thebes! He was always in the thick of battle!"

Diomedes heard the reproof of his king in silence; his friend Sthenelus answered for him. "You know better, son of Atreus," he said. "We can boast of greater prowess than our fathers, for we conquered that very Thebes before which they failed." But Diomedes interrupted his friend and said sternly: "Say no more. I do not blame the king for urging the Danai on to battle. It is he who has the glory if we win; it is he who bears loss and grief if we fail. So let us keep off defeat!" With that Diomedes leaped down from the chariot, and his bronze breastplate rang.

Troop after troop, like waves rushing in upon the shore, the Argives fared forth to battle. The leaders shouted commands; the men marched in silence. The Trojans, on the other hand, were as noisy as a flock of bleating sheep, and the tongues of many different peoples could be heard from their ranks. And through all that clamor rang the battle cry of the gods. Ares, the war-god, rallied the courage of the Trojans, and Pallas Athene fired the hearts of the Argives.

THE BATTLE. DIOMEDES

Soon the hosts, surging foward, met face to face. Shield clashed on shield; spear crossed spear, and everywhere was the clamor of voices: here lament and there jubilation. As in late spring two swollen streams fuse and plunge down the mountain side, so the shouts of the armies merged to a single roar. The first hero to fall was Echepolus of Troy, who ventured out too far, so that Nestor's son Antilochus pierced his forehead, and he toppled over like a tower. Swiftly Elephenor, one of the princes of Greece, caught hold of the foot of the fallen warrior to pull him away from his comrades and strip him of his armor. But as he bent down to drag him over, his shield shifted a little, and Agenor, the Trojan, seeing his advantage, brandished his spear and pierced his side, so that the Argive sank dead in the dust. Over him raged the battle, and the warriors fell on one another fiercely as wolves.

Simoisius, in the flower of youth, darted forward and was struck above his right breast by Ajax the Great. The spear came out through his shoulder, and he sprawled on the ground. Instantly Ajax threw himself upon him and took his breastplate. Straightway Antiphus of Troy threw his lance, but it missed Ajax and hit Leucus, the friend of Odysseus, just as he was dragging off the youthful dead. This filled Odysseus with fury and grief; looking about him cautiously, he hurled his javelin, but the Trojan recoiled from it. He struck Democoon, a bastard son of Priam; the pointed spear passed through each temple. He fell with a great thud, and the first row of Trojan fighters, Hector among them, retreated. At that the Danai shouted with joy, shoved aside the dead bodies, and penetrated farther into the ranks of the Dardanians.

This angered Apollo, and he urged the Trojans on. "Do not give up the battlefield to the Argives," he cried, and his voice rang out above the tumult. "They are not made of stone or iron, and Achilles, the best of them, is not even fighting! He remained behind near the fleet, where he is nursing his grudge." On the other side, Athene was spurring the Danai to battle, and many heroes fell in both armies.

Then Pallas gave Diomedes, son of Tydeus, such valor and strength that he stood out among the Achaeans and won undying glory. She made brighter his shield and helmet, so that they glittered like stars on an autumn night, and drove him into the thick of the foe. Now among the Trojans was Dares, a priest of Hephaestus, a rich and powerful man who had sent two sons, Phegeus and Idaeus, both dauntless warriors, into this war. These guided their chariot out from the ranks of their men and straight toward Diomedes, who fought on foot. First Phegeus cast his lance; it grazed the shoulder of the son of Tydeus but did not wound him. But Diomedes' spear pierced the breast of Phegeus who fell from his chariot. When his brother Idaeus saw this, he did not dare stop to screen his brother's body but leaped from his chariot and fled, while Hephaestus, his father's protector, spread darkness about him, for he did not want his priest to lose both sons.

And now Athene took her brother Ares, the war-god, by the hand, saying to him: "Brother, shall we not leave the Trojans and Argives to their own devices for a time, and see to whom our father will grant the victory?" So Ares let his sister take him from the battlefield, and the mortals were left to themselves. But Athene knew that Diomedes, her favorite, was fighting with the strength she had conferred upon him.

Now the Achaeans pressed hard upon the foe, and a Trojan fell before the onslaught of every Argive commander. Agamemnon thrust his spear into the shoulder blade of Hodius; Idomeneus pierced Phaestus and plunged him headlong from his chariot; Scamandrius, the skillful hunter, was struck down by the sharp lance of Menelaus; Meriones slew Phereclus, who had built Paris the ships for his marauding expedition; and many other Trojans fell at the hands of the Danai.

The son of Tydeus raged through the army of the foe like a mountain stream swollen with rains, and it was difficult to guess whether he belonged to the Argives or the Trojans, for he was now here and now there. While he was darting back and forth with the tide of battle, Pandarus, son of Lycaon, fixed him carefully with his eye, aimed his bow at him, and shot him in the shoulder, so that blood flowed over his armor. Pandarus, seeing this, exulted and called back to his comrades: "Come, Trojans, goad on your horses! I have hit the bravest among the Argives! Soon he will have raged his last and lie in the dust, for Apollo himself called me from Lycia to do battle with this man!"

But Diomedes was not fatally wounded. He rose, stood in front of his chariot, and called to Sthenelus, his friend and charioteer:

"Come down from the chariot, dear comrade, and draw the arrow out of my shoulder." Sthenelus hurried to do as he asked, and the clear red blood spurted from between the links of the armor. Then Diomedes prayed to Athene: "Blue-eyed daughter of Zeus! You were ever wont to protect my father; now be gracious to me as well! Guide my spear to that man over there who has wounded me and who would rejoice in my death. Let him not see the light of the sun for long!" And Athene heard his prayer and quickened his limbs. His body grew light as that of a bird, his wound no longer throbbed, and he raced back into battle.

"Go!" she said to him. "I have healed you and taken the human darkness from your eyes, so that now you can see who on the field is mortal and who is immortal. Do not lift your hand against a god should you see one coming toward you. But should Aphrodite approach—you may wound her with your spear."

Diomedes, hearing this, rushed to the forefront, fierce as a mountain lion, for his courage and strength were trebled. He felled Astynous by a thrust at the shoulderjoint; he pierced Hypiron with his lance and slew the two sons of Eurydamas and the two late-born sons of Phaenops, who now had nothing left in all the world but his grief. Then he hurled from their chariot Chromius and Echemmon, sons of Priam, and stripped them of their armor while his men seized the chariot and took it to the camp.

Aeneas, King Priam's bold son-in-law, saw the ranks of the Trojans thinning under the strokes and thrusts of the son of Tydeus. He hurried through the storm of missiles until he reached Pandarus. "Son of Lycaon," he said to him, "where is your bow? Where are your arrows and that glory which, up to now, no one from Lycia and no one from Troy has equalled? Aim a shaft at that man who is making such havoc among the Trojans!—unless, of course, he is a deathless god in the guise of a mortal!"

Pandarus replied: "If it is not a god, then it must be Diomedes, son of Tydeus, whom I thought I slew. But if it is Diomedes, then a god must have shielded him and is still giving him protection and aid. Alas for my ill luck in this war! I have shot at two Argive princes, wounded both without killing them, and only fanned their anger. It was in an evil hour that I took my quiver and bow and strode through the gates of Troy. If ever I return home, then let any stranger strike off my head, if I do not break my useless bow and arrows with these hands and toss them into the fire!"

Aeneas tried to console him. "It were better for you to mount my chariot," he said, "and learn how agile Trojan horses are in flight and pursuit. If Zeus is bent on honoring Diomedes by granting him the victory, they will carry us safely back to Troy. But I shall dismount and fight on foot." Pandarus, however, begged him to drive the horses himself, since he was not practiced in this art. So he mounted the chariot, and the nimble horses bore them toward the son of Tydeus.

Sthenelus saw them coming. "Look!" he called to his friend. "Two fearless men are making straight for you, Pandarus, and

Aeneas, the demigod, son of Aphrodite! Against these all your rage and power will be of small avail. This time let us flee in the chariot!"

But Diomedes frowned and said: "Talk not to me of fear! To shrink from battle—to yield—is not my way! My strength is still unbroken. To stand inactive in the chariot would only vex me. No, just as you see me here, on foot—that is how I shall go to meet them. If I succeed in slaying both, then stop our horses, tether the reins to the edge of the car, and take the steeds of Aeneas to our ships as our rightful booty." While he was still speaking, the lance of Pandarus flew toward the son of Tydeus, pierced his shield, and rebounded from his breastplate.

"Missed!" shouted Diomedes at the Trojan, exulting, and cast his spear. It sped through the air and straight into the face of his foe, under the eye, cutting through teeth and tongue; the point came out below the chin. Pandarus fell from his chariot with a clash of arms, doubled up on the ground in all his glitter· ing array, and quivered in the throes of death. His horses shied, breaking away. But Aeneas leaped down from the chariot and paced around the dead body like an angry lion, holding out his shield and spear, ready to slay anyone who dared to touch his friend. Now Diomedes grasped a stone lying in the field, a stone so large that two ordinary men could not have lifted it. With this he struck the son of Anchises on the hip-joint, crushing it and tearing the sinews, so that the hero sank to the earth and lost consciousness. He would have died, had not Aphrodite wound her white arms around her cherished son, covered him with the silvery folds of her robe, and carried him from the field.

In the meantime, Sthenelus, obedient to his friend's command, had taken the horses and chariot of Aeneas to the ships, and now returned to Diomedes in his own chariot. With the clear vision Athene had given him, the son of Tydeus had recognized Aphrodite. He followed her through the din of battle and soon caught up with her as she bore away her son. The hero thrust at her with his lance, and the point pierced the skin of her soft hand, so that it began to bleed. The wounded goddess screamed and let Aeneas fall to the ground. Then she hurried to Ares, her brother, whom she found seated on the left of the battle, his chariot and horses hidden in cloud. "O brother!" she pleaded. "Take me away! Give me your horses, that I may quickly flee to Olympus. My hand hurts! Diomedes, a mortal, has wounded me. I believe he would fight against our father Zeus himself!"

Ares let her have his chariot, and when Aphrodite reached Olympus, she threw herself weeping into the arms of Dione, her mother, who caressed and comforted her and guided her to the father of the gods. He received her with a smile. "Now you see, sweet daughter," he said, "why the business of war was not entrusted to you. Let your work be to arrange weddings, and leave battles to Ares." But her sister Pallas and Hera looked at her askance and taunted her. "What is it all about?" they asked maliciously. "That beautiful and false woman from Greece most probably lured our sister to Troy. There she must have passed her hand over Helen's gown and scratched herself on a clasp."

Down on the battlefield, meanwhile, Diomedes had thrown himself upon Aeneas. Three times he lunged forward to deal him the deathblow, and three times wrathful Apollo, who had hurried to the spot after Aphrodite's departure, held his shield over the wounded man. When Diomedes lifted his sword a fourth time, the god threatened him in a terrible voice: "Mortal, do not venture to vie with gods!" Abashed, Diomedes faltered and drew back.

Apollo bore Aeneas out of the battle and carried him to his temple in Troy, where Leto, his mother, and Artemis, his sister, took him into their care. On the ground where the hero had lain the god shaped a phantom in his image, and Achaeans and Trojans alike began to fight for it with savage blows and thrusts. Then Apollo bade Ares try to remove from battle the insolent son of Tydeus who fought against the immortals themselves, and the war-god, in the shape of Thracian Acamas, mingled with the crowd of warriors and approached the sons of Priam to reprove them: "How much longer, O princes, will you permit that Argive to commit his murders? Will you wait until the fighting reaches the very gates of your city? Do you not know that Aeneas has fallen? Come! Let us save our comrade from the hands of our foe!"

In this way Ares moved the hearts of the Trojans. And Sarpedon, king of the Lycians, went up to Hector. "What has become of that famous courage of yours?" he asked. "Only a

little while ago you boasted that without allies, yes, even without an army, you with your brothers and brothers-in-law would
be enough to defend Troy. Yet now I do not see a single one of
them in the battle. They are all crouched like dogs before a lion,
and we allies are forced to keep up the fight alone." In his heart
Hector felt that he deserved reproof. He sprang down from his
chariot, brandished his lance, strode through the ranks, inciting
all who crossed his path, and set the conflict blazing afresh. His
brothers and the other Trojans again turned their faces toward
the foe. And Apollo healed Aeneas, filled him with new strength,
and sent him back to the field where he appeared among his men
quite suddenly and wholly sound. They all rejoiced; no one
took the time to ask questions but all rushed forward to battle.

The Argives with Diomedes, the two Ajaces, and Odysseus in
their van awaited the impact, calm and motionless as a bank of
clouds, and Agamemnon hurried through the ranks calling:
"Now, my friends, be men, and have faith in your own powers.
When a people has faith in itself, more men stand than fall, but
for him who flees there is neither help nor glory." So he spoke
and was the first to fling his spear at the Trojans. It struck the
friend of Aeneas, Deicoon, who always fought in the forefront.
But the mighty hand of Aeneas slew two of the bravest Achaeans:
Crethon and Orsilochus, sons of Diocles, who in Pherae, in the
Peloponnesus, had grown up together, sturdy as mountain lions.
And Menelaus grieved for them as he raised his spear and flung
himself into the fight. Ares spurred him onward, for he hoped
Aeneas would fell him to the ground, but Antilochus, son of
Nestor, fearing for the life of the king, sprang to his side at the
very moment the two were preparing to rush at each other with
their lances. When Aeneas saw two heroes confronting him, he
drew back. Menelaus and Antilochus saved the two bodies from
the hands of their foes and put them in the care of friends. Then
they returned to the onslaught. Menelaus stabbed Pylaemenes
and Antilochus drove his sword into the temple of Mydon, his
charioteer, so that he fell from the chariot and stood head first
in the deep dust until his own horses, which Antilochus was driving toward the Argives, knocked him over and trampled him
underfoot.

Hector stormed forward with the bravest of the Trojan warriors, and the war-god accompanied him, going now before and now behind him. When Diomedes saw Ares coming he paused in wonder, as a traveller stops to marvel at a thundering waterfall, and called to the people: "Do not be amazed at Hector's fearlessness, my friends. For a god is at his side, shielding him from harm. And so, if we are forced to retreat, we shall be retreating from the gods!" While he was speaking, the Trojans came nearer and nearer, and Hector slew two bold Achaeans, Anchialus and Menesthes, both in one chariot. Ajax, son of Telamon, wanted to avenge them. With his lance he struck Amphius, an ally of the Trojans, under the belt, and he crashed to the ground. Then he pressed his foot against the body and drew out his lance, but a hail of spears prevented him from stripping his victim of his armor.

In another part of the field, evil chance drove Tlepolemus, a descendant of Heracles, toward Sarpedon, to whom he called from afar: "Why are you still here, shaking with terror, you weakling from Asia, who lyingly boast that you are a son of Zeus, like Heracles, my father? You are a coward, but even if you had courage, you should not escape Hades!"

"Had I won no glory before this," Sarpedon replied, "I should now gain it by your death." As the last word left his lips, the two heroes raised their lances, and Sarpedon pierced his overbearing foe right through the throat. The weapon's point came out at the nape of his neck, and he sank dead upon the earth. But the spear of Tlepolemus pierced Sarpedon's left thigh to the bone; he would have died had it not been for Zeus, his father, who wanted his son to live. His friends led him from the battlefield. He was trembling with pain, but they went so swiftly that no one noticed he was still dragging with him the lance stuck in his leg. The Argives, in the meantime, carried off the body of Tlepolemus.

While Odysseus raged through the leaderless troops of the Lycians and came close to Sarpedon as he withdrew from the fight, the son of Zeus caught sight of Hector and called to him in a weak voice: "Son of Priam! Do not leave me here as the prey of the Argives! Defend me, so that if I cannot return to the land of my fathers, to my wife and my little son, I may at least breathe my last undisturbed in your city." Hector did not take time to answer. He drove back the Argives around Sarpedon with such vigor that even Odysseus did not venture to advance. The Trojan warriors laid Sarpedon down near the Scaean Gates, under a tall beech tree sacred to Zeus, and Pelagon, the friend of his youth, drew the spear from his thigh. For a moment the wounded man lost consciousness, but soon he revived, and a cool wind blowing from the north freshened his languid spirit.

And now Ares and Hector pressed upon the Argives until they were forced to retreat to their ships. Hector unaided slew six splendid heroes. Stricken with horror, Hera gazed down from Olympus and saw the slaughter the Trojans were accomplishing with the help of Ares. Then the mother of all the gods ordered her chariot made ready, the chariot with its bronze wheels rimmed with gold, the silver shaft, and the golden yoke to which Hera harnessed her fleet-footed horses. Athene meanwhile girt on her father's armor, set the gold helmet on her head, took the shield blazoned with the Gorgon's head, grasped the spear, and mounted the silver car bound to the axle with chains of gold. Hera stood beside her and used her goad, so that the horses moved with even greater speed. The gates of heaven, guarded by the Hours, opened of themselves, and the great goddesses passed the jagged slopes of Olympus. On the highest peak sat Zeus. Reigning in her team for an instant, Hera, his wife, called to him: "Are you not angry that Ares, your son, is harassing the Achaeans contrary to the will of Fate? Aphrodite and Apollo exult because they have succeeded in rousing the war-god to do as they wish. Now surely you will permit me to strike that impudent wretch a blow that will send him flying from the field!"

"You may try," Zeus answered her from his peak. "Send my daughter Athene against him, for she is vehement and strong and knows how to fight." And now the chariot sped on between starry heaven and earth, until it descended where the Simois and the Scamander join their waters; there the horses touched ground.

The goddesses at once hastened into the midst of battle where warriors bold as lions and boars were fighting around the son of Tydeus. Hera, in the shape of Stentor, mingled with them and called aloud in the tone of the hero whose form she had assumed, and her voice rang like bronze · "Shame on you, Argives! Are you a terror to your foes only when Achilles fights at your side? Now that he stays with the ships, you cannot succeed!" Her taunts rallied the courage of the Argives. And Athene fought her way to Diomedes himself. She found him standing beside his chariot, trying to bind up the wound he had received from the shaft of Pandarus. His broad shield weighed on him, the sweat streamed from his body, and his hands were powerless. It was an effort for him even to loosen the strap and wipe away the blood.

Athene leaned on the horses' yoke and said to him: "The son of Tydeus is most unlike his father! He was small of stature and yet the bravest of fighters. Before the walls of Thebes he fought against my will, but such was his pluck and daring that I could not deny him my aid. You too could claim my protection and help, were it not for—but I cannot say just what is the matter with you! Are you stiff with striking blows, or has fear clouded your mind and numbed your limbs? Whatever the cause may be, to me you do not seem the son of fiery Tydeus."

At her words Diomedes raised his eyes to her face and looked at it wonderingly as he said: "I recognize you, daughter of Zeus, and I shall tell you the plain truth. Neither fear nor slackness hold me back, but one of the mightiest among the gods. You yourself opened my eyes that I might know him. It is Ares, the god of war, whom I have seen directing the attack of the Trojans. That is why I fell back and commanded the other Achaeans to gather here about me."

Then Athene replied: "Diomedes! My chosen friend! From now on you shall fear neither Ares nor any other immortal, for I shall be at your side. Guide your horses straight toward the raging god himself." Thus she spoke and lightly touched Sthenelus, his charioteer, who willingly dismounted so that she herself could ride beside Diomedes. The axle groaned under the weight of the goddess and the boldest among the Argive heroes.

She at once took reins and goad and drove the horses at Ares. He was just stripping off the armor of Periphas, the hardiest of the Aetolians. When he saw Diomedes coming toward him in his chariot—the goddess had veiled herself in impenetrable mists— he let Periphas lie and hastened toward the son of Tydeus, leaning forward over the yoke and the reins of his horses and aiming his lance. But Athene, unseen by anyone, laid her hand on it and gave it a different course, so that it slanted off into the empty air. And now Diomedes aimed, and Athene herself directed his spear so that it pierced Ares in the groin. The god of war roared as loudly as ten thousand mortals put together, and Trojans and Argives alike trembled, for they thought that though the sky was blue and serene they were hearing the thunder of Zeus. Only Diomedes saw Ares sheathed in cloud and riding up to heaven as if carried on a great gust of wind. There the war-god seated himself beside Zeus, his father, and showed him the blood running from his wound. But the Thunderer looked at him sternly and said:

"My son, do not whine complaints to me. Of all the Olympians you displease me most. You have always been fond of fighting and quarrels, and more than any other you resemble your mother in your stubborn, rebellious ways. It must be she who is responsible for this trouble of yours. All the same, I cannot bear to see you suffer. The healer among the gods shall tend you." And he called Paeëon, who examined the wound and treated it so that it closed, and soon he was whole and well again.

In the meantime, the other gods had also returned to Olympus and left the Trojans and Danai to themselves. First Ajax, son of Telamon, broke the ranks of the Trojans and cleared a way for his men by piercing between the eyes Acamas, greatest among the Thracians. Then Diomedes slew Axylus and his charioteer. Three other Trojans fell by the hand of Euryalus, Pidytes by that of Odysseus. Teucer slew Aretaon, Antilochus killed Ablerus, and Agamemnon Elatus. Menelaus caught hold of Adrastus just as his horses stumbled and threw him to the ground, running off toward the city with other leaderless horses and dragging the chariot with them. The foe, lying in the dust, clasped the king's knees and implored him: "Take me prisoner, son of Atreus! You shall have a ransom of bronze and gold from the stores of my father who will gladly give it to you if only he can clasp me alive in his arms again."

The heart of Menelaus was moved, but just then Agamemnon came toward him and said reproachfully: "Have you pity on your foes, Menelaus? Not one shall escape our revenge, not even the child at the mother's breast. All whom Troy has reared must die without mercy." When Menelaus heard these words he thrust pleading Adrestus from him, and Agamemnon pierced his body with his lance.

Incessantly Nestor's call rang out among the Argives: "Friends, do not stay behind to strip or loot! Now all that counts is to kill. Later on we can take the weapons of the dead at our leisure!"

The Trojans would have been vanquished and forced to flee back to their city, had not Helenus, Priam's son, who could predict the future from the flight of birds, turned to Hector and Aeneas and said to them: "All now depends on you. If you can stop the men before they enter the gates, we shall still be able to resume the battle with the Argives. Aeneas, the gods have chosen you for this task. And you, Hector, shall go to Troy and give a message to our mother. Tell her to assemble the noblest women on the acropolis, in the temple of Athene, to place her most precious robe on the knees of the goddess, and vow to sacrifice to her twelve unblemished heifers if only she will take pity on the Trojan women, their children, and their city, and ward off the terrible son of Tydeus." Willingly Hector sprang from his chariot, strode through his battalions, spurring their courage, and then hastened toward the city.

GLAUCUS AND DIOMEDES

On the battlefield, Glaucus of Lycia, a grandson of Bellerophon, and Diomedes, son of Tydeus, had stormed forward from the ranks and were facing each other, eager for the struggle. When Diomedes saw his opponent at close quarters, he measured him with his eyes and said: "Who are you? I have not encountered you before, yet now I see you standing out from the rest. I must warn you that those who cross my path in war are destined to disaster. But should you be a god who has taken mortal shape, I renounce combat, for I do not wish to raise my hand against an immortal. If you are mortal, come! You shall not escape death!"

The son of Hippolochus replied: "Diomedes, why ask my lineage? We men are like leaves in the forest which fall and are scattered in the wind, and in the spring the branches bud afresh. But if you wish to know, then hear. My forbear was Aeolus, son of Hellen, and he begot crafty Sisyphus. Sisyphus begot Glaucus, Glaucus Bellerophon, Bellerophon Hippolochus, and I am his son. It is he who sent me against Troy that I might excel in battle and not disgrace my ancestors."

When his opponent had ended, Diomedes thrust the shaft of his lance into the ground and spoke in a friendly voice. "Noble prince," he said, "we are bound by ties of hospitality from the days of our fathers! For twenty days Oeneus, my grandfather, had your grandfather Bellerophon as a guest under his roof, and they honored each other with splendid gifts. My grandfather gave yours a crimson belt, and yours gave mine a golden cup with handles which I still have in my house. And so I must be your host in Argos and you mine in Lycia, should I ever journey there. Let us avoid each other in the turmoil of battle. There are enough Trojans left for me to kill, and Argives enough for you to slay. Let us exchange weapons so that the others may see we are proud to be bound by these ties of old." And lightly they dropped from their chariots, took each other by the hand, and vowed friendship. But Zeus who turned all that chanced in favor of the Achaeans, blinded the spirit of Glaucus, so that he exchanged his golden armor for the brazen cuirass of Diomedes. It was as if a man had given a hundred bullocks for only nine.

HECTOR IN TROY

Hector, meanwhile, had reached the beech tree of Zeus and the Scaean Gates. Here the wives and daughters of the Trojans crowded around him and anxiously asked about their husbands, their sons, brothers, and kinsmen. He could not tell everyone what she wished to know, but counselled all to pray to the gods. Even so, what he had said filled many with gloom and anguish. And now he had come to his father's palace. It was a beautiful structure flanked by spacious colonnades. Within were fifty chambers with walls of polished marble, one built close to the next. Here lived the sons of the king with their wives. On the other side of the inner court were twelve adjoining marble halls which housed the king's daughters and their husbands. The whole was circled by a high rampart and was in itself a stately citadel. Here Hector met Hecuba, his mother, who was on her way to Laodice, the fairest of her daughters and the one she loved most dearly.

The aged queen hastened toward Hector, took him by the hand, and said, full of love and concern: "Son, how is it that you come to us in the midst of battle? It must be that the Argives

are besetting us sorely and that you have come to raise your hands to Zeus in supplication. Wait until I bring you wine, fragrant and rich, that you may pour a libation and then refresh your own spirit with a sparkling draught. For nothing revives a weary fighter like wine."

But Hector answered her: "Have no wine brought, dear mother, lest my mind blur and my limbs grow unsteady. Nor would I bring Zeus a libation with unclean hands. But you and the noblest women in Troy shall go to the temple of Athene, bearing incense, lay on the knees of the goddess your most beautiful robe, and vow to sacrifice to her twelve heifers without blemish, if she will take pity on us. I, meanwhile, will go to summon my brother Paris to battle. I wish the earth would swallow him where he stands, for he was born to our destruction!"

The mother did as her son had asked. She entered the perfumed chamber where she kept the fair silken robes Paris himself had brought her from Sidon when he was journeying home with Helen by slow and devious ways. One of these, the most beautiful, worked in an intricate pattern, she took from the very bottom of the chest and went to the acropolis, to the temple of Athene, accompanied by the noblest of the Trojan women. Theano, wife of Antenor, the Trojan priestess of Pallas, opened the house of the goddess. The women encircled the statue of Athene, lifted their hands to her, and made lament. Then Theano took the robe from the queen's hands, laid it on the knees of the image, and implored the daughter of Zeus: "Pallas Athene! Protectress of cities, great and powerful goddess, shatter the spear of Diomedes! Let him fall headlong and writhe on his face in the dust before the gates of Troy. Have pity on this city, on the women and young children. In the hope that you will do all this, we dedicate to you twelve unblemished heifers."

But in her heart Pallas Athene refused their request. By this time Hector had arrived in the palace of Paris which stood high on the acropolis, near the king's palace and Hector's own. For both princes had their houses separate from that of Priam. In his hand Hector carried his spear. It was eleven cubits long and the shaft, where it joined the brazen point, was bound with a ring of gold.

He found his brother examining weapons and smoothing the curve of a bow. Helen sat among her women directing them, and all were busily occupied with their day's work. When Hector saw his brother he reproved him, saying: "It is wrong for you to loiter here at your ease. It is because of you that men are fighting before our walls. You yourself would blame anyone you saw idle at a moment such as this. Come and help us defend our city before it bursts into flame from the firebrands of the foe."

Paris replied: "You are wrong to chide me, brother. I am sitting here idly because I am grieved. But now that Helen has warmly urged me to return to battle, I shall go. Wait until I gird on my armor. Or if you want to go, I shall soon follow you."

Hector answered nothing to this, but Helen said to him humbly: "O brother-in-law! I am, indeed, a woman who brings calamity in her wake. I wish the sea had closed over me before ever I set foot on this coast with Paris! But now that things are as they are, would I were the wife of a better man, of one who felt the disgrace and the contempt he has brought upon himself. He has no heart, and the fruit of his cowardice will not be long in coming. But enter, Hector. Come in and rest from those labors which, because of me and that idle husband of mine, now weigh heavily on your shoulders."

"No, Helen," said Hector. "Do not bid me be seated, for indeed I must not. My heart yearns to help the men of Troy. Your task shall be to fire Paris to action. Let him hasten, so that he may join me before I am beyond the city walls. But first I must go to my own house to see my wife, my little son, and my servants." So said Hector and hurried away. But he did not find his wife at home. "When she heard that the Trojans were hard pressed and the Argives were winning," the woman who watched the doors told him, "she left the palace beside herself with anxiety, to climb one of the towers, and the nurse had to carry the child after her."

Quickly Hector turned and again traversed the streets of Troy. When he reached the Scaean Gates, Andromache, his wife, the lovely daughter of Eetion, king of Thebe in Cilicia, came swiftly toward him. A serving-woman followed her, clasping to her breast the boy Astyanax, radiant as a star. The father looked at his son with a quiet smile, but Andromache went up to him with tears in her eyes, took his hand tenderly, and said: "Surely your courage will be the death of you! Have you no pity on your child or on your unhappy wife whom you will soon leave widowed? If I am deprived of you, it were best I sank into the earth. Achilles slew my father, my mother fell by the arrow of Artemis, and my seven brothers were also done to death by the son of Peleus. You are all I have, Hector. You are father, mother, and brothers to me. And so, take pity on me and stay here in the tower. Do not make an orphan of your child! Place your battalions over there, on that hill overgrown with fig trees. For there the wall is open to attack and easiest to scale. Three times already the bravest of the Argives—the two Ajaces, Idomeneus, the sons of Atreus, and Diomedes—have turned their steps in that direction, guided perhaps by the words of a soothsayer or by their own intuition."

Tenderly Hector replied: "All this weighs heavily on me too, beloved. But I should disgrace myself before the men and women of Troy if I stayed here, like a coward, and watched the battle from afar. Nor does my own courage permit me such a course; it has always driven me on to the front. My heart tells me the day will come when sacred Troy shall lie in ruins and Priam and all his people be destroyed. But neither the sufferings of the Trojans nor those of my own parents and brothers, falling under the sword strokes of the Argives, will give me the pain I shall feel for you. An Achaean will carry you off into captivity. You will weep and lament. In Argos you will sit at the loom or fetch water, and someone seeing your tears may say: 'That was Hector's wife!' Let the burial mound cover me rather than that I should hear your moans when they take you away."

So he spoke and held out his arms to the child. But the child screamed and hid his head in his nurse's breast, for he was frightened by his father's warlike appearance and by his brazen helmet with its terrifying crest of fluttering horsehair. Hector smiled at the child, took off the gleaming helmet, laid it on the ground, and kissed his little son and rocked him in his arms. Then he prayed to heaven: "Zeus, and all the gods! Let this boy become like his father, a leader of the people. Let him grow mighty and govern the city, and when he returns from battle laden with spoils, let them say: 'He is even braver than his father was.'" With these words he laid his son in his wife's arms, and she pressed him to her, smiling through her tears.

Hector sorrowfully stroked her hand and said: "Do not be sad! No one will kill me if it is not my fate to die. But no mortal can escape his destiny. Go to your distaff and loom and see to your women. The men of Troy must bear the brunt of this war— and most of all myself." And Hector set his helmet on his head and left her.

Andromache went toward her palace, looking back many times, and weeping tears of sorrow. When her women saw her, they too were overcome with sadness, and in his own palace Hector was mourned as though he were already dead.

Paris did not delay. Armed with shining weapons of bronze he strode through the city like a stately stallion which breaks loose from the halter when it has eaten its fill and races toward the river. He reached his brother just as he turned from Andromache. "I have kept you waiting, haven't I?" he called to Hector from afar. "I have made my elder brother wait because I did not come promptly enough."

But Hector answered him kindly: "My good brother, in fairness I must say that you are a brave fighter, only that you often hang back and idle away the hours. And then it cuts me to the heart when I must listen while the Trojans, who have suffered so much for you, speak of you with derision. But we shall talk of all this another time, when we have chased the Achaeans from our coast, sit at ease in the palace, and drain the cup of freedom."

HECTOR AND AJAX IN SINGLE COMBAT

When Athene, looking down from Olympus, saw the two brothers striding to battle, she herself impetuously hastened to the city of Troy. Under the beech tree of Zeus she met Apollo who had left the ramparts of the citadel and was directing the fighting of the Trojans. "What fiery zeal has driven you here from Olympus?" he asked his sister. "Are you still ruthlessly bent on the fall of Troy? If only you would listen to me and allow this day to pass without decisive warfare! Let them fight another time, for I know that Hera and you will not rest until lofty Troy lies in ruins."

Athene replied: "Far-Darter, let it be as you say. It was with this very thought in mind that I came down from Olympus. But tell me how you expect to stop all these men from fighting?"

"What we must do," said Apollo, "is to swell the courage of mighty Hector until he challenges one of the Danai to single combat. Then let us watch and see how they acquit themselves." Pallas Athene agreed.

The spirit of Helenus, the soothsayer, had heard this conversation of the immortals. Swiftly he went to Hector and said: "Wise son of Priam, obey my counsel this once, for I am your brother who loves you! Bid all the others, Trojans and Argives alike, call a truce. But you yourself shall challenge the bravest among the Argives to single combat which will decide the war. You may do this without danger. Believe me, for I am a seer and know that your time to die is not yet come."

Hector rejoiced at these words. He halted the Trojan army and, holding his spear in the middle, stepped forth between the two hosts. They marked this sign, and now the fighting stopped on both sides, for Agamemnon too ordered his men to refrain. Athene and Apollo meanwhile perched in the beech tree of Zeus in the shape of two vultures and delighted in the turmoil. At last all were seated with shields, helmets, and lances bristling about them, moving no more than the sea when the least breath of the west wind just ruffles its waters. And now Hector, standing in the center, began to speak.

"Trojans and Danai, hear what my heart bids me undertake. Zeus has not approved the treaty we recently made. Rather has he incited both your men and mine not to rest until either Troy is vanquished or you are driven back to your ships. The bravest heroes of all Greece have come with your host. Whichever of these dares to fight me in single combat, let him now come forward. This is what I propose, and may Zeus be my witness: if my opponent slays me with his spear, he shall have my armor and carry it to his ship as the spoils of war, but let him send my body to Troy, so that it may be honored in death and may burn on a pyre heaped on native soil. But should Apollo grant me the victory, should I slay my opponent, I shall hang his armor up in the temple of Phoebus in Troy, and you may bury your dead with all splendor and pile his burial mound at the Hellespont, pile it so high that in times to come sailors will say: 'See! Here is the burial mound of a man who died long since, one who was killed in combat with glorious Hector.' "

So he spoke, but the Argives were silent, for it was shameful to refuse this challenge and dangerous to accept it. Finally Menelaus rose and chided his people. "Alas!" he said. "What cowards you are! Women rather than men! It would be a disgrace we could never live down if no Argive dared confront Hector. You who sit there with cringing hearts that do not thirst for glory, I wish you were all turned back to water and mud! I myself shall prepare for combat and commend the outcome to the gods." With this he girt on his armor, and his death would have been sealed, had not the Argive princes started up and held him back.

Agamemnon seized his right hand and said: "Brother, wait! What are you thinking of? You are mad to fight one stronger than yourself, one of whom those mightier than you are afraid, for even Achilles hesitated to measure his strength against Hector's. We all beg you to think better of it!"

In this way Agamemnon persuaded Menelaus to alter his resolve. And now Nestor addressed the people and told them the tale of a combat he had fought with Ereuthalion of Arcadia. "If I were young," he said in conclusion, "if my strength were still as unbroken as in those days, Hector would not have long to wait for an opponent." After these words, intended as censure, nine princes arose and offered to do single combat with Hector. First among these was Agamemnon, then came Diomedes, and after him the two Ajaces; then Idomeneus, Meriones, his friend, Eurypylus, Thoas, and Odysseus. "The lot shall decide," said Nestor. "And no matter on which of you it falls, the Argives will rejoice and so will he himself when he issues victorious from this conflict."

Each marked his own lot, and they were tossed into Agamemnon's helmet. Nestor shook it, and out leaped the lot of Ajax, son of Telamon. A herald took it in his hand and passed it to each of the eight heroes before Ajax, but no one recognized it until it reached him who had marked it himself. Joyfully Ajax threw down the lot and cried: "It is mine! And I am glad, for I hope to vanquish Hector. Do you all pray silently or aloud while I make myself ready!"

The people obeyed. Ajax girded on his shining armor and stormed into battle like the war-god himself. A smile lit his grave face as he strode forward, brandishing his heavy lance. All the Argives rejoiced at sight of him, and a shudder of fear rippled through the Trojan battalions. Even the heart of great Hector hammered against his ribs, but now he could not draw back, for he himself had given the challenge to combat.

Ajax approached him, covering his body with the shield of bronze and seven oxhides, which Tychius, a peerless craftsman, had once made for him. When he was quite close to Hector, he said threateningly:

"Hector, now you can well see that the Danai have other heroes besides the lion-hearted son of Peleus, other and many! So let us begin!"

And Hector answered: "Godlike son of Telamon, do not try to frighten me as though I were a weak child or a woman faint of spirit. For I am experienced in fighting with men. I know how to shift the shield left and right, I know how to foot the dance of the terrible war-god and guide the horses through the tumult.

Come then! Not with hidden ruse but openly will I launch my spear at you."

With these words he cast his lance, and it flew in a bold curve straight into the shield of Ajax through six layers of hide and stopped only at the seventh. Now the son of Telamon flung his lance, and it shattered Hector's shield, cut his cuirass, and would have entered his groin had not Hector swerved to one side. Both drew their spears and ran at each other again and again like tireless boars. Hector aimed at the middle of Ajax's shield, but the point of his lance bent and did not penetrate the bronze. Ajax pierced his opponent's shield and grazed his neck, so that the dark blood spurted out. Now Hector drew back a few steps; his sinewy right hand gripped a stone lying in the field and with it he hit the buckle of his enemy's shield so that the bronze rang. Then Ajax picked up a bigger stone and hurled it at Hector with such force that the shield caved in and Hector was wounded in the knee and fell on his back. But he did not let go his shield; Apollo, who stood beside him invisible to all, quickly raised him from the earth. And now these two would have rushed at each other with their swords to decide the combat once and for all, had not the heralds of both peoples—Idaeus for the Trojans and Talthybius for the Argives—run forward and held their staves between the combatants. "Do not fight any more," called Idaeus. "You are both courageous and both favored by Zeus. All of us have seen this. But night is coming! Obey the bidding of night!"

"Speak to him who belongs to your own people," Ajax answered the herald. "It is he who challenged the bravest among the Argives to single combat. Let him stop if he wants to!"

And now Hector addressed his opponent: "Ajax, a god gave you your strong limbs, your power, and your skill in casting the spear. Today let us rest from the combat. We will renew it another time and fight until Zeus confers victory and fame on one or the other of our two peoples. But now let us honor each other with gifts, so that the Trojans and the Argives one day may say: 'They fought with each other as foes but they parted as friends.' "

So said Hector and gave his opponent his sword with the silver hilt, together with the scabbard and the sword strap. And Ajax undid his crimson belt and offered it to Hector. Then they parted. Ajax returned to the Argive battalions, and Hector went back to the Trojans who were happy to see their hero emerge alive from the hands of terrible Ajax.

THE TRUCE

The Argive princes assembled in the house of Agamemnon, their commander-in-chief, and to them came Ajax, exulting at his prowess and heralded by loud acclaim. A fat bull five years old was sacrificed to Zeus, and the victor was given the best pieces, cut from the back. When they had eaten and drunk their fill, Nestor opened the assembly of princes with the proposal not to fight on the following day but call a truce, fetch the bodies of fallen Argive heroes with wagons drawn by oxen and mules, and burn them near the ships, so that when they returned to their own country each could bring the children of his kinsmen the bones of those who had belonged to them. His words were greeted with a burst of applause.

The Trojans, on their part, assembled in front of the king's palace on the acropolis. They were bewildered and dismayed at the outcome of the combat. Wise Antenor was the first to speak. "Mark my words, Trojans and allies!" he said. "We have broken faith! As long as we persist in fighting contrary to our solemn oath, the oath which Pandarus violated, no good can come to our people. I, for one, shall not hide what I think, and herewith counsel you to hand over to the Argives Helen with all her treasure."

When he had spoken, Paris rose and replied: "If you have proposed this in all seriousness, Antenor, then the gods must, indeed, have robbed you of your senses. As for me, I shall say straight out that I do not intend ever to give up Helen. Let them have the treasure we took from Argos, for all I care. And I shall gladly add to it from my own stores as much as they demand in recompense."

After his son, Priam, the aged king, spoke in calm tones: "Do not let us undertake anything further this day, my friends. Distribute their evening fare to the men, place your guards, and give yourselves up to sleep. Tomorrow Idaeus, our herald, shall go to the Argive fleet, convey the peaceable words of my son Paris, and at the same time discover whether they are willing to call a truce until we have burned our dead. If we cannot come to an agreement, let war be resumed when the burial mounds are heaped."

And so it was done. The next morning Idaeus, the herald, appeared before the Achaeans and reported the offer of Paris and the king's proposal. The Argive heroes listened to what he had to say and remained silent for a long time. At last Diomedes spoke. "Fellow Argives," he said, "do not so much as dream of taking the treasure; not even if they give you Helen along with it. The most credulous among you can easily see from this proposal that the Trojans know they are doomed."

All the princes shouted approval, and now Agamemnon turned to the herald. "You have heard what the Danai have resolved in regard to your offer. But we shall not deny you the burning of your dead. The Thunderer himself shall bear witness to our consent." And saying this, he raised his scepter toward heaven.

Idaeus returned to Troy and found the Trojans gathered in assembly. When he had reported the reply, the city was quickly astir. Some fetched the bodies of the dead, others felled trees on the mountain slopes. And the same was happening in the Argive camp. Peacefully foe met foe in the beams of the morning sun, each looked for his dead on the other's side of the field. As for the fallen warriors, lying on the ground stripped of their armor and covered with blood, it was difficult to distinguish friend from enemy. Their lids red with tears, the Trojans washed the blood from the limbs of the corpses—and there were more slain Trojans than Argives. But Priam had forbidden loud lament, so they lifted them silently into the wagons, heaped the pyres, and locked their sorrow in their hearts. The Achaeans did the same. They too were sad, and when the blaze had died down they returned to their ships. The work had taken up the whole day; it was time for the evening meal. From Lemnos, Euneus, son of Jason and Hypsipyle, had sent cargo ships laden with fragrant wines, many thousand jars, for the Argives to whom he was bound by ties of hospitality. These arrived at a very opportune moment. A great banquet was spread, and when the Argives had seen to their dead they sat down at the festal board.

The Trojans too wanted to refresh themselves from the toils of battle, but Zeus left them no peace. All through the night he startled them with crashes of thunder, repeated at intervals, and each seemed to forebode new disaster. Terror gripped their hearts, and they did not dare touch their lips to the cup without first pouring a libation to the angry father of gods.

A TROJAN VICTORY

But for the moment Zeus withheld decision. "Mark my words well!" he said to the assembled gods and goddesses on the following morning. "If, on this day, one of you dares to help either the Danai or the Trojans, I shall seize the rebel and hurl him into the chasm of Tartarus, as far below earth as earth lies beneath heaven. Then I shall bolt the iron gate which guards the brazen threshold of the underworld, and never again shall the evildoer see the light of Olympus. If you doubt my power to carry out this threat, fasten a golden chain to heaven, hold fast to it, every one of you, and see if you can pull me down to earth! But more likely I shall draw you upward, and the land and sea with you, and knot the chain to the peak of Olympus, so that the whole earth will float in air."

The gods grew humble at these imperious words. But Zeus himself mounted his thunder chariot and drove to Mount Ida, where a grove and an altar were sacred to him. There he seated himself on the summit and surveyed the city of Troy and the Achaean camp with exultant pride. Everywhere men were girding on their armor. The Trojans were fewer in number, but they too were impatient for battle, for they were fighting in defense of their women and children. Presently their gates flew open, and the host thronged out swiftly in chariots and on foot, with clatter and cries. That morning both sides shared the fortunes of war equally, and both Argive and Trojan blood dyed the earth. But when the sun was steep in the sky at noon, Zeus placed two lots of death in his golden scales, held them in the middle, and weighed them in air. And the part which held doom for the Argives dropped earthward, while the part holding the Trojan lot rose to heaven.

With thunder and lightning he warned the Danai of the change in their fate. When they saw this they shook with foreboding, and even the strongest quailed. Idomeneus, Agamemnon, and the two Ajaces faltered where they stood. Aged Nestor alone still fought in the van, but only because he could not retreat; for Paris had hit one of his horses between the forelocks, and the animal reared high in terror and then writhed on the ground with the pain of the wound. While Nestor attempted to cut loose the reins of the second horse with his sword, Hector, who was pursuing the Greeks, rode up to him in his chariot.

And now the life of noble Nestor would have been forfeit, had not Diomedes hastened to his aid. The son of Tydeus shouted reproach to Odysseus who had turned his back on the foe and was fleeing to the ships, and tried in vain to urge him back. Then he placed himself in front of Nestor's horses, entrusted them to Sthenelus and Eurymedon, and took the old man in his own chariot which he drove straight at Hector. He cast his spear and, though he missed Hector himself, shot his charioteer Eniopeus through the breast, so that he fell to the ground. Deeply as Hector mourned the death of his friend, he let him lie and called another to drive the horses. Then he rushed at Diomedes. Now had Hector measured swords with the son of Tydeus he would have been doomed, and the father of gods knew very well that

with his fall the tide of battle was bound to turn and that the
Argives would take Troy that very day. Zeus did not wish this
to happen, so he tossed a bolt of lightning to earth, close to the
chariot of Diomedes. In terror Nestor dropped the reins and
cried: "Flee, Diomedes! Did you not see that Zeus does not want
you to conquer today?"

"You are right," answered the son of Tydeus. "But my heart
would burst if, in time to come, Hector could say in an assembly
of Trojans: 'The son of Tydeus was afraid and retreated to the
ships!'"

But Nestor said: "And do you think that the Trojan men and
women whose friends and husbands you killed will believe Hector
when he calls you a coward?" With these words he guided the
horses away from the battlefield, and Hector, racing after them
with his Trojans, cried: "Son of Tydeus, up to now the Argives
have honored you at their banquets and in assembly. From this
moment on they will scorn you. It is not you who will vanquish
Troy and take our women away on your ships!" Diomedes
wavered. Three times he turned over in his mind whether or not
he should head for the field again and drive straight at derisive
Hector. But three times Zeus thundered up on Ida with an echoing crash, and so Diomedes continued to flee and Hector to
pursue.

Hera watched and was dismayed. In vain she tried to move
Poseidon, the special patron of the Danai, to help his people,
but he did not venture to act contrary to the command of his
powerful brother. By this time the fugitives had reached the
trench and wall in front of the fleet, and Hector would surely
have invaded their camp and tossed a firebrand on the ships, had
not Agamemnon, heartened by Hera, gathered the frightened
Danai about him. He boarded the great ship of Odysseus which
towered far above the rest. Here he stood erect on the deck, flung
his mantle of shimmering crimson across his shoulder, and called
down to the one side where the house of Ajax, the son of Telemon,
stood, and to the other where the son of Peleus was encamped.
"Shame on you! Where is that great courage you vaunted when
you emptied your cups? We have yielded to a single man, to
Hector alone! Soon he will set our ships afire. O Zeus, what curse
have you laid upon me! If ever I have honored you with prayers

and offerings, do not let the Trojans vanquish me here by our own ships." So he spoke with tears, and the father of gods had compassion on him and sent the Argives a happy omen: an eagle which gripped in its claws a fawn and dropped it before the altar the Achaeans had reared to Zeus.

The hearts of the Argives beat high at this sign, and again they bounded forward to confront the invading foe. Ahead of all the rest was Diomedes who leapt the trench with his horses and drove his spear into the back of Agelaus of Troy who had wheeled his chariot about for flight. After him came Agamemnon and Menelaus, and then the two Ajaces; after them Idomeneus and Meriones; then Eurypylus. Teucer was the ninth. Protected by the shield of Ajax, his half brother, he shot one Trojan after another into the dust. He had just mowed down the eighth when Agamemnon looked at him with flashing eyes and exclaimed: "That is the way, my friend! Go on like this and be a beacon among the Argives. If Zeus and Athene grant us the conquest of Troy, you shall be the first to receive a gift of honor from me."

"I need no promises, my king," Teucer replied. "I shall not spare myself. I am putting forth all my strength, but as yet I have not succeeded in shooting down that mad dog." And he launched his arrow at Hector. It missed and struck a bastard son of King Priam, Gorgythion, whose head, weighed by the helmet, sank to one side, just as the poppy bends under a spring shower. Teucer sent a second arrow after the first. But Apollo diverted it from its mark, and it pierced the breast of Archeptolemus who was driving Hector's horses. This friend too Hector let lie, though he was filled with bitter sorrow for him, and called a third to his chariot. Then with burning zest he dashed forward, and just as Teucer was again bending his bow, Hector hit his collarbone with a long jagged stone; the bowstring snapped, his wrist grew numb, and he sank to his knees. But Ajax took care of his brother. He circled him, keeping him covered with his shield until two friends lifted him from the ground and carried him moaning to the ships.

And now Zeus again kindled the courage of the Trojans. Eyes glowing with rage, Hector stormed after the Argives as a hound pursues a boar over the wooded hills and slew everyone who came within hurling distance. Again the Argives were crowded back to their ships and prayed to their gods in anguish of soul. Hera heard them and was moved to pity. She turned to Athene. "The Danai are dying," she said. "Has not the time come for us to save them? See how Hector is harassing them—what carnage he has wrought!"

"Yes, my father is cruel," Athene replied. "He has forgotten how faithfully I helped his son Heracles in all his quests. Now Thetis has bribed him with her flattery and her caresses, and I am hateful in his eyes. Yet I think the time will soon come when he shall again call me his dear blue-eyed daughter. Help me harness the horses, Hera. I myself will go to Mount Ida to speak to my father."

When Zeus became aware of her intentions, he scowled and bade his messenger Iris, fleet as the wind, halt the chariot with the two goddesses as it was passing through the foremost gate of Olympus. When they heard his command they turned back; soon after, Zeus himself appeared in his thunder chariot, and the mountain of the gods quaked at his coming. He did not relent to his wife and his daughter though both pleaded with him. "The Trojans shall win a far greater victory tomorrow," he said to Hera. "Great Hector shall not rest from battle until the Argives fight at the very rudders of their ships and Achilles rises in his house at their clamor. This is the will of Fate." Hera fell silent and her face was sad.

It was dusk and the fight around the ships died down. Hector summoned his warriors to one side of the battlefield; they sat in council near the waters of the Scamander. "Had night not come," he said, "the enemy would be destroyed by now. But even though darkness has overtaken us, let us not return to the city. Some shall go and bring from it horned cattle and sheep, wine and bread. Watchfires will protect us from sudden attack while we eat or tend our wounds. And at break of day we will renew the onslaught against the ships. Then we shall see whether Diomedes thrusts me from the wall or whether I strip his dead body of its armor!" A wave of applause ran through the ranks of the Trojans. They did as he had counselled. All night they rested, and many fires were lit. Fifty at a time they regaled themselves with food and wine. Their horses stood near the harness and fed on spelt and barley.

THE ARGIVES SEND A MESSAGE TO ACHILLES

The terror and confusion of flight had not yet subsided in the Argive camp when Agamemnon had the princes summoned to a council, each one by name, but without noisy ado. Weighed with care and grief they came together, and the son of Atreus addressed them, sighing between his words. "Friends and guardians of our people, Zeus has been harsh with me. He who gave me so gracious an omen that I should conquer Troy and return home a victor has deceived me and now bids me return to Argos inglorious and leave behind on the field of battle many brave warriors. It is useless for us to resist the will of him who has shattered so many cities and will shatter many more. We are not destined to conquer Troy. So let us board our swift ships and sail to the land of our fathers."

Long after they had heard these mournful words, the heroes of Greece sat in silence. Then Diomedes spoke. "Only a short while ago," he said, "you mocked me before the Achaeans. You jeered at my lack of courage, O king. Yet now it seems to me that when Zeus conferred the scepter on you, he did not give you the valor that should go with it. Do you believe in all seriousness that the men of Greece are as unwarlike as would appear from your words? If your heart yearns for home, go! The way lies open, your ship is ready. But the rest of us, we other Argives, will remain until the palace of Priam lies in ruins. And even if everyone chose to leave, I and my friend Sthenelus would stay, in the faith that a god has guided us here!"

When he had ended, the heroes shouted acclaim, and Nestor said: "You are as young as my youngest son, yet every word you spoke was right and weighty. Come, Agamemnon, give a feast for these leaders of men. There is wine enough in your house. Those who keep the watch shall have their fare by the wall which skirts the trench, but we shall pass the cup here and listen to the counsel of the wisest among us."

And so it was done. The princes feasted with Agamemnon and were comforted, and after the banquet Nestor again rose and addressed the gathering. "Agamemnon, you know all that has happened since the day when against our judgment you carried the lovely daughter of Briseus from the house of Achilles. I, for one, warned you against this with great earnestness. Now we must think how we may persuade the offended son of Peleus to give up his grudge and anger."

"You are right," Agamemnon replied. "I am at fault, and I do not deny it. But I am willing to make good my mistake and offer ample recompense as well: ten talents of gold, seven tripods, twenty cauldrons, twelve horses, seven fair women from Lesbos whom I myself carried from their homes as spoils, and lovely Briseis herself. Though I took her from Achilles, I have not touched her, and I will swear to this with a solemn oath. When Troy is vanquished and the time to divide the spoils of victory is come, I myself will fill his ship with gold and bronze, and he may choose for himself those twenty women of Troy who, after Helen, are fairest. When we return to Argos, he shall take one of my daughters to wife. I will cherish him as my son-in-law, and Orestes, my only son, shall not be honored more or held more dear. Seven cities will I give him as dower with the bride. All this I promise to do as soon as he gives up his grudge."

"Truly," said Nestor, "these are no mean gifts you are willing to offer Achilles. Let us at once send chosen men to the house of the hero: Phoenix in the lead, then Ajax the Great, Odysseus, and with them the heralds Hodius and Eurybates."

After making solemn libation, the princes Nestor had named left the gathering and set out for the ships of the Myrmidons. They found Achilles plucking the strings of a lyre delicately curved and fitted with a silver crossbar. He had taken it as spoils from Eetion's city and was easing his heart by singing of the glorious exploits of heroes. His friend Patroclus sat opposite, silently waiting until he had ended his song. When the son of Peleus saw the men coming with Odysseus in the lead, he rose in surprise, keeping his lyre in hand. Patroclus too got up. Both went forward to meet the emissaries, and Achilles took Phoenix and Odysseus by the hands, saying: "Greetings, my friends! I suppose you have come because you are in need of something or other, but so great is my love for you, so much greater than for any among the Argives, that you are welcome to me even when I am in an angry mood."

Swiftly Patroclus fetched out a bowl of wine. Achilles himself fastened on a spit the back of a goat and a sheep and the shoulder of a fatted pig, and roasted these with the help of Automedon. Grouped about the board they ate their meal. When they had refreshed themselves with meat and wine, Ajax signed to Phoenix, but Odysseus anticipated him. He filled his cup and drank to Achilles, then clasped his hand and said: "Hail to you, son of Peleus! This feast was, indeed, abundant. But it is not your rich fare we have come for; overwhelming misfortune has driven us to you! For now it is a question of our rescue or our fall, according to whether you do or do not support us. The Trojans are threatening the wall and the ships. Hector's eyes flash with the lust to murder, and he rages at will, putting his trust in Zeus. Rescue the Argives at this late hour when their fortunes are at an ebb! Curb your pride! Believe me that a friendly spirit avails more than destructive feud. Your own father Peleus gave you such counsel when you set out against Troy." And then Odysseus counted up all the magnificent gifts Agamemnon offered to placate him.

But Achilles replied: "Noble son of Laertes, to your fair words I must answer 'no,' without an instant's hesitation. Agamemnon is as hateful to me as the gates of Hades, and neither he nor the Danai will ever induce me to fight in their ranks again. For have I had thanks for my labors and toils? Like a mother bird who brings her fledgling the morsels she finds, even if she herself goes hungry, I spent many troubled nights and days when the blood ran in rivers to conquer a woman for that ungrateful prince, and whatever I gained I brought the son of Atreus. He took everything and kept most of it for himself. Only a small part of his treasure did he distribute among the rest of us! And my own spoils, my beautiful prize, he tore from me. That is why tomorrow at dawn, after I have made sacrifice to Zeus and the other gods, my ships will be moving along the waters of the Hellespont. In three days I hope to be home in Phthia. Agamemnon has cheated me once. He shall not trick me again! Let him be satisfied with what he has. Go and give him my message, but if Phoenix likes he may stay and sail home with me to the land of our fathers."

In vain Phoenix, his old teacher, tried to shake the resolve of the young hero. Achilles only signed to Patroclus to prepare a bed for his friend. Then Ajax rose and said: "Odysseus, let us go. The cold heart of this man knows no kindness. Friendship does not move him. He is harsh and implacable." Odysseus too rose from the board, and after pouring a libation to the gods, they left the house of Achilles together with the heralds. Only Phoenix remained behind.

DOLON AND RHESUS

When Odysseus returned with Achilles' reply, Agamemnon and the princes fell silent. All night long sleep did not touch the lids of the sons of Atreus. Long before daybreak they rose with troubled heart and divided the work between them. Menelaus strode from hut to hut to wake the men and strengthen their courage. But Agamemnon went to the house of Nestor. He found the old man resting on his couch, his armor, shield, helmet, belt, and two lances at his side. He started from sleep, supported his head on his elbow, and called to the son of Atreus: "Who are you, walking alone through the ships at dead of night when others sleep, as though you were looking for a friend, or a mule gone astray? Speak, silent one! What is it you want?"

"Don't you know me, Nestor?" the son of Atreus said softly. "I am Agamemnon, whom Zeus has plunged into unfathomable grief. I cannot sleep. My heart throbs, and my limbs tremble with fear for the Achaeans. Let us go down to the guards to see if they are awake. For no one can tell if our enemies will not attack this very night."

Nestor quickly put on his woolen tunic, cast his crimson mantle about him, and accompanied the king on his way through the ships. First they wakened Odysseus who instantly slung his shield over his shoulder and followed them. Then Nestor approached the house of the son of Tydeus, touched his foot with his heel, and woke him with harsh words. "Tireless old man," the hero answered, still half asleep, "can you never rest? Are there not enough younger men to go through the camp by night and rouse the host? But you are never content to let be."

"What you say is true and right," answered Nestor. "I have enough people of my own, not to speak of my sons, who could perform this work for me. But the plight of the Argives is so grave that I myself must do as my heart bids me. Now death and life are balanced on the point of the sword. So rise, and help us waken Ajax and Meges, son of Phyleus." Instantly Diomedes rose, cast his lion's skin about his shoulders, and called the heroes Nestor had named. Together they went to look after the guards, but not one was asleep; all were wide-awake, armed, and ready.

Little by little all the princes gathered, and soon the council met. Nestor was first to speak. "How would it be," he said, "if someone ventured to go to the Trojans and should try to capture one of their men lying asleep at the very edge of the camp, or to eavesdrop at their council to find out whether they intend to remain on the battlefield or return to their city as victors? The man who proves hardy enough to do this should be rewarded with precious gifts."

When Nestor had ended Diomedes rose and offered to undertake this daring enterprise, provided someone accompanied him. And many were willing: both Ajaces, Meriones, Antilochus, Menelaus, and Odysseus. Then Diomedes said: "If you leave the choice of my companion to me, how can I fail to choose Odysseus, whose heart is steadfast in danger and who is beloved by Pallas Athene? If he goes with me, I think we could escape from fire or flood, for he always finds a way out sooner and better than anyone else."

"Do not blame or praise me too much," said Odysseus. "Remember that you are speaking before experienced men. But let us go. The stars have travelled far, and only a third of the night is left."

Then both girt on their strong armor and disguised themselves. Diomedes left his own sword and shield on the ship and borrowed the two-edged sword of Thrasymedes, his oxhide shield, and his helmet which had neither a crest of feathers nor plumes of horsehair. And Meriones gave Odysseus his bow, his quiver, a sword, and a helmet of leather topped with the tusks of a boar. Thus equipped, they left the Argive camp and went out into the night. From the right, they heard a heron cry as it flew past, and they rejoiced in the happy omen Pallas Athene had sent them and implored her to favor their undertaking. On they strode through the darkness, over weapons and corpses, through pools of blood, and their courage was like that of two lions.

While the Achaeans were planning to spy on the Trojans, Hector had made the very same proposal in the Trojan council and promised a chariot and two of the best horses from his share of prospective Argive spoils to the man who would undertake to report conditions in the enemy camp. Now among the Trojans was a man named Dolon, son of the herald Eumedes, who was well-known and respected. Dolon had stores of gold and bronze. He was ungainly and slight of build, but a swift runner. His heart leaped at Hector's words, and at the promise of the finest Argive chariot and horses—those of Achilles—he offered to enter the enemy camp and go to Agamemnon's ship, there to spy on the council of the Achaeans. Quickly he slung his bow over his shoulder, set on his head his helmet of otterhide, gripped his lance, and jauntily set out on his way. But the path he had chosen took him close to the two Argive heroes who were bound on a similar expedition.

Odysseus heard steps approaching and whispered to his companion: "Diomedes, someone is coming from the Trojan camp! Either he is a spy or he is out to strip the corpses of their armor. Wait until he passes, and then let us pursue and capture him or chase him toward our ships."

Both cowered down among the dead on one side of the path, and Dolon sped by unsuspectingly. When he was a bowshot past them, he heard the sound of their pursuit and stopped, for he thought that Hector was perhaps recalling him through a friendly messenger. But when the heroes were within a spear's throw of him, he saw that they were foes. Then he bent his supple knees and ran like a hare before the hound. "Stand, or I cast my lance at you!" Diomedes thundered and hurled his spear. But he missed the target on purpose, and the brazen point flew over the runner's shoulder and buried itself in the ground. Dolon halted, pale with terror. His chin shook and his teeth chattered.

"Take me alive," he pleaded tearfully as the heroes panted up to him and seized him. "I am rich and will ransom myself with as much bronze and gold as you may want!"

"Be of good courage," Odysseus said to him. "Do not think of death. But tell us truthfully what was taking you this way." And when Dolon had confessed all with fear and trembling, Odysseus said smilingly: "If your soul yearns for the horses of the son of Peleus, you have, indeed, good taste! But now tell me without delay: Where did you leave Hector? Where are his horses? His armor? And the rest of the Trojans and their allies?"

Dolon replied: "Hector and the princes sit in council near the gravemound of Ilus; the warriors are sleeping around fires and have no more guards than usual; and the allies from far away, who have no wives and children to care for, sleep apart from the rest of the host without any guards. When you enter the Trojan camp, the first people you will find are the Thracians, but lately arrived. They are grouped around Rhesus, their king, the son of Eioneus. His horses are dazzling white, the largest and swiftest I have ever seen. His chariot is decorated with silver and gold, and he himself wears armor of glittering gold, armor like that of an immortal rather than of a mere man. Now that you know all there is to know, either take me to your ships, or leave me here bound and prove to yourselves that I have spoken the truth."

But Diomedes scowled at his captive and said: "Liar, I know you are planning to flee, but I shall see to it that you will never again be a menace to the Argives!" Tremblingly Dolon started to raise his right hand to touch Diomedes' chin in supplication, but the sword of the son of Tydeus cut his throat, and his head rolled in the dust. Then the heroes took his helmet of otterhide, drew the wolf's skin from his body, loosed the bow, took the spear from his dead hands, and laid the armor on a tamarisk bush as a sign to show them the way home. After that they went forward until they came upon the Thracians, sleeping peacefully. Beside each stood his team of restless-hooved horses. Their weapons lay on the ground well-ordered, in three gleaming rows. In the center slept Rhesus, and his horses stood behind his chariot, tied to it with the reins.

"These are the men we are looking for," Odysseus whispered to Diomedes. "Now let us be swift to act. You untie the horses— or rather, you kill the men and leave the horses to me."

Diomedes did not stop to reply. As a lion rages among goats and sheep so he lunged wildly about him, and wherever his sword flashed, a death rattle sounded and the earth grew red with blood. Soon he had slain twelve Thracians. But wise Odysseus took each body by the foot and dragged it to one side to make way for the horses. And now Diomedes slew the thirteenth, King Rhesus, who was just moaning in the midst of a bad dream the gods had sent him. In the meantime, Odysseus had loosed the horses from the chariot; holding them by the reins and using his bow for a goad, he drove them out of the camp. Then he whistled softly as a sign to his companion. Diomedes was hesitating whether to draw the beautiful chariot away by the pole or carry it on his shoulders, when Pallas Athene approached him warningly and bade him hasten. Quickly Diomedes mounted the one horse. Odysseus, running beside, urged both horses on with his bow, and thus they sped back to the ships.

Apollo, the patron god of the Trojans, had seen Athene join Diomedes. This vexed Phoebus. He descended into the very midst of the Trojan host and wakened Hippocoon, the friend of Rhesus. When he noticed that the place where the king's horses had been standing was empty and that men were writhing on the earth in the throes of death, he called loudly on his friend in a griefstricken voice. The Trojans stormed to the aid of their allies and halted, numbed with fear, before the dreadful sight.

In the meantime, the two Greek heroes had reached the place where they had killed Dolon. Diomedes jumped down from his horse, but mounted again as soon as he had put the armor in the hands of his friend. Odysseus leaped on the other horse, and they flew over the ground toward the ships. Nestor was the first to catch the sound of fleet hooves and to tell the princes, but before they could stop to listen the heroes arrived, dismounted, clasped the hands of their friends, and related their adventures, a tale which the warriors heard with shouts of joy. Odysseus drove the horses through the trench, and the other Argives followed him to the house of the son of Tydeus. There they tied up the team by a manger filled with grain. The bloodstained armor, however, Odysseus laid down behind his ship until such a time as he could bring it, clean and bright, as a thank offering to Athene. And now the two heroes washed the sweat and blood from their limbs in the sea, sat in tubs filled with warm water, rubbed their bodies with oil, and enjoyed the morning meal, at which full cups abounded; and they did not forget to pour a libation to Pallas Athene.

ANOTHER ARGIVE DEFEAT

Day had dawned. Agamemnon bade his men don their armor, and he himself girt on his splendid cuirass, on which ten rows of bluish metal alternated with twelve of shining gold and twenty of white tin. The part shielding the neck was worked in the shape of serpents gleaming like rainbows. It was a gift from Cinyras, king of Cyprus. Then he fastened his sword to his shoulder by a strap buckled with gold. The scabbard was of silver and the hilt adorned with golden studs. He took his curved shield round which ran ten circles of bronze, and on it sparkled twenty bosses of white tin. In the center, blazoned on the dark azure field, was the head of the terrible Medusa, and the strap was in the shape of a purple dragon with three heads interlaced. On his head he set a helmet with four horns. Plumes of horsehair fluttered about it, and the crest nodded menacingly. Last he gripped two great lances with points of luminous bronze, and thus he strode into battle. From heaven Hera and Athene greeted the king with joyful thunder. And now the host sped forward. First the foot soldiers crossed the trench. After them came the chariots, and all moved forward with deafening clamor.

On the other side of the battlefield the Trojans had occupied a hillock. Their leaders were Hector, Polydamas, and Aeneas.

Next in importance were Polybus, Agenor, and Acamas, the three sons of Antenor. Like a star shining out between the clouds on a dark night, Hector appeared now in the van, now in the rear of the host and ordered the battalions. His brazen armor shone like a flash of lightning flung by Zeus. As reapers cut swathes in a field upright with grain, so Trojans and Achaeans, storming against one another, hewed their way through the mass of warriors. The Achaeans were first to break through the ranks of the foe, and Agamemnon, plunging forward, struck down Prince Bienor and his charioteer. Then he threw himself on the two sons of King Priam, Antiphus and his charioteer Isus. Antiphus he pierced with his sword, Isus he pushed from the chariot with his lance. Quickly he stripped them of their armor. And now he encountered the two sons of Antimachus, the Trojan prince who, beguiled by Paris' gold, had dissuaded the others from surrendering Helen.

The youths let the reins slip from their hands, crouched in the depths of the chariot, and pleaded for mercy. But Agamemnon, thinking of their father, slew one with his spear and cut off the hands and head of the other. And the Argives, on foot and in chariots, penetrated deeper and deeper into the ranks of the enemy, even as a fire lashed by the wind spreads through the dense forest.

Out of the turmoil and rivers of blood Zeus himself guided Hector, shielding him from missiles, and the prince fled past the slope covered with fig trees to the grave of old King Ilus and on toward the city. But Agamemnon, his hands spattered with Trojan blood, pursued him with loud shouts. Near the beech tree of Zeus, not far from the Scaean Gates, Hector and all those fleeing with him finally came to a stand. And Zeus sent Iris to command him to keep back as long as Agamemnon raged in the van and to leave the fighting to others until the son of Atreus was wounded. Then the father of all gods would lead him to victory. Hector obeyed. He spurred his warriors forward to fresh onslaught, and the battle opened anew.

Agamemnon rushed forward and again entered the lines of the Trojans and their allies. The first he came upon was Iphidamas, son of Antenor, a great and valiant hero who had grown up in Thrace, reared by his grandfather, and had just wed when he left to battle in the land of his birth. Agamemnon's lance missed him, and the spear of Iphidamas bent against the silver belt of his assailant. Swiftly Agamemnon gripped the shaft, wrenched it from his opponent's hand, and cut his throat with his sword. Thus Iphidamas died fighting for his people, far from his young wife, and there was no one to look with pity on his body, stark in the sleep of death. Agamemnon took his armor and flourished his splendid spoils as he strode through the rows of Argives. When Antenor's elder son Coon, one of the best of the Trojan warriors, saw him, he was filled with intolerable grief for his slain brother. But his sorrow did not lessen his caution. Coming from the side, unobserved by the son of Atreus, he suddenly thrust his spear deep into his arm, close to the elbow. Agamemnon felt a shudder course through him but would not stop fighting. As Coon tried to drag his brother from the field by the foot, Agamemnon's lance struck him under the shield, and he sank dead over the corpse.

Although the warm blood was still flowing from his open wound, Agamemnon went on making havoc among the Trojans with lance, sword, and stones. But when the blood began to clot, a sharp pain warned him to leave the field. Quickly he mounted his chariot and bade the charioteer take him back to the ships. Soon the chariot, in a swirl of dust, was speeding toward the Argive camp.

When Hector saw the son of Atreus leave, he remembered the message of Zeus and hurried to the front ranks of Trojans and Lycians, where he cried aloud: "Now take heart, my friends, and hold the Argives at bay. The bravest of the Danai has left the battlefield, and Zeus will give us victory. Forward! Rush among the Argives with your horses, that our glory may be the greater." So cried Hector, and he was the first to sweep on like a tempest. Not long after, nine Achaean princes and many of the common soldiers had fallen beneath his strokes. He had almost succeeded in driving the enemy back to their ships when Odysseus roused the son of Tydeus.

"Is it possible," he cried, "that we have forgotten how to fend off the foe? Come closer, friend, and stand beside me. Let us not live through the disgrace of seeing Hector capture our camp!" Diomedes nodded and hurled his dart at Thymbraeus of Troy; it shattered his left breast, and he rolled from his chariot and lay in the dust, while Odysseus slew Molion, his charioteer. On they dashed against the Trojans, and the other Achaeans began to breathe more freely. Zeus, who was still watching from the peak of Ida, held the fortunes of Argives and Dardanians in balance. But now Hector had recognized the two heroes and stormed straight at them with his battalion. Diomedes only just saved himself and cast his lance at the crest of Hector's helmet. It did, indeed, glance off, but Hector recoiled and fell on one knee. He broke his fall with his right hand, but the world went black before his eyes. By the time the son of Tydeus had run after his spear, the Trojan had swung himself back on his chariot and escaped death in the throng of his warriors.

Sulkily Diomedes turned to another of the Trojans, felled him to earth, and prepared to strip him of his armor. Paris took advantage of this opportunity. He hid behind the mound of Ilus and, pressed close to the stone, shot the kneeling hero in the right heel; the arrow went through the sole and stuck fast. Then with a laugh he leaped from ambush and scoffed at his victim. Diomedes looked around, and when he saw who the archer was he called to him: "So it is you, the favorite of women! Out in the open you could not prevail against me, and now you boast because you have scratched my foot from behind! But it irks me as little as if a girl or a mere boy had struck me." Odysseus, meanwhile, had hastened to the spot and shielded his wounded friend with his body, so that Diomedes could draw the arrow from his sole. It was painful, but his fingers were deft and sure. Then he mounted the chariot beside his friend Sthenelus and allowed him to take him back to the ships.

Now Odysseus was alone in the midst of his foes, and no Argive ventured to come to his aid. The hero considered whether to flee or remain steadfast where he was, but it quickly became clear to him that he who would win fame in battle must stay to slay or be slain. While he was pondering this, the Trojans surrounded him, even as hunters and their hounds circle the boar as he rages and whets his tusks. But Odysseus stood firm, and before long five Trojans measured their length in the dust. Then came a sixth, Socus, whose brother had just been slain, and cried: "Odysseus, today you will either go from here with the glory of having killed both the sons of Hippasus and taken their arms as spoils, or die from the thrust of my lance!" And with that he shattered the shield of the son of Laertes with his spear and flayed the skin from his ribs. But Athene did not let the point go deeper. Odysseus, who knew very well that the thrust had not been fatal, drew back a few steps and then lunged at his adversary who turned to flee; he pierced him in the back between the shoulders, so that the spear came out through his breast and he crashed to the ground. Not until then did Odysseus draw the lance out of his own wound. When the Trojans saw his blood spurt forth they thronged closer, and he retreated and called for help three times.

Menelaus was the first to hear and said to Ajax beside him: "Let us force our way through the thick of the battle. I heard the cry of Odysseus." Soon the two reached the unflinching fighter just as he was brandishing his lance against countless foes. But when Ajax held his shield like a towering wall in front of the hero the Trojans trembled with fear. Menelaus seized this moment to take the son of Laertes by the hand and help him mount his own chariot. Ajax, meanwhile, sprang into the very midst of the Trojans and swept corpses before him, just as a mountain stream swollen in winter uproots the dry oaks and pines. Hector did not see him. He was fighting on the left side of the field, on the shore of the Scamander, and sowing destruction among the youths who pressed about Idomeneus. The warriors would not have yielded to him, had not a three-barbed arrow launched by Paris wounded the right shoulder of Machaon, the great physician of the Argive host. At that Idomeneus called out in alarm: "Nestor! Come and help our friend into your chariot. A man who can cut out arrows and apply soothing salves is worth a hundred others!" Swiftly Nestor leaped to his chariot, lifted wounded Machaon beside him, and hurried toward the ships.

Hector's charioteer now drew his attention to the confusion in that wing of the Trojan army where Ajax was forcing his way through the foe. In an instant they were there with the chariot, and Hector began to attack the Argives; but he avoided Ajax, for Zeus had warned him not to measure his strength against a man of even greater daring than his own. Zeus also put terror into the soul of Ajax, so that when he saw Hector, he slung his shield over his shoulder and, fearing for the ships, left the Trojan battalions. Seeing him run, his enemies hurled their

lances at the shield hanging down over his back. But whenever
Ajax turned his face toward them, they shrank back. When he
came to the path that led to the ships, he stopped and fended off
his attackers. Their spears either clung in his shield covered
with seven oxhides, or buried themselves in the earth without
touching his body. When brave Eurypylus saw him so hard
pressed, he hastened to his aid and pierced the breast of Trojan
Apisaon. While Eurypylus was taking the armor from his dead
foe, Paris shot him in the right thigh, and he retreated to his
friends who protected him with raised lances and shields.

In the meantime, Nestor's mares bore him and wounded
Machaon out of battle and past glowering Achilles who sat
in the stern of his ship and calmly watched the Trojans pursue
his countrymen. Not dreaming that his words would bode ill to
his friend, he called to Patroclus: "Go and ask Nestor whom he
is bringing in from the field, for suddenly—I do not know why
—my spirit is moved with pity for the Argives."

Patroclus did as he was bidden and ran to the ships. He
reached Nestor just as he had dismounted from the chariot and
was handing the horses over to Eurymedon, his servant, and entering his house to refresh himself and Machaon with food which
Hecamede served them. When the old man saw Patroclus standing in the door, he rose from his chair, took him by the hand,
and urged him to sit with him. But Patroclus refused. "There
is no time," he said. "Achilles sent me to see who it is you brought
back from the field with you. Now that I myself have recognized
Machaon, versed in the skill of healing, I must hurry back to
tell him. You know my friend and how impetuously he is apt to
accuse even those who are guiltless."

Nestor replied, and his tone betrayed a shaken spirit. "Why
is the heart of Achilles now troubled in behalf of the Argives who
are wounded and almost dead? All the bravest men lie hurt on
the ships: Diomedes struck by an arrow, Odysseus and Agamemnon by spears, and this man I have just brought here, matchless
Machaon, by a dart from the bowstring. But Achilles is merciless. Is he going to wait until our ships go up in flame and we
bleed to death, one after another? Oh, that I had the strength
of my youth or my prime, when I came to the house of Peleus as
a victor! That was the time I saw your father Menoetius and

you and the child Achilles. His father, a hero turned gray, urged him always to be first and foremost, to strive ahead of all the rest, while yours told you to be friend and guide to the son of Peleus, because, though he was the stronger, you were the older. Tell this to Achilles. Perhaps now he will listen to your words." So said the old man, calling up fair memories from the time of his own brave youth, until the heart of Patroclus beat fast in his breast.

When, on his way back, he passed the ships of Odysseus, he met Eurypylus, wounded in the thigh by an arrow and painfully limping home from battle. He called on the son of Menoetius to soothe his pangs with the arts of Chiron, the centaur, which Achilles had taught him. Patroclus took pity on him and led him into the house, supporting him under the arm. There he laid him down on an oxhide and with a sharp knife cut the arrowhead from his thigh. Then he washed the dark blood away with warm water, ground a bitter herb between his palms, and held it to the wound until the blood began to clot. Thus he tended the wounded hero.

THE FIGHT AT THE WALL

The Argives had erected the trench and the wall around their ships without making offerings to the gods, and so it was that these fortifications were not destined to protect them. Now, in the tenth year of the siege, Poseidon and Apollo finally resolved to destroy the whole structure by loosing the mountain streams on it and by churning up the sea. They decided to do this immediately after the fall of Troy.

The din of battle swelled around the camp, and the Argives, dreading Hector's fury, crowded against their ships. Hector raged among his men like a lion, bidding them cross the trench. But the horses were afraid. When they reached the edge they reared and snorted, for it was too wide to leap, too steeply sloped to cross, and set with pointed stakes besides. Only foot soldiers could venture the crossing. When Polydamas saw this he took counsel with Hector, saying: "If we forced our horses, we should all be lost and perish ingloriously at the bottom of the trench. So let the charioteers halt at the brink, but we ourselves with our brazen armor will cross on foot under your leadership and break through the wall."

Hector approved this plan. At his command all the heroes except the charioteers alighted from the chariots and ranged themselves in five groups: the first under Hector and Polydamas; the second under Paris; Helenus and Deiphobus led the third; Aeneas was in charge of the fourth; Sarpedon and Glaucus headed the fifth, the group of the allies. Of all the warriors only one, Asius, refused to leave his chariot. He turned it to the left where the Argives had reserved a passageway for their own horses and chariots. Here he found the gate wide open, for the Danai were waiting to see if perhaps one of their number would come belatedly to seek refuge in the camp. Asius drove straight for this passage, and other Trojans followed him on foot. But in the entrance were two formidable guards: Polypoetes, son of Pirithous, and Leonteus. They stood at the gate like tall mountain oaks which grip the earth so firmly with roots long and broad that neither winds nor scourging rains can shake them from their place. And suddenly these two hurled themselves at the advancing Trojans, while at the same time a shower of stones rattled from the squat towers of the wall.

While Asius and his comrades were engaged in this unexpected combat and lost many men, others pressed through the trench on foot and battled for other gates of the camp. Now the Achaeans were concentrating all their strength on defending their ships, and those of the gods who favored them gazed sadly down from Olympus. Only one of the Trojan battalions, that most numerous and with the bravest men, led by Hector and Polydamas, delayed undecided in front of the trench, for they had seen an evil omen: an eagle flying on the left above their host. In his talons he clutched a red snake which squirmed and, curving backward, bit the bird in the neck. Stung with pain, he dropped it and flew away, and the snake fell in the very midst of the Trojans. With horror they watched it writhing in the dust, and they accepted the whole occurrence as a sign from Zeus.

"Let us stop!" Polydamas, son of Panthous, called to his friend Hector in alarm. "The fate of the eagle who did not succeed in carrying home his prey may be in store for us, too."

But Hector said scornfully: "How do birds concern me? Let them fly right or left! I rely on the pledge of Zeus. For me, all that counts is to rescue our country. Why shudder at the thought of the fight? Even if all of us lose our lives at the ships, you still need have no fear of death, for you have not the courage to face the foe. But let me tell you that should you really flee, my own lance will slay you." So said Hector and strode forward, and all the rest followed him and shouted the savage war cry. Down from the mountains of Ida Zeus sent a great wind that whipped up the dust and swept it on the ships, so that the confidence of the Argives ebbed, while the Trojans, trusting the sign of the Thunderer and their own strength, prepared to destroy the wall of the Danai by tearing down the battlements and digging up the stakes of the palisade.

But the Argives never faltered. Firm on the ramparts they stood with their shields and greeted the attackers with stones and missiles. The two Ajaces made the rounds on the wall. They spoke to the fighters in the towers, kindly to the brave and menacingly to the slackers. And all the while the stones flew here and there as thick as snowflakes. But Hector could not have broken the massive bolts of the gate had not Zeus incited his son Sarpedon, the Lycian with his gold-rimmed shield, to spring on his enemies like a hungry mountain lion and swiftly say to Glaucus, his friend: "Why should we Lycians have seats of honor at the banquet or why should the brimming cups be offered first to us, as if we were gods, if we do not distinguish ourselves when the fight goes hardest? Come, let us heighten our own glory, or by our death, the glory of others!"

Glaucus heard and kindled at his comrade's words, and both stormed straight ahead with their Lycian warriors. Menestheus, looking down from his tower, started when he saw them rage forward, a terror to his countrymen. Timidly he looked about for support. In the distance he could see the two Ajaces, and close at hand Teucer returning from the huts. But his call for help could not reach him. It was thrown back by the clash of helmets and shields and drowned in the roar of battle. So he sent Thootes, the herald, to the two Ajaces with a message for the son of Telamon and his brother Teucer to come to his aid. Ajax the Great did not delay an instant. With Teucer and Pandion who carried his bow he hastened toward the tower along the inside of the wall. They reached Menestheus just as the Lycians were beginning to scale the ramparts. Ajax at once pried loose a jagged piece of rock and with it crushed the helmet and head of Epicles, a friend of Sarpedon's, so that he plunged from the wall like a diver. And Teucer wounded the bare arm of Glaucus while he was climbing the wall. At that Glaucus secretly left, lest the Achaeans see him and jeer at his wound.

Stricken with grief, Sarpedon saw his friend steal out of battle, but he himself climbed the wall, pierced Alcmaon, son of Thestor, with his lance, and then shook the rampart so mightily that it gave way, and a path lay open to the Trojans. Ajax and Teucer met the onslaught. Teucer shot an arrow into Sarpedon's shield strap, while Ajax pierced the shield itself, and the thrust of his lance was so forceful that for a moment the Lycian recoiled. But he regained his position almost at once and turning to his men, cried aloud: "Have you forgotten to join in the attack? I cannot break through alone, not if I were the bravest man in the world. Only by keeping together can we open a path to the ships." And the Lycians rallied around their king and came up faster. From within, the Argives doubled their resistance, and so the foes stood, separated by nothing but the rampart, lunging savagely at one another, like farmers who, at the border of their fields, fight over their boundaries. Right and left, from towers and ramparts, blood flowed in rivers.

For a long time the battle was undecided, but at last Zeus gave Hector the upper hand. He reached the gate in the wall, and his men followed him or climbed past on either side. At the gate whose portals were locked by two bolts that met on the inside was a thick stone, pointed at the top. This Hector wrenched from the earth with superhuman strength and beat it against the hinges and planks until the bolts gave way. The gate crashed open, and the heavy stone fell inside. Terrible to behold in the glitter of his brazen armor, like a night of thunder and lightning, Hector leaped through the gate with flashing eyes, brandishing two shining lances. His warriors swarmed after him. Others had scaled the wall by the hundreds. The entrance to the camp was in an uproar, and the Danai fled to their ships.

THE STRUGGLE FOR THE SHIPS

When Zeus had furthered the fortunes of the Trojans to this point, he left the Achaeans to their misery and, seated on Mount Ida, turned his eyes from the ships and allowed his gaze to rove over the land of Thrace. Poseidon, meanwhile, was far from idle. He sat on one of the highest peaks of wooded Samothrace. Below him lay the summits of Ida, Troy, and the ships of the Danai. Sorrowfully he watched the Argives yield to the Trojans. He left the jagged cliffs, and with four steps—a god's steps that made the hills and forests quake—he was down on the shore of the sea, near Aegae, where, under the restless waters, stood his palace of gold, bright and imperishable. Here he girt on his golden armor, harnessed his light-maned horses, grasped his glittering goad, swung himself into his chariot, and drove through the tide. The sea monsters recognized their king and, slipping from rifts in the rock, glided about him. Willingly the waves parted to let him pass, and not a drop touched the brazen axle. Quickly he reached the Argive ships. He arrived in a grotto between Tenedos and Imbros. There he unyoked his horses, hobbled them with golden thongs, and fed them on ambrosia. Then he sped into the fury of the fight, where the Trojans were clustered around Hector like storm-clouds and preparing to master the ships.

Poseidon mingled with the Argives in the shape of Calchas, the soothsayer. First he called to the two Ajaces who needed no urging, for the joy of battle burned fiercely within them. "You two," he said, "could save your people if only you took stock of your strength. Though the Trojans are crossing the walls in other places too, I have no misgivings, for there our combined forces will be able to fend them off. I fear for us only here, where Hector is raging like a firebrand. O that a god would put into your heads the thought of centering your resistance in this place and inciting others to do likewise!" With these words the Earth-Shaker struck them lightly with his staff. Their courage rose and their limbs grew light, while the god went from them swift as a hawk.

Ajax, son of Oileus, was the first to know who he was. "Ajax," he cried to his namesake, "that was not Calchas! It was Poseidon! I know him by his stature and his gait, for the gods are easy to discern. Now my heart longs for the fight that will decide the issue. My feet and hands are tingling."

And the son of Telamon replied: "My hands too grasp the spear now firmer. My spirit soars and my feet yearn to fly. I am wild with desire to do single combat with Hector!"

While they were talking, Poseidon went among the heroes who stood listless and weary by the ships. He stirred their courage until they roused themselves, joined the two Ajaces, and awaited Hector and his Trojans, composed and steadfast. So close they stood that lance crowded on lance, shield on shield, and helmet brushed helmet. The fluttering plumes touched, and the spears quivered in their hands. But the Trojans too were coming in full force, Hector in the van, rushing headlong like a rock pried loose from the peak of a mountain and tearing up trees as it crashes down with unrestrained force.

"Hold firm, Trojans and Lycians!" he called back over his shoulder. "That well-ordered army over there will scatter before my spear, as surely as the Thunderer is my aid!" So he cried out, spurring the courage of his men. Among them was Deiphobus, Priam's valiant son, covering himself with his shield and striding defiantly forward, though with muffled tread. Meriones chose him as a target for his lance, but Deiphobus held his great shield well away from his body, and the point broke against it. Vexed at his failure, Meriones turned toward the ships to fetch a sturdier spear from his hut.

Meanwhile the fight went on and battle cries rose from many throats. Teucer smote Imbrius, son of Mentor, under the ear, and he fell like a towering ash on a mountain top, struck by the axe of a woodsman. Hector strove with Teucer for the body, but instead of him he felled Amphimachus, and as he bent to strip off his helmet the lance of Ajax the Great struck the boss of his shield so that he recoiled; Menestheus and Stichius together bore the body of Amphimachus from the field, while the Ajaces, like two lions snatching a goat from the hounds, carried that of Imbrius back to the Argive ranks.

Amphimachus was a grandson of Poseidon, and the sea-god was angered by his death. Hastily he went to the huts to fan the flame of Achaean valor. There he found Idomeneus who had taken a wounded friend to the physicians and was just fetching another spear from his house. In the shape of Thoas, son of Andraemon, the god approached him and spoke in ringing tones. "King of the Cretans," he said, "what of all your threats? Let no one who of his own free will withdraws from battle on this day ever return home from Troy! Sooner shall dogs rend his flesh."

"So let it be, Thoas!" Idomeneus called after the vanishing god, and he armed himself with stronger weapons and dashed out of his hut, magnificent as the lightning which Zeus flashes through the sky. At that moment he met Meriones whose spear had broken against the shield of Deiphobus and who was about to get himself a fresh lance. "Valiant hero, I know what you need," Idomeneus said to him. "You will find at least twenty spears I have won in battle leaning against the wall of my house. Take the best for yourself." And when Meriones had selected a tall lance, the two returned to battle together and joined those of their friends who were fending off Hector's onslaught.

Although Idomeneus was turning gray, he rallied the Argives with youthful fire. The first foe his spear wounded under the belt was Othryoneus, who fought on the side of the Trojans because he was courting Cassandra, the daughter of King Priam. While he was dragging his victim off by the foot, Idomeneus shouted jubilantly: "Now go and wed the daughter of Priam, happy bridegroom! Had you been our ally we would have given you the fairest daughter of the son of Atreus. Come with me to the ships. There we can discuss the marriage; you shall have a fine dowry!" While he was taunting him thus, Asius flew toward him in his chariot to avenge the dead man. Already his arm was raised to smite, when the spear of Idomeneus pierced his throat just under the chin; the point came out through the nape of his neck, and he fell from his chariot and measured his length on the ground. When his charioteer saw this, he was numbed with fear. His hands refused to drive the horses away from the scene, and the lance of Antilochus, son of Nestor, tumbled him from the chariot as well.

Now Deiphobus advanced toward Idomeneus, determined to avenge the death of Asius, his friend. He cast his spear at the Cretan, but he shifted his shield so deftly that the weapon flew over, grazing the rim with a metallic clang, and on into the liver of Prince Hypsenor, who fell to his knees. "Asius, you are avenged!" sang out the Trojan. "For I have sent you an escort on your way!" Hypsenor, groaning aloud, was carried from the field by two of his companions.

And still Idomeneus did not lose courage! He slew Alcathous, the son-in-law of Anchises, shouting: "Have we evened our accounts, Deiphobus? I give you three for one! Come and see for yourself whether or not I am sprung from the line of Zeus!" Idomeneus said this because he was the grandson of King Minos and thus the great-grandson of Zeus. For an instant Deiphobus turned over in his mind whether to dare single combat or to call some other brave Trojan to help him. This latter course seemed best, and soon he and Aeneas, his sister's husband, rushed at Idomeneus. Seeing those warriors coming against him, he did not falter with fear, but awaited them as a boar awaits the hounds. But he too called to friends fighting nearby. "Come and help me who stand alone!" he cried. "For I dread Aeneas, who

is great in battle and in the heyday of youth besides." At his call
came Aphareus, Ascalaphus, and Deipyrus, supporting their
shields on their shoulders.

Meanwhile Aeneas too called to his friends Paris and Agenor,
and the Trojans followed him as sheep follow the bellwether.
Bronze clashed on bronze, and instead of single combat a fight
of many men ensued. Aeneas cast his spear at Idomeneus, but it
missed and went into the ground. Idomeneus smote Oenomaus in
the belly, so that he toppled and, dying, clawed the earth with
his hand. The victor only just had time to draw out his spear,
for missiles came so hard and fast that he was forced to retreat.
But his old feet moved slowly, and Deiphobus, glowering with
rage, hurled a lance after him which, missing its mark, felled
Ascalaphus, son of Ares. The war-god, who by decree of Zeus
was held captive in the golden clouds of Olympus along with
the other immortals, did not know that a son of his had fallen.
As Deiphobus reached for the gleaming helmet of Ascalaphus,
Meriones wounded him in the arm, and the helmet rolled to the
ground. Meriones sprang forward, snatched his spear from the
arm of the wounded man, and darted back into the throng of his
comrades. Polites put his arm about the waist of his brother
Deiphobus and carried him out of battle, through the trench, and
to the waiting chariot which took him, bleeding and weak with
pain, to the city.

The others fought on and on. Aeneas smote Aphareus, and
Antilochus, Thoon. Adamas, the Trojan, rushed at Antilochus,
but bled to death from the spear thrust of Meriones. Of the
Argives, Deipyrus was struck in the temple by the sword of
Helenus and rolled along the ranks of the Danai. Full of grief,
Menelaus brandished his spear at Helenus who at this moment
launched an arrow at the son of Atreus. Menelaus smote the son
of Priam, but the spear rebounded from his cuirass. The arrow
of Helenus also went astray, and now Menelaus buried his lance
in the hand which still held the bow, and Helenus, fleeing toward
his friends, dragged the weapon with him. Agenor, his comrade-
in-arms, drew the point from his palm and took the woolen sling
of one of his companions to bind up the seer's wound.

Now evil chance guided Pisander, the Trojan, toward dauntless Menelaus. The son of Atreus missed with his lance; his

adversary aimed his spear at Menelaus' shield, but the shaft
broke near the point. Then Menelaus lunged forward with his
sword. Pisander drew his long battle-axe from under his shield,
and they ran at each other. But the Trojan only grazed the crest
of his assailant's helmet, while the other split his forehead above
the nose. His eyes dropped out of their bleeding sockets, and he
died racked with anguish. Menelaus set his heel on his breast and
said with bitterness and rejoicing: "Dogs! You carried off my
young wife with all her treasure, after she had received you with
due hospitality. And now you want to throw firebrands among
our ships and murder the Argive host! Will you never leave off,
insatiable fighters that you are?" Thus he spoke, and he stripped
the bloodstained armor from the corpse and gave it to his friends
for safekeeping. Then he forged to the front again and with
his shield caught the lance which Harpalion hurled at him.
Meriones smote him who had cast it in the thigh, and the dying
Harpalion was lifted into the chariot by his father Pylaemenes.
This roused Paris, and furiously he shot at Euchenor of Corinth,
who happened to cross his path, and the arrow pierced his ear
and cheek.

So they fought, but Hector was unaware that on the left of
the ships the Danai were close to victory. At the very place where
he had first leaped through the gate, where the wall was lowest,
he penetrated farther and farther into the ranks of the Achaeans.
In vain they tried to check him. Boeotians, Thessalians, Locrians,
Athenians—none could force him back. Like oxen teamed at the
plough, the two Ajaces strode breast to breast, and the warriors
of the son of Telamon were steadfast and stayed close. But the
Locrians who could not endure this form of fighting did not
follow on the heels of Ajax, son of Oileus. For they had gone
against Troy full of confidence, without helmets or shields or
lances, armed only with bows and woolen slings. Earlier in the
war they had scattered many a Trojan battalion with their missiles. Now too they harried the Trojans, standing in ambush
and shooting from a distance, and in this way they threw confusion among them.

The Trojans would surely have been driven from the huts
and ships and ingloriously forced back to their city, had not
Polydamas addressed stubborn Hector. "Do you spurn counsel,

friend, just because you are boldest in battle? Do you not see that the flames of war are closing over your head, that the Trojans are either retreating with the spoils they have won, or fighting in isolated groups near the ships? Go from here and summon the noblest of your people to an assembly to decide whether we should rush into the labyrinth of the ships or retreat unharmed. I myself fear the Argives will pay back their yesterday's debt, while their most indomitable warrior still waits on his ship."

Hector agreed and asked his friend to call an assembly. He himself hastened back into battle, and wherever he met a commander, he bade him go to Polydamas. He looked for his brothers Deiphobus and Helenus, Asius, son of Hyrtacus, and Adamas in the foremost ranks and found the first two wounded, the others dead. When his eyes fell on Paris, he shouted at him angrily: "Where are our heroes, you seducer of women? Soon it will be all up with our city, and then you yourself will not escape awful Fate. But now come and fight while the others are gathering for the council."

"I will follow you with a glad heart," said Paris soothingly. "You shall not complain of lack of courage on my part." Together they stormed into the heart of the fight, where the bravest of the Trojans were surging ahead like gusts of wind in sullen weather. Soon Hector was in the van. But the Argives did not recoil from him in terror as before, and mighty Ajax challenged him to combat. The Trojan, however, ignored his taunts and rushed toward the ships.

POSEIDON STRENGTHENS THE ACHAEANS

While arms were clashing outside, old Nestor sat quietly in his hut, sipping his wine and playing the host to wounded Machaon, the physician. But when the battle cry drew close and sounded louder and louder in their ears, he gave the care of his guest over to Hecamede and bade her prepare a warm bath for him. Then he took shield and lance and left the hut. He saw the ominous turn the encounter had taken, and while he was still hesitating whether to fight or seek out Agamemnon and confer with him, the king himself with Odysseus and Diomedes came toward him from the ships. All three were wounded and leaned on their lances. They had only come to watch the further course of the battle without hope of sharing in it themselves. With deep concern they discussed the fate of their army with Nestor.

"We have nothing more to hope for," said Agamemnon. "Since the trench we dug with such labor and the wall we thought could resist any attack have not served to protect the ships, since our enemies are in our very midst, I must believe that unless we Argives leave of our own accord, Zeus will let us perish here, far from Argos, and that we shall die an inglorious death. So let us drag down the ships which are nearest the shore, launch them, and wait for night. Then, if the people of Troy turn back to their city, we can return and push the rest of the ships down to the water and escape all danger when protecting darkness falls."

Odysseus listened to this proposal with a scowl. "Son of Atreus," he answered, "you should be at the head of warriors less valiant than ours! At the peak of battle you bid us launch the ships? The poor Danai would be stricken with dismay, the lust for fight would ebb from their hearts, and they would withdraw themselves from battle!"

"Far be it from me," said Agamemnon, "to do this against the will of the Argives and without hearing what they have to say. And I shall gladly withdraw my proposal if anyone knows a better way out."

"The best way of all," cried the son of Tydeus, "is to return to battle at once and—though we are wounded and cannot fight ourselves—stir the hearts of those who can, as true leaders should!"

Poseidon, protector of the Argives, who had been listening to the heroes, heard these words with approval. In the shape of an old warrior he came up to them, clasped Agamemnon's right hand, and said: "Shame to Achilles who is rejoicing in the flight of the Argives! But take courage! The gods do not hate you, and soon you will see the dust swirl under the heels of fleeing Trojans." So said the god and stormed from them straight for the field. As he ran he shouted his battle cry to the Argive host so loudly that it sounded like the voices of ten thousand mortals, and the heart of every hero grew staunch and daring.

When Hera, surveying the struggle from the heights of Olympus, saw Poseidon, her brother, take a hand in the fight in favor of her friends, she too could no longer bear to watch inactively. In the depths of her soul she burned with resentment for Zeus, sitting hostile on the peak of Ida, and pondered how she might trick him and divert his thoughts from the battle. At last she devised a scheme. She hastened to a hidden chamber which her son Hephaestus had built for her in the palace of the immortals. He had fitted the doors with bolts no other god could open. Hera entered this chamber and locked herself in. Then she bathed and anointed her lovely body with perfumed oils, smoothed her shining locks, put on a rich and delicate robe which Athene had made for her, and fastened it over her breast with a brooch of gold. About it she wound her shimmering girdle, clasped in her ears a pair of precious earrings set with jewels, cast a soft, sheer veil about her, and bound slender sandals to her shining feet. Radiantly beautiful she left her chamber and visited Aphrodite, the goddess of love.

"Do not bear me a grudge, my sweet," she said caressingly, "just because I am helping the Argives and you the Trojans. And do not deny me what I beg of you with all my heart. Lend me your magic girdle of love which beguiles both men and gods. For I am bound for the utmost ends of the earth to see my foster parents, Oceanus and Tethys. They live in constant feud with each other. I want to see whether I cannot reconcile them with gentle words, and for this I shall need your girdle."

Aphrodite, who did not see through Hera's ruse, readily complied. "Very well," she said. "You are the wife of the king of gods. It would not be fitting to refuse your request." And with that she loosed her embroidered girdle wherein were seduction and enchantments. "Hide it in your bosom," she counselled, "and you will not return without having accomplished what you desire."

And now the queen of gods went to far-off Thrace and from there to Lemnos, the dwelling of Sleep, brother of Death, and implored him to lull to sleep the bright eyes of Zeus. But Sleep was afraid. Once before, at Hera's command, he had numbed the thought of the Thunderer. It was when Heracles was on his way home from ravaged Troy, and Hera, his enemy, wanted to drive him from his course and to the island of Cos. When Zeus awoke and saw that he had been tricked, he hurled the gods about in his palace and would have destroyed Sleep, had he not fled into the arms of Night, who restrains both men and immortals. The god of sleep reminded Hera of this, but she calmed him. "What are you thinking of!" she exclaimed. "You cannot really believe that Zeus' zeal in behalf of the Trojans is as great as his love for Heracles, his son! Be wise and obey my wish. If you do as I say, the youngest and loveliest of the Graces shall be your wife." The god of sleep had her seal this promise with an oath on the Styx and then gave her his word to do as she asked.

Hera left him and soared to Mount Ida in all her shimmering beauty. When Zeus beheld her, his heart was overcome with fervent love, and he instantly forgot the Trojan War. "How did you come here from Olympus?" he asked her. "Where are your horses and chariot, my love?"

Craftily Hera replied: "I am going to the ends of the earth to reconcile Oceanus and Tethys, my foster parents."

"Must you always differ with me?" exclaimed Zeus. "You can take this journey another time. Stay with me, and let us delight in each other while we watch this battle of two great peoples."

When Hera heard this she was dismayed, for she saw that even her beauty and the magic girdle of Aphrodite could not make her husband forget the struggle on the plain below and his resentment for the Achaeans. But she concealed her alarm and twined her white arms around him. "I shall do as you say," she said docilely, but secretly she beckoned Sleep who had followed her, invisible to all, and was standing behind the king of gods, awaiting her command. And Sleep silently weighed the lids of Zeus. The king of gods did not even answer, but laid his drowsy head in Hera's lap and was soon slumbering deeply. Now Hera quickly dispatched Sleep as her messenger to Poseidon and had him tell her brother: "This is the time to carry out your purpose and give glory to the Argives, for thanks to my ruse Zeus lies asleep on the summit of Ida."

Swiftly Poseidon stormed to the front and assuming the shape of an Argive hero called aloud: "Shall we give Hector such easy victory? Shall we let him conquer our ships and win undying fame? I know he is relying on the anger of Achilles, but what a disgrace if we were vanquished just because the son of Peleus is not with us! Take your tallest shields, set on your heads your most flashing helmets, brandish your mightiest lances! Let us go, I myself in the lead! We shall see if Hector can stand against us!" Obedient to the ringing, rousing voice, the warriors rallied. The wounded princes ordered the battalions and distributed the weapons, the best to the strong, the less good to the weaker. Then all pressed forward. First went the Earth-Shaker, and in his right hand was a terrible sword that flashed like lightning. He cleared the way, for all dispersed before him, since no one dared face him in fight. And as he advanced the sea rose and the waves towered behind the ships of the Argives.

But Hector did not allow this to intimidate him. As a forest fire roars through a valley winding between mountains, he tore ahead, and the two hosts clashed in new encounter. First Hector aimed at Ajax the Great, and his lance sped to its mark. But the shield and the sword straps which crossed over the breast protected the son of Telamon, and Hector, vexed by the loss of his weapon, drew back into the ranks of the Trojans. Ajax hurled an enormous stone after him, and he fell in the dust; lance, shield, and helmet flew in all directions, and his bronze armor clanged. The Danai shouted with joy, loosed a hail of spears, and hoped to drag Hector away. But the foremost heroes among the Trojans came to his aid: Aeneas, Polydamas, noble Agenor, Sarpedon of Lycia, and Glaucus, his comrade-in-arms. They held up their shields to fend the missiles from him and lifted him and placed him in a chariot which took him safely back to the city.

When the Achaeans saw Hector fleeing, they drove against the foe with increased force. Ajax was the center of great tumult, for his spear and his lance struck and smote on all sides. Even so Argive heroes fell, and in their fall saddened their friends. Ajax avenged the death of Prothoenor, whom Polydamas had slain, by killing Archelochus, son of Antenor. Promachus of Boeotia, felled by Acamas, the brother of Archelochus, was avenged by Peneleus, who slew Ilioneus. Ajax pierced Hyrtius, Antilochus took the weapons of Mermerus and Phalces, and Meriones did to death Hippotion and Morys. Teucer's arrow pierced Prothoon and Periphetes. Agamemnon wounded Hyperenor in the groin. But Ajax the Less, the agile fighter from Locris whose great moment had come, made the most havoc among the Trojans who had already retreated from the walls and were beginning to flee through the pointed palisade of the trench.

APOLLO REVIVES HECTOR

The Trojans did not stop until they had reached their chariots. They were bewildered and pale with fear. And now Zeus awoke on the peak of Ida and lifted his head from Hera's lap. Abruptly he sprang up and at a glance took in the scene below: Trojans fleeing, Argives in hot pursuit. In their ranks he saw his brother Poseidon. He saw Hector on his way to the city, and now the chariot halted; he was taken from it and laid on the ground, and his friends surrounded him. The wounded son of Priam was unconscious. His breath came in gasps and he spat blood, for it was no mean hero who had struck him!

Full of pity the eyes of the father of gods and men rested upon him. Then he turned to Hera, and his face darkened. "Deceiver!" he said to her threateningly. "What have you done? Are you not afraid that you will be the first to suffer for your crime? Have you forgotten how you once hung in mid-air, your feet bound to two anvils, your hands tied with a golden chain, and no dweller on Olympus could draw near to you without being hurled down to earth by me? That was your punishment for inciting the god of the north wind against my son Heracles. Are you so anxious to endure such a penalty a second time?"

For a time Hera said nothing. Then she spoke. "Heaven and earth and the waters of the Styx be my witnesses," she said, "that it was not I who roused the Earth-Shaker against the Trojans. It must have been his own heart that prodded him to this. As for me, I should rather try to induce him to obey the command of Zeus who rules all heaven."

The face of Zeus cleared, for Aphrodite's girdle which Hera had with her was still doing its work. After a pause he spoke, and his voice was gentler. "If you were in agreement with me in the council of immortals," he said, "Poseidon would be compelled to alter his plans in accordance with our wishes. But now, if you are, indeed, serious in trying to please me, call Iris who shall summon my brother home from battle, and Apollo who shall heal Hector and breathe fresh courage into his soul."

Hera obeyed. She sped to the halls of Olympus where the immortals were gathered about the board. When she entered, they rose up from their places, and each offered her his cup. She took that of Themis, sipped of the nectar, and told them the bidding of Zeus. Fleet as the wind Iris floated down to the field of battle. Hearing his brother's command from her lips, Poseidon was ill pleased. "Those are not brotherly words," he said sulkily. "Nor should he try to break my will, for I am as good as he. It is true that when we cast lots for sovereignty, I was apportioned only the gray sea, Pluto the underworld, and Zeus heaven. But earth and Olympus are common to us all."

"Shall I repeat your defiant words to the father of gods, just as you have said them?" Iris asked hesitantly.

But the god thought better of it, and leaving the ranks of the Danai, he grumbled: "Very well, then. I shall come with you. But one thing is certain, and Zeus shall hear of it: if he opposes me and the other gods who favor the Argives and refuses to decree the fall of Troy, implacable enmity will flare up between us." So he said and dipped down into the sea, and immediately the Achaeans missed his presence among them.

To Hector Zeus dispatched Phoebus Apollo. The sun-god found the son of Priam no longer lying on the ground but sitting up, for Zeus had revived him. The sweat of anguish had ceased; his breath came more easily; life had returned to his limbs. When Apollo approached him full of pity, he looked up mournfully and said: "Who are you, best of the immortals, who are come to inquire after me? Have you not heard that Ajax the Great cast a stone at me near the ships and struck me in the breast and stopped me just as I was about to conquer? I thought that this very day I should have to behold black Hades."

"Be of good courage," Apollo replied. "Zeus has sent me, his own son Phoebus, to you. I shall shield you at his command, as I did before of my own accord, and brandish in your behalf the golden sword you see in my hands. Mount your chariot again. I myself will go on ahead, clear the way for your horses, and help you put the Argives to flight."

Scarcely had Hector heard the voice of the god when he leaped up like a horse who has eaten his fill at the manger and breaks his tether impetuously. He swung himself on his chariot, and when the Achaeans saw him flying toward them, they stood still and ceased pursuing, like hunters and dogs who have followed a stag into the thick of the forest and suddenly halt at the sight of a shaggy lion which crosses their path. The first to see Hector was Thoas of Aetolia, a man of ready words, who at once told the Argive princes among whom he was fighting what he had beheld. "Woe is me!" he cried out. "What miracle is this! Hector, whom all of us saw struck down by the stone of the son of Telamon, is there, upright in his chariot, hastening into battle joyful and eager. Zeus, the Thunderer, must be giving him aid! If you take my advice, you will order the bulk of our warriors to retreat to the ships, while we, the bravest, fend him off. For though he is raging forward with the lust to kill, he will hesitate to break through our ranks."

The heroes obeyed his wise counsel. They called on the noblest of their number, and these swiftly gathered about the two Ajaces, Idomeneus, Meriones, and Teucer, but all those behind them

withdrew to the ships. The Trojans, meanwhile, advanced in
serried ranks. Hector, high in his chariot, was leading them, and
he himself, in turn, was led by Apollo sheathed in cloud, holding
in his hand the aegis. Standing shoulder to shoulder, the Argives
awaited the enemy, and loud shouts sounded from both hosts.
And now arrows whirred from the string and spears cut the air.
But it was the Trojans who always hit the mark. Their missiles
quivered in the flesh of their foes because Phoebus Apollo was
with them, and every time he shook his aegis in the faces of the
Danai and sent forth a terrible shout from his dark cloud, the
hearts of the Argives quaked, and they forgot to defend themselves.

First Hector slew Stichius, the leader of the Boeotians, then
Arcesilaus, friend of Menestheus. Aeneas killed and stripped
of their armor Iasus of Athens and Medon, half brother of
Ajax of Locris. Mecisteus fell by the hand of Polydamas. Polites
slew Echius and Agenor Clonius. Paris shot Deiochus through
the back as he was fleeing from the field, and the point of the
lance came through his breast.

While the Trojans were seizing the weapons of their victims,
the Argives fled in utter confusion, dashing toward the trench
and the palisade, swerving hither and thither. Some, goaded by
terror, were already crossing the wall. Then Hector called to
his men, and his voice rang across the field: "Let the bodies lie
in their bloodstained armor and make straight for the ships. If
I come on anyone bound elsewhere, I shall do him to death!" Thus
he cried out, lashing on his horses, and drove toward the trench,
while all the heroes of Troy followed him in their chariots. With
his feet full of godly strength, Apollo stamped down the steep
banks of the trench and made a bridge for them as long as a
spearcast. On this path the god himself crossed first, and with
one thrust of his aegis he demolished the wall of the Argives,
just as a child playing on the shore of the sea scatters the forts
of sand he has only just built. The Achaeans were again crowded
into the passageways between their ships and lifted their hands
to the gods in supplication. And when Nestor made his prayer,
Zeus answered with thunder that boded mercy.

The Trojans interpreted the sign from heaven to their own
advantage. They raged across the wall with horses, chariots and

men, and fought from the chariots, but the Danai fled to the ships and defended themselves from the decks.

While Argives and Trojans were still fighting for the wall, Patroclus sat in the splendid house of Eurypylus, whose wound he was tending, anointing it with the balm of soothing herbs. But when he heard the Trojans crashing the wall and the Achaeans fleeing with loud cries of distress, he struck his thigh with the flat of his hand, and his voice was troubled. "Eurypylus," he said, "much as I want to help you back to health, I cannot stay here any longer, for the din outside is coming too close. Your comrade-in-arms will have to help you now. I myself will go to the son of Peleus and with the aid of the gods try to induce him to take part in battle again at long last." Hardly had he ended before his swift feet bore him away.

All the while the struggle for the ships went on, and the fortunes of war were equally divided. Hector and Ajax were fighting for one of the ships, and the son of Priam could not force him from his stronghold nor throw a firebrand into the vessel. And the son of Telamon could not drive Hector back. Ajax's spear felled Caletor, a kinsman of Hector who had been fighting at his side, and Hector slew Lycophron, comrade of Ajax, with his lance. As he fell, Teucer sprang to his brother's aid and sped a shaft into the neck of Clitus, charioteer of Polydamas. Polydamas, fighting on foot, caught at the reins of the horses as they plunged away. A second arrow of Teucer's flew toward Hector, but Zeus broke the bowstring, and the missile swerved to one side. Sorrowfully the archer recognized the interference of a hostile god. Ajax counselled his brother to lay aside his bow and arrows and fight with shield and spear. This he did and set on his head a stately helmet. Hector, on the other hand, called to his men: "Take courage! I just saw the Thunderer break the shaft of the bravest of the Argives. So on to the ships, for the gods are with us!"

On the other side Ajax exhorted his warriors. "Shame on you, Achaeans!" he cried. "We must save the ships or die! There is no other course. If mighty Hector burns them to their keels, do you intend to walk home across the ocean? Or perhaps you think Hector is bidding you to a dance rather than to battle? Better to hasten the choice between life and death than loiter in shameful uncertainty, downed by men less worthy than ourselves, men who fight shielded by gods!" So spoke Ajax and felled a Trojan hero, but for every man he laid low Hector slew one of his own comrades. After a little, the struggle centered about the body and armor of Dolops whom Menelaus had killed. Hector called on all his brothers and kinsmen, but Ajax and his friends guarded the ships with a veritable wall of shields and lances.

Then Menelaus urged forward Antilochus, Nestor's son, saying: "There is no one younger and swifter than you in the entire host, and no one braver! It would be a praiseworthy deed if you leaped from the ranks and slew one of the Trojans!" Thus he incited Antilochus, and the youth instantly sprang forward from the throng, looked threateningly about him, and hurled his gleaming spear. As he aimed, the Trojans flew apart, but he struck Melanippus, son of Hicetaon, under the nipple. He fell, and his weapons clattered around him. Antilochus raced to him like a hound to the fawn the hunter has shot from ambush, but when Hector advanced on him, he fled like a beast of prey which has mangled the herdsman or the dog and, well aware of what he has done, runs away when he sees men coming toward him. Trojan missiles sped in his wake, and Antilochus did not turn until he was safely on his own side again.

And now the Trojans rushed on the ships like bloodthirsty lions. Zeus seemed resolved to grant the merciless wish of Thetis, whose anger was long and unrelenting like that of her son Achilles. Nevertheless, as soon as the first ship burst into flame, he visited flight and pursuit on the Trojans and again rewarded the Argives with triumph and glory. Hector fought with bitter rage. He foamed at the mouth, his eyes glittered under his beetling brows, and the fierce crest of his helmet streamed in the air. Because he was destined to live only a few more days, Zeus gave him strength and splendor beyond all other men for one last time. Already Pallas Athene was preparing grim death for him. But now he tried to break through the ranks of his foes wherever he saw the densest throngs and the finest armor. For a long time he fought without success. The Danai stood man beside man in a solid mass, like a cliff in the sea against which the tide pounds in vain, while the spray of the surf spatters its sides. But he threw himself on the warriors as, in a storm, a wave rushes on a ship, and the Argives were stricken with terror and fled. One—it was Periphetes of Mycenae, son of Copreus, and a better man than his ugly father—stumbled against the lower rim of his shield and fell backwards, and Hector's lance stabbed him in the breast.

The Achaeans were retreating from the foremost ships, but they did not scatter through the streets of the camp. Shame and dread kept them together. They crowded around the huts and exhorted one another, above all old Nestor who quickened their hearts with his battle cry. Ajax, son of Telamon, strode over the ships, and in his right hand he wielded a pole twenty-two cubits long and bound with iron rings. As an agile rider leaps from horse to horse while the spectators stare in amazement, so he sprang from ship to ship and called down to the Argives in a terrible voice. But Hector too was not content to rest in the safe haven of the ranks. As an eagle flashes through the sky and swoops on flocks of cranes or swans resting on the margin of a stream, he rushed on one of the ships, and Zeus himself pushed him on from behind so that he flew forward and all his men after him.

Then the battle for the ships broke out afresh. The Argives were ready to die rather than flee, and there was not a Trojan who was not in high hopes of being the first to fling a firebrand into the ships. And now Hector laid hold of the stern of the fair ship which had brought Protesilaus to Troy but was not destined to take him back, since he had fallen in the battle which took place shortly after the landing. The struggle focused around this ship. It was not a matter of shooting the bow or casting the spear. Fighting at close quarters, the men used sharp hatchets, battle-axes and swords against one another, and thrust with their lances, keeping them in their hands. Many a good sword slipped from lifeless fingers or fell from the shoulder of a fighter, and the earth ran with blood. But Hector, once having seized the stern, held fast to it and cried: "Now bring the brands and raise the battle cry! For Zeus has given us a day which shall make return to us for all that has gone before. On, and take the ships which have caused us so much suffering! Not one of our elders would restrain us from using this moment to the full. Zeus himself bids us go!"

Even Ajax could no longer withstand Hector's attack. The missiles came too hard and fast. He drew back a little and swung himself to the bench at the rudder. But never did he cease watching where he might fend off the foe, and he brandished his lance against the Trojans drawing closer with the brands. At the same time he spoke to his friends in a thundering voice. "Be men!" he called to them. "Or do you think there are others beyond the ships, others who will help you, or a stronger wall to shelter you? You have no city to flee to like the Trojans. We are on enemy soil, crowded to the edge of the sea, far from the land of our fathers. Our safety depends on the strength of our arms." Thus he spoke and thrust with his lance at every Trojan advancing with a brand, so that soon twelve bodies lay on the ground before him.

THE DEATH OF PATROCLUS

While the ship on which Ajax stood had become the center of a struggle to the death, Patroclus, leaving wounded Eurypylus, had hastened to Achilles. When he entered his house the tears gushed from his eyes like a torrent which pours its dark waters over a steep cliff. Compassionately the son of Peleus gazed at him and said: "You are crying like a child, Patroclus, a girl child who runs after her mother and screams 'take me, take me!' and clings to her gown until the mother lifts her into her arms. Have you bad news from Phthia? And do they concern my Myrmidons, or me, or yourself? I know that your father Menoetius and my father Peleus are alive. Or is your sorrow for the people of Argos, who are perishing miserably as a result of their own presumptuousness? Tell me what is in your heart and let me know all."

First Patroclus only sighed, but then he spoke: "Do not be angered with me, noblest of heroes. It is true that the fate of the Argives weighs heavily on my soul. All the bravest lie among the ships, laid low by missiles launched or thrust. Diomedes is wounded; Odysseus and Agamemnon gashed with lances; Eurypylus struck in the thigh by an arrow! None of these fight in our ranks now; they have been given over to the physicians. But you are implacable! Your parents are not Peleus and Thetis, the mortal and the goddess! The dark sea or the stony mountain must have borne you, for your heart is relentless. Well then, if you are held back by your mother's words or by some message from the gods, let me at least go with your warriors and bring comfort to the Achaeans. Let me gird on your own armor. Perhaps the Trojans, seeing me and thinking it is you, will stop fighting and give us time to rally our strength."

But Achilles scowled and said sulkily: "It is not my mother nor the voice of gods that keeps me here. It is the bitter pain gnawing at my soul, pain that an Argive has dared to rob me, his peer, of what was mine by right. But I never intended to cherish my grudge forever, and from the outset resolved to give it up when the battle came close to my ships. Now, while I cannot make up my mind to take part in the fight myself, you may take my armor and lead our fighters. Rush on the Trojans with all your might and drive them from the ships. There is only one you shall not attack, and that is Hector. And be careful not to fall into the hands of a god, for Apollo loves our foes. As soon as you have saved the ships, turn back. Let the rest slaughter one another in the open field. For I should be willing to let all the Argives perish, so that we two might be the only ones left to tear down the walls of Troy."

While they were talking, Ajax was more and more sorely pressed near the ships, and his breath grew labored. Spears and arrows rattled against his helmet. His shoulder, burdened by his shield, began to stiffen. The sweat of anguish poured from his limbs, but he could not rest. When Hector's sword struck off the top of his lance so that only the broken shaft was left in his hand and the brazen point clattered to the ground, Ajax knew that the Argives were confronted with the powers of a god, and he drew back in dismay. Then Hector and his men tossed a huge brand into the ship, and the flames leaped up and closed over the stern.

When Achilles saw the flare of fire, his stubborn heart winced with pain. "O Patroclus!" he cried. "Keep them from taking the ships and barring our men from escape. I myself shall go to assemble my warriors." Patroclus rejoiced and swiftly girt on the greaves of Achilles. About his breast he bound his spangled cuirass, slung his sword over his shoulder, set on his head the helmet with its streaming horsehair crest, seized the shield with his left hand and with his right two mighty lances. He would have liked to take the enormous spear of his friend Achilles. Chiron, the Centaur, had once given it to Peleus. It was carved from an ash of Mount Pelion in Thessaly, and it was so large and so heavy that no one except the son of Peleus could handle it. And now Patroclus bade Automedon, his friend and charioteer, harness the horses Xanthus and Balius, the immortal offspring the harpy Podarge had borne the god of the west wind, and besides these the horse Pedasus, which the son of Peleus had once taken as spoils from Thebe in Cilicia. Achilles, meanwhile, called together his Myrmidons, and they came like hungry wolves, fifty men from each of the fifty ships. And their five leaders were Menesthius, son of the river-god Spercheus and Polydora, the fair daughter of Peleus; Eudoras, son of Hermes and Polymele; Pisander, son of Maemalus and, after Patroclus, the best fighter of them all; and last Phoenix, gray about the temples, and Alcimedon, son of Laerces.

As they were leaving, the son of Peleus called to them: "Let my Myrmidons not forget how often they threatened the Trojans and reproached me for my wrath which compelled them to refrain from battle. The hour you have yearned for has come. Now fight to your hearts' content!" When he had spoken, he withdrew to his house and from a chest filled with tunics, mantles, coverlets, and other precious possessions his mother Thetis had given him to take on the journey, he fetched a cup, artfully wrought, from which no one but himself had ever drunk the sparkling wine and from which no god but the Thunderer had received libation. Now he stepped outside, poured a libation to Zeus, and prayed that the Argives might win and Patroclus, his comrade-in-arms, return to the ships in safety. The first request Zeus heard with a nod; at the second he shook his head, but all this was unseen by Achilles. He returned to his house to put away the cup. Then he went out to watch the battle between Achaeans and Trojans.

Like a swarm of wasps the Myrmidons sped in the wake of Patroclus, their leader. When the Trojans saw him coming, their hearts hammered with terror and their companies faltered in confusion, for they thought it was Achilles. They looked desperately about for a way to escape destruction. Patroclus took advantage of their fear and cast his shining lance into their midst where the press was thickest about the ship of Protesilaus. It struck Pyraechmes of Paeonia and pierced his right shoulder. Moaning he tumbled on his back, and the Paeonians around him were bewildered with dread and fled before Patroclus. He quenched the fire, and the ship was only half-burned. Now all the Trojans took to flight, and the Danai pursued them through the passageways between the ships. But soon the Dardanians rallied, and the Argives were forced to fight on foot, man for man. Patroclus shot Areilycus in the thigh; Menelaus thrust his lance into the breast of Thoas; Meges, son of Phyleus, stabbed Amphiclus in the calf; Antilochus, son of Nestor, pierced the groin of Atymnius. Then Maris, enraged by the fall of his brother, rushed at Antilochus, placed himself in front of slain Atymnius, and brandished his lance. But Thrasymedes, Nestor's other son, gored his shoulder and upper arm with his spear, so that he sank dying to the ground. When brothers had thus killed brothers, Ajax the Less leaped nimbly forward and smote Cleobulus in the neck with his sword. Peneleus and Lycon ran at each other with their lances but lunged past, each missing his mark; when they took to their swords, however, the Achaean triumphed. Meriones hit Acamas as he was mounting his chariot and pierced his right shoulder. Down from the chariot he toppled, and darkness veiled his eyes.

Ajax the Great was intent on one thing alone: to strike Hector with his spear. But the son of Priam was a skillful and experienced warrior and covered himself so deftly and well with his shield that arrows and lances bounded off the oxhide. He was, of course, aware that victory was turning from him and his men, but he remained steadfast, thinking at least to protect and save his dear companions. Not until the onslaught swelled to resistless fury did he turn his chariot and goad his splendid steeds back across the trench. The other Trojans were not so fortunate. Many of the horses broke the poles and left the chariots shattered between the stakes of the palisade. But whoever cleared the trench sped toward the city, swirling up the dust, and Patroclus, sounding the battle cry, pursued them. Many plunged headlong, falling under the wheels, and the chariots overturned. At last the immortal horses of the son of Peleus leaped the trench, and Patroclus lashed them on, for he wanted to overtake Hector's speeding chariot. On the way he killed whomever he found in the field between the wall and the river. As he stormed ahead, Pronous, Thestor, Eryalus and nine other Trojans fell by his spear, the thrust of his lance, or the stones he hurled. Sarpedon of Lycia saw this with grief and bitterness, reproved and incited his men, and sprang from his chariot in full armor. Patroclus did the same, and now they rushed at each other with loud cries like eagles with sharp talons and curved beaks.

Seated on Olympus, Zeus looked pityingly on Sarpedon, his son. But Hera reproached him. "What are you thinking of?" she said. "Would you spare a mortal who is long since forfeit to death? If all the gods removed their sons from battle, what would become of the destinies you yourself are resolved to fulfill? Believe me, it is better to let him perish in the field, to give him over to Sleep and Death, and let his people bear him away, bury him, and heap him a mound." Zeus let the importunate goddess have her way, but from his heavenly eyes there dropped a tear for his son.

The two heroes were now within casting distance. But first Patroclus struck at Thrasydemus, Sarpedon's brave comrade-in-arms. Sarpedon's spear missed Patroclus but went into the right flank of Pedasus, the mortal horse, who, as he fell, the breath rattling in his throat, startled the two deathless horses. The harness creaked, the reins tangled and would have torn, had not Automedon, the charioteer, quickly drawn his sword from his hip and cut the thong of the dead horse.

Sarpedon cast a second time and again missed his adversary. But this time Patroclus' spear struck the Lycian in the belly, and he fell like a mountain pine under the axe, ground his teeth, and clawed at the bloodstained dust with his hand. With the last remnant of his strength he called to Glaucus, his friend, telling him to protect his body with his Lycians. Then he died. Glaucus begged Phoebus Apollo to heal his arm which Teucer had wounded with an arrow at the storming of the walls and which still hurt and disabled him. And the god took pity on him and instantly eased his pain. He strode through the ranks of the

Trojans and called on Polydamas, Agenor, and Aeneas to guard the body of Sarpedon. The princes mourned when they learned of his death, for though he was of an alien line, he had been a pillar of strength to their city. But their sorrow did not make them idle. Savagely they stormed against the Danai, Hector in the lead.

Patroclus, meanwhile, roused the courage of the Argives, and they ran at the Trojans, uttering battle cries and fighting for the body of Sarpedon. Then Hector hurled a stone which struck Epeigeus, son of Agacles, and for the first time the Myrmidons recoiled. But Patroclus, grieving bitterly at the death of his friend, dashed to the van, broke the back of Sthenelaus of Troy, and drove the Trojans to retreat. Glaucus was first among them to forge ahead again, and he pierced the breast of Bathycles, the Myrmidon, with his lance. Meriones then struck Laogonus, whose father Onetor was a priest of Idaean Zeus. But when Aeneas cast his spear at Meriones, he missed. While these two were scoffing at each other, Patroclus called to them: "Why waste time with words! War is decided by arms!" And with that he led his men toward the corpse of Sarpedon, but the Trojans fended them off fiercely, so that the body was covered with blood and dust from the head to the soles of the feet.

Zeus, who had been watching the conflict attentively, pondered a little on whether or not Patroclus should die, but for the time being he thought it better to grant him victory. And so the friend of the son of Peleus succeeded in driving Trojans and Lycians alike back toward the city. The Danai stripped Sarpedon of his armor, and Patroclus was just about to hand it over to the Myrmidons when, at the bidding of Zeus, Apollo descended from the mountains, took the body on his shoulders, and bore it away to the shores of the Scamander. Here he washed it in the clear water, anointed it with ambrosia, and gave it to Sleep and Death, the twin brothers. High they rose on their wings and carried it to his native land of Lycia.

But Patroclus, driven by Fate, exhorted his charioteer to greater speed and raced after the Trojans and Lycians, straight to his own destruction. Nine Trojans he slew and stripped of their armor, and he plied his lance with a hand so savage and sure that he would have conquered Troy with all her towers, had

not Apollo stood on the highest rampart, intent on saving the Trojans and destroying the hero. Three times the son of Menoetius scaled the wall, and three times Apollo held out toward him the shield in his immortal hand and cried: "Go back!" And knowing this for the command of a god, Patroclus withdrew in haste.

At the Scaean Gates, fleeing Hector stopped his horses and hesitated whether to urge them back into the tumult of battle or bid his people lock the gates and retreat behind the safe walls of their city. While he was still wavering, his fingers slack on the reins, Phoebus in the semblance of Asius, brother of Hecuba, approached him and said: "Hector, why do you shun encounter? If I were as much stronger as I am weaker than you, I should send you to the underworld for your hesitation. But come! If you do not like to hear such words, swing your chariot around and spur the horses toward Patroclus. Who knows but Apollo may send you victory?" So the god, in the form of Asius, whispered in his ear and vanished. Then Hector spoke words of courage to Cebriones, his charioteer, and he headed for the field. Apollo, running on before, wrought confusion in the ranks of the Achaeans. But Hector did not stop to slay a single Argive. He made straight for Patroclus.

When the friend of Achilles saw him coming, he leaped down from his chariot. In his left hand he brandished his spear and with his right he picked up from the ground a jagged stone and threw it at Cebriones. It struck him in the middle of the forehead, and he fell to earth, Patroclus calling after him jeeringly: "By the gods, a nimble man! How easily he plunges into the dust! Perhaps he was versed in the art of diving and was a trader in oysters!" Like a lion he sprang toward the body he was deriding, but Hector fended him off from his half brother. He gripped the head of the slain, while Patroclus clutched the foot. And from both sides Trojans and Danai raged at one another as when the east wind clashes with his brother from the south.

Toward evening the Argives gained the advantage. They took possession of the corpse of Cebriones and stripped it of its armor. And now Patroclus fell on the Trojans with redoubled fury and slew three times nine of them. But at his fourth onslaught, Death lay in ambush, for Phoebus Apollo himself fought in this encounter. Patroclus did not observe him, because he was wrapped in a heavy mist. But Apollo came up from behind and struck his back with the flat of his hand, so that everything blurred before his eyes. Then the god knocked the helmet from his head, and it clattered to the ground and rolled under the hooves of the horses, so that the crest was soiled and draggled with dust and blood. And now he broke the lance in his hand, loosed the shield-strap from his shoulder and the cuirass from his breast, and numbed his heart, so that he stood motionless and staring. Then Euphorbus, son of Panthous, a brave warrior who that day had felled twenty Argives, pierced his back with a lance and returned to the ranks. But Hector running forward thrust his spear into the groin of the wounded hero, and the brazen point went clear through his body. Hector vanquished him as a lion downs the boar at the mountain spring to which both have come to quench their thirst. He seized the lance to wrench it from the flesh of Patroclus and cried jubilantly: "Patroclus! You were going to turn our city to a heap of ruins and carry our wives away on your ships to be slaves in your country! Now I have at least put off the evil day of servitude; as for you—the vultures will feast on your flesh. What does your friend Achilles avail you now?"

Dying Patroclus answered him, but his voice was faint. "Rejoice as much as you wish, Hector," he said. "Zeus and Apollo have granted you effortless triumph, for it was they who deprived me of my weapons. Had it not been for the gods, my lance would have tamed you and twenty more like you. In the face of the gods, it was Phoebus who struck me down, in the face of men, Euphorbus. You may strip me of my armor. But one thing I predict: not for long will you go proudly on your way, for disaster lurks at your side, and I know by whose hand you will fall." When he had gasped out these words, the soul left his body and flew to the underworld. But Hector called after him: "Why predict my coming fate, Patroclus? Who knows but that Achilles himself may first be slain by my spear!" And with these words he dug his heel into the earth, pulled the brazen spear from the wound, and cast the dead man back on the ground. Then he turned his lance, dripping with Patroclus' blood, against Automedon, his charioteer. But the immortal horses bore him out of danger.

Next Euphorbus of Troy and Menelaus, son of Atreus, fought for the body of Patroclus. "You shall atone!" shouted the Trojan. "Atone for having slain Hyperenor, my brother, and widowed his wife!" And he drove his lance at the shield of the son of Atreus. But the iron point bent double. Then Menelaus lifted his lance and thrust it deep into his enemy's throat, so that the point came out at the nape of his neck and his black locks, adorned with gold and silver, streamed with blood. Down he sank, and his weapons clattered as he fell. Instantly Menelaus stripped him of his armor and would have borne it away, had not Apollo envied him his spoils. Assuming the shape of Mentes, king of the Cicones, he came to Hector and persuaded him to leave off pursuing the immortal horses of Achilles which Automedon was driving off, as spoils too difficult to attain, and go back to the body of Euphorbus. Hector turned and suddenly saw Menelaus bending over the bleeding corpse and taking the splendid armor. The son of Atreus heard the ringing cry of the Trojan hero and had to admit to himself that he could not withstand Hector dashing toward him with his battalions. Reluctantly he retreated, leaving the body and armor behind, but as he fled he glanced back from time to time, or paused to look for Ajax the Great. He finally found him to the left, where the tumult was thickest, and hurried toward him to ask his help in the struggle for the body of Patroclus. When the two drew near the place where the son of Menoetius had fallen, they saw that Hector had already taken the armor and was drawing the body toward him to hew the head from the shoulders and drag the trunk away as a feast for the dogs. But when he saw Ajax coming under cover of his shield of seven oxhides, he gave up his prey and quickly fled to the ranks of his comrades. There he sprang into his chariot and handed the armor of Patroclus to friends who were to take it to Troy for him, to be preserved as a token of his glory. Meantime Ajax stood guard over the body like a lion over its young, and by his side Menelaus kept watch.

Glaucus of Lycia meanwhile glowered at Hector and reproached him. "What avails your fame," he said, "if you falter and flee from a hero. Think now how to defend your city single-handed. No Lycian, at all events, will fight beside you from now on. For how can we expect you to aid a lesser man, now that you have let Prince Sarpedon, your comrade-in-arms, to whom you were bound by ties of hospitality, lie unprotected, the prey of the Danai and the dogs! If the Trojans had our courage, we should soon have the body of Patroclus inside the walls of Troy. When the Argives would be ready enough to give us the corpse of Sarpedon, if only to get back the splendid armor." Glaucus said this not knowing that Apollo had removed the body of Sarpedon from the hands of the Argives.

"You are foolish, Glaucus," said Hector, "if you think I am afraid of powerful Ajax. Never yet have I shrunk from the fight. But the will of Zeus is mightier than all our power. Watch me now, though, and judge whether I am as timid as you have just said." With these words he raced after his friends who were carrying toward the city the armor of Achilles which Patroclus had worn. When he reached them, he exchanged his own cuirass for that of Achilles and girt on the immortal armor the gods themselves had given Peleus at his wedding with Thetis, goddess of the sea. When Peleus felt himself growing old, he had given it to his son, but he, alas! was not destined to grow old in it.

The king of men and immortals looked down from the heights and saw Hector girding on the arms of godlike Achilles. Gravely he shook his head and spoke in his heart's depth: "Unhappy Hector, you do not even dream that Death already stalks at your side. You have slain the cherished friend of the hero before whom all others tremble; you have stripped his body, snatched the helmet from his head, and now you walk adorned with the im-

mortal armor of the son of a goddess. But because you will never
return from this encounter, because Andromache, your wife, will
never greet you again, nor undo these splendid arms, I shall give
you one last and glorious victory." When Zeus had ended, the
cuirass clung closer about Hector, the spirit of Ares flamed
within him, and his limbs swelled with strength and power. With
a shout he rejoined his allies and led them against the foe.

The struggle for the body of Patroclus broke out afresh. So
furiously did Hector rage that Ajax said to Menelaus: "I am
now less concerned for dead Patroclus who will be food for the
birds and dogs of Troy, than for our own heads. For Hector
and his men surge about us like a cloud. Lift your voice and see
if the heroes among the Danai will hear your cry." Menelaus
called as loudly as he could, and the first to hear was Ajax of
Locris, the swift son of Oileus. He ran to the spot, and after him
came Idomeneus with Meriones, his comrade-in-arms, and countless others, so that the corpse was again fenced about with shields
of bronze. The Trojans pressed them so hard that the body was
almost dragged from their midst. But at last Ajax the Great came
to the rescue. As Hippothous, the Pelasgian, an ally of the Trojans, was tying the ankles of the body with a thong to pull it by,
the son of Telamon hurled his spear through the round top of
his helmet. It cracked, and brains and blood from the wound
spattered the point. Hector aimed at Ajax but hit Schedius, the
Phocian. Ajax countered and pierced the cuirass of Phorcys, son
of Phaenops, who was fighting for the body of Hippothous, and
the lance dug into his entrails.

Now the Trojans, and even Hector himself, recoiled, and the
Argives would have conquered against the decision of Zeus, had
not Apollo, in the guise of Periphas, the aged herald, goaded
mighty Aeneas on to battle. Aeneas knew him for a god. He fired
his men with ringing shouts and himself sprang forward in the
lead. At that the Trojans once more turned their faces to the
foe. Aeneas slew Leocritus, friend of Lycomedes. He, in turn,
avenged the death of his comrade by killing Apisaon of Paeonia.
And now the Argives again held out their lances to ward their
adversaries from the body of Patroclus.

In other parts of the field too the fighting went on ever more
furiously, until the sweat poured from the struggling warriors.

"Rather shall the earth swallow us," cried the Danai, "than that we leave this body to the Trojans and return to our ships without having won glory!"

"Even if we die to the last man," the Trojans roared on their side, "let no one hang back!"

While they were fighting, the immortal horses of Achilles stood apart. When they heard that Patroclus, their charioteer, had died at Hector's hand, they began to weep as men do. In vain did Automedon try to urge them on, now with the goad, now with caressing words, and now with threats. They refused to stir either toward the ships or to the battling Argives. Motionless as a monument on the mound of the dead they stood before the chariot and hung their heads to the ground. Soiled with dust, their manes streamed thick and curling beneath the ring in the yoke, and hot tears dropped from their eyes. Even Zeus, gazing down from above, could not but feel pity for them. "Poor creatures!" he said to himself. "Why did we give you, eternally young and immortal, to mortal Peleus? That you too might suffer sorrow like luckless men? For of all that breathes and moves on earth, there is nothing more wretched than man! And as for Hector, vain is his hope of taming you and yoking you to his chariot. I shall never permit it. Is it not enough that he vaunts his ownership of the armor of Achilles?" And Zeus filled the horses with courage and strength.

At once they shook the dust from their manes and quickly drew the chariot into the throng of Trojans and Achaeans. But Automedon, alone in the chariot, could not guide the horses and hurl his lance at the foe as well. While he was still in this predicament his friend Alcimedon, son of Laerces, caught sight of him and was astonished that he should expose himself in this way without a charioteer. "Who except Patroclus was ever your equal in bridling horses?" Automedon called to him. "If you will take the reins and the goad, I can leave the horses to you and use my strength for fighting."

When Automedon gave his place to another, Hector observed it and said to Aeneas beside him: "Look over there! The horses of Achilles are rushing into battle with an inexperienced charioteer. Are you willing to tackle those two with me? The spoils are well worth the trouble!" Aeneas nodded assent, and both stormed forward under their shields, with Chromius and Aretus following them.

But Automedon prayed to Zeus, and the Cloud-Gatherer filled his heart with unwonted strength. "Drive close behind me, Alcimedon!" he cried, and then: "Here Ajax! Here Menelaus! Leave the dead to other defenders and keep us, the living, from destruction. Hector is bearing down on us, Hector and Aeneas, the two bravest heroes of Troy!" With this he swung his lance at Aretus, and it pierced his entrails. Caught in full advance, the hero fell backward in the dust. Then Hector hurled his spear at Automedon, but it flew over his head, and stood with quivering shaft fixed in the ground. And now they would have used their swords against each other, had not the two Ajaces come between them and turned the Trojans back to the body of Patroclus.

There the battle raged most hotly. Zeus was now of another mind. Hid in a dark cloud, he sent Athene as his messenger down to earth, where she appeared in the semblance of aged Phoenix and went up to Menelaus. Seeing the old man, he said: "O Phoenix! If only Athene would give me strength today, so that I might avenge my slain friend! For I understand the reproach in your eyes." The goddess rejoiced that, unknowing, he had sought her aid, poured strength into his shoulders and knees, and in his heart she put defiance and steadfastness. Brandishing his lance he ran to the body, and as Hector's friend Podes, son of Eetion, turned to flee from him, the spear of Atreus' son struck him under the belt so that he crashed to earth.

Now Apollo, in the shape of Phaenops, approached Hector and taunted him. "Who among the Danai will fear you, if Menelaus can frighten you away? He slew your most cherished friend, and now he, the least manly of the Argives, will deprive you of the body of Patroclus as well!" These words bowed Hector's heart with dark grief, and he dashed forward again, shining in his brazen armor. Then Zeus shook his aegis, veiled Mount Ida in cloud, and with lightning and thunder crowned the Trojan's victory.

Peneleus of Boeotia, whose shoulder Polydamas had grazed with his spear, was the first to turn and flee. Leitus was rendered unfit for the fight by Hector, who pierced his hand at the knuckles. Idomeneus, who had just come from the ships on foot, missed Hector when he hurled his spear, and Hector missed him with his counter cast but shattered the ear and cheek of Coeranus who, fortunately for Idomeneus, had preceded him with Meriones in his chariot. The spear knocked out his teeth and cut his tongue, and the hero fell. Meriones gathered the reins up from the dust and gave them to Idomeneus who quickly swung himself into the chariot and drove the horses back to the ships. When Ajax saw this, he lamented so loudly to Menelaus who fought beside him that Zeus had pity on him, scattered the clouds, and shed full sunlight over the battlefield. "Menelaus," said Ajax, "try to find Antilochus, son of Nestor. See if he is still alive. He would be a fitting messenger to tell Achilles that Patroclus, his dearest friend, is dead." With watchful eyes, like an eagle who peers for the hare flat against the earth among bushes, Menelaus went about and soon saw Nestor's son to the left of the field.

"Have you not heard, Antilochus," he called to him, "that a god has given victory to the Trojans and disaster to the Danai? Patroclus has fallen, and all the Argives feel the loss of that dauntless hero. Only one lives who is braver: Achilles. Go quickly to his house, bring him the sorrowful news, and summon him to rescue the corpse which Hector has stripped of its armor."

A shudder ran through the youth. His eyes filled with tears when he heard these words. For a long time he was speechless. Then he gave his armor to Laodocus, his charioteer, and ran toward the ships on flying feet. When Menelaus had again reached the body, he and Ajax took counsel how they could bear away their slain friend, for they did not expect too much of Achilles, even if he could be prevailed on to come, since he no longer had the armor of the immortals. With a mighty straining of muscles they lifted the body from the earth, and though the Trojans burst into shouts of rage and followed with brandished swords and spears, Ajax had only to turn and they paled and dared not contest his burden. Thus they bore the body from the field and toward the ships, and with them the rest of the Argives fled from battle. Hector and Aeneas were close on their heels, and here and there one of the fleeing dropped a shield or a lance as he retreated across the trench in frantic haste and confusion.

THE GRIEF OF ACHILLES

Antilochus found the son of Peleus in front of the ships, brooding on a fate which was already fulfilled, though he did not know it. When he saw the Argives approaching the ships, he was troubled and said to himself: "Why are the Achaeans running from the field as if routed and flocking toward the camp? I hope the gods have not accomplished what my mother once predicted: that while I was still alive the bravest of the Myrmidons would die at the hands of the Trojans!"

While he was still in thought, Antilochus came toward him, weeping because of the terrible message he had to bear, and called to him from afar: "Alas, son of Peleus! Oh, that what I am forced to tell you had never happened! Patroclus has fallen! And now they are fighting for his naked body, for Hector stripped him of his armor." When Achilles heard this, the world turned dark before his eyes. With both hands he took up the brown dust and scattered it over his head, his face, and his tunic.

Then he threw himself on the ground, measuring his great length, and tore his hair. Seeing their lord and master stretched on the earth, the handmaids whom Achilles and Patroclus had borne away as spoils rushed out of the house trembling. When they learned what had happened, they beat their breasts with loud lament. Antilochus too shed bitter tears and gripped the hands of Achilles, holding them fast, for he feared he would cut his throat with his sword.

Achilles himself moaned so greatly with grief that his mother heard his voice in the depths of the sea, where she sat beside her gray-haired father, and she too began to weep. At the sound of her sobs, the Nereids glided into her silvery grotto and beat their soft breasts and joined in the wails of their sister. "How unhappy I am," she said to them, "that ever I bore so brave and splendid a son! He grew up like a sturdy young fruit tree, tended and cherished by the hand of the gardener. Then I sent him against Troy. But never again will he return to the palace of Peleus! While he still lives in the light of the sun he must suffer great grief, and I cannot help him! But I will go to my beloved child and hear what sorrow has overtaken him." So said the goddess, and with her sisters she rose through the waves which parted at her coming and went ashore where her son sat groaning in front of the ships.

"Why do you weep, my child?" she asked him, clasping his head. "Who has stricken your heart with sorrow? Tell me and hide nothing! Has not everything come about as you wished? Are not the Argives thronged in the camp and begging your help?"

With a heavy sigh Achilles answered: "Mother, what is all this to me, now that Patroclus, who was dearer to me than my eyes, is slain and lies in the dust? My own finely wrought armor, the gift which the gods gave Peleus at his wedding with you, Hector has taken from his body. Oh, if only you had stayed forever in the depths of the sea! For had Peleus wedded a mortal wife, you would not have to bear immortal grief for your son who is doomed to die. I shall never return to my native land, for my heart forbids me to breathe and live on among men unless Hector falls by my lance and suffers for robbing me of Patroclus."

Thetis replied in a voice choked with tears. "My son," she

said, "then you too will be cut off in the flower of your life, for it is decreed that soon after Hector dies your own end is near."

At that Achilles cried in anger: "Would I could die this very instant, since Fate did not allow me to shield my murdered friend! He died far from his home, and I did not come to his aid. How can my brief life avail the Argives now? I have brought misfortune to Patroclus, misfortune to countless slain friends. Here I sit by the ships, a worthless burden on earth, I who am supposed to be the best fighter among the Achaeans, though in council others surpass me. Cursed be anger, whether it spring in gods or men, for first it is sweet as honey to the heart, but then it grows acrid as smoke." Suddenly he curbed his grief and roused himself and said: "What is past, is past! I go to strike down the man who slew the friend I cherished above all. I go to kill Hector. Let my fate overtake me when Zeus and the gods decree. Because of me, many a Trojan woman will put both her hands to her soft face to dry bitter tears of mourning, and her breast will heave with sighs. The Trojans will find that I have rested long enough. Do not hold me back, dear mother!"

"You are right, my child," answered Thetis. "Your shimmering armor is in Trojan hands. Hector himself wears it boastfully. But he shall not vaunt his pleasure in it for long! Tomorrow, as soon as the sun comes up, I shall bring you new arms, made by Hephaestus himself. Do not go to battle until I return." Thus spoke the goddess and bade her sisters dive back into the depths of the sea. But she herself hastened up to Olympus to find Hephaestus, the smith among the immortals.

Meantime the Trojans once more attacked the body of Patroclus which his friends were bearing away, and Hector, sweeping forward like fire, came so close that three times he seized the corpse by the foot to drag it off, but three time the two Ajaces thrust him away from the dead. He withdrew to one side and then halted again and cried aloud that he would never retreat. Then the two Argive heroes who bore the same name tried to frighten him off from the corpse like herdsmen who try to drive a hungry mountain lion from the flesh of a mangled bullock. But Hector would have carried off the body, had not Iris, at Hera's command, flown to the son of Peleus and bidden him arm secretly, unseen by Zeus and the other gods. "How can I go into battle?" Achilles asked the messenger of the gods. "My enemies have my weapons. And my mother forbade me go before she herself brought me new armor, made by Hephaestus. There are no arms which would suit me, unless perhaps the great shield of Ajax, and he needs that himself."

"We know very well that you have been deprived of your glorious weapons," Iris answered him. "But meanwhile approach the trench just as you are, so that the Trojans may see you. Perhaps they will pause when they catch sight of you. The Achaeans, weary as they are, need a breathing space."

When Iris had sped away, godlike Achilles rose. Athene herself slung her shield across his shoulder and shed radiance on his features. Swiftly he strode, crossed the wall, and stood by the trench. But mindful of his mother's warning he did not mingle in battle. He only watched from afar and shouted, and Athene joined her cry to his, so that in the ears of the Trojans it sounded like the blare of a war trumpet. When they heard that voice like ringing bronze, their hearts filled with fear, and they turned back their horses and chariots. And the charioteers shuddered to see the head of the son of Peleus circled with flame. Three times he shouted, and three times Trojans scattered. Twelve of their bravest men fell in the confusion and were killed by the chariot wheels and the lances of their own companions. And now the corpse of Patroclus was out of reach of the missiles. The heroes laid him on a bier, and his friends stood around it lamenting. When Achilles saw his beloved comrade-in-arms, he went among the Argives again for the first time and threw himself over the body with many tears. And on these two, the living and the dead, the setting sun shed its last glow.

ACHILLES NEWLY ARMED

Both armies rested from the stubborn battle. The Trojans loosed their horses from the chariots, but before they even thought of eating, they assembled in council. Upright they stood in a circle, and no one dared sit, for they were still trembling with terror at Achilles and feared he might reappear. At last wise Polydamas, son of Panthous, who could see both the future and the past, ad-

vised them not to wait for the dawn but to return to the city with all possible speed. "When Achilles is full-armed and finds us here in the morning," he said, "those who escape and reach Troy will be favored by Fortune, but many will be food for dogs and vultures. May Heaven avert such fate! Therefore I counsel you and all your warriors to spend the night in the market place of Troy, where high walls and solid gates will guard us on all sides. When dawn comes let us man the ramparts, and woe to him when he rushes from the ships to attack us."

Now Hector spoke, and his eyes were stern. "Your words, Polydamas, strike harshly on my ears. What—now that Zeus has granted me victory, now that I have pressed the Argives back to the sea, your timid counsel must seem folly to the people, and not a single Trojan will heed you. I, for my part, bid everyone eat and keep watch. If there is any who fears for his stores and his wealth, let him spend all for a feast to be held in common. Better our men take pleasure in it than the Achaeans! When the day dawns we shall resume our attack on the ships. If Achilles has really returned to the field, he has chosen an unenviable lot, for I shall not stop fighting until he or I bear off the crown of victory." These ill-advised words of Hector weighed heavier with the Trojans than the sound counsel of Polydamas. They burst into joyful acclaim and hungrily fell on their food.

The whole night long the Argives mourned Patroclus, and Achilles, more than all, made lament. Laying his hands, which had slain so many foes, on the breast of his friend, he said: "What idle words I spoke that time when I tried to comfort old Menoetius by promising him to bring his son back to Opoeis, rich in spoils and glory, after the fall of Troy! Now Fate wills that both he and I pour out our blood on alien soil, for I too shall never return to the palace of my father, gray-haired Peleus, and of Thetis, my mother; the earth of Troy will cover me. But since it is appointed that I die after you, Patroclus, I shall not hold your funeral until I have brought you the armor and the head of Hector, your slayer. And twelve of the noblest sons of Troy I shall offer up at your pyre as well. Until this has been done, rest here by the ships, beloved friend." When he had spoken, Achilles bade his companions set a great cauldron filled with water on the fire, and wash and anoint the body of the fallen hero. Then they laid him on a bier and spread fine linen over him from head to foot, and over this a white robe.

Thetis, meanwhile, had arrived at the bronze palace which lame Hephaestus had built for himself. It shone like stars, beautiful and everlasting. She found the god sweating at the bellows. He had forged twenty tripods, and at the base of each he had fastened golden wheels which, without the touch of a hand, rolled into the halls of Olympus to the feet of the immortals and returned to his workshop again. They were wonderful to see, complete save for the handles, and these he was just making ready, wielding his hammer to rivet them in their proper place. And while he worked, Charis, his wife, one of the Graces, took Thetis by the hand, led her to a silver chair, set a foot-stool beneath her feet, and fetched her husband Hephaestus. When he saw the goddess of the sea he called out joyfully: "How happy I am that the noblest among the immortals has come to my house, she who saved me from destruction when I was just born! For because I was lame, my mother cast me out, and I should have perished miserably, had not Eurynome and Thetis taken me and reared me in a cave in the sea until I was nine years old. There, in a vaulted grotto, I fashioned works, curious and cunning, clasps and rings, brooches and necklaces, and about me foamed the surging stream of the ocean. And now she who rescued me is visiting me in my own house! See to her entertainment, sweet Charis, while I clear away this welter of work and tools."

Thus spoke the sooty god, and he rose limping from beside the anvil, took the bellows from the fire, locked his delicate implements in a silver chest, and with a sponge wiped his hands and face, his neck and shaggy chest. Then he put on his tunic and, helped by his handmaids, limped back into the room. These maids, however, were not living creatures born of women, but only the image of such. They were fashioned of gold and furnished with the charms of youth, with strength and skill, with reason and voice. Moving on swift feet they hastened from their master, who seated himself beside Thetis, clasped her hand, and said: "Dear and honored goddess, why have you come to my house today, you who visit me so rarely? Tell me what you desire, and whatever I am able to do, I shall surely do for you."

Then Thetis told him all her sorrow and, clasping his knees, begged him to fashion for her son Achilles, destined to die so soon, a helmet and shield, a cuirass and greaves fitted with ankle pieces, since the armor which the immortals had given Peleus had been lost when Patroclus fell before Troy. "Be of good courage, and do not let this upset you, dear goddess," said Hephaestus. "If only I could save your son from the power of Death as surely as I shall now make him armor so strong and so splendid that he will rejoice, and every mortal who looks at it will be filled with wonder!"

So saying he left Thetis and turned his bellows toward the fire. Twenty of these of their own accord blew upon the melting-vats, in which he placed bronze and tin, silver and gold. Next he set his anvil on the anvil block. With his right hand he seized his mighty hammer, and with his left gripped the tongs. First he made a shield, great and strong, in five layers, adorned with a triple gleaming rim and a shield strap of silver. On the shield he wrought the earth, the tiding sea, and heaven with the sun, the moon, and all the constellations; and further two fair cities, the one gay with bridal rites and torch-lit feasts, with an assembly of the people, citizens arguing about the blood price of a slain man, heralds and elders. The other city was besieged by two armies. Within the walls were women, young children, and old men with faltering feet. Outside were warriors lying in ambush where the herdsmen watered their cattle. On another side was the tumult of battle, with wounded men and the fight for bodies and armor. He also wrought a field with loosened clods and ploughers and oxen; waving barley and reapers cutting swathes with their sickles; and further a vineyard, the dark-golden clusters of swelling grapes hanging from stakes of silver, and round about a trench of bluish metal and a fence of tin. A path led to the vines, and the time of vintage had come: youths, sturdy and gay, and lovely maids bore the fruit away in fair baskets. Among them went a boy with a lyre, and some danced to his music. Furthermore he wrought cattle of gold and tin, pastured beside a flowing river by four gold shepherds and nine dogs. Two lions had fallen on the foremost in the herd and seized a bullock, and the herdsmen set on them their dogs who stood baying within springing distance of the beasts of prey. And further he devised a gentle valley with silver sheep scattered over the slopes, with folds and houses and the huts of the shepherds; and a dance of youths and maidens in shining array; the girl dancers wore wreaths and the boy dancers daggers of gold suspended from silver straps. Two tumblers whirled about to the sound of a harp, and many had come to watch the dance and the merriment. And around the uttermost rim of the shield, the river Oceanus twined like a glittering serpent.

When he had finished the shield, he forged a breastplate brighter than blazing fire; then the massive helmet, fitted well to the temples and topped with a crest of gold; then greaves of pliant tin. When all was complete, he laid it before the mother of Achilles. She seized the armor as a falcon its prey, thanked the smith, and in her slender hands bore away the shimmering pieces.

With the first glimmer of dawn she was back with her son who was still weeping over the body of Patroclus. She laid the arms down before him, and they rang aloud in their splendor. The Myrmidons trembled at the sight, and no one dared look the goddess straight in the face. But under their wet lashes, Achilles' eyes flashed with fierce joy. One after another he lifted the glittering gifts of Hephaestus and feasted his heart on them. Then he girt on his armor. "Look to it," he told his friends in parting, "that flies do not settle in the wounds of my fallen comrade-in arms and defile his beautiful body!"

"Let that be my care," said Thetis, and through the half-open lips of Patroclus she poured ambrosia and nectar. The balm of the gods suffused his flesh, and he looked like one who was alive.

Achilles strode down to the seashore and with thunderous voice called to the Achaeans. Whoever could stand on his feet ran to his call, even the helmsmen who had never yet left their ships. And though they were wounded, Diomedes and Odysseus limped up to him, leaning on their lances, and after them came all the heroes, last of all Agamemnon, still faint from the wound he had suffered at the spear of Coon, son of Antenor.

ACHILLES AND AGAMEMNON RECONCILED

When all the Argives were assembled, Achilles rose and said: "Son of Atreus, I wish Artemis had killed the daughter of Briseus by the ships that day I took her as my share of the spoils of Lyrnessos, rather than that so many Achaeans should have died while I was cherishing my anger. Let the past be forgotten, even if our souls still smart with it. I, at least, have given up my grudge. And now, to battle! We shall see if the Trojans still crave our ships!"

At his words the air rang with the applauding shouts of the Achaeans. Then Agamemnon rose, but he did not come into the middle of the circle like other speakers. "Cease your tumult!" he said. "Who can talk or hear in such an uproar? I shall explain my action to the son of Peleus, and you others listen well and mark my words. The sons of Hellas have often upbraided me for what I did on that day which set such disaster afoot. But the fault was not mine. It was Zeus and the Furies who blinded my reason in that fateful assembly of our people. That I erred was their doing! But all the time Hector was killing hosts of Argives by the ships I was reminded of my fault and grew aware that Zeus had darkened my spirit. Now I am most willing to make amends and offer you, Achilles, whatever you desire. Only fight with us again, and I shall give you all those gifts Odysseus, who came to you as my messenger a short time past, promised in my name. Or, if you prefer, remain here until my slaves have brought them from the ships, so that with your own eyes you may see how I fulfill my pledge."

"Great Agamemnon," the hero replied, "whether you give me those gifts or withhold them rests with you. Let us not waste time but think of battle, for much is still undone, and I yearn to be in the forefront of the fight again!"

But wise Odysseus intervened, saying: "Godlike son of Peleus, do not goad the Achaeans toward Troy unfed! Let them refresh themselves with meat and wine, for only this lends strength and force. Agamemnon, meanwhile, may bring his gifts into this circle, so that all the Danai may delight in them. And after that he shall be your host and serve you with sumptuous fare."

"Joyfully have I heard your words," answered the son of Atreus. "And you, Achilles, shall choose the noblest youths in our host to bear the gifts from my ship; and Talthybius, the herald, shall fetch forth a boar to sacrifice to Zeus and the sun-god, and seal the bond of friendship between us."

"Do as you like," said Achilles. "As for me, neither food nor drink shall touch my lips while my friend lies slaughtered in my house. All that I crave is carnage, blood, and groans of dying men."

But Odysseus tried to calm him, saying: "Noblest of all Argive heroes! You are far stronger than I, and braver in fighting with the spear. But in counsel I am, perhaps, your better, for I have lived longer and had more experience. So bend your stubborn spirit and heed my words. The Danai need not mourn their dead with the belly! When a man dies, we bury him, and bewail him for one day. But those who have escaped death must sustain their strength with food and drink, to fight more fiercely."

Thus he spoke and went to Agamemnon's quarters, taking the sons of Nestor with him, and also Meges, Meriones, Thoas, Melanippus, and Lycomedes. There they collected the promised gifts: seven tripods, twelve horses, twenty cauldrons, seven women of flawless beauty; fair Briseis was the eighth. Odysseus weighed out ten talents of gold and walked on ahead of the youths who followed with the other gifts. When they had entered the circle of the assembly Agamemnon rose in his seat, and Thalthybius, the herald, seized the boar, prepared it for sacrifice, prayed, and cut its throat. He took the slain animal and cast it into the sea as food for the fish, and the waters swirled about it. Then Achilles cried out before all the Achaeans: "Father Zeus, how

great is the blindness you often visit on us mortals! Never would
the son of Atreus have roused my heart to wild anger, or been so
ruthlessly determined to carry off spoils which were mine, had
you not willed the death of many Argives. But now let us eat and
then prepare for the fight."

When the hero had spoken, the assembly dispersed. The
daughter of Briseus, lovely as Aphrodite, entered the house of
her former lord and saw Patroclus with his deep spear-wounds,
stretched on a bier. She beat her breast, tore her cheeks, and
threw herself weeping over the body. "O Patroclus," she cried,
"you were a tender friend to me in my exile. When I left you
here, you were radiant with life, but now that I return, I find you
dead! For me, disaster always follows disaster! Before my very
eyes my bridegroom was killed with a spear; three brothers of my
own blood, brothers dearly cherished, were snatched from my
side on the same day. But after Achilles had slain my promised
husband and ravaged my city, you were sorry to see me weep.
You gave your word that you would urge the son of Peleus to
marry me as soon as he had brought me to Phthia, and that we
should have our wedding feast among the Myrmidons. Never
shall I cease to grieve for you, you of the tender heart." Thus she
spoke, weeping, and the captive women around her sighed with
her; but while they sighed for Patroclus, each, in the secret of
her heart, wept her own misery.

In the meantime, the princes of the Danai surrounded the son
of Peleus, begging him to take food and drink. But he refused
them: "If you love me, my friends, do not ask me to eat and
drink, for my sad heart will not suffer it. Let me be as I am until
the sun sinks into the sea." With these words he dismissed them,
and only the two sons of Atreus, Odysseus, Nestor, Idomeneus,
and Phoenix stayed behind. Vainly they tried to cheer the soul
of the mourner. He remained silent and aloof, and whenever he
spoke at all, it was with a sigh, and the words were for the friend
who was dead. "In days gone by," he said, "ah, how often and
with what eager haste you brought the morning meal to my
house when the Argive host made ready to go to battle! And now
you lie slain before me, and no rich store of food can refresh me.
No bitterer thing could have happened, not even the death of
my father Peleus or my dear son, Neoptolemus, who—if he still

lives—is being reared for me in Scyros. I was glad in the thought that I alone should die here, and that you would return to Phthia, fetch my son home from Scyros, and show him all that was mine. My father Peleus, I think, must have died long ago. If he still lives, he must be bowed by age and grief, for he lives in fear of the messenger who will tell him that I am dead." This he said with tears, and the princes around him sighed too, for each thought of the loved ones he had left behind.

Full of compassion Zeus gazed down on the mournful men below, and turning to Pallas Athene, said: "My daughter, are you no longer concerned for the noble hero who, while the others have gone to eat the morning meal, remains sunk in his grief and touches neither food nor drink? Go at once and bathe his breast with nectar and ambrosia, lest hunger overtake him in the midst of battle."

Like a broad-winged falcon the goddess, who long had yearned to help her friend, sped through the air, and while the warriors prepared for the struggle, softly and secretly she anointed the breast of Achilles with ambrosia and nectar. Then she returned to the palace of her all-powerful father.

And now the Achaeans poured out of their ships, helmet close to helmet, cuirass to cuirass, shield to shield and lance to lance. The earth shone with bronze and rang under their tread. While they hastened on, Achilles girt on his armor, and as he did so he gnashed his teeth, and his eyes blazed. First he fitted to his legs the greaves with the ankle pieces; then he covered his breast with the cuirass, slung over his shoulder the sword, and gripped the shield which sent forth a gleam like that of the moon. Next he set on his head the heavy helmet with the tall crest and golden plumes; it glittered like a star. Then he tested his armor to see whether it fitted freely to his limbs. And it seemed like wings impatient to lift him up from earth. From its stand he drew the lance of his father Peleus, the great spear which no other Argive could wield. Automedon and Alcimus yoked his horses, put the bits in their jaws, and stretched the reins to the chariot. Into it sprang Automedon and grasped the polished goad. Gleaming in his armor, Achilles mounted beside him.

"Immortal horses!" he called to the steeds of his father. "When we are sated with battle, bring us home. Do not treat us like Patroclus, whom you left dead in the field!" And as he spoke the gods sent him a terrible omen, for Xanthus, the horse, bowed its head, till his mane, streaming from under the yoke pad, touched the earth. And gifted with speech by Hera, it answered him sadly: "O mighty Achilles! This time we shall bring you back alive and sound, but the day of disaster is near. It was not because we were careless or slow that Patroclus died and Hector won; it was the will of the gods. We can vie with Zephyr, the swiftest of the winds, and never tire. But Fate has appointed that you shall fall by the hand of a god." Thus spoke the horse and wanted to say still more, but the Furies stifled the voice in its throat.

Achilles was troubled and answered: "Xanthus, why speak to me of death? I do not need your prophecies, for I already know that my fate will overtake me here, far from my father and mother. But even so, I shall not rest until I have slain innumerable Trojans!" And with a shout he drove forward his prancing horses.

THE BATTLE OF GODS AND MEN

On Olympus Zeus had called an assembly of the immortals in which he gave them permission to help both the Trojans and the Argives, as their hearts prompted them. For if Achilles fought the Trojans without the gods taking a part in the battle, he would surely conquer the city of Troy against Fate herself. As soon as the immortals knew that they might do as they wished, they ranged themselves into groups which went opposite ways: Hera, the mother of gods, Pallas Athene, Poseidon, Hermes, and Hephaestus hastened to the Argive ships; Ares set out for the Trojans, and with him were Phoebus and Artemis, Leto, their mother, Aphrodite, and Scamander, the river-god, whom the gods called Xanthus.

As long as the gods had not yet joined the advancing hosts, the Achaeans held high their heads because dread Achilles was again in their midst. And the limbs of the Trojans shook with fear when from afar they saw the son of Peleus who, in his glittering array, resembled the war-god himself. But now the gods had mingled with both armies, and again the outcome was uncertain. Athene was now here, now there, outside the wall at the trench, or by the shore of the sea, and wherever she appeared she sounded her battle cry. On the other side Ares roared encouragement to the Trojans, now from the highest point in their city, now flying through their ranks at the river Simois. Through both hosts alike stormed Eris, the goddess of discord. Zeus, the ruler of battles, thundered terribly down from Olympus, and Poseidon shook the earth from beneath until the peaks of all mountains and the very roots of Ida quaked, and even Pluto, the lord of shades, was startled and leaped from his throne, for he feared that a rift in the earth might discover to men and gods his secret kingdom below. And now the gods confronted one another in actual encounter: Phoebus Apollo launched his arrows against Poseidon; Pallas Athene fought the god of war; Artemis used her bow against Hera; Hermes opposed Leto, and Scamander Hephaestus.

While gods thus advanced against gods, Achilles was intent on one thing alone: on finding Hector in the throng. But Apollo, in the semblance of Lycaon, son of Priam, urged toward him Aeneas, whom he had fired with such courage that he went swiftly forward in his armor of shimmering bronze. Through all that tumult Hera saw him. Quickly she summoned those gods who were her allies, and said: "Poseidon and Athene, I beg you to consider what is to come of this! There is Aeneas, whom Phoebus has roused, storming against the son of Peleus. Either we must thrust him back or one of us must increase the strength of Achilles until he feels that the mightiest of the gods are supporting him. Today he shall be safe from the Trojans. Only for this have we all descended from Olympus! Later he must suffer the Fate decreed at his birth."

"Think of the outcome, Hera," Poseidon replied. "I do not think that we should attack the other gods with combined strength. That would be unfair, since we are by far the most powerful. Rather let us sit apart in some high place and watch the struggle. But if Apollo or Ares begin to fight, if they hinder Achilles and keep him from moving freely, then we shall have the right to take part in the conflict, and surely our adversaries will quickly yield to our strength and return to Olympus." The sea-god did not wait for an answer but shook his locks and led the way to the wall of Heracles which Pallas and the Trojans had built long ago. To that place Poseidon hastened, and the other gods followed him; there they sat, their forms shrouded in impenetrable mist. Opposite them, on the hill called Callicolone, were Ares and Apollo. And so the immortals camped not far from one another, separate, but ready to fight, only pausing a little to reflect.

Meantime the field was filling with warriors and glistened with the bronze of their armor and chariots, and the earth echoed beneath their feet. It was not long, however, before two sprang forward from among the rest: Aeneas, son of Anchises, and Achilles, son of Peleus. Aeneas came first. The plumes swayed from his massive helmet. With his great shield of oxhide he covered his breast, and threateningly he brandished his spear. When the son of Peleus saw him, he too forged ahead impetuously, like an angry lion. The moment they were within hailing distance, he shouted: "How dare you come so far in advance of your men, Aeneas? Do you cherish the hope that after slaying me you will rule Troy? What folly, for never will Priam accord you this honor! Has he not sons enough of his own? And besides, he himself, old as he is, does not dream of giving up the throne. Or perhaps the Trojans have promised you a fine country estate in reward for killing me? If I remember rightly I pursued you once before! Do you recall how, when you were alone with the herds, I chased you down the steep slopes of Ida? You did not even take time to look back over your shoulder as you fled, and never stopped until you reached the city of Lyrnessos. But I, with the aid of Pallas and Zeus, laid it in ruins, and only the mercy of my immortal allies saved you, while I bore off plenty of spoils and captives. But the gods will not rescue you a second time. So I counsel you to draw back and mingle with your men. Have a care! Do not advance against me—not unless you want to be hurt."

And Aeneas retorted: "Do not think you can frighten me with mere talk, as though I were a child. I too could give you words that cut to the heart. Each of us is acquainted with the glory and lineage of the other: I know that Thetis, goddess of the sea, bore you, but I can boast of being the son of Aphrodite and the grandson of Zeus. Besides, we will surely not part with childish threats. So let us not stand on the battlefield chattering like silly boys. Let us rather try each other with our brazen lances." So he said and hurled his spear. It struck the strong shield of Achilles, and the air rang with the sound. But it pierced only the first two layers of bronze. The next layer was of gold, and it stopped the lance before it reached the last two layers which were of tin. And now the son of Peleus cast his spear, and it struck the shield of Aeneas at the outermost rim where the bronze and oxhide were thinnest. Aeneas crouched down and held up his shield in terror as the lance sped through the shield and struck behind him in the ground; the son of Aphrodite trembled at the great danger he had escaped. Already Achilles was running at him with the sword, uttering a fierce shout. Aeneas picked up a stone lying in the field, a stone so large that two ordinary men could not have lifted it, but he swung it easily in his hand. Then he would have struck Achilles on the helmet or the shield, and the son of Peleus would have slain Aeneas with the sword in close combat, had not Poseidon been quick to see what was happening.

For though the gods who sat on the wall of Heracles were hostile to the Trojans, they were sorry for Aeneas. "It would be a pity," said Poseidon, "if the son of Anchises descended to Hades, because he relied on Apollo's words. Besides, I fear Zeus' wrath, for while it is true that he hates the line of Priam, he does not wish to let it perish completely, and it is through Aeneas that this race of kings shall endure, through his sons and his sons' sons."

"Do as you like," replied Hera. "As for Pallas and myself, we have sworn a solemn oath not to avert misfortune from the Trojans, come what may."

And now Poseidon flew into battle. Invisible to mortals, he drew the spear from the shield of Aeneas, laid it at the feet of Achilles, and shed a fog before the hero's eyes. Then the sea-god lifted the Trojan from the earth and, holding him high, hurled him over chariots and warriors to the edge of the field where the Caucones, allies of Troy, were arraying themselves for the fight. Here Poseidon upbraided the hero he had rescued. "What immortal blinded you, Aeneas," he said, "that you ventured to strive against the darling of the gods, against the son of Peleus who is so much stronger than you? From now on, withdraw whenever you catch sight of him. Once Fate has overtaken him, you may fight in the foremost ranks."

Then the god left him and dissolved the mist from before the eyes of Achilles. In great astonishment the son of Peleus saw his lance lying on the ground, and his enemy gone. "Let him escape—with the help of a god," he said to himself sulkily. "I am used to having him flee from me." Then he sprang back into the ranks of his men and urged them on. On the other side, Hector was stirring up his warriors, and a fierce encounter followed. When Phoebus Apollo saw Hector making so eagerly for the son of Peleus, he whispered a word of warning in his ear, and Hector heard and drew back into the throng. But Achilles stormed at his enemies, and at the first cast of his spear split the skull of brave Iphition, so that he fell and was mangled by the chariot wheels of the Achaeans. Then he thrust his spear into the temple of Demoleon, son of Antenor. Hippodamas he bored in the back with his lance, just as he was dismounting from his chariot, and one of the sons of Priam he caught in the spine beneath the belt clasp, just as the youth passed him; he screamed with pain and sank to his knees.

When Hector saw his young brother writhing on the ground, his eyes darkened with rage. He could no longer bear to keep aloof from battle and, despite the warning of the god, made straight for Achilles, brandishing his spear like a flash of lightning. Achilles saw him and rejoiced. "This is the man," he said, "who has grieved me to the core of my heart. Do not let us avoid each other, Hector. Come close, that you may die the sooner."

"I know how brave you are," Hector replied unafraid, "and that I am less mighty than you. Still the gods may favor my spear! It may slay you, even though it is launched by a weaker man." So saying, he cast his spear. But Athene stood behind the son of Peleus and breathed against the weapon; it swerved back to Hector and fell powerless at his feet. And now Achilles stormed to the spot to pierce his opponent with a thrust of his spear. But Apollo shed a thick mist about Hector, and three times the son of Peleus lunged into empty air. When he dashed forward in vain a fourth time, he cried in threatening tones: "Dog, again you have cheated death—surely because you have prayed to your guardian Apollo. But if I too have an ally among the immortals, we shall meet again and you shall not escape death at my hands! Now I shall seek more Trojans and kill all of them." So he spoke, and his lance hit the neck of Dryops, who tumbled at his feet. Next he wounded Demuchus in the knee and threw down from the chariot Laogonus and Dardanus, sons of Bias, one with the lance, the other with the sword. Although young Tros, son of Alastor, clasped his knees in supplication, asking him to spare his youth, he pierced him through the liver. Then he thrust his lance into one ear of Mulius; the brazen point came out at the other. Echeclus, son of Agenor, he struck in the skull with his sword. Deucalion he gashed in the elbow with the point of his lance and then struck off his head; it rolled into the dust together with the helmet. Rhigmus, the Thracian, his flying lance pierced in the belly, and Areithous his spear threw from the chariot. Thus godlike Achilles raged like a forest-fire whipped on by swift winds. His horses pranced over shields and bodies; the axle dripped with blood, and the drops spattered onto the wheels and the chariot itself.

ACHILLES FIGHTS THE RIVER-GOD SCAMANDER

When the fleeing Trojans reached the waters of the swift-flowing Scamander, they separated. One part poured toward the city, to the field where, the day before, Hector had won his victory over the Argives. Over them Hera spread a thick drift of cloud to hinder them from fleeing farther. But the others, crowded close to the margin of the river, threw themselves into the swirling current; the shores roundabout echoed with the sound. There they floundered like locusts which fire has driven into the water, so that the whole river filled with a tangle of horses and men. At that the son of Peleus leaned his lance against a tamarisk on the bank and only with his sword in his hand rushed after them like a god. Soon the water grew red with blood, and under his thrusts groans and gasps rose up from the waves. He raged like an enormous dolphin that hurtles through a bay devouring what fish he can. And even when his hands were numb with killing, he seized twelve youths still alive in the waters, dragged them to shore, almost out of their minds with panic, and handed them over to his warriors. These were to fall in atonement for the death of Patroclus, his friend.

When the hero again rushed to the river, greedy for new kill, Lycaon, son of Priam, struggled up through the water, and Achilles paused at sight of him. Once, in an assault by night, the son of Peleus had surprised him in his father's orchard as he was carving a rim for his chariot from the shoots of the wild fig. On that occasion Achilles had taken him by force and sent him to the island of Lemnos, where Euneus, son of Jason, bought him as a slave. And when Eetion, Prince of Imbros, another son of Jason's, visited his half brother in Lemnos, he ransomed the youth, so delicately fair, for a high price and had him brought to Arisbe, his city. For a time Lycaon lived there, but then he ran secretly away and managed to reach Troy. This was the twelfth day since he had returned from captivity, and now he fell into the hands of Achilles for the second time! When the son of Peleus saw that his knees failed him, that he was floating weakly with the current, he said to himself in amazement: "What miracle is this? Now that this boy I sold as a slave has reappeared, I suppose all the Trojans I slew will crawl forth out of the night of death again. Well then, let him taste the point of this lance, and we shall see whether he can come up even from under the earth!" But before Achilles had time to aim, Lycaon swung himself ashore, clasped his knees with one hand, and touched his spear with the other.

"Have pity on me, Achilles!" he cried. "For once I was put in your care. At that time I got you one hundred bullocks. Now the ransom will be three times that number. Only for twelve days have I been free from the pain of long captivity, but Zeus must hate me, for he has again delivered me into your hands. Do not kill me! I am the child of Laothoe and not of Hecuba, the mother of Hector, who slew your friend."

But Achilles frowned, and his voice was relentless. "Do not speak of ransom, you fool. Before Patroclus died, my heart was ready to spare, but now all shall die, you too! Do not look at me so pitifully. Did not Patroclus die who was infinitely more glorious than you? And I myself—see how tall I am and how strong, and yet I know I shall soon meet my fate at the hands of my foes, one dawn or dusk." When Lycaon heard him in this way, he let go the spear, spread wide his hands, and received the sword thrust in his neck. Achilles took the body by the foot, tossed it into the water, and cried mockingly: "Now let us see if the river, to which you have made so many vain offerings, will save you."

These words roused Scamander, the river-god, who sided with the Trojans, and he pondered on how he could trouble this dread hero and save his charges from those implacable hands. Achilles, meanwhile, leaped at Asteropaeus of Paeonia, son of Pelegon, who was just coming out of the river holding high two spears. And the river-god suffused him with pride and courage. Angrily he surveyed the merciless doing of the son of Peleus and ran to him boldly. "Who are you who dares oppose me?" asked Achilles. "Only the sons of unhappy parents measure their strength against mine!"

Asteropaeus replied: "Why do you ask my lineage? I am the grandson of the river-god Axius. Pelegon begot me. Eleven days ago I came here with my Paeonians, to aid the Trojans as their ally. Now fight with me, great son of Peleus!"

Achilles brandished his lance, but the Paeonian cast both spears at once, one with each hand, for he could use his left as deftly as his right. One cracked three metal layers of his adversary's shield, the other grazed his right arm at the elbow, and the blood spurted from it. And now Achilles hurled his lance, but it missed his opponent and drove into the earth to half its length. Three times Asteropaeus pulled at it with his sinewy hand, but he could not wrench it out of the ground. When he tried a fourth time, Achilles fell on him with his sword and plunged it into his body until the bowels gushed out, and he sank in the throes of death. With jubilant shouts the son of Peleus stripped him of his armor and let the body lie as food for the eels which swarmed near the shore. Then he rushed on the Paeonians who were straying fearfully along the bank. Seven he slew with his sword, and he had not nearly sated his lust to kill when suddenly Scamander, the angry lord of the river, rose up through a swirl of waves in the guise of a hero, and called: "Son of Peleus, you are working evil beyond the measure of man. My waters are clogged with the bodies of the dead and can hardly find a way to the sea. Leave off!"

"I obey you, because you are a god," said Achilles. "But my arm shall not cease from slaying Trojans until I have chased them back into their city and tested my strength against Hector's." So saying he rushed in pursuit of the Trojans and drove them toward the river. But when they tried to save themselves by leaping into the water, he forgot the river-god's command and sprang in behind them. Then the river grew swollen with wrath, churned its turbid waters, and flung the dead on the shore with bellow and crash. The torrent clashed against the shield of Achilles. He tottered and grasped an elm-tree, but it fell uprooted and tore away the bank. And now he raced over the field, but the river-god surged after him with wild waves and caught up with him, even though he was so fleet of foot. Whenever he tried to resist, the waves washed over his shoulders and swept the ground from under his feet. Then the hero complained to heaven. "Father Zeus," he lamented, "will not one of the immortals have pity on me and rescue me from this angry river? My mother deluded me when she said that I should die by the shaft of Apollo. Had Hector only slain me, had the strong but killed the strong! Now it seems I am to die ingloriously, like a boy herding swine who wades through a mountain stream in winter and is swept away by the turbulent waters."

As he moaned and wailed, Poseidon and Athene in the semblance of mortals came to him, took him by the hand, and comforted him, saying that it was not his fate to drown in the river. And before the gods left him, Athene filled him with such strength that he bent his knees and bounded out of the water until he again stood on dry land. But Scamander still cherished his anger and reared to taller and taller crests, calling aloud to Simois, his brother. "Come, brother! Let both of us together tame the power of this man, or he will raze Priam's citadel to the ground this very day! Call the springs from the mountains; urge on the torrents; lift high your waters and sweep great blocks of stone in your tide. Neither his strength nor his armor shall avail him. Deep under the flood let him lie, with mud and slime for his burial mound. I myself shall heap over him shells and pebbles and sand, so that the Argives will not even find his bones." When he had spoken, Scamander made for Achilles, churning with foam and blood and corpses, and the waves soon towered over the hero's head, for Simois had joined his waters with those of his brother.

When Hera saw this, she screamed aloud in fear for her favorite and then called to Hephaestus: "My son, dear lame son! Nothing but your fires can cope with the strength of the river. Rush to the aid of the son of Peleus! I myself will rouse the west and the south winds from the sea and raise up a blast that will fan your flames and utterly consume the Trojans. You, meanwhile, shall set afire the trees on the bank of the river and flame through Scamander himself. Let neither flattery nor threats hold you back, for only fire can halt this destruction." Obedient to her words Hephaestus, turned to flame, winged his way over the field. First he burned the bodies of the Trojans Achilles had slain. Then the field grew dry, and the waters were stopped. On the banks the elms, the willows, the tamarisks, and the grass began to burn. The eels and other fish grew weak in that fiery breath and gasped for fresh water. Finally the river itself was a river of flame, and out of the depths Scamander, the god, cried humbly: "Blazing god, I do not wish to fight you! For how am I, after all, concerned with the quarrel of the Trojans and Achilles?"

So he pleaded, while his waters hissed like fat in a cauldron over the fire. And he turned to the mother of gods and implored her: "Hera, why does your son Hephaestus torment me? Am I more at fault than the other gods who come to the aid of the Trojans? But I shall be still, if you wish it so, only let him too leave me in peace."

Then Hera said to her son: "Hold, Hephaestus! No longer shall you beset an immortal god for love of a mortal." And the god of fire quenched his flame. Scamander returned to his bed, and far away Simois calmed his riotous waters.

THE BATTLE OF THE GODS

The other gods were bitterly at odds. Their hearts beat high with hatred, and they had at one another until the whole earth clanged and the air rang as if with the blare of trumpets. Zeus heard on the peak of Olympus, and his heart leaped with delight when he saw the immortals rushing at one another in battle. The first to advance was Ares, the god of war, who made for Athene with his brazen spear, taunting her as he came. "Why, O gadfly," he called to her, "do you incite gods against gods with stormy insolence? Do you remember how you spurred on the son of Tydeus to pierce me with his lance, how you yourself dealt my immortal body a wound with your shining spear? But now, I think, we shall settle our accounts!" So he said, and struck her awful aegis with his spear. Evading his thrust, she reached for a huge rough stone which lay in the field and hurled it at Ares' neck. He sank to the ground with a great clashing of armor, covering seven rods in his fall, and his immortal locks were soiled with dust.

Then Athene laughed and said triumphantly: "O foolish one, when you dared to measure your strength against mine, you did not stop to think that I am the stronger! Now feel the full force of Hera's curse, for she is angry that you have withdrawn your favor from the Argives and are protecting the haughty Trojans." Thus she spoke and turned from him her radiant eyes. He was still gasping. His breath slowly returned, and Aphrodite, daughter of Zeus, led him out of battle.

When Hera saw them approaching she turned to Athene.

"Alas, Pallas!" she said. "Do you see how boldly that softhearted goddess of love is leading the ruthless killer out of the turmoil of the battle? Go—pursue them swiftly!" Pallas Athene stormed forward and struck delicate Aphrodite a blow in the breast, so that she fell and dragged wounded Ares down with her.

"Let all who dare help the Trojans fall like these!" exclaimed Athene. "If all who fight on my side had acted as I have, we should have had peace long ago, and Troy would be nothing but a heap of ruins." When Hera saw and heard this, a smile touched her lips.

Then Poseidon, the Earth-Shaker, spoke to Apollo: "Phoebus, why do we hold aloof, now that others have begun to fight? How disgraceful it would be if we two returned to Olympus without having measured our strength! You shall be first to strike, for you are the younger. Why do you hesitate? Have you forgotten how much we two, above all other gods, have already endured for the sake of Troy? How we served proud Laomedon by building the wall, and how he refused to give us our promised reward? Surely this must have slipped your memory, otherwise you would try to destroy the Trojans as I do and not give aid to the people of that crafty king!"

"Ruler of the sea," answered Phoebus, "I should be taking leave of my senses if, for the sake of mortals who perish lightly as the leaves of forest trees, I fought you, a god who commands reverence." So said Apollo and turned away, reluctant to raise his hand against his father's brother.

Then Artemis, his sister, mocked him, saying contemptuously: "Are you fleeing battle at the very outset, Far-Darter, and giving easy victory to boastful Poseidon? Then what is the use of the bow you carry over your shoulder? Is it only a child's toy?"

But Hera was displeased by her jeers. "Because you carry a quiver full of arrows on your back, do you venture to try your strength against me, shameless one?" she asked. "Better you went to the forest to shoot a boar or a stag, then insolently oppose the high gods. But since you are so defiant, you shall feel my hand." Thus reproving her, with her left hand she took Artemis by the wrists and with her right snatched her quiver from her shoulder and beat her about the ears with it while she turned this way and that, until the arrows dropped out. Like a timid dove pursued by a falcon, Artemis let lie her shafts and fled weeping. Leto, her mother, would have come to her aid, had not Hermes lurked close by. But when he saw her he withdrew, saying: "Far be it from me to pick a quarrel with you, Leto. For it is dangerous to quarrel with a woman whom the Thunderer has given his love. And so in the circle of immortals you may brag of having defeated me." Thus he spoke, and instantly Leto gathered up the bow and the arrows where they lay scattered in the dust and hastened after her daughter to Olympus. There Artemis, still in tears, seated herself on her father's knee, her dainty robe, fragrant with ambrosia, still trembling with the shaking of her limbs. Zeus took her tenderly in his arms and asked: "Who of the gods has dared abuse you, sweet child?"

"Father," she replied, "it is your wife who has done this to me, angry Hera, who incites all the gods to battle." At that Zeus only laughed and patted her cheek.

But down below, Phoebus Apollo had entered the city of Troy, for he feared that the Danai, defying Fate, would tear down the wall of the city that very day. The other gods hastened back to Olympus, some exulting, others filled with wrath and grief, and seated themselves in a circle around the Thunderer, the father of them all.

ACHILLES AND HECTOR BEFORE THE GATES

On a high tower of his city stood old King Priam and looked down on the mighty son of Peleus driving the fleeing Trojans before him, with neither god nor mortal to halt his progress. Lamenting, the king came down from the tower and exhorted the guards at the wall: "Open the gates and hold them so until all the fugitives have entered the city, for Achilles is pursuing them. As soon as our people are inside, lock the double doors, or the fierce son of Peleus will invade Troy." And the guards drew back the bolts, the gates flew apart, and a way to safety lay open.

As the Trojans, covered with dust and parched with thirst, fled from the battlefield and Achilles pursued them with his lance like a madman, Apollo left the open gates of Troy to come to the aid of his wards. He roused the courage of Agenor, brave son of Antenor, and enfolded in cloud, stood at his side at the foot of the beech tree of Zeus. Thus it came about that Agenor was the first of the Trojans to halt, collect his wits, and say to himself, full of shame at his flight: "Who is it that is following you? Cannot his flesh be wounded with a point of iron? Is he not mortal like other men?" He regained his composure, awaited Achilles, held out his shield, and cried to him, brandishing his lance: "Do not think you can raze the city of Troy so quickly! There are still those among us who will fight to defend the citadel for their parents, wives, and children." With this he cast his spear, and it struck the greaves of the hero at the knee, but rebounded without harming him. And now Achilles threw himself on his assailant, but Apollo carried Agenor off in a veil of mist and, by a ruse, kept Achilles from pursuing him. For the god assumed the shape of Agenor and ran through a field of barley toward the river Scamander. Achilles flew after him, hoping at every step to overtake him. Meantime the Trojans hurried through the open gates and poured into the city which soon filled to overflowing. No one waited for the other; no one turned to see who was saved or who had fallen; each rejoiced in his own rescue, in his safety behind the firmly built walls. They cooled their sweating limbs, quenched their thirst, and rested on the battlements.

But the Achaeans shouldered their shields and thronged toward the wall. Of all the Trojans, only Hector had remained outside the Scaean Gates, for this was appointed by Fate. Achilles was still pursuing Apollo whom he took for Agenor, until suddenly the god halted, turned, and said in his divine voice: "Why do you dog me so stubbornly, son of Peleus, and allow me to make you forget to go after the Trojans? You thought you were chasing a mortal, but you are running after a god whom you can never slay."

At that the scales fell from the eyes of Achilles; he was vexed and cried: "Cruel and tricking god! So you have lured me away from the wall! Had it not been for you, many a man would have bitten the dust before the Trojans entered Ilium. But you stole conquest from me and saved them without any danger to their ranks, for you are immortal and need have no fear of vengeance, much as I should like to avenge myself for what you have done to me!"

And Achilles faced about and flew toward the city like an impetuous chariot horse accustomed to victory. The first to see him was aged Priam who had again ascended his lookout in the tower, and he saw him blaze forth just as the Dog Star, bringing draught, glitters in the night sky, foretelling a poor harvest to the farmer. The old man beat his breast with his hands and called sorrowfully down to his son who was standing outside the Scaean Gates, waiting for the son of Peleus: "Hector, will you recklessly deliver yourself into the very hands of this murderer who has already robbed me of so many of my children? Come into the city and defend the men and women of Troy! Do not increase the glory of Achilles by letting him add your death to the tale of his numberless victims. Have pity on me, your old father, while I still breathe, for Zeus has condemned me to loiter long on the uttermost rim of old age and to suffer intolerable grief. Must I see my sons slain, my daughters torn from me and made captive, the halls of my palace plundered, young children hurled to the ground, the wives of my sons carried off? In the end I too will be laid low by a spear or a lance, laid low at the very door of my palace, and the very dogs I have reared will mangle my flesh and lap my blood."

So the old man called from the tower and tore his white hair.

Hecuba appeared at his side, and she too wept and cried: "Hector, remember that I fed you at my breast. Have pity on me! Drive off that dread hero from behind the wall, but do not meet him in front of the gates, for that would be madness!"

But neither the tears nor the entreaties of his parents could turn Hector from his purpose. Motionlessly he waited for Achilles and said to himself: "There was a time when I ought to have retreated. That was when my friend Polydamas advised me to take the Trojan army back into Ilium. Now that so many are slain because of my rashness, I fear the men and the women of Troy will some day say of me: 'Hector trusted his strength and in so doing delivered up his people!' Better that I win or die in fighting terrible Achilles. Or should I put my shield and helmet down on the ground, lean my spear against the wall, meet him unarmed, and offer to him Helen, all the treasure Paris took with her, and rich stores of gifts besides? What if I made the princes of Troy swear to keep nothing back, to divide our treasures and other possessions into two equal parts? But what thoughts are these! I, supplicate him? He would strike me down mercilessly! And how would it look if I went up to him and spoke sweet words, like a youth to a maiden? Better rush toward each other in battle, for soon we shall see to which of us two the Olympians will grant the victory." Such were the thoughts which passed through Hector's mind.

THE DEATH OF HECTOR

Nearer and nearer came Achilles, awful and splendid as Ares himself. On his right shoulder quivered his lance with the shaft of ash, and his brazen weapons blazed about him like the rising sun. When Hector saw him, he trembled against his will and turned toward the gate. But after him flew the son of Peleus, even as the hawk swoops on the dove which tries to slip to this side and that, but the bird of prey darts straight in ruthless pursuit. So Hector ran along the walls of Troy, along the wagon track and past the two bubbling springs of the Scamander, the warm and the cold, and on and on. A strong man fled, but a stronger followed. In this way they circled the city of Priam three times, and from Olympus the gods watched the spectacle with anxious hearts. "Weigh this well, O gods!" said Zeus. "The hour of decision has come. Shall Hector, who brought us so many sacrifices, escape death once more, or fall, brave though he be?"

And Pallas Athene answered: "Father, what are you saying? Would you redeem from death a mortal whom Fate has doomed long since? Do as you think best, but you must not expect the gods to approve."

Zeus nodded to his daughter in token of his willingness to let her follow her own counsel, and like a bird she flew down to the battlefield from the rocky heights of Olympus.

There Hector was still fleeing from his pursuer who gained on him like a hound on the deer he has startled from its hiding place and which he allows neither rest nor escape. And as he ran so fleetly, Achilles signed to his men that no one was to aim a missile at Hector, for he wanted the glory of being the first and the only one to slay the most dreaded enemy of the Argives.

When for the fourth time they had circled the walls and reached the springs of the Scamander, Zeus rose on Olympus, held out his golden scales, and placed in them two death lots, one for the son of Peleus and one for Hector. Then he held the scales in the middle and weighed. Hector's lot sank low toward Hades, and instantly Phoebus Apollo left him. But to Achilles came Pallas Athene and whispered: "Stand and compose yourself while I go to persuade your enemy to take courage and face you in fight." Obedient to the goddess, Achilles halted and leaned on his ashen spear, while she, assuming the shape of Deiphobus, approached Hector and said: "Ah! elder brother of mine, how relentlessly the son of Peleus besets you! Come, let us make a stand and beat him off."

Hector rejoiced at sight of his brother and answered: "I always loved you better than my other brothers, Deiphobus. But now that you have ventured out of the city to goad me on while the rest sit behind the walls, I honor and cherish you still more." And Deiphobus, who was Athene, led Hector on to where Achilles was resting, and she went before, raising her lance.

Hector was the first to speak. "I shall not flee from you any longer, son of Peleus," he said. "My heart urges me to confront you and fight until I slay you or am slain myself. But let us swear an oath before the gods: if Zeus grants me the victory, I shall not abuse you after death, but after I have stripped you of your armor I shall give your body back to your people. And you shall do likewise."

"I make no covenants!" Achilles replied sullenly. "As little as lions can make friends of men, as little as lambs and wolves can live peaceably together, just as little can there be friendship between us two. One of us shall sink bleeding to the ground. Muster what skill you have. You may cast the spear and fence with the sword. But you shall not escape me. For now you shall atone for all the grief you have brought my warriors with your weapons." So saying, Achilles hurled his lance. But Hector bent his knees, and the missile flew over him and into the earth. Athene took hold of it, drew it out, and returned it to Achilles, unseen by Hector. And now Hector poised his lance and cast angrily. It struck the shield of Achilles but rebounded from the bronze. Then Hector, in despair, looked back for his brother Deiphobus, for he had no other lance, but Deiphobus was gone. And suddenly Hector knew that Athene had tricked him and that his last hour had come. Unwilling to sink into the dust ingloriously, he drew his mighty sword from the sheath at his hip and, swinging it in his right hand, rushed forward as an eagle swoops on a lamb or a hare flattened against the earth. The son of Peleus did not wait for the thrust. He too swung forward, covering himself with his shield. The plumes on his helmet fluttered, and the spear he brandished in his right hand was bright as a star. Carefully he studied Hector to find a place where he could deal him a wound. From head to foot he was protected with the shining armor he had taken from Patroclus. There was only one small opening where shoulder and neck join at the collarbone. Achilles aimed carefully at this vulnerable part of his throat and pierced it with such violence that the point came out at the back of his neck. But the spear had not cut the windpipe, so that Hector could still speak, even though he had fallen, while Achilles jubilantly proclaimed that he would leave his body for dogs and birds to devour. At that Hector pleaded with him, though his breath grew fainter and fainter: "By your life, Achilles, I implore you! By your knees, by your parents—do not let the dogs mangle my flesh by the ships of the Argives! Take bronze and gold, as much as you want, but send my body to Troy, that the men and women of Priam's city may heap a pyre for me with due rites!"

But Achilles scowled, shook his head, and replied: "Do not entreat me by my knees and my parents, you who have murdered my friend! No one shall drive the dogs from your flesh, not if your countrymen pledged me twentyfold ransom, not if Priam gave me your own weight in gold."

"I know you," Hector moaned, dying. "I knew that you would be implacable. Your heart is of iron. But you will remember my words when the gods avenge me, when at the high Scaean Gates you fall from the deadly shaft directed by Phoebus Apollo, when you sink into the dust, even as I." As the last prophetic word left his lips, the soul of Hector departed from his body and winged its way down to Hades.

But Achilles shouted after it: "Die! My fate shall befall me when Zeus and the other gods decree!" So saying, he drew the spear from the body, laid it aside, and stripped slain Hector of his bloodstained armor.

And now from the Argive host many warriors came out and admired the stature and face of Hector and how goodly were his limbs, and many a one touched him and said: "Strange, how much gentler he is now than when he hurled the firebrand into our ships!"

Then Achilles stood up among the Achaeans and said: "Friends and heroes! Now that the gods have permitted me to vanquish this man who did us more harm than all the others put together, let us approach the city and try to discover whether they will surrender the citadel, or dare to offer resistance even without Hector. But why do I waste time in talking? Does not my friend Patroclus still lie unburied by the ships? Let us sing the song of victory and bring my friend the victim I have slain to avenge his death."

With these words, Achilles again bent down to Hector's body, pierced the tendons of both feet between ankle and heel, threaded thongs of oxhide through the opening, and made them fast to his chariot. Then he leaped in and goaded his horses toward the ships, letting the corpse trail on the ground. Clouds of dust rose about the dragged body, and the head, which only a little before had been so fair, drew a furrow through the sand, and the hair was matted and soiled. Looking down from the wall, Hecuba beheld her son and tore off her shining veil. King Priam too wept and made lament, and the city resounded with the cries and moans of the Trojans and their allies. In his anger and grief the old king could scarcely be restrained from rushing out of the Scaean Gates in pursuit of the slayer of his son. He threw himself on the ground and cried: "Hector, Hector! I forget all my other sons whom the enemy has killed in my sorrow for you. Oh, had you but died in my arms!"

Andromache, Hector's wife, knew nothing of all this, for no messenger had come to her, and she thought her husband was still within the walls of Troy. Serenely she sat in her chamber and embroidered stuff of Tyrian purple in bright colors. She had just bidden one of her handmaids set a great tripod on the fire to prepare a warm bath for Hector's return, when she heard moans and wails from the tower. Her heart full of dark forebodings, she cried: "Alas! I fear that Achilles has cut my husband off from his men, for Hector is so brave that he always rushes ahead of all the rest." Her heart beating painfully, she ran through the palace, climbed to the tower, and, looking down over the wall, saw the horses of the son of Peleus dragging her husband's body, bound to the victor's chariot, over the plain. Andromache fainted, and her kinswomen caught her in their arms. From her head fell her precious array, the frontlet and band and the veil Aphrodite had given her on her wedding day. When she regained consciousness, she sobbed and cried in broken tones: "Hector! Hector! You, ill-fated as I, both of us born to sorrow! Lonely and sad shall I sit in my house, a widow with a little son who has no father, who grows up with lowered eyes, his lashes wet with tears. He will have to beg among his father's friends and pull this one and that one by the cloak, that he may give him food and drink. And sometimes a child whose parents are both living will thrust him from the board, saying: 'Go away! Your father is not at the feast!' And then he will weep and seek refuge with his mother who has no husband. For the dogs will devour Hector and the worms take what is left. Of what use now are the fine and splendid tunics stored in my chests? I shall burn them, for never again will they adorn my husband." So she said weeping, and her women joined in her lament.

THE FUNERAL OF PATROCLUS

As soon as Achilles reached the ships with the corpse of his foe, he laid the body, face downward, in the dust beside the bier of Patroclus. The Danai, meanwhile, put off their armor and, by the thousands, sat down to the funeral feast. Oxen were slaughtered, and sheep, and boars, and the son of Peleus had rich and ample fare prepared for the warriors. Only reluctantly did he allow his friends to take him from the bier of his friend and lead him to the house of Agamemnon. Here a great cauldron of water was set over the fire, and they tried to persuade Achilles to wash the blood and sweat of battle from his limbs. But he stubbornly refused and swore a mighty oath: "No, by Zeus on Olympus! Water shall not touch me before I have laid Patroclus on the pyre, shaved my head, and heaped him a monument. Now the funeral feast shall be held. But tomorrow, Prince Agamemnon, let trees be cut in the forest and everything brought which is needed, that the fire may swiftly take from us the mournful sight of my friend. After that, the men may again turn to war." The princes let him do as he wished and sat down to the meal. Then each went to his own house. But the son of Peleus, surrounded by his Myrmidons, lay down on the shore of the sea, where the waves had washed it clean.

Long on the stony strand he sighed for his friend who was

slain. When at last he fell asleep, the soul of Patroclus came to him in a dream. It resembled Patroclus in stature and voice and eyes, and the tunic it wore was like his. The form leaned over him and said, "Are you asleep? Have you already forgotten me, Achilles? You always loved the living, but you are unmindful of the dead! Give me a grave, for I yearn to pass through the gates of Hades. Until now I have only wandered near them, for phantoms sit there as guards and drive me away. I cannot find rest until my body is burned on the pyre. And, my friend, you must know that Fate has decreed that you too shall fall near the walls of Troy. Therefore let the grave be so that we, who grew up together in your father's house, may have our bones buried side by side in death."

"I shall do all you say," said Achilles and stretched out his arms to that shadowy form, but it vanished into earth like mist. Achilles leaped up amazed, struck together his hands, and said mournfully to his companions: "So it is true that souls live on in Hades, for this night I saw before me the soul of Patroclus, sad and making lament, but like him in all things!" And his words again wakened the yearning of the heroes for him who was no more.

When dawn reddened the sky, Agamemnon bade men and mules go forth, Meriones in the lead. The beasts came first, and after them men with axes and ropes. Then on the wooded slopes of Ida the tallest trees were felled and the wood split and loaded on the mules which dragged the trunks down to the ships. And the men too carried logs on their shoulders, and on the shore all was laid in rows. Now Achilles bade his Myrmidons gird on their armor of bronze and yoke the horses to the chariots. Then the funeral procession began to move. First in the chariots came the princes and warriors with their charioteers, and after them followed a vast throng of men on foot. In the midst, his friends and comrades bore Patroclus. His body was covered with locks they had cut from their heads. Following it came Achilles, bowing his head in his hands, and he was sunk in sorrow.

When they came to the place Achilles had chosen they set down the bier, and a whole forest of trees was heaped for the pyre. The son of Peleus stood apart, cut off one of his golden locks, gazed into the dark tide of the sea, and said: "O Spercheus, river of Thessaly, my country, in vain did my father Peleus vow that if I returned I should shear my hair for you and offer fifty rams at your springs, where your grove stands and your altar. You were deaf to his pleading, O river-god! You will not let me return. And so do not be angry with me if I give this lock to Patroclus, to carry down with him to Hades." With these words he put the lock in the hands of his friend and said to Agamemnon: "Tell the people to disperse and eat their meal, O prince. After that they shall mourn and bury my friend."

At Agamemnon's command the warriors went their ways among the ships, and only the princes remained. From the trunks of the trees which had been felled they built a great pyre, a hundred feet square, and with heavy hearts laid the body on it. Numberless sheep and horned cattle they flayed beside the pyre, heaped the bodies around, and covered the corpse with the fat. Against the bier they leaned jars of honey and oil and led four living horses to the pyre. They also slaughtered two of the nine dogs of Patroclus and then slew with the sword twelve noble Trojan youths chosen from among the captives. Thus Achilles took terrible vengeance for the death of his friend.

Then he bade them kindle the pyre, and as they obeyed he called to the dead: "May happiness attend you even in Hades, Patroclus! What I pledged you I have fulfilled! Twelve victims have been slain and shall burn on your pyre. Hector alone shall not be consumed in the flames. His flesh shall be food for the dogs!" He spoke threateningly, but the gods willed otherwise. Day and night Aphrodite kept the ravening dogs from the body of Hector and anointed it with ambrosia, fragrant as roses, until all trace of the dragging had vanished. And Apollo poised a dark cloud over the place where he lay, so that the sun might not shrivel his flesh.

And now, though the wood was lit, it would not burn. Then Achilles again turned from the pyre and vowed offerings to the winds, to Zephyr and Boreas, poured wine for them from a cup of gold, and begged them to quicken the sparks to a blaze. Iris brought his message to the winds, and with awful clamor they stormed across the sea and flung themselves on the pyre. All night they roared through the wood and lashed the flame, while Achilles never ceased pouring libations for the soul of his dead friend. When the sky grew saffron with dawn the winds rested, the fire died down, and the embers crumbled to ash. In the midst of charred wood and cinders lay the bones of Patroclus, and at the uttermost edge the bones of animals and men intermingled. At the command of the son of Peleus, the heroes quenched the heat of the ashes with red wine. With many tears they gathered up the white bones of their comrade, covered them with a two-fold layer of fat, and placed them in a golden urn which they carried to the house of Achilles. Then they measured the place, set a foundation of stones where the pyre had been, and heaped earth for the burial mound.

When all was done, the funeral games began. Achilles had the Argives assemble and sit in a wide circle. Then he brought as prizes tripods, cauldrons, mules, strong oxen, and, arrayed in costly robes, women who were trained in crafts, and precious gray iron. First came the chariot races. In these he himself did not take part, for he had lost his beloved charioteer. But up rose Eumelus, son of Admetus, a hero most skilled in the art of driving. Then came Diomedes, who yoked the splendid horses he had taken from Aeneas. Third was Menelaus with his horse Podargus and Agamemnon's mare Aethe. The fourth to enter the race was Antilochus, Nestor's young son, to whom his father gave advice concerning the race. Fifth, Meriones yoked his glossy-flanked steeds. Then the five heroes mounted their chariots, and Achilles shook the lots to decide in what order they were to stand. First the lot of Antilochus leaped from the helmet, then that of Eumelus, Menelaus, Meriones, and last that of the son of Tydeus. As umpire Achilles chose gray-haired Phoenix, his father's comrade-in-arms.

All five together raised their goads, called to their horses, struck their backs with the reins, and stormed across the plain. The dust whirled high under the horses' hooves, their manes fluttered, and the chariots now rolled on the ground, now leaped through the air. Taut and upright stood the drivers, and their hearts beat high with longing for victory. As the horses approached the end of the course which was near the sea, each seemed fleetness itself as it strained toward the goal. The mares of Eumelus flew in the van; but hot on their flanks blew the breath of Diomedes' steeds, when suddenly Apollo snatched the goad from the hands of the son of Tydeus, and the speed of his creatures lessened. Athene observed the trick, returned the goad to the hero, and broke the yoke of Eumelus, so that the mares sprang apart and the driver plunged headlong from the chariot and doubled up in pain beside the wheel. Past him sped the son of Tydeus; after him Menelaus; next came Antilochus, urging on his horses with panting cries. And then, where the rains had washed away the soil, Menelaus stopped his horses, but Antilochus boldly drove past him. As the Argives watched, trying to distinguish the horses and cars through moving clouds of dust, Diomedes left the others behind. His chariot, overlaid with shining tin and gold, had arrived at the goal. From the necks and breasts of his horses sweat poured in streams. And the son of Tydeus sprang to the ground and leaned his goad against the yoke. His friend Sthenelus took the prizes—a fair woman and a tripod—and gave them to his comrades to carry away. Then he loosed the horses from the yoke.

After him came Antilochus, and almost at the same moment, Menelaus. Somewhat slower, a spear's throw behind, Meriones reached the goal, and last of all injured Eumelus with his damaged chariot. But though he came last, Achilles wished to give him the second prize, because he was the most skilled in driving and his misfortune was due to no fault of his own. But Antilochus disputed this heatedly. "The second prize is mine," he said. "That beautiful mare is my prize! If you are sorry for Eumelus, surely you have enough gold and bronze, horses and women in your house to give him something." Achilles smiled, awarded the mare to his younger friend, and gave Eumelus the magnificent breastplate he had seized from Asteropaeus. But now Menelaus accused Antilochus of having got in the way of his horses, and he bade him swear by Poseidon if this was untrue. Antilochus did not dare swear a false oath. He admitted his ruse and led the mare he had won over to the son of Atreus. But Menelaus was satisfied to let the youth have his mare and accepted the third prize, a cauldron. The fourth prize, two talents of gold, fell to the share of Meriones, and the fifth, a two-handled bowl, though it was unclaimed, Achilles gave to Nestor as a memorial of the funeral of Patroclus.

Next came the boxing match. The prize for the victor was a

mule, that for the vanquished, a two-handled cup. When this was proclaimed, a tall and mighty man arose, Epeius, son of Panopeus. He put his hand on the mule and cried: "This is mine! Let him who will, have the cup! But I give him fair warning: my fist will shatter his body, and his bones will be crushed!" Silence met this grim announcement, but then Euryalus, son of Mecisteus, girded himself and faced his opponent ready for the fight. Then they raised their arms, fists landed on jaws, and sweat flowed from straining limbs. Finally Epeius struck his adversary on the cheek, and he fell to the ground like a fish which a wave has flung on the sandy shore. Epeius helped him up by the hands, and as his friends led him away he spat blood, and his head drooped.

Next Achilles announced the prizes for the wrestling match: for the victor, a great tripod, equal in worth to twelve oxen; for the vanquished, a woman lovely to look at and skilled in handiwork. Then Odysseus and Ajax the Great clasped each other with supple arms, and they were as closely interlocked as timbers joined by a builder. The sweat poured from them, their bones creaked, and their sides and shoulders were marked with bloody weals. The Argives were beginning to mutter with impatience when Ajax lifted Odysseus from the ground, but he crooked his knee and thrust at his opponent, threw him on his back, and fell on his chest. But he could move him only very little, and the two rolled in the dust. "You have both won!" cried Achilles. "I shall give you prizes of equal value."

For the foot race to follow, a mixing bowl of silver, delicately wrought and so large that it held six measures, was destined for the victor. The second to reach the goal was to have an ox, the third, half a talent of gold. Ajax, the swift Locrian, Odysseus, and Antilochus offered to run. Achilles gave the sign, and Ajax stormed ahead. But close to him as the weaving rod to the breast of a woman came Odysseus. Ajax felt his breath fanning his neck, and all the Danai called encouragement to the fleet runner. When they were almost at the goal, Odysseus prayed to Athene with all the fervor of his heart. And she made his limbs light and let Ajax stumble over the filth left over from the sheep and cattle which had been slaughtered for Patroclus, and he fell and soiled his face.

The Argives roared with laughter when, a moment later,

Odysseus seized the mixing bowl and Ajax, gagging and spitting, laid his hand on the ox. Smilingly Antilochus took the third prize and said: "The gods give honor to older men. Ajax is, indeed, only slightly older than I in years, but he is of an older line."

"It is to your profit that you have spoken words so free from envy," said Achilles, and added half a talent of gold to the prize of the handsome youth.

And now the son of Peleus brought into the circle the beautiful lance of Sarpedon, which Patroclus had carried off as spoils, and laid it down together with the shield and the helmet. For these, two of the bravest heroes were to fight fully armed and receive the prize jointly. Achilles was to feast both in his house, and the victor was to have a sword, studded with silver, the Thracian sword of Asteropaeus. Three times with flashing eyes Ajax, son of Telamon, and Diomedes ran at each other with their arms. Ajax pierced the shield of the son of Tydeus, but Diomedes aimed at his throat. In grave concern for Ajax, the Argives separated the two, but it was the son of Tydeus who received the sword.

Next came the contest with the iron discus which Eetion, king of Thebes, whom Achilles slew, had often thrown. Epeius swung it and threw, but with so little skill that the Danai burst out laughing. Then Leonteus threw, and next mighty Ajax, and it flew beyond the mark. But Polypoetes hurled it farther than all others, as a herdsman flings his crook over his grazing kine, and he bore off the prize.

Ten double axes and ten hatchets of bluish iron Achilles set as prizes for the archers. A pigeon was bound to the mast of a ship with a thin cord. Whoever hit the bird was to have the double axes. And whoever missed the bird but hit the cord was to have the smaller hatchets. Teucer and Meriones cast lots for the first shot. Teucer's lot leaped from the helmet, but because Apollo did not favor him, he missed the bird and cut the cord with his shaft, so that the pigeon soared into the air. As Teucer watched it, vexed and disappointed, Meriones snatched the bow from his hands, fitted his arrow to the string, and shot the pigeon through the wing, in flight, and this he achieved because he had quickly vowed a hecatomb as thank offering to Phoebus. The wounded dove perched on the mast; its neck and wings drooped, and a moment later it fell down dead. The Achaeans shouted with joy and amazement. Meriones took the axes, and Teucer carried off the hatchets.

Lastly a spear and a cauldron carved with tendrils and flowers were brought into the ring as prizes for casting the javelin. First Agamemnon, ruler of many peoples, arose, and after him Meriones. But Achilles said: "Son of Atreus, from watching you in battle, we all know how far you excel all others in casting the lance, so leave the spear to Meriones and take the cauldron without competing for it." Agamemnon consented. He handed the lance to the Cretan and took the cauldron. This was the end of the games.

PRIAM VISITS ACHILLES

When the participants separated, each man ate and slept. Only Achilles did not sleep, for he spent the night thinking of the friend he had buried. First he lay on his side, then on his back, then on his face. Finally he got up and roamed along the shore. In the early morning he harnessed his horses, bound Hector's body to his chariot, and dragged him three times around the burial mound of Patroclus. But Apollo held his golden aegis over the corpse and saved it from being disfigured. Achilles left it sprawled on its face in the dust. All the gods on Olympus, except Hera, grieved at the sight, and Zeus sent for Thetis, the mother of Achilles. He ordered her to go to the Argive camp with all possible speed and tell her son that all the gods, even Zeus himself, were consumed with anger because he was holding Hector's body without ransom.

Thetis obeyed. She entered the house of her son, came close to him, gently caressed his hair, and said: "How long are you going to eat out your heart with sorrow and forget food and sleep? It would be better if you turned to the pleasures of living again, for you will not be on earth for long. Dark Fate already lurks at your side. Listen to what Zeus bade me tell you. He and all the gods are indignant that you have maltreated Hector's body and are keeping it by the ships. Let it go, my son, let it go for a rich ransom."

Achilles looked up, fixed his eyes on his mother's face, and answered: "So be it. What Zeus and the council of the immortals have resolved must be done. Whoever brings me the ransom shall carry away the corpse."

While Thetis was with her son, Zeus sent fleet-footed Iris, the messenger of the gods, to the city of Priam to announce his decision. When Iris reached Troy, she found nothing but wailing and weeping. In the court of the palace was Priam in the circle of his sons, and their robes were wet with tears. The old man sat stiff and still, wrapped in his mantle; his head and shoulders were strewn with dust. In their chambers his daughters and the wives of his sons loudly lamented the heroes who had been slain. Suddenly and softly the messenger of Zeus came up to the king and spoke to him in a low voice. A shudder ran through his limbs. "Contain yourself, son of Dardanus," she said. "Do not despair. I bring you good news. Zeus has mercy upon you. He bids you go to Achilles, bearing rich gifts, with which to ransom the corpse of your son. You shall go alone, accompanied by no one except one of the older heralds to guide the wagon with the mules and bring the body back to the city. You need not fear death or dangers of any kind, for Zeus is giving you an escort. Hermes will take you to the son of Peleus and protect you while you are with him. Besides, Achilles is not so blind as to disobey the gods. He will spare the suppliant of his own accord and keep all harm from you."

Priam had faith in the words of the goddess. He told his sons to yoke the mules to the wagon, while he went to the chamber panelled with fragrant cedar-wood, where he kept his treasures. He summoned Hecuba there and said to her: "Zeus sent me a message. I am to go to Achilles, to his house near the ships, propitiate him with gifts, and so ransom the body of Hector, our beloved son. What do you think of this? I myself am most eager to go to the ships." So said the old man, but his wife sobbed and replied: "Alas! Priam, where is your good sense, for which you have been famed? You, an old man, go alone to the Argive ships and meet the foe who has killed so many of your brave sons! Do you think that false, bloodthirsty wretch will feel pity at your sight? Rather let us mourn from afar for our son who, from the hour of his birth, was destined to be killed and devoured by dogs."

"Do not try to hinder me," Priam said resolutely. "Do not be a bird of ill omen in my house. Though death may await me at the ships, let that madman kill me if only I can hold the body of Hector in my arms and ease my heart with tears." Then he raised the lids of the chests and selected twelve sumptuous festal robes and a like number of tunics and costly mantles. After this he weighed out ten talents of gold and took four gleaming cauldrons and two tripods. And he added a priceless cup the Thracians had given him when he came to them an an envoy. Nothing was too much to ransom his cherished son! He drove away the Trojans who wanted to hold him back, and said threateningly: "You good-for-nothings! Have you no griefs at home that you come here to add to my sorrow? Is it not enough that Zeus has taken my son from me? You will soon find out what it means! Rather would I go to Hades than see the heap of ruins and ashes your city will become." And he drove them out of the hall with his scepter.

Then he turned to his sons. "Cowards!" he cried. "Idlers! If only you lay by the ships in Hector's stead! All the best and bravest are dead. What is left is the scum—the liars, the cheats, the dancers, who wallow in the fat of the land. Now, this very instant, you shall make ready a wagon and lay all these things in baskets, so that I can start on my way." The sons were taken aback and afraid of their father's anger. They yoked the mules to the wagon and loaded it with the ransom. Then they harnessed the well-groomed, glossy horses to Priam's chariot and called the herald who was to go with him. With heavy heart Hecuba handed the king the golden cup for the libation. A slave approached with a basin and pitcher, and when Priam had bathed his hands in clean water, he took the cup, stood in the center of the court, poured the wine, and raised his voice in prayer to Zeus.

"Father Zeus," he implored, "ruler of Ida, let the son of Peleus show mercy and grace to me. Give me a token, let a bird fly on my right, so that I may go to the Argive ships without fear." He had barely finished speaking when an eagle with black wings spread wide soared over the city, flying from the right. The Trojans hailed the sign joyfully, and full of confidence the old man mounted the chariot. In front of him went the four-wheeled wagon, heavily loaded, drawn by mules which Idaeus, the herald, drove. As Priam touched his horses with the goad and they began to move, his people followed him with troubled eyes and wailed as though he were going to his death.

When Priam and his herald were outside the city and passing the monument of old King Ilus, they stopped to let the horses and mules drink at the river. It was evening, and twilight hung over the plain. Then Idaeus saw a man standing close by and warned Priam. "Look, master," he said. "We must be cautious. See the man over there. I fear he is waiting to kill us. We have no arms, and both of us are old. Let us either turn and flee back into the city or clasp his knees and beg him to spare us." The king shook with terror, and his hair stood up on his head. And now the man approached; it was not a foe, but Hermes, the messenger of Zeus, the bringer of help to men, whom the father of the gods sends to accompany chosen mortals on their ways. Priam did not recognize him, but the god took the old man's hand and said:

"Where are you driving your horses and mules at dead of night when other mortals sleep? Are you not afraid of the angry Argives? If one of them saw you taking so many precious wares through the darkness, would it not be dangerous for you? Do not think for an instant, though, that I shall harm you! Quite on the contrary—I shall protect you from others! All the more because you are so very like my own dear father. But tell me, are you fleeing and taking all these choice things to an alien land? Perhaps you are leaving Troy, now that the city has lost the bravest of its defenders, Hector, whom no Argive surpassed in courage?"

Priam breathed more freely and answered: "Now I see that I must be under the protection of a god, for he has sent me a wise and gentle companion who speaks tenderly of the death of my son. Tell me who you are and the name of your parents."

"Polyctor is my father," Hermes replied. "I am the youngest of seven sons, a Myrmidon, a comrade of Achilles. That is how I happened to see your son driving the Argives back to their ships while we stood by our angry king and admired Hector from afar."

"If you are a comrade of dread Achilles," said Priam, full of anxiety, "then tell me if my son still lies by the ships, or whether the son of Peleus has already hacked him to pieces and thrown him to the dogs."

"He has not," said Hermes. "Hector still lies in the house of Achilles, and no decay has touched his flesh, though this is the twelfth morning and though the son of Peleus drags him around the grave of his friend at every dawn. You would be amazed if you saw him, for his body looks as fresh as if he were alive. All his wounds are closed and there is not a bloodstain on him! Even in his death, the gods cherish and tend him."

Joyfully Priam reached for the priceless cup which he had in the chariot. "Take it," he said. "In return, give me your protection and take me to your master's house." Hermes refused the cup, as though he hesitated to accept gifts without the knowledge of Achilles. But he mounted the chariot beside Priam, took reins and goad, and soon they reached the trench and the wall. The guards were just having their evening meal, but the god lifted his hand, and they sank into deep sleep. A mere touch of his fingers and the bolts opened. In this way Priam came safely and quickly to the house of Achilles.

It loomed high, built of timbers and roofed over with reeds. A spacious court was all around it, and this in turn was protected by a close-set palisade. A single bolt of pine wood closed the door, but it was so heavy that only three strong men could push it back or forward. No one but Achilles could handle it alone. But Hermes opened the door effortlessly, dismounted, and revealed himself as a god after he had advised the old man to clasp the hero's knees and beseech him by his father and mother. Now Priam too dismounted and left the horses and mules in the care of Idaeus. He himself went straight into the house and found Achilles sitting apart from his comrades. He was resting after the meal. The board still stood before him, and only Automedon and Alcimus were close by.

No one noticed the entrance of Priam. He hastened to Achilles, clasped his knees, kissed his hands, those terrible hands which had slain so many of his sons, and gazed into his face. The son of Peleus and his friends regarded him with amazement. And then the old man began to plead. "Godlike Achilles," he said, "think of your father, who is as old as I. Perhaps hostile neighbors are threatening him and he is as frightened and helpless as I myself. Still, day after day, he lives in the hope of seeing his dear son once more. But I, who had fifty sons when the Argives came to this coast, nineteen of them from one and the same wife, have lost most of them in this war, and now you have killed the only one who could have saved our city and all our people. That is why I have travelled to the ships. I have come to buy the body of Hector from you, and I bring immeasurable ransom. Fear the gods, son of Peleus, have pity on me, and remember your own father! I am worthier of compassion than he, for I have suffered what no mortal has suffered, and I press to my lips the hand which has slain my children." So he spoke and aroused in the hero longing and sorrow for his father. He gently loosened the old man's clasp; then Priam, prostrate at Achilles' feet, shed bitter tears for Hector, and Achilles also wept for his father and for his friend. The house resounded with lament.

At last the son of Peleus rose from his seat and raised the old man, filled with pity for his gray hair and beard, and said: "How much you have suffered, and now, what courage to come alone to the Argive ships and into the presence of the man who has killed so many of your sons! You must have an iron heart! But come, sit down, and let us quiet our grief, though it gnaws at the soul. This is the fate decreed by the gods for mortal men, while they themselves are free from care. At the door of Zeus stand two great urns. One is filled with disaster, the other with good fortune. He to whom the god gives a little of both alternates between unhappiness and joy. But he to whom Zeus deals nothing but anguish is pursued over all the earth by grief that eats at his heart. To Peleus the gods did, indeed, give marvellous gifts, power and possessions, and even an immortal to wife. But he was also allotted a share of distress, for he has an only son who is destined to die young, so that he will not be able to tend his father in his old age. And here I am, far from home, fighting before the gates of Troy and grieving you and yours, old man. You too were famed through the world for the fortune attending your house, you and your many sons, but now the Olympians have sent war and death to your city. Endure your lot and do not mourn incessantly, for even years of lament will not give you back your glorious son."

Priam replied: "Favorite of Zeus, do not bid me be seated while Hector lies in your house unburied. Let me have him quickly, for I long to see him. Accept the rich ransom I have brought you, spare me, and return to your native land."

Achilles frowned at his words and said: "Do not press me, old man. I myself wish to give Hector to you, for my mother brought me the message of Zeus. Besides, I know quite well that a god must have led you to our ships. For how could a mortal, were he ever so young and brave, get by the guards or draw back the bolt from the gate? But do not trouble my sad heart still more, or I might forget the command of Zeus and fail to spare you, no matter how humbly you plead."

Priam trembled and was silent. But Achilles leaped from the house like a lion, and after him his comrades. They unyoked the mules and admitted the herald. Then they took the ransom from the wagon, but they left in it two mantles and a tunic, so that the body of Hector might be fittingly covered. After this Achilles had the corpse washed, anointed, clothed, and laid on a bier. As his companions lifted it on the wagon, he called the name of his friend and said: "If, in the night of the underworld, you should hear that I gave Hector's body to his father, do not be angry with me, Patroclus. He brought no mean ransom, and you shall have your share of it."

He re-entered the house, seated himself opposite Priam, and said: "Your son has been ransomed, as you desired. He lies properly clad, and as soon as the sky reddens with dawn, you may see him and take him away with you. But now let us eat the evening meal. You will have time enough to lament your son when you return to Troy, and he well deserves all the tears you will shed for him." So saying, the hero rose from his seat, hastened out, and slaughtered a sheep. His friends flayed it, cut the meat into pieces, and roasted them on a spit. Then they sat down at the board. Automedon passed each his share of bread in a basket skillfully plaited; Achilles dispensed the meat, and all satisfied their hunger and thirst. Priam watched his host wonderingly, for in beauty and strength he was like the immortals. But Achilles too marvelled whenever he looked at Priam's face, full of majesty and command, or heard the wise words he uttered. When the meal was over, Priam said: "Now assign me a couch, noble Achilles, that I may refresh myself with sleep, for since my son died, my lids have not closed, and this is the first time I have tasted meat and wine."

Instantly Achilles bade his handmaids prepare a couch with crimson mats and spread it with soft coverlets. The herald had a couch of his own. Then Achilles said: "And now lie down and sleep, old man. For if you went to your couch later in the evening, one of the Argive princes who have the custom of assembling in my house might see you prowling through the dark and report it to Agamemnon. And he might question my right to dispose of Hector's body as I wish. But tell me one thing more: how many days will you spend on the burial of your son? I ask because during all that time I shall keep my people from attacking your city."

"If you permit me to bury my son with all honors," Priam replied, "then allow me eleven days. You know that we live in a city and must fetch wood for his pyre from the mountains, and that is a long way. We shall need nine days for our preparations. On the tenth we shall bury him and hold the funeral feast and on the eleventh heap the burial mound. On the twelfth—if it must be so—we shall be ready to fight again."

"It shall be as you say," answered Achilles. "I shall restrain my warriors for the number of days you ask." As he spoke he clasped his hand around the old man's right wrist, in order to take from him all fear. Then Priam went to his couch, and Achilles lay down in the innermost room of his house.

All were asleep except Hermes, and he pondered in his mind

how he could lead the king of Troy back from the ships unseen. At last he went to Priam where he lay asleep, stood at the head of his couch, and said: "Old man, is not your sleep among hostile men a little too untroubled? They have spared you, it is true. They took your rich ransom and consented to give you the body of your son. But if Agamemnon and the other Argives knew of it, your sons at home would have to ransom you, the living, with three times as much." The old man sat up in alarm and woke the herald. Hermes himself yoked the horses and mules and mounted the chariot with the king. Idaeus drove the wagon on which the body lay. Unnoticed they rode through their enemies, and soon the camp of the Achaeans lay behind them.

HECTOR'S BODY IN TROY

Hermes accompanied the king as far as the ford of the Sca-mander. There he left the chariot and soared to the peak of Olympus. Priam and the herald went on alone, sighing and groaning with grief. It was early morning when they reached the city. All were asleep, and no one saw them coming except Cassandra. She had climbed to the ramparts of the palace and, from afar, saw her father standing in the chariot, saw the herald with the wagon drawn by mules, and on it the body of Hector. At the sight which met her eyes she began to weep and cried so loudly that the silent city rang with her lament: "Come, you Trojan men and women! Here is Hector—alas! only the body of Hector! If ever you rejoiced in him while he was alive and returned victorious from the battlefield, then greet him now too, now that he is dead!"

At her call, every man and woman in the city came from his house, and the hearts of all were bursting with grief. At the gates the people of Troy, Hector's mother and wife in their van, met the herald. Hecuba and Andromache tore their hair and rushed toward the wagon to clasp Hector's head. Weeping throngs sur-rounded them, and they would have held the wagon there until evening, had not Priam spoken to them from his chariot. "Make way and let the mules pass. When the body lies in my palace, you may weep your fill." The people reverently fell to the right and left and let the wagon proceed.

When it reached the palace of Priam, the body was laid on a couch, richly adorned. Singers were called to chant dirges, and the women wailed in chorus. Andromache uttered the bitterest lament. In the flower of life she stood before the corpse and touched his head with her hands. "My husband," she mourned, "you have lost your life and left me behind, a widow with a little son, who, I fear, will never grow into a youth. For now that you, the defender of our city, the protector of women and children, are gone, Troy will be destroyed! All will be taken captive and led to the ships, and I among them. And you, my darling Astyanax, will share the disgrace of your mother. Both of us will have to work under a harsh lord. Or perhaps an Argive will take you by the arm and hurl you from the tower, because your father slew his father or brother or son. For Hector did not spare his foes in battle! You have caused your parents bitter grief, and bitterest of all to me. I could not hold your hand as you lay dying. You did not give me a single word of farewell, a word of wisdom which night and day I might have treasured in my heart with fond memories and tears."

After Andromache, Hecuba spoke. "Hector," she lamented, "my cherished son! The gods too loved you, for they did not forget you in the cruel death you suffered. You were slain with the sword and dragged over the ground, and yet you look unharmed, as if an arrow from Apollo's silver bow had struck you, swiftly and mercifully." So she spoke, comforting herself and shedding many tears.

Then Helen spoke. "Hector," she cried, "you were dearest to me of all my husband's brothers. Twenty years have passed since Paris took me from my native land, and in all that time I never heard a harsh word from your lips. It is true that King Priam was also gentle with me, but when anyone else in the house, a brother or sister of my husband, his mother or the wife of one of his brothers reproached me, it was you who calmed their anger, you who always smoothed my way. In you I have lost a helper and a friend. Now everyone will turn from me in disgust."

So she spoke weeping, and all the countless people about her sighed. But now Priam raised his voice above the throng of mourners. "Fetch wood for the pyre, Trojans," he ordered. "And be careful not to fall into an ambush, for Achaeans may be lurking in wait for you, even though the son of Peleus promised me that no harm would come to us for eleven days."

The people quickly obeyed. They harnessed oxen and mules to their wagons, and all assembled before the city. For nine days they fetched wood from the forested mountain slopes. On the tenth morning Hector's body was carried out with loud lament. They laid it on the pyre and set it aflame. And all the people stood about and watched it burn to the ground. Then they quenched the glowing ashes with wine, and the brothers and comrades-in-arms of the dead gathered his white bones from among the ashes, wrapped them in cloths of soft crimson stuff, put them in a golden chest, and lowered this into a grave. Blocks of stone were laid on it, and a burial mound heaped over these. All the while men kept watch, for fear the Argives might suddenly attack and disturb the rites. When the earth was piled high over the grave, the people returned to the city, and a solemn feast for the dead was held in Priam's palace.

PENTHESILEA

When Hector's burial was over, the Trojans again stayed behind their walls, for they feared the impetuous strength of the son of Peleus and shrank from going anywhere near him, like oxen that balk and shy away from the den of a mountain lion. The city still resounded with lament for the hero who was dead, and the anguish of the people was as great as though Troy itself were already burning with the firebrands of the conqueror.

In the midst of all this grief and terror, help came to the besieged from an unexpected quarter. From the region around the river Thermodon in Pontus, Penthesilea, queen of the Amazons, arrived with a small group of her warrior women to aid the Trojans in their war. She had embarked on this enterprise partly because she had that love of danger and battles peculiar to the Amazons, and partly because she was guilty of a crime she had committed unknowingly, and which had lessened the esteem she commanded among her people. For once, on a hunt, when she had aimed her spear at a stag, she had killed her own beloved sister Hippolyte. And now the Furies pursued her wherever she went, and no offering she had made so far had appeased them. She hoped that an expedition pleasing to the gods would end her disgrace, and so she had left for Troy with twelve chosen companions, all of whom shared her thirst for strife and danger. But compared with Penthesilea these companions of hers, lovely though they were, seemed like slaves. As the radiance of the moon dims the light of the stars, so greatly did she outshine her maidens in beauty and splendor. She was glorious as the goddess of dawn when, with the Hours about her, she leaves the heights of Olympus and floats to the rim of the earth.

When the Trojans looked down from their walls and saw Penthesilea, strong and yet delicately made, clad in brazen armor and gleaming greaves, approaching at the head of her women, they streamed together from all sides. And when the little train drew nearer, they marvelled at the beauty of the queen, for in her face majesty and charm were curiously blended. Her lips smiled, and under her long lashes her eyes were shining and young. Her rosy cheeks looked girlish, but her features were more spirited than a girl's, lively and afire for action. At sight of her, the Trojans forgot their despair and shouted with delight. Even Priam's heart was gladdened when he saw Penthesilea, and he felt like one who has been in darkness for a long time and now sees the longed-for light. But his joy was dulled by the memory of the many sons he had lost. He conducted the queen to his palace, honored her as though she were his own daughter, and received her as a cherished guest. At his command priceless gifts were spread out before her, and he promised her even more, should she succeed in saving Troy.

Then the Amazon queen rose from the seat of honor to which the king had bidden her and dared swear an oath which no other mortal would have dreamed of taking. She pledged the king the death of godlike Achilles. She and her women, she said, would destroy the Argives; their firebrands would eat their way through all the enemy ships. In ignorance and folly Penthesilea swore this oath, for she did not yet know the terrible arm of peerless Achilles. When Andromache, Hector's widow, heard her words, she thought to herself: "Poor creature! You do not know what

you have said, or what, in your pride, you are venturing upon. How could you have the strength to overcome that hero? You are out of your mind! You do not even see Death who already confronts you. Hector, my husband, was honored by his people as though he were a god, and yet the son of Peleus pierced his neck with the spear. Oh, that earth would open to devour me!"

These things Andromache said to herself. Meantime the day was drawing to a close. Penthesilea and her retinue were served with food and drink and shown to the couches prepared for them. The Amazon queen soon fell fast asleep. And then, at Athene's command, she had a dream sent to hasten her destruction. Ares, her father, appeared to her and urged her to battle with Achilles as soon as possible. At his words her heart leaped in her breast, and she thought that on that very day she would accomplish what she had sworn to Priam. She woke, sprang from her couch, and girt on the shining armor Ares himself had given her. She fastened the golden greaves to her legs and donned the glittering cuirass. Across her shoulder she slung her sword in its scabbard of silver and ivory. Then she took her shield, bright as the moon when it rises from the mirror of the sea, and set on her head her helmet with its crest of yellow gold. In her left hand she held two spears and in her right a double axe which she had received from the goddess of discord. When she stormed out of the palace, slender and dazzling in all her array, she looked like a flash of lightning flung to earth from Olympus.

Jubilant and eager she ran to the wall and urged the Trojans to fight and win glory for themselves and their city. At her call, men who had not dared face dread Achilles quickened with new courage and prepared for battle. But Penthesilea herself, impatient for the onslaught, leaped on her beautiful horse, fleet as the harpies. The wife of Boreas, king of Thrace, had made her a gift of it. Her women also mounted their horses and followed her to the field. Many battalions of Trojan warriors accompanied them. King Priam, who had remained behind in the palace, raised his hands to heaven and prayed to Zeus: "Today, O father Zeus, let the Achaeans roll in the dust before the daughter of Ares, but guide Penthesilea herself safely back to my city. Do this in honor of Ares, your mighty son! Do it for love of her who sprang from a god and is herself so like an immortal. And do it for my sake too, for I have suffered much and lost so many of my sons to the Argives. Do it while some are left of the noble line of Dardanus, while the ancient city of Troy still stands!" But hardly had he finished when an eagle screamed at his left. With powerful strokes of his mighty pinions he cut the air, holding in his talons a mangled dove. At this evil omen the old man shuddered and gave himself up to despair.

In the meantime, the Argives, to their great surprise, saw the Trojans whom they had come to regard as cowards rush forward like beasts of prey who run from the mountains to throw themselves on the herds grazing in the valley. Full of astonishment one said to the other: "Who can have rallied the Trojans? Since Hector's death they seemed to have lost all heart to fight us. It must be a god who had pity on them! But we too have gods on our side; we have kept the enemy at bay up to now, and we shall fend them off today as well." With this they seized their arms and swept from the ships to the battlefield. And now with clang and clatter of shields and spears the fight began, and soon there was blood underfoot. Penthesilea and her women raged among the Argive warriors. She herself slew Molion and seven others. But when the Amazon Clonia felled Menippus, the friend of mighty Podarces, he became infuriated and pierced her hip with his lance. Penthesilea slashed at his hand with her sword, but she was too late to save her friend. And now Fortune favored the Argives. Idomeneus dealt a death blow to Bremusa, Meriones slew

Euandra and Thermodoa. Derione died from a wound inflicted by Ajax, son of Oileus. The son of Tydeus killed Alcibia and Derimachia at the same instant, for his sweeping swordstroke cut both their heads from their shoulders. When they had done with the women, they turned to the Trojans. Sthenelus slew Cabirus of Sestos, but himself escaped death, for the arrow Paris aimed at him missed. The ruthless Fates guided its flight to a fellow Argive, to Euenor of Dulichium. His death roused Meges, the leader of the Dulichians, son of King Phyleus, to grief and fury. Like a lion he sprang at the Trojans and slew two of their bravest allies, Itymoneus and Agelaus of Miletus, and as many others as his spear could reach.

But Penthesilea was still unhurt and fought so fiercely that the Argives retreated before her thrusts. Drunk with success she called to them: "Today, you dogs, you shall atone for the suffering you have inflicted on Priam! Beasts and birds shall feed on your rotting flesh. Not one of you shall ever see his wife and child again, and no burial mound will be heaped above your bones. Where is Diomedes? Where is Ajax, son of Telamon? And where is the son of Peleus, where is Achilles? The best in your host do not dare measure their strength against mine! And why? Because they know that I should make corpses of them!" When she had spoken these arrogant words, she went on fighting, full of contempt for her foes. Now she wielded the axe, now the lance, or she reached for her quiver full of arrows, which her swift horse carried for her. In her wake came the sons of Priam and the best among the Trojans. At first the Danai could not stand against this massed attack. They fell like leaves in the wind or drops of rain; the field was covered with their bodies, and the horses of the Trojan war chariots trod them underfoot as if they were threshing grain. The Trojans felt as though an immortal had come from heaven to help them curb their foes, and they gave themselves up to foolish joy, to the belief that they had already vanquished the Argives.

But the clash and cry of battle had not yet reached mighty Ajax or Achilles, the son of a goddess. Both were far away, at the grave of Patroclus, and were letting their thoughts dwell on their slain friend. For such was the will of Fate who had appointed a few hours of brilliant victory for the Amazon queen, so that she might die wreathed in glory. The women of Troy stood on the walls of their city and acclaimed the deeds of Penthesilea. One of them, Hippodamia, the wife of Tisiphonus, was suddenly infected with the desire to fight. "My sisters," she cried to those about her, "why do we not fight like our men? Why do we not defend our city and our children? We are not so much weaker than the youths of Troy. Our eyes are just as keen, our knees as supple as theirs. Light and air and food we share with them. Why should we not share their battles as well? Look at that woman in the field! She looms above all the men. And she does not even belong to our line, but is fighting for a king not her own, for a city which is not her home. Yet see how savagely she mows down her opponents! Now, if we fought, it would be for our own welfare and to avenge the wrong done to our own people. Is there a single one of us who has not lost a father, a husband, a child, a brother, or a near kinsman? And if our men are defeated, what awaits us but serfdom? So let us not loiter here a moment longer. Rather die than be carried off as spoils with our little children, when our husbands are killed and the city has gone up in flames!"

Thus spoke Hippodamia, and at her words all the women burned with the zeal to fight. They tossed aside their wools and their weaving, scattered like a swarm of bees, and girded themselves with whatever weapons they found in their houses. And all would have died, victims of ill-considered enthusiasm, had not Hecuba's sister, Theano, the wife of Antenor, she who was wiser than the rest, opposed their headstrong ardor. She tried to reason with them: "What folly!" she cried as they prepared to stream through the gates. "You think you can fight the Achaeans, fight men practiced in the use of weapons, in the art of war? How can you even dream of competing with them! You have not been trained to fight like the Amazons! You have not learned to handle horses and to excel in the other occupations of men. And besides, Penthesilea is the daughter of the war-god, and you the children of ordinary mortals. That is why you must keep to the life of woman, shun the battlefield, stay in your houses, and ply the spindle. Leave war to our men. They are still unconquered! They are still defending Troy. Things have not come to such a pass that they need help from their womenfolk."

With her wise words, aged Theano gradually succeeded in calming the excited women. Reluctantly they returned to their lookout on the wall and contented themselves with watching the battle from afar. Penthesilea fought untiringly, and the Argives fled from her and scattered here and there, some fully armed, while others had thrown their weapons to the ground. Horses and chariots, deprived of their charioteers, blundered in all directions. The groans of the wounded and the screams of the dying resounded over the field, for the spear of the Amazon queen dealt death wherever she appeared.

Nearer and nearer the Trojans came to the Argive camp. They had reached the ships and were about to burn them when Ajax, son of Telamon, at last heard the roar of battle. He raised his head from the burial mound of Patroclus and said to Achilles: "I hear the clash of arms and a confused din as if a battle were being waged nearby. Let us go to fend off the Trojans, for we want to keep them from our camp and from burning the ships!" Achilles roused himself at his words and listened, and now he too heard the clatter and the cries. Quickly the two girt on their shining armor and hurried toward the sounds.

A tremor of hope quickened the broken ranks of the Argives when they saw the bravest of their heroes running toward them. Ajax and Achilles threw themselves wholeheartedly into the battle. They divided the work between them: Ajax slew the Trojan leaders, while Achilles set upon the Amazons. Four of these quickly fell before his onslaught. Then both stormed against the bulk of the enemy army with united strength; soon the ranks of the foe showed great gaps, and those who remained were thrown into confusion.

When Penthesilea saw this, she ran to meet Ajax and Achilles as furiously as a panther rushes at the hunters. But they only stretched until their brazen armor creaked, and brandished their lances. The Amazon chose Achilles as her first target and hurled her spear at him, but it rebounded from his shield and splintered. And now she aimed her second lance at Ajax and called to both: "Even though I missed at the first throw, my second shall drain strength and life from the two of you who boast of being the strongest in the Argive host. Soon you will discover that a woman can do more than both of you put together!" Her words did little

more than amuse the heroes, but her lance grazed the silver
greaves of Ajax. Much as she would have liked to revel in his
blood, she had not even scratched the skin, for the metal repelled
her weapon, and it glanced off. Ajax did not deign to notice the
Amazon, but rushed at the Trojans, leaving Penthesilea to
Achilles, for he never doubted that his friend could slay her
unaided, as easily as a hawk kills a dove.

When Penthesilea saw that her second throw had also failed,
she heaved a great sigh, but Achilles measured her with his glance
and called to her: "Tell me, woman, how did you summon courage to confront us, the most powerful heroes on earth, sprung
from the blood of the Thunderer himself, us, before whom Hector
trembled and fell? You must be mad to threaten us with death,
for your own last hour is come." With these words he cast the
lance which Chiron, his teacher, had made for Peleus, the lance
which never missed its mark. It struck the Amazon above the
right breast; the dark blood gushed from the wound, and her
strength failed her. The axe fell from her hand, and her eyes

dimmed. But with a great effort she retained consciousness and looked straight at her enemy, running toward her to drag her from her horse. For a moment she hesitated whether to draw her sword and defend herself, or dismount and buy her life from the victor with gold and bronze. But Achilles left her no time to decide one way or the other. In his blind rage at her pride, he pierced horse and rider with one mighty thrust. And she slipped down in the dust, impaled on the spear, quivering and leaning back against her horse which also lay dying. She was like a slender pine which the north wind has broken.

When the Trojans saw that she had fallen, they retreated to their city, lamenting her death as if she had been one of their own kinswomen. But the son of Peleus cried exultantly: "Lie there, poor creature, where dogs and birds can feed on your flesh! Who set you on to fight with me? Priam probably promised you priceless gifts as a reward for slaying Argives. But your reward was quite different from what you expected!" So he said and drew the spear from her body and the horse's, and one last shudder ran through both. Then he took off her helmet and looked at the face of the foe he had slain. Although it was stained with dust and blood, her features were noble and lovely even in death, and the Achaeans who stood around the body marvelled at her great beauty; she looked like Artemis, sleeping after the heat of the chase over the wooded mountain slopes. Achilles could not take his eyes from her lips and brow. He grew more and more sorrowful, for he was struck by the thought that, instead of slaying, he should have taken her to wife and brought her back with him to Phthia.

But Ares, Penthesilea's father, was more than all others saddened by her death. Swift as lightning and with the roar of thunder he descended from Olympus fully armed and strode across the peaks and chasms of Mount Ida. The heights and valleys shook beneath his tread. And he would have brought sure destruction to the Argives had not Zeus warned him off by unleashing a tempest over his head. Through the howl of the gale and the booming in the clouds, Ares recognized the voice of the father of gods, the friend of the Danai, and stopped halfway to the battlefield. He stood here irresolute, not knowing whether to return to Olympus, or, in defiance of Zeus, to stain his hands with the blood of Achilles. But he remembered how many of his sons Zeus had killed for rebelling against his command, and how even he, the war-god, had not been able to save them from death. So he thought better of it, for he had no wish to be silenced forever by lightning and hurled down to the underworld to bear the Titans company.

In the meantime, many Achaeans had crowded around the body of Penthesilea and began to strip her of her arms. But Achilles stood by silently, he who had been willing to leave her exposed to dogs and birds only a short time ago. With aching grief he looked down at her, and the anguish in his heart was as bitter as his mourning for Patroclus, his friend.

Among the Argives who had thronged to the spot was ugly Thersites who now began to taunt the son of Peleus. "What a fool you are," he exclaimed. "A fool to regret the death of this woman who pursued us and brought misfortune with her. You are a weakling, a lover of women, to stand there filled with regret and longing for her beauty. It should have been her lance that slew you in battle, you who never have enough, who think that all women must fall to your share!" When Achilles heard such words from the lips of so wretched a man, he was filled with uncontrollable fury. With his bare fist he struck Thersites on the cheek so hard that his teeth flew out of his mouth, a stream of blood gushed from his throat, and he doubled up on the ground and breathed his last. Not one of all those who watched was sorry for him, for his only business had been to make mock of others, though both in the field and in council he had proved himself a coward and a fool, over and again. Achilles voiced the feeling of all when he said: "Here you shall lie, here in the dust, and forget your folly. For it is folly for a base man to place himself on a level with his betters. Just as you sneered at me now, you sneered at Odysseus before me, only that he was too generous to punish you. But now you have learned that the son of Peleus cannot be taunted with impunity. Go now, and mock the shadows in Hades."

In the entire Argive army there was only one who was galled at the death of Thersites: Diomedes, son of Tydeus, and he was angry because the dead man was of his own blood, for his grandfather Oeneus and the father of Thersites had been brothers. This was why Diomedes blazed with wrath at the son of Peleus.

He would have raised his sword against him, had not some of the noblest among the Achaeans intervened.

Out of pity and admiration for the slain Amazon queen, the sons of Atreus granted Priam's request to surrender her body to him, so that he might bury her bones with all honors in the tomb of King Laomedon. Before the city the king of Troy had a great pyre heaped for her and laid the corpse on it, and many splendid gifts besides. Then he lit the pile of wood, and the flames darted up. When the body was consumed, the Trojans quenched the fire with fragrant wine. Then they collected her bones, put them in a precious chest, and in solemn procession bore this to the tomb of King Laomedon which was situated near one of the towers of the city. With her they buried her twelve women who had fallen in battle.

The Argives also buried their dead and mourned them, above all Podarces who had now followed his brother Protesilaus whom Hector had slain. His burial mound was heaped apart from the rest; it loomed so high that it was a landmark visible far and wide. Last of all they buried Thersites and then returned to their ships, full of gratitude to mighty Achilles who again had proved himself the rescuer of his people. When night came the noblest of the heroes banqueted in the house of the sons of Atreus, and the other Argives too feasted in the camp and then slept until dawn reddened the sky.

MEMNON

When the sun rose over Troy it shone on a troubled city. On the ramparts were the Trojans, keeping anxious watch, for they feared that at any moment the victor might come, set ladders against the walls, and burn up the town. Then an old man by the name of Thymoetes rose in the council and said: "Friends! In vain have I tried to think of some way to ward off destruction. Now that Hector has died at the hands of indomitable Achilles, I believe that even if a god fought on our side he would fall in the fight. Did not the son of Peleus kill the Amazon, before whom the other Argives trembled? And this in spite of the fact that she was so strong and gallant that all of us took her for a goddess and rejoiced at the mere sight of her! And so we must consider whether it might not be best for us to leave this unfortunate city, which is doomed to destruction, and settle elsewhere, in some safe place which the vengeful Danai could not reach."

So said Thymoetes. Then Priam rose in the assembly and answered him. "You, my friend," he said, "and all you Trojans and allies: let us not give up our beloved city and face even greater dangers than here by trying to fight our way through the foes who surround us on all sides. At least let us wait until Memnon comes, Memnon the Ethiopian, from the land of black men. He is already on his way to bring us help with a countless host. Much time has passed since I dispatched a messenger to him. Wait just a little longer. For even if we all should die in the battle for our city that would be better than leading a poor and inglorious life among strangers."

And now Polydamas intervened between these two who held such opposing views. He was both shrewd and deliberate and expressed his opinion in well-chosen words. "I shall be glad to see Memnon. But I fear that he and all the men he brings with him will fall in our behalf and only plunge us into still greater distress. All the same, I do not believe we should leave the land of our fathers. My suggestion is that even at this late day we surrender the cause of the whole war—Helen and everything she brought with her from Sparta! Let us give her back to the Argives before they divide all our possessions between them and set fire to our city."

In their hearts the Trojans agreed with these words and applauded them, but they did not dare contradict their king openly. Paris however, Helen's husband, accused Polydamas, the well-wisher of the Argives as he called him, of rank cowardice. "The man who gives such counsel," he said, "would be the first to flee in battle. Think well, Trojans, if it is really wise to follow the counsel of such as he."

Polydamas knew very well that Paris would not relinquish Helen and would rather rouse the army to revolt, rather die than renounce her. So he said nothing in reply, and all the assembly sat in silence. While they were still sunk in thought, news came that Memnon was approaching. The Trojans felt like sailors when, after a storm which promised sure death, they see the stars shining in the sky once more. But King Priam was gladdest of all, for he did not doubt that with the aid of the Ethiopians, the Trojans would succeed in burning the Argive fleet.

So when Memnon, the son of Eos, arrived, the king honored him and his men with precious gifts and festive banquets. And the hearts of the Trojans grew lighter as they talked of the deeds of their fallen heroes. Memnon, on his part, told them about his immortal parents, Tithonus and Eos, about the boundless sea and the ends of the earth, the rising of the sun and the long, long way he had journeyed from the shores of the ocean to the peaks of Ida and the city of King Priam, and all the adventures of travel which he had met boldly and well. It cheered Priam to listen to him. Full of friendly warmth he seized his hand and said: "Memnon, how I thank the gods for having let me, an old man, live to see you and your army, and to entertain you in my palace! You, more than any other mortal, are like the gods, and that is why I am confident that you will slaughter our foes." And the king lifted his golden cup and drank to his new ally.

Memnon marvelled at the beautiful cup, the work of Hephaestus, an heirloom passed from one Trojan king to his son. Then he replied: "It would not be proper for me to boast at the feast and to make too-confident promises. So I shall not give you my answer now but enjoy this banquet in peace and think over the preparations which are necessary for our enterprise. It is in battle that a man must show his valor. Let us retire early and sleep, for too much wine and a giddy night would be an ill beginning for the fight which awaits us." With this he rose from the board, and Priam was careful not to urge him to stay. The other guests followed Memnon's example.

Now, while mortal men were asleep, the gods were still feasting in the palace of Zeus and discussing the war of Troy. Zeus, son of Cronus, who saw the future as clearly as the present, was the last to speak. "It is useless to concern yourselves, some for the Argives, others for the Trojans! For you will see countless men and horses fall on both sides. And though one or the other of you may have the welfare of this or that hero at heart, do not dream of coming to me and pleading for a son or a friend, for the goddesses of fate are just as implacable toward me as toward you!"

Not one of the immortals dared contradict the father of gods.

Silently they left the feast. Each went to his own house and threw himself sadly on his couch until at last Sleep had pity on the gods as well as on men.

The next morning Eos rose in the sky reluctantly, for she too had heard the words of Zeus and divined the fate in store for her son. Memnon had wakened early. The stars were just paling when he shook sleep—his last on earth—from his lashes and leaped from his couch impatient to fight the Argives. Trojans and Ethiopians girt on their armor, and like a train of dark clouds driven by the wind the battalions streamed out of the gates and into the field. The whole road was jammed with a moving throng, and their feet stirred up the dust.

The Achaeans saw them coming and were amazed. In great haste they too seized their weapons and came forward from the ships, Achilles, in whom they placed their trust, in the center. Erect and proud he stood in his chariot, like the thunderbolt in the hand of Zeus. But in the middle of the Trojan army, no less proud and menacing than Achilles, came Memnon, and he resembled Ares himself. Round about him were his many men, all of them obedient to his word and eager to begin the fight. The hosts were like two seas which rolled toward each other and clashed wave on wave. Swords hissed through the air, spears whirred, and battle cries mingled with the moans of the dying. Trojan after Trojan fell from the thrusts of Achilles who raged like a tempest which tears up trees by the roots and topples houses and walls. But Memnon also sowed destruction among the Achaeans. He slew two comrades-in-arms of Nestor, and now he was close to the old man from Pylos himself and would have slain him, for one of his horses had been wounded by an arrow from the bow of Paris; this slowed the chariot just as Memnon came running with lifted lance. In alarm Nestor called to his son Antilochus, and his cry was heard. Quickly Antilochus came, placed himself in front of his father, and cast his spear at the Ethiopian. He sprang to one side, and the missile hit Ethops, his friend, the son of Pyrrhasus. At that, Memnon rushed at Antilochus like a lion at a boar. The youth hurled a stone at his assailant, but it bounded back from his helmet. And now Memnon's lance pierced him to the heart, and Antilochus bought his father's rescue at the cost of his own life.

When the Achaeans saw him fall, they were deeply distressed, but his father grieved most bitterly because it was for his sake that his son had been killed before his very eyes. But he had enough presence of mind to call Thrasymedes, one of his other sons, to drive the murderer away from his brother's body. Above the din of battle he heard the call, and Phereus went with him. Memnon was so sure of himself that he let them come quite close. All the spears they hurled at him flew past his armor, on which his mother Eos had laid a spell. They did, indeed, reach a target, but never that at which they were aimed. While they were striking down other enemy warriors, Memnon began to strip Antilochus of his armor, and the Argives circled their slain companion, just as howling jackals prowl about the stag which the lion is tearing. When Nestor saw that their efforts were in vain, he groaned aloud, called to other friends, and even dismounted from his chariot in a desperate attempt to save the body of his son. But when Memnon saw him, he met him reverently, as though he were his own father. "Old man," he said, "for me to fight you would not be fitting. From a distance I took you for a young warrior, and that is why I aimed my lance at you. Now I see that you are far older than I thought. Leave the battlefield, for my heart rebels against striking you down into the dust beside your son. As for you, men would call you a fool for daring so unequal a combat."

But Nestor replied: "What you have just said, Memnon, is untrue. No one in the world would say 'fool!' to the man who fights for the body of his son, who tries to drive the cruel slayer from it. Oh, had you only known me when I was young! Now, to be sure, I am like an old lion which every dog can keep from the herd. But you will see that I can still hold my own with many a man, that my old age forces me to yield only to the hardiest." Thus said Nestor and retreated, leaving his son on the ground. Thrasymedes and Phereus went with him, and now Memnon and his Ethiopians forged ahead unhindered, and the Argives fled before their thrusts.

Nestor turned to Achilles. "Protector of the Argives!" he addressed him. "See, there lies my son—dead. Memnon has taken his weapons. Soon the dogs will tear his flesh. Come and help! For the only true friend is he who defends the body of his slain comrade." Achilles listened intently, and profound sadness weighed his spirit when he saw the Ethiopians felling the Danai in droves. Up to this moment the son of Peleus had been fighting the Trojans, many of whom he had slain. Now he abandoned them and turned his attention to Memnon alone. When the son of Eos saw him coming, he grasped a huge stone and flung it at the shield of his foe, but the stone rebounded and Achilles, who had left his chariot behind the lines, had at Memnon on foot and wounded his right shoulder with his spear. The Ethiopian ignored the thrust and ran forward and lunged at Achilles with his mighty lance. It struck the hero's arm, and the blood flowed from the wound. At that Memnon exulted and cried: "You wretch! You slew the Trojans without mercy, but now you are face to face with the son of a goddess, with a foe you are not equal to, for Eos, my mother, who dwells on Olympus, is more powerful than Thetis, your mother, who lives in the sea with fish and monsters."

But Achilles only smiled and said: "The outcome will show which of us is descended from better parents. For now I shall avenge the death of young Antilochus as once I took vengeance on Hector for the death of Patroclus, my friend."

With that he gripped his long spear in both hands, and Memnon did the same with his. They rushed at each other, and Zeus made them taller and stronger and more tireless than ordinary mortals, so that neither could down the other. They came so close that the crests of their helmets touched. In vain they tried to wound each other above the greaves or below the cuirass. Their armor clanged. Ethiopians, Trojans, and Argives sounded their battle cries to heaven. The dust danced under their

feet, and while their leaders fought, the men too flung about in
fierce battle. The Olympians watched from their lofty lookout
and took pleasure in the undecided struggle. Some rejoiced in
the strength of the son of Peleus, others in Memnon's steadfast
resistance, according to whether they were friends or kinsmen of
one or the other of the two heroes. And a quarrel would have
broken out among the gods, had not Zeus summoned two of the
Fates and ordered the dark goddess to go to Memnon, the shining
one to Achilles. At this command loud cries rang out on Olympus,
cries of delight and of despair.

But the two fought on unaware of the presence of the goddesses of Fate. They used swords, lances, and stones. Neither
yielded. Both stood solid as rock. And the combat of their men
was just as stubborn. Blood and sweat streamed from their
bodies, and the earth was littered with the slain. But in the end
the Fates swayed the issue. Achilles thrust his lance into Memnon's breast, thrust so deeply that the point came out at his back
and he crashed to the ground in a pool of blood.

And now the Trojans fled, and Achilles pursued them like
a tempest while his friends stripped his fallen foe of his arms.
Up in heaven Eos uttered a mournful sigh. She veiled herself in
heavy cloud, and the earth was covered with darkness. At her
command her children, the winds, flew down to the field, seized
the body of her son from under the hands of his enemies, and
bore it away through the air. All that was left of him on earth
were the drops of blood which fell from him as he was carried
through space. These merged to a crimson river which every
year, on the day of Memnon's death, lapped the base of Mount
Ida and flowed through the plain with a stench of decay. The
winds carried their burden low over the earth, and the Ethiopians, who could not bear to part from their dead king, followed
along the ground groaning with sorrow, until the corpse vanished
from the sight of both Trojans and Argives. The winds set it
down on the bank of the Aesepus, and the lovely daughters of
the river-god prepared a burial place in a quiet grove. Then Eos
descended from heaven, and she and the nymphs buried Memnon
and heaped the mound, weeping and sighing. The Trojans, who
had returned to their city, also mourned the Ethiopian king with
true sorrow. Even the Argives could not take unalloyed pleasure

in their victory. They praised Achilles for his prowess and called him the pride of their host, but they wept with Nestor for his dear son Antilochus. And so that night the battlefield resounded with cries of triumph and grief.

THE DEATH OF ACHILLES

In the morning the Pylians carried the body of Antilochus, the son of their king, to the ships and buried him on the shore of the Hellespont. Old Nestor curbed his anguish, and his spirit remained steadfast and calm. But Achilles found no peace. At crack of dawn his fury over the death of his friend drove him toward the Trojans who had already left the shelter of their walls. They too were eager for the fight, even though they trembled at the thought of godlike Achilles. And again the two hosts joined in battle. The son of Peleus slew countless foes and pursued the Trojans to their very gates. There, conscious that his powers were more than human, he prepared to lift the gates from their hinges, break the bolts, and lay the city of Priam open to the Argives.

But Phoebus Apollo, looking down on the plain strewn with corpses, felt anger rise within him. Like a beast of prey intent on its quarry he descended from Olympus and slung over his shoulder was his quiver jangling with deadly arrows. Thus he faced the son of Peleus. His eyes darted flame, and the earth quaked under his tread. And now he raised his voice and thundered at Achilles: "Let the Trojans be, son of Peleus! Make an end of this slaughter! Beware, lest one of the immortals destroy you!"

Achilles recognized the voice of the god perfectly, but he did not recoil in fear. Ignoring the warning he replied: "Why do you spur me on to fight with gods, by always favoring the Trojans? Once before you roused me to fury by snatching Hector out of my hands. Now I advise you to go back to the other gods, for if you do not, my spear will surely strike you, even though you are immortal!"

With these words he turned from Apollo and back to the Trojans. But Phoebus, in grim resentment, shrouded himself in cloud, fitted an arrow to his string, and through the impenetrable mist shot the son of Peleus in his vulnerable heel. A stinging pain darted from his foot to the heart of Achilles, and he toppled like a tower from under which men have dug the foundation. Lying on the ground he glared angrily in all directions and shouted: "Who was it shot that arrow at me from far away? Oh, if only he faced me in open combat, I should drag out his entrails and spill his cursed blood until his spirit fled to the underworld! But cowards always kill the brave from ambush! Let him hear that— even if he be a god! For alas! I fear it was Apollo. Thetis, my mother, once told me that I should die from the shaft of Phoebus, and I fear that now her words have come true."

Thus moaning, Achilles drew the arrow from the wound which could not be healed. When he saw the black blood spurt from it, he flung the dart furiously from him. Apollo picked it up and took it back to Olympus, and a cloud hung about him as he went. When he reached the heights of heaven, he shed his garment of mist and mingled with the other gods. Hera, the friend of the Argives, noticed his presence and began to upbraid him for what he had done. "That was an evil deed," she said. "Did you not feast at the wedding of Peleus like the rest of the gods? Did you not sing and raise your cup and drink to the children he would have? But in spite of it all you have just killed his only son. And you slew him because you envied him! Foolish Apollo! How, after this, can you face the daughter of Nereus?"

Apollo was silent. He seated himself a little apart from the other gods and bowed his head. Some of the Olympians were indignant at what he had done, others thanked him in their heart of hearts. But down on earth the dark blood of Achilles still seethed in his mighty limbs. He burned with the lust to fight, and not a Trojan dared approach him, even though he was wounded. Once more he leaped from the ground, brandished his spear, and rushed at his foes. He struck Orythaon, the friend of his old enemy Hector. The point pierced the left temple and went through to the brain. Then he thrust his spear into the eye of Hipponous, gored the cheek of Alcathous, and slew many more besides. Suddenly he felt a coldness creeping through his limbs. He stood still and leaned on his lance. But the Trojans kept on fleeing before him, for his voice pursued them even after his feet could not. "Run for all you are worth!" he roared. "It won't help you any. My weapons will reach you just the same, for when I am dead the gods of vengeance will punish you!" And they trembled as they ran, for they thought he was still whole and sound. But now his limbs stiffened. He fell among the other dead. The earth shook, and his armor clanged upon him.

The first to see him down was Paris, his deadly enemy. With a shout of joy he told the Trojans, and instantly many who had only just been trying to avoid his lance and sword gathered about him to take his armor. But Ajax circled the body and with spear raised high drove off all who approached; anyone who defied him he dealt the deathblow. Soon Ajax was no longer content with merely fending off the Trojans. He plunged into offensive action. Glaucus, the Lycian, fell at his hands, and Aeneas was wounded. Side by side with Ajax Odysseus fought and other Achaeans. But the Trojans staunchly resisted, and Paris even dared aim his spear at Ajax himself. He, however, always on the watch, saw the attack coming, took a stone, and hurled it with such force that it smashed the helmet of Paris and threw him to earth; the arrows dropped out of his quiver and scattered over the ground. He was still breathing, though very faintly. His friends barely had time to lift him into the chariot drawn by Hector's horses and take him back to Troy. Now when Ajax had driven all the Trojans back to their city, he strode to the ships, and his feet trod over corpses and weapons. From the walls of Troy to the shore of the Hellespont the field was littered with bodies.

Meantime the kings had carried slain Achilles to the ships, and his people surrounded his bier, pouring out grief too great to bear. Ajax joined them, and his plaint was loudest as he mourned the fallen hero, the son of his uncle. Old Phoenix too broke into wails of sorrow and clasped the strong body of Achilles in his arms. He thought of the day when Peleus had put the child into his hands and entrusted him with his rearing and teaching. He also recalled the hour he and his pupil had set out for Troy. And now both father and teacher were destined to survive the child!

At last Nestor, mindful of his own son, put an end to their lamentations. He reminded them to wash the corpse and give it the honors due to the dead. This was done. The body of the son

of Peleus was washed with warm water and attired in the rich
robes his mother Thetis had given him for this expedition. And
when he lay in the house ready for the pyre, Athene looked down
at him from Olympus, and her heart filled with pity for her
favorite. Quickly she sprinkled on his head a few drops of ambrosia, the balm of the gods which is said to guard the dead from
disfigurement and decay. Hardly had they touched him when
he looked like one alive. The anguish and rage which had distorted his features ever since Patroclus, his friend, had been
slain were smoothed away. All the Argives who came to look
at him were amazed when they saw him lying on the bier in all
his lordly length, his face beautiful and serene as though he
were sleeping and would soon waken.

The loud lament the Argives had raised at the death of the
greatest among them was carried to the depths of the sea, where
Thetis, his mother, lived with the other daughters of Nereus.
Sorrow swelled their hearts to bursting, and they moaned so
despairingly that the Hellespont echoed with their cries. By
night they set out in a great company. The tide parted before
them, and they went ashore where the Argive fleet was beached.
In their wake the sea monsters groaned and sighed in sympathy
with their sorrow. They approached the corpse, and Thetis put
her arms around her child, kissed him, and wept until the ground
was wet with her tears. Reverently the Danai withdrew at the
coming of the goddesses who had risen from the sea, and they did
not return to the body until, at the first pale light of dawn,
Thetis and her sisters vanished in the waves.

Then down from the slopes of Ida they dragged great logs
and stacked them into a pyre. They laid on it the arms of all
the slain, many slaughtered victims, gold, and precious metals.
The Argive heroes cut strands of hair from their heads, and
Briseis, Achilles' favorite, sheared off one of her lovely locks as
a last gift to her lord. Over the wood they poured many flasks of
oil, and among the logs they placed bowls of honey, of wine
fragrant as nectar, and of sweet-smelling spices. On the top they
placed the corpse. Then, fully armed, on foot and on horseback,
they circled around the pyre. Finally it was lit, and the flames
crackled and licked through the pile. At the command of Zeus,
Aeolus sent his swiftest winds. They blew through the stacked

wood and lashed the fire so that in a very few hours the wood and the body were wholly consumed and turned to ashes. The Danai quenched the last flickering flames with wine. And there, easily recognizable from everything that had been burned with him, lay the bones of great Achilles. Sighing, his friends collected them, laid them in a coffer of hammered gold and polished silver, and lowered it next to the remains of his friend Patroclus, on the highest point of the shore. Then they heaped the burial mound.

The immortal horses of the son of Peleus sensed that he was dead. They tore the thongs which tethered them, unwilling to share the toils and cares of men now that their master was gone. It was difficult to catch them and to calm their restlessness and alarm.

FUNERAL GAMES FOR ACHILLES

In Troy too they were doing honor to a slain hero. Glaucus, the Lycian, the loyal ally of the Trojans, had fallen in the last struggle with the Argives, and his body which his friends had snatched from the hands of his foes was burned and buried.

The following day Diomedes, son of Tydeus, rose in the Argive assembly and proposed that at once, at this very moment when their enemies were rallying their courage because Achilles was dead, they must attack the city with chariots and foot-soldiers and storm the walls. But Ajax, son of Telamon, opposed him. "It would not be right," he said, "to offend the goddess of the sea who is mourning her son. Should we not, before all things, have splendid funeral games for glorious Achilles? Yesterday, when Thetis sank back into the waves, she begged me not to leave her son unhonored and declared that she herself would appear at the celebrations. As for the Trojans, even though the son of Peleus has fallen, it is unlikely that they will marshal sufficient courage to resume the fight as long as you, Diomedes, and I, and Agamemnon, son of Atreus, are among the living."

"I shall agree with you, provided Thetis really comes today," Diomedes replied. "Her wish must take precedence over the demands of war."

As the last word left his lips, the waves parted, and the wife of Peleus, frail as the breath of dawn, rose from the sea and advanced toward the Argives. With her came the nymphs, her handmaids, and from the veils which floated about them they drew magnificent prizes and spread them out before the eyes of the Achaeans. Thetis herself bade the heroes begin the games. Then Nestor, son of Neleus, rose, not to fight, for old age had left his limbs stiff and feeble, but to honor the lovely daughter of Nereus with fitting words. He told of her wedding with Peleus: how the gods themselves had attended as guests; how the Hours had come with dainty and rich foods in golden baskets and served them with hands scented with ambrosia. The nymphs had blended the wine in golden bowls while the Graces danced and the Pierides sang. Air and Earth, mortals and immortals, all had shared in bliss and delight.

This was what Nestor related. And then he went on to tell of the great deeds of the son of Peleus who had sprung from this union. His words were balm to sorrowful Thetis; and though the Argives were restive and eager to resume the conflict, still they listened intently and joined in the praise of the hero. Thetis gave Nestor two of her son's horses. Then she selected as a prize for the foot race twelve stately cows, each with a suckling calf. Her son had captured them while he was fighting on the slopes of Ida and brought them back to the camp as spoils.

And now Teucer, son of Telamon, and Ajax of Locris, the fleet-footed son of Oileus, stripped to the belt. Agamemnon set up the goal, and they darted forward like two hawks. To the right and left of them stood the Argives, watching and shouting applause. Both were close to the goal when a tamarisk shrub blocked the path of Teucer; he stumbled and fell. The Danai shrieked with excitement as Ajax of Locris outstripped him, touched the goal post, and triumphantly led off the cows to his ships. Teucer's friends took him to his house limping. Physicians washed the blood from his foot and carefully bound it up.

Two other heroes volunteered for the wrestling match, Diomedes and Ajax the Great, son of Telamon. Both wrestled with equal strength, but in the end Ajax locked the son of Tydeus in his sinewy arms and almost throttled him. But Diomedes who was deft as well as muscular slipped slantwise out of that terrible grip, straightened his shoulders, lifted his mighty opponent straight into the air, so that he was forced to relinquish his hold, and with a thrust of his left foot threw him to the ground. The spectators shouted their applause, but Ajax pulled himself together and the struggle began afresh. They raged like two bulls who fight in the mountains and butt each other with heads as hard as iron. This time Ajax took Diomedes by the shoulders and tossed him to earth as if he were a rock, and he rolled a little way. Again acclaim rang through the circle. But Diomedes too picked himself up and prepared for a third bout. Then Nestor stepped between them and said: "Stop wrestling, my children. For there is not one among us who does not know that, since the death of Achilles, you are the bravest of the Argives." A cry of approval came from the spectators. The wrestlers wiped the sweat from their foreheads, embraced, and kissed each other. Thetis gave them four lovely women whom Achilles had captured in Lesbos, each distinguished for her goodness and skill. The first was versed in the arts of cookery, the second tasted the wine at the board, the third poured water at the close of the meal, and the fourth carried the platters from the table. Only Briseis surpassed them in beauty. Each wrestler chose those he wanted and sent them to his ships.

Then came the boxing match, for which Idomeneus, the hero most skilled in all the intricacies of this form of fighting, volunteered. Because of this, and also because he was one of the older men, no one offered to compete with him, and so Thetis gave him the chariot of Patroclus as a gift, while Phoenix and Nestor tried to persuade some of the younger men to volunteer for this contest. Epeius, son of Panopeus, and Acamas, son of Theseus, were willing to make the attempt. They bound the boxing thongs to their hands and examined them to see if they were flexible. Then they raised their hands, circled each other on their toes, step by step, until suddenly they rushed together like wind-driven clouds, full of thunder and lightning. Through the air rang the smack of the thongs on their cheeks, and blood flowed under the sweat. The son of Theseus fended off his assailant by craftily dodging his blows, and then, when he was least expecting it, struck him over the eyes with his fist, down to the bone, and blood spurted forth. And now Epeius hit him in the temple so that he slumped to the ground. But he rose to his feet again, and the match went on until friends interposed and made it clear to these two grim opponents that this was not a matter of Argive fighting Trojan to the very death. Thetis gave them two beautiful silver mixing bowls which her son had received in Lemnos. And the two young heroes reached for them eagerly, not waiting to stanch their wounds.

Now Ajax of Locris and Teucer, who had already measured their strength in the foot race, also competed for the prize of shooting with the bow. As a target, Agamemnon set up a helmet with a fluttering mane. He whose arrow cut the horsehair was to be the victor. Ajax was first. He launched his arrow from the string and hit the helmet so that the metal rang. Then Teucer let fly his arrow, and the point cut the crest. All acclaimed him loudly, for though his foot was still lame from his earlier bout, he had aimed surely and well. Thetis rewarded him with the armor of Troilus, the princely youth of Troy, whom Achilles had slain in one of the first years of the war.

The shooting match was followed by throwing the discus. Many of the heroes tried their strength, but no one could throw the heavy disk as far as Ajax, son of Telamon. He tossed it as lightly as though it were a dry branch. Thetis gave him Memnon's armor, and he girt it on at once. The Danai were astonished to see that piece for piece it fitted him as though it had been made to measure.

In the jump, Agapenor, brandisher of lances, was victorious, and he received the weapons of Cycnus whom Achilles had defeated. Euryalus won in casting the hunting spear, and his prize was the silver bowl Achilles had carried off from Lyrnessos.

Next came the chariot races. Five heroes harnessed their horses: Menelaus, son of Atreus, Euryalus, Polypoetes, Thoas, and Eumelus. Then each drove his chariot to the starting post. At a given sign they swung their goads, and all five at once sped across the plain; the air grew thick with dust and sand. Soon the horses of Eumelus outstripped all the rest. After him came Thoas, and then Menelaus. The other two had fallen far behind. But the horses of Thoas soon tired; those of Eumelus stumbled in their swift course, and when their driver wanted to drag them to their feet by force, they reared, threw over the chariot, and he tumbled into the sand. The spectators shouted and screamed, and now the horses of the son of Atreus were far in the lead and halted at the goal. Menelaus exulted in his victory, but he was not arrogant in his joy, and Thetis gave him the golden cup her son had once taken from the palace of Eetion.

THE DEATH OF AJAX THE GREAT

So ended the funeral games in honor of godlike Achilles. Odysseus was the only one of all the princes in the Argive host who had not taken part in them, for as he was fending off the Trojans from the body of Achilles, Alcon had dealt him a painful wound from which he had not yet recovered.

And now Thetis offered as a prize the armor and weapons of her son: his glittering shield, on which Hephaestus had worked graceful pictures, and the heavy helmet carved with the image of Zeus standing on the vault of heaven battling with the Titans; also the curved cuirass which had clasped the breast of the son of Peleus, dark and impenetrable; and the massive greaves which he had worn as though they were light as feathers. Close by lay his indomitable sword in its silver scabbard, with a golden knob and handle of ivory. Beside it was the weighty spear, as long as a felled pine, and still red with Hector's blood.

Behind the weapons stood Thetis, her head covered with a dark veil. Sadly she said to the Danai: "All the prizes offered at the funeral games in honor of my son have been won. Now let the best among the Argives, he who saved the corpse, come forward, for to him I shall give the splendid weapons of Achilles. All of them were gifts from the gods, and the immortals themselves delighted in them."

It was then that two heroes at once laid claim to the arms, Odysseus, son of Laertes, and Ajax the Great, son of Telamon. Radiant as the evening star Ajax drew the weapons to him and called on Idomeneus, Nestor, and Agamemnon to testify to his valiant defense. But Odysseus called on the very same three, for they were the most wise and just in the entire host. Nestor took the other two aside and said in a troubled voice: "It is most unfortunate for us that the two best warriors we have are vying for the weapons of slain Achilles. Whichever of them is denied will be offended and withdraw from the fight, and all of us will suffer the consequences of his anger. So do as I say, for I am old and experienced. We have here in our camp a number of Trojans who were captured only recently. Let them decide the quarrel between Ajax and Odysseus, for they have no preference and are not biased in favor of either of the heroes." The others agreed and set up as judges the noblest of the Trojans, even though they were prisoners of war.

Ajax was the first to appear before them. "What demon has blinded you, Odysseus," he cried, "that you dare to contend with me? You are as much inferior to me as the dog to the lion. Have you forgotten how reluctant you were to leave your home in Ithaca? And you were the one who persuaded us to leave behind in Lemnos Philoctetes, son of Poeas, in his sickness and misery. It is you who are guilty of the death of Palamedes who was stronger and wiser than you! And now you are willing to forget all the services I performed for the Argives, to forget that I saved your life when all the rest had abandoned you, and you were alone in the field and looked about you in vain for an opportunity to flee! When the fight for Achilles' body started, was

I not the one who carried off the corpse together with the armor?
You would never have had the strength to carry the weapons,
let alone the hero himself! That is why you should yield to me.
In any case, I am stronger than you, of a nobler family, and related to the hero for whose arms we are competing."

So spoke Ajax, and his excitement grew as he talked. But
Odysseus replied with a mocking smile: "Why waste so many
words, Ajax? You call me weak and cowardly and forget that
only wisdom is true strength. It is wisdom that teaches the sailor
to ride through a stormy sea, that tames wild beasts, panthers
and lions, and compels oxen to serve man. And that is why both
in times of need and in the council a man of sense is worth more
than a foolish giant who has nothing but bodily strength. That
was why Diomedes chose me when he wanted a companion for his
expedition to the camp of Rhesus. He did it because I am more
crafty and resourceful than anyone else. It was due to my wisdom that the son of Peleus was won for the fight against the
Trojans. And if ever the Danai require a new hero for their host,
believe me, Ajax, that neither your clumsy size nor the wit of
another will secure him; he will come because of my smooth, persuasive words! But in addition to my wisdom the gods also lent
me sturdy limbs, and it is not true that I was fleeing when you
saved me from the enemy. I was facing them boldly and killing
those who attacked, while you stood apart, intent on your own
safety."

In this way they quarrelled for a long time. But finally the
Trojans, who had been set up as judges, were impressed with
the reasoning of Odysseus and unanimously awarded him the
magnificent arms of the son of Peleus.

When Ajax heard the verdict, the blood boiled in his veins.
His brain throbbed with anger, and he trembled in every fiber.
For a long time he stood motionless and fixed his eyes on the
ground. At last his friends succeeded in taking him back to the
ships. He walked slowly, and every step expressed stubborn
reluctance.

In the meantime dark night rose out of the sea. Ajax sat in his
house. He would not touch food. He would not sleep. Finally he
girt on his armor and gripped his double-edged sword, considering whether to cut Odysseus to pieces, burn the ships, or rage

among all the Argives together. And he surely would have done one of these three things, had not Athene who was concerned for Odysseus, her friend, and hostile to mighty Ajax, sent madness on him as he brooded on the harm he would do. Anguish pricked his heart, and he rushed from his house and among the flocks of sheep which, because he was blinded by the goddess, he took for Argive battalions. The shepherds saw him coming and hid in the bushes on the shores of Xanthus. And he slaughtered the sheep right and left. With his spear he killed two great rams, one after another, and taunted them: "Writhe in the dust, you dogs! Lie as the prey of birds! Never again will you two sons of Atreus confirm an unjust decision. And you," he continued, "you, who are lurking there in the corner and hiding your head because you have a bad conscience, now the arms of Achilles which you stole from me and which you vaunt will avail you nothing, for what good is the armor of a hero when a coward wears it?" With that he seized another huge wether, dragged him away to his house, bound him to a door-post, and took a goad and began to beat the creature with all his might.

At this moment Athene approached him from behind, touched his head, and bade the madness leave him. Unhappy Ajax found himself goad in hand, staring at the wether, its back torn to shreds. The goad fell from his fingers, his strength left him, and he sank to the ground, divining that he was the victim of a god's anger. Boundless sorrow filled his spirit. When he rose from the dust he was overcome with such hopeless despair that he could move his feet neither forward nor backward but stood motionless as a tower on the peak of a mountain. Finally he heaved a deep sigh and said: "Alas! Why do the immortals hate me? Why have they humiliated me for love of crafty Odysseus? Here I stand, a man who has never returned from a fight dishonored; here I stand soiled with the blood of guiltless sheep, an object of ridicule, a target for the taunts of my foes!"

While he was lamenting his disgrace, Tecmessa, the daughter of the king of Phrygia, whom Ajax had taken from her country as spoils of war, and whom he honored and loved as if she were his wife, had been looking for him all over the camp and by the ships. Her little son Eurysaces clung in her arms. She had seen that her master was brooding and sad, but she did not know the reason, for he refused to answer when she questioned him. Soon after he left she was troubled with dark forebodings, and she followed him and saw the sheep scattered dead over the field. She hurried back to the house and there found Ajax ashamed and desperate, calling now for Teucer, his half brother, now for his child Eurysaces, and praying for a death befitting a noble hero. Tecmessa approached him in tears, clasped his knees, and implored him not to leave her alone, a captive among enemies. She reminded him of his old father and mother in Salamis, and held out the child to him, picturing his lot if he were forced to grow up without his father, governed by harsh taskmasters.

Impulsively Ajax stretched out his arms to his son, took him and caressed him, saying: "Child, surpass your father in happiness, but resemble him in all else; then everything will be well with you. My half brother Teucer will rear you and cherish you. But now my shield-bearers shall take you to my parents, Telamon and Eriboea, in Salamis, so that you may delight the last years of their life, until they too descend to Hades." With that he handed the boy over to his servants and commended Tecmessa too to his half brother. Then he tore himself from her embrace, drew the sword which Hector, his foe, had once given him, and fixed it firmly in the ground. Finally he raised his hands to heaven and prayed: "It is a little thing I ask of you, Father Zeus: when I am dead, send my brother Teucer quickly. Do not let my foes reach me before him and throw my body to the dogs and birds of prey. And I call on you, Furies: as you see me here, the slayer of myself, so let those others fall, done to death by their own, by their dearest kin. Come! Show no mercy! Satisfy your hunger! But you, O sun-god, shining through the heights of the sky, when your chariot circles over Salamis, my native land, slow your journey and bring my old father and my poor mother news of my bitter fate. Farewell, sweet light! Farewell Salamis! Farewell Athens, the home of my ancestors, with your rivers and springs! And farewell, region of Troy, where I have lived so many years. And now, come Death, and may your eyes hold pity for me!" With these words he ran on his sword and fell as if struck by lightning.

When the Danai heard of his death they came in throngs, threw themselves on the ground, lamented, and strewed dust over their heads. Teucer, whom Telamon had forbidden to return from Troy without Ajax, wanted to kill himself and would have done so had not his friends taken his sword from him. So he only threw himself over the corpse and wept with more abandon than a fatherless child on the day which has taken his mother from him. But with a great effort he composed his soul and turned to Tecmessa who sat beside Ajax in numb despair, holding to her breast the child the servant had put back in her arms. He promised to protect her and care for the boy like a father, even though he could not accompany them to Salamis for fear of Telamon's anger.

Then he prepared to bury the body of his beloved half brother. But Menelaus, son of Atreus, interfered. "Do not dare bury this man," he said, "who has proved worse than our enemies, the Trojans. By his wicked plan to do murder he has forfeited honorable burial." Agamemnon, who had just joined them, sided with his brother and in the course of their heated discussion called Teucer the son of a slave. It was in vain that Teucer reminded them of all the benefits the Argives owed to Ajax, of how he had saved the host when the firebrand flung by the Trojans was setting the ships aflame and Hector leaped to the decks. "And why do you call me a slave?" he cried. "My father Telamon is one of the most glorious heroes of Greece, and my mother's father was King Laomedon! I am descended from the noblest parents and have nothing to be ashamed of! If you dishonor this fallen hero, you will also disgrace his wife, his son, and his brother. Would such a deed win you fame among men and blessing from the gods?"

In the midst of this quarrel came crafty Odysseus, turned to Agamemnon, and asked: "May a loyal friend tell you the truth without bringing ill will on himself?"

"Say what you wish," Agamemnon replied, looking at him in surprise. "I do, indeed, regard you as my best friend in all the Argive host."

"Then listen," said Odysseus. "By all the gods I beg you not to leave this man unburied. Do not let your power blind you so that you hate unjustly. If you dishonor a hero such as this, you will not degrade him, but make mock of the law and will of the gods."

The sons of Atreus listened, and for a long time they were speechless. At last Agamemnon cried: "Are you, Odysseus, willing to quarrel with me for the sake of Ajax? Have you forgotten that he was your deadly enemy too?"

"He was my enemy," Odysseus replied. "I hated him while he was alive. Now that he is dead, I can no longer cherish bitterness against him. We must mourn the loss of so noble a man. I myself am ready to help his brother fulfill the sacred duty of burying him."

When Teucer, who had turned away at the coming of Odysseus, heard these words, he went up to him and held out his hand. "You, his grimmest enemy," he exclaimed, "are the only defender of the dead! And still I do not dare let you handle the corpse, for the spirit of Ajax, which left his body while you and he were unreconciled, might resent your touch. But in all other things you shall be my helper, for there is enough to be done!" And he pointed to Tecmessa who was still mute with grief. Odysseus spoke to her kindly. "You shall not be the slave of another," he said. "As long as Teucer and I live, you and your child shall be safe and cared for, as though Ajax himself were at your side."

The sons of Atreus did not venture to object to the fair decision of Odysseus. It took the combined strength of many warriors to lift the great body of Ajax. They carried him to the ships, cleansed him of blood and dust, and burned him on a pyre as stately as that of Achilles, who by his death had caused the loss of a second Argive hero whom no one could replace.

MACHAON AND PODALIRIUS

The next day the Danai thronged to a council called by Menelaus. When all were assembled, he rose. "Princes of the people," he said, "my heart bleeds when I see our men falling in droves. They embarked on this war because of me, and now it looks as if no one will be alive to return to his home and greet his kin. It shall not come to this! Let us leave these shores. Let those who have survived sail to their own country. Now that Achilles and Ajax are dead, our undertaking is hopeless. I, for my part, am less troubled about Helen, my wife, who has proved herself unworthy of me, than about you. Let her remain with Paris, for all I care."

This was what Menelaus said, but he was only trying the Argives, for in his heart of hearts he still longed to destroy the Trojans. But Diomedes, son of Tydeus, who did not perceive his ruse, started up impatiently and said: "I do not understand you! What shameful fears have taken hold of you that you propose so cowardly a course? But I am not at all disturbed! Never will the brave sons of Greece follow you before they have razed Troy to the ground. And should there be one who did, this sword of mine would sever his head from his trunk!"

Hardly had Diomedes seated himself again when Calchas, the soothsayer, rose and gave wise counsel to calm the apparent difference between the two. "Do you remember," he asked, "that many years ago, when we first sailed to these shores to lay siege to this cursed city, we abandoned Philoctetes, the friend of Heracles, on the waste island of Lemnos? We did so because we could not endure his constant cries of pain and the stench from his poisoned wound. Nevertheless, it was unjust and pitiless on our part to leave him there helpless. Now one of our captives, a seer, has told me that Troy cannot be vanquished without Philoctetes and the aid of the unerring arrows he got from Heracles, nor without Pyrrhus, the young son of Achilles. Perhaps the Trojan only said this because he was sure the conditions could not be fulfilled. For he must consider it out of the question for Philoctetes, who probably loathes us for deserting him, to join us and use his unfailing arrows against the Trojans. Now my advice is to send Diomedes, the strongest of our heroes, and Odysseus, the most eloquent, to Scyros without a moment's delay to fetch the son of Achilles who is being reared there by his grandfather. With his help we shall then persuade Philoctetes to come to us and bring with him the weapons of Heracles by which Troy shall fall."

The Argives shouted their approval, and the two heroes at once left in their ships. Meantime the army again prepared for battle. Eurypylus of Mysia, son of Telephus, had come to the aid of the Trojans, bringing many warriors with him, and the Dardanians quickened with fresh courage. The Argives, on the other hand, had been deprived of two of their mightiest heroes. And so it was inevitable that they suffered grave losses in the fight. Nireus, the most beautiful of the Danai, fell beneath the thrust of Eurypylus and lay in the dust like a young olive tree which a river has torn up by the roots and washed ashore, and there it lies covered with buds. But Eurypylus only mocked him and bent down to strip off his shining cuirass. Then Machaon, brother of Podalirius, who had seen Nireus die, fended off the robber. Into his massive shoulder he plunged his spear, and the blood gushed out in a stream. Like a wounded boar Eurypylus ran at Machaon. He tried to keep him at a distance by hurling a stone, but it rebounded from his brazen helmet. Then the son of Telephus stabbed the Argive through the breast with his spear. The bloodstained point came out at the spine, and Machaon doubled up on the ground. Eurypylus drew his lance from the body and looked about for another victim.

Teucer, who had seen the two Argive heroes fall, called for aid to protect their bodies. But in the end the Trojans captured them. After Aeneas wounded Ajax of Locris with a pointed stone, his friends carried him off, gasping for breath, and the other Achaeans flew toward the ships hotly pursued by the Trojans. They would have set the fleet afire, had not night fallen. As it was, the victor from Mysia withdrew to the mouth of the Simois where he pitched camp in the gathering darkness. But the Danai lay on the sandy shore close to their ships and moaned with the pain of their wounds and sorrow for the countless companions they had lost in the fight.

Scarcely had dawn shed a glow over the heavens when they started up, burning with eagerness to take revenge on Eurypylus. But first they buried beautiful Nireus and Machaon, the wise physician and great warrior. While the din of battle sounded in the distance, Podalirius, the brother of Machaon and like him a skilled physician, had thrown himself in the dust beside his grave and would taste neither food nor drink. Now he laid his hand on his sword, now he reached for a strong poison he always had with him, for he wanted to kill himself. His friends took hold of his hands and spoke words of comfort, but he would have carried out his resolve, had not old Nestor approached. He saw Podalirius strew dust over his head, beat his breast, and cry aloud the name of his cherished brother, while his companions and servants

stood by in helpless distress. Then Nestor spoke to him lovingly:
"Put an end to this bitter grief! A man should not weep for the
dead unrestrainedly, like a woman. Your moans will not bring
him to life again. His flesh has been consumed by flame, and his
bones rest in the earth. He went as he came. But you must bear
your great sorrow as I bore mine when the son of Eos killed my
son, killed the dearest of my children, who loved his father more
than all the others. Nevertheless, when he died, I ate and drank
just as before. I endured the light of day, for I remembered that
all of us must travel the same way to Hades."

Podalirius listened to the old man, and the tears ran down his
cheeks. "Father," he said, "I cannot help grieving for my
brother. For when our father Aesculapius died and was welcomed on Olympus, Machaon took care of me, though I was the
older. We shared everything, our food, our couch, our possessions, and he instructed me in his wonderful art, the art of healing. Now that he is dead I do not wish to see the lovely light of
earth any longer."

But the old man insisted. "Remember," he continued earnestly,
"that our lot, whether good or bad, comes from the gods. Dark
Destiny governs all and deals out her judgment blindly. That is
why great misfortune often descends on good and forthright
men, and no one at all is secure. Life changes incessantly. At
times it is somber, and then again it is radiant. People say that
the souls of the brave rise to heaven while those of men who could
not cope with life descend to darkness. Your brother was dear to
mortals and immortals alike. He was, moreover, the son of a god.
And so I believe he has joined the gods." With such words Nestor
raised Podalirius from the dust and led him away from the burial
mound. But as he went, he looked back at it over his shoulder
many times.

In the meantime Eurypylus of Mysia raged on the battlefield.
The Danai fled to their camp and fought back from behind the
shelter of the wall.

NEOPTOLEMUS

While this was taking place in Troy, Odysseus and Diomedes, the envoys for the Argives, arrived safely on the island of Scyros. Here, in front of his grandfather's house, they met Pyrrhus, the young son of Achilles, whom the Argives later called Neoptolemus, which means "the young warrior." He was practicing shooting with the bow, casting the spear, and riding the chariot with its swift horses. They watched him a while and noticed signs of grief in his face, for he had already been told of his father's death. As they came closer they were amazed to see how greatly the youth resembled Achilles in stature and face. Pyrrhus hailed them first. "Welcome, strangers," he said. "Who are you and where have you come from? What is it you want of me?"

Odysseus replied: "We are friends of Achilles, your father, and have no doubt that we are speaking to his son. You are so like him! I am Odysseus of Ithaca, the son of Laertes, and this is Diomedes, son of immortal Tydeus. We have come because Calchas, the soothsayer, told us that the war of Troy would end in our favor, provided we brought you to the battlefield. The Achaeans will give you splendid gifts, and I myself the weapons which Hephaestus made for your father and which were awarded to me."

Joyfully Pyrrhus answered: "If the Achaeans have called me because a god commanded them to do so, then let us put to sea tomorrow morning! But now come with me and refresh yourselves at my grandfather's board." When they reached the palace, they found Deidamia, the widow of Achilles, brooding in sorrow with tearful eyes. Her son went up to her, but though he told her who the strangers were, he concealed the reason for their coming, for he did not want to add to her grief. The heroes satisfied their hunger and thirst and then lay down to sleep. But Deidamia did not close her eyes. She could not forget that the very men she was forced to lodge as guests under her roof were those who had persuaded Achilles to go to war, and that it was because of them she was now widowed and lonely. She divined that her son would be taken from her too, and that they had come to fetch him. At

break of day she rose, went to him, pressed her head against his
breast, and broke into lament. "O my child," she cried, "I know
without your telling me! You want to accompany these strangers
to Troy, where so many heroes have fallen, where your father
met his death. But you are so young and inexperienced in warfare! Listen to your mother! Stay at home with me, for otherwise I shall surely hear one day that my son has fallen in battle,
just like his father."

But Pyrrhus replied: "Mother, do not bewail what has not
yet happened. And besides, no man falls in battle against the will

of Fate. If death is allotted to me, what better thing could I do
than to die a death worthy of my ancestors, to die for the people
of Greece?"

Then Lycomedes, his grandfather, rising from his couch, confronted his grandson and said: "I know that you are just as
gallant as your father was. But even should you survive the battle
of Troy, who knows what dangers may lurk on your homeward
journey, for the sea is never safe!" Then he kissed the boy, but
he did not try to dissuade him from his purpose. And Pyrrhus
smiled, a young and happy smile. He gently disengaged himself
from his mother's embrace and left the palace behind him. Striding ahead on his strong slender legs, he looked as radiant as a
star. After him came Odysseus and Diomedes and twenty of
Deidamia's trusted servants. When they reached the shore they
at once boarded the ships.

Poseidon granted them a good voyage, and soon, in the first faint light of dawn, they saw the peaks of Ida, then the city of Chrysa, the promontory of Sigeum, and the grave of Achilles. But Odysseus did not tell the boy whose burial mound they were passing. Silently they sailed by the island of Tenedos and on toward Troy. They neared the coast just as the fight for the wall which protected the ships was fiercest, and Eurypylus would have torn it down, had not Diomedes leaped ashore and called to the others to follow him.

They hurried to the nearest house, that of Odysseus, and armed themselves with his own weapons and with the arms he had captured. Neoptolemus girt on the armor of Achilles, his father, which was too large for the other Achaeans. But the cuirass and the helmet fitted him as though they had been made for his body and head. He handled the heavy spear, the sword and the shield with the utmost ease and stormed to the field, the rest in his wake. And now the Trojans were forced to retreat from the wall. Like children who have been frightened by thunder and flee to their father, they crowded around the son of Telephus. But every missile Neoptolemus hurled brought death to a Trojan, and in their despair they though they saw Achilles risen from the grave. And surely his father's spirit was with Neoptolemus, and Athene, who had always helped Achilles, now protected his son as well. As snowflakes sift around a cliff, so the enemy missiles rained about him without so much as scratching his skin. One victim after another he slew to avenge his father. The two sons of rich Meges, twin brothers, born in the same hour, now died within the same hour, for Neoptolemus thrust his spear into the heart of one of them and threw a stone at the other with such force that his heavy helmet was crushed and the brains spurted through his shattered skull. He slew so many Trojans that Eurypylus finally ordered the retreat, and toward evening the son of Achilles put his foes utterly to rout.

While Neoptolemus was resting from the furious fight, old Phoenix, the friend of his grandfather Peleus and his father's teacher, visited the young hero, and he too was astonished at the likeness between him and Achilles. He was torn between sadness and joy, for his delight in this strong young man was clouded by the memory of his father's death. With tears in his eyes he threw his arms around Neoptolemus and kissed his forehead and breast. "O son!" he exclaimed. "I feel as if your father were again among us, alive and well. But do not let me dampen your high spirits with sad thoughts of him who is gone. I want your heart to overflow with anger. You must help the Argives and kill the son of Telephus who has done us such immeasurable harm. For you are as much his better in strength as your father surpassed his father!" Modestly the youth replied: "The fight will decide who is bravest!" With these words he turned back to the ships, for night had fallen, and the warriors went to their huts to rest for the coming battle.

At daybreak the fight began anew. Spear touched spear, sword clashed on sword. For a long time the battle was undecided. Eurypylus saw one of his friends fall, and his fury doubled. He felled the Achaeans as a man hews trees on a densely wooded slope, hews so many that the trunks fill a whole gully. Last of all he came on Neoptolemus, and the two brandished their lances at each other. "Who are you?" Eurypylus asked. "Where have you come from to fight with me? Fate has driven you here to sure destruction, for I kill every Achaean who ventures to resist me!"

Neoptolemus replied: "Why do you, my enemy, wish to know who I am? But I shall tell you: I am the son of Achilles, who wounded your father in times gone by. The horses which draw my chariot are the swift children of Zephyrus and a harpy, and they can race even across the foaming sea. My lance comes from the peak of Pelion; it is my father's lance, and now you shall feel its force!" So spoke the hero, and he leaped from his chariot with lifted spear. Eurypylus hurled a huge stone at his golden shield, but it did not so much as dent the metal. Like two beasts of prey the two ran at each other, and to the right and left of them the battle raged through the long rows. Eurypylus and Neoptolemus fought on and on, striking each other now on the greaves, now on the helmet, and their strength grew as they strove with each other, for both were descended from immortals. In the end Neoptolemus pierced the throat of his assailant, the crimson blood gushed from the fatal wound, and Eurypylus fell.

And now the Trojans would have fled from Neoptolemus like calves from a lion, had not Ares, the terrible god of war, lent them his aid. Unobserved by the other gods, he had left Olympus and driven his chariot with its fire-breathing steeds down to the battle-field. Here he swung aloft his tremendous lance and called to the Trojans to down their foes. They were startled to hear his thundering voice, for he himself was invisible, veiled in mist. Helenus, the soothsayer, son of Priam, was the first to recognize the voice of a god. "Do not be afraid!" he cried to his people. "A friend is among us, the great war-god himself! Do you not hear the call of Ares?"

This stiffened the backs of the Trojans, and the fight on both sides gained in momentum. Ares stirred his favorites to such feats of strength that the Argive ranks wavered. Neoptolemus was the only one who stood firm and undauntedly thrust right and left. The god fumed at his boldness and was about to emerge from his veil of mist and face the young hero in single combat when Athene, the patron of the Argives, descended from Olympus. The earth and the waves of the Xanthus trembled at her coming. Her weapons sparkled, and the snakes on her Gorgon shield flashed dazzling flames. Though the feet of the goddess stood solidly on earth, her helmet touched the sky; but no mortal could see her. And now the immortals would have lifted their hands against each other, had not Zeus warned them off with a clap of thunder. They understood their father's wish. Ares withdrew to Thrace, while Athene turned to Athens. The Argives and Tro-jans were left to themselves once more, but now the great strength Ares had lent the Dardanians ebbed from them again. They re-treated to their city, and the Achaeans pursued them to the very gates. And they would have broken them down, had Zeus not hidden Ilium in veils of cloud. At that, wise Nestor advised the Argives to return to the ships and bury their dead.

The next morning the Danai were astonished to see the acrop-olis of Troy clearly limned against deep-blue sky. Then they knew that the heavy mists of the evening before had been a miracle wrought by the father of gods. This was a day of truce which the Trojans used to bury Eurypylus of Mysia. Neoptole-mus, however, visited the burial mound of his father, kissed the tall pillar upon it, and said with sighs and tears of sorrow: "I shall never forget you, father! If only you had been alive when I joined the Argives! But you never saw your child, and I have never seen my father, though in my heart I longed for him. Still, you live within me, and you live on in your spear. For both I and your spear spread terror among the enemy, and the people of Greece look at me with joyful eyes and say that I resemble you in appearance and in deeds."

So saying, he returned to the ships of Achilles. The whole next day they fought for the walls of Troy, but the Argives did not succeed in invading the city, and on the shores of the Scamander, where Neoptolemus did not fight, they fell in droves. For there Deiphobus, Priam's brave son, was harassing his foes. When Neoptolemus heard of this, he bade Automedon, his charioteer, guide his immortal horses to that place. The Trojan prince saw him coming and was uncertain whether to flee or face this terrible opponent. But Neoptolemus called to him from far off: "Son of Priam! What havoc you have made among the trembling Danai! No wonder you regard yourself the bravest hero on earth. Well, then, try your luck with me too!" As he spoke he rushed at him and would have slain him and his charioteer, had not Apollo hastened from Olympus in a drift of cloud and carried Deiphobus back to the city. The rest of the Trojans fled after him. When Neoptolemus felt his spear stabbing the empty air, he called out angrily: "Dog, you have escaped me! But it was not through your own power. A god stole you from me." Then he threw himself into the fight again. But Apollo remained within the walls of Troy and protected the city. And Calchas, the soothsayer, guessed this and counselled the Danai to return to their ships and rest. There he addressed them: "It is useless for us to batter against the walls of Troy until the second part of the prophecy I told you of has been fulfilled. We must fetch Philoctetes and his unconquerable arrows from Lemnos."

After taking brief counsel with one another, the Argives decided to send wise Odysseus and fearless Neoptolemus to Lemnos, and they instantly boarded the ship which was to take them there.

PHILOCTETES ON LEMNOS

They landed on the uninhabited coast of the island of Lemnos. It was here that nine years ago, not long after the Argives had departed for Troy, Odysseus had abandoned Philoctetes, son of Poeas, who was suffering from an incurable wound. He had left him in a cave with two entrances. One part of it was warm in winter, the other afforded coolness from the hot summer sun. Close by was a spring of fresh water. The two heroes quickly located the place, and Odysseus found everything just as it had been. But the cave was deserted. A bed of leaves, pressed flat, as if someone had risen from it only a short time ago, a cup crudely carved of wood, and some tinder indicated that it was inhabited. And left to dry in the sun were rags bearing the stains of a wound, so that there was no doubt Philoctetes still lived there.

Odysseus sent a servant out to watch for him, for he did not want to be surprised by a man who was bound to be his enemy. "Let us make the most of his absence," he said to Achilles' young son, "to think up some sort of plan, for we shall not be able to win him over to our cause unless we invent a good reason. I must not be here when you first meet him, for he hates me, and he is right! When he asks you who you are and where you come from, tell him the truth. But add what is not true: that you have turned from the Argives in anger and are bound for home. Complain to him that we fetched you from Scyros to help us win the war, and then refused you your father's weapons. Say that they were given to me, to Odysseus. Malign me as much as you please—the more the better. It will not hurt me, and unless we do something of the sort, we shall not be able to win over this man and obtain his much-needed weapons. You must get hold of those arrows, in any case!"

Neoptolemus interrupted him. "Son of Laertes," he said, "the mere thought of doing this fills me with loathing. I could not possibly steal his arrows. Neither my father nor I were born to be crafty. I am willing to take Philoctetes captive by force, but do not try to persuade me to do it by guile. Besides, how could one man alone, and one who has only one sound foot, get the better of us?"

"With those arrows of his!" Odysseus answered calmly. "I know very well that you were not born with the gift of trickery. I myself had an honest father, and in my youth I was slow and awkward in speech and swift and sure with my arm. But experience has taught me that words often succeed more readily than deeds. If you stop to think that only the bow and the shafts of Heracles can vanquish Troy, and that you will gain the reputation of wisdom in addition to that of courage by obtaining them, you will surely not refuse to use a little shrewdness."

Neoptolemus gave in to his older friend, and Odysseus left. Not long after, loud groans announced the coming of Philoctetes. From far off he had seen the ships riding at anchor near the coast which had no real harbor; he hurried toward Neoptolemus and those with him. "Who are you?" he cried. "Who are you who have come ashore on this barren island? I recognize the dress of fellow Argives, but I long to hear you speak. Do not recoil from me because I look wild and unkempt. I am an unhappy man, deserted by my friends and tormented with pain. If you have not come here with hostile intent, speak!"

Neoptolemus answered as Odysseus had prompted, and Philoctetes broke into cries of delight. "O beloved sound of the native tongue I have not heard for so long! O son of noble Achilles! O Lycomedes and fair Scyros! And you, his foster child, what was it you said? Evidently the Danai have treated you no better than me! I am Philoctetes, son of Poeas, whom Odysseus and the sons of Atreus abandoned when I was racked with pain. They landed me here while I slept and left me with a few beggar's rags and a little food. Imagine my awakening! My fright when I found myself alone, the ships gone, no physician at hand, no help, nothing but solitude and pain! Days and years have passed since then, and I have had to see to my own needs. My bow here kept me fed. But though the arrows unerringly hit the quarry, I had to drag myself to the place where it fell. I had to fetch water from the spring, wood from the forest. And for a long time I had no fire. At last I found the right kind of stone—flint which gives out a spark when you strike it against iron. Once I had fire, I had all I needed for bare living, all except health! As for this island, it is the poorest bit of earth in the world. No seafarer comes here of his own free will. There are no good landing places. There are no men here with whom a merchant could barter his wares. Whoever lands here does so because he must. And there were a few such men. They pitied me and gave me food or clothing, but not one of them would consent to take me home. Ten years I have been leading this wretched lonely life, and this is the fault of Odysseus and the sons of Atreus. May the gods requite their evil deed with evil!"

Neoptolemus was moved to great pity as he listened to the story of Philoctetes, but mindful of his friend's warning he suppressed his emotion. Instead, he told Philoctetes of the death of Achilles and whatever else he wanted to hear about his countrymen. In the course of his tale, he wove in all the lies Odysseus had suggested. Philoctetes listened with rapt attention and now and then interrupted the story with expressions of sympathy. Then he took Neoptolemus by the hand, wept, and said: "I implore you by your father and mother! Do not leave me behind. I know that I am unwelcome cargo, but please take me just the same. You can stow me away wherever you wish, near the rudder, in the bow of the ship, or down in the hold where I should cause the least possible disturbance to your crew. Only take me out of this dreadful loneliness! Take me to your home. From there it is not far to Mount Oeta and the land where my father lives. I have sent messages to him through those who landed here, but have never had one in return. Perhaps he is dead. Well, I shall be content if I may see his grave and rest there."

With a heavy heart, Neoptolemus gave the man pleading at his feet a promise he did not mean to carry out. "We shall go to the ships whenever you like," he said. "May a god permit us to leave this island quickly and reach our appointed destination." Philoctetes jumped up as well as he could with his wounded foot. He clasped the young man's hand in deep gratitude. At this moment the servant they had sent out appeared, disguised as an Argive sailor. With him was another sailor who belonged to their crew. Turning to Neoptolemus, the servant brought the fictitious news that Diomedes and Odysseus were on the way to take captive a man called Philoctetes, for Calchas, the soothsayer, had said that his presence was necessary if Troy was to fall. At these words Philoctetes put himself entirely at the mercy of Neoptolemus. Hastily he gathered up his immortal arrows, gave them to the youth for safekeeping, and went with him through the mouth of the cave. And then Neoptolemus could no longer restrain himself. Before they reached the shore he told Philoctetes the truth. "I cannot bear to conceal it from you," he said. "You must come to Troy with me, to the sons of Atreus, to the Argives." Philoctetes stopped. He trembled, he cursed, he prayed. But before Neoptolemus had time to yield, Odysseus left the cover of bushes where he had been hiding and ordered his servants to take the unhappy old hero prisoner. Philoctetes had recognized him at the first word he spoke. "Alas!" he exclaimed. "I am betrayed! This is the man who abandoned me nine years ago, and now his wiles have deprived me of my arrows!" Then he turned to Neoptolemus. "Son," he said, "return them to me. Give me back the bow and the arrows which belong to me!"

But Odysseus did not allow him to continue. "Never!" he shouted. "Not even if the boy wanted to! You must come with us, for there is much at stake—the welfare of the Argives, the fall of Troy!" With that Odysseus drew Neoptolemus away with him and left the old man in the hands of his servants. He stood outside his cave and bewailed the trick which had been played on him. He was just about to call on the gods to avenge him when he saw Odysseus and Neoptolemus coming back. They were quarrelling. He heard the younger cry out: "No, it was wrong! I got the better of him through shameful deceit. You shall not take this man to Troy against his will, not unless you kill me first!" They drew their swords. But Philoctetes intervened. He threw himself at the feet of the son of Achilles. "Promise to save me," he cried, "and I, in turn, give my word that the arrows of my friend Heracles shall ward all attacks from your country."

"Follow me," said Neoptolemus, raising the old man from the ground. "This very day we leave for Phthia, my native land."

Suddenly the blue air over their heads grew dark. They looked up, and Philoctetes was first to recognize his friend, immortal Heracles, floating above them in a heavy cloud. "You shall not go!" he called down from heaven in a voice that echoed across the earth. "My lips, friend Philoctetes, shall tell you the wish of Zeus, and you must obey. You know the labors I had to perform before I could attain to immortality. Fate has decreed that you too must suffer before you attain to glory. If you go to Troy with this youth, your sickness will leave you. Then, when you are whole and sound again, the gods will choose you to destroy Paris, the cause of this war. After that you will raze Troy to the ground. It is you who will have the most precious spoils. Laden with treasure you will return to Poeas, your father, who is still alive. And should you have something left over from your spoils, bring it as an offering to my burial mound. Farewell!" Philoctetes stretched out his arms to his friend as he disappeared in heights too great for human eyes to follow. "Very well, then," he cried. "Let us board the ships. Give me your hand, noble son of Achilles. And you, Odysseus, walk beside me without misgivings, for what you wanted was, after all, the will of the gods."

THE DEATH OF PARIS

When the Argives saw the eagerly awaited ship, which carried the heroes and Philoctetes, running into port in the Hellespont, they thronged to the coast with loud rejoicing. Philoctetes held out his thin arms, and his two companions lifted him ashore. Painfully he limped toward the Danai waiting to welcome him. They were full of pity when they saw him ill and suffering. But one of them sprang forward, gave a quick sharp glance at the wound, and promised that with the help of the gods he would heal Philoctetes. It was Podalirius, the physician, an old friend of Poeas. The immortals blessed the undertaking, the wound closed, and the old man's limbs grew sound and strong. He revived like a field of barley which the rains have beaten down but which gentle summer winds raise once more. The sons of Atreus were amazed to see what seemed like a rebirth. When Philoctetes had refreshed his body with food and drink, Agamemnon went up to him, took him by the hand, and said: "My friend, it is true that we were blinded in spirit when we left you in Lemnos, but it was also the will of the gods. Do not bear us a grudge any longer. We have been pnnished enough for what we did. For the time being, accept these gifts we have set aside for you—seven Trojan girls, twenty horses, and twelve tripods. Feast your eyes on these and live in my own house with me. At the board, and in every other way as well, you shall have the honors due to a king."

"My friends," Philoctetes replied kindly, "I cherish no grudge, neither against you, Agamemnon, nor against any other Argive who has wronged me. For I know that the spirit of a noble man must be flexible, gentle as well as stern. But now let us sleep. For those who love the fight do better to sleep by night than feast." So he said and went to his couch to rest until morning.

The next day the Trojans were still burying their dead outside the walls when they saw the Argives coming toward them in full battle array. Polydamas, the wise friend of slain Hector, advised them to retreat into their city and fend off the foe from behind the walls. "Troy," he said, "is the work of gods, and what they have made is not easy to destroy. We have enough food and drink, and King Priam, in the vast halls of his palace, has stores enough to feed three times as many people as live in our city for years to come." But the Trojans rejected his counsel and acclaimed that of Aeneas who urged them to conquer or die on the battlefield.

Soon the fight was raging with full fury. With his father's spear Neoptolemus slew twelve Trojans, one after another. But Eurymenes, the comrade-in-arms of bold Aeneas, and Aeneas himself made great gaps in the Argive host, and Paris killed the friend of Menelaus, Demoleon of Sparta. Philoctetes raged among the Trojans like Ares himself or like a beating rain which floods the fields and pastures. If an enemy so much as saw him from afar he was already lost. The very armor he wore, the armor of Heracles, seemed to terrify the Trojans as if they saw a Gorgon's head on his cuirass. Finally Paris dared approach him with lifted bow. Quickly he launched an arrow, but it whirred past Philoctetes and wounded Cleodorus, who stood beside him, in the shoulder. Cleodorus retreated, defending himself with his lance, but a second arrow shot by Paris killed him. And now Philoctetes took his bow in hand and cried in a voice like thunder: "You Trojan thief! You are the cause of all our woe. You shall mourn your insolent wish to measure your strength against mine. And once you are dead, destruction will come on swift feet, and your line and your city will fall." So speaking, he drew the twisted string of his bow close to his breast and fitted the arrow so that the point projected only a little beyond the curved bow. The arrow hissed through the air and did not miss its mark. But it only scratched the tender skin of beautiful Paris at the wrist, and he aimed again. A second arrow from the bow of Philoctetes hit him in the groin; trembling from head to foot, he fled like the dog from the lion.

The struggle continued while physicians tended the painful wound of Paris. At nightfall the Trojans went into their city, and the Danai returned to their ships. Paris moaned through the darkness. He could not sleep. The shaft had pierced to the marrow, and the poison which tipped the arrows of Heracles had blackened the wound with decay. The physicians could not help him, though they tried every known means to lessen his pain.

Then, in his great anguish, Paris recalled an oracle which had said that in his utmost need only Oenone, the wife he had put aside, could enable him to escape death. He had spent serene and happy days with her when he was still a shepherd, pasturing his flock on the slopes of Ida. When he left for Greece, she herself had told him of the oracle. And so now he had himself carried up Mount Ida where Oenone still lived, but he was reluctant and full of qualms. Birds of ill omen croaked from the trees as his servants climbed toward the peak with him. Their voices filled him with horror, but his will to live was so strong that he tried to ignore them. When they reached Oenone's house, he fell at the feet of the wife he had deserted. "Do not hate me now, in my agony," he cried. "I left you only because it was the will of the Fates that I go to Helen. I wish I had died before bringing her to my father's palace! But now I implore you by the gods, by the love we bore each other, pity me and put balm on my wound, for you yourself once predicted that you alone would be able to save my life."

But his words did not soften Oenone. "How dare you come to me, whom you abandoned and left to loneliness and sorrow, while you took pleasure in Helen's eternal youth!" she said angrily. "Why don't you go and fall at her feet and ask her to help you? For you certainly will not move my spirit with your weeping and lamenting." And she let him go from her house, not dreaming that her own fate was bound to his. He leaned heavily on his servants and dragged himself painfully away. They carried him down the wooded slopes of Ida, and Hera on Olympus revelled in his despair. Before he reached the foot of the mountain, he died of his poisoned wound, and Helen never saw him again.

A shepherd brought his mother Hecuba word of his death. Her knees shook at this message, and, losing consciousness, she fell to the ground. But Priam heard nothing of this fresh misfortune. He sat at the grave of Hector, lost in grief, and did not know what went on in the world. Helen, on the other hand, burst into tears, but her sadness was less for her husband than for herself, and she was confused by a feeling of guilt she had long suppressed.

Oenone, alone in her house, far from the city of Troy, was seized with deep remorse. Now she permitted herself to remember

Paris in the freshness of youth, and the delights of their young love. As the ice in the woods and the sunless gorges thaws at the soft breath of the west wind and flows in swift streams, so her harshness melted in sorrow, and tears poured from her eyes. She sprang from her couch, tore open the door, and rushed out like a tempest. From cliff to cliff she hurried through the night, over jagged rocks and mountain streams. Pityingly Selene looked down at her from the dark blue sky and shed light on her path. At last she reached that part of the woods where the body of her husband lay on a pyre. The logs burst into flame, and the shepherds of that region stood around, paying honor to their friend and prince. When Oenone saw Paris dead, she was speechless with grief, and veiling her lovely face in her gown, she cast herself on the pyre. Before anyone could move to help her, her hair had caught fire, and with her husband she was consumed in the flames.

THE STORMING OF TROY

While this was taking place on the slopes of Ida, the two armies had resumed the fight. Apollo breathed courage into Aeneas, son of Anchises, and Eurymachus, son of Antenor, and they drove the Achaeans back. They suffered great losses, and Neoptolemus rallied his men with almost superhuman effort. But he could not stop the Trojans until Pallas Athene herself came to his help. Now Aphrodite also took part in the battle, for she feared for the life of Aeneas, her son. Finally she hid him in dense mist and bore him away from the battlefield.

Only a few Trojans escaped death, and these retreated to their city, wounded and exhausted. Weeping women and children took their bloodstained weapons from them and loosened their heavy cuirasses, and physicians hastened to their aid. The Danai too were tired and weakened, for they had defeated their enemies only after a long and desperate struggle. But the next morning they woke refreshed. Leaving a guard with their wounded, they marched courageously toward the walls of Troy. They distributed their forces, so that one battalion was stationed at each gate. But the Trojans resisted from every part of the wall and from every tower. The Scaean Gates bore the brunt of the attack. Sthenelus, son of Capaneus, and Diomedes were the first to rush against it. But tireless Deiphobus and strong Polites, with many others, fended their foes off with arrows and stones, and their shields and helmets rang with the striking missiles. Neoptolemus fought at the Idaean Gates. His Myrmidons were experienced in all the methods of storming a wall. On this part of the ramparts Helenus and Agenor kindled the hearts of the Trojans and fought for their city. Those gates which led to the plain and the Argive camp had been assigned to Eurypylus and Odysseus. They attacked again and again, but Aeneas kept them at a distance by incessantly hurling great stones at them. Teucer, meanwhile, fought on the banks of the Simois. So the fighting went on everywhere, and there was no decisive action. Finally Odysseus had a happy thought. He had his warriors lift up their shields so that they formed a compact and vaulted roof under which the men went forward, keeping close to each other. And now the stones and arrows and javelins launched from the walls rained on the shields without wounding a single man. In this way, like a solid mass of threatening cloud, they approached the walls. The earth groaned beneath their steps, the dust whirled about their heads, and under the roof of shields their talk sounded like the buzzing of bees in a hive. The hearts of the sons of Atreus brimmed with joy when they saw this unshakable procession. They urged their men forward toward all the gates and prepared to lift them from their hinges or batter them in with two-edged axes. The new invention of Odysseus seemed to assure victory.

But the gods who sided with the Trojans put new and greater strength into the arms of Aeneas. With both hands he grasped an enormous stone and hurled it down on the roof of shields with desperate fury. This stone caused disaster to the besiegers, and they fell like mountain goats mowed down by a tumbling rock. But Aeneas stood on the wall, his limbs swelling with strength, and his armor flashed like lightning. Beside him was Ares, hidden in cloud, and every time Aeneas cast a missile the war-god guided it, spreading terror and death among the Achaeans. Through it all Aeneas kept sounding his battle cry, firing his men to action, while down below Neoptolemus shouted to his Myrmidons to stand fast. And so they fought all day without respite.

The Argives were luckier at another part of the wall, where Ajax of Locris swept the defenders down with his arrows and spears. He actually cleared a space, so that Alcimedon, his comrade-in-arms, set up a ladder and began to climb it, trusting to his youth and courage. He held his shield over his head. But Aeneas had been watching him from far off, and just as he mounted the topmost rung, just as his first and last glance fell on the city of Troy, he was hit in the forehead by a stone flung by the powerful hand of the son of Anchises. The ladder broke under the impact of the falling hero. He whirled through space like an arrow shot from the bow and died before he struck the ground. The men of Locris cried out when they saw him lying there crushed and mangled.

Now Philoctetes fixed his eyes on the son of Anchises, who was raging along the wall like a wild beast. He aimed one of his inescapable arrows at him, but only scratched the leather of his shield and instead felled Medon, who dropped from the rampart like quarry shot down by the huntsman. In return, Aeneas cast a stone at Toxaechmes, the bold friend of Philoctetes, and cracked his skull. Furiously Philoctetes looked up at his foe and exclaimed: "Aeneas! You think yourself brave when you throw down stones from your post on the tower. But any weak woman could do as well. If you are a man, come out of the gate in full armor and measure your strength and skill in the use of bow and lance with me, the son of Poeas!" The Trojan did not stop to reply, for he was summoned to another part of the wall which was endangered at that moment, and Philoctetes too was drawn back into the battle.

THE WOODEN HORSE

For a long time the Argives fought for the gates and walls of Troy, but they were repulsed on all sides. Then Calchas summoned the heroes to an assembly, and this is what he told them: "The hardships you are going through are utterly in vain. You will never take Troy by force. It would be far better to devise some ruse to accomplish your purpose. Yesterday I saw a sign —a falcon chasing a dove which deftly slipped into a cleft in a rock. For a long time her pursuer waited in front of the crack, but she did not come out. Then he hid in a bush nearby, and the foolish little dove fluttered out unsuspectingly. Thereupon the falcon swooped down on her and clutched her in his talons. Let us follow the bird's example. Let us stop fighting for Troy and see what can be achieved by craft."

When Calchas had finished, the heroes tried to think of some scheme or other to end this grim war, but they racked their brains to no purpose. Finally Odysseus had a clever idea. "Let us build an enormous wooden horse and hide in its belly as many of the bravest Argives as it will hold. The rest shall take the ships to the island of Tenedos. Before sailing, they must burn everything in the camp, so that the Trojans see the fire and smoke from their towers, forget caution, and scatter over the field. But one of us— and it must be one whom the Trojans do not know by sight— shall go to Troy pretending he is a fugitive, and tell them that he has escaped the Achaeans who were going to slaughter him as a victim to insure their safe return home. He shall say that he hid under the wooden horse which the Argives had dedicated to Pallas Athene, the enemy of the Trojans, and crawled out only after the ships had left. The man who undertakes this must be able to repeat this story in answer to all questions the Trojans will put to him, and speak with such a semblance of truth that they forget their suspicions. They will then pity the poor stranger and take him into their city. There he shall see to it that the Trojans drag the wooden horse inside the gates. When our enemies are asleep, he shall give us a sign we have agreed on. We will rush out of the horse, signal to our friends in Tenedos with a burning torch, and destroy the city with fire and sword."

When Odysseus had finished unfolding his plan, all praised his inventiveness. Calchas was loudest in expressing his approval, for shrewd Odysseus had hit on a scheme exactly in keeping with the soothsayer's wish. He drew the attention of the assembly to favorable omens read from the flight of birds, and to the sound of thunder in heaven which signified the consent of Zeus. The Argives were just going to begin building the horse when the son of Achilles rose and said: "Calchas! Brave men face their enemies in open warfare! Let the Trojans be cowards and fight down from their towers and walls. But we surely must not take

to hidden ruse or to any method but pitched battle. That is the only way to prove that we are better men."

His voice rang with courage and fearlessness, and even Odysseus was forced to admire his unbroken strength and pride. But he retorted: "You are the noble son of a noble father, and you have spoken like a hero. But remember that even your father, who matched the gods in power and daring, was unable to shatter these massive fortifications. Not all things can be achieved by courage alone. And so I beg you and all you other heroes to accept the counsel of Calchas and get to work at once to carry out my project."

Everyone except Philoctetes applauded the son of Laertes. The son of Poeas, however, sided with Neoptolemus, for he craved battle, and his heart was far from sated. In the end these two almost persuaded the rest of the Danai. But Zeus showed his disapproval and anger. Lightning flashed, and thunder shook the earth at the very feet of the Argives, so that they could not but understand that Zeus favored the plan of Calchas and the wily son of Laertes. And so Neoptolemus and Philoctetes yielded, though with inner reluctance.

They all returned to the ships, but before beginning the work they gave themselves up to deep refreshing sleep. And at midnight Athene sent a dream to Epeius, an Argive hero. She ordered him, who was skilled and deft with his hands, to build the great horse, promising her help, so that it might quickly be completed. The hero recognized the goddess. Joyfully he sprang up from his couch. He thought of only one thing—building the horse—and he pondered how to accomplish the task which had been set him.

At break of day, he told the Argives of the dream he had had. Instantly the sons of Atreus sent men to the slopes of Ida and had them cut the tallest trees. These were quickly dragged to the Hellespont, and there many young men offered to help Epeius. Some of them chopped the branches from the trunks. Others sawed the timbers. Epeius himself shaped the horse. First he carved the feet, then the belly. Over this he arched the back. Then he formed the flanks, and the neck with a mane, so delicately fashioned that it seemed to flutter in the wind. The ears were pointed, and the eyes sparkled with life. The whole horse seemed to breathe and move. With Athene's help, all this was finished in only three days, and the entire host marvelled at the great work of art made by Epeius. They expected to hear it neigh at any moment. But the artist lifted his hands to heaven and prayed before the army: "Hear me, Pallas Athene, great goddess! Save your horse and save me!" And all the Achaeans joined in his prayer.

The Trojans remained quietly behind their walls, weary and frightened by what they had suffered at the hands of the Argives. But up on Olympus there was great tumult. For now that Troy's doom was sealed the gods divided into two factions, the one favorable, the other hostile to the Argives. They descended to earth and stood in battle array on the shores of the Xanthus. But no mortal could see them. Even the deities of the sea joined the ranks of the immortals. The Nereids who were kin to Achilles sided with the Argives. Other gods of the ocean took the part of Troy, and they lashed the waves to angry crests and drove them toward the ships and the horse. Had Fate permitted, they would have destroyed both. In the meantime the fight on the plain had begun. Ares rushed at Athene. This was a sign for the rest, and soon all the gods were joined in conflict. Their golden armor rang at every move, and the sea surged and pounded on the sand. Under the feet of the immortals the whole earth quaked, and their battle cry was so piercing that it reached the underworld, and the very Titans trembled in Tartarus.

Now the gods had chosen the moment for battle at a time when Zeus was away on a journey. He had gone to the cave of Tethys and the waters of Oceanus at the utmost edge of the earth. But even at so great a distance his keen spirit knew everything that was happening before Troy. Hardly had he grown aware of the battle of the gods before he returned to Olympus, borne by the four winds. Iris was his charioteer, and his steeds reached the goal in an instant. With swift, strong hands he flashed lightning upon the gods below, and they dropped their arms and stood motionless. Themis, the goddess of justice, the only one of the immortals who had not taken part in the fight, went down to them and proclaimed that Zeus was resolved to destroy them unless they obeyed his will and gave up their struggle with one another. And now, fearing for their immortality, they subdued the enmity in their hearts and returned to their homes, some to heaven, others into the depths of the sea.

While this was going on, the wooden horse had been completed, and Odysseus rose in the assembly. "The time has come," he said gravely. "Now, O leaders of the Danai, we shall see who is really strong and fearless. For now we must enter the belly of this horse and go toward the unknown. Believe me, it takes more courage to crawl into this hiding place than to face the foe in open battle. So let only the very bravest come. The rest can sail to Tenedos. Only one unafraid man must remain near the horse and do as I have counselled. Who will volunteer for this?"

No one came forward. The heroes hesitated. Then Sinon went up to Odysseus and said: "I am ready to do what must be done! Let the Trojans maltreat me! Let them throw me into fire alive! My decision is made!" His words were greeted with jubilant shouts, and many an old hero said to himself: "Who is this young man? We have never even heard his name! He has no particular deed to his credit. He must be possessed of a demon who wants to destroy either us or the Trojans."

But Nestor rose and encouraged the Danai. "Let us marshal all our strength," he cried. "For the gods have placed in our hands the means of putting an end to ten years of hardship. Quickly now! Into the horse! My old limbs feel as strong as when

I wanted to board Jason's Argo, and I would have done so, had not King Pelias held me back."

So speaking, the old man attempted to precede all the rest through the wooden door let into the horse's belly, but Neoptolemus, son of Achilles, implored him to leave this honor to him who was young, and content himself with guiding the others to Tenedos. It was difficult to persuade Nestor, but at last he gave in, and Neoptolemus, in full armor, was first to enter the hollow horse. After him came Menelaus, Diomedes, Sthenelus, and Odysseus. Then Philoctetes, Ajax, Idomeneus, Meriones, Podalirius, Eurymachus, Antimachus, Agapenor, and as many others as the wooden belly would hold. Last to enter was Epeius, the maker of the horse. When he too was inside, he pulled the ladders up after him, drew them into the opening, shut the door, and bolted it from within. In utter darkness and deep silence the heroes huddled in the horse, not knowing what awaited them, whether victory or death.

The rest of the Argives set afire their huts and whatever utensils they did not take with them. Then they boarded their ships, which were under the command of Agamemmon and Nestor, and sailed for Tenedos. This was done according to the decision of the assembly which did not wish these two to enter the horse, the one because of his great majesty, the other because of his old age. At Tenedos they weighed anchor, went ashore, and longingly waited for the fire signal which had been agreed on.

It did not take the Trojans long to notice that the air was heavy with smoke, and when they peered down from their towers, they saw that the Argive ships were gone. Joyfully they thronged to the shore, but stopped to gird on their armor, for they had not given up all their fears. When, in place of the hostile camp, they found the gigantic wooden horse, they surrounded it in wide-eyed wonder. First they admired this amazing work of art to their heart's content, and then began to argue what to do with it. Some were in favor of dragging it into the city and setting it up on the acropolis as a monument of victory. Others mistrusted this strange gift the Argives had left behind and advised throwing it into the sea or burning it. All the while the heroes, hidden in that great belly, suffered pangs of anguish at each new proposal. And now Laocoon, the Trojan priest of Apollo, made his way through the crowds. But even before he had reached the horse, he cried: "What folly, what madness is this! Do you think the Danai have really sailed? How can you believe that any gift of theirs is without trickery? You know Odysseus! Either some danger lurks in that horse, or it is a war machine which our enemies, hidden somewhere nearby, will direct against our city. In any case, do not trust the horse!" With these words he grasped the heavy lance of the warrior standing nearest him and thrust it into the horse's belly. The spear quivered in the wood, and the sound which issued from the belly was like an echo from a hollow cave, but the spirit of the Trojans was blind, and their ears did not hear.

While this was going on, some curious shepherds, who had come close to the horse, detected Sinon who had hidden under it; they dragged him out and took him to King Priam. And now all those who had surrounded the horse went to see this new spectacle. Sinon stood there, unarmed and apparently numb with fright, and played the part Odysseus had invented for him. He lifted pleading hands, now to heaven, now to the spectators, and sobbed: "Alas! What land shall I turn to, what sea? For the Argives have banished me, and the Trojans will surely kill me!" The very herdsmen who had seized him were moved by these words, and a number of warriors went up to him, asked him who he was and where he came from, and told him that if he were really guiltless he should be of good courage.

Finally Sinon gave up his show of fear and said: "I am an Argive. I do not deny it. Misery shall not succeed in making a liar of me. Perhaps you have heard of Palamedes, prince of Euboea? At Odysseus' instigation he was stoned to death, simply because he had counselled his countrymen against waging war on Troy. I am a poor kinsman of his, and ever since his death I have had no one to turn to. You see, I dared threaten vengeance for the murder of my kinsman, and the son of Laertes began to hate me and has persecuted me all the years of this war. He did not rest until together with false Calchas he had plotted my death too. For when the Argives at last decided to flee—a plan they had weighed so often—and this wooden horse was already made, they sent Eurypylus to the oracle of Apollo, because they had seen ominous signs in the sky. And this was Apollo's answer: 'When you left for this war, you propitiated the angry winds with the blood of a virgin. Now you must buy your safe return with blood. You must sacrifice one of your own people.' The Argives shuddered at these words. But Odysseus summoned Calchas, the soothsayer, to the assembly, and begged him to reveal the will of the gods. For five days Calchas, hypocritical Calchas, refused to designate any particular warrior for the offering. Finally, pretending that Odysseus was forcing his hand, he called my name. And everyone agreed readily, for each was glad to escape death himself. The terrible day dawned. They wreathed me as a victim and bound the sacred fillet about my head. The altar, the wine, the flour—everything was prepared. But I broke the thongs that bound me, fled, and hid in the reeds of a swamp until they had sailed away. Then I crept out and took shelter under the belly of the sacred horse. I cannot return to my country or to my people. I am in your hands. You must decide if you wish to be generous and let me live, or kill me as my fellow Argives threatened to do."

The Trojans were moved by these lies. Priam spoke kindly to Sinon. He told him to forget his cruel comrades and promised him refuge in his city. All he asked in return was information about the wooden horse which the prisoner had just called "sacred."

Sinon's hands were freed of their bonds. He lifted them to heaven and prayed with false fervor: "You gods, to whom I was consecrated! O altar, and sword which menaced me, be my witnesses that the ties which bound me to my countrymen are severed, that I am not doing wrong in revealing their secrets!" Then he began his tale. "During the whole course of this war the Achaeans had staked their hopes on the help of Pallas Athene. But ever since her image, the Palladium, was stolen from the temple you reared for her in Troy, all has gone wrong. You Trojans probably do not know that it was taken by some of our men! The goddess was angry and withdrew her favor from the Argives. Then Calchas, the soothsayer, declared that we must launch our ships immediately and return to our own country to find out what the gods wished us to do. He said it was useless to expect victory until the Palladium was restored to its proper place. This was why the Danai at last resolved to sail home. But at Calchas' advice they first built this great wooden horse as a gift for the goddess. He claimed it would calm her anger. They made it tall and wide so that you Trojans could not wedge it through the gates and take it into your city, because if you did, Athene's favor and protection would go to you instead of to the Achaeans. If, on the other hand, you injured the sacred horse in any way—and the Danai hoped you would!—Athene would surely destroy your city. They intend to return as soon as they have learned the will of the gods in Argos, and expect to give the Palladium back to a city which has already been condemned by its own impious deeds."

This web of lies was so cleverly devised that Priam and his warriors believed it and trusted Sinon. And Athene watched over the fate of her friends who sat within the horse shaken with anxiety, for ever since Laocoon had voiced his warning, they had been consumed with the fear of death. But an almost matchless miracle freed the heroes at least from this one danger. After the death of Poseidon's priest, Laocoon, who was the priest of Apollo, had been chosen by lot to fill the vacant post, so that he was now priest of Poseidon as well. Just as he was about to sacrifice a splendid bull to the sea-god, two enormous snakes, coming from the direction of Tenedos, swam through the glassy water toward the shore. Their heads topped with scarlet crests loomed high above the surface of the sea. The rest of their bodies writhed through the water which moved and splashed with their passage. And now they crawled ashore, darted out their tongues, hissed, and looked about with eyes like flame. The Trojans, who were still thronged around the horse, grew pale as death and took to their heels. But the serpents made straight for the altar where Laocoon and his two young sons were busy with the sacrifice. First they wound themselves around the two boys and sank poisonous fangs into their tender flesh. When the children screamed and their father came running with drawn sword, they looped their heavy coils twice about him and reared their crests above his head. The fillet of the priest dripped with venom. In vain he tried to loosen the noose of their bodies with his hands. In the meantime the bull, which Laocoon had already struck with the axe when he heard his sons cry for help, shook the blade from his neck and fled bellowing from the altar. Laocoon and his children died from the bite of the snakes, and the creatures slithered along the ground until they reached the temple of Athene. There they hid at her feet, under the shield of the goddess.

The Trojans interpreted this awful event as punishment inflicted on the priest for the doubt he had expressed. Some hurried to the city and made a breach in the wall, large enough to admit the wooden horse. Others fastened wheels to its feet and twisted strong ropes to throw over its lofty neck. Then they pulled it to Troy in triumph. Girls and boys followed in solemn procession and chanted hymns. Four times the horse caught on the raised threshold of the gates before it finally rolled over, and four times the belly resounded as though bronze had struck on bronze. But still the Trojans did not hear, and they conducted the wooden image to the acropolis amid waves of thundering acclaim. In all this ecstasy of joy, only Cassandra, King Priam's daughter, whom the gods had lent the power of foretelling the future, remained aloof. With unclouded vision she saw what was to be. Never had she spoken a word which had not come true, but she had the misfortune always to be doubted. Now too she recognized danger and ran from the palace, driven by the spirit of prophecy. Her hair fluttered wildly, her eyes were glazed, and her slender neck swayed like a twig in the wind. She cried aloud through the streets: "People of Troy, do you not realize that we are travelling the road to destruction? That we stand at the verge of death? I see the city filled with fire and blood. I see death breaking out of the belly of that horse you have brought here so exultantly. But why do I speak? If I used thousands of words you still would not believe me. You have fallen prey to the Furies who will take vengeance on you for Helen's marriage."

But the Trojans only laughed at the girl or mocked her. At best one would stop and say: "Have you grown so shameless, Cassandra, that you, a girl, run around in the streets alone? Don't you see that everyone is ridiculing your foolish talk? Better go home before anything happens to you."

THE DESTRUCTION OF TROY

Late into that night the Trojans gave themselves up to feasting
and celebrating. Flute boys moved among the revellers. Again
and again the cups were filled with wine, seized in both hands,
and drained to the last drop. At midnight, when tongues and lids
grew heavy and all were dulled with sleep, Sinon, who had feasted
with the rest, pretended to grow drowsy. He rose from his couch,
walked softly out of the gates, lit a torch, and waved it so that
it could be seen on the shores of Tenedos. Then he extinguished
it, crept up to the horse, and knocked gently on the belly, as
Odysseus had told him to do. The heroes heard the sound. But
they only turned in silence to receive the command of the son of
Laertes. He bade them go out as quietly as possible, and warned
those who were most impatient. Noiselessly he slid back the bolts,
put out his head, and looked around to make sure no one was
awake. Then, as a ravening wolf prowls softly to the sheeppen,
between watchful shepherds and dogs, he climbed down the rungs
of the ladder which Epeius had made along with the horse. One
hero after another followed him, his heart thudding against his
ribs. When the wooden belly had disgorged all its inmates, they
brandished their lances, drew their swords, and scattered through
the city. And now dreadful slaughter overtook the Trojans,
dazed with sleep and wine. Firebrands were tossed into their
homes, and soon the roofs began to burn over their heads. At the
same time, a favorable wind carried the fleet from Tenedos into

the harbor on the Hellespont, and soon after the entire Argive host rushed into the city through the broad breach the Trojans themselves had cut for the horse. The already vanquished city was filled with screams of agony. The maimed and wounded crawled among corpses, and anyone who still ran unharmed was hit in the back with a lance. Dogs yelped and howled above the moans of the dying, and the clamor was swelled bv the wails of women and children.

But the Argives too had heavy losses, for although the greater part of their enemies were unarmed, they fought as well as they could. Some hurled their cups at the foe. Others snatched burning brands from the hearth, or hacked about with spits, hatchets, axes, or whatever they could lay hands on. So the Danai had to be on their guard. Stones were thrown at them from the roof tops, and some were crushed by burning walls which collapsed as they passed. When they had fought their way to the acropolis, many Trojans issued fully armed from the palace of Priam, so that the Argives had to fight for their very lives.

In the course of the battle the city grew lighter and lighter, though it was still night, for the many torches carried by the Achaeans and the brilliance of the spreading conflagration made Troy as bright as day. And now that the Argives no longer feared to mistake friend for foe in the dark, they became bolder and went purposefully for the noblest among the Trojan heroes. Diomedes killed Coroebus, son of great Mygdon, by driving his lance through his stomach. Then he slew brave Eurydamas, the son-in-law of aged Antenor. Soon after he met Ilioneus, one of the oldest among the Trojans, who fell on his knees and, catching at the victor's sword, cried in a trembling voice: "Whoever you may be, give up your anger! For only victory over the young and strong brings glory. Spare an old man, for you too will some day be old and look for mercy." For an instant Diomedes stayed his sword and hesitated. But then he pierced his enemy's throat, saying: "I do, indeed, hope to grow to honored old age, but first I must use my young strength to send all my foes to Hades!" And he rushed on and killed many other Trojans.

Ajax of Locris and Idomeneus were also pursuing the Trojans relentlessly. But Neoptolemus picked out the sons of Priam as his victims and slew three of them, and after that Agenor, who had dared fight with Achilles, his father. Finally he came on Priam himself. The old man was praying at an altar of Zeus built out in the open. Eagerly Neoptolemus lifted his sword. Priam looked him fearlessly in the eye. "Slay me, O son of brave Achilles," he said. "I have suffered much; many of my children have died before my eyes. Why should I still see the light of the sun? I wish I had died long before this. I wish your father had killed me. Since he did not, satisfy your own fierce heart and release me from my griefs."

"Old man," Neoptolemus answered, "you urge me to do what my own soul bids," and he cut off the old king's head lightly and swiftly as the reaper in the heat of summer mows the grain in the sun-baked field. The head rolled along the ground, and the body lay among the corpses of other Trojans.

The common warriors in the Argive host were far more cruel. In the king's palace they had found Astyanax, Hector's little son. They snatched him from his mother's arms, and, full of hatred against Hector and his line, hurled him down from the ramparts. When they wrested him from his mother, she cried: "Throw me from the wall too! Or cast me into the flames! Since Achilles killed my husband, I have been living only for my child. Take from me the agony of a life without him!" But the men did not even listen to her and stormed away.

So Death prowled about, entering now this house, now that. He spared only one, the home of old Antenor who had been so generous and kindly a host to Odysseus and Menelaus and saved their lives long ago when they came to Troy as envoys. For this the Danai now spared him and left him all his possessions.

As long as Troy was under siege, Aeneas had fought from the walls with unbroken strength. But when he saw the city burning in all quarters, when he realized that further resistance was useless, he acted like a brave sailor in a storm who defends his ship against the raging sea as long as possible, but when he knows that sinking is inevitable, abandons it to the waves and tries to save himself in a boat. So now Aeneas took his father Anchises on his broad shoulders, his son Ascanius by the hand, and hastened away. The boy pressed close to his father, and his feet hardly touched the earth as Aeneas leaped across the count-less bodies which littered the streets. And Aphrodite never left

her son's side, for wherever he went the flames receded, the clouds of smoke parted, and the arrows and spears the Danai hurled at him fell harmlessly to the ground.

In all other places, murder was abroad. Just outside the chamber of faithless Helen, Menelaus, her first husband, found Deiphobus, son of Priam. Since Hector's death he had been the pillar of his house and his people; after Paris was slain, Helen had fallen to his share. He was still drowsy and numb with the evening's carousal as he staggered to his feet and fled through the corridors of the palace. But Menelaus overtook him and killed him with his sword. "Die here, at my wife's doors!" he cried in a voice like thunder. "If only I could have killed Paris in this place! But just as he had to die, so you too shall not take delight in Helen and go unpunished! You shall learn that no one who does wrong can escape the hands of Themis, goddess of justice." And Menelaus rolled the corpse to one side with his foot and started on a search through the palace, for his heart, torn with emotions, yearned for Helen. Fearing her husband's anger, she had hidden herself in the farthest corner of the house, and it took him a long time to find her. When he first caught sight of her, jealousy prompted him to slay her, but Aphrodite, who had made her even fairer than before, struck the sword from his hand, dispelled his rage, and woke the old love sleeping in his heart. He was bewitched by Helen's beauty, and again and again his hand refused to raise the sword. Suddenly he forgot all the wrong she had done him. But when he heard the battle cry of the Argives, he felt ashamed to think that he was standing in front of false Helen, not as an avenger, but as her slave. Against his will he picked up the sword which had fallen to the ground, curbed his passion, and aimed a blow at his wife. But in his heart he hated to harm her, and so he was relieved when Agamemnon came up to him, laid his hand on his shoulder, and said: "Wait, Menelaus! It is not proper for you to slay your lawful wife, for whose sake we have endured so much suffering. She is far less at fault than Paris who broke the laws of hospitality. But he and all his line and all his people have now been punished. They have paid with their lives." So spoke Agamemnon, and Menelaus obeyed him with seeming reluctance but inner joy.

While this was happening on earth, the immortals veiled themselves in cloud and mourned the fall of Troy. The only ones to rejoice so greatly that they shouted with satisfaction were Hera, the deadly enemy of the Trojans, and Thetis, the mother of Achilles who had died in the flower of manhood. Pallas Athene could not restrain her tears, even though she had constantly worked for the fall of Troy, for she saw Ajax, the wild son of Oileus, enter her temple. There he seized Cassandra, her priestess, who had sought refuge in the sanctuary and was clasping her image, and dragged her away by the hair. The goddess did nothing to help the daughter of her foes, but her cheeks burned with anger, and her image gave forth a sound that shook the floor of the temple. Turning her eyes from this scene of crime, she swore to avenge the wrong done to Cassandra.

The conflagration and slaughter went on for a long time. Like a pillar the flames soared to heaven and announced the fall of the city to all those who lived on islands nearby, and to the ships which plied back and forth on the sea.

MENELAUS AND HELEN. POLYXENA

By morning, most of the inhabitants of the city were either dead or captured. The Danai could roam through Troy at will and take what they wanted of the boundless treasure stored in it. They carried their spoils to the ships: gold, silver, precious stones, many costly utensils, and captive women, girls, and children. In the midst of the throng was Menelaus, leading Helen out of the confusion. He was still a little ashamed and yet very happy to have her back. Beside him walked Agamemnon with Cassandra whom he had rescued from the rough grasp of Ajax. Neoptolemus guided Hector's wife, Andromache, from the burning city. Queen Hecuba, who walked with difficulty and tore at her grey hair which she had strewn with ashes, was the prisoner of Odysseus. Countless other Trojan women followed, young and old, and behind them girls and children. Handmaids mingled with the daughters of kings, and all alike sobbed and wailed with anguish. Only Helen was silent. She kept her eyes on the ground, and a blush of shame flooded her face. Then she thought of the fate which awaited her on the ships, and she shivered and paled. Swiftly she drew her veil over her head and walked tremblingly at her husband's side.

But when she reached the ships, the Achaeans were so dazzled by the flawless beauty of her face and the grace and loveliness of her body that they told themselves it had been well worth while to follow Menelaus to Troy for such a prize, and to endure dangers and hardships for ten long years. No one at all thought of hurting Helen in any way. They left her to Menelaus who, moved by Aphrodite, had forgiven her long ago.

And now the feasting began. All the heroes lay couched around the board, and in the middle was a bard who struck chords on his lyre and sang the deeds of Achilles, the greatest of all the Argives. Until nightfall they made merry.

Now when Helen was alone with Menelaus, she threw herself at his feet, clasped his knees, and said: "I know that you have the right to punish me, your faithless wife, with death. But remember that I did not leave the palace in Sparta of my own free will. Paris, that trickster, took me by force at the very time you were absent from home, and I had no husband to protect me. And when I wanted to kill myself, when I lifted the sword or laid the noose around my neck, my tirewomen held me back and begged me to think of you and of our little daughter. Do as you like with me. I lie at your feet as a penitent, as a suppliant."

Menelaus raised her tenderly and answered: "Forget the past, Helen, and lay aside your fears. What was done is over. I shall never cherish a grudge against you for any fault you may have had." With that he took her in his arms, and tears of sad and sweet emotion glistened in her eyes.

Neoptolemus, son of Achilles, was fast asleep. In his dream he saw his father, looking just as he had in life, the terror of the Trojans and the delight of the Danai. He kissed his son on the throat and eyes, and said: "Do not grieve that I am dead, dear son, for now I am in the company of the gods. Do not give yourself up to mourning! Do as I did while I lived. Always be first in battle, but in council do not hesitate to yield to the wisdom of men older than yourself. Strive for glory, enjoy the light of earth, and do not let misfortune rest too heavily on your spirit. My early death has taught you how near to the doors of Hades is every mortal. For men are like the flowers in spring: they bloom and they fade. And now, tell Agamemnon to sacrifice the most precious and noblest of all the spoils, that my heart may rejoice in the fall of Troy, and nothing be lacking to my content on the heights of Olympus."

When he had given his son this command, Achilles vanished from Neoptolemus, lightly and fleetly as wind. He woke and felt as happy as if his father were still alive and had talked to him.

In the morning the Danai rose from their couches full of impatience to be off on their journey, for their longing for home had grown overgreat after the sack of Troy. They would have dragged their ships into the sea at once, had not the grandson of Peleus gone among them and detained them with his words. "Argives!" he called in his strong young voice. "Last night my immortal father came to me in a dream and bade me tell you to make him an offering of the best you carried off as spoils from Troy, so that he too might have his share of the prizes of war and sate his heart with joy at the fall of the hated city. You shall not leave these shores until you have fulfilled your duty toward dead Achilles, to whom you really owe your conquest. For had he not defeated Hector, we should never have reached our goal."

Reverently the Argives resolved to obey their slain hero. Out of love for Achilles, Poseidon quickened the sea to a tempest, and the breakers rose so high that even had the Danai wished to leave, they would not have been able to. And when they saw the towering waters and heard the howl of the wind, they whispered to one another: "Yes, Achilles is indeed descended from Zeus himself. See how the elements are supporting his commands!" And they were all the more willing to do as he had bidden and thronged to his burial mound, looming high above the shores of the sea.

But now came the question, what to sacrifice? What was best and noblest among all the spoils taken from Troy? Of his own accord, every Argive brought his treasures and captives. When everything had been examined, gold and silver and precious stones, the glory of these as well as of all other possessions paled before the beauty of Polyxena, Priam's daughter, and a cry rose up from the throng that it was she who was best and noblest of the spoils. The girl did not blanch when she saw all eyes fixed on herself. She remained steadfast even when Hecuba, her mother, pressed forward from the crowd of captives and wailed aloud. For Polyxena was willing to die for the sake of Achilles. She had seen him from the walls, and although he was the enemy of Troy, his beauty and strength had stirred her inmost being. There was even a rumor that once, when the battle had been carried to the very gates of the city, Achilles had seen Polyxena on the ramparts. His heart had quickened with love, and he had called to her: "Daughter of Priam, if you fell to my share, who knows if I should not try to make peace between your father and the Argives!" It seems that the hero regretted his words the moment they were spoken, for he remembered what he owed to Greece. But Polyxena—so they say—was deeply touched by them and from that day on had burned with secret love for the foe of her people.

Be that as it may, the girl did not falter when all eyes fastened on her and all lips proclaimed her the only offering fit for the greatest of heroes. An altar had been reared at the burial mound of Achilles, and the utensils for the sacrifice lay in readiness. And then, before anyone knew what was happening, the princess sprang forward from among the other captive women, seized a dagger, and, clinging to the altar like a victim, drove it into her heart. She fell to the ground without a word or a sigh.

A wave of lament ran through the Argive host. Old Queen Hecuba threw herself over her daughter's body with many tears, and her women wailed with pity and sorrow.

The moment Polyxena sank to the earth and the crimson blood spurted from her breast, the sea grew as calm and smooth as a mirror. Overcome with compassion, Neoptolemus hurried to the altar, helped them carry Polyxena away, and saw to it that she was buried with the honors due a princess. But Nestor rose in the council of the Argives and said: "At last the hour for our journey home has come. The lord of the sea has bridled the breakers. As far as the eye can reach not a crest of foam is to be seen, not even a ripple. Achilles is content. He has accepted the sacrifice of Polyxena. Let us launch our ships and sail!"

DEPARTURE FROM TROY. AJAX OF LOCRIS DIES

At Nestor's advice all this was done, and the men shouted lustily as they loaded the ships with stores and the many spoils of war. First the captives were put aboard, sobbing and wailing. Then the Argives themselves entered the ships. Calchas, the soothsayer, was the only one to remain ashore. His prophetic spirit had divined a terrible disaster lurking in wait for the Achaeans near the Capharean Rocks of the promontory of Euboea, which the Argive fleet had to pass on the journey home. He warned them not to sail, but no one paid any attention to his words because all hearts were overcome with longing for home. Only Amphilochus, son of Amphiaraus, the famed seer whom the earth of Thebes had swallowed, drew back the foot with which he was about to board his ship. For something of his father's gift of

prophecy stirred within him, and suddenly he had the same premonition as Calchas and decided to stay behind with him. Fate
had decreed that neither Calchas nor Amphilochus were to return to Greece. They settled in the cities of Cilicia and Pamphy-
lia, in Asia Minor.

But the other Achaeans loosed the ropes which bound the ships
to the shore and weighed anchor. The wind bellied out the sails,
and the open sea lapped the keels. The bows of the ships were
laden with the weapons of slain foes. Countless trophies of victory hung from the masts. The ships were wreathed with flowers,
and the victors had garlanded their shields, their helmets and
lances. Joyful and triumphant, they poured libations of wine into
the shining sea and begged the gods for a safe return. But their
prayers never reached Olympus; the winds swept them from the
decks and scattered them among the drifting clouds.

While the heroes were looking ahead full of hope and longing,
the captive Trojan women and girls gazed back at Troy, where
the smoke was still curling from the ruins. They tried to hide
their sorrow by stifling the sobs which rose in their throats, and
they eased their grief with silent tears. Some of the girls had
clasped their hands around their knees, others covered their
faces with their palms. The young women held children in their
arms, but these thought of nothing but their mother's breast and
did not know the unhappiness in store for them. Cassandra stood
among them, taller than the rest. Her eyes were tearless, and
she was too proud to give way to sighs. What had happened was
only what she had foretold long ago, and her fellow citizens had
jeered at her for it. Now she spoke contemptuous words to her
countrywomen, but though her lips mocked them, her heart bled
for her city which had been sacked and burned.

The only people left in the ruins of Troy were the old and the
wounded. Antenor urged them on to the mournful task of burying their dead. It was slow work, for there were so many corpses
and so few living men. These built one gigantic pyre, laid the
bodies on it side by side, and lit the wood with weeping and
lament.

The Argives, in the meantime, had already left behind them
the coast of Troy and the grave of Achilles. But their joy was
tempered with grief at the thought of how many of their com-

rades had fallen, how many friends they were leaving in alien earth. Coast after coast, island after island slipped past: Tenedos, Chrysa, the temple of Apollo Smintheus, sacred Cilla, Lesbos, and the promontory of Lecton, where Mount Ida juts out into the sea. The wind filled the sails, and the surging sea was dark except for the trail of white foam in the wake of the ships.

The victors would have reached the coast of Hellas safely, had not Pallas Athene been angry with them because of what Ajax of Locris had done. So when they approached the stormy shores of Euboea, the goddess prepared a sad and cruel death for the son of Oileus. She had complained to Zeus that her priestess Cassandra had been dragged from the sanctuary of her temple, and she demanded the right to take vengeance on the perpetrator of the crime. And the father of gods not only gave her the permission she asked but lent his daughter thunderbolts which the Cyclopes had just forged, and let her stir up a deadly tempest for the Argive fleet. Then Athene girt on her armor. In the middle of her shimmering aegis was the Gorgon's head in a tangle of serpents. She grasped one of her father's thunderbolts, which no other god except Zeus could lift, filled Olympus with the crash of thunder, poured clouds about the mountains, and wrapped the sea and the land in darkness. Then she sent Iris, her messenger, to Aeolus, god of the winds. He kept them imprisoned in a cave in a rift of earth, next to his palace.

Iris found the lord of storms at home with his wife and his twelve sons. He at once set about obeying Athene's command. With powerful hands he thrust his huge trident into the hill which covered the cave of the winds and tore it open. And out darted the winds like hounds eager for the hunt. He bade them unite to a single black tempest and fly to the surf which pounds the Capharean Rocks on the coast of Euboea. The words had scarcely left his lips before they were on their way. The sea groaned under their impact. The waves swelled to mountains, and the courage of the Argives sank when they saw towering walls of water rolling toward them. They could no longer ply their oars. The storm had torn their sails to tatters. At last even the helmsmen gave up. Night fell, the darkest night they had ever experienced, and with it the last shred of hope vanished.

Poseidon helped Pallas, his brother's daughter, and unceasingly she tossed fresh lightning and thunder down from Olympus. Screams and groans sounded through the ships. The wood cracked with the force of the gale. The timbers were wrenched apart, and those who tried to escape the impact of the wrecks driving through the waters were sucked beneath the waves. Finally Athene hurled her mightiest thunderbolt into the ship of Ajax of Locris, and the next instant it was nothing but a mass of splinters. Earth and air rang with the tremendous crash, and the waves licked at the wreckage. The crew struggled and drowned, but Ajax himself was still alive. Now he clutched a timber, now he parted the tide with the strong strokes of an expert swimmer. Now he rode the crest of a wave, now he was dashed into the trough. All the while lightning blazed about him, but Athene did not want him to die just yet. Such a death would have been too merciful. Nor was his courage broken by all these terrors. He gripped an edge of rock protruding from the sea, clung to it stubbornly, and boasted he would save himself even if all the gods combined to destroy him.

Poseidon, the Earth-Shaker, who was close to Ajax, heard his vaunts with anger. Furiously he shook earth and sea at the same time. The crags of Caphareus trembled, and the shores quaked under the trident of the sea-god. And then the rock which Ajax was clutching with both bleeding hands was uprooted from the bottom of the sea, and he was thrust helpless into the swirling waters. His head and beard were white with foam. As he sank, Poseidon flung at him a cliff he had pried loose from the promontory, and it covered the king of Locris as Aetna had once covered Enceladus. And so Ajax perished, shattered both by the earth and the sea.

The ships of the other Danai tossed about on the waves. Some were in pieces, many had sunk. The storm raged on, and the rain poured in such torrents that it resembled the flood in the days of Pyrrha and Deucalion. And now the Argives had also to suffer vengeance for the stoning of Palamedes. For King Nauplius, the father of this hero, was still in Euboea. When he saw the Argive fleet battling with the tempest near the coast of his country, he thought of the malicious murder of his son whom he had been mourning so many years. The lust for revenge had never weakened within him, and here was a chance to satisfy it. He hurried to the shore and had his servants set up burning torches all along the promontory of Caphareus, opposite the most dangerous cliffs in the sea. The Achaeans, thinking that the torches were beacons of safety put up by the compassionate inhabitants of the island, made for those very cliffs with haste and hope. And here many more of their ships were wrecked.

While this was happening to the Danai on their homeward journey, Poseidon commanded the sea to tear down the walls and towers they had put up around their camp near Troy. And so of all that great undertaking, nothing was left but the ashes of Troy and a small number of ships with returning heroes and captive Trojan women. The tempest had scattered them. It was only after terrible toil and many hardships that they reached the coast of Greece, and even there only a very few found the unalloyed happiness which all had yearned for during the long years of warfare.

THE LAST TANTALIDES

TROY had fallen. A tempest had overtaken the homeward
bound Argive fleet and destroyed more than half of it. The
survivors continued their journey on a calm sea and steered for
their native lands. Agamemnon, whom Hera had protected from
the dangers of the sea, made for the coast of the Peloponnesus.
But when he was quite close to the steep promontory of Malea in
Laconia, a fresh tempest rose with dark fury and drove all his
ships back to the open sea. He groaned and, lifting his hands,
begged the gods not to let him drown within sight of home after
all the hardships he had suffered to obey the wishes of the immortals. He did not know that this new storm had been sent to
him as a warning from Olympus, for it would have been better
for him to live as a castaway in a distant country, among barbarians, than set foot in his own palace in Mycenae.

There was a curse on Agamemnon's house. It went back to
the days of his ancestor Tantalus, and new crimes had strengthened its intensity. The ruthless violence inherent in his line had
lifted some of his forebears to power and magnificence and
had hurled others to their destruction. And now Agamemnon was
to be the victim of a plot conceived in his own palace. His great-
grandfather Tantalus had served the gods, who had come to dine
with him, a horrible dish—his own son Pelops, whom he had
killed and cooked. Only a miracle had restored the boy. Pelops,
who was otherwise guiltless, murdered Myrtilus, the son of
Hermes, and so did his share toward keeping alive the curse hanging over his house. The story of Myrtilus was this: he was the
charioteer of King Oenomaus, whose daughter Hippodamia Pelops had won by carrying off the victory in a chariot race with her
father. Now this had been possible only because Pelops induced
Myrtilus to remove the brazen bolts from his master's chariot
and replace them with fastenings of wax. This caused the chariot
to fall apart, and so Pelops won the race and the king's daughter.

But when Myrtilus came for the reward which he had been promised, Pelops cast him into the sea because he did not want the witness of his trickery to be alive to testify against him. It was in vain that he tried to placate angry Hermes by building him a temple and heaping a high burial mound for Myrtilus. The god swore to take revenge on him and his descendants.

Pelops had two sons, Atreus and Thyestes, and they too increased the power of the curse. Atreus was king of Mycenae, while Thyestes ruled the southern part of Argolis. The elder brother had a ram with a fleece of gold which the younger coveted. He seduced Aerope, his brother's wife, and she gave him the golden ram. When Atreus learned of his brother's twofold crime, he did not stop to reflect. He followed his grandfather's example; secretly he seized Tantalus and Pleisthenes, Thyestes' two little sons, slaughtered them, and set the meat before his brother at a banquet he gave in his honor. The children's blood he blended with wine and served the draught to their father. The sun-god, who was watching the gruesome feast, was so horrified that he guided his chariot backwards. Thyestes fled from his inhuman brother and took refuge in Epirus with King Thesprotus. The land governed by Atreus was visited with drought and famine. When the king questioned an oracle, he received the reply that his country would not prosper until the brother whom he had driven away was recalled.

Atreus himself set out to search for Thyestes and brought him and his son Aegisthus back to their old home. Aegisthus had been born in Epirus, and his father had begotten him by committing a crime. Now he swore to avenge his brothers on Atreus and his children. The first part of his vengeance he accomplished soon after Atreus and Thyestes returned to Mycenae. Their friendship was of brief duration. Atreus had Thyestes thrown into prison. Then Aegisthus went to his uncle, pretended indignation at the horrors attending his birth, and offered to murder his own father. In this way he gained admittance to the dungeon, and there he and his father made a plan. Aegisthus showed Atreus a bloody sword, and when he rejoiced over his brother's death and made a thank offering at the shore, his nephew thrust that very blade into his body. Thyestes left his prison and seized his brother's realm, but not for long. Agamemnon, the eldest son of

Atreus, slew his uncle to avenge his father. Aegisthus was spared. The gods preserved him to carry on the curse, and he ruled his father's kingdom in the south of Argolis.

When Agamemnon had left for Troy and his wife Clytaemnestra was at home in her palace, nursing her grief and rage at the sacrifice of her daughter Iphigenia, Aegisthus felt the time had come to avenge his father on the son of Atreus. He suddenly appeared in Mycenae, and Clytaemnestra's hatred for her husband and her wish to wrong him were so great that she finally yielded to the importunities of Aegisthus, lived with him as her husband, and shared the realm with him. At that time three of Agamemnon's children were living in the palace: Electra, nearest in age to Iphigenia, Chrysothemis, her younger sister, and Orestes, who was still a little boy. Before their very eyes, Aegisthus usurped their father's place, both in their mother's affections and in the country at large. As the battle for Troy approached its end, the guilty couple trembled at the thought of Agamemnon's return and the punishment he and his warriors would mete out to them. Years ago they had stationed special watchmen on the palace ramparts, who were to report the instant a signal, given by beacon fires flashed from coast to coast, announced the fall of Troy and the king's return. They planned to make festive preparations for Agamemnon's reception and to lure him into a trap before he had time to discover what went on in his palace and kingdom.

At last a golden flame shot through the night. A watchman hurried down from the ramparts and reported it to his queen. Impatiently Clytaemnestra and her lover waited for the dawn. Shortly after sunrise a herald, dispatched by Agamemnon, ran toward the palace, his temples wreathed with olive sprays. The queen met him with hypocritical joy, but saw to it that he did not mingle with others. She interrupted the long flow of his speech, saying: "Do not trouble to relate the whole story. I shall hear everything from the lips of the king, my husband. Go, tell him to hasten. Tell him how overjoyed I am, how all Mycenae rejoices. I shall go to meet him myself and welcome not only my beloved and honored husband, but the splendid conqueror of a world-famous city, with the solemnity and splendor due to a hero."

AGAMEMNON'S END

When the storm threw Agamemnon back from the promontory of Malea, the wind drove his ships to the southern coast of the land where his uncle Thyestes had once ruled and Aegisthus now held sway. He cast anchor in a safe harbor and waited for a favorable wind. The spies he had sent ahead brought back the news that Aegisthus, the king of this country, had been living in Clytaemnestra's palace ever since her return from Aulis, and that he had been ruling Mycenae in Agamemnon's name for a number of years. Agamemnon was glad to hear of this and suspected no evil. He thanked the gods that the ancient spirit of vengeance had vanished from his house. He himself had shed so much blood at Troy that his thirst for blood vengeance had abated, and he did not dream of punishing his father's murderer, who, after all, had taken only a just revenge. He was, moreover, guileless enough to think that during this long interim his wife had given up her grudge against him. And so, when a fair wind rose, he weighed anchor with a light heart and sailed for his home harbor.

As soon as he had made a thank offering to the gods for having brought him safely home, he and his men followed the herald whom the queen had sent to meet him. Before the gates of Mycenae, he was met by all his people, headed by his cousin Aegisthus whom the country regarded as the king's deputy. Then came Clytaemnestra, accompanied by her tirewomen and her children, carefully guarded. As is usual when happiness is not genuine but pretended, she received her husband with exaggerated reverence and with all possible demonstrations of delight. Instead of clasping her arms about him, she threw herself on her knees and poured out a flood of praise and congratulations. But Agamemnon lifted her to her feet with simple happiness, took her to his heart, and said: "What are you doing, daughter of Leda! You must not receive me lying in the dust, as a slave receives her barbarian lord! And why these embroidered tapestries spread beneath my feet? This is a welcome for gods, not for mortal men. Give me only such honors as the immortals may not envy!"

When he had greeted his wife and embraced his children, he turned to Aegisthus who stood a little to one side with the elders of the city. He gave him his hand in brotherly fashion and thanked him for having governed his city so carefully during his absence. Then he unbound the thongs of his sandals and walked over the costly tapestries on his bare feet until he reached the palace. In his retinue was Cassandra, the prophetic daughter of Priam, whom Agamemnon had freed from the rough hands of Ajax of Locris and brought home as part of his spoils. With bowed head, her eyes cast down, she sat on a high wagon laden with other booty. When Clytaemnestra saw her, the nobility of her appearance filled her with envy, but even more with terror, for she had heard the name of the captive and learned that the soothsaying priestess of Pallas was to live in her palace which she had desecrated by her faithlessness toward Agamemnon. She realized more than ever that it would be most dangerous to put off the execution of her plot and instantly resolved to murder the alien captive at the same time as her husband. But she carefully concealed her thoughts, and when the procession reached the palace of Mycenae, she went up to the wagon and spoke kindly to Cassandra: "Come, give up your sadness! Even Heracles, the indomitable son of Alcmene, was once forced into servitude and bent his head under the yoke of an alien mistress. Since Fate has decreed exile for you, be happy that you have come to those who have been rich and prosperous for generations. For he who has got his wealth suddenly and recently is apt to be harsh and over-bearing to his servants. Be at ease! You shall have fair treatment from us, and all that is your due!"

Cassandra's face did not change at these words. For a long time she sat motionless, and her handmaids had to urge her to dismount. Then she leaped from her place like a frightened doe. Her spirit divined all that was to happen. She was certain that nothing could be altered. And even had she been able to change the decree of Fate, she would not have wanted to save the foe of her people from the goddess of vengeance. But because he had saved her, she was not unwilling to die with Agamemnon.

The king was completely deceived by the preparations for the sumptuous banquet which Clytaemnestra had ordered for his homecoming. Her original intention had been to have him slaughtered at this feast, slaughtered like a bull at the manger by the hirelings of Aegisthus. But the arrival of the seeress moved the queen and Aegisthus to act more quickly and without taking anyone into their confidence.

Agamemnon was weary and dusty from his journey and called for a warm bath. Clytaemnestra told him she had given orders to have it ready for him. Unsuspectingly the king entered the chamber where the bath was prepared, laid aside his weapons, took off his armor and clothing, and stepped into the tub. The moment they saw him unarmed and at their mercy, Clytaemnestra and Aegisthus rushed out of hiding, threw a close-meshed net over his head, and drove their daggers into his body again and again. Since the baths were in subterranean chambers, his cries for help were not heard in the palace above. Soon afterward Cassandra, wandering alone through the dark halls, divined the murder and announced it in strange words with hidden meanings. She too was done to death.

When Aegisthus and Clytaemnestra had accomplished their twofold crime, they decided not to conceal it, for they trusted to the loyalty of their followers. The two corpses were displayed in the palace. Clytaemnestra summoned the city elders and addressed them without reserve. "Do not bear me a grudge for deceiving you up to now, my friends," she said. "I had to do this to my deadly enemy, to the murderer of my darling child. Yes, it is true: I lured him into the net; I caught him like a fish. Three times I pierced him with my dagger in the name of Pluto, lord of the underworld. I have avenged my daughter's death with my own hand. I have slain Agamemnon, my husband. I do not deny it. Did he not slaughter his child as if she were a sacrificial animal? Was it not my anguish, was it not a mother's sorrow which calmed the Thracian winds for the Argive fleet? Did so ruthless a man deserve to live and rule his devout people? Is it not more just that you be governed by one whose conscience is not weighed by child murder, by Aegisthus, who by killing Atreus and his son did no more than take revenge on his father's foes? It is only right that I should become his wife and share the palace and the throne with him who helped me dispense justice. He is the shield for my courage. As long as he and his men protect me, no one will dare take me to account for what I have done. As for that slave—" and here she pointed to Cassandra's body, "she was the mistress of your faithless king. She had to be killed because she was an adultress, and her corpse shall be thrown to the dogs!"

The elders said nothing. To fight was out of the question. The palace was surrounded by Aegisthus' men. The ominous clash of weapons and threatening cries broke the stillness. Agamemnon's warriors, greatly reduced in numbers by the war of Troy, had put off their armor and scattered through the city. Now the insolent followers of Aegisthus strode through Mycenae and felled every man who dared breathe a word against the murderers of his lord.

Clytaemnestra and Aegisthus immediately did all they could to strengthen their position as rulers. They distributed important posts and military commands among their most faithful friends. They did not trouble about Agamemnon's daughters, for they regarded them as harmless women. Later—too late—they remembered that Orestes, Agamemnon's young son, might grow up to be his father's avenger. Although he was not yet twelve years old, they would have liked to kill him, in order to free themselves from all fear of punishment. But his clever sister Electra had thought more quickly than the murderers. Immediately after her father's death, she had entrusted the boy to a slave who had secretly taken him to Phanote in Phocis. Here he was received by King Strophius who had been a friend of Agamemnon's, and brought up with Pylades, the young prince, as if he were his brother.

AGAMEMNON IS AVENGED

Electra in the meantime spent mournful days in the palace of her murdered father. She lived in the hope that when her brother had grown to manhood he would return and avenge his father. Her own mother was bitterly hostile to her. The girl had to share the palace with her father's murderers and submit to their wishes. It was in their power to feed her or let her starve. She saw Aegisthus sit on Agamemnon's throne, adorned in the dead king's most magnificent robes, taken from his own storerooms. She saw him pouring libations to the gods of the house whose head he had slain. She was forced to witness the caresses her mother lavished on this usurper. Clytaemnestra passed over the horrors she had committed with a smile and ordered a splendid feast held on the anniversary of the day on which she had killed her husband. Besides this, she sacrificed many victims every month to the gods who had saved her from Agamemnon's anger.

The girl ate out her heart in secret sorrow, for she was not even allowed to let her tears flow freely. "Why are you crying?" her mother would call to her. "Are you the only one who has lost a father? Is no one entitled to mourn except yourself? I wish your foolish griefs would be the death of you!" And when vague rumors that Orestes was alive and preparing to go against Mycenae reached her, she poured out her terror and sense of guilt on her unhappy daughter. "It would be your fault if he came!" she cried. "Did you not steal him from under my very hands? But you will not live to rejoice in the fruit of your plots! The punishment you so richly deserve will overtake you sooner than you think!" Whenever such scenes occurred, Aegisthus aided and abetted his queen, and Electra fled from them and tried to hide in the remotest chamber of the palace.

Years had passed, and still she waited for Orestes to come, for even though he had been so young when she sent him away, he had promised his sister to return as soon as he was strong enough to bear weapons. But that was long ago, and now hope was slowly dying in Electra's heart.

Her younger sister Chrysothemis did not have her staunch, brave spirit. She could not further her plans or ease her sorrow, not because she was careless of Electra's grief, but because she was too soft and tenderhearted. Chrysothemis obeyed her mother and constantly opposed Electra's wishes. One day she came out of the palace carrying offerings for her dead father and utensils with which to perform sacrifice. Clytaemnestra had sent her, but when she crossed Electra's path, her sister reproved her for her obedience and for her forgetfulness of Agamemnon. "Will you never learn to give up your useless grief?" Chrysothemis answered. "I too am hurt by what I see around me, and I give in only because I have to. But you—unless you stop lamenting, they will imprison you in a cave, far away, and you will never again see the light of day. I heard them talking about it. Remember this, and if misfortune overtakes you, do not blame me!"

"Let them do with me as they like," said Electra coldly and proudly. "I shall be best off wherever I am farthest away from all of you. But for whom are those offerings intended, sister?"

"My mother told me to sacrifice them at the grave of our dead father."

"For her murdered husband!" Electra cried in amazement. "Whatever put that into her head?"

"A dream," Chrysothemis replied. "They say she saw our father in her sleep. With his hand he seized the scepter he once owned and which Aegisthus carries now. He planted the scepter in the earth, and out of it grew a tree with sturdy branches which soon cast their shade over all of Mycenae. This dream frightened her, and so today, while Aegisthus is not at home, she sent me to placate our father's soul with these offerings."

"Dear sister," Electra said pleadingly, "do not let the gifts of this wicked woman touch our father's grave! Scatter them to the winds, or bury them secretly in the sand where no smallest part can reach our father's resting place. Do you think that the murdered man wants to receive a gift from his murderess? Throw all this away, and instead cut a few locks from your head and take my locks as well and bring these and my girdle—the only thing I possess—to our father. And when you reach his grave, throw yourself on the ground and beg him to come out of the depths of the earth to aid us against our foes and his; beg him to let the proud footsteps of his son soon sound in our ears, of Orestes, who will dispatch his murderers. Then we shall adorn his grave with rich offerings!" For the first time Chrysothemis was stirred by her sister's words. She promised to do as she said and hastened away with the offerings her mother had given her.

She had not been gone long when Clytaemnestra came from the inner halls of the palace and began to jeer at her elder daughter as usual. "You seem quite gay today, Electra," she said. "I suppose it is because Aegisthus, who keeps you within bounds, is away. You should be ashamed to appear in front of the door! This is not proper for a girl! But perhaps you are here to complain of me to the servants? Are you still accusing me of killing your father? I do not deny that I did this deed, but I was not unaided. The goddess of justice stood at my side, and if you had any sense, you would hasten to be her ally. Did not this father of yours, whom you weep for all the time, have the insolence to sacrifice your sister for his own advantage and the sake of Menelaus? Has such a father not forfeited all claim to reverence? If my dead daughter had the power of speech, I am sure she would say I am right. But whether you approve of me or not, foolish girl, is a matter of indifference to me."

"Listen," Electra replied. "You boast of having murdered my father. That is shameful enough! Whether or not the murder was justified has nothing to do with it. You did not kill him for the sake of justice! You were driven to it by the flattery, by the caresses of that man who now owns you. My father sacrificed his daughter for the Argive army, not for his personal welfare. He did it reluctantly. He did it under compulsion and only for the sake of the people of Greece. But even if he had done it for his brother and himself, is that any reason why he should die by the hand of his wife? Did you have to marry your accomplice and so let disgrace follow on the heels of crime? Or was that also included in the vengeance you think you owed your daughter?"

"Insolent girl!" screamed Clytaemnestra. "By Artemis, you shall repent your defiance as soon as Aegisthus returns! Will you stop annoying me and let me make my offerings in peace!"

Clytaemnestra turned from her daughter and went up to the altar of Apollo which stood in front of the palace, as before every Argive house, to protect the walls and the street. Her sacrifice was intended to propitiate the god of prophecy who had sent her the dream which had frightened her during the past night. And it seemed that the god wished to favor her. Hardly had she completed the rites when a stranger approached the tirewomen who had accompanied her and asked for the palace of Aegisthus. When they pointed the queen out to him, he bowed to her and said: "Hail, Clytaemnestra! I have come with welcome news for you and your husband and your friends. I am sent by King Strophius of Phanote. Orestes is dead. That is what I have been sent to tell you."

"These words mean death to me," moaned Electra and sank down on the steps.

"Repeat what you said!" cried Clytaemnestra, hastily leaving the altar. "Do not mind that foolish girl. Tell me everything. Tell me!"

"Your son Orestes," said the stranger, "went to the sacred games at Delphi, for he was driven by the thirst for glory. When the herald announced the beginning of the foot races, he stepped forward, and he was so radiant that all marvelled at him. Before anyone even saw him start he had reached the goal, running like wind or lightning. He won, and the name of Argive Orestes, son of Agamemnon, conqueror of Troy, was proclaimed as the victor. This was on the first day of the games. But the strongest man cannot escape his fate if the gods choose to bewilder him. The next morning, when the chariot races were to begin at rise of sun, he was again among the contestants. They were an Achaean, a Spartan, and two men from Libya with great experience in the driving of horses. Orestes, with his four Thessalian horses, was the fifth. After him came an Aetolian with four bays. The seventh contestant in the races was from Magnesia, the eighth, with white horses, an Aenian. The ninth came from Athens, and the tenth from Boeotia. And now the judges shuffled the lots, the chariots were lined up in order, a trumpet gave the signal, and all ten stormed forward, shaking the reins and calling to their horses. The brazen chariots clanged, dust whirled from under the wheels, and no one spared the goad. Close behind every chariot were the snorting horses of the next. They had already started on the seventh round. Whenever Orestes circled the turning post he almost touched it with the axle, for he had taken the curve very close by drawing tight the rein of the left horse and leaving slack that of the right. Up to this point the chariots had all run smoothly, but now the hard-mouthed horses of the Aenian shied and ran against the chariot of one of the contestants from Libya. This one slip immediately caused the wildest confusion. Chariot crashed on chariot, and soon the field was covered with shattered cars. The Athenian was the only one wise enough to drive on the outer side of the course. He reined in his horses and left the clutter of chariots in the inner circle. Close behind him came Orestes. When he saw the tangle of men, beasts, and chariots, and realized that only the Athenian was left to compete with him, he beat his horses with the goad, and now, both standing erect, the bold pair set out to finish the race. The turning post around which they had to drive for the last time, was near. Orestes had made good progress on the long course. Overconfident in his luck, he gradually slackened the rein of the left horse too. This caused the animal to turn too soon. The axle barely grazed the post, but still the impact was so great that it broke. Orestes fell and was dragged along the ground. The moment he toppled from the chariot his horses ran over the sand in frantic flight. The spectators screamed with pity, for the Argive now trailed on the earth, now hurtled through the air. At last the other charioteers succeeded in stopping his horses and cutting him loose. But he was so disfigured and covered with blood that even his own friends would not have recognized the body. The Phocians quickly burned it on the pyre, and envoys from Phocis are on their way with an urn which contains his bones, so that these may be buried in his native earth."

The messenger paused. Clytaemnestra was shaken with conflicting emotions. She wanted to rejoice wholeheartedly at the death of her son whose coming she had feared. But her mother's grief tempered the feeling of relief which the message had given her. Electra, on the other hand, felt nothing but boundless sorrow. "Where shall I flee?" she cried, after Clytaemnestra had taken the stranger from Phocis into the palace. "Now I am utterly alone. Now I must go on and on serving the murderers of my father! But I cannot! I will not live under the same roof with them any longer. Rather will I leave the palace and perish miserably. And if anyone within begrudges me this slow death, let him come out and kill me at once! Life can mean nothing but grief to me. Death is more than welcome!"

Gradually she fell silent and gave herself up to dull despair. She must have been sitting on the marble steps of the palace for hours, her head bowed in her lap, when her younger sister Chrysothemis ran up to her and roused her from her brooding. "Orestes has come!" she cried. "He is just as much alive as you or I!"

Electra raised her head and stared at her sister with wide-open eyes. "Have you lost your wits, sister?" she asked. "Are you jeering at my sorrow and yours?"

"I can only report what I found," said Chrysothemis between smiles and tears. "Listen, and I shall tell you how I discovered the truth. When I came to our father's grave, overgrown with grass, I saw the traces of a fresh offering of milk and garlands of flowers. I looked around in terror and amazement, and when I had made sure that no one was there, I came closer. Then, at the edge of the mound, I saw a lock of hair, newly cut. And suddenly—I hardly know why—I thought of our brother Orestes, and I guessed that the lock must be his. I took it in my hand with tears of joy, and here it is! It must—I am sure it must have been cut from his head!"

Electra shook her own head doubtfully. All she had heard seemed too vague, too fantastic. "I am sorry for you because you are so credulous," she said to her sister. "But then you do not know what I know." And now she told her sister everything she had heard from the Phocian, and at every word Chrysothemis grew sadder and sadder, until she joined in her sister's lament. "The lock," said Electra, "is probably from the head of some friend who offered it up for dead Orestes at his father's grave." But in spite of her bitterness and unbelief, Electra had gained control of herself while she spoke to her sister, and now she proposed that since the last hope of vengeance by the hand of Orestes was gone, the two girls together should do the great deed and kill Aegisthus, the murderer. "Think well, Chrysothemis," she said. "You cling to life and its joys. Do not imagine that Aegisthus will ever permit us to marry and bring forth children who could be future avengers of Agamemnon. But if you do as I say, you will prove your faithfulness to your father and brother, win glory, live in freedom, and be happy with a husband worthy of you and your line. For who would not be glad to court the daughter of so noble a house? And all the world will praise what we have done. At the feast and in the assembly we shall be honored for a deed brave enough for a man. Give me your help! Save me, save yourself from the joyless and humiliating life we are leading!"

But Chrysothemis regarded the plan her sister had unfolded with such passionate intensity as unwise, incautious, and unfeasible.

"What have you to rely on?" she asked. "Have you the strong arm of a man? Are you not a woman? Are you not opposed by powerful foes whose position grows more and more secure every day? It is true that our lot is hard, but if you are not careful it will become insufferable. We could, indeed, win glory, but it is far more likely that we should die a shameful death. And perhaps dying would not be the worst to befall us. There are more terrible things than death. Let me beg you, sister—do not destroy us! Curb your anger! I shall guard everything you have said and keep it secret."

"I am not surprised to hear you say this," Electra sighed. "I knew very well that you would reject my plan. Then I must do it alone, do it unaided. And perhaps it is better so!" Chrysothemis put her arms around her and wept. But her elder sister did not relent. "Go," she said coldly. "Tell all you have heard to our mother." And when her sister shook her head, she called after her: "Go, go! I shall never follow in your footsteps."

She was still sitting motionless on the steps when two young men came toward her. They were carrying a small urn of bronze, and with them were other youths. The one with the noblest bearing turned to Electra and asked her where he might find Aegisthus. He told her that he was one of the envoys from Phocis. At that Electra sprang up and stretched out her hand for the urn. "By the gods, stranger," she cried, "give me the urn, so that, in shedding my tears on the bones of Orestes, I can mourn my whole unhappy house."

"Whoever she may be," said the youth, looking at the girl attentively, "give her the urn. She cannot be a foe of the dead. She is his friend, or perhaps he was her kinsman." Electra took the urn in both hands and pressed it to her heart again and again. And softly she moaned: "O remains of the dearest I had on earth! How great were the hopes with which I sent you away, and now you come back to me like this! I wish I had died rather than let you go to another land. Then you would have been slaughtered as your father before you, and would not have perished miserably in exile, burned on a pyre heaped by the hands of strangers. All my care of you, all my sweet pains have gone for nothing! Now that you have died, everything is dead for me, even I have died, since you are no longer alive. Our enemies exult. Our mother can give herself up entirely to her pleasures, for she has nothing more to fear. If only I could share this small urn with you!"

While the girl was uttering her bitter lament, the youth who was leading the envoys could no longer curb his tongue. "Can this be Electra?" he cried. "But how distorted by sorrow! Who has done this to her?"

Electra looked at him in surprise. "It is because I am forced to serve the murderers of my father," she answered. "This urn means the death of my hopes."

"Put it down!" said the youth, his voice choked with tears. And when Electra refused and only clutched it more tightly, he said: "Put it away. It is empty!"

Electra flung the urn down in despair. "Then where is his grave?" she asked pleadingly.

"Nowhere," he answered. "The living need no grave."

"He is alive—he lives?"

"He is alive—just as alive as you and I. I am Orestes, I am your brother. See, you can recognize me by the signet ring our father once gave me. Do you believe me now?"

"O light in the darkness!" cried Electra and threw herself into his arms.

Just then the messenger who had given Clytaemnestra the false news of her son's death came out of the palace. He was the servant of young Orestes, the man to whom Electra herself had entrusted the child and who had accompanied him to Phocis. When he revealed himself to the girl, she greeted him and said joyfully:

"You have saved our line. What great service these faithful hands of yours have performed! But how was it possible that you were not discovered? How did you accomplish all this?"

The man did not take time to answer her impetuous questions. "The day will come," he said, "when I can tell you at my leisure everything that happened. But now we must hurry. The hour for revenge has come. Clytaemnestra is still alone. She has no one to protect her, for Aegisthus has not yet returned. But if we hesitate even for a moment, we may have to fight the guards— more guards than we can cope with." Orestes agreed, and with his faithful friend Pylades, son of King Strophius of Phocis, he rushed into the palace. His companions followed. Electra flung herself down at Apollo's altar in supplication and then followed her brother.

A few minutes later Aegisthus returned. He entered the palace and immediately asked for the men from Phocis who had brought the happy news of Orestes' death. The first to cross his path was Electra, and he put his question to her with contemptuous pride. "Well, speak!" he said. "Where are those strangers who have crushed your dearest hopes?"

Electra suppressed her true feelings and answered quietly: "They are inside. They have been taken to their dear hostess."

"And have they really reported his death?" he continued.

"Yes," said Electra. "Not only that, but they have brought the dead with them."

"These are welcome words I hear from your lips," he said jeeringly. 'But look! There they come, bringing the dead!"

Joyfully he went to meet Orestes and his companions, who were carrying a shrouded corpse from the inner part of the palace into the court. "O happy sight!" cried the king, and fixed his eyes on their burden. "But hurry now and lift the covering. It is, after all, only proper that I mourn him who was my kinsman."

Orestes replied: "Lift the covering yourself. It is fitting that you alone see and mourn what lies under this pall."

"That is right," said the king. "But first call Clytaemnestra, so that she too may see what she will rejoice to see."

"Clytaemnestra is not far away," said Orestes. And now the king raised the covering, but he recoiled with a cry of horror. For under it was not the corpse of Orestes, which he had hoped to see, but the bloodstained body of Clytaemnestra. "Into what trap have I stepped!" he cried in terror.

Orestes answered in a voice like thunder. "Did you not know that you have been talking to him you thought dead? Do you not see that Orestes, his father's avenger, stands before you?"

"Let me explain," gasped Aegisthus, sinking to the floor. But Electra implored her brother not to listen to him. Orestes forced Aegisthus to precede him back into the palace, and in the very same place where he had once murdered King Agamemnon, he himself now fell a victim to the sword stroke of the avenger.

ORESTES AND THE FURIES

In avenging Agamemnon by the slaying of Clytaemnestra and her lover, Orestes had done the will of the gods, for an oracle of Apollo had commanded him to do this deed. But his piety toward his father had made him the murderer of his mother. Hardly was she dead before filial love stirred in his heart, and the crime he had committed against nature made him the prey of the Erinyes or Furies, the goddesses of vengeance, whom the Greeks —to propitiate them—gave the name of Eumenides, which means "the Gracious Ones," or "those we implore to be gracious toward us." The Eumenides were the daughters of Night, and as dark as their mother. They were taller than any human being. Their eyes were bloodshot, their hair was a mass of writhing serpents. Holding a torch in one hand and a scourge plaited of snakes in the other, they pursued the murderer of his mother wherever he went and tormented him with the pangs of remorse.

Immediately after the deed, the Furies afflicted Orestes with madness. He left his sisters, Mycenae, and his native land in frantic flight. In a lucid moment he had betrothed his faithful friend Pylades to Electra, and now Pylades did not return to his father, Strophius, king of Phocis, but shared the wanderings of mad Orestes. He was the only mortal to stand by him in his wretchedness. But an immortal also came to his aid. Apollo, at whose command he had slain his mother, remained near him, now visible, now invisible, and fended off the raging Erinyes. The spirit of Orestes grew calmer whenever he felt the god at his side.

After long wanderings the fugitives came to Delphi, and Orestes took refuge in the temple of Apollo which the Furies were not permitted to enter. He threw himself on the floor, exhausted with weariness and terror, and the god looked at him full of compassion. Then he revived his hope and courage with the words: "Unhappy son, take comfort. I shall not betray you. Whether I am near or far, I shall guard you and never give you up to your enemies. At this very moment I have poured leaden sleep on the lids of those terrible old goddesses who rise from the depths of Tartarus and are abhorred by immortals, mortals, and even animals. For the present they are tamed and dare not approach my temple. But do not depend too much on their slumber! It will not last long, for Fate permits me only brief ascendency over these ancient deities. You must soon resume your flight, but you shall, at least, not wander without a goal. You shall go to Athens, to the stately city of my sister, Pallas Athene. There I shall see to it that you come before a just court, where you can speak and defend your cause. Do not be afraid. Though I myself must leave you now, my brother Hermes will guard you and protect you from all harm."

So said Apollo. But before he left his temple and Orestes, the shade of Clytaemnestra had appeared to the sleeping Furies in a dream and whispered to them angrily: "Why are you asleep? Have you abandoned me so utterly that I must hover unavenged in the bleakness of Hades? My closest kin have wronged me, and no god cares that I was slain by my own son! I have poured you many libations, and you drained them all. How many offerings have I brought you by night! And now you forget all this and let your prey escape like a deer which slips from the snare! Hear me, gods of the underworld! It is I, Clytaemnestra, whom you swore to avenge, and who now troubles your dream to remind you of your oath."

But the sinister goddesses could not shake off the magic sleep which held them spellbound. Not until they heard the words: "Orestes, the murderer of his mother, is escaping you!" did one of them rouse herself and wake the others. Like wild beasts they leaped from their lair, stormed boldly to the temple of Apollo, and set foot on the threshold of the sanctuary. "Son of Zeus," they shouted at him, "you are a cheat! You, the younger god, tread underfoot the older goddesses, the daughters of Night, and dare withhold from our wrath this scorner of the law, this slayer of his mother! You have stolen him from us! Is it right for a god to do that?"

But Apollo drove the black Furies out of his sunlit temple. "Away with you, terrible sisters!" he cried. "Your place is in the lion's den where beasts lap blood, you, the hounds of the Fates, not here on the site of my pure and sacred oracle." In vain the Furies reminded him of their office, of their rights. Apollo declared that Orestes was under his protection because he had avenged Agamemnon at his and Zeus' command. At last the Eumenides quailed before his power, backed away from the threshold, and fled.

Then Phoebus entrusted Orestes and his friend to Hermes, the protector of travellers, and returned to Olympus. The friends took the road to Athens, as Apollo had bidden them, and the Furies, fearing the golden rod of Hermes, followed only at a safe distance. But gradually they grew bolder. When the two arrived in the city of Pallas Athene, the Eumenides came close on their heels, and hardly had Orestes and Pylades entered Athene's temple before the dark sisters rushed after them through the open gates.

Orestes had thrown himself on the ground before the image of the goddess, flung wide his arms, and prayed in wild despair: "Athene, I have come to you at Apollo's command. Receive me mercifully, for my hands are not stained with innocent blood. I am weary of wandering and begging at the doors of strangers. Obedient to your brother's oracle I have fled through towns and open country, and now I lie at your feet and await your judgment."

But the Furies, who stood close behind him, raised their voices in solemn chorus. "We are on your trail, murderer!" they cried. "We have tracked your steps, dripping with blood, as the hound tracks the wounded stag. You shall find no asylum and no rest. We shall suck the red blood from your body, and when nothing is left but a living shadow, we shall take you down to Tartarus with us. Then neither Apollo nor Athene shall free you from unending torture. You are our quarry, a victim for our altar. Come, sisters, let us dance around him, and with our songs cloud his spirit with madness!"

They were just about to begin their awful chant, when a light from above flooded the temple. The image of Pallas Athene had vanished, and in its place stood the goddess herself. Her stern blue eyes gazed on those before her, and she opened her lips to speak.

"Who is disturbing the peace of my sanctuary?" she asked. "What visitors do I see here? A stranger is clasping my altar, and women who do not look like mortals throng behind him with menacing eyes. Tell me who you are and what you want!"

Orestes was speechless with fear. He trembled and could not rise. But the Erinyes did not hesitate to reply. "Daughter of Zeus," they said, "we shall tell you everything just as it is. We are the daughters of Night and are called Erinyes."

"I know you," said Athene. "Word of you has come to me often. You are the avengers of perjury and of the murder of kinsman by kinsman. But what can have brought you to my temple?"

"This man, who lies at your feet and soils your altar with his presence!" they answered. "He has slain his own mother. Judge him! We shall honor your verdict, for we know that you are stern and just."

"If I am to make judgment," said Pallas Athene, "I must first hear what the stranger has to say. How can you defend yourself against the accusation of these goddesses? What is your country, your line? What has befallen you? You shall cleanse yourself of the crime you have been accused of. I permit this because you are lying before my altar and clasping it as a suppliant. But now answer me and be unafraid."

At last Orestes ventured to raise his eyes. He half rose, so that he was still on his knees, and said: "Athene! You need not fear for your temple. I have not committed a murder which cannot be atoned for. I am not clasping your altar with hands that desecrate. I was born in Argos. You must have known my father. He was Agamemnon, the ruler of many peoples, the man who guided the Argive fleet to Troy and whom you helped destroy the citadel of proud Ilium. When he returned from his conquest, he did not die a natural death. My mother and her lover tangled him in a net and slew him in his bath. For a long time I lived in a foreign land, but when I returned, I avenged my father. I do not deny it. I avenged the murder of my beloved father by slaying my mother. And it was your own brother Apollo who urged me to do this deed. His oracle threatened me with unending anguish if I did not punish my father's murderers. Now judge, O goddess, whether I have done right or wrong. I shall bow to your verdict."

The goddess was silent and thoughtful. Finally she said: "The matter which I am to judge is so strange and involved that no law-court on earth would know what to do about it. Although

I am going to choose mortal judges, it is right that you have turned to an immortal for help. For I shall summon the judges to my temple and preside over the court. If the judges find they cannot arrive at a verdict, I myself shall decide the issue. In the meantime this stranger shall live in my city unmolested. But you, you implacable goddesses, shall not taint these precincts any longer. Return to Tartarus and do not come back to this temple until the day of the trial. Both parties shall collect evidence and summon witnesses, while I call on the wisest and best men in my city to solve this difficult problem."

When the goddess had set a day for the trial, Orestes and Pylades, as well as the Furies, were dismissed. The Eumenides obeyed Athene without demurring. They left the city and returned to the underworld. Orestes and his friend were hospitably received in Athens.

When the day of the trial dawned, a herald called those citizens whom Athene had chosen to a hill opposite the acropolis. This hill was sacred to Ares, and for this reason it was called Areopagus, or Ares-hill. The goddess was already there, and both the accusers and the accused had arrived. But a stranger had also appeared and taken his place beside the accused. When the Erinyes saw him, they cried out in alarm: "Phoebus Apollo, do not interfere with our concerns! What are you doing here?"

"This man is under my protection," replied the god. "He came to Delphi to seek refuge in my temple. I have purified him of the blood he spilled, and so it is only right that I should help him. I have come to testify for him, and also to defend him before the court which my sister Athene has summoned. For it was I who counselled him to murder his mother and told him that in the eyes of the gods this would be a devout act and pleasing to them."

As he spoke, the god came closer to Orestes. And now Athene opened the court and asked the Erinyes to state their accusation. "We shall be brief," said the eldest of them, who had been chosen to speak for them all. "You, whom we accuse, answer us. First, did you or did you not murder your mother?"

"I do not deny it," said Orestes, who had paled at the question.

"And how did you commit the crime?"

"I pierced her throat with my sword."

"At whose advice or instigation did you do this?"

"At his who stands beside me," said Orestes. "Apollo gave me his commands through an oracle, and he is here to confirm my words." Orestes then went on to explain that in killing Clytaemnestra he had not thought of her as his mother, but only as the murderess of his father. Apollo seconded him in a long and eloquent speech. The Furies countered his words. The god first painted the murder of Agamemnon in dark colors, but they argued that Clytaemnestra had not killed a kinsman but only her husband, while Orestes had murdered his mother. Then the eldest said: "Now we have launched all the arrows we had in our quiver, and we shall await the verdict of the judges in silence."

Athene had the stones for voting distributed among the judges. Each was given a black stone to indicate guilt, and a white one for innocence. The urn which was to hold the stones was set up in the middle of the fenced-off space. And now Athene rose from the raised seat she occupied as the head of the court and addressed the judges before they cast their votes. Standing erect in all her divine majesty she said: "Citizens of Athens, listen to what the founder of your city has to say to you on this first occasion you have assembled to give judgment at a murder trial. This tribunal shall remain within your walls for all time to come. Here, on the sacred hill of Ares, where the Amazons once camped when they waged war on Theseus, where they brought sacrifice to the god of war, here the Court of the Areopagus shall assemble and keep the citizens of Athens from doing wrong. I herewith establish this court, made up of the best men of this city. They shall be stern, just, and incorruptible. They shall not take bribes nor look to their profit, but protect the rights of everyone in the land. The citizens shall reverence its dignity and uphold it as a pillar of strength, such as no other people in Greece or elsewhere on earth can boast of. This is my will as to the future. And now, judges, remember that you have sworn to serve the law; put your votes into the urn, so that this issue may be decided."

Silently the judges rose from their seats. One after another approached the urn and dropped into it a stone. When all had voted, chosen citizens, who were also under oath, counted the stones. And then it appeared that there were just as many black as white, and that the goddess, who had reserved the right of decision for herself, would have to give the verdict. Again she rose and said: "I was not borne by a mother. I, a virgin, sprang from the head of Zeus, my father, and I protect the rights of father and son against those of the mother. And so I shall not take the part of the woman who slew her husband to please her wicked lover, but cast my vote for Orestes, who killed his mother because she murdered his father." With that she left her place, took a white stone, and added it to the rest of the white stones. "This man," she then said solemnly, "is herewith, by a majority of votes, pronounced 'not guilty.' "

When she had given the verdict, Orestes turned to her. He was deeply moved. "O Pallas Athene," he cried, "you have saved my line and given me back my native land. All Greece will exalt you for what you have done, and say: 'Argive Orestes is again living in the palace of his fathers, rescued by the justice of Athene and Apollo and of the Thunderer, without whose will this could not have come about.' And now, before I start for home, I swear to this country and this people that no Argive in all time to come shall ever make war on the devout Athenians! And if, after my death, one of my countrymen should break this oath, I myself shall rise from my tomb to punish him, send misfortune to dog his footsteps, and prevent him from carrying out his cursed plans against this city. Farewell, noble protector of justice, and people of Athens. May victory and welfare attend you in war and all else you undertake."

Then Orestes left the sacred hill of Ares, and his friend Pylades, who had never left his side during the entire court proceedings, went with him. The Furies did not venture to oppose the verdict of Athene, and besides they feared the strength of Apollo, who was prepared to see that the judgment of the court was upheld. But the eldest, who spoke for the rest, rose from the plaintiff's seat and confronted the god and the goddess. In a deep hoarse voice, she defiantly questioned the verdict. "Woe to us!" she cried. "Younger deities have trodden underfoot the age-old laws; they have wrested the power from our hands, from us who are the elder. We are scorned. We cannot vanquish them with all our anger. But you, Athenians, shall live to regret your judgment! On this ground, where justice has been scoffed at, we shall pour out the venom seething in our hearts. Blight shall attack your fields, destruction shall overtake all that is living.

With famine and plague we shall haunt this land and this city, we the offended and derided goddesses of night."

When Apollo heard this terrible curse, he intervened and tried to appease the mighty deities. "Be gracious," he said to them. "For you were neither defeated nor dishonored. The number of black stones and white was the same. The judges did not override you. The accused, who was forced to choose between two sacred duties, and in choosing was bound to neglect one, has been

saved through the will of Zeus who guarded him. So do not vent your anger on the innocent people of this land. For in their name I promise you a worthy sanctuary in this country. The citizens of Athens shall bring you offerings year after year and revere you as the implacable goddesses of just revenge."

Athene confirmed his words. "Believe me, majestic goddesses," she added. "If you make your home in another country you will regret it and long for the earth you have spurned. The citizens of Athens are ready to hold you in high honor. Choruses of men and women clad in crimson robes will sing your glory. Your sanctuary shall be in the sacred cave beside the temple of King Erechtheus, and every house that does not honor you will be unblessed."

As they listened to these promises, the Furies gradually grew calmer. They consented to remain in that country and were pleased to think that they, as well as Athene and Apollo, were to have a sanctuary in the most famous of all cities. In the end they grew so gentle that they, on their part, solemnly swore to shield the city from wild weathers, from drought and plague, to guard the herds, to bless marriages, and, with the Fates, their half sisters, to work for the welfare of the entire region. They went so far as to wish everlasting peace and prosperity to the people. Then the dark sisters left the Areopagus and the city. Athene and Apollo gave them thanks, and all the citizens of Athens accompanied them with blazing torches and chants of praise.

IPHIGENIA IN THE LAND OF THE TAURI

After leaving Athens, Orestes and Pylades again went to the oracle of Apollo in Delphi. Orestes had indeed been acquitted, but he had not recovered from his madness and asked the god what he was now to do. The priestess said that the prince would be restored to health and happiness in Mycenae, but that first he was to sail to the peninsula of the Tauri, where Artemis, Apollo's sister, had her temple. There he was to carry off the image of the goddess, which, according to a legend of the barbarian people of that region, had fallen from heaven and had been reverenced there ever since. When he had taken it by force or ruse, he was to bring it to Athens, for the goddess had grown tired of the savage people of that alien land, and longed for gentler worshippers. As soon as this was accomplished, his madness and exile would be at an end.

Pylades did not desert his friend but accompanied him on this dangerous quest. The Tauri were in the habit of sacrificing to Artemis all the shipwrecked or other strangers who came to their shores. In war, they cut off the heads of their captured enemies, fastened them to poles, and fixed these on the roofs of their houses, as guardians to keep watch over the land.

Now the reason the oracle was sending Orestes to this cruel tribe was this. In Aulis, when Agamemnon was about to sacrifice his daughter Iphigenia at the advice of Calchas, the soothsayer, a hind had appeared at the altar just as the priest brandished the blade above the girl's throat. Artemis had removed Iphigenia from the eyes of the Argives and carried her off across the sea, through shining clouds, to her own temple in the land of the Tauri. There Thoas, the king of this barbarian people, found her and made her the priestess of Artemis. Her service required her to see to the sacrifice of every stranger who set foot in that land, and these were, for the most part, her own countrymen! It is true that she had only to consecrate the victim. It was the task of others to drag it to the altar and do the slaughtering. Still, her lot was sad and hopeless.

The girl had been performing her distasteful office for many years. The king held her in high esteem, and the people reverenced her for her charm and gentleness. So she lived, far from her home, utterly unfamiliar with the destinies of her house. But one night she dreamed she had left the land of the Tauri and was home in Argos, sleeping surrounded by her handmaids. Suddenly the earth began to tremble and heave, and she saw herself fleeing from the palace, standing outside, while the roof shook and the colonnade swayed and crashed to the ground. Only one column of her father's house remained upright. And all at once it seemed to her that it was turning into a man. The capital became a head ringed with blond locks, and the head spoke to her in her own language, but what it said the girl had forgotten when she awoke. All she knew was that in her dream she had obeyed the demands of her priestly office. She had sprinkled the man, who was a pillar of her father's palace, with holy water to consecrate him for death, and while she did this, she wept. When she roused herself from her dream, her cheeks were wet with tears.

On the morning after this night, Orestes and his friend Pylades landed on the shore of the Tauri, and went toward the temple of Artemis. Soon they reached the structure the barbarians had put up to the goddess. It resembled a prison rather than the dwelling of a deity, and they looked at the high and solid wall in silent amazement. Orestes was the first to speak. "My faithful friend," he said, "you have shared the dangers of this journey with me. But what shall we do now? Shall we climb the spiral stairs around the wall? I fear that, when we reach the top, this unknown building will seem like a labyrinth to us. Undoubtedly we shall find the doors to the rooms locked with iron bolts, and if our attempts to get in rouse the guards who must be placed all around the sanctuary, they will seize us and kill us. For we have heard that much Argive blood has already spattered the altar of this implacable goddess. Would it not be wiser to return to the ship which brought us here?"

"If we did that, it would be the very first time we have taken to flight," answered Pylades. "Let us hold sacred the oracle of Apollo. But we must, indeed, leave this place. The best thing would be to hide in a grotto on the shore, far from our ship, so that no one, seeing it, will be able to tell the cruel ruler of this country anything about its crew. But when night falls, let us venture out. We know the position of the temple. Through some ruse or other we shall get in, and once we have the image in our hands, I am sure we shall be able to get back to the shore. Brave men court danger! We have come a long way. Would it not be shameful to turn back when we are so close to the goal, and go home without the prize the god has commanded us to seize?"

"We shall do as you say," Orestes exclaimed. "Let us hide through the day, and may night bring us success!"

The sun was high in the heavens when a herdsman came running from the shore, straight toward the priestess of Artemis, standing on the threshold of her temple. He brought her the news that two youths, welcome victims for the goddess, had landed on that coast. "Prepare for the sacred rites, priestess," he said. "The sooner the better!"

"Where do the strangers come from?" Iphigenia asked mournfully.

"They are Argives," answered the herdsman. "That is all we know so far, except that one of them is called Pylades. They are our captives."

"Tell me about it," said the priestess. "How did it happen, and where did you capture them?"

"We were just bathing our cattle in the sea. One after another we drove into the swirling waters. There is a grotto there, wavewashed, where the fishers go to collect purple snails. Here one of us saw two young men. They seemed so radiant to him that he took them for gods and wanted to throw himself on the ground before them. But another who stood near, a pert, inquisitive fellow, was not so foolish. He laughed when he saw his companion bending his knees, and said: 'Don't you see that these are shipwrecked strangers who have hidden in the cave because they

know of our custom of sacrificing all who reach these shores?'
Most of us agreed with him, and we prepared to seize the two
men. Just then, one of the strangers came out of the grotto,
shook his head wildly, and flung out his arms. He groaned aloud
in the throes of madness and cried: 'Pylades, Pylades, look over
there! See the dark huntress, the dragon from Hades, who wants
to murder me! She is coming at me, and her head is ringed with
hissing snakes. And there—another—she is breathing fire! She
is carrying my own mother in her arms, and now she is threatening to hurl a rock at me! Help! She is killing me!' But we could
see nothing of all the horrors he raved about," the herdsman
continued. "He must have taken the bellowing of our cattle and
the barking of the dogs for the voices of the Furies. And now
we were alarmed, because the stranger drew his sword, rushed
at our cows, and slashed right and left until the sea was red with
their blood. At last we managed to gather our wits, blew into
our conch shells to summon the peasants, and advanced on the
armed stranger in a solid mass. His madness was slowly leaving
him, and he fell on the ground, foaming at the mouth. We threw
stones at him while his companion wiped the froth from his lips
and put his own mantle around him. In another instant the youth
seemed to be fully conscious of what was happening. He jumped
up and defended himself and his comrade. But there were so
many of us that soon the two strangers had to give up. We surrounded them and made them drop their weapons, and finally
they yielded in sheer weariness. Then we captured them and took
them to Thoas, our king. He had barely glanced at them when he
ordered us to take them to you. O priestess, pray for many more
such splendid victims, for if you sacrifice these men of Argos,
Greece will atone for all the pain you were forced to suffer, and
you will be avenged for their attempt to kill you as an offering
for Artemis at Aulis."

The herdsman had ended and awaited the commands of the
priestess. She told him to bring her the strangers, but when she
was alone, she said to herself: "I have always felt pity for my
countrymen and wept whenever Argives fell into my hands. But
now that a dream has given me the certainty that Orestes, my
beloved brother, no longer sees the light of day, now all Achaeans
who approach this coast shall find me merciless. For the unhappy

are always hostile to the happy. The Argives dragged me like a lamb to the altar where my own father was willing to see me slaughtered! Never shall I forget my terror! If Zeus drove Menelaus, who urged that I be sacrificed, and Helen, who caused the siege of Troy, to these shores, I should rejoice, and—"

But here she was interrupted by the approach of the captives. "Loosen their hands," she commanded. "The consecration they are to receive demands that they be free of all bonds. And now go into the temple and make the necessary preparations." Then she turned to the strangers and asked: "Who is your father, your mother, your sister, if you have a sister, who is to be robbed of such strong, fine brothers? Where have you come from? You must have a long journey behind you, but now you must prepare for one still longer, for you are going to the underworld."

Orestes answered her: "Whoever you may be, do not speak to us in so compassionate a voice. It is not fitting for the executioner to comfort his victim before he strikes him dead. If death is inevitable, then lament is useless. No tears, either from you or from us! Let Fate take her course."

"Which of you two is Pylades? Tell me that first of all," said the priestess.

"This is he," said Orestes, pointing to his friend.

"Are you brothers?"

"Through friendship, not by birth," Orestes replied.

"And what is your name?"

"Call me an exile," he answered. "Better I die nameless, for then no one can taunt me."

The priestess was vexed by his defiance and pressed him at least to tell her what city he came from. When she heard the name of "Argos," she trembled and exclaimed excitedly: "By Zeus, do you really come from there?"

"Yes," said Orestes. "I come from Mycenae, where Fortune once favored my house."

"If you come from Argos, stranger," cried Iphigenia with growing suspense, "you must have news of Troy. Is it true that the city lies in ruins? Did Helen return to her husband?"

"It is as you say."

"And how is the commander of all Argives—I think his name is Agamemnon, son of Atreus?"

Orestes shuddered at her question. He turned his head from her and said: "I do not wish to speak of him, O priestess." But she begged him in such pleading words that he gave in to her. "He is dead," he said in a low voice. "His own wife killed him."

The priestess of Artemis uttered a cry of distress. But she collected herself and continued questioning the stranger. "And is that woman still living?"

"She is no longer alive," was his reply. "Her own son killed her. He took on himself the burden of avenging his father, but he is suffering for it."

"Is any other child of Agamemnon's alive?"

"Two daughters, Electra and Chrysothemis."

"And what is known of his eldest daughter, of the one who was sacrificed?"

"That a hind died in her stead. She herself vanished. She must be dead long since."

"And is the son of murdered Agamemnon still alive?" the girl asked hesitatingly.

"Yes," said Orestes. "He is an exile, and wanders without rest through all of Greece."

"Away with you, beguiling dream!" Iphigenia said to herself. Then she bade the servants withdraw, and when she was alone with the two youths, turned to Orestes and said in a low voice: "Listen to what will be of profit to you and me. I shall save your life if you agree to take to Mycenae, which is both your home and mine, a letter I shall write to my people."

"I do not care to save myself unless my friend is also saved," said Orestes. "He did not leave me in my misery, and I shall never leave him!"

"How noble and brotherly a friend!" Iphigenia exclaimed. "If only my brother were like you! For you must know that I too have a brother, only that he is very far away. But I have not the power to save both of you. The king would never permit it. So let your friend Pylades return to Greece in your stead."

"Who will sacrifice me to Artemis?" asked Orestes.

"I myself. Such is the command of the goddess," Iphigenia replied.

"Will you, a frail girl, slay men?"

"No. My office is to sprinkle your hair with sacred water. The temple servants take care of the rest. Your body will be burned in a rocky gorge."

"Oh, that my sister could bury my bones!" sighed Orestes.

"That cannot be, since she lives in far away Argos," answered the girl, much moved. "But I myself shall quench the glowing ashes of your pyre and pour on it offerings of oil and honey. I shall adorn your grave as though I were, indeed, your sister." With that she left them to write the letter.

When the two friends were alone—for the men who guarded them stood at some distance—Pylades could no longer restrain himself. "No!" he cried. "I cannot live if you die! Do not ask me to consent to so disgraceful a proposal. I shall follow you to death, just as I followed you across the sea. Phocis and Argos would brand me a coward. All the world would say that I betrayed and killed you to inherit your realm—and all the more so because I am to become your brother-in-law and courted Electra without asking a dowry. But aside from all this, I cannot live without you. If you die, I die!"

Orestes tried to dissuade him from his purpose, and they were still disputing when Iphigenia returned with the letter in her hand. First she made Pylades swear to deliver it and in return she gave her word to save him. Then she decided to tell him the contents, in case the letter were lost in the course of the journey, in an accident perhaps, and the bearer himself survive. "Tell Orestes, son of Agamemnon," she said, "that Iphigenia was taken from the altar in Aulis by Artemis, that she is alive, and—"

"Where is she?" broke in Orestes. "Can the dead awaken?"

"She stands before you," said the priestess, "but do not interrupt me." Then she continued her message: "My dear brother shall take me home to Argos, away from these barbarians, from this altar where I am forced to murder strangers. If he does not do this, a curse shall rest on him and his house."

The friends were speechless with amazement. At last Pylades took the letter, turned to his friend, and gave it to him with the words: "I shall immediately perform what I have sworn to carry out. Here, Orestes, take the letter your sister Iphigenia sends you!" Orestes let it fall to the ground and locked his sister in his arms. She pushed him from her, unable to believe the truth, until he told her incidents from the history of her house which only one of the family could know. Then she cried out joyously: "So you are here and mine, my only brother! How young you were when I left you in the arms of your nurse, how carefree and happy! Yes, as happy as we are now that we have found each other again!"

But Orestes' brow had clouded. He had remembered the danger threatening him and his friend. "We are happy now," he said. "But for how long? Are we not faced with death?"

And now Iphigenia too was seized with terror. "What can I do to save you?" she asked. "How can I send you back to Argos? How rescue you and your friend from falling as victims at the altar? Oh, that the gods would give me counsel! But quickly now—before Thoas becomes impatient at the delay in sacrificing you. Tell me, tell me everything that has happened at home."

Orestes hastily told her the tale of horror, lightened by only one piece of good news, the betrothal of Electra to Pylades. While she listened, the girl cast about for some possibility of saving her brother. When he had ended she had found a way. "I have thought of a plan," she said. "The madness which attacked you when you were taken captive on the shore shall serve me as a pretext. I shall tell the king what is entirely true: that you have come from Argos, where you murdered your mother; that you are unclean because you have not atoned, and are therefore not acceptable to the goddess; that you must first be purified in the sea to wash the blood of murder from your body. And I shall tell him that because you touched the image of the goddess with supplicating hands, it too is unclean and must be cleansed in the waves. Since I, the priestess, am the only one allowed to handle the image, I myself shall carry it down to the shore, and you shall both accompany me, for I shall say that Pylades is an accomplice in your crime. I must convince the king of all this with crafty words, for he is too shrewd to be deceived easily. And once we reach the shore and board your ship, you and your men must do the rest."

They had been talking in the court of the temple, far from the servants and guards. Now the captives were again handed over to the attendants, and Iphigenia conducted them into the interior of the temple. Shortly afterwards, Thoas, the king of the Tauri, arrived with his retinue and asked for the priestess, for he could not understand why the bodies of the strangers were not already burning at the altar of the goddess. As he reached the doors of the temple, Iphigenia crossed the threshold with the image of Artemis in her arms. "What are you doing, daughter of Agamemnon?" the king exclaimed in surprise. "Why have you taken the image from its sacred pedestal? Why are you carrying it away?"

"A terrible thing has happened, O king," said the priestess, her face drawn with emotion. "The victims who were captured near the shore are not pure. When they approached the goddess to clasp her in supplication, the image turned of itself and lowered its lids. For these two are guilty of an awful crime." And now she told her tale which in all essentials was the truth, and asked the king's permission to purify the image of the taint the strangers had put on it, and to cleanse the victims themselves, that they might be fit for sacrifice. To make her story seem more plausible, she had the strangers fettered again and their faces veiled from the rays of the sun, as it was customary to do with those who were unclean. She also begged the king to leave with her the slaves he had brought in his retinue, for greater security. He—so she said with shrewd forethought—was to send a messenger to the town, bidding the citizens remain within the walls until the purification was over, so that they might not be exposed to the contaminating presence of guilty men. The king himself was to stay in the temple during her absence and see to it that the entire building was filled with cleansing fumes, so that on her return she might find it ready for the sacred rites. The moment the strangers issued from the gates of the temple, the ruler was to hide his face in his robe, lest the mere sight of them should stain him. "And if I stay down at the shore for a long time, O king," she said, "do not grow impatient. Remember that it is a very great and terrible crime which must be washed from the victims."

The king consented to everything. He veiled his face when Orestes and Pylades were led out of the temple, and soon Iphigenia, together with the captives and some of the king's slaves, was on her way to the sea. Thoas entered the temple and had it purified, as the priestess had demanded.

Several hours passed, and suddenly a messenger came running

from the direction of the shore. He was panting. "Faithless women!" he gasped to himself, as he knocked at the closed gates. "Ho there, inside!" he cried. "Open! And tell the king that I am the bearer of bad news!"

The gates swung open, and Thoas himself stood on the threshold. "Who dares disturb the peace of these halls with such clamor?" he asked with a frown.

"Hear, O king, what I have to tell you," the man replied. "The priestess of this temple, that Argive woman, has fled with the captives, and they have stolen the image of the revered patron goddess of our country! Her long tale of needed purification was nothing but lies!"

"What is this you say!" cried the king who could not believe his ears. "What evil spirit possessed this woman? Who are the men with whom she fled?"

"She has fled with her brother Orestes," said the messenger. "With the very man whom she pretended to purify as a victim. Listen to the whole story, and then find a way to pursue the fugitives, for they have a long distance to go and are still within reach of your revenge! When we came to the shore, Iphigenia motioned us to halt, for we were not to stand too close to the sacred rites. She herself loosed the bonds of the strangers and bade them precede her. This in itself seemed suspicious to us, but we thought we had to obey the commands of your priestess, O king! And then it seemed that the rites of purification were really under way, for Iphigenia chanted magic spells and prayed in solemn tones and with curious words. We lay on the sand and waited. But all at once it occurred to us that the captives, who were no longer shackled, might have killed the unarmed priestess and escaped. So we jumped up and rounded the wall of rocks which had hidden Iphigenia and the victims from our sight. And then we saw an Argive ship with fifty rowers sitting at the oars! On the shore, not far from the stern, stood the strangers, no longer captive! Some of the crew weighed anchor, others coiled the ropes, and still others were letting down ladders for the two youths. We no longer hesitated. We saw through the whole web of lies and seized the woman who was still on the shore. But Orestes, loudly proclaiming his identity and purpose, defended his sister with Pylades. We could not succeed in dragging her off. Since neither we nor the strangers were armed, we fought with our fists. But in the end we were forced to retreat, for the men in the ship were launching arrows at us. At the same instant, a huge wave drove the ship still nearer the shore, and it was all but shattered. At that Orestes took the priestess in his arms—she still carrying the image—waded through the water, and quickly climbed the ladder into the ship. There he laid his sister with her sacred burden down on the deck. Pylades came close after, and when all were safely aboard, the crew broke into triumphant cries and began to row swiftly away. While the ship was crossing the bay, it glided gently through the water, but as soon as it reached the open sea, a gust of wind drove it back to the shore, in spite of the straining of the oarsmen. Then Agamemnon's daughter rose and pleaded aloud: 'O Artemis, daughter of Leto, you yourself, through the oracle of Apollo, your brother, demanded to return to Greece. Take me there with you, and forgive your priestess the bold deceit I practiced against the ruler of this country whom I was forced to obey for so many years. You too have a brother whom you love! Then be gracious to the mortal brother and sister who love each other!' And when she had ended, all the crew at her command stopped rowing and sang the song of supplication which they call a paean. But the ship continued to drive toward the shore, and I hurried to tell you what had happened. If you send men to the coast at once, you will recapture them. For unless the angry sea grows quickly calm, the strangers cannot escape. Poseidon is angry. He remembers the destruction of Troy, his favorite city. He is the sworn enemy of all Argives and of the line of Atreus in particular. Unless I am very much mistaken, he will put Agamemnon's children in your power this very day."

Thoas had waited impatiently for the messenger to finish. The moment he had ended, the king commanded all his people to mount horses and ride to the coast. They were to take the ship as soon as the waves hurled it ashore, and with the help of offended Artemis capture the fugitives. They were to sink the ship with all the crew, but the two strangers and the priestess were to be thrown into the sea from a tall cliff, or impaled alive on a pole.

The cavalcade was already storming toward the shore when a dazzling apparition halted them. Against his will, the king reined in his horse. Pallas Athene, encircled with shining clouds, floated between heaven and earth in all her majesty and splendor and her voice sounded like thunder in the ears of the Tauri. "Where are you going, King Thoas?" she cried. "Where are you going in such breathless haste? Mark the words of a goddess. Stop your people in their hot pursuit, and let my wards leave your country unmolested. Apollo's oracle proclaimed the will of Fate. It is the Fates who brought Orestes to these shores, so that he might be cured of his madness and take his sister back to her native land, and with her the image of Artemis who also wishes to dwell in my beloved city. For my sake, Poseidon will quiet the sea and carry the ship home. Orestes will build a new and splendid temple for the goddess in Athens, and Iphigenia will continue to be the priestess of Artemis. The daughter of Agamemnon shall die and be buried in her own country. And you, Thoas, king of the Tauri, shall not begrudge her this happiness. You shall give up your anger."

King Thoas reverenced the gods devoutly. He threw himself on the ground before the vision and said: "O Pallas Athene, base is he who hears the will of the gods and does not obey, or even tries to resist. Your wards shall take the image of Artemis where they will and set it up in its new shrine. I lower my lance at the command of the gods." Then he turned to his men. "Back to our city!" he ordered.

And what Athene had predicted came true. Tauric Artemis was lodged in a temple in Athens, and Iphigenia continued to be her priestess. In Mycenae, Orestes ascended the throne of his fathers. He married Hermione, the only daughter of Menelaus and Helen. She had been betrothed to Neoptolemus, son of Achilles, but Orestes slew him and was made king of Sparta. Even before that he had taken over the rule of Argos, so that he now had a greater realm than his father had ever ruled. Electra became the wife of Pylades and shared the throne of Phocis with him. Chrysothemis died unwed. Orestes himself grew very old, but in his ninetieth year the curse of the Tantalides struck once more: a serpent bit him in the heel, and he died of its venom.

ODYSSEUS

TELEMACHUS AND THE SUITORS

THE war for Troy was over, and all the Argive heroes who had
escaped death on the battlefield and survived the storms on
the homeward journey had reached their native shores. Only
Odysseus, son of Laertes, the king of Ithaca, had not returned.
A strange fate had overtaken him. After many wanderings he
had landed on a lonely island covered with wild forests. It was
the island of Ogygia, and there the nymph Calypso held him
captive in her grotto, because she wished to have him for her husband. But he was faithful to Penelope, the wife he had left behind
in Ithaca, and at long last the gods on Olympus pitied his sad
lot—all but Poseidon, the sea-god. He was the ancient enemy of
Odysseus, and while he did not dare destroy him, he put every
possible obstacle in his way and drove him wandering over the
sea. It was he who had cast him ashore on the island.

But now, while Poseidon was feasting with the Ethiopians,

the immortals resolved that Odysseus was to be released by Calypso. At Athene's request, Hermes, the messenger of the gods, went to the lovely nymph to announce the decision of Zeus. Athene herself, meanwhile, bound to her feet the golden sandals which carried her over lands and seas, took in her hand the sharp-pointed lance with which she had overcome many a hero in battle, and descended from the rocky peak of Olympus. She flew to the island of Ithaca, on the west coast of Greece. There she assumed the form of Mentes, leader of the Taphians, and went to the palace of Odysseus.

Here there was sad confusion. Beautiful Penelope, daughter of Icarius, and her young son Telemachus had not been able to remain masters in their own house. When Odysseus failed to return, long after the news of the fall of Troy and the homecoming of other heroes had reached Ithaca, the rumor of his death spread and was given more and more credence. Penelope was looked on as a young and wealthy widow, and she attracted many suitors. Twelve rich lords came from Ithaca alone, twenty-four from the neighboring island of Same, twenty from Zacynthus, and from Dulichium fifty-two. Besides these, there were among their retinue a singer and a herald, two expert cooks, and a large following of slaves. All the lords courted Penelope and used up the stores of absent Odysseus. For over three years they had eaten, drunk, made merry, and lived on the fat of his land.

When Athene arrived in the shape of Mentes, she found the suitors playing draughts in front of the palace. They were seated on the hides of cattle they had taken from the stalls of Odysseus. Heralds and servants went among them, mixing wine and water in bowls, cutting and serving meat, and cleaning the tables with sponges. Telemachus, the son of the house, sat among the suitors with a sad heart and thought of his father. He longed for him to come and drive out the throng of arrogant wastrels. When he saw Mentes, he ran forward to greet him, clasped his right hand in welcome, and asked him into the house. They entered the great hall, and Telemachus took the stranger's lance and leaned it against the spear rack. Then he led his guest to a chair covered with soft tapestry and put a footstool under his feet. He himself sat beside him. A woman slave brought water in a golden pitcher for the stranger to wash his hands. Then meat and bread were served and the cups filled with wine. Soon after, the suitors joined them and began to eat and drink with much gusto. Then they demanded music. The herald handed Phemius, the singer, his graceful lyre, and he plucked the strings and chanted his tale.

While the suitors listened, Telemachus turned his head to his guest and whispered in his ear: "My friend, I shall unburden my heart to you, if I may. Do you see how these men are wasting the fortune of my father, whose bones are perhaps at the bottom of the sea, or rotting on an alien shore? I fear he will never return to punish them. But tell me where you come from, who you are, and the names of your parents. Perhaps you were a friend of my father's?"

"I am Mentes, son of Anchialus," answered Athene. "I rule the island of Taphos and have come here by ship to barter iron for copper in Temese. Ask Laertes, your grandfather, who, they say, is eating out his heart in sorrow far from the city, and he will tell you that from time immemorial our houses have been bound by the ties of hospitality. I came because I thought your father had returned. I see he has not, but I am sure he is living! Perhaps he has been shipwrecked on some savage island and is held captive there. But my spirit, which can look into the future, tells me that it will not be for long. He will soon be released and return to his country. You are your father's true son, dear Telemachus! How you resemble him in your features, above all your eyes! I knew your father well before he left for Troy. Since then I have not seen him. But tell me, what are all these people doing in your house? Are you celebrating a wedding, or is this some other festive banquet?"

Telemachus answered him with a sigh: "All these men you see are courting my mother and eating us out of house and home. We may have been prosperous once, but now everything is changed. My mother cannot bear the thought of marrying again, but while she refuses her consent, she cannot get rid of her suitors, who are consuming our substance and will soon bring me to ruin."

The goddess replied in sorrowful but angry tones: "How much you need your father! Let me counsel you how to drive this swarm of wooers from your palace. Speak to them tomorrow and bid them return to their homes. Tell your mother that if she wishes to marry again, she should go to her father. In his house, the

wedding can be arranged, and there they can see to her dowry.
You yourself, however, make ready your best ship. Take twenty
oarsmen and set out to look for your father. First go to Pylos
and question Nestor. If he cannot tell you anything, go on to
Sparta, to Menelaus, for he was the last of the Argives to reach
home. If you learn from him that your father is alive, then have
patience one more year. But if you hear that he has died, return
home, make offerings to the dead, and heap him a burial mound.
If the suitors are still in your house, you must kill them openly
or by guile. For you are no longer a boy who needs a guardian.
Have you not heard of the glory Orestes won by slaying Aegisthus, who had murdered his father? You are tall and strong.
Conduct yourself accordingly and see to it that later generations
have nothing but praise for you!" Telemachus thanked his guest
for his fatherly counsel and wanted to give him a gift in parting.
But Mentes promised to come again and take it with him on his
way back to his own country. Then he, who was Athene, vanished.
Like a bird she flew upward, and Telemachus trembled, for now
he guessed that he had been talking to an immortal.

In the meantime, Phemius had been singing of the perilous
homeward journey of the Achaeans. Lonely Penelope sat in her
chamber, and the song drifted up to her. She veiled herself and
with two of her tirewomen descended to the great hall. There she
went up to the singer and said: "You know many joyful tales,
Phemius. Gladden the hearts of my guests with them, but do not
sing of matters which torment me and wring my soul. For even
without your song, I do nothing but think of the man whose fame
has travelled over all of Greece, and who has not come home."

But Telemachus spoke kindly to his mother. "Do not reprove
the singer for giving voice to what kindles his soul at the moment," he said. "Let him sing of the Danai. Odysseus is not the
only one who has not returned. Think how many others have
perished. And you, dear mother, go back to your chamber and
direct your women in spinning and weaving. Giving orders is the
business of men and above all mine, for I am master in this
house."

Penelope was surprised to hear such determined words from
her son who seemed suddenly to have ripened into manhood. She
returned to her room and mourned her husband in solitude. When

she was gone, Telemachus joined the suitors, who were reeling and shouting over their cups, and called aloud: "Enjoy the feast, but do not make so much noise! It takes silence to delight in song. Tomorrow I shall call an assembly of the Achaeans, and then I shall demand that each of you return to his own home before you have entirely used up my father's property."

The suitors scowled and bit their lips at the resolute speech of the young man. But they stubbornly rejected his suggestion to woo Penelope at the house of her father, Icarius. After much wrangling and jeering they retired to their couches, and Telemachus too went to rest.

The next morning he rose early, slung his sword over his shoulder, left his room, and ordered the herald to summon the citizens of Ithaca to a council. The suitors were also asked to attend. When the people had gathered, the young prince appeared before them, lance in hand. Pallas Athene had made him taller and so handsome that all those who saw him were struck with wonder. Even old men reverently made way for him as he strode toward the chair of his father Odysseus. The first to speak was Aegyptius, who was bent with age and rich in experience. His eldest son Antiphus had gone to Troy with Odysseus and been killed on the journey home. His second son Eurynomus was one of the suitors, and his two youngest sons still lived in their father's house. Aegyptius faced the assembly and said: "We have not come together since Odysseus went away. Who is it that has summoned us now? Is it an old or a young man, and why has he called us? Has he heard of foes approaching? Has he something to propose for the welfare of our country? In any case, I believe he has honest intentions, and I ask Zeus to bless his purpose."

Telemachus rejoiced in the happy omen he saw in these words. He rose and took the scepter which Peisenor, the herald, handed him. Then he turned to Aegyptius and said: "Noble old man, he who has summoned you stands before you. It is I who am in trouble and need. First, I lost my father who was once your king, and now my heritage is being wasted so that soon nothing will be left. My mother Penelope is pressed by unwelcome suitors. They refuse to woo her in her father's house, as I have proposed to them. Day after day they slaughter our cattle and sheep and drink the wine sealed in our jars. What can I do against so many? You suitors, do you not realize you are wrong? Do you not fear these citizens and the vengeance of the gods? Did my father ever offend you? Have I myself ever done you harm which would entitle you to take what is mine in recompense? No, you have caused me sorrow through no fault of my own."

So said Telemachus, and bursting into angry tears he threw his scepter on the ground. The suitors had listened in silence, and no one except Antinous, son of Eupeithes, ventured to reply. He, however, rose and cried: "Defiant boy, how dare you malign us! It is not we who are to blame, but your mother! She has been deceiving us! Three years have passed; the fourth is almost up, and still she scoffs at our wooing. She shows favor now to this one and now to that, but her true thoughts are quite different. We have discovered her ruse! She began weaving a large web and announced to us, her assembled suitors: 'The wedding shall wait until I have finished weaving the shroud for my husband's old father, Laertes, so that no Achaean woman can ever say his body was not clad as befits a king.' This devout pretext of hers won us over. We consented to wait. She really sat at her loom all day and worked at her weaving, but at night, by torch-light, she secretly unravelled everything she had woven by day. In this way she put us off for three years. But finally one of her handmaids, who spied on her, told us the truth, and then we ourselves surprised her as she was undoing her work, and forced her to finish the shroud. So our answer to you, Telemachus, is this: send your mother to her father, if you wish. But command her to marry the man her father and she herself may choose. If she prefers to go on deceiving us and putting us off, we shall go on living on your stores. In any case, we shall not return to our homes until your mother has taken a husband."

Then Telemachus replied: "I cannot compel my mother, who bore and reared me, to leave my home against her will, Antinous. Neither Icarius, her father, nor the gods would approve such a course. If you have any sense of fairness at all, provide your banquets from your own stores. Let each take his turn in feasting the rest. If it pleases you better to devour the means of one man without attempting to pay back what you have taken—do so. But I shall implore Zeus and the immortals to help me deal out to you your just deserts."

While Telemachus was speaking, Zeus sent him a sign. Two eagles soared down from the mountains on widespread pinions. First they flew side by side, and then they circled each other. When they were directly above the assemblage, they looked down threateningly and began to tear at each other's throats and heads. Then they swept upward to the right and winged over Ithaca. Halitherses, the aged soothsayer versed in reading the future from the flight of birds, interpreted this as an omen of destruction for the suitors. He claimed Odysseus was alive and near, and that his coming would spell death for them. But Eurymachus, son of Polybus, scoffed at the old man and said: "Go home and tell your own children what fate is in store for them, foolish old man! You will not trouble us with your prophecies. Many birds fly around in the beams of the sun, and they do not all foretell something. There is nothing more certain than that Odysseus has died far from his native land." And the other suitors applauded his words and insisted that Penelope should go to her father's house and choose a husband.

Telemachus made no further effort to persuade them otherwise. He asked the people of Ithaca for a swift ship with twenty oarsmen, for he wanted to set out for Pylos and Sparta to seek news of his father. If he were alive, Telemachus would wait another year. If he were dead, he would urge his mother to marry again. And now Mentor, the friend of Odysseus, to whom he had entrusted the welfare of his house while he was fighting for Troy, rose in council. Angrily he turned toward the suitors and said: "It would be no wonder if a king lost his sense of justice and treated his people with cruelty! They do not deserve any better! Who among you remembers Odysseus, who was always kind to you and ruled over you like a father? Are you not letting these suitors squander his substance unhindered? They are hardly to blame, for they are encouraged by rumors that Odysseus will never return. But the people of Ithaca are to blame because they are silent and do not even attempt to curb the suitors with a single word, although they are in the majority."

At that, Leocritus, one of the boldest of Penelope's wooers, jeered at Mentor and said: "Just let Odysseus come if he likes, old mischief-maker! We shall see if he can get the better of us! And believe me, Penelope herself, much as she yearns for him, would be least pleased if he were actually to appear. Ill luck would soon overtake him! And now let us leave this meeting. Mentor and Halitherses will do to speed Telemachus on his journey. But what do you wager that he will be here for weeks to come, and wait safe in Ithaca for news of his father? I am sure he will never start for Pylos!"

The assembly broke up speedily and with a great deal of noise. The people of Ithaca returned to their houses and occupations, and the suitors sat at their ease at the board of Odysseus.

TELEMACHUS AND NESTOR

Telemachus went down to the shore. He washed his hands in the surf of the sea and called to the god who had come to him in human shape the day before. At his prayer, Pallas Athene approached him in the shape of Mentor, his father's friend, and said: "If the spirit of your father, wise Odysseus, has not wholly forsaken you, stir up your soul to action and carry out your decision. I, your father's friend, will see to it that a swift ship is prepared for you, and I will accompany you myself." Telemachus, who thought he had heard the counsel of Mentor, hastened toward the palace, firmly resolved to set out on his journey. On the way he met Antinous, who caught at his hand laughingly and said: "Why so rebellious and gloomy? Come, eat and drink with us as you did before. Let the citizens see to your ship and its crew, and when everything is ready, sail to Pylos if you like."

But Telemachus replied: "No, Antinous. I can no longer sit at the same board with you. I am not a boy any more. From now on, whether I go or stay, you shall deal with a full-grown man. But I will go, and nothing shall keep me!" And as he spoke, he withdrew his hand and hurried to his father's storerooms where gold and bronze were kept, where costly tunics filled the chests and flasks of fragrant oil and big jars of old wine were set up around the walls. All these things were under the care of Euryclea, an old serving-woman. When he had entered and closed and bolted the doors behind him, he said to her: "Quick, fill twelve two-handled jars with the choicest wine and seal them well. Then pour twenty measures of barley-meal into well-sewn skins, and put everything together. Before nightfall, but after my mother has gone to her sleeping-chamber, I shall fetch everything. Do not tell her that I have gone to look for my father until twelve days have passed, unless she asks for me before that." Euryclea wept at his going, but promised to do as he had asked.

Meantime Athene had assumed the shape of Telemachus, enlisted men for the journey, and borrowed a ship from Noemon, a wealthy citizen of Ithaca. Then she dazed the minds of the suitors. The cups dropped from their hands, and they fell into a deep sleep. When she had done this, she again appeared as Mentor, joined Telemachus, and urged him not to put off his departure. Swiftly they went to the shore where they found the ship and the crew. They had ample provisions stored in the hold and then went aboard. When the waves were already lapping the keel and the wind swelled the sails, they poured a libation to the gods and all night sped over the sea with a favorable breeze.

At sunrise, Pylos, Nestor's city, lay before their eyes. The people had come down to the shore in nine groups, each of which sacrificed nine black bulls to the god of the sea. They burned the offering to Poseidon and prepared to feast on the meat. When the men from Ithaca landed, Athene in the guise of Mentor led

Telemachus into the center of the ring where Nestor sat with his sons.

Servants went back and forth preparing the board, while others turned the meat on the roasting-spits. As soon as the Pylians saw strangers come ashore they thronged to meet them, clasped their hands in greeting, and pressed Telemachus to sit beside their king. Peisistratus, Nestor's son, who was as young as Telemachus, greeted him and Mentor with the warmest hospitality and bade them take a seat of honor on the thick, soft fleeces, between Nestor and his son Thrasymedes. Then he set before them the choicest pieces of meat, filled two golden cups with wine, drank to them, and said to the old man who was Athene: "Pour a libation to Poseidon, O stranger, and tell your younger friend to do likewise. For mortals are in need of the favor of the gods." Athene took the cup, begged Poseidon to bless Nestor, his sons, and his people, and prayed that he might help Telemachus accomplish what he had set out to do. Then she poured the wine out on the sand and told the son of Odysseus to do the same.

When they had eaten and drunk, old Nestor graciously asked the strangers where they had come from and what was the object of their journey. Telemachus replied to both questions, and when he began to speak of his father he sighed and said: "Up to now our attempts to find out what has happened to him have been in vain. We do not know whether he died on the mainland, at the hands of foes, or drowned in an angry sea. And so I beg you to tell me what you know. Perhaps you yourself witnessed his death, or heard of it from travellers. Do not spare us from a sense of pity, but tell us the truth."

"Now that you speak of those mournful years, I shall tell you the whole tale," answered Nestor. And—after the fashion of old men—he began very far back. First he named the heroes who had died near the walls of Troy. He told of the quarrel between the two sons of Atreus, and finally of his own journey home. Of Odysseus he knew just as little as Telemachus himself. But he related the story of Agamemnon's death in Mycenae, and the vengeance of Orestes. In the end he advised Telemachus to go to Sparta, to King Menelaus, who had only just returned from a distant land on whose coast a storm had wrecked his ship. Since he had been on his homeward journey longer than any other Argive hero, he was the most likely to have heard something, somewhere, of the fate of Odysseus.

Athene approved Nestor's counsel and said: "While we have been talking with one another, darkness has fallen. Permit my young friend to accompany you to your palace and sleep there. I myself will see to the ship and spend the night aboard. In the morning I shall sail to the Cauconians, where I have a debt to collect. But I beg you to send my friend Telemachus to Sparta with one of your sons and to give him your swiftest horses."

So saying, Athene suddenly changed into a sea-eagle and soared into the sky. All gazed after her in astonishment and Nestor took Telemachus by the hand and said: "You have no cause to be sad, for, young as you are, gods protect you and walk at your side. Your companion was Athene, the daughter of Zeus, who also favored your father above all the other Achaeans." Then the old man prayed to the goddess, promised to sacrifice a yearling heifer to her the next morning, and, with his sons and the husbands of his daughters, conducted his guest to the palace in Pylos. Here a last libation was poured and the cup passed from one to the other. Then they lay down to sleep. For Telemachus, a couch had been prepared in the great hall, and next to him lay Peisistratus, Nestor's brave son.

At the first pale light of dawn Nestor rose, went to the threshold, and seated himself on one of the polished stones which were placed on either side of the door. His own father, Neleus, had liked to sit there. Presently his six sons joined him, and the last to come, Peisistratus, brought with him the guest from Ithaca, lordly Telemachus. And now the heifer, which Nestor had pledged the goddess, was led to the palace. Laerces, the goldsmith, was summoned to gild her horns. Slaves fetched wood and fresh water and prepared the sumptuous board. Up from the shore came the comrades of Telemachus. Two of Nestor's sons held the cow by her gilded horns. Another brought a basin and barley for the offering, a fourth the ax to strike down the victim, a fifth held the bowl to catch its blood. When the animal had been felled with the ax, Peisistratus, the sixth son, cut its throat, while Nestor's wife and daughters prayed to the gods. The best pieces were burned as an offering to Athene, and on them dark wine was poured. The rest was put on spits and roasted.

Meanwhile Telemachus refreshed himself in a warm bath, and now appeared clad in a splendid tunic and a costly mantle. While all feasted, the best and fleetest horses were harnessed to take the guest to Sparta. A servant put wine and provisions into the chariot which Telemachus mounted. Up beside him sprang Peisistratus, and he took the reins and swung the goad. The horses flew along the road, and soon Pylos was left behind. All day long they drove, and the horses did not tire.

When the sun was about to set and all the roads grew dark, they came to the city of Pherae, where an Argive hero by the name of Diocles, son of Ortilochus, had his house. He received the two with warm hospitality and they spent the night with him. The following morning they drove on between fields of wheat and on the next evening came to the great city of Lacedaemon or Sparta, flanked on all sides by steep, jagged mountains.

TELEMACHUS IN SPARTA

King Menelaus was holding a feast in his palace in Sparta. Among the throng of his neighbors and relatives a singer was plucking the strings of his lyre. Tumblers kept the guests amused with their agile leaps and somersaults. Menelaus was celebrating the betrothal of two of his children, Hermione, Helen's daughter, who was to be the bride of Neoptolemus, son of Achilles, and Megapenthes, Menelaus' son by a slave woman, whom the king was giving in marriage to a well-born Spartan girl. In the midst of the joyful tumult, Telemachus and Peisistratus arrived and were announced to Menelaus by Eteoneus, one of his warriors, who asked whether the horses of the strangers were to be unharnessed, or whether, because of the great crowd of guests, the two young men should be sent to the house of another. "Eteoneus!" exclaimed Menelaus. "What foolish talk is this? You know how many times I have enjoyed the hospitality of others, and that I should never turn a stranger from my door for any reason whatsoever. Have their horses unyoked at once, and invite them in to the feast."

Eteoneus quickly left the hall with a number of servants. They unharnessed the sweating horses and walked them to the stable, where the manger had already been filled. The chariot was set against the white wall near the entrance. The guests were conducted to the palace, where a bath had been prepared to cleanse them of the dust of the journey. Then they were taken to King Menelaus, who bade them sit beside him at the board. Telemachus was astonished at the splendor of the hall and the abundance and richness of the fare set before them. "Look, Peisistratus," he whispered to his friend. "Look at all that flashing bronze, gold, silver, and ivory! What priceless treasure! Zeus' palace on Olympus cannot be more magnificent!"

Telemachus had lowered his voice, but Menelaus had caught the last few words. "No mortal can compete with Zeus," he said smilingly. "His palace and all he possesses is imperishable. But it is true that among mortals it might be difficult to find one who could vie with me in wealth. For what I have, I have collected by wanderings and hardships. It took me eight years to come home. I was in Cyprus, Phoenicia, Egypt, Ethiopia, and Libya. Now there is a country for you! The lambs are born with horns on their heads. The sheep bear young three times a year, and neither masters nor herdsmen ever lack meat or milk and cheese. But while I was collecting treasure in many lands, my brother in Mycenae was killed by the guile of his faithless wife, so that I cannot enjoy these possessions with a light heart. You must have heard all these things from your fathers—whoever they may be. Believe me, I should be satisfied with a third of what I own, if only the heroes who fell at Troy were still alive! And there is one, in particular, whom I mourn so bitterly that the thought of him makes food lose its savor and troubles my sleep. For no Argive had to suffer as greatly as Odysseus. I do not even know whether he is living or dead. Perhaps his people are mourning his death by now—his old father Laertes, Penelope, his faithful wife, and his son Telemachus, who was a small child when his father left for the war."

So spoke Menelaus, and he moved the heart of Telemachus so that the tears fell from under his lashes and he hid his eyes in his crimson robe. At that the king of Sparta knew that he must be the son of Odysseus.

While he was pondering this, Helen came from her fragrant chamber, and her beauty was like that of a goddess. A throng of lovely handmaids surrounded her. One placed a chair for her, another spread a fleecy rug beneath it, while a third brought her the silver basket she had once received from the queen of Thebes in Egypt. It was filled with spun yarn, and a spindle with violet wool lay on top. The queen seated herself in the chair, put her feet on a stool, and began to ask her husband about the strangers who had recently arrived. "Nowhere in the world have I seen any-one who looked so exactly like noble Odysseus as does this youth," she said softly to Menelaus, and he answered: "That is just how it seems to me! Hands and feet, the expression of the eyes, the way the hair grows—all resembles him! Besides, the young man wept a short time ago when I spoke of Odysseus."

Peisistratus had heard them talking and now said aloud: "You have guessed right, King Menelaus. This is Telemachus, the son of Odysseus. But he is too modest to tell you himself. Nestor, my father, sent us here together to see if Telemachus cannot find out what has become of his father."

"Indeed!" exclaimed Menelaus. "Then my guest is really the son of my dearest friend, of the man whom I should receive with the warmest hospitality if he were here on his way home, in his own person!" And as the king went on to speak of Odysseus with words of love and longing, all who heard him shed tears—Helen, Telemachus, Menelaus himself, and even the son of Nestor who was reminded of his own brother Antilochus, who had died in saving his father before the walls of Troy.

But after a time they remembered how useless and joyless a thing it is to grieve at a feast. They finished their meal, and after the servants had poured water for their hands, prepared to go to their couches. But Helen, the daughter of Zeus, who was versed in magic, cast into the last round of wine a herb which blots out the memory of pain and eases all sorrow. Anyone who drank of the draught so blended would shed no tear for a whole day, not even if his father or mother died, or if his son or brother were slain by a foe before his very eyes. So they all grew merry and talked far into the night. Crimson blankets were spread for the guests on the couches in the portico, but Menelaus and Helen slept in the inmost chamber of the palace.

The next morning the king asked his guests the purpose of their journey. When he heard about the suitors and the state of affairs in Ithaca, he said indignantly: "And those wretches plan to take the place of great Odysseus! Even as the lion returns to his lair, in which a hind has laid to sleep her young while he was away in a fertile valley, so Odysseus will come back and put an end to them—an end full of terror! Listen, and I will tell you what Proteus, the old man of the sea, told me in Egypt. Under my hands he took on one shape after another, but finally I got the better of him and forced him to reveal the destinies of the Argive heroes who were on their homeward journey. 'In my mind's eye,' said the god, 'I see Odysseus shedding tears of longing on a lonely island. The nymph Calypso is keeping him there against his will, and he has neither a ship nor oarsmen to take him home to his native land.' This is all I can tell you about your father. Stay with us eleven or twelve days, and when you go we shall give you precious gifts in parting."

Telemachus thanked him, but he did not consent to remain. Then Menelaus gave him a mixing-bowl of silver, with a rim of gold. It was of incomparable beauty, the work of Hephaestus himself. And an abundant morning meal of the meat of goats and sheep was prepared for the guests.

THE SUITORS' PLOT

While Telemachus was away in Pylos and Sparta, the suitors on the island of Ithaca, in the palace of Odysseus, continued their bouts and amused themselves with throwing the discus and the spear. One day, when Antinous and Eurymachus, the strongest and handsomest among them, were sitting a little apart from the rest, Noemon, son of Phronius, went up to them and said: "Do you know when Telemachus is expected back from Pylos? The ship on which he is making his journey is mine. I lent it to him, but now I need it myself to sail to Elis. I keep mares there for breeding, and I want to fetch a colt to tame it and train it."

The two suitors were surprised, for they did not even know that Telemachus had left. They thought he had retired to his property in the country, where he had herds of goats and swine. Now they jumped at the conclusion that he had forced Noemon to give him his ship. But the man denied this. "I gave it to him of my own free will," he said. "Who would refuse an act of friendship to one who is in trouble? That would have been unfeeling and harsh. Besides, he was accompanied by noble youths, and Mentor went with them as their guide—or was it perhaps a god in the guise of Mentor? For now that I come to think of it, I saw Mentor himself here only yesterday!" So saying, Noemon left the suitors and went back to his father's house.

But Antinous and Eurymachus were astonished and vexed at this unexpected news. They rose and joined the others who were seated in a circle, resting from their games. Seething with anger, Antinous cried to them with flashing eyes: "This Telemachus has gone on his quest. He has undertaken the journey we refused to believe in. May Zeus destroy him before he does us any harm! Give me a swift-sailing boat, friends, with twenty oarsmen, and I shall lie in wait for him in the strait between Ithaca and Same, so that his voyage of exploration may end in death." All acclaimed his plan and promised to get him everything he required. Then the suitors withdrew into the palace.

But there was one who spied on the council they held there. It was Medon, the herald, who hated the shameless suitors, even though he performed services for them. He had stood outside, but close enough to hear every word they said, and now he hurried to Penelope to report their plot to the queen. Her knees shook as she listened. For a long time she was speechless with distress. Her breath failed her, her eyes filled with tears. "Oh, why did my son have to go?" she burst out at last. "Is it not enough that his father has perished? Shall the name of our house be blotted from the earth?" And when Medon could give her no explanation, she sank weeping on the threshold of her chamber, and her handmaids lamented with her. "Why did he go without telling me?" cried Penelope. "I would have advised him against this journey! Call Dolius, my old servant, and tell him to go to Laertes and give him this sad news. Perhaps that old and experienced man will think of something we can do."

Then Euryclea, the old serving-woman, opened her lips and said: "I shall not hide it from you any longer, my queen, even if you kill me for keeping silence up to now. I knew of his going. I myself gave him everything he needed for his voyage. He made me swear not to tell before the twelfth day, unless you yourself noticed his absence. But now I advise you to bathe and adorn yourself, and to pray for protection for your son at the altar of Athene, daughter of Zeus."

Penelope did as the old woman had counselled. When she had pleaded for the safety of Telemachus in solemn prayers, she lay down to sleep. And in a dream Athene sent her Iphthime, her sister, the wife of the hero Eumelus. Iphthime comforted her and promised that her son would return. "Be of good courage," she said. "Your son has a guide whom all other men would envy him. Pallas Athene herself goes at his side. She will protect him against the suitors. It is she who has sent me to you in your dream." So said the vision and vanished through the bolted door. And Penelope woke from her sleep filled with courage and gladness.

Meantime the suitors had prepared their ship, and Antinous boarded it with twenty sturdy oarsmen. A rocky island with many jutting cliffs lay in the middle of the strait which separated Ithaca and Same. Toward this island the suitors steered and waited for Telemachus, hidden from sight in an inlet.

ODYSSEUS LEAVES CALYPSO AND IS SHIPWRECKED

Hermes, the messenger of Zeus, stepped from the upper air and swooped down upon the sea, skimmed the waves like a sea-gull, and sped to Ogygia, Calypso's realm, as the gods had commanded. He found the fair-tressed nymph at home. A fire was burning on her hearth, and the spicy fragrance of split cedar logs drifted over the island. Calypso was singing sweetly in her chamber, while she wove an exquisite web with a shuttle of gold. Her grotto stood in a grove green with alder, poplar, and cypress, and in the trees nested bright-colored birds and also hawks, owls, and crows. Vines clung to the vaulted rock, and clusters of ripening grapes glistened on the thick-leafed stalks. Four springs rose close to one another and ran a twisting course through meadows strewn with violets, parsley, and pungent herbs.

Hermes stood for a moment and marvelled at the beauty of the island. Then he entered the grotto. Calypso recognized him at once, for though they may live far apart, the gods know each other the moment they meet. Odysseus, however, was not there. He was sitting on the shore, as usual, gazing out over the vast ocean with tears in his yearning eyes.

When Calypso heard Hermes' message, she was silent for a time and then said mournfully: "O cruel and jealous gods! Do you not suffer an immortal to love a mortal and choose him for her husband? Do you begrudge me the companionship of a man whom I saved from death when he was flung ashore here, clinging to a plank? His ship had been struck by lightning, and all his friends had sunk to the bottom of the sea. I received the poor castaway with great kindness. I fed him and tended him and held out to him the boon of immortality and eternal youth. But since it is impossible to disobey the command of Zeus, let him go out to sea again. But do not expect me to send him away myself, for I have neither ships nor oarsmen. I can give him nothing but good advice on how to reach his native land unharmed."

Hermes was well-pleased with her answer and hastened back to Olympus. But Calypso went to the shore, came close to Odysseus, and said: "You need no longer sorrow here, your eyes clouded with tears. I shall let you go. Come, hew timbers for a raft. Fasten cross-planks upon it and build a raised deck. I myself shall provide you with water, wine, and food. I shall give you clothing and launch a favorable wind from the land. And may the gods send you safely home!"

Odysseus looked at the goddess suspiciously and said: "I fear you have something quite different in mind! Never shall I board a mere fragile raft until you swear to me with the oath of the gods that you are not plotting to do me harm."

But Calypso smiled, gently passed her hand over his hair, and replied: "Do not torture yourself with idle fears. The earth, the sky, and the Styx shall be witness to my oath that I do not wish you ill. I am only advising you to do what I myself should do were I in your position." With these words she turned to go, and Odysseus followed her. In the grotto she bade him a tender farewell.

The raft was soon built, and on the fifth day Odysseus embarked with the wind in his sails. He himself sat at the rudder and steered carefully and well. Sleep did not lower his lids. Steadfastly he gazed at the constellations and charted his course according to the signs Calypso had explained to him in parting. For seventeen days his way was smooth. On the eighteenth he sighted the mountains of Scheria. The land lay like a shield in the dull sea.

But now Poseidon, who was just returning from Ethiopia, saw him from the hills of the Solymi. He had not attended the last assembly of the gods, and now realized that they had used his absence to free Odysseus from Calypso's snares. "Well," he said to himself, "he shall have plenty of trouble!" And with that he summoned the clouds, churned up the sea with his trident, and called to the tempest to wrap land and sea in darkness. The winds howled around the raft, and Odysseus trembled and groaned aloud that he would rather have died at the hands of the Trojans. While he was lamenting, a wave broke over him and swept his raft into a whirlpool. The rudder slipped from his grasp. The mast, the yards, and the planks drove here and there across the angry waters. Odysseus was washed under, and his wet tunic dragged him down. At last he came up, spat out the brine he had swallowed, and swam toward the floating timbers. He reached the biggest of them and swung himself on it. And as he was cast hither and thither like a thistle in the autumn wind, Leucothea, a sea-goddess, saw him, and her heart filled with pity. Like a sea-fowl she rose up from the deep, perched on the raft, and said: "Listen to what I advise you, Odysseus. Take off your clothes, leave the plank to the storm, wind my veil about you, here under your breast, and then swim, and scorn the terrors of the sea." Odysseus took the veil, and the goddess vanished. Though he had small faith in her words, he obeyed her directions. Like a rider he sat astride his plank, drew off the tunic Calypso had given him, wound the veil around his body, and slipped into the wild waves.

Gravely Poseidon shook his head when he saw the bold swimmer. "Well then," he said, "wander through the sea until Zeus sends you aid. You shall still have more than enough to suffer." With these words the god left the sea and withdrew to his palace. For two days and nights Odysseus was driven through the ocean. At last he saw a wooded shore where the surf pounded against high cliffs. A wave carried him toward the coast before he had time to come to any decision. With both hands he gripped a jutting rock, but another wave cast him back into the sea. He began swimming again, and after a long and almost despairing effort found a small, shallow bay, where a river emptied into the sea. Here he prayed to the god of the river, who heard him and calmed the current and made it possible for him to reach the land. Breathless and exhausted Odysseus sank down. The water gushed from his nose and mouth, and, numb with fatigue, he lost consciousness. When he woke from his faint, he unwound Leucothea's veil and gratefully flung it back into the waves, that it might return to its owner. Then he threw himself down among the reeds and kissed the earth. He was naked and cold, and he shivered in the grey dawn. Searchingly he looked around and saw a wooded hill. This he climbed and bedded himself under two twisted olive trees, one wild and one tame, and so thickly leafed that neither wind, nor rain, nor the rays of the sun could penetrate the foliage. Here he heaped a bed of leaves, lay down, and covered himself with more leaves. Quickly he fell asleep and forgot the hardships he had suffered, nor did he think of the dangers still in store for him.

NAUSICAA

While Odysseus slept, Pallas Athene, his patron, busied herself in his behalf. She hastened to the island of Scheria, where the Phaeacians had built their city. They were governed by wise King Alcinous, and it was to his palace that the goddess turned her steps. Here she went to the chamber of Nausicaa, the king's young daughter, who in loveliness and charm was like the immortals. She was sleeping in a spacious room, and at the doors were two handmaids who kept watch over her. Athene approached the girl's couch as quietly as a breath of air. She assumed the shape of one of her playmates and said to her in her dream: "What an idler you are! Your mother will not be pleased with you! The cupboard is full of unwashed clothing. What would you do if you were betrothed tomorrow? You would lack clean garments for yourself and for those who escort the bride. So rise with the dawn to wash robes and tunics. I myself will help you, so that the work goes more quickly. You know you will not be single for long. Have not the noblest among your people been courting you these many months?"

The dream came to an end. Swiftly Nausicaa rose from her couch and went to her parents. Her mother was already seated at the hearth, spinning purple thread with her handmaids, but the king met his daughter at the door. He was about to go to a council of lords he had called for that morning. But the girl stopped him, took him by the hand, and said coaxingly: "Dear father, have them make ready a wagon, so that I can take my clothing down to the river to wash it. You too must have clean garments for the council, and your five sons, three of whom are still unwed, always want to look trim and fine for the feast and the dance. And it is I who must attend to all these things."

So said the girl, for she was too shy to speak of her own betrothal. Her father, however, guessed what was in her mind, and said with a smile: "Go, my child. You shall have a big wagon and mules to draw it. Tell the servants to harness them at once." Soon after, the girl and her handmaids loaded the wagon. Her mother gave her a goatskin of wine, bread, and other food for the day, and when Nausicaa had swung herself up on the wagon, she added a flask of oil so that she and her maidens could anoint their bodies after the bath. Nausicaa herself took the reins and the goad and guided the mules to the pleasant shore of the river. Here she and her companions unyoked them, let them pasture on the thick grass, and took the clothes to the washing-place, where they put them into trenches dug in the earth for this purpose, which filled with water from the river. Her handmaids washed the clothes and stamped on them to remove the stains. Then they rinsed them and spread them on the bank where the clean pebbles formed a shelf of stone. When all was done, the girls bathed, rubbed their bodies with fragrant oil, merrily ate the food they had brought with them, and waited for the sun to dry their washing.

They decided to while away the time with playing ball in the meadow. They laid aside their headgear, which was a hindrance to swift motion, and Nausicaa, who was taller and fairer than all the others, sang as they played. Finally Nausicaa threw the ball to one of her playmates, but Athene changed its direction so that it fell into the river, where the current was swift and strong. At this the girls gave little shrieks of distress, and Odysseus, who was lying nearby under the olive trees, awoke. He half rose and listened. "Where am I?" he asked himself. "Have I come to savage shores peopled with robbers and murderers? But those are surely the voices of girls, or perhaps nymphs of springs or hills. It may be that I am among friendly people, after all."

As he was pondering these things in his mind, he reached out with his sinewy right arm and broke a thick-leafed bough from the twisted tree to cover his nakedness. When he emerged from the thicket, holding it in front of him, he seemed like a shaggy lion among all those delicate girls. His hair was still matted with salt foam and seaweed. Taking him for a monster, the girls fled in all directions. Only the daughter of Alcinous remained. Athene had breathed courage into her heart, and bravely she faced the stranger. Odysseus did not know whether to clasp her knees or keep at a distance and ask her to give him clothing and point him the way to the houses of men. He decided that this latter course might be better, and so he called to her: "I do not know whether you are a goddess or a mortal, but whoever you may be,

I implore your protection. If you are a goddess, you must be Artemis, for you are lithe and beautiful as she. But if you are a mortal, then your parents and brothers are blessed indeed. Their hearts must dance with delight to have so lovely a daughter and sister. And how happy will he be who takes you home as his wife! But look graciously on me, for I have suffered almost unendurable hardships. Twenty-one days ago I left the island of Ogygia. A storm tossed me about on the ocean and finally cast me ashore here, where I know no one, and no one knows me. Have pity on me. Give me clothing; show me the city you live in, and may the gods give you what your heart desires—a husband, a home, and quiet happiness."

Nausicaa answered him: "Stranger, you do not look like a base or foolish man. You have turned to me and my country, and you shall lack neither clothing nor whatever else a suppliant has the right to expect. I shall take you to our city and tell you the name of our people. These shores and these fields are inhabited by the Phaeacians, and I am the daughter of Alcinous, their king." So she spoke and called to her maidens, assuring them that there was no cause to fear the stranger. But they hesitated, and each urged the other to go first. Finally they obeyed their mistress, and while Odysseus washed the salt water from his limbs in a hidden cove, they laid out for him a tunic and a mantle. After he had bathed and anointed himself, he put them on. And Athene made him more stately and handsome. She smoothed his hair, and it curled like the petals of hyacinths, and she shed radiance over his features. Tall and beautiful he left the shelter of the bushes and seated himself at some distance from the girls.

Nausicaa looked at him with wonder and said to her companions: "Surely, all the gods cannot be against this man. One at least must be for him, and has brought him to our coast. How insignificant he seemed when first we caught sight of him, but now he looks like an immortal. If only he were one of our people and Fate had chosen him to be my husband! But now quickly, girls, let us give him food and drink." And Odysseus satisfied the hunger and thirst he had suffered for so long.

Then the wagon was loaded with the clean garments, the mules were yoked once more, and Nausicaa again took the reins. But she asked the stranger to follow on foot in the company of her

handmaids. "Do this," she said to him with all kindness, "while we go through the fields and meadows. Soon you will see the city. It is circled by a high wall on all sides except where it faces the sea, and there it is protected by a wide harbor with a narrow entrance to it. You will find the market place and a splendid temple to Poseidon, beside which ropes, sailcloth, oars, and other wares for seamen are made and sold. For our people have not much use for bows and arrows; they are a nation of sailors. Now when we approach the town, I should like to avoid cause for idle talk. A peasant might meet us and say: 'Who is that tall, handsome man following Nausicaa? Where did she pick him up? Most likely she intends to marry a stranger.' And that would mean disgrace for me. I myself would not like it if a friend of mine were seen with a stranger before the day of her marriage. And so when you come to the grove of poplars which is sacred to Athene, and to the spring which rises there and winds through the meadow, wait for a little while, just until you think we have reached the city. The grove is no farther away than a herald's call can travel. Then go on. You will easily recognize my father's palace. Go there, and clasp my mother's knees. If she feels kindly disposed toward you, you may be certain that you will see the land of your fathers again."

So said Nausicaa and drove her wagon slowly, so that her companions and Odysseus could follow. At Athene's grove the hero fell behind and said a fervent prayer to his protectress. The goddess heard him, but she feared the anger of her father's brother, Poseidon, and so she did not appear.

ODYSSEUS AND THE PHAEACIANS

When Odysseus left the sacred grove, the girl had already arrived in her father's palace. Athene protected him all the way to the city. For fear that a bold Phaeacian might offend the unarmed stranger, she veiled him in mist, though he himself did not notice this. When he drew near the gates she could not refrain from confronting him, so she assumed the shape of a young girl carrying a pitcher to draw water. "My child," said Odysseus to her, "would you show me the way to the palace of King Alcinous? I am a stranger from a faraway land, and no one knows me here."

"Gladly," said the goddess in the guise of the girl. "My own father lives close by. But walk quietly at my side. The people here are not very fond of strangers. Their adventurous seafaring life has made them bold and defiant." With these words Athene led the way and Odysseus followed, and no one at all could see the two. He could admire the harbor, the ships, and the high walls undisturbed. Then Athene spoke: "This is the house of Alcinous. Enter without fear. He who is brave, succeeds! But let me give you one piece of advice. Go to the queen before all! Her name is Arete, and she is her own husband's niece. For our former king, Nausithous, son of Poseidon, and Periboea, daughter of Eurymedon, king of the Giants, had two sons, Alcinous, our king, and Rhexenor. Rhexenor did not live long and left one daughter, Arete, our queen. Alcinous honors her as much as a man can honor a wife, and all the people hold her in reverence too, for she is wise and understanding and can even judge in the quarrels of men. If you can win her favor, all will be well with you."

So said Athene and hastened away. Odysseus stood motionless, entranced by the beautiful palace before him. It was high, and dazzling as sunlight. On either side of the gate the walls were of solid bronze with a cornice of bluish metal. A golden door closed off the inner house. Its silver posts rose from a threshold of bronze. The lintels were also of silver, and the handle of gold. Dogs of silver and gold, the work of Hephaestus, stood right and left, like palace guards. When Odysseus entered the hall, he saw chairs covered with rich and delicate tapestries. On these the lords of that country sat at the board. The Phaeacians loved much feasting and drinking. On high bases stood the golden statues of youths. Their hands were extended and held burning torches to light the banquet. Fifty women servants were in the palace. Some ground grain in a handmill; others wove, and still others sat and turned the spindle. The women in that country were as good at weaving as the men at sailing. Outside the court was an orchard four acres in size, circled by a fence and planted with trees bearing juicy pears, figs, pomegranates, apples, and olives. There was fruit both winter and summer, for the warm west wind always blew over the land. Often, in the same season, some trees were just bursting into bloom while others were already covered with fruit. Near the orchard was a vineyard with clusters of grapes swelling in the sun. Others were being harvested, and some were still quite green and hard, or just taking on color. At the other end of the garden flowers bloomed and shed their sweet odors, and a spring gushed from the ground and wound through the shrubs and blooms in a crystal stream. Another spring rose at the very threshold of the palace court, and here the people came to fetch water.

When Odysseus had gazed his fill at all these splendors, he entered the palace and went to the king's great hall. Here the nobles of the land had gathered at a banquet, but because the day was drawing to a close, they were beginning to feel drowsy and were about to end the feast by pouring a libation to Hermes. Shrouded in mist Odysseus traversed the rows of banqueters, but when he reached the king and queen, Athene lifted her hand and the cloud melted from about him. He threw himself down before Queen Arete, clasped her knees, and said: "O Arete, daughter of Rhexenor, as a suppliant I lie before you and your husband. May the gods give you life and happiness as surely as you will give me help to return to my native land! For it is a long time that I have been wandering in exile, far from my own people."

So said the hero and sat down in the ashes of the hearth, close to the glowing fire. The Phaeacians looked at him in wondering silence. But finally gray-haired Echeneus, oldest among the guests and versed in the ways of the world, turned to the king and spoke. "Truly, Alcinous," he said, "it is not fitting anywhere on earth that a stranger should sit in the ashes. I am certain that all agree with me and are only awaiting your command. So raise the stranger from the dust and seat him in a comfortable chair, like ourselves. The heralds shall blend wine for a libation to Zeus, the guardian of hospitality, and the servants offer our new guest food and drink."

The king was well-pleased with these words. He took the stranger by the hand and led him to a chair at his own side, which Laodamas, his favorite son, had to vacate. All was done as Echeneus had advised, and Odysseus feasted with the rest as an honored guest. When a libation to Zeus had been poured, the assemblage broke up, and the king invited them back for the next day. He did not ask the stranger his name or his line, but promised him hospitality in the palace and a safe return home. But as he looked at the hero, on whom Athene had shed a glow of unearthly radiance, he added: "Should you, however, be one of the immortals, who sometimes visit the feasts of men in human form, you will not need our help, and it is we who must ask your protection!"

"Do not believe that for an instant, O king," said Odysseus. "Neither in stature nor in shape do I resemble the gods of Olympus. I am a mortal like yourself, but an unhappy mortal! Show me the man you think the most luckless on earth, and I shall prove to you that my misfortune exceeds his. When I entered the palace, I thought of nothing but satisfying my hunger at your board, and from this alone you can see that I am a poor mortal man."

When the guests had left and the king and queen were alone in the hall with the stranger, Arete studied his tunic and mantle and recognized her own workmanship. "I must ask you a question, stranger," she said. "Will you tell me who you are, from whence you come, and who gave you these garments you are wearing?" Odysseus replied with a truthful account of his stay with Calypso on Ogygia, his disastrous journey, and his encounter with Nausicaa, who had dealt so generously with him.

When he ended, Alcinous smiled. "My daughter did quite right," he said. "But she was remiss in one point: she should have brought you to us herself."

"Do not reprove her for that, O king," said Odysseus. "She was eager to do as you say, but I myself refused, partly out of shyness, and partly because I thought that you might be vexed. For mortals are full of mistrust."

"Never should I be vexed without reason," said the king. "But order is good in all things. Now, if it were the will of the gods that a man like yourself should ask my daughter to wife, how gladly would I give you a house and possessions! I shall, however, not keep you here by force. Tomorrow you shall have help to go wherever you wish. I shall give you a ship and oarsmen who will take you to your country, even if it is as far away as the most distant island we traffic with."

Odysseus received this promise with deep gratitude, bade his royal hosts goodnight, and rested from his hardships on a soft couch.

Early the following morning King Alcinous summoned his people to an assembly in the market place of his city. He took his guest there with him and sat side by side with him on polished stones. In the meantime, Athene, in the shape of a herald, went through the streets, calling the citizens to the council. They streamed from all directions, and the market place soon filled with an eager throng. Admiringly they looked at the son of Laertes, whom Pallas Athene had lent more than human majesty and stature. In a solemn speech, the king commended the stranger to his people and asked them to put at his disposal a good ship with fifty-two Phaeacian oarsmen. He also invited the lords to a banquet in honor of his guest and gave orders that Demodocus, to whom Apollo had given the power of song, should attend to gladden the hearts of his guests with his verses.

When the assembly was dissolved, the oarsmen made ready the black ship, as the king had commanded. They brought the mast, attached the shining sails and spread them wide, and rested the oars in leather loops. Then they went to the palace. The halls and the courts were already swarming with guests, for young and old had come. Twelve sheep, eight boars, and two oxen had been slaughtered for the feast, and the smell of roasting meat hung in the air. The singer too had arrived, led by the herald, for to Demodocus the Muses had given both good and ill. They had taken from him the light of his eyes, but had lit his heart with song. The herald guided him to a chair at the pillar in the middle of the hall. He put his lyre where the blind man could easily reach it, and set before him a table with food and a brimming cup. When the feasting was over, the singer began his tale. He sang of the heroes of Troy whose fame had already spread over the world, and above all of the courage of two heroes whose names were on all lips, Achilles and Odysseus.

When the son of Laertes heard his own name celebrated in song, he hid his face in his mantle that no one might see the tears which rose to his eyes. Whenever Demodocus paused, he lifted his head and reached for the cup. But when the singer went on with his story, he again veiled his face. No one noticed this except the king who sat beside him and heard him heave a deep sigh. Since he did not wish to sadden his guest, he bade the singer put an end to his recital and announced that there were also to be contests in honor of the stranger. "Our guest," he said, "shall tell his people at home that the Phaeacians excel in wrestling and boxing, as well as in jumping and racing." At that, everyone left the board and hastened to the market place. There was a throng of noble youths, among them three sons of Alcinous, Laodamas, Halius, and Clytoneus. These three opened the games with a foot race on the sand-strewn course which stretched as far as eye could reach. At a given sign they stormed forward, and the dust swirled under their flying feet. Clytoneus soon outstripped his brothers and was first to reach the goal. Next came the wrestling match, and here young Euryalus was victorious. In the jump, Amphialus outdid his rivals; in hurling the discus, Elatreus won, and in boxing, Laodamas, the king's favorite son.

And now Laodamas rose and said to the young men: "Should we not ask if the stranger is versed in one or another of our sports? His body, his thighs, and his feet promise well. His arms are sinewy, his neck is strong, and he is of powerful build. It is true that hardship and grief have left their mark on him, but he still seems full of the strength of youth."

"You are right," said Euryalus. "Ask him yourself, O prince, and invite him to join in the games." This Laodamas did with courtesy and warmth.

But Odysseus replied: "Are you doing this to mock me? Sorrow gnaws at my soul, and I have no heart for games. I have worked and suffered enough, and now I want nothing but to return to my native land."

Euryalus was ill-pleased with this answer. "Stranger," he said, "you do not act like a man who is skilled in our games. You are, most likely, a captain or a merchant, but certainly no athlete!"

Odysseus frowned at him and said: "These are rude words, my friend, and you are a forward boy. But the gods do not give beauty and grace, and wisdom and eloquence besides, all to one man! Many a person is insignificant to look at, but his words cast a spell, so that all who hear him are enchanted. Such a man stands out in assembly and is honored like an immortal. On the other hand, there are those who look like gods, but their words lack charm and spirit. Still, I know something about contests, and when I was young and strong, I did not hesitate to measure my strength with the boldest. Now, to be sure, battles and sufferings have weakened me. But you have challenged me, and so I shall try."

So said Odysseus and rose from his seat without laying aside his mantle. He chose a discus, larger, thicker, and heavier than any the Phaeacian youths had thrown, and hurled it with such vigor that the stone hummed through the air. The men near him drew back as he cast, and the discus flew far beyond the target. Quickly Athene, in the guise of a Phaeacian youth, made a mark where it had fallen and cried: "A blind man could find this mark, for it is far beyond all the rest. In this contest you will surely be the victor!"

Odysseus felt glad to think that he had such a true friend among the people and said with a lighter heart: "Well, young men, cast as far as that, if you can! And you, over there, who insulted me, come here, and I shall take part in whatever contest you like. I shall compete with each and every one, but not with Laodamas—for who wants to fight his host? My special accomplishment is shooting with the bow, and no matter how many competed with me, I should be the first to hit the target. I know of only one who can do better than I—Philoctetes. He often beat me at Troy when we practiced shooting. And I am just as expert at throwing the javelin. I can cast it as far as another shoots an arrow. But in the foot race, some of you will probably excel me. The sea has sapped too much of my strength, especially those many days I sat on my raft without food."

When the young men heard this, they fell silent. But now the king spoke. "You have shown us your strength, stranger," he said. "And from this moment on, no one shall question your power. But when you sit at home with your wife and children, remember that we too are sturdy and skilled. We are not great boxers and wrestlers, but we are splendid runners and excellent sailors. As for feasting, plucking the strings, and dancing—we are past masters at that! With us you will find the most beautiful garments, the most refreshing bath, and the softest couch. Come then, dancers and singers! Show this stranger what you can do, so that he may praise you when he reaches his country. And do not forget to bring the lyre of Demodocus!"

Nine chosen men levelled the ground for the dance and staked off the space for the performance. The lyre player advanced toward the center, and the dance began. Boys in the first bloom of youth moved in perfect rhythm, leaping on light feet. Odysseus was filled with wonder. Never had he seen so charming a dance. And the singer, meanwhile, chanted merry episodes from the lives of the gods. When the dance was over, the king bade his son Laodamas dance with lithe Halius, for these two were the best, and no one dared vie with them. They took a purple ball. One leaned backward and threw it high up, and the other leaped and caught it in the air before his feet touched the ground again. Then they swung around each other with effortless grace, always casting the ball, and the other young men, who formed a ring about them, clapped their hands in time. Odysseus was full of admiration. He turned to the king and said: "Alcinous, you may, indeed, boast that you have the most agile dancers in the world. There is no one who can surpass your people in this art."

Alcinous was well-pleased with his guest's praise. "Did you hear?" he called to the Phaeacians. "Did you hear what this stranger has to say about you? He is a man of good judgment and certainly merits a substantial gift. Each of the twelve princes of our land—and I myself as the thirteenth—shall bring a mantle, a tunic, and a talent of gold. Then let us put all these things together and present them as one parting gift, which will surely gladden his heart. And in addition to this, Euryalus shall address friendly words to him, so that he may not bear us the slightest grudge." All the Phaeacians loudly acclaimed his words.

A herald was sent to collect the gifts. And Euryalus took his sword with the silver hilt and sheath of ivory and offered it to the guest, saying: "If I have said anything to offend you, let the winds blow it away. And may the gods grant you a safe journey home. We all wish you welfare and happiness!"

"May you never repent of this gift!" said Odysseus as he slung the beautiful sword over his shoulder. It was sunset by the time the presents were all gathered in and laid down before the queen. Alcinous asked her for a well-wrought chest, and into this the garments and the gold were laid. Then it was carried into the palace for Odysseus, and the king, who had gone there with all his retinue, added still more sumptuous robes and an exquisite cup of gold. While a bath was being prepared for the guest, the queen showed him the contents of the chest and then said: "See how the lid is fastened, and then close the chest yourself, so that

no one can rob you while you sleep." Odysseus closed the lid carefully and secured the chest with intricate knots. Then he refreshed himself in the bath and was just about to join the men,
who were already seated at the board, when, at the entrance to
the hall, he found Nausicaa standing beside the doorpost. He had
not seen her since his arrival in the city, for she had kept to the
women's chambers, apart from the banquets of the men. Now,
before his departure, she wanted to see the distinguished guest of
her house once more. She cast a glance of wondering admiration
at his tall form and handsome face, detained him gently, and
said: "All happiness to you, noble stranger! And think of me
sometimes when you reach the land of your fathers, for I had the
privilege of saving your life."

Odysseus was deeply moved. "Nausicaa," he said, "if Zeus
grants me a safe return, I shall address you with prayers every
day, as if you were a goddess." With this he entered the hall and
took his place at the king's side. The servants were just cutting
the meat and pouring wine into the cups from the mixing-bowl.
Blind Demodocus was led in and seated himself by the central
pillar of the hall, as before. Then Odysseus summoned the herald,
cut the best piece from the back of a roasted boar lying in front
of him, put it on a platter, and said: "Herald, give this to the
singer. Although this is not my home, I should like to do him a
courtesy, for singers are honored all over the world. The Muse
herself has taught them the art of song and watches over them
with favor." Gratefully the blind singer received the gift.

When the meal was over, Odysseus again turned to Demodocus. "I prize you beyond other mortals," he said to him. "How
well you have sung of the fate of the Argive heroes—as if you
yourself had been with them and seen and heard everything!
Now chant us the tale of the wooden horse and the part Odysseus
had in that adventure." Joyfully the singer obeyed, and all
listened to his song. When Odysseus heard his own praises, he
again wept and hid his tears, but Alcinous noticed it. He bade
the singer be silent and said to the Phaeacians: "Better let the
lyre rest now, for not everyone is rejoicing in this tale Demodocus
has sung. Our guest is saddened by it, and our company does not
cheer his heart. But a man should love his guest like his brother!
Tell us at last, stranger, who your parents are, and what country

you are from. Everyone, whether he be a noble or a common man, has a name! And if my Phaeacians are to take you home, we must know the name of your country and of your city. That is all they require. They do not need a pilot. If you only tell them the name of the place, they will find their way through fog and darkness."

At this friendly request, the Argive hero replied: "Do not think, O king, that your singer has not pleased me. It is delight to listen when such a man lifts his godlike voice, and I know of nothing pleasanter than when guests at a feast hang on the words of the singer while they sit at the board heaped with bread and meat and the cupbearer pours wine from the full bowl. But now, my dear hosts, you wish to hear about me, and I fear my own tale is bound to sadden me still more. Where shall I begin? Where shall I end? But first of all I shall tell you my name and my country."

ODYSSEUS TELLS THE TALE OF
HIS WANDERINGS TO THE PHAEACIANS

The Cicones. The Lotos-Eaters. The Cyclopes. Polyphemus

I am Odysseus, the son of Laertes. I am known among men, and the fame of my wisdom has spread over the earth. My country is the sunny island of Ithaca, in the midst of which rises the wooded mountain Neriton. Scattered in the sea around Ithaca are many smaller inhabited islands, Same, Dulichium, Zacynthus. My country is rugged, and it rears vigorous men—but everyone thinks his own native land best and sweetest! And now listen to the tale of my unfortunate journey home from Troy. The wind carried me from Ilium to Ismarus, the city of the Cicones, which I sacked with my friends. We killed the men and divided the women and other spoils among us. My advice was that we leave as quickly as possible, but my companions were less cautious and insisted on lingering at their revels. In the meantime those Cicones who had fled at our coming had won allies among their comrades farther inland, and now they fell on us as we sat at the banquet. There were too few of us to resist them. They defeated us. Six men from each of our ships lost their lives in the city. The rest of us escaped death only by frantic flight.

We steered toward the west, but our hearts were sad for the friends we had lost. And then Zeus sent a tempest from the north. Earth and sea were wrapped in clouds and darkness. We lowered our masts, but before we could draw in the sails the yards cracked and the sailcloth hung in tatters. We managed to reach the coast and lay at anchor two days and two nights, until we had repaired the yards and spread new sails. Then we set out again, full of glad hope of reaching our native land. But when we rounded the promontory of Malea, at the southern tip of the Peloponnesus, the wind suddenly veered and drove us out to sea. For nine days we were beaten and battered by the blast. On the tenth we reached the coast of the Lotos-Eaters who feed on nothing but the fruit of the lotus. We went ashore for a supply of fresh water and sent two of our number to explore the lay of the land. A herald accompanied them. They happened on the assembly of the Lotos-Eaters and were courteously received by this gentle people who did not dream of doing us harm. But the fruit of the lotus which they gave our envoys has a strange effect on men. It is sweeter than honey, and whoever tastes of it wants to remain in that country forever and refuses to return home. We had to fetch our comrades back to the ship by force while they wept and struggled.

In the course of our further journey we came to the cruel and savage people of the Cyclopes. These do not work the land, but leave everything to the gods. And, actually, everything grows there without ploughing or sowing, wheat, barley, and vines bearing huge clusters of heavy grapes. Zeus sends gentle rains and blesses the soil. The Cyclopes have no laws and hold no assembly. They live in vaulted caves on the tops of rocky mountains. Each leads his life with his wife and children, just as he pleases, and no one pays any attention to his neighbor. A short distance from the land of the Cyclopes a wooded island lies in the bay. It serves as a pasture for wild goats which breed there, untroubled by the huntsman. No human being lives on it, and the Cyclopes, who know nothing of the art of shipbuilding, cannot cross to it. Men could make a fruitful place of this island, for the ground is very fertile. Lush green meadows run along the coast, and farther inland the soil is crumbly and good. The low hills would make excellent vineyards. And there is a harbor so sheltered from winds that one would need neither anchors nor ropes to secure his ships. Right where you land pure water gushes from a stony gorge, and tall poplars circle the spring. To this place a friendly god guided our ships in the darkness of night. When day dawned, we went ashore and shot so many goats that there were nine for each of my twelve ships, and I kept ten for myself. The livelong day we sat on that pleasant shore and refreshed ourselves with goat-meat and the strong red wine which we had taken from the city of the Cicones and brought with us in jars.

But the next morning I grew curious about the opposite shore. I did not know anything about the Cyclopes then. Many of my companions boarded the ship with me and we rowed across. When we landed we saw a high cave overgrown with laurel, and around it many sheep and goats. Great stones had been rammed into the earth to wall in a court, and tall firs and oaks formed an impenetrable fence around it. Later we discovered that within this enclosure lived a man of gigantic stature. He pastured his herds on distant meadows and had nothing to do with his kind. He was a Cyclops, lonely and lawless. When we had surveyed the shore, I chose twelve of my boldest companions and told the rest to stay aboard, row the ship out of sight, and wait at anchor. I took with me a skin of the best wine. A priest of Apollo had given it to me in Ismarus because I spared him and his family. I thought that this wine and the abundant provisions we had taken with us in a basket would win over whoever might be living in this place.

When we reached the cave we found no one there, for the Cyclops had taken his sheep to pasture. We entered, notwithstanding, and marvelled at what we saw. All along the walls were enormous cheeses. In the pens were lambs and kids, and each kind of creature was in its own stall. The floor was covered with baskets, milking-pails, jugs of whey, and casks. My comrades urged me to take as many of the cheeses as we could carry, drive the lambs and goats to our ship, and return to our friends on the island. Oh, if only I had followed their advice! But at the time I was eager to find out who inhabited the cave, and I wanted to receive a gift from my host, rather than leave with stolen goods. So we lit a fire and made an offering. Then we ate a little of the cheese and waited for the master of the house to return.

At last he came. On his massive shoulders was an enormous

load of dry wood which he had collected to cook his evening meal. He threw it on the ground, and the crash was so great that we started up and then hid in the farthest corners of the cave. We watched him drive in those of his herd he wanted. The rams and the he-goats had to stay in the outside enclosure. And now he closed off the entrance with a tremendous rock. Twenty-two four-wheeled wagons could not have budged it from its place. After that, he sat down at his ease, milked the ewes and the she-goats, let the little lambs and kids suck at the udder, curdled half the milk, and placed it in wicker baskets. The other half he poured into large vessels, for this was his daily draught. When he had finished his work he poked the fire, and now he spied us in our distant corners. This was the first time we had got a good look at him too. Like all the Cyclopes he had a single flashing eye in the middle of his forehead. His legs were like the trunks of thousand-year-old oaks, and his arms and hands were big and powerful enough to play ball with blocks of granite. "Who are you?" he thundered at us in his great rough voice. "Where have you come from? Are you pirates, or what trade do you ply?"

Our very hearts trembled at his roaring, but I managed to collect myself and replied: "We are no pirates! We are Achaeans on the way home from the war of Troy, and we have lost our way on the sea. We come to you to beg your protection and help. Fear the gods and hear us! For Zeus is the patron of suppliants and avenges any wrong done to them!"

But the Cyclops only burst into hideous laughter. "You are a fool, stranger!" he said. "You do not know the men you are dealing with! Do you think we are concerned with gods and their vengeance? What do the Cyclopes care about the Thunderer and all the rest of the immortals put together? We are mightier than they! Unless my own heart prompts me to mercy, I shall spare neither you nor your friends. But first of all, tell me where you have hidden your ship. Where have you cast anchor? Is it nearby?"

This was a shrewd question, but I was ready with a shrewder reply. "My ship," I told him, "was smashed on the cliffs of this island by Poseidon the Earth-Shaker. These twelve men and myself are the only ones who escaped destruction."

The monster said nothing in reply. All he did was to put out his huge hands, grab two of my companions, and dash them to the ground so that blood and brains spurted through their shattered skulls. Then he chopped them up for his evening meal and satisfied his hunger like a lion devouring his prey in the mountains. And he ate not only their flesh, but their entrails as well, and he crunched their bones to the marrow. All we could do was lift our hands to Zeus and lament this awful crime.

After the giant had filled his belly and quenched his thirst with milk, he threw himself on the floor of the cave to sleep. And now I prepared to have at him, to thrust my sword into his side, between his midriff and liver. But I quickly gave up the idea. For how could this have helped us? Who could roll the enormous stone from the mouth of the cave? We should all have died a miserable death. So we let him snore on and waited for the dawn in fear and trembling. When morning came the Cyclops rose, fanned the fire, and did his milking. Then he reached for two more of my companions and ate them for his breakfast, while we watched in speechless terror. After that he drove his well-fed herd out of the cave. He himself went last and put the stone back in its place, as one puts the lid on a quiver. Finally he whistled shrilly to his beasts and strode off with echoing tread. We remained behind, and each thought of how he might be next to die. But I kept turning plan after plan over in my mind. At last I hit on a scheme which I thought might work. Beside a sheeppen lay the Cyclops' mighty club. It was of green olive wood, and he was waiting for it to season before carrying it with him. In length and thickness it was like the mast of a ship. From this club I split off a staff about six feet long. My comrades smoothed it for me and then I sharpened it to a point and hardened it in the fire. This staff I carefully hid in a pile of manure at the side of the cave. Then we cast lots as to who was to help me pierce the monster's eye while he lay asleep. The lot fell on the four bravest, those whom I myself would have chosen.

At nightfall the loathsome shepherd returned with his flock. This time he did not leave any of the animals in the court but drove them all into the cave. Perhaps he was vaguely suspicious; perhaps a god had decided to help us. After that, everything took its course just as on the evening before: he put the stone back in its place and ate two of our number. While he was busy with this, I had filled a wooden jug with the dark wine from our wineskin. Then I approached the Cyclops and said: "Here, take it and drink. Wine tastes good after human flesh. I want you to know what a precious brew we carried with us on our ship. I took it with me to offer you in return for hospitality and for helping us to get to our country. But you have dealt very differently with us. May no mortal ever visit you hereafter!"

The Cyclops took the jug without deigning to reply and emptied it at one gulp. It was easy to see how delighted he was with the strength and sweetness of the wine. For the first time he spoke in cordial tones. "Stranger," he said, "give me another drink. And tell me your name, so that I may offer you a gift. For we Cyclopes also have good wine. And now I shall tell you whom you see before you: I am Polyphemus."

So said the Cyclops, and I was only too glad to give him more of my wine. Three times I filled the jug, and three times he was stupid enough to drain it to the last drop. When the draught began to do its work and his mind clouded, I said: "You want to know my name, Cyclops? I have a rather odd name. It is No Man. All the world calls me No Man. My father and my mother and all my friends use this name."

The Cyclops replied: "Well then, here is the gift I have in mind for you. No Man is the one I shall eat last of all his companions. Are you pleased with the gift, No Man?"

But the last words sounded blurred. His tongue was heavy. He leaned back and then sprawled on the floor. His thick neck was bent, and in his drunkenness he vomited human flesh and wine. And now I quickly held my staff in the glowing ashes until it caught fire. When it began to glow I drew it out, and with my four comrades I pierced his great eye and turned the staff like a carpenter drilling timber for a ship. His lashes and brows were scorched, and his eye hissed like hot iron in water. He leaped up with a howl so loud that the whole cave shook, and we fled into its farthest corners.

Polyphemus jerked the staff out of his eye and flung it away, while the blood streamed from the socket. Then he began to rage around like a madman. He shrieked and shouted and called on his fellow Cyclopes who lived scattered over the mountains. They came running from all sides, surrounded the cave, and asked what had happened. "No Man is murdering me!" he cried. "No Man has tricked me!" When the Cyclopes heard this, they said: "Well, if no man is hurting you, what are you shouting about? You must be out of your mind. But that is a sickness we have no remedy for." They went away, and my heart swelled with satisfaction.

And now the blind Cyclops began to stumble through the cave, still moaning with pain. He took the stone from the opening, but he himself sat down in the entrance and groped about with his hands to catch any one of us who tried to go out with the sheep. For he thought me dull enough to attempt such a thing. But I was again busy with plans and finally found a way. All around us were many large rams with thick, heavy fleece. These I bound together in threes with the willow withes of the Cyclops' sleeping mat. Every middle ram carried under his belly one of our men, while the rams on either side protected this secret burden. I myself chose the bellwether, who was bigger than all the rest. I gripped his back, worked myself down under his belly, and clung to his curly wool. Thus concealed under the beasts we waited for morning. At dawn the rams were the first to go out to pasture.

The ewes bleated in the stalls with stiff, full udders, waiting to be milked.

Polyphemus carefully passed his hands over the backs of the rams to make sure no one was on them, but he never thought of reaching around under them. My wether came last, for he was slowed by the burden he bore. Polyphemus stroked him too and said: "My good bellwether, what makes you go out of the cave so slowly? Usually you do not let any of the rest of the flock get ahead of you. You are always first on the meadow and at the brook, and in the evening first to return to your stall. Are you sad because your master has lost his eye? If you could talk, I am sure you would tell me where that scoundrel and his companions are hiding. Once I have dashed out their brains against these stone walls, I could recover from the sorrow which No Man has brought me."

So said the Cyclops and let the wether pass. And now all of us were outside! The moment we were a short distance from the cave, I let myself drop to the ground and then loosed my companions. Alas! There were only seven of us left! We embraced and lamented for those we had lost. But I signed to them not to weep aloud, but to drive the rams quickly to our ships. And when we sat on the rowing benches, safe and sound, when the ships slid smoothly over the waters and we were a herald's cry from the shore, I called to the Cyclops who was climbing the hill with his herd: "Let me tell you, Polyphemus, that you have eaten the companions of a man who is by no means insignificant! At last your evil deeds have been requited, and you have felt the punishment of Zeus and the other gods!"

When Polyphemus heard this, he broke into a savage fit of rage. With a violent wrench he tore a huge rock from the mountain and hurled it at our ship. And his aim was so accurate that he missed the stern by only a very little. Even so the waves rose high from the splash of that huge block of stone and our ship was driven back to the shore, so that it took all our strength to row forward and away from the giant. And now I called to him a second time, although my friends feared another rock and tried to prevent me. "Listen, Cyclops!" I shouted, "if anyone should ever ask you who blinded you, you shall give a more correct answer than you gave the Cyclopes. Tell them that you were blinded by the conqueror of Troy, by Odysseus, son of Laertes, who lives on the island of Ithaca."

At this the Cyclops howled with fury and grief and called: "So the ancient prophecy has been fulfilled! Years ago a soothsayer, Telemus, son of Eurymus, lived in our land and grew old there. It was he who told me that Odysseus would deprive me of my sight. I always thought this Odysseus would be a huge fellow like myself, that he would challenge me to single combat. But now it is this little chap who came, this weakling, who fuddled me with wine and put out my eye while I was drunk! I beg you to return, Odysseus! This time I shall be a good host to you and ask the sea-god to take you home safely. For you must know that I am the son of Poseidon, and he and no other can heal me." With that he began to pray to his father Poseidon to keep me from reaching my country. "And should he return," he ended, "let it be after many years. Let him be sad and alone on the ship of strangers, and let him find nothing but unhappiness when he reaches his home."

So he prayed, and Poseidon granted his prayer. When he had done talking, Polyphemus gripped another rock and tossed it toward us, and this time too he almost hit us. But we managed to row out of the swirl of waters and soon reached the island where the rest of our ships were riding safely at anchor. Our friends, who had been greatly troubled at our long absence, received us with cries of joy. As soon as we landed, we distributed the sheep we had stolen from the Cyclops. But in addition to my share, my companions agreed to give me the wether who had carried me out of the cave. I immediately offered him up to Zeus and burned the legs of the beast in his honor. But the god spurned the sacrifice and refused to be propitiated. It was his will to let all our ships and all my companions perish.

But we did not know this at the time. We were carefree and gay, and feasted and drank until the sun set in the sea. Then we lay down on the shore and fell asleep to the sound of the surf. When the sky reddened with dawn, we boarded our ships and rowed on toward home.

ODYSSEUS CONTINUES HIS TALE

The Leather Bag of Aeolus. The Laestrygonians. Circe

After this we came to an island which was the dwelling of Aeolus, son of Hippotes, a cherished friend of the gods. This island floated about in the sea. It was circled by a wall of bronze built along the edge of steep rock which rimmed the land. On it was the palace of Aeolus. He had six sons and six daughters, and with them and his wife he feasted day after day. This good ruler was our host for a full month. He asked us all about Troy, about the Argives and their return from Ilium. We told him everything in great detail; when we finally begged him to help us on our way home, he was very willing. Among other things he gave us a taut leather bag. In it were many winds which blow across the earth, for Zeus had made Aeolus the keeper of the winds, and he had the power to loose those he wanted and to bid them fly or stay. He himself bound the bag to the ship with a silver cord and tied it up so well that not a breath of air could escape. But he had not imprisoned all the winds. For when we set out, the gentlest west wind swelled our sails and would have brought us safely home had not our own folly plunged us into disaster.

We had been travelling for nine days and nine nights; on the tenth night we were so near the coast of Ithaca that I could see the watch fires burning on the shore. And then—of all times—I had to grow irresistibly sleepy! I had been up and managing the sails the entire voyage, for I wanted to get home as quickly as possible and did not wish to entrust this important business to anyone else. Now, while I slept, my companions began to discuss what might be in the bag King Aeolus had given me in parting. And it seemed that all of them thought it must be filled with silver and gold. In the end, one of them, an envious fellow, said: "This Odysseus is honored and made much of wherever he goes. Look at the spoils he carried off from Troy alone! But we, who endured exactly the same hardships and dangers, are going home empty-handed. To crown it all, Aeolus has given him a whole sack of gold and silver! How about looking into it, at least, and finding out how much treasure it contains?" The others instantly

agreed to this unfortunate suggestion. They untied the bag, but hardly had it been opened before the winds all rushed out and drove our ship back to the high seas.

The noise of the gale woke me. When I saw the disaster which had overtaken me, I felt like jumping overboard and drowning in the waves. But I thought better of it and decided to bear up under whatever might come. The rage of the tempest drove us back to the island of Aeolus. Here I left my men on the ships and went to the palace with one friend and a herald. We found the king, his wife, and his children at their midday meal. They were amazed to see us, but when they heard the cause of our return, the ruler of the winds rose from his chair and cried: "Vilest of mortals! It is clear that the gods are pursuing you with their wrath. But a man whom immortals hate must not be my guest, and I shall not assist him any further. Leave this house, you who are accursed!" And with that he drove me from his threshold. With heavy hearts we again boarded our ships and sailed on. For seven days we rowed, but saw no land. Then we gave up hoping.

At last we sighted a coast and a city with many towers. Its name was Telepylus, and the people were called Laestrygonians, as we learned later on. We entered an excellent harbor, protected on all sides by rock, so that the waters in the bay were smooth as a mirror. I anchored my ship, climbed to a rugged height, and looked around. Nowhere did I see ploughed fields, farmers, shepherds, or cattle. All I could detect was smoke from a great city mounting to the sky. So I sent two friends and a herald to recon-

noitre. They found a path leading through woods and walked toward the smoke until they were near the city. Here they met a girl carrying a pitcher. She was the daughter of Antiphates, king of the Laestrygonians, and was on her way to the spring called Artacia, from which the inhabitants of that place drew water. The girl was so tall that they marvelled at her stature. She spoke to them in a friendly manner and told them what they wanted to know about her father's palace, the country, the city, and its people. But when they actually reached the city and approached the palace, they froze with horror, for the queen of the Laestrygonians confronted them, tall as a mountain. It seemed that the Laestrygonians were man-eating giants! She lost no time in calling her husband, who at once seized one of my envoys and gave orders to prepare him for the evening meal. The two others fled in mortal terror. But the king roared orders to pursue them, and over a thousand giants, fully armed, came and hurled stones at our ships, so that the air was filled with the crash of timbers and the groans of the dying. I had anchored my own ship in the shelter of a cliff, where it was safe from the missiles. Now I took into it those who were still alive and made off with all possible speed. The other ships sank, and with them, alas! many of my comrades.

Crowded into a single ship, we rowed on and came to the island of Aeaea. This was the home of a beautiful goddess, child of the sun-god and Perse, daughter of Oceanus and sister to King Aeetes. Her name was Circe, and she lived in a splendid palace. But when we entered the bay of the island we did not know who lived there. We cast anchor, and, almost dead with fatigue and sorrow, lay down and slept for two days and nights on the grassy shore. On the third day, I took my sword and lance and set out to explore the island. Soon I saw smoke rising, but mindful of the terrible adventure we had only just survived, I decided to return to my friends. It was a long time since we had had sufficient food. One of the gods must have taken pity on us, for suddenly I saw a stag with broad antlers running out of the woods and down to the stream. I cast my lance at him, and it struck him in the back, coming out at the belly. Then I planted my foot against the animal, drew out the spear, twisted myself a rope of willow withes, bound together its ankles, and carried it to the ship on my back. It was so heavy a burden that I had to lean on my lance in walking.

My companions started up joyfully when they saw the fine beast on my shoulders. We roasted the stag, fetched what bread and wine we still had on the ship, and sat down to eat. Not until now did I report the column of smoke I had seen mounting from some habitation. But my men received the news dejectedly, for they remembered the cave of the Cyclops and the land of the Laestrygonians. I was the only one who kept up his courage, and I divided the crew into two groups, one of which I was to lead, the other Eurylochus. Then we shook lots in a brazen helmet. The lot fell on Eurylochus, and so he, with twenty-two men, set out toward where I had seen the smoke.

They soon came to the stately stone palace of Circe, lying in a fair green valley. But imagine their amazement when they saw shaggy-maned lions and wolves with long sharp teeth prowling around in the walled court in front of the palace! They looked at these beasts in terror and were just going to flee from that uncanny place when the animals surrounded them. But, oddly enough, they advanced slowly, wagging their tails like dogs who go to meet their master to receive a tidbit he has brought them from a feast, and they behaved in an altogether gentle and docile fashion. Later we discovered that they were really men whom Circe had changed into animals.

Since these beasts made no motion to stop my companions, they took courage again and approached the gates of the palace. From within, they heard the beautiful voice of Circe. She was seated at her loom, weaving a mantle such as only a goddess can contrive, and singing as she worked. The first to see her and to rejoice in what he saw was Polites, my particular friend. At his advice, the rest called to Circe to come out, and she came to the gate and smilingly invited them in. All followed her except Eurylochus. He was a cautious man, tempered, moreover, by bad experience, and he suspected some trickery or other.

The rest entered the palace where Circe bade them be seated on sumptuous chairs. She had cheese and flour, honey and Pramnian wine brought, and proceeded to mix these ingredients to a custard. But as she worked, she secretly added baneful drugs which would make her guests forget their native land and rob them of their true form. And the dish did its work! As soon as my men had eaten of it, they were turned into bristly swine. They commenced to grunt, and Circe drove them into sties and threw to them acorns and wild cherries.

Eurylochus had watched part of what happened and guessed the rest. He hurried back to the ship as fast as he could to tell us of what had befallen our comrades. But when he reached us, his terror was still so great that he was unable to utter a single word. The tears gushed from his eyes, and he was speechless with grief.

At last, when we pressed him to talk, full of concern and surprise, he broke his silence and told us what he had seen. The moment he had ended I slung my sword and bow over my shoulder and asked him to lead me to the palace. He, however, clasped my knees with both hands and pleaded with me to give up my plan, or at any rate not to take him with me. "Believe me," he said in a voice choked with tears, "you will not return, nor will you bring back our friends. Oh, let us flee this accursed island!" I permitted him to stay, but I myself resolved to do what I could to save my companions.

On the way I met a beautiful youth. He held out to me a golden staff by which I recognized Hermes, the messenger of the gods. Clasping my hand, he said: "Why do you wander through the woods where you do not know the way? Circe, the sorceress, has turned your friends into swine and shut them up in sties. Do you think you can rescue them? More likely she will add you to the list of her victims. But I have been sent to help you. If you carry with you this herb"—and here he dug a black root bearing a milk-white bloom out of the earth—"she will not be able to harm you. What she will do is prepare a wine custard and blend into it some magic potion. But this herb will prevent her from turning you into a beast. Should she, however, try to touch you with her long magic wand, rush at her with your sword as if you intended to kill her. Then it will be easy to compel her to swear a sacred oath not to trick you in any way. After that, stay with her if you like. There will be no further danger. And once you have made friends with her, she will not refuse your request to return your companions to their proper shape."

So said Hermes and left to return to high Olympus, while I walked toward Circe's palace. At my call, she opened the gates and bade me enter. I followed her, seething with anger, sat down in a sumptuous chair, and let her put a footstool under my feet. Under my very eyes she prepared her wine custard in a cup of gold. She could hardly wait for me to finish eating, and when I had emptied the cup she touched me with her wand, without the faintest doubt of her powers, and said: "Out to the pigsty to join your friends!" But I snatched my sword from its scabbard and rushed at her as though I meant to kill her. At that she screamed, threw herself on the floor, clasped my knees, and moaned: "Who are you, great and mighty man, whom my potion has left untransformed? No other mortal has ever been able to resist my witchcraft. Can it be that you are Odysseus, whose arrival, on your way home from Troy, Hermes predicted to me long ago? If it is you, put up your sword and let us be friends."

But I did not lower my threatening hand and replied: "How can you, Circe, ask me to be friends with you, who have turned my companions into swine! Am I not forced to think that you are using kindly words only to lure me into some trap? I cannot be your friend until you swear a sacred oath not to harm me in any way." She instantly swore the oath I had demanded of her, and now I felt at ease and spent a carefree night. In the early morning, her handmaids, who were lovely and gentle nymphs, busied themselves in ordering the chambers of their mistress. One spread the chairs with soft crimson mats, another placed silver tables beside them and golden baskets on the tables. A third mixed wine and water in a silver bowl and set out cups of gold; and the fourth fetched clear water from the spring and poured it into a cauldron which she placed over a flame. When the water was warm, I took a refreshing bath, rubbed my body with perfumed oil, and dressed. Then I was bidden to the morning meal which I was to take in Circe's company. Now although I was served with

good and abundant food, I did not put out my hand to eat, but sat opposite my beautiful hostess silent and sad. When she finally asked me the cause of my sorrow, I said: "What man who has not lost all feeling for what is just and fair could enjoy food and drink while he knows that his friends are unhappy? If you want me to take pleasure in your company, restore my dear companions to their proper shape, that I may feast my eyes on them."

This was enough for Circe. She left the room, holding her wand in her hand. Outside, she opened the door of the sty and drove out my friends. I followed her, and they crowded around me as swine. But now she anointed each with a salve, and suddenly they shed their bristly hides and became men again, only younger and handsomer than before. They rushed up to me full of joy and clasped my hands. But when they recalled what they had just been through, their eyes filled with tears. Then Circe said to me: "I have done what you asked! And now do what I beg of you: beach your ship, store its cargo in one of the rock grottoes on the shore, and be my honored guest, together with all those who are with you!"

Her courteous words won my heart. I returned to the shore and the friends I had left behind. They had given me up, and now rushed toward me with tears of joy. When I suggested that we beach the ship and remain with the goddess a while as her guests, all were willing except Eurylochus, who objected vehemently. "Do you really want to go to that witch of your own free will?" he cried. "Are you longing to be turned into lions, wolves, and swine, and guard her palace in these horrible shapes? Have you forgotten how the Cyclops dealt with us when Odysseus was unwise enough to let us fall into his power?" When I heard him say this about me, I had the greatest desire to draw my sword and strike his head from his trunk, even though he was a kinsman of mine, but my friends saw my sudden movement toward the hilt; they took hold of my arm, and brought me back to my senses.

And now we all started on our way inland. Even Eurylochus, whom my threatening gesture had frightened, no longer refused to join us. In the meantime Circe had ordered baths prepared for our friends. They had anointed themselves with perfumed oil and put on the splendid tunics and mantles she had provided for them. When we arrived they were feasting at the board. What a happy reunion! Clasping of hands, embraces, tears of joy! Circe bade us all be of good courage and was so kind to us that our hearts grew lighter from day to day, and we stayed with her for many months. But when the year drew to a close, my comrades begged me to set out on the journey home. Their words moved me, and that very evening I clasped Circe's knees and implored her to keep her word and send us home. "You are right, Odysseus," she replied. "I must not try to force you to remain here with me. But before you return to Ithaca you must travel to Hades, to the bleak realm of Persephone, and ask the soul of Tiresias, the blind soothsayer of Thebes, to foretell the future, for Persephone has allowed him to retain the gift of prophecy even after death. The souls of the other dead are only like hovering shadows."

When I heard this, I lost heart and began to weep. I shuddered at the thought of visiting the dead and asked her who was to be my guide, for no man of flesh and blood had ever sailed to the underworld. "Do not worry about your ship or look for a guide," Circe answered. "Raise your mast and hoist the sails. The north wind will take you there, and once you have crossed Oceanus, the waters which encircle the earth, land on the low shore at the point where you will see tall poplars and willows growing side by side. That is the grove of Persephone, and there you will find the entrance to the underworld. In a valley, near a rock where the roaring currents of Pyriphlegethon and Cocytus, a branch of the Styx, flow into Acheron, you will find a cleft which leads into the land of shades. There you must dig a hole and offer honey, milk, wine, water, and flour to the dead. You must also promise to sacrifice a heifer to them when you reach Ithaca, and to offer a black ram to Tiresias besides. After that, slaughter two black sheep, a ram and a ewe, and look through the cleft at the pointed streams, while your companions burn the animals in honor of the gods and pray to them. Then you will see the souls of the dead, and these phantoms shaped of air will try to approach and taste the blood of the victims. But you must fend them off with your sword and not permit them to come closer until you have consulted Tiresias, for he will soon appear and tell you about your journey home."

These words gave me some comfort. The next morning I summoned my friends in order to prepare for our departure. Now one of them, Elpenor, the youngest of them all, but a man who was neither very brave nor very wise, had drunk a little too much of Circe's sweet wine, left the others to cool his hot face, and lain down on the flat roof of the palace. There he had fallen asleep and spent the night in undisturbed rest. When the noise and bustle of my companions woke him, he started up in a daze, forgot where he was, and instead of making for the stair, walked to the edge of the roof and fell off. He broke his neck, and his soul descended to the underworld.

I gathered my friends about me and said: "I know you think we are setting out for our beloved native land. But this, alas! is not so, for Circe has bidden us go elsewhere first. We must visit Hades and there ask the soul of the soothsayer Tiresias concerning our journey." When my companions heard this, their hearts almost broke with sorrow. They tore their hair and broke into loud lament. But there was no help for it. I commanded them to go to the ship with me. Circe had preceded us to put aboard the two sheep we were to sacrifice, together with the honey, wine, and flour. When we reached the shore, she slipped past us in silence. We pushed the ship into the water, raised the mast, spread the sails, and mournfully sat down on the rowing benches. Circe sent us a fair wind. It swelled our sails, and soon we were out on the high seas.

ODYSSEUS CONTINUES HIS TALE

The Realm of Shades

The sun dipped into the sea. A steady wind drove our ship to the end of the world, to the land of the Cimmerians, which is wrapped in eternal mists and never lit by the rays of the sun. And there was Oceanus, the river which bounds the earth. We came to the rock and the streams which join their waters, and there we made our offerings, just as Circe had bidden us. The moment the blood from the throats of the sheep flowed into the pit we had dug for the sacrifice, the souls of the dead emerged from the cleft. Young men and old, girls and children came, and many heroes with gaping wounds and bloodstained armor. They thronged about us with sobbing sighs and hovered over the pit. Terror almost got the better of me. I told my companions to burn the sheep quickly and pray to the gods. Then I drew my sword and kept the shades from lapping the blood, for Circe had said that first I was to put my question to Tiresias.

But before him came the soul of our friend Elpenor, whose body still lay unburied in Circe's house. With tears in his eyes he complained of his sad lot and pleaded with me to sail back to the island of Aeaea and bury him with all due honors. I promised him that I would, and he seated himself opposite me. Thus we sat and conversed sorrowfully, the shadowy form of Elpenor and I, holding my sword across the pool of sacrificial blood. Soon after this, the shade of my mother, beautiful Anticlea, joined us. She had still been alive when I left for Ilium. Silently she seated herself and stared at the blood. Never once did she look at me, her son.

And now the shade of Tiresias appeared, a golden staff in his right hand. He recognized me at once and said: "Son of Laertes, what prompted you to leave the light of the sun and visit this place of dread? But since you are here, take your sword from the pit, that I may drink of the blood and so be able to foretell your fate to you." At his words I withdrew from the pit and thrust my sword into the earth. The shade drank the dark blood and began to speak: "You hope, Odysseus, that I shall predict a happy homecoming for you. But a god will put obstacles in your way, and you cannot evade the hand of the Earth-Shaker, whom you have deeply offended by putting out the eye of his son Polyphemus. Still, in the end you will return, so do not give way to despair. First you will land on the island of Thrinacia. If you want to reach home, do not touch the sacred herds of the sun-god which are pastured there. Should you harm them, your ship and your friends will be destroyed. And even if you yourself escape, you will arrive in Ithaca only after many years, alone, poor, and on an alien ship. Even then you will not find happiness, but will encounter arrogant men who are squandering your property and wooing your wife Penelope. You will slay them openly or by guile. But soon after you shall take your oar on your back and wander on and on until you come to men who do not know the sea, who have no ships, and do not season their food with salt. When, in that faraway land, you meet a man who tells you that you are carrying a winnowing fan on your back, thrust your oar into the ground, make an offering to Poseidon, and go home again. Your realm will prosper, and at long last you will die an old man's death, far from the sea."

This was what he told me. I thanked the seer and asked him another question I had in my heart. "Tell me this: there sits the shade of my mother. How can I make her recognize me?"

"Let her drink of the blood," the soothsayer replied, "and she will break her silence."

Then I let my mother approach, and she drank. Suddenly she knew me, gazed at me with wet eyes, and said: "Dear son, how could you, who are still alive, enter this place of death? Did not Oceanus and the other rivers keep you back? Have you been wandering about since the fall of Troy? Can you not return to Ithaca?" When I had answered her questions, I asked her how she had died, for she had been still alive when I left for Troy. And then, my heart beating with fear, I inquired about the others I had left behind. "Your wife," she told me, "is unshakably faithful and weeps for you day and night. Your son Telemachus sees to your property, and no one has taken over your scepter. Your father Laertes leads a peasant's life in the country and never comes into the city any more. He does not live in a royal chamber or sleep on a soft couch. Like a slave he lies in the ashes beside the hearth, throughout the winter, and his clothing is of

the poorest sort. In summer he sleeps on a heap of fallen leaves
under the open sky. And all this he does for grief at your fate. I
myself died of sorrow for you, dear son. It was not sickness that
took me from the earth."

As she spoke I trembled with yearning. But when I tried to
take her in my arms, she dissolved like the shapes in our dreams.
And now other shades came, many of them women famed on
earth. They all drank of the blood of the victims we had slaughtered and told me their story. When they had vanished, I saw a
sight that made my heart turn over. I saw the soul of great
Agamemnon! Slowly he moved toward the pit and drank of the
blood. Then he looked up, recognized me, and began to weep. In
vain he reached for me with his strengthless hands. Then he
answered my eager questions. "Noble Odysseus," he said, "perhaps you think that the sea-god destroyed me, or that enemies
got the better of me while I was drinking at a feast. But this
is not so. Just as one slays an ox at the stall, so Clytaemnestra
and her lover Aegisthus killed me in the bath, killed me who had
journeyed toward home so full of longing for my wife and children! That is why I now counsel you, Odysseus, not to trust your
wife too much. Do not let affection lead you to tell her all your
secrets! But I forget! Penelope is virtuous and wise. And the
child she nursed when you and I left for Greece, the child Telemachus, is now a youth who will receive his father full of filial
love. Clytaemnestra did not even let me feast my eyes on my
son Orestes before she murdered me. In any case, I advise you
to land secretly on the coast of Ithaca, for no woman can be
wholly trusted."

With these somber words the shade of Agamemnon turned and
vanished. After him came the shades of Achilles and his friends
Patroclus and Antilochus and Ajax the Great. Achilles was the
first to drink. He recognized me in amazement. I told him why
I had come. But when I said to him that he, the most renowned
of all the Argives, must be happy even in Hades, as the greatest
among the dead, he answered mournfully: "Do not try to find
comforting words about death, Odysseus! Rather than be lord
over all the throngs of the dead, I should choose to till the fields
like a serf who has no property and no heritage." Then he begged
me to tell him about the feats of his son Neoptolemus, and when

he had heard of his courage and glorious deeds, he grew more content. Finally he strode from me with mighty steps and was lost from sight.

All the other souls who had drunk of the blood were willing to speak to me. Only Ajax, whom I had once conquered in the fight for the weapons of Achilles and who had taken his life because of this, stood to one side and nursed his grudge. I addressed him with gentle words: "Son of Telamon, can you not forget your anger even in death, your anger about the weapons of Achilles which the gods gave to the Argives only to put a curse on them? For because of them we lost you who were like a tower in battle. Not we were guilty of your death! It was Fate. Then curb your wrath, noble prince, and speak!" The shade did not reply, but turned away into the darkness.

And now I saw the shades of heroes long dead: of Minos, who judges the dead; of the great hunter Orion, who stood, club in hand, driving away the phantoms of lynxes and lions; of Tityus, on whose liver two vultures fed, in punishment for his crime; Tantalus, who thirsted amid waters rising to his chin. Whenever he leaned to drink they receded, and the trees laden with fruit, which grew at his side, whipped upward with the wind whenever he reached for them; his hand clutched the empty air. I also saw Sisyphus straining to roll a huge boulder up a mountain. He pressed his whole weight against it and worked with his arms and legs, but whenever he got near the top the stone rolled down, and he had to begin his labors all over again. The sweat poured from his limbs, and dust rose in clouds about his head. Near him was Heracles, that is, the shade of Heracles, for he himself dwells on Olympus, and his wife is the goddess of eternal youth. But his shade was dark as night and fitted an arrow to the bow, ready to launch it at an enemy. A gold sword strap, decorated with the shapes of many different animals, hung over his shoulder.

He too disappeared, and throngs of other shades hovered around me. I should have liked to see Theseus and his friend Pirithous. But suddenly those shadowy hosts filled me with terror, as if the Medusa had turned her dreadful head to look at me. Quickly I left with my companions and went back to the shore of Oceanus. And first I fulfilled my promise to Elpenor; we sailed back to Circe's island.

ODYSSEUS CONTINUES HIS TALE

The Sirens. Scylla and Charybdis. Thrinacia and the Herds of
the Sun-god. Shipwreck. Odysseus and Calypso

When we had burned the body of our comrade and buried his
bones in the earth of Aeaea, we heaped a burial mound for him
and set a pillar on it. Circe received us with warm hospitality
and provided us with ample stores for our further journey.

The first adventure—of which we had been forewarned by
Circe—awaited us on the island of the Sirens. These are nymphs
who sing so sweetly that all listen spellbound to their song. They
stand on a green shore and lift their lovely voices whenever a ship
comes by. But he who is beguiled and lands is destroyed, for the
coast of their island is strewn with bleaching bones. When we
approached the realm of the Sirens, the fair wind which had
floated us gently on suddenly stopped, and the sea lay smooth
as a mirror. My comrades lowered the sails, folded them, laid
them down in the ship, and began to row. But I thought of
Circe's words. "When you are close to the island of the Sirens,"
she had told me, "stop up the ears of your companions with wax,
so that they can hear nothing. But if you yourself desire to hear
the song, have them fetter your hands and feet and bind you to
the mast. The more you implore them to let you go, the more they
shall tighten the ropes."

This I remembered. I cut a slab of wax, kneaded it until it was soft, and with it stopped up the ears of my men. They, in turn, tied me to the mast, plied their oars, and calmly rowed through the waters. When the Sirens saw the ship, they came to the edge of the shore in the shape of beautiful girls and raised their clear-toned song:

> *Come, famed Odysseus, glory of all Greece,*
> *Turn from your course and hearken to our song!*
> *Ere now has never dusky ship sailed by*
> *But that its helmsman paused at our sweet voice,*
> *Took his full joy of it, and went his way*
> *Made wiser by the tale of what he heard.*
> *For we know all the toils that in wide Troy*
> *Trojan and Argive by gods' will endured,*
> *And in our wisdom know all things besides*
> *That come to pass upon the fruitful earth.*

As I listened, my heart almost burst with the yearning to go to them. I motioned with my head that I wished to be loosed from the mast, but my comrades, who could hear nothing, rowed the faster, and two of them, Eurylochus and Perimedes, came and tightened the cords as I had bidden them. Not until we were safely out of reach of the Siren song did my companions take the wax out of their ears and cut my bonds. I thanked them for remaining steadfast in ignoring my entreaties.

After a short while I sighted a fountain of spray and heard the roar of surf. This was Charybdis, a whirlpool which three times a day shot out from under a cliff and in the backwash sucked down any ship which happened to pass at that moment. My men dropped their oars in horror, and the tide threatened to carry them away. The ship did not move. Then I jumped from my seat and went from man to man, speaking words of courage. "My friends," I said, "we are old hands at meeting danger! Come what may, nothing worse can befall us than what happened in the cave of the Cyclops; but even there I found a way out. Now too you must do as I say. Grip your oars"—for they had caught them up from the sea—"and make straight for the surf. I have faith that Zeus will help us. You, our helmsman, shall guide the ship as well as you can. Keep to the rocks, so that we will not be caught in the whirlpool." In this way I warned my friends of Charybdis, but I said nothing of Scylla, the monster Circe had described to me, for I feared they would again drop their oars and lose them. And in my concern I forgot another piece of advice Circe had given me. She had told me not to gird on armor for the fight with this monster. I, however, put on my cuirass, took two spears, went to the bow, and prepared to meet Scylla. But though my eyes ached with peering about I could not discover her, and I waited in deadly fear as the ship came closer and closer to the narrows. This is how Circe had described Scylla to me: "She is no mortal foe, but rather immortal disaster. Courage cannot prevail against her. The only possibility of escape lies in flight. Her house is opposite Charybdis: a steep rock whose jagged point is always hidden in gray cloud. In the middle of this rock is a cave as black as night. Here Scylla lives and proclaims her presence by a loud barking and whining which seems like that of a young dog. This monster has twelve shapeless feet and six snaky necks. At the end of each is a hideous head with three rows of gnashing teeth, ready to crush her prey. Half of her is concealed in her cave, but her heads she puts out of the cleft and fishes for seals, dolphins, and other large creatures of the sea. Never has a ship passed her without losing some of its crew. Usually she snatches a man with each pair of her toothy jaws before anyone is even aware of her nearness."

This was the picture I saw in my mind's eye. And now the ship had come close to Charybdis, which was sucking in the sea with greedy mouth and spewing it out again. The water seethed like a kettle over the fire, and white spray filled the air. But when the tide was drawn in the sea looked turbid, the rock seemed to thud with thunder, and one could look far down into a cavern of black slime. While we stared spellbound and our helmsman steered left and away from the whirlpool, we inadvertently came too near Scylla. At one gulp she snapped up six of my comrades. I saw them struggling in the air between her teeth. One moment they moved their arms and legs convulsively and cried to me for help, the next they were ground to pulp. I have suffered much on my wanderings, but never have I seen a more pitiful sight.

And now we were safely through the narrows between Charybdis and Scylla, and before us lay Thrinacia, shining in the sun. The roar of the surf died away, and we heard the lowing of the sacred cattle of the sun-god and the bleating of his sheep. Misfortune had freshened my memory, and I immediately told my companions that both Tiresias and Circe had bidden me flee the island of Helios. This grieved and annoyed my companions beyond measure, and Eurylochus said angrily: "Odysseus, you are a cruel man. You are made of iron and inflexible. Do you seriously intend to deprive us of the rest we need so much? Are you going to prevent us from setting foot on this island and refreshing ourselves with food and drink? Must we ride on over the black sea through the long night? Suppose a tempest overtakes us in the darkness! Let us at least anchor near this friendly shore until the sun rises again."

When I heard him rebelling against my counsel, I knew very well that a hostile god was planning our destruction. All I said was: "Eurylochus, it is not difficult for you to persuade me, for I am one man against many. I shall yield to you. But first you must all swear a sacred oath not to slaughter a single one of the sun-god's animals, no matter how many herds of cattle or sheep you may see. Let us be content with the provisions Circe has given us in such abundance." They were all willing enough to take the oath. We entered the bay from which the fresh water poured into the salt, set foot on land, and prepared our meal. When we had eaten, we began to lament our friends whom Scylla had devoured, but we were so tired that we fell asleep in the midst of weeping.

Perhaps two thirds of the night had gone by, when Zeus sent a roaring gale. At dawn we rowed our ship into a safe grotto. Again I warned my friends not to touch the sun-god's creatures, for I realized that the stormy weather would force us to remain on the island longer than we had expected. It turned out to be a solid month. The south wind alternated with storms from the east, and both were against us. As long as the food and the wine Circe had given us lasted, there was no trouble. But when we had eaten up all we had and began to feel hungry, my comrades went fishing and hunting birds, while I walked along the shore, hoping to meet a god or a mortal to help us in our distress. When I was well away from the rest, I washed my hands in the sea, so that I could pray with clean palms outstretched, and begged the immortals to rescue us. But all they did was to make me drowsy. I fell asleep.

While I was gone, Eurylochus rose and gave dangerous counsel to my companions. "Listen to me!" he said. "We are in great need. Death is terrible in any form, but the worst death is by starving. Why should we hesitate to sacrifice the finest of the cattle to the gods and satisfy our hunger on the remaining meat? As soon as we reach Ithaca, we can propitiate Helios by building him a splendid temple and filling it with precious gifts. But should he be so angry that he sends a tempest and sinks our ship on the way, well, I for my part would rather die instantly by drowning than drag out my life famishing slowly on this island."

My hungry comrades were well-pleased with these words. They immediately singled out the best cattle from the herds of the sun-god, prayed to the gods, slaughtered the beasts, wrapped the entrails and haunches in fat, and offered them up to the immortals. Since they had no wine left, they sprinkled them with water from a spring. The rest of the meat they put on spits. They were just about to eat when I awoke and smelled the odor of roasting from far-off. I raised my hands to heaven. "O father Zeus!" I cried. "You made me drowsy to destroy me! What crime have my men committed while I slept?"

In the meantime the sun-god had already been told what had occurred in his sanctuary. Angrily he summoned the immortals and complained of the wrong done to him. He threatened to drive the sun chariot down to the underworld to shine among the dead and never again light the earth if the evildoers were not sternly punished. Zeus rose from his seat in majesty. "Do not stop shining for gods and men, Helios," he said. "I myself shall shatter the ship of those robbers with a thunderbolt and sink it to the bottom of the sea." These words of Zeus were reported to me by Calypso who had heard them from Hermes, the messenger of the gods.

When I joined my friends I reproved them bitterly. But it was too late. The cattle had been slaughtered, and frightful signs made it clear that a crime had been committed: the hides of the bullocks crept about as if they were alive; the meat on the spits bellowed. But my hungry men paid no attention to these evil portents. For six days they feasted. On the seventh, when the storm seemed past, we boarded our ship and steered for the sea. When we were out of sight of land, Zeus massed a roof of blue-black clouds right over our heads, and the water grew darker and darker. Suddenly a furious gale swept on us from the west. The mast broke and fell, sweeping the sails with it. The whole weight landed on our helmsman and cracked his skull. Like a diver he plunged headlong into the waves, and the waters swallowed his body. And now lightning struck the ship and filled the air with sulphurous fumes. My companions fell from the deck and struggled in the surf like sea-crows, until they all sank. I was the only one left on the ship, and I paced the deck until the sides broke away from the keel. But I had my wits about me, seized the backstay made of oxhide, and lashed the mast to the keel with it. On this raft I sat, called on the gods, and let the sea toss me hither and thither.

At last the storm abated, and the west wind died down. But the south wind began to blow in its stead and filled me with new terror, for it threatened to drive me back to Scylla and Charybdis. And this really happened! At dawn I saw Scylla's pointed cliff dwelling and the swirling waters of Charybdis. The whirlpool swept my mast into the abyss. I myself seized the bough of a fig tree growing on the rock, clung to it, and hung in the air like a bat until my mast and keel were spewed up again. The instant I saw them, I let myself drop on my raft and used my hands to row frantically away from those angry waters. But I should have been lost, had not Zeus floated me past Scylla and guided me safely out of those narrows.

For nine days I was tossed about on the sea. On the tenth night the gods had pity on me and cast me ashore on the island of Ogygia. There Calypso gave me food and drink and nursed me back to health. But this, my last adventure, I have already told you, O king.

ODYSSEUS BIDS THE PHAEACIANS FAREWELL

Odysseus had ended the tale of his adventures and fell silent, weary with the long telling of it. The Phaeacians, who had listened with delight, were also silent, for they were still under the spell of what they had heard. Alcinous was the first to speak. "Hail to you," he said, "the noblest guest this palace has ever sheltered! And now, since you are in my realm, I hope your wanderings are over, and that you will soon be in the house of your fathers and forget all you have suffered." Then he turned to his friends. "Listen to what I have to say to you," he said. "A chest has been filled with beautiful tunics and mantles for our guest, and with wrought gold and many other gifts. Let each of us add to these a large tripod and a cauldron. It is much to give, but the people will recompense us."

All applauded this suggestion, and the gathering dispersed. On the following morning the Phaeacians brought tripods and cauldrons to the ship, and Alcinous himself helped stow them under the rowers' benches in such a way that the oarsmen would not be hindered by them. After that, the farewell feast was held in the palace. Zeus received his share of the slaughtered cattle, and blind Demodocus sang his most beautiful songs while the guests ate at the board laden with rich and delicate food.

But Odysseus was not there in spirit. His glance kept straying to the window to look at the sun, and he yearned for the hour of its setting as fervently as the peasant who has guided the ploughshare through his fields the livelong day and yearns for his evening meal. At last he could no longer restrain his eagerness and said to his kingly host: "Great Alcinous, pour the libation, and let me go! You have done for me all that my heart could desire. The gifts are on my ship, and all is ready for departure. May the immortals heap blessings on you! And may I find waiting for me faithfully my wife, my son, my kinsmen and friends."

All the Phaeacians joined him in this wish. Alcinous bade Pontonous, the herald, fill the cups for a last time, and each man poured a libation to the gods of Olympus for the safe and joyful return of their guest. Then Odysseus rose, gave his cup to Queen Arete, and said: "Live in happiness, O queen, and may old age and death, which overtake all mortals, come to you late and lightly. I am leaving for my home. May you have joy of your husband, your children, and your people!"

So said Odysseus, and he crossed the threshold of the palace. Alcinous commanded a herald to accompany him to the ship, and Arete sent three of her servants. One carried the tunics and mantles, the second the closed chest, and the third food and wine. All these things were taken aboard. Then a thick mat was laid on the deck and smooth linen spread over it. Silently Odysseus lay down to sleep. The rowers took their places. The ship was loosed from its moorings and sped over the waters to the steady beat of the oars.

ODYSSEUS REACHES ITHACA

The sleep of Odysseus was sweet and peaceful as death. The ship glided across the sea as swiftly and safely as a four-horse chariot speeds over the plain or a hawk flies through the air. It seemed to know it was carrying a precious burden, a man who in wisdom was the peer of gods, and who had borne more than mortal suffering, though now his slumber had blotted out the memory of battle and shipwreck.

When the brightest of the stars shone in the sky, announcing the coming of day, the ship approached Ithaca, and soon it entered the bay consecrated to Phorcys, the old man of the sea. Here two rocky promontories jutted out into the waters, one on each side, and formed a safe harbor. Midway between them grew an old olive tree, and beside it was a twilit cave, the dwelling of nymphs. In it were rows of bowls and jars of stone where bees stored their honey. There were also looms of stone, strung with purple thread, which the nymphs wove into beautiful garments. Two springs, which never ran dry, gushed through the cave. It had two entrances, one toward the north wind for mortals to enter, the other, a hidden door toward the south wind, for the immortal nymphs. Near this cave the Phaeacians landed. They lifted Odysseus with the linen sheet and the mat on which he lay, and laid him down in the sand under the olive tree, still overpowered by sleep. Then they unloaded all the gifts Alcinous and Arete had sent to the ship and put them a little to one side, so that a passerby might not see them too readily and perhaps rob the sleeper. Since they dared not wake him, thinking that his deep slumber was sent by the gods, they took to their oars again and steered for home.

But Poseidon, the sea-god, was angry at the Phaeacians, because with the help of Pallas they had gone contrary to his wish that Odysseus suffer many woes; so he asked Zeus for permission to take vengeance on them. The father of gods granted his request. As their ship approached the island of Scheria and sped toward the home coast with billowing sails, Poseidon rose through the waves, struck it with the flat of his hand, and then sank back into the sea. Instantly the ship and everything on it was turned to stone and rooted fast. The Phaeacians, who had sighted the ship and run to the shore to welcome their countrymen, were amazed to see it stop in full course. But Alcinous guessed what had happened. He called an assembly and said: "I fear this is the fulfillment of an ancient prophecy of which my father told me. Poseidon—so he said—hates us because, good sailors that we are, we bring all strangers who ask our help safely back to their native lands. And one day, he went on to tell me, one of our ships, returning from such a journey, would be turned to stone and would be rooted fast before our city like a rock. From this day forward we must give up our custom of seeing strangers home. But now let us sacrifice twelve bullocks to the angry sea-god, lest he surround our city with a solid wall of stone." When they heard this, the Phaeacians shuddered with terror and hastened to prepare the victims.

Odysseus, meanwhile, had wakened. But he had been away from Ithaca so long that he did not recognize his own country. Besides, Pallas Athene had shed a mist over the land, because she did not want him to reach his palace before preparing him for what he would find there. And so everything, the winding paths, the bay, the cliffs, and the tall trees, looked unfamiliar to him. He sat up, struck his forehead with his hand, and lamented: "To what new and strange land have I come? What new monsters shall I find here? If only I had stayed with the Phaeacians, who received me so hospitably! But it seems they have betrayed me, for they promised to take me home to Ithaca, and now they have abandoned me on a foreign coast. May Zeus avenge me for this! They have, most likely, stolen the gifts I had aboard."

He looked around and saw tripods, cauldrons, gold, and clothing in orderly piles. He began to count his goods, but nothing was missing. While he was still hesitating what to do, Athene came up to him in the shape of a youth, a shepherd, but delicately formed as the son of a king. Her mantle fell in folds from her shoulders, and she wore sandals and carried a spear in her hand. Odysseus was glad to see a human being and courteously inquired where he was and whether this were the mainland or an island. "You must be from far away," the goddess replied, "if you do not know the name of this country. All the world has heard of it. It is, to be sure, a hilly region, and we cannot raise horses as they do in the land of the Argives. But we are not poor. The earth yields a plentiful harvest of grain and grapes. We have countless herds of cattle and goats, tall forests, and pure springs. And those who live here have helped make the land famous. Even in Troy, which is surely a distant city, people have heard of the island of Ithaca!"

How Odysseus rejoiced to hear the name of his own country! Still, he was careful not to blurt out his name to the unknown shepherd. He pretended to have come from the far-off island of Crete with half his property. The other half, so he said, he had left there for his sons. He had slain a man who tried to rob him—so he spun out his tale—and had been forced to flee from his native land. When he had finished his story, Pallas Athene smiled and passed her hand caressingly over his face. And suddenly she changed into a tall, beautiful woman. "Really!" she said to him. "Even among the gods themselves it would take a cunning knave to outdo you! Even in your very own realm you will not cease dissembling! But let us say no more about it. I agree that you are the craftiest of men, just as I am the wisest of the immortals. Yet you did not recognize me! You did not dream that I was beside you and saw to it that the Phaeacians met you courteously and hospitably. And now I have come to help you hide the gifts they gave you, to warn you that trouble awaits you in your palace, and to discuss with you the best way to meet it."

Odysseus looked at the goddess in astonishment and answered: "Noble daughter of Zeus, how could a mortal recognize you who can assume so many different shapes? I have not seen you in your own form since the fall of Troy. But now I beg you to tell me whether it is really true that I am in Ithaca, or whether you deceived me to comfort me in my distress?"

"Use your eyes!" Athene replied. "Do you not recognize the bay of Phorcys, that olive tree, the cave of the nymphs where you offered up many a sacrifice in days gone by, and those dark-wooded mountains, the range of Neriton?" So spoke Athene, and she dissolved the mist so that the hero saw his country clearly before him. Joyfully he threw himself on the earth, kissed it, and prayed to the nymphs, the patron deities of that place. Then the goddess helped him hide his treasure in the recesses of the cave. When they had rolled a stone in front of it, Odysseus and Athene sat down under the sacred olive tree to devise death for the suitors of whose insolence Athene told him, as well as of the faithfulness of Penelope.

"Had you not reported all this to me," said Odysseus when he had heard what had happened, "I should have been killed on my arrival home, just as surely as Agamemnon was murdered in Mycenae. But if you, gracious goddess, give me your aid, I shall not be afraid to stand alone against three hundred foes!"

"Be of good courage, my friend," the goddess replied. "I shall never desert you. Above all I shall see to it now that no one on this island recognizes you. The flesh shall shrivel on your stately limbs, the brown hair vanish from your head. I shall clothe you in rags which everyone will regard with loathing. Your shining eyes shall lose their luster. Not only the suitors, but even your wife and son will take you for an old and ugly stranger. And now I want you to seek out your most honest and loyal subject, the man who tends your swine and is devoted to you from the bottom of his heart. You will find him at the rock of Corax, near the spring Arethusa, where he is pasturing the herd. Sit down beside him and ask him about everything that is going on here. In the meantime I shall hasten to Sparta and recall your son Telemachus, who went there to inquire about you of Menelaus."

"Since you knew all about me," said Odysseus with some annoyance, "why did you not tell him in the first place? Did you want him to wander over the sea like myself, while strangers waste his substance?"

But the goddess comforted him, saying: "Do not fear for your son! I myself guided him, and my purpose in urging his journey was to mature the youth through travel and let him win glory, so that on his return he might face the suitors as a man. Rest assured that he is not suffering the slightest discomfort. He is lodged in the palace of Menelaus and has all his heart could wish. It is true that the suitors are lying in ambush for him and want to kill him before he reaches home, but I do not think this will come to pass. Long before that, many of them will sprawl dead on the ground."

So said the goddess and lightly touched the hero with her staff.

Instantly his flesh shrivelled, his back grew bent, and he looked like a ragged and dirty beggar. She handed him a staff and a patched sack which he slung over his shoulder by its frayed cord. Then she disappeared.

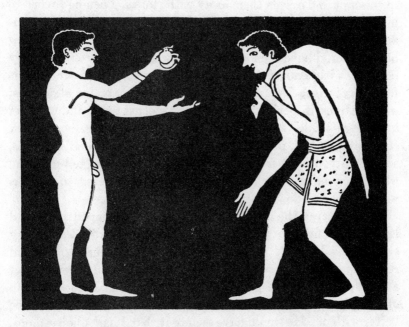

ODYSSEUS VISITS THE SWINEHERD

In this shape Odysseus walked over the hills to the place his patron goddess had described, and there he found Eumaeus, the swineherd, the most faithful of his servants. He was pasturing his herd on a wide piece of ground which he had hedged about with heavy stones. Within this enclosure were twelve pens, in each of which fifty sows were kept for breeding. The boars—only three hundred and sixty against six hundred sows!—were outside the pens. The reason there were so few of these was that day after day the suitors demanded a fatted boar for their feast. Four dogs, which looked as savage as wolves, guarded the herd.

The old man was cutting oxhide for sandals. He was alone. Three of his helpers were scattered over the meadow with the animals, and a fourth had gone to the city to deliver the daily boar to the palace.

The dogs were the first to notice Odysseus. They rushed at him with fierce barks, but all he did was to put aside his staff and sit down. And now he might have suffered the disgrace of being attacked by his own dogs, had not the swineherd hurried to the spot and driven them away with stones. Then he turned to his master, whom he took for a poor beggar, and said: "In another moment the dogs would have torn you to pieces, and a new burden would have been added to the weight of sorrow I already bear. It is bad enough that I must mourn for my master who is far away! Here I sit and have to fatten boars for strangers, while he himself, perhaps, has not even a crust to eat and wanders in foreign lands—that is, if he is still among the living! But come into my hut, poor old man. Let me give you food and wine, and when you have satisfied your hunger, you can tell me from where you have come and what you have suffered to look as wretched as you do."

They entered the hut of the swineherd. He heaped twigs and leaves on the floor for a pallet and covered it over with the shaggy skin of a wild goat. When Odysseus thanked him for his kind reception, Eumaeus replied: "Old man, one should never neglect a guest, not even the poorest. To be sure, I have not much to offer. If my good master had stayed at home, things would be better with me. He would have seen to it that I had a house, land, and a wife. Then I could play the host in quite another fashion! But he is away—perhaps dead. And I wish ill luck to all of Helen's line, she who is responsible for the death of so many brave men!"

So saying, the swineherd bound up his tunic with his belt and went to the pens where there were countless young pigs. He took two and slaughtered them, to have something to set before his guest. Then he cut up the meat, sprinkled it with white flour, roasted it on spits, and handed it to Odysseus. From a large jug he poured honey-sweet wine into a wooden bowl, seated himself opposite him, and said: "Eat now, stranger! This is the best I have to offer. It is only the meat of young pigs, for the suitors get all the fatted boars. They are insolent men with even less fear of the gods than pirates! They must have heard that my master is dead, for they do not woo his wife according to the custom of righteous men. They never return to their own homes at all, but stay here squandering the property of Odysseus. They do not slaughter his cattle once or even twice a day, but every hour, and they eat and drink day and night! My lord is as rich as twenty other kings put together. He has twelve herds of cattle and as many herds of sheep, swine, and goats on his farms where his herdsmen and servants tend them for him. Here alone, he has eleven flocks of goats watched over by faithful men, but each man is forced to deliver a he-goat to the suitors day after day. I take care of his swine, and every morning I too must send those greedy guzzlers a boar."

As the herdsman talked, Odysseus quickly ate the meat and drained his cup without answering, like one who is not thinking of what he is doing. His mind was already intent on the revenge he was going to take on the suitors. When he had satisfied his hunger and thirst and Eumaeus had filled his bowl again, he drank to his health and said in a kind voice: "Describe your master to me in greater detail, my friend. It is quite possible that I know him, that I have met him somewhere, for I have been around in the world a good bit."

But the swineherd had small faith in this possibility. "Do you think it would be easy for a stranger, a wayfarer, to make us believe what he tells us about our master?" he said. "During the past years, vagabonds who wanted food and shelter have frequently come to my mistress and her son and told them tales of our dear lord which moved them to tears. But I am certain they lied to get food or clothing, and that dogs and birds have devoured his flesh, or fish have eaten it, and that his bare bones are bleaching on some alien shore. Never again will I have so good a master! He was a kind and thoughtful man! When I think of him it is less as my lord than as an elder brother."

"Well then, because your doubting heart denies so firmly that he will return," Odysseus said, "I swear to you that he will! I do not lie like those other men who only wanted to get a new tunic or mantle with their tales! I shall not expect rewards until he returns. Though I am in rags and tatters, I shall tell only the truth: before the year is up—I swear it by Zeus, by your hospitable board, and by the herds of Odysseus!—your master will enter his house and punish the suitors who dare to make the life of his wife and son a burden to them."

"Old man," said Eumaeus, "I shall not have to reward you for your prediction, for Odysseus will not return. Do not spin out your foolish fancies. Drink your wine and let us talk of other things. I shall not hold you to your oath. I have no hopes concerning Odysseus, but I am troubled about Telemachus. I hoped to see him like his father both in body and spirit. But a god or a mortal has addled his brain, for he has gone to Pylos to make inquiries about my master. In the meantime, the suitors are lying in ambush, waiting to kill him, the last scion of the age-old line of Arcisius. But now tell me your own griefs. Who are you, and what has brought you to Ithaca?"

Odysseus amused himself by telling the swineherd a long story in which he presented himself as the impoverished son of a rich man on the island of Crete and invented the wildest adventures. He claimed to have been in the war of Troy and to have come across Odysseus there. On the way home, he said, a tempest had cast him ashore on the coast of the Thesprotians, whose king had given him news of Odysseus. The king said that he had been his guest a short time ago and that he had left to travel to the oracle of Dodona to hear the bidding of Zeus.

When Odysseus had finished his web of lies, the swineherd said: "Unhappy stranger! How you have touched me to the quick with the descriptions of your wanderings! The only thing I do not believe is what you have told me about Odysseus. An Aetolian assured me years ago that he had seen my master on Crete, where he was mending his ship. He said Odysseus was certain to come home that very summer, or in the autumn at the latest. And he invented all those lies because he was being hunted for murder and wanted to ingratiate himself with me. Ever since then I have been suspicious of anyone who claims to have seen Odysseus! You shall enjoy my hospitality without being driven to lies."

"Let us make a bargain," said Odysseus. "If your master really returns, you shall give me a tunic and mantle and send me to Dulichium, where I want to go. If he does not, bid your helpers cast me from a cliff into the sea, as an example to other beggars given to lying."

"That would be small glory for me!" the swineherd objected.

"How could I kill the guest I took into my own hut? If I did that, I could never pray to Zeus any more. But it is time for our supper. The rest will soon be here, and then we shall make merry together." Shortly after this the other herdsmen arrived, and Eumaeus had them slaughter a five-year-old boar in honor of his guest. Part of it was offered up to the nymphs and the god Hermes. The men had an ample share, but the best piece, cut from the back, was given to the guest, even though he looked like a beggar to his host.

This moved Odysseus, and he cried out gratefully: "May Zeus cherish you, Eumaeus, as you have cherished me, though I am sorry enough to look at!" The swineherd thanked him and pressed him to eat. While they feasted, clouds drove across the moon, the west wind howled around the hut, and rain began to fall in torrents. Odysseus felt cold in his beggar's rags, and, in order to attract his host's attention to his plight and induce him to offer his own warm mantle, he began to tell a story he invented on the spur of the moment.

"Listen, Eumaeus, and you other herdsmen," he said. "Your wine has loosened my tongue, and I am tempted to relate what had perhaps better be left unsaid. Once, during the siege of Troy, when the three of us, Odysseus, Menelaus, and myself, together with our warriors, lay in ambush in a reedy swamp close to the walls of the city, night fell, and it became very cold. The north wind blew flurries of snow about us, and soon our shields were rimmed with ice. This did not matter to my friends. They wrapped themselves in their mantles and slept warmly enough. But I had left my mantle behind in the camp, since I had not counted on such weather. Now a good part of the night was still to come, and I knew that it would be coldest just before dawn. So I nudged Odysseus, who lay beside me, with my elbow and said to him: 'If this cold keeps up, I shall freeze to death! An evil god prompted me to set out in nothing but my tunic.' When Odysseus heard this, he whispered back: 'Don't let anyone hear you! You shall soon have what you need!' He crooked his elbow, raised his head a little, and called softly to the others: 'Friends, the gods have sent me a warning dream! It seems we have ventured too far from our ships. Will not one of you go and ask Agamemmon to send us more men?' At his words Thoas, son of

Andraemon, jumped up, eager to do his bidding, flung his mantle to the ground, and ran off to the camp. I picked it up, wrapped it around me, and slept comfortably until morning. If I were as young and strong now as I was then, perhaps some herdsman here would lend me his mantle to shelter me from the cold of night. But old and poor as I am, no one cares how much I freeze in these rags of mine!"

"That was a fine hint you gave us in your tale," said Eumaeus laughing. "We shall certainly take it, and you shall lack neither clothing nor anything else. Tomorrow you must put on your rags again, though, for we have no mantles to spare. But should the son of Odysseus return safely, he will surely give you a tunic and mantle and have you conducted wherever you wish to go." And with that, Eumaeus took soft fleeces and heaped them near the hearth. When Odysseus lay down on them the swineherd covered him with his own thick mantle. While the others also settled down to sleep, he himself took his weapons in hand and prepared to spend the night near the pens. He took a shaggy goatskin to shield him from the wind, and another to serve as bedding. In his hand he carried a sharp spear to fend off thieves or dogs. Odysseus watched him leave the hut and felt glad that he had a faithful servant who cared for his master's possessions so conscientiously, even though he thought him dead.

TELEMACHUS LEAVES SPARTA

In the meantime Pallas Athene flew to Sparta, where she found the two youths from Pylos and Ithaca on couches in the palace of King Menelaus. Peisistratus, son of Nestor, was sound asleep, but Telemachus lay awake, worrying about his father. Suddenly he saw the daughter of Zeus standing at the foot of his bed. "Telemachus," she said, "you do not do well in staying away from home while wanton suitors are feasting and drinking in your palace. Do not delay any longer, but ask Menelaus to let you return to Ithaca before your mother is compelled to marry against her will. For her father and brothers are urging her to choose Eurymachus for her husband. He has outdone all the rest in bringing splendid gifts and has promised a large marriage settlement besides. Hasten home, and—if worst comes to worst—entrust your property to a loyal servant until such a time as the gods help you find a wife worthy of you. And one more thing: the strongest of the suitors are lying in wait for you in the strait between Ithaca and Same. They intend to kill you before you can reach your country. So steer away from there and travel only by night. A god will provide you with a fair wind. When you reach Ithaca, tell your companions to go to the city, but you yourself first visit Eumaeus who tends your swine. Stay with him until the following morning and from there send word of your safe arrival to Penelope, your mother."

When she had spoken thus, the goddess returned to high Olympus. But Telemachus touched his friend's boot with his heel and said: "Wake up, Peisistratus! Let us yoke the horses and start for home!"

"What was that?" the other answered drowsily. "You surely don't want to leave now, at dead of night? Wait until morning. King Menelaus will give us gifts in parting and speed us on our way with words of friendship." They were still discussing their journey when dawn came. Menelaus was up even before his guests. When Telemachus saw him walking through the hall, he quickly put on his tunic, slung his mantle over his shoulder, approached the king, and begged him to let him leave for home that very day.

"I shall not keep you if you long for your country," Menelaus replied. "A host who burdens his guest with too insistent hospitality is a foe rather than a friend. It is just as discourteous to hold back one who wishes to hasten away as to remind one who lingers of departure. Wait just long enough for me to put gifts into your chariot, and for the women to prepare a meal for you."

"Noble Menelaus," said Telemachus, "the only reason I wish to return to Ithaca is that I myself may not be killed while I am making inquiries about my father. It seems that dangers are in store for me, and that I am much needed in my palace."

When Menelaus heard this, he hurried to have the food made ready, and went to his storeroom together with Helen and his son Megapenthes. Here he selected a cup of gold and a silver pitcher. Helen looked through her chest and fetched out the most beautiful of the garments she herself had woven. With these gifts the three returned to their guest. Menelaus offered him the cup, Megapenthes set the pitcher before him, and Helen went up to him, carrying the garment, and said: "Take this gift, dear Telemachus, as a remembrance of Helen's art. Your bride shall wear it on her wedding day. Until then, let it lie in your mother's chest. But for you I wish a glad heart and a safe return to your father's house."

Telemachus accepted the gifts with courteous words of thanks, and his friend Peisistratus admired them and stowed them away in the chariot. Then Menelaus feasted with the two youths for the last time. When they had already mounted the chariot, the king came with a full cup, poured a libation to the gods, imploring them to give the youths a happy homecoming, and bade them farewell and sent his greetings to his old friend Nestor. While Telemachus was still thanking his host, an eagle flew up from the court, to the right of the horses, carrying a white goose in his talons, and a crowd of men and women followed shouting. All rejoiced in this sign of good omen, and Helen said: "Listen to my prophecy, my friends! As the eagle flew from his mountain aerie and snatched the goose fattened on the food of our house, so Odysseus will return from his long wanderings and avenge the wrong done him by the suitors who have grown fat on his provisions."

"May Zeus make this come true!" cried Telemachus. "And if he does, we shall pray to you as to a goddess, Queen Helen."

And now the two set out in their chariot. They spent the night with Diocles in Pherae, who again received them with warm hospitality, and on the second day reached the city of Pylos. As they approached the gates, Telemachus turned to his young friend and said: "Dear Peisistratus, even though our fathers know and value each other, and though this journey we have taken together has made us such good friends, I do not want to enter the city with you. Do not be angry with me for this! It is only that I fear your father will want to keep me as his guest out of the kindness of his heart, and you know yourself how important it is for me to get home as quickly as possible."

Peisistratus agreed that this would be the better course, and he guided the horses around the city confines and straight to the shore and the ship of Telemachus. Here he bade his friend a

tender farewell and said: "Now board your ship and leave as soon as you can, for if my father heard you were here, he would come and urge you to spend the night in our palace." Telemachus did as Nestor's son had bidden him. His companions boarded the ship and seated themselves at the oars. He himself stayed ashore near the stern just long enough to make an offering to Athene, his protectress.

While he was still praying to the goddess, a man came toward him in great haste, stretched his hands out toward him, and cried: "By your offering, O youth, by the gods, and by the welfare of your house and your people, tell me who you are and where you live!" When Telemachus briefly told him what he wanted to know, the stranger continued: "I too am on a journey. I am Theoclymenus, the soothsayer. My family comes from Pylos, but I myself lived in Argos. There I slew a man in a fit of anger. He has powerful kinsmen, and I am fleeing from his brothers and other male relatives, who have sworn to kill me. Henceforth I have no choice but to roam through the world as an exile. Regard me as a suppliant, and let me board your ship with you, for my pursuers are at my heels!"

Telemachus, who was of a kindly disposition, gladly asked the stranger into his ship and promised to see to it that he wanted for nothing when they reached Ithaca. He took the spear from the soothsayer's hands and laid it on the deck. Then he went aboard with Theoclymenus and sat down beside him in the stern. The ropes which bound the ship to the shore were loosed, the mast, carved of pine, was fitted into its socket, and the white sails were fastened to the yards. A fair wind bellied out the cloth, and through the rushing waves the ship sped out to sea.

WITH THE SWINEHERD

On the evening of that very day Odysseus had his meal with Eumaeus and the other herdsmen. To try his host and to find out how long he would give shelter to a poor beggar, Odysseus said to him after they had finished eating: "Tomorrow, my friend, I shall take my beggar's staff and set out for the town, for I do not want to be a burden to you. Tell me the best way to go, and give me a guide as far as the gates; then I shall wander about and see where I can get a little bread and wine. I should also like to go to the palace and tell Penelope what I know about Odysseus. Who knows but that the suitors may give me food and shelter in return for a little work? For I am very good at splitting wood, making a fire, turning the spit, serving meat and wine, and doing other things the rich expect from the poor."

But Eumaeus frowned and replied: "What talk is this! Do you want to walk straight to your own destruction? Do you really think those arrogant suitors want such as you for servants? They have quite other persons to see to their needs. Boys with blooming faces, with perfumed hair and dainty tunics walk among the tables loaded with meat, bread, and wine, and pass the platters. Better stay with us—you are no burden—and wait until Telemachus returns and supplies you with clothing and food."

Odysseus accepted this offer with thanks and then begged the herdsman to tell him about his master's parents—whether they were still living or had gone the dark path to Hades. "Laertes, his father, is still alive," said Eumaeus. "But he mourns Odysseus and Anticlea, his own wife, who died of sorrow for her lost son. I too lament the death of that good woman, for it was she who brought me up with her daughter Ctimene, almost as if I had been her own child. Later, when her daughter married a man from Same, the mother fitted me out and sent me here, to the country. Now, to be sure, I have been deprived of many things, and live by my work as well as I can. Penelope, who is queen now, can do nothing at all for me. She is surrounded and spied on by her suitors, and an honest servant is not even admitted to her presence."

"But where do you come from, and how did you happen to get to the palace in Ithaca?" Odysseus asked.

The swineherd filled his guest's bowl and answered: "Drink, old man, while I tell you a story which I hope will not tire you. This is the season when the nights are long, and there is time both for talk and for sleep. Beyond Ortygia lies the island of Syria. It has not a large population, though the soil is fertile. Two cities are on it. Both were governed by a mighty king, by my father Ctesius, son of Ormenus. When I was quite a small boy, dishonest seamen from Phoenicia landed there. They had all sorts of fine wares for sale on their ship and stayed near our coast for a long time. Now in our palace was a woman from Phoenicia. My father had bought her as a slave. She was slender and lovely, skilled in crafts, and well-liked by everyone in our household. She fell in love with one of the traders from her own country, and the man promised to take her to Sidon. The faithless slave, on her part, pledged him certain things in return. Not only would she bring him gold to pay her passage, but something better! For—so she told him—she was the nurse of the little prince! He was bright for his age and went with her whenever she had to do errands for the house. It would be easy to get him to come to the ship, and he should sell well enough to fetch the trader a substantial profit.

"So the woman made a bargain with him and returned to the palace. The traders remained on our island for a full year. When they finally loaded their ship and prepared to sail for home, one of them came to the palace with a necklace of gold and amber beads for sale. My mother and her tirewomen were grouped around him, passed the charming trinket from hand to hand, examined it, and offered him their price. While this was going on, the man nodded to the Phoenician, and hardly had he left the house before she took me by the hand and led me out. As we passed through the room which lay before the great hall, she saw the board spread for my father's guests. I watched her take three gold cups and hide them in the folds of her mantle, but I was too unsuspecting to give it a thought and followed her. The sun was just setting when we reached the harbor and boarded the ship with the rest of the crew.

"We left with a favorable wind, but when we were about six days out at sea, the false woman fell dead, struck by an arrow of Artemis, so they said, dead as a sea-fowl shot by the hunter. They threw her overboard as food for the fish, and I, a little child, was left alone among strangers, not one of whom had pity on me. After a time they landed in Ithaca, where Laertes bought me from the traders. That was the first time I ever saw this island."

"Well," said Odysseus, "you need not lament your fate too bitterly! For along with the bad, Zeus gave you much good. He put you into the hands of a good man who took care of your needs and on whose land you are still living well. I, on the other hand, am a beggar, wandering about in eternal exile."

While they were talking, the hours had sped. There was only a little time left to sleep before the dawn woke them.

TELEMACHUS RETURNS

That very morning Telemachus and his companions landed on the coast of Ithaca. Following Athene's advice he ordered them to row on to the city, while he himself went ashore to visit the swineherd. He promised the men their pay and a merry feast on the following day. "But where shall I go, my son?" asked Theoclymenus. "Who will give me shelter in the city? Shall I go straight to your mother's palace?"

"If things at home were as they should be," Telemachus replied, "I should urge you to go there without more ado. But as it is, the suitors would never admit you, and my mother keeps to her room. It would be wiser for you to go to the house of Eurymachus, son of Polybus of Ithaca, a man highly esteemed by his countrymen. Besides, Eurymachus is the most reasonable of my mother's suitors."

While he was speaking, a hawk flew by on his right. In its talons was a dove whose feathers it was plucking as it flew. When the soothsayer saw this, he took the young man aside and whispered to him: "If my knowledge of signs does not trick me, this is a happy omen for your house! Never will another line rule in Ithaca. It is you and yours who will govern this land forever!"

Before bidding farewell to Theoclymenus, Telemachus commended him to the care of his best friend, Peiraeus, son of Clytius, to whom he sent word to take the seer into his house until he, Telemachus, came to the city. Then he left the ship and went his way on foot.

In the meantime Odysseus and the swineherd were preparing the morning meal, while the helpers drove the herd to pasture. They had just begun to eat when they heard steps and the dogs jumped up. They did not snarl, but rather seemed to bark a joyful welcome. "A friend must be coming to see you," said Odysseus. "The dogs would not act this way toward strangers."

Hardly had the last word left his lips when he saw his own dear son Telemachus standing on the threshold. The herdsman dropped his bowl in glad excitement and ran to his young master. He embraced him and covered his head, his eyes, and his hands with kisses, weeping with joy, as though he were seeing someone he loved who had escaped from death. An old father welcoming his late-born son when he comes home after ten years in foreign lands could not have been happier! Telemachus did not enter the hut until Eumaeus had told him that nothing of importance had happened in the palace during his absence. Then he handed the swineherd his lance and went in. Odysseus wanted to give him his seat, but Telemachus waved him back with kindly words: "Stay where you are, stranger," he said. "Eumaeus will find a place for me." And the herdsman was, indeed, already heaping a pile of twigs and leaves and spreading over these a soft fleece. And now Telemachus sat down, and the swineherd served him with roast meat and bread, and mixed wine and water in a wooden bowl. While the three ate, Telemachus asked Eumaeus about the stranger, and the old man gave him a brief outline of the long tale Odysseus had invented about himself. "And now," he concluded, "he has fled from a Thesprotian ship and taken shelter with me. I shall put him in your hands. Do with him as you please."

"I am alarmed at the very idea," Telemachus replied. "How can I take this man home with me—old and weak as he is? It will be better for you to keep him here a while longer. I shall send him a tunic, a mantle, sandals, and a sword, and food enough so that you and your helpers need not share your stores with him. But he must not appear before the suitors, for they are so insolent that even a powerful man could not prevail against them."

Odysseus expressed his amazement at the fact that the suitors dared defy the son of the house. "Can it be," he asked Telemachus, "that your people hate you? Or have you a quarrel with your brothers? Or do you let those men oppress you of your own free will? If I were as young as you and the son of Odysseus, I should rather let myself be knocked senseless or die in my own house than passively watch such goings on!"

Telemachus answered quietly: "The people do not hate me, and I have no brothers. I am an only son. But many men from the surrounding islands and from Ithaca itself are wooing my mother and regard me as their enemy. She has been evading them, but they stay, and soon I shall have nothing left to my name." Then he turned to the swineherd and said: "And now do me the favor of going to the city and telling my mother that I have returned. But do not let the suitors hear you!"

"Would it not be better for me to go by way of your grandfather Laertes?" Eumaeus asked. "They say that since you left for Pylos, he has neither eaten nor drunk, and has not even gone out to watch over the work done in his fields. He just sits there overcome with grief and grows feebler every day."

"In spite of that I cannot let you go the long way around," said Telemachus. "My mother must be the first to hear of my homecoming. She will send a servant to bring the news to my grandfather." And he urged the old man out of the hut. Eumaeus bound his sandals to his feet, took a lance in his hand, and hastened away.

ODYSSEUS REVEALS HIMSELF TO HIS SON

Pallas Athene had only waited for Eumaeus to leave the hut. The instant he was gone she appeared on the threshold in the form of a tall, beautiful woman. She did not reveal herself to Telemachus, but only to his father and the dogs, who did not bark but whined and ran to the other side of the court. The goddess motioned to Odysseus. He understood what she wanted and went outside. She met him at the wall and said: "Odysseus, you need no longer conceal your true self from your son. It will be better if both of you go to the city together to bring doom to the suitors. I shall not fail to join you, for I burn with eagerness to punish those scoundrels." So said the goddess and touched the beggar with her golden staff. And a miracle took place. He grew taller, his face became smooth and tanned, and his hair and beard were thick and curled. A fine tunic and mantle clothed his strong, bronzed limbs. When she had brought about this change, the goddess vanished.

Odysseus reentered the hut, and his son gazed at him in amazement. Then he turned away his face, for he thought he was in the presence of a god, and said: "Stranger, you look very different now than before! You have other clothing, and your very features have changed. You must be one of the immortals! Let me bring you an offering and implore your favor."

"I am no god," Odysseus replied. "Look at me, Telemachus! Do you not recognize your own father, for whom you have grieved so many years?" And as he spoke the tears gushed from his eyes. He hastened toward his son and clasped him in his arms.

But Telemachus found it difficult to believe the truth. "No, no," he cried. "You are not Odysseus, my father! A god is tricking me only to plunge me deeper into despair. How could a mortal bring about such a change in his appearance with his own mortal powers?"

"Do not be so astonished, dear Telemachus," said Odysseus. "It is really I who have returned to my country after an absence of twenty years—I and none other. It was Athene who transformed me, first into a stooping old beggar, and then back into a strong man. For the gods find it easy to make a man seem noble or base." So said Odysseus and seated himself. And now Telemachus took courage and put his arms around his father. Both father and son were stirred by the long years of sorrow they had suffered, and they lamented as loudly as parent birds whose unfledged young have been stolen from the nest. When they had wept their fill, Telemachus at last asked his father on what ship he had come home. Odysseus told him the story and then said: "And now that I am here, my son, Athene wants us to take counsel as to the best way to revenge ourselves on our foes. Name the suitors to me so that I may know how many of them there are and whether the two of us are enough to cope with them, or whether we should look around for allies."

"Your glorious deeds have been told me over and over, father," Telemachus answered. "I know that you are both strong and wise. Nevertheless, we two could never prevail against the suitors. It is not as if there were ten or even twenty of them. There are many more: fifty-two of the boldest young men from Dulichium alone, and six servants to boot; twenty-four from Same; twenty from Zacynthus, and twelve from Ithaca. And then there is Medon, the herald, a singer, and two cooks. So, if it is at all possible, let us try to get others to help us."

"Do not forget," Odysseus replied, "that Athene and Zeus have allied themselves to our cause, and that once the fight breaks out in my palace, they will not let us wait long for their help. Now my plan is this. You must return to the city tomorrow and take your place among the suitors as though nothing had happened. By Athene's touch I shall again assume the shape of a beggar, and the swineherd will conduct me to the palace. No matter what they do to me there, even if they throw things at me and drag me across the threshold, you must curb your heart and bear it. You may try to calm them with words, but they will not listen to you. At a sign from me you shall take all the weapons hanging in the great hall and hide them in one of the upper chambers of the house. If the suitors notice they are gone and ask about them, say you have had them removed because soot from the hearth has dimmed the gleam they had when Odysseus still used them. Leave out only two swords, two spears, and two oxhide shields for us to fight with when our enemies, in the blind confusion the gods will send upon them, try to attack us. For the rest, no one must know that Odysseus has returned, not Laertes, not the swineherd, and not even Penelope, your mother. In the meantime I shall test the servants and find out who still honors and fears me, and who has forgotten me and does not reverence you."

"Dear father," said Telemachus, "I shall certainly do just as you say. But I do not think testing the servants will help us. It will take too long. It will be easy enough, of course, to find out about the women in the palace, but as for the men on your farms, let us leave that for the time when you are again king in your own palace." Odysseus agreed with his son and rejoiced in his clear-headed thinking.

THE CITY AND THE PALACE

In the meanwhile the ship which had brought Telemachus and his companions home from Pylos had run into port, and a herald had been sent on ahead to the palace to tell Penelope of her son's return. The swineherd arrived with the same news, and the two met in the king's house. The herald was first to speak. He said aloud to the queen in the presence of her tirewomen: "Your son, O queen, has returned." But Eumaeus spoke to her alone, without eavesdroppers, and repeated what his young master had said; he also begged her to send on the good news to his grandfather Laertes. As soon as the swineherd had delivered his message he hastened home to his herd. Some of Penelope's handmaids reported the brief words of the herald to the suitors, and they gathered dejectedly outside the gates and seated themselves on the polished stones to take counsel with one another. Eurymachus opened the assembly. "We surely would never have believed that this boy would carry out his purpose and accomplish this journey," he said. "Let us quickly prepare a swift-sailing ship and send a message to our friends who are lying in ambush, so that they wait no longer but return."

While Eurymachus was speaking, Amphinomus, another suitor, had looked toward the harbor which was easily visible from the forecourt of the palace. And there he saw the ship with those suitors who had gone to lie in ambush coming in with full sails. "We need not send a message," he cried. "There they are! Either a god has told them of the return of Telemachus, or they have been pursuing his ship and could not catch up with him."

All the suitors rose and hurried down to the shore. Then, together with those who had just arrived, they went to the market place where they held an assembly. Antinous, leader of the party which had set out for the strait, defended himself and his comrades. "It was not our fault that he got away," he said. "We had spies watching from the hills the livelong day, and after sunset we did not stay ashore but crossed and recrossed the strait, thinking only of capturing Telemachus and putting an end to his life. One of the immortals must have guided him, for we did not even catch sight of his ship! But to make up for this failure, we must destroy him here, in the city, for the boy is growing too clever and will soon be too much for us. In the end he will make the people rebellious too. If they find out that we have lain in ambush to murder him, they will drive us out of the country. Rather than have that happen, let us get him out of the way, divide up his possessions among us, and leave the palace to his mother and her husband-to-be. But if my plan does not appeal to you, if you want him to live and keep his estates, then let us stop using up his stores. Let each one of us go to his home and from there woo the queen with gifts, and let her choose the one who is most generous, or the one whom Fortune favors."

When he had finished, there was a long silence. Finally Amphinomus, son of Nisus, the noblest among the suitors, whose wisdom and courteousness had commended him even to Penelope, rose and stated his opinion to the gathering. "My friends," he said, "I do not think we should murder Telemachus. It is a terrible crime to kill the last descendant of a kingly line. At any rate, let us first ask the gods about this. If Zeus favors the enterprise, I myself shall be willing to kill him, but if the immortals do not consent, I counsel you to give up the plan."

The suitors agreed to do as he had advised. They postponed carrying out their scheme and returned to the palace. But this time, too, Medon, the herald, who kept secret faith with Penelope, had eavesdropped at their meeting and told the queen everything he had heard. Instantly she veiled herself and hastened down into the great hall, where she addressed the originator of the plot in a voice trembling with emotion. "Antinous," she cried, "Ithaca is wrong in regarding you as the wisest among your countrymen. You are not really wise. You are deaf to the words of the wretched, to whom even Zeus gives ear, and insolent enough to conspire against the life of my son Telemachus. Have you forgotten that your father once fled to our house as a suppliant, because he was being hunted for having practiced piracy on our allies? His pursuers wanted to kill him, but Odysseus held them back and quieted their rage. And now you, in thanks for the help given your father, waste the goods of Odysseus, woo his wife, and want to murder his only son! You would do better to keep your companions from impious actions!"

Before Antinous could reply, Eurymachus broke in. "Have no fears for your son, Penelope," he said. "As long as I live, no man shall dare lay hands on him. When I was a child, Odysseus sometimes took me on his knee and gave me tidbits. And so his son is dearest to me of all men. He need not be afraid of death, at least not of death at the hands of the suitors. But if the gods want him to die, their will cannot be evaded." So said that false man with the kindliest face in the world, but his heart was black with hatred.

Penelope returned to her chamber, threw herself on her couch, and wept for her husband until Athene shed sleep on her eyes.

TELEMACHUS, ODYSSEUS, AND EUMAEUS REACH THE CITY

That evening, when the swineherd returned to his hut, he found
Odysseus and Telemachus occupied in preparing a pig for the
evening meal. Since Athene had again turned the hero into a
ragged beggar, Eumaeus did not recognize him. "Have you come
at last?" Telemachus called to him as soon as he had crossed the
threshold. "And what news have you brought from Ithaca? Are
the suitors still lying in wait for me, or have they given up and
left their hiding-place?" Eumaeus told him of the ship he had
seen returning, and Telemachus smiled knowingly at his father,
but so that the swineherd did not notice it. Then the three of
them ate and lay down to sleep.

The next morning Telemachus prepared to go to the city and
said to Eumaeus: "Old man, I must look after my mother now. I
want you to take this poor stranger to the city so that he may
beg his food from house to house. I cannot possibly assume the
burdens of the whole world. I have enough troubles of my own.
If the old man is offended at this, so much the worse for him!"

Odysseus, who was pleasantly surprised at his son's ability to
to dissemble, answered in the swineherd's stead: "Young man, I
myself do not wish to remain here any longer. A beggar is always
better off in a town than in the country. Just you go, and when I
have warmed myself a little at the fire, and the sun is higher in
heaven, your servant here shall guide me to the city."

Telemachus hastened on his way. It was still fairly early in
the morning when he reached the palace, and the suitors had not
yet appeared. He leaned his lance against a pillar at the entrance
and crossed the stone threshold of the great hall. Here Euryclea
was just spreading the chairs with soft fleeces. When she saw
the youth, she ran toward him with tears of joy and welcomed
him home. The other servants too kissed his head and shoulders.
And now Penelope came down from her chamber, slim as Artemis
and lovely as Aphrodite. "Have you come back to me, dear son?"
she cried, clasping him in her arms and kissing his eyes. "I despaired of seeing you again ever since I knew you had left for
Pylos. But tell me—what did you find out about your father?"

"O mother," said Telemachus mournfully, though it was very difficult for him to conceal his true feelings, "I have only just escaped death myself. Do not revive my grief for my father the moment I enter this house. Go to the bath, put on festal garments, and pledge hecatombs to the gods when they have granted us revenge. I myself must go to the market place to bring home a stranger who accompanied me on my voyage and whom I left with a friend until I should call for him."

Penelope did as her son had said, while he took his spear in hand and went toward the market place with his dogs at his heels. Athene had shed such grace about him that the citizens marvelled at his beauty; the suitors overwhelmed him with flattering words, though in their hearts they brooded on their wicked plans. But Telemachus did not stay with them. He joined three of his father's old friends, Mentor, Antiphus, and Halitherses, and told them as much as he was allowed to. And now Peiraeus brought to him Theoclymenus, the soothsayer, and Telemachus greeted both. Peiraeus at once begged him to send servants to his house to fetch the presents Menelaus had given Telemachus in parting. But Telemachus said: "The gifts are safer in your house, for I do not know what turn my affairs will take. If the suitors murder me and divide up my possessions, then I should like you to have those beautiful things rather than they. But if I succeed in punishing and destroying them, why then, come gayly and bring the treasures to your glad friend."

So saying, Telemachus took Theoclymenus by the hand and led him toward the palace. There both had a refreshing bath and ate the morning meal in Penelope's company. Then she sat at her spindle and said sadly to her son: "There is really no reason why I should not return to my lonely chamber and wet my couch with tears, as I have done all these years, for it seems you will tell me nothing you have heard about your father."

"Dear mother," Telemachus said to her, "I shall gladly tell you all I have heard and only wish it were news that could be of comfort to you. Old Nestor received me well in Pylos, but he knew nothing at all of my father. So he sent me to Sparta with his son. There I was entertained by Menelaus and Helen, for whose sake the Argives and Trojans suffered so much and so long. There I learned the scant bit which Proteus, the sea-god, had told Menelaus. It was that he had seen Odysseus sorrowing on the island of Ogygia, where Calypso is keeping him in her grotto against his will. He has neither a ship nor oarsmen to take him home."

When Theoclymenus, the soothsayer, saw that Penelope was deeply moved by these words, he interrupted his young host and said: "He does not know everything, O queen! Listen to my prediction: Odysseus is already in his native land, waiting or prowling about secretly and plotting the death of your suitors. This I know from the flight of birds, and I told your son the moment I saw the omen."

"May your prediction come true!" said Penelope with a sigh. "I shall not fail to give you rich rewards."

While these three were talking, the suitors were amusing themselves in the court as usual. They threw the discus and hurled the javelin until the herald summoned them to the midday meal. Eumaeus and his guest had, in the meantime, set out for the city. Odysseus had slung his beggar's scrip across his shoulder, and the swineherd had put a staff in his hand. Soon they came to the city well which the ancestors of Odysseus had walled in with stone. All about it was a grove of poplars, and the water gushed forth in a clear stream. Here they met the goatherd Melantheus with two of his helpers, driving the best goats in his herd to the city as food for the wooers.

When Melantheus saw Eumaeus and his companion, he began to revile them both. "There you are!" he exclaimed. "Birds of a feather flock together! There is one scoundrel leading another. Where are you taking that hungry beggar, swineherd? To the city, to go from door to door, lazily begging a crust? If you handed him over to me, he could sweep out the pens and carry young shoots to the kids. Who knows but that he might fatten up a bit on a diet of goat cheese? But he has, of course, learned nothing and can do nothing but beg to fill his belly." So he spoke and kicked the beggar in the hip. But Odysseus did not stumble. He did, to be sure, turn over in his mind whether to strike this insolent fellow over the head so hard that he would never rise again. But he curbed his anger and suffered the insult without a word.

Eumaeus, however, did not restrain his rage. He scolded the goatherd soundly and then turned to the well. "Holy nymphs, daughters of Zeus," he said, "if ever my lord has brought you precious offerings, grant my prayer that he may soon return. He would quickly punish this churlish man! He is the worst goatherd in the world, and all he can do is idle away his time in the town."

"You dog!" Melantheus retorted. "All you are good for is to be sold on the islands as a slave! You might fetch a pretty penny. For the rest, I wish Apollo's arrow or the spear of a suitor might strike that Telemachus of yours, so that he joined his father in the underworld." With this parting shot he went on to the palace and seated himself right opposite Eurymachus, for he was well-liked among the suitors who permitted him to share their feasts.

A little later the swineherd and Odysseus reached the palace. When the hero saw the house from which he had been absent so long a time, his heart beat high. He took his companion by the hand and said: "Eumaeus, this must be the house of Odysseus! How splendid it is, and how many rooms it has! How solid is the wall around the court, and what tall, wide gates flank the entrance! It seems a strong fortress as well as a palace. And feasting must be going on inside, for I can catch the scent of roast meat, and can hear the voice of a singer who is seasoning the banquet with his songs."

They took counsel with each other and decided that Eumaeus should go first and reconnoitre in the hall, while Odysseus waited in front of the gate. They were still conferring about this, when an old dog lying at the door lifted his head, pricked his ears, and rose. His name was Argus. Odysseus himself had bred him before setting out for Troy. He had been a good hunting dog, but now, in his old age, the men neglected him and let him sleep on a dung-heap, swarming with flies. When Argus noticed Odysseus, he seemed to recognize him in spite of his disguise, for he dropped his ears and wagged his tail. But he was too weak to go up to him. Odysseus quickly wiped away a tear, but he hid his sadness and said: "That dog was not a bad sort in his prime. You can still see that he is a thoroughbred."

"He is indeed," Eumaeus replied. "He was my master's favorite hound. You should have seen him racing through the valley and following the scent of game in the underbrush! But now, since his master is gone, no one pays any attention to him. He is utterly neglected, and the servants do not even bother to feed him." And Eumaeus entered the palace. But the dog, who had seen his master again after twenty years, put his head down between his paws and died.

ODYSSEUS, THE BEGGAR, IN THE HALL

Telemachus was the first to see the swineherd come into the hall, and with a nod he called him to his side. Eumaeus looked around cautiously and took a stool that was standing near, on which the carver sat when carving for the wooers. This he placed at Telemachus' table and seated himself opposite him, and the herald immediately served him with meat and bread. Soon after, Odysseus tottered in, leaning heavily on his staff, and sat down on the ashen threshold. The instant Telemachus saw him, he took a whole loaf from the basket in front of him, as well as a large piece of meat, and gave these things to the swineherd with the words: "Take these gifts to the stranger, my friend, and tell him not to be ashamed, but to beg among the suitors."

Odysseus received the gifts and raised both hands to bless the giver. Then he placed the food on the sack at his feet and began to eat.

All through the feast Phemius, the singer, had charmed the guests with his song. Now he fell silent, and the wild carousing of the banqueters filled the hall. This was the moment Athene chose to approach Odysseus, invisible to all. She urged him to beg crusts from the suitors so that he might learn which were brutal and which more kindly. Not that the goddess did not plan death for all alike, but some were to suffer less than others. Odysseus did her bidding and went from man to man, holding out his hand in pleading as if he had been a beggar all his life. A few were compassionate and gave him food, and the question arose where he had come from. Then Melantheus, the goatherd, said: "I have seen that old fellow before. Eumaeus brought him along with him."

Angrily Antinous turned to the swineherd. "Why did you bring him to this city?" he shouted at him. "Haven't we loafers

enough? Do you think we need another mouth to feed in this hall?"

"You are a harsh man," Eumaeus answered quietly. "All great men vie in calling to their palaces seers, physicians, builders, and singers who gladden us with their song. But no one ever invites a beggar. He comes of his own accord, but that is no reason to throw him out. And this shall not be done here as long as Penelope and Telemachus live in the house."

But Telemachus bade him be silent, saying: "Do not trouble to answer, Eumaeus. You know that this man is in the habit of uttering insults. As for you, Antinous, let me tell you that you are not my guardian and therefore have no right to make me drive a stranger from my door. Better give him all he needs. But I know, of course, that you prefer to eat all you can yourself, rather than share with others."

"Listen to that boy gibing at me!" cried Antinous. "But I say that if all the wooers would hand that beggar as much as I, he would not have to beg for three months running." And with that he lifted a stool threateningly. Odysseus was just coming toward him to ask for alms and, as he did so, he began to complain of his long wanderings through Egypt and Cyprus. Antinous answered him sourly: "What god has sent us this greedy, forward fellow? Go away from this table, or I'll Egypt and Cyprus you!" And when Odysseus withdrew, grumbling at his inhospitable manner, Antinous threw the stool at him, and it struck his shoulder close to the neck. But Odysseus stood unshaken as a rock and silently shook his head, pondering evil in his heart. Then he returned to the threshold, set down his full scrip, and complained aloud of Antinous to the rest of the company. But Antinous cut him short.

"Silence!" he roared. "Shut your mouth and stuff your belly, or I shall catch hold of you and drag you over the threshold by hands and feet and flay you alive!"

Such coarseness was too much even for the suitors. One of them rose and said: "Antinous, you have not done well to throw things at this unfortunate stranger. What if he were a messenger of the gods who has assumed mortal shape—for that sometimes happens?" But Antinous paid no attention to this warning. Telemachus said nothing at all at this abuse of his father. He nursed his anger in silence.

Through the open window of her chamber, Penelope could hear everything that was taking place in the great hall, and she felt sorry for the beggar. She had Eumaeus brought to her in secret and commanded him to conduct the stranger to her. "Perhaps," she added, "he can tell me something about my husband. He may even have seen him, for it seems he has wandered all over the world."

"Yes," said Eumaeus. "Had the suitors been quiet, he could have told them many things. He has been staying with me for three days, and his tales delighted me as if they were recited by a singer. He comes from Crete, and he claims that his father and the father of Odysseus were bound by ties of hospitality. He asserts that Odysseus is now in the land of the Thesprotians and will soon return laden with treasure."

"Go quickly," said Penelope, deeply moved. "Bring the stranger here, and let him tell me! Oh, these insolent suitors! What we lack is a man like Odysseus. If only he were here, he and Telemachus would soon take revenge for what they have done!" She had hardly finished speaking when Telemachus sneezed so loudly that the hall echoed with the sound. Penelope smiled and said to Eumaeus: "Did you hear my son sneeze when I said that? Surely that is a good omen, so call the stranger at once."

Eumaeus told the beggar of Penelope's wish, but he replied: "I should very much like to tell the queen whatever I know about Odysseus, and I know a great deal! But the behavior of the suitors fills me with dread. When that man over there hurled a stool at me and hit me in the shoulder, neither Telemachus nor anyone else took my part. So ask Penelope to wait until sunset. Then, if she will let me, I shall sit at her warm hearth and tell her many things." When Penelope heard his reply she saw that he was right, and resolved to curb her impatience.

Eumaeus returned to the hall, mingled with the suitors, and managed to whisper to Telemachus: "I am going back to my hut now, master. You will see to matters here, but I beg you to see to yourself above all, for the suitors are shrewd and vicious and are out to harm you." But Telemachus begged him to stay until after the evening meal. He did so, and then left, promising to return on the following day and bring with him the best fatted boars he had.

ODYSSEUS AND THE BEGGAR IRUS

The suitors were still seated at the board when a notorious beggar from the town entered the hall. He was known as a big eater, but though he was tall and broad-shouldered, his muscles were weak and flabby. His real name was Arnaeus, but the young people in the city called him Irus, playing on the name of Iris, messenger of the gods, since for a small sum he carried messages from one to another. Envy had brought him to the palace, for he had heard that a rival beggar had come. Now he advanced with the intention of driving Odysseus out of his own house. "Get away from the door, old man," he shouted. "Don't you see that they are all winking at me to drag you out by the feet? Better go of your own accord, and do not force me to speed you on your way!"

Odysseus gave him a black look. "There is room on the threshold for both of us," he said. "You seem to be as poor as I. Do not envy me, for I do not begrudge you your share. And do not rouse my anger or challenge me to fight. Old as I am, the blood would soon flow from your breast and mouth, and the people in this house would not be disturbed by your presence tomorrow."

This infuriated Irus, and he shouted louder: "See how glibly the wretch talks—like an old fish-wife! I'll hit you right and left until your teeth drop out, as though you were a swine spilling corn! Do you want to fight me, even though I am much younger than you?"

The suitors burst out laughing when they heard the beggars quarrelling, and Antinous said: "I'll tell you what, my friends. Do you see those goat paunches, stuffed with blood and fat, roasting on the fire? Let us use them as a prize for these noble heroes. The victor shall eat of them as much as he can, and in the future no beggar but he shall enter this hall."

All the suitors were well-pleased with this proposal. But Odysseus played the timid old man, weakened by hardships. He begged the suitors to promise not to intervene in favor of Irus, and they promised him this without hesitation. Then Telemachus rose and said: "Stranger, if you down this fellow, then fear no man among the Achaeans. I am the host in this house, and whoever attacks you will have to reckon with me!" The suitors applauded these words. Odysseus girded up his tatters, and then all saw his sinewy thighs, his muscular arms, his broad shoulders and chest, for Athene had made him even mightier than he was.

The suitors were amazed, and one said to the other: "What sturdy limbs that old man has under his rags! Irus won't have an easy time of it!" And Irus himself began to regret his challenge. The servants had to force him to gird himself for the fight, and his knees shook. Antinous, who had looked forward to a very different situation, said crossly: "Big-Mouth, I wish you had never been born! How can you tremble before such a feeble old man? But let me tell you that if he defeats you, you shall be put aboard ship and taken to Epirus, to King Echetus, who is the terror of all men. He will cut off your nose and ears and throw them to the dogs!" The more Antinous raged at him, the more Irus trembled. But they thrust him forward, and now both beggars raised their hands and began to fight. Odysseus deliberated whether he should kill the wretched fellow at the first blow, or strike gently, in order not to arouse the suspicions of the suitors. This seemed the wiser course to him, so when Irus struck him on the right shoulder, he only gave him a little tap under the ear. But slight as it was it crushed the bone, the blood spurted from his mouth, and Irus dropped to the floor, writhing and with teeth chattering. While the suitors howled with laughter and clapped their hands, Odysseus pulled Irus away from the threshold, out to the court and out of the gate. There he propped him against the wall, put a staff in his hands, and said mockingly: "Stay there and keep away the dogs and pigs!" Then he returned to the hall and again seated himself on the threshold.

His victory had made an impression on the suitors. They

laughed, hailed him, and said: "May Zeus and the other immortals give you whatever you desire, stranger, for you have rid us of a troublesome fellow whom we shall now ship off to King Echetus." Odysseus accepted their words as a good omen. And now Antinous gave him the big goat paunch stuffed with blood and fat, and Amphinomus added two loaves from the basket, filled a golden cup with wine, and drank to the victor. "To your health, old man," he said. "May you be free from care in times to come!" Odysseus looked him gravely in the eyes and answered: "Amphinomus, you seem to be a reasonable young man, and I know you have a distinguished father. Take to heart what I am going to say to you: nothing on earth is more frail and uncertain than the life of man. While the gods favor him, he thinks the future can hold no danger, but when sorrow overtakes him, he finds he has not the courage to bear it. I know all this from experience. There was a time when I, too, trusting to the strength of youth, did much that I should not have done. And so I warn everyone not to be lawless at any time, but to accept the gifts of the gods in silent gratitude. For this reason it is not wise for the suitors to be so wanton and headstrong, and to offend the wife of a man who, I believe, cannot be far from home. Perhaps he is already quite near. May some god take you away from this house, Amphinomus, before he reaches his home." So saying, Odysseus poured a libation, drank, and returned the cup to the youth. The suitor grew thoughtful, bowed his head, and walked through the hall with a heavy heart, as if he guessed what was in store for him. But he was not to escape the punishment Athene had decreed.

PENELOPE AND THE SUITORS

And now the goddess breathed into Penelope the wish to appear before the suitors, to fill their hearts with longing, and to prove her true worth and faithfulness in front of her son and husband, of whose presence, to be sure, she was not aware. Her old and loyal servant applauded her decision. "Go, daughter," she said, "and speak words of counsel to your son while there is still time. But they must not see you down there as you are now, your lovely face stained with tears. First bathe and anoint yourself, and then confront the suitors."

But Penelope shook her head and replied: "Do not expect that of me. Ever since my husband shipped for Troy, I have had no pleasure in adorning myself. But now call my handmaids Autonoë and Hippodamia. They shall come with me, for I do not wish to appear before those men unaccompanied."

While Eurynome went to fetch the tirewomen, Athene lulled Penelope, reclining in a chair, into a sweet sleep which lasted no more than a few moments. But this was long enough for the goddess to endow her with unearthly beauty. She refreshed her face with ambrosia, with which Aphrodite anoints herself when she goes to dance with the Graces. She made her taller and lither and shed over her skin the whiteness of new ivory. Then Athene vanished. As her two handmaids hurried into the room, Penelope awoke, rubbed her eyes, and said: "How sweetly I slept! I wish the gods would this very instant send me so sweet a death that I would no longer have to grieve for my husband and endure what goes on in this house." With these words she rose from her chair and descended to the suitors below. She stood in the doorway of the great hall, her beauty shining through her veil, and when the suitors saw her, their hearts beat high, and each longed to have her as his wife. But the queen turned to her son and said: Telemachus, I am surprised at you. Even as a boy you showed more sense than you do now that you are tall and grown. Why did you sit there and say nothing when the poor stranger who came to us for shelter was mocked and insulted? This will disgrace us in the eyes of the world."

"I do not wonder at your distress, dear mother," Telemachus replied. "And I know quite well what is right, but these men are all against me; there is not one who would support me in anything I did. As for this fight, it did not end as the suitors hoped. I only wish that they were forced to hang their heads like that miserable fellow out in the court." Telemachus had spoken in so low a voice that the suitors could not hear him, and now Eurymachus, quite unaware of what had been said, called to the queen: "Daughter of Icarius! If the Achaeans in the whole of Greece could only see you, there would be many more suitors here tomorrow, for you excel all other women in beauty and wisdom."

"Ah, Eurymachus," Penelope answered, "my beauty paled when my husband left for Troy. If he came back, if my life were once more protected by his arm, I might bloom again. But now I am stricken with sorrow. When Odysseus bade me farewell, when he clasped my right hand at the wrist for the last time, he said: 'Not all the Achaeans will return from Troy unharmed. They say that the Trojans know the art of war, that they are good at casting the javelin, shooting with the bow, and guiding their chariots. And so I do not know whether I am destined to return, or to die before Troy. Watch over the house and take care of my father and mother even more tenderly than you have been doing. And if I am not home by the time our son is grown, then marry if you like, and leave our house.' That was what he said, and now it is all coming true. The terrible day of the wedding draws near, and I think of it with dread, for these suitors behave very differently from other wooers. If a man desires the daughter of a distinguished father as his wife, it is customary for him to bring cattle and sheep for the feast, and gifts for the bride, but not to waste the stores of another man without offering compensation."

It gave Odysseus keen pleasure to hear her speak with such wisdom. But Antinous replied in the name of all the suitors: "Noble queen, we shall gladly bring you costly gifts and ask you to accept them. But we shall not go home until you have chosen one among us for your husband." All the suitors applauded these words. Servants were dispatched, and soon they returned with the promised gifts. Antinous presented her with a robe, woven in many colors and fastened with twelve clasps of gold fitted to widely curved catches. Eurymachus offered a necklace of amber beads, strung on gold, and it shone like the sun. Eurydamas held out to her earrings set with three mulberry colored jewels, and Pisander gave her a pendant exquisitely wrought. The other suitors also brought costly gifts which the servants carried up after Penelope as she returned to her chamber.

ODYSSEUS MOCKED AGAIN

The suitors amused themselves riotously until nightfall. When it grew dark, handmaids brought in three braziers to light the hall and filled them with dry oak wood and resinous pine. As they were fanning the flames, Odysseus went up to them and said: "Listen to me, servants of Odysseus, of a master who has been absent from his house all too long: you should be upstairs with your noble mistress, turning the spindle and carding wool. Let me tend the fire in this hall. I shall not tire, even if the suitors stay until dawn. I am accustomed to hardship."

The girls exchanged glances and laughed among themselves. Finally Melantho, a young handmaid whom Penelope had reared like her own child, but who now was the mistress of Eurymachus, said haughtily: "Miserable beggar! What a fool you are! You should spend the night at a smithy or with some other host of humble birth, instead of trying to lay down the law to us here, where there are men of noble family. Are you drunk, or is it just that you have no sense? Or did your victory over Irus go to your head? If you don't look out, someone here will strike you until the blood pours from you, and then drive you from this palace."

"You shameless thing!" said Odysseus angrily. "I shall tell Telemachus what you have just said, and he will cut you limb from limb!" At that the girls grew frightened and fled from the hall. Then Odysseus took his place at the braziers and fanned the flames as he brooded on revenge. Athene, meanwhile, spurred the suitors on to make fun of him. Eurymachus turned to his companions and said: "That man has surely been sent here to light up the hall with his wisdom. Just look at his head—not a single hair on it! Doesn't it shine like a torch?" His words were greeted with bawdy laughter. Encouraged by applause, he turned to Odysseus. "How about hiring out to me as a servant, fellow?" he asked him. "You could plant trees in my orchard and weed out the thornbushes. In return you should have all you can eat. But I see that you prefer to beg and fill your belly with gifts that cost you no sweat."

"Eurymachus," said Odysseus in a steady voice, "I wish it were spring and that we could match ourselves in mowing the meadow, both with scythes in our hands and working on an empty stomach until dark. Then we would see who had the greater endurance! And if we stood at the ploughshare, you would see whether or not I could cut a furrow straight through a four-acre field! Or if we were off at war, I would show you that I can carry shield, helmet, and two brazen lances, and fight in the front line. Then it would not occur to you to taunt me with this belly of mine! Now you think you are great and powerful because you have measured your strength with a few, but certainly not with the best men. But should Odysseus once return to his home, I fear that these doors, wide as they are, would prove too narrow for your escape!"

At this Eurymachus grew very angry. "Scoundrel!" he shouted. "Now, this very instant, you shall be repaid for your drunken impudence!" And with that he seized a footstool, but Odysseus ducked at the knees of Amphinomus; the heavy missile hurtled over his head and struck a cupbearer in his right hand, so that the wine jug fell to the floor with a clatter, and the boy groaned and toppled over backwards.

The suitors cursed the stranger for the disturbance he had caused, but went on carousing nonetheless until Telemachus courteously but firmly asked them to retire for the night. At that Amphinomus rose and said: "You have heard what is certainly a fair request, my friends. Let us not quarrel with the young man. And in the future let us not offend this stranger or any servant in the palace with deeds or words. Fill your cups and pour a libation, and then let us go to our couches. Let this beggar stay here under the protection of Telemachus; for at his hearth he has taken shelter." All was done as Amphinomus had said, and soon after the suitors left.

ODYSSEUS ALONE WITH TELEMACHUS AND PENELOPE

Only Odysseus and Telemachus remained. "Quick, let us put away the weapons!" the father said to his son.

Telemachus called Euryclea, his old nurse, and said: "Keep the girls inside until I have taken my father's weapons away from all this smoke and soot."

"It is a good thing, my child," answered Euryclea, "that you are concerned for what is yours. But who shall carry the torch to light your way if you do not take one of the girls?"

"That stranger over there," said Telemachus. "Whoever eats of my bread shall do me some service." And now father and son carried helmets, shields, and lances to a storeroom. Before them went Athene, a golden lamp in her hand to spread light on their way.

"This is a great marvel," Telemachus whispered to his father. "How the walls of the palace shimmer! Every beam, every pine post, every pillar—everything glows like fire! A god must be with us, one of the immortals from Olympus."

"Silence, my son," said Odysseus, "and do not probe into these things. The gods forbid mortals to pry into their doings. Go to bed now. I myself shall stay up a little longer and try your mother and the handmaids."

Telemachus left, and now Penelope came into the hall, beautiful as Artemis or Aphrodite. Her own chair, inlaid with silver and ivory, and spread with a thick fleece, was placed at the hearth for her, and she seated herself on it. Servants cleared the food and cups from the tables, set these to one side, and then tended the fire and saw to the lighting of the room. And now Melantho mocked Odysseus a second time. "Stranger," she said, "surely you are not going to spend the night here and spy about the palace? Let what you have had be enough for you, and get out of the door this instant unless you want a firebrand to fly at your head."

Odysseus scowled at her and replied: "You are hard to understand. Are you so hostile toward me because I am in rags and beg for my food? Is not that the common fate of those who wander homeless over the earth? Once I was happy. I lived in a fine house, had ample stores, and gave wandering strangers whatever they needed, regardless of how they looked. And I had servants and handmaids in plenty too. But all this Zeus has taken from me. Remember, girl, that a like fate may overtake you! What if the queen became seriously angry with you, or if Odysseus returned? There is still hope of that! Or if Telemachus, who is no longer a child, punished you in his stead?"

Penelope heard the beggar's words and scolded the arrogant

girl. "Shameless creature," she said. "I know your base soul, and I know what you are up to. But I shall make you sorry for what you have done. Did you not hear me say that I wish to honor this stranger, that I want to ask him about my husband, and do you yet dare jeer at him?" Melantho was abashed and crept from the hall. Eurynome, the old housekeeper, placed a chair for the beggar, and Penelope began to question him. "First tell me your name and who your parents are," she said to Odysseus.

"Queen," he replied, "you are a wise and virtuous woman, and the glory of your husband is great. Your people and your country are also well spoken of in the world. As for me, ask me whatever you like, but not my lineage or my native land. I have suffered too greatly and cannot bear to be reminded of my home. If I were to tell you everything I have been through, I should break into loud and long lament, and then your handmaids and even you yourself might reprove me—and with good reason."

At this Penelope said: "I too have had much to endure since my husband left Ithaca. You saw the great numbers of men who are courting me against my will. For three years I evaded them through a ruse which I have had to give up." And she told him about the web and how her own handmaids had betrayed her. "And now," she concluded, "I can no longer put off taking a second husband. My parents are urging me, and my son is angry because his inheritance is being wasted. You see the trouble I am in, so you need not keep secret who you are. You were, after all, not born from a fabled oak or rock!"

"Since you insist, I shall tell you," said Odysseus, and he began his old tale about Crete. It sounded so like the truth that Penelope wept with compassion, and Odysseus was filled with pity for her. But he restrained his tears, and his eyes stood fixed between his lids as though they were horn or iron, and revealed nothing of what he felt.

When the queen had wept her fill, she spoke again. "I must test you, stranger," she said, "to see if what you say is really true, if you really entertained my husband as a guest in your house. Tell me what he was wearing, how he looked, and who was with him."

"That is difficult to remember after so long a time," said Odysseus. "It is almost twenty years ago that your husband landed in Crete. But I seem to recall that he wore a mantle of crimson wool fastened with a double clasp of gold embossed with a dog holding a writhing fawn in his forepaws. A tunic of fine white linen showed under the mantle. With him was a herald, a round-shouldered fellow, by the name of Eurybates, and he had curly hair and a dark skin."

Penelope wept anew because in her mind's eye she saw everything the beggar had mentioned. Odysseus comforted her with a fresh tale in which he blended imaginary adventures with the truth, such as his landing on Thrinacia and his stay in the land of the Phaeacians. The beggar pretended to know all about the king of the Thesprotians, who had been host to Odysseus just before he had gone to consult the oracle at Dodona. There he had left great treasure for safekeeping. The beggar claimed to have seen it with his own eyes, and thought there was no doubt whatsoever that the king of Ithaca would soon return to his country.

But all this could not convince Penelope. "I do not believe that will ever be," she said, bowing her head. She was about to bid her handmaids wash the stranger's feet and prepare a comfortable couch for him; but rather than accept the services of those faithless girls, Odysseus asked for a pallet of straw. "Unless," he added, "you have some good and faithful old woman who has suffered as much as I. Let her wash my feet!"

"Come, Euryclea!" Penelope cried. "It was you who brought up Odysseus. Now wash the feet of this man who must be just about as old as your master."

Euryclea looked at the beggar and said: "Ah! perhaps Odysseus has just such hands and feet! For when people suffer, they age before their time." And as she spoke, the old woman was choked with tears. Now when she approached to wash the stranger's feet, she looked at him more closely, and said: "Many men have visited this house, but never have I seen one who resembled Odysseus as you do! You have his stature, his legs, and his voice."

"Yes, that is what everyone who has seen both of us says," Odysseus replied carelessly, while she mixed hot and cold water in a basin. But when she had completed her preparations, he moved out of the light, for he did not want her to see the scar above his right knee, where a boar had thrust his tusk into the flesh long ago, when he had hunted as a youth. He feared that the moment Euryclea noticed it, she would recognize him. But though his legs were in shadow, she knew the scar when her palm touched it, and in the first shock of joy let his foot slip from her hand and into the basin, so that the metal rang and the water splashed over the rim. Her breath faltered and her eyes filled with tears. Tremblingly she touched his knee. "Odysseus, dear child, it is you!" she cried. "I have felt the scar!" But out shot Odysseus' right hand and caught her by the throat, and with his left he drew her toward him. "Do you want to destroy me?" he whispered. "What you say is true, but no one in the palace must know. If you do not keep silence, you shall share the fate of those worthless girls!"

"No need to threaten me!" said Euryclea softly, when he had released her throat. "My heart is firm as rock and iron. But beware of the other handmaids in this palace. I shall tell you the names of all who have no respect for you."

"You do not have to," said Odysseus. "I already know who they are." When Euryclea had washed and anointed his feet, Penelope began to speak. She had not noticed what had passed between them, for Athene had turned her thoughts elsewhere.

"My heart sways to and fro in doubt, stranger," she said pensively. "Shall I remain with my son and administer the palace for my husband who may still be alive, or shall I marry the noblest among my suitors, him who offers the most splendid bridal gifts? While Telemachus was still a child, I refused to marry. Now that he is a youth, he himself wishes me to go from here, for he fears that his possessions will be utterly wasted. And I have had a dream. Perhaps you, who seem so wise, can explain it to me. I have twenty geese, and I like to watch them eat their grain. Well, I dreamed that an eagle came flying down from the mountains and broke the necks of all my geese. They lay dead, scattered about on the ground, and the bird flew off through the air. I began to sob aloud, but the dream went on. I thought I saw women coming from the city to comfort me in my grief. And suddenly the eagle came too, perched on the sill, and began to speak to me in a human voice. 'Be of good courage, daughter of Icarius,' he said. 'This is no dream; it is a vision.

The suitors are the geese, and I, the eagle, am Odysseus, returned to put an end to them.' That is what the bird said, and then I awoke. I immediately went to look after my geese, and they were feeding quietly at the trough."

"Queen," the beggar replied, "in your dream Odysseus himself has told you what will come to pass. The vision can have no other meaning. He will come, and not a suitor will remain alive."

But Penelope sighed and said: "Dreams are like ripples on the waters, but tomorrow is the dreaded day on which I am to leave my husband's house. I shall arrange a contest for the men who court me. Odysseus sometimes used to set up twelve axes, one behind the other. Then he would step back and shoot an arrow through the holes of all twelve of them. Now what I have decided is this: I shall marry that suitor who can accomplish this feat with Odysseus' bow."

"That is right," said Odysseus in a firm voice. "Do not fail to arrange the contest tomorrow. For Odysseus will come before the suitors can bend the bow and shoot the arrow through the holes of the axes."

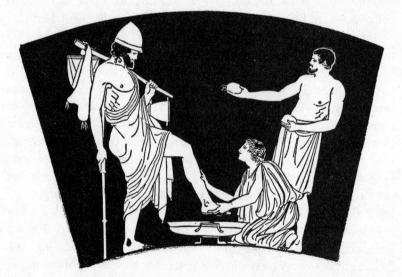

NIGHT AND MORNING IN THE PALACE

The queen bade the stranger goodnight, and Odysseus lay down on the couch Euryclea had prepared for him. She had spread thick fleeces over an untanned hide, and provided a warm mantle for covering. For a long time he tossed about sleepless. He heard the shameless girls carrying on with the suitors and mocking him with impudent words. He beat his hand against his breast and said to himself: "Bear this too, heart of mine, and remember that you have suffered worse things! Have you forgotten the time you were in the cave of the Cyclops and were compelled to sit by inactive while he devoured your friends? Wait then, and endure!" In this way he curbed his heart, but still he could not sleep, for he cast about for some way of taking sure revenge on the suitors. He was troubled to think how many of them there were, and he doubted whether he could prevail against them. As he was turning such thoughts over in his mind, Athene came to him in the shape of a beautiful woman, bent over his couch, and said: "You have small faith in me! A man often depends on a friend, a mere mortal, but you have me, a goddess, to shield you from harm. If fifty armies, all eager to kill, were to encircle us, you would still find a way to conquer. And now sleep, and forget your griefs." So she spoke and touched his lids with sweet slumber.

But Penelope, for her part, woke after a brief sleep, and sitting up on her couch, began to weep. In a voice choked with tears she prayed to Artemis. "Sacred daughter of Zeus," she pleaded, "if only you would aim an arrow at my breast! If only a tempest would snatch me away and fling me down on the farthest shores of Oceanus, before I am forced to break faith with my husband and marry a man who is base compared with him! Sorrow can be borne, though the day be spent in weeping, if only night bring sleep and forgetting. But even in my sleep a god torments me with evil dreams. Just as I awoke I seemed to see my husband at my side, tall and majestic as he was when he left for Troy, and my heart beat high with happiness, for I believed he was really here." Penelope sobbed these words aloud, and Odysseus, hearing her weep, feared that she might recognize

him before the time was ripe. So he quickly left the palace and
under the open sky implored Zeus to send him a favorable omen.
Straightway a sudden clap of thunder sounded above the palace.
In the mill near the house was a woman who had been grinding
barley all night. She stopped working, looked out, and cried
aloud: "How Zeus is thundering, and yet there is not a cloud to
be seen far and wide! He must be giving a sign to some mortal.
O father of gods and men, grant my request too, and kill those
accursed suitors who force me to grind day and night so that
they may have enough flour for their feasting!" Odysseus rejoiced in the good omen, and he lay down and fell asleep.

At dawn the palace was astir. Servants came and made up the
fire. Telemachus, when he had risen, dressed and went up to
the threshold of the women's chamber and called to Euryclea:
"Did you give our guest food and drink, or has no one seen to
his wants? My mother seems to have lost her sense of right and
wrong. She accords honor to her good-for-nothing suitors and
refuses it to a man far better than they."

"You do my mistress wrong," Euryclea replied. "The stranger drank as much wine as he pleased, and he ate all he wanted
as well. He was even offered a sumptuous couch, but he spurned
it, and it was only with difficulty that we prevailed on him to
accept a humbler one."

When Telemachus had been thus reassured, he hastened to
the assembly in the market place. Euryclea, meanwhile, ordered
the handmaids to prepare for the feast of Apollo. Some spread
the chairs with crimson stuffs; some cleaned the tables with
sponges, while others washed the pitchers and cups; twenty were
needed to fetch water from the well. The servants of the suitors
also took part in these preparations and split wood in the forecourt. The swineherd came with his fattest boars and greeted
his former guest with joy and affection. Melantheus and two
of his helpers brought the choicest she-goats, which they tied to
posts in the portico. In passing, he addressed Odysseus in scornful tones. "Are you still here, old beggar?" he asked. "Are you
still glued to the threshold? We certainly shall not part until
you have felt my fists. Are there no other feasts you could go to?"
Odysseus did not answer. He only shook his head.

And now an honest man entered the palace, Philoetius, who

from the mainland had brought the suitors a bullock and fatted goats. When he saw Eumaeus, he said: "Who is the stranger who came here a short time ago? He looked very much like Odysseus, our king. It can well happen, you know, that suffering makes beggars of kings." Then he went up to Odysseus and greeted him, saying: "Though you seem wretched enough now, I hope the future may bring you ease and happiness. When I first saw you, I broke into a sweat and tears came to my eyes, because you made me think of Odysseus, who, if he is still alive, may also be wandering around somewhere in the world, dressed in tatters. When I was quite young, he made me the herdsman over his cattle, and they are thriving, but I am forced to supply them for the feasts of others. I should have left the country long ago in anger and grief if I did not still hope to see Odysseus come back and put an end to the scoundrels we are forced to entertain here."

"Herdsman," said Odysseus, "you seem neither base nor foolish. And I swear to you by Zeus that while you are still in the palace Odysseus will come home, and your eyes will see him take vengeance on the suitors."

"May Zeus make your words come true!" said Philoetius. "And when the time comes, I shall not stand by and twiddle my thumbs!"

THE FEAST

The suitors, who had been plotting the murder of Telemachus, began to arrive in the palace. They laid their mantles aside. Meat was roasting on the spits, and the servants were mixing the wine. Eumaeus passed around the cups, and Philoetius served bread in baskets. Melantheus poured, and the feasting began.

Telemachus purposely assigned to Odysseus a place near the threshold and set before him a mean stool and a little table. He had him served with meat, filled his cup with wine, and said: "Eat here in peace, and I do not advise anyone to molest you!" Even Antinous warned his companions not to trouble the stranger, for it was evident to him that he was under the protection of Zeus. But Athene secretly goaded the suitors to words of contempt. Among them was a malicious man named Ctesippus from the island of Same. "Listen to me, you suitors," he said with a mocking smile. "It is true that the stranger has already got his share, and it would, indeed, have been unpardonable for Telemachus to have neglected so noble a guest, but I want to give him a special gift. He can use it to pay the old nurse who scraped the filth from his body!" And with that he drew from a basket the hoof of an ox, and flung it at the beggar with all his might. But Odysseus dodged it and hid his anger behind an ominous grin. The missile struck the wall.

And now Telemachus rose and cried: "Consider yourself fortunate not to have hit the stranger, Ctesippus! Had you done so, I should have thrust my lance through your chest, and your father would have had to prepare for your burial instead of your wedding. Let no one else permit himself such actions in my house. Rather kill me than insult a guest!"

The suitors were silenced by these grim words, and Agelaus, son of Damastor, rose and said: "Telemachus is right! But now he and his mother must listen to reason. As long as there was the slightest hope that Odysseus would return to his country it was all very well to hold off us suitors. But now there is no doubt that he will never come back. So talk to your mother, Telemachus. Urge her to choose the noblest among us, him who brings the best gifts, and then you will be able to enjoy your inheritance in peace."

Telemachus rose from his chair and said: "By Zeus! I too do not wish to postpone this matter any longer. On the contrary, I have been begging my mother to choose among her suitors. The only thing I refuse to do is to force her to go from my palace."

These words were greeted with loud bursts of laughter, for Pallas Athene was turning their wits awry. They grinned and grimaced, and stuffed their mouths with uncooked meat until the blood dripped from their lips. But then suddenly their eyes filled with tears, and instead of bawdy merriment they felt only dejection. Theoclymenus, the seer, noticed the change which had come over them. "What is wrong with you?" he cried in surprise. "Your heads are shrouded in night, your eyes are wet, and lament pours from your lips. And what do I see? The walls are oozing blood, the hall and the forecourt swarm with ghosts from the underworld, and the sun is blotted out in the sky!" So he spoke, but the suitors all laughed at him.

Then Eurymachus said to them: "This foreign soothsayer who has been with us for only a short time is nothing but a fool! If he sees only darkness in this hall, take him out and let him stay in the street or the market place."

"I do not need your servants to guide me from here," said Theoclymenus indignantly. "My eyes and ears and feet are sound, and my reason is unimpaired. I shall leave of my own accord, for I foresee the destruction which will overtake you and which not one of you will escape." So he said and swiftly left the palace to go to Peiraeus, his former host, who was glad to welcome him back.

The suitors, meanwhile, went on taunting Telemachus. "No one in the world has ever lodged worse guests than you," said one of them. "A dirty beggar and a fool who makes predictions! What you should do is travel through Sicily with them and exhibit them in the market place for money." Telemachus said nothing in reply. He glanced at his father, for he was only waiting for the sign to begin.

THE CONTEST WITH THE BOW

And now Penelope too realized that the time had come. She took in her hand a brazen key with an ivory handle and, accompanied by her handmaids, went to a storeroom where many precious utensils of bronze, gold, and iron, the property of Odysseus, were kept. Among these were his bow and a quiverful of arrows, gifts he had once received from a host in Lacedaemon. When Penelope had unlocked the door, she slid back the bolts, and their creak was loud as the bellow of a bull in the pasture. The door flew open and Penelope entered. The bow and quiver were hanging on the wall. She stood on her toes, reached up for them, and took them down. But when she held them in her hands, grief overwhelmed her. She threw herself in a chair and gave way to tears. At last she rose and left the room. The servants followed carrying the bow and quiver. She went straight to the suitors, called for silence, and said: "You who have been wooing me so long a time, listen to what I have to say. Let him who wishes to win me hold himself in readiness, for now we shall have a contest. Here is the great bow of my noble husband. Whoever can bend it and shoot an arrow through the holes of twelve axes, set up one behind the other, shall take me to wife, and with him I shall leave this palace, the house of my first husband."

When she had spoken, she bade the swineherd lay the bow and the arrows before the suitors. As Eumaeus took the weapon, his eyes were wet, and Philoetius, the cowherd, wept too. This angered Antinous. "Stupid peasants!" he grumbled. "Why do you make the queen's heart heavy with your tears? Eat all you want in silence, or lament outside. We suitors have to go about this trying contest, for I do not think it will be easy to bend that bow. Not one among us is as strong as Odysseus. I remember him perfectly, though I was only a little boy when he left." So said Antinous, but in his heart he already saw himself bending the bow and shooting the arrow through the holes of the axes. But to him Fate had allotted the first shaft to be launched by the hand of Odysseus.

And now Telemachus rose and said: "Zeus must have addled my brain! Here is my mother declaring her willingness to leave this house to follow a suitor, yet I am standing by with a smile. Well then, you suitors, you are about to wage a contest for a woman who has not her equal in all of Greece. But you know that yourselves, and I need not din my mother's praises in your ears. Begin then, and bend the bow! I wish I could take my turn with you, for if I won, my mother would not go from here." When he had finished speaking he unslung his sword and cast off his crimson mantle. Then he drew a straight furrow along the floor of the hall and fixed the axes in the ground, one after the other, and stamped the earth hard around them. Everyone admired his strength and the sureness and accuracy of his movements. Then he himself gripped the bow. Three times he strained to bend it, but three times he failed. When he tried a fourth time, he was about to succeed when his father motioned to him and stopped him. "Gods of Olympus!" Telemachus cried. "Either I am a weakling or too young, and not yet able to fend off an attacker. You are stronger than I, so you try it!" And so saying, he leaned the bow and quiver against the doorpost and seated himself in his chair.

With an air of great triumph, Antinous rose and said: "Come, my friends, let us take turns from left to right, the way the cup-bearer goes." Then Leiodes rose. He was the one who poured the libations and always sat in the innermost part of the hall, by the big mixing-bowl. Of all the suitors he was the only one who was dismayed by their wanton deeds, and he hated the noisy mob of feasters. Quietly he went to the threshold and attempted to bend the bow, but he could not.

"Let another try," he said, letting his delicate hands drop to his sides. "I am not the right man for this, and perhaps no one here will succeed." With these words he leaned the bow and the quiver against the post.

But Antinous reproved him, saying: "That was an unpleasant speech, Leiodes. Just because you could not bend the bow, is that sufficient reason to claim that no one else can? Come, Melan-theus," he continued, turning to the goatherd. "Light a fire, put a chair in front of it, and bring us a thick slice of fat from the kitchen. We shall warm this dried-out bow and grease it, and then it will be easier to handle." All was done as he had bidden, but the bow was just as inflexible as before. In vain one suitor after another tried to bend it. Finally only two were left— Antinous and Eurymachus.

ODYSSEUS REVEALS HIMSELF TO THE GOOD HERDSMEN

Now it happened that, in leaving the palace, the cowherd and the swineherd met, and close on their heels came Odysseus. He caught up with them just as they closed the door to the forecourt behind them, and said to them in a low voice: "I should like to tell you something, my friends, but only if I can rely on you; otherwise I had better keep silence. So first let me ask you some-thing. If a god suddenly brought Odysseus home from alien lands, whom would you side with, him or the suitors? Tell me quite frankly!"

"O Zeus on Olympus!" exclaimed the cowherd. "If my dearest wish were granted, if Odysseus really returned—you should see me fight for him!" And Eumaeus too called on all the gods to send his master home.

When Odysseus had thus made sure of their faithfulness, he said: "Well then, this is what I have to tell you: I myself am Odysseus! After twenty years, after unbearable hardships, I have returned to my native land and find only you two of all my servants ready to welcome me, for I have not heard anyone else implore the gods to send me home. As soon as I have destroyed the suitors, you shall have your reward for this! I shall give each of you a wife, and fields, and a house built close to my own. And Telemachus shall treat you like brothers. But to convince you that I am telling the truth, I shall show you the scar from the wound a boar once dealt me while I was out hunting." With that he pushed aside his rags and bared the long scar. And the two herdsmen began to weep, clasped their arms about their king, and kissed his head and shoulders. Odysseus kissed them too, and then said: "Do not give way to past grief or present joy, for no one in the palace must know I am here. Let us return to the hall singly. The suitors will not want to give me a turn at bending the bow, but you, Eumaeus, shall take it up boldly and hand it to me. When you have done this, order the handmaids to lock themselves into the women's chamber. No matter what they hear from the hall, shouts or groans, let none of them dare rush out, but let them stay at their work. You, dear Philoetius, shall see to the outer gate. Bolt it well and secure it with a rope."

When Odysseus had given these directions, he returned to the hall, and the herdsmen followed him in. Eurymachus was turning the bow this way and that over the fire, but he could not bend it. He sighed and said: "This really grieves me! Not so much because of Penelope, for there are plenty of other Achaean women in Ithaca and elsewhere. But it is annoying that we should appear so weak compared with Odysseus. Our very grandsons will taunt us with our failure!"

Antinous, however, reproved his friend for these words. "Do not talk like that, Eurymachus," he said. "Today is the feast of Apollo, and a holiday is really not the proper time to wage a contest. Let us put aside the bow and go back to our cups. The axes can stay where they are. Tomorrow we shall make an offering to the archer Apollo and try again."

But now Odysseus turned to the suitors and said: "You do well to rest today. Tomorrow Apollo, the Far-Darter, will, let us hope, grant victory. In the meantime let me try the bow and see if there is anything of my old strength left in this miserable body."

"Stranger," shouted Antinous, "have you lost your mind? Or are you drunk with wine? Do you want to start a fight, like Eurytion, the centaur, at the wedding of Pirithous? Remember

that he was the first to fall, and so you too shall be killed the instant you take the bow in hand, and no one among us will defend you!"

Here Penelope intervened. "Antinous," she said in her gentle voice, "how unbecoming it would be to exclude the stranger from the contest! Do you really think that this beggar could bend the bow and claim me as his wife? Surely he himself is thinking of no such thing. It would be quite impossible, so you need not be in the least disturbed."

"What we are afraid of, O queen," answered Eurymachus, "is the gossip that will spread through all of Greece. They will say that only inferior men, not one of whom was able to bend the bow of immortal Odysseus, courted his wife, but that in the end a beggar from heaven knows where bent the bow effortlessly and shot the arrow through the twelve axes."

"The stranger is not as base a man as you seem to think,"

said Penelope. "Look well at him, and you will see how tall he is and how solidly built. Besides, he claims he is the son of a noble man. Give him the bow! Should he bend it, his only reward shall be a tunic and mantle, sandals, a spear, and a sword. When I have given him these, he shall go wherever he likes."

Telemachus interposed at this point and said: "Mother, no one but I has the right to give or withhold this bow. Even if I chose to give it to this stranger to take with him on his wanderings, no one could prevent me. As for you—go to your chamber, to your spindle and loom, for the bow is the business of men." Penelope heard her son's firm words with amazement, but did as he said.

And now the swineherd took the bow in his hands, even though the suitors broke into angry cries. "What are you doing with that bow, you fool?" they roared. "Are you itching to be thrown to your own dogs near the sties?" Eumaeus laid the weapon down in alarm, but Telemachus called in a threatening voice: "Bring it, old man! I am the only one who gives orders here. If you do not obey me, I shall drive you out with stones, even though I am much the younger." The suitors' fury changed to amusement, and they laughed as the swineherd brought the beggar the bow. Then Eumaeus secretly bade Euryclea lock in the girls, and Philoetius hastened out of the palace and carefully made fast the gate of the forecourt.

Odysseus, meanwhile, examined the bow from all sides. He looked to see whether, in all the years he had been gone, worms had got into the horn, or if anything else had happened to it. The suitors nudged one another, and someone said: "The man seems to know something about bows. Perhaps he has one like this at home, or else he wants to copy this one for himself. Just look at him fingering it!"

When Odysseus had examined the huge bow from every angle, he bent it, and strung it as easily as a singer strings his lyre. He plucked the string with his right hand to see if it was taut, and it twanged with a high clear sound, like the tone of a swallow. When they heard it, the suitors winced and grew pale. But Zeus sent thunder down from heaven as a happy omen. Then Odysseus took an arrow which had fallen from the quiver and lay on the table before him, gripped the bow, drew back the string, fitted the arrow and loosed it, aiming with a sure eye. And the shaft flew through every hole of the twelve axes, from the first to the last! Then the hero said: "Well, Telemachus, the stranger you took into your palace has not disgraced you. My strength, it seems, is unbroken in spite of the taunts of the suitors. But now the time has come to serve these Achaeans their evening meal. Let us see to it before it grows dark, and later we can have lyre playing and singing and whatever else befits a feast." And as he spoke, Odysseus gave his son the sign they had agreed on. Quickly Telemachus slung his sword over his shoulder, took his spear, and hurried over to his father, armed with gleaming bronze.

VENGEANCE

Then Odysseus stripped off his tatters and sprang to the raised threshold, holding the bow and the quiver full of arrows. There he poured them out at his feet and called down to the suitors: "The first contest is over. Now for the second! But this time it is I who will choose a mark such as no archer has ever hit, and yet I do not think I shall miss!" And as he spoke he aimed at Antinous, who was just lifting his two-handled cup of gold to his lips. The arrow pierced his throat, and the point came out at the nape of his neck. The cup dropped from his hand as a thick jet of blood spurted from his nostrils, and he fell, dragging down with his foot the table and everything on it. When the suitors saw him fall, they leaped from their chairs and ran to the walls to seize weapons, but there was neither spear nor shield to be seen. Then they broke into a storm of abuse. "Why do you shoot at men, accursed stranger?" they shouted. "You have killed our companion, but it is the last arrow you will ever launch! The vultures shall tear your flesh!" They said this thinking that he had shot Antinous by accident, not dreaming that the same fate was in store for them all. But Odysseus thundered down at them: "Dogs! You thought I would never return from Troy, and so you wasted my stores, seduced my servants, courted my wife without having any certainty that I had really died, and feared neither men nor gods! But now your hour is come!"

The suitors heard and grew pale. Fear gripped their hearts. Each looked about, silently wondering how he could escape from the hall. Eurymachus was the only one to gather his wits. He said: "If you are really Odysseus of Ithaca, you have every right to be angry with us, for both in the palace and on your farms much wrong has been done. But he who was most to blame is already dead. It was Antinous who was behind all these doings, and he was not even courting Penelope in earnest. All he wanted was to be king of Ithaca in your stead, and to this end he plotted the murder of your son. Now that he has received his just punishment, give up your anger against us! Spare your equals in rank! Every one of us shall bring you twenty bullocks in recompense for what we have eaten, and you shall have all the bronze and gold it will take to win back your favor."

"No, Eurymachus," said Odysseus, scowling at him. "Even if you offered me everything you have inherited from your fathers, I should not rest until all of you have atoned for your misdeeds with death. Do what you will, fight or flee—not one of you shall escape me!"

And now the suitors shook with uncontrollable terror. Once more Eurymachus spoke, but this time to his companions. "No one can stop this man," he said. "Draw your swords and use the tables as shields against his arrows. Try to throw yourselves at him and thrust him from the threshold. Then let us go throughout the city to call on our friends for aid." So saying, he whipped his sword from its sheath and leaped forward with a shout. But at the same instant an arrow pierced his liver. The sword slipped from his grasp, and cups and platters rolled down with him as he fell over a table and struck his head on the floor. He beat his head on the ground in agony, but a second later a tremor ran through him and he died. And now Amphinomus rushed against Odysseus to try to force a way out for himself with his sword. But Telemachus hurled his spear at him. It struck him in the back, between the shoulder blades, and he plunged forward on his face. Then Telemachus sprang free of the throng and stood on the threshold beside his father, to whom he brought a shield, two lances, and a helmet of bronze. Quickly he slipped out of the door to fetch more weapons. Four shields, eight spears, and four helmets with crests of horsehair he brought for himself and his

friends. He and the two faithful herdsmen armed themselves;
the fourth set of weapons he brought to Odysseus, and now the
four stood shoulder to shoulder.

While the arrows lasted, Odysseus shot suitor after suitor, and
one victim tumbled on top of another. Then he leaned his bow
against the doorpost, slung the shield over his shoulder, set the
helmet on his head, and took two great lances in hand. In the

hall was a side door which opened into a passage leading to the
back of the palace. But this door was so narrow that only one man
at a time could pass through. Odysseus had told Eumaeus to
watch there, but when the swineherd went to arm himself it was
momentarily unguarded. One of the suitors, Agelaus, at once
seized the advantage. "Why not flee through the side door," he
asked those near him, "and hasten to the city? There we can get
help and soon put an end to this man!"

"Impossible!" said Melantheus, the goatherd, who sided with
the suitors. "The door and the passage are so narrow that they
admit only one man at a time. It will be better if I alone slip out
quietly and fetch weapons for the rest of you." And he immediately began to carry out his own suggestion. Time after time he
went out and in, unobserved in the crowd, and brought back with
him twelve shields and as many spears and helmets. Odysseus

suddenly found himself confronted with armed foes, brandishing their lances. He was startled and said to Telemachus: "One of the faithless handmaids or the disloyal goatherd is responsible for this!"

"I am afraid it is my own fault," answered Telemachus. "When I brought the weapons for us, I was in such a hurry that I did not fasten the door of our storeroom."

Quickly Eumaeus hastened to repair his young master's neglect. Through the open door he saw the goatherd taking more spears and shields. He came back to tell Odysseus. "Shall I take him alive or slay him?" he asked.

"Take the cowherd with you," said Odysseus. "Fall on that scoundrel, bind his hands and feet behind his back, and let him hang from the central pillar by a stout rope. Then fasten the door and return."

The two herdsmen did as he had bidden. They hurled themselves on the goatherd just as he was snatching more arms. They threw him to the floor, bound his arms and legs behind his back, looped a long rope about a hook in the ceiling, slung it around his body, and hoisted him up the tall pillar until he hung close to the rafters. "We have couched you in a comfortable position," said Eumaeus. "Sleep sweetly!" They locked the door and returned to their posts near Odysseus.

A fifth ally unexpectedly joined the four friends. It was Athene in the shape of Mentor, and Odysseus joyfully recognized the goddess. When the suitors noticed the newcomer, Agelaus called to him angrily: "Mentor, I warn you not to let Odysseus persuade you to fight us suitors, for if you do, we shall kill you and all yours along with this father and son!"

These words made Athene seethe with rage. She spurred Odysseus to greater effort, saying: "You do not seem to me as brave as in those nine years you fought at Troy. It was your counsel that caused the fall of that city, but now, when it is a question of defending your own palace and property, you are hesitant and slow." This she said to goad his courage, for she did not intend to take part in the actual fighting. Hardly had she finished speaking when she flew up in the form of a swallow and perched on the sooty rafters.

"Mentor has left!" Agelaus called to his friends. "The four

are by themselves again. Now let us plan our attack. Do not all cast your spears at once. The six of you over there shall be first, and be sure that all of you aim only at Odysseus. Once he is down the rest will be easy to manage." But Athene turned the course of those six lances: one stuck in the doorpost, another in the door, and the rest hit the wall.

Then Odysseus cried to his friends: "Aim carefully and cast well!" All four hurled their spears, and not one missed. Odysseus struck Demoptolemus, Telemachus Euryades, the swineherd hit Elatus, and the cowherd Pisander. When they saw their companions rolling in the dust, the other suitors fled to the farthest corners of the hall, but an instant later they advanced again, drew the spears from the corpses, and cast once more. Again the missiles went astray, all except the spear of Amphimedon, which grazed one of Telemachus' wrists, and that of Ctesippus, which scratched the swineherd's shoulder just above the shield. But neither of the wounded men was in the least disabled, and they repaid their would-be slayers with death. When Eumaeus cast his spear, he cried: "Take this for the hoof you threw at my master when he was a beggar in this hall!"

Odysseus had killed Eurydamas. Now he hurled his lance and killed Agelaus, son of Damastor, while Telemachus drove his spear through the belly of Leiocritus. Then Athene shook her aegis and filled the suitors with such panic that they fled through the hall like cattle stung by a gadfly, or like small birds trying to escape the talons of a hawk. Odysseus and his friends left the threshold and raged through the hall. And wherever they strode sounded the death rattle, and blood flowed in torrents.

Leiodes, throwing himself at Odysseus' feet, clasped his knees and cried: "Have mercy on me! I never wronged you or yours! I tried to check the rest of the suitors, but they would not listen to me. All I did was to pour the libations. Must I die for that?"

"If you poured libations in their behalf," Odysseus answered with a frown, "you prayed for them!" And he picked up the sword Agelaus had dropped as he fell and struck off Leiodes' head while his lips were still pleading.

Near the side door stood Phemius, the singer, his lyre in his hands. He was badly frightened and wondered whether he should try to slip through the door and save himself by flight, or clasp

the knees of Odysseus. He decided for the latter, laid his lyre
down between the mixing bowl and a silver-studded chair, and
threw himself on the ground before Odysseus. "Have pity on
me!" he cried, clasping his knees. "You yourself would feel regret if you killed a singer whose song delights gods and men.
A god taught me my art, and like a god I shall celebrate you in
song. Your son shall be my witness that I did not come here of
my own free will, but that they forced me to sing for them."

Odysseus raised his sword, but he hesitated. And then Telemachus ran toward him and cried: "Stop, father! Do not hurt
him! He is guiltless! And if the herald Medon has not already
been killed by you or the herdsmen, let him live too. He took
such good care of me when I was a little boy, and always wished
us well!" Medon, who had wrapped himself in an oxhide and lay
hidden under a chair, when he heard this plea in his behalf unwound himself and clasped the knees of Telemachus. At that,
even Odysseus had to smile. "You have nothing to fear, you two,"
he said to the singer and the herald. "Telemachus has saved you.
Leave the hall and tell the people outside that it pays to be loyal
rather than faithless." Phemius and Medon hurried away and
sat down in the forecourt by the altar of Zeus, still trembling
with terror.

THE SERVANTS ARE PUNISHED

Odysseus looked about him. Not one of his enemies was alive to
confront him. They lay on the ground like fish which the fisher-
man has shaken from the net, and the bright sun takes their life.
Then Odysseus sent Telemachus to fetch the old nurse. She
found her master standing among the dead bodies like a lion
who has torn oxen limb from limb, whose fierce eyes sparkle
while the blood drips from his jaws over his breast. He was terrible and great to see, and Euryclea was ready to break into cries
of joy. But Odysseus checked her. "Be glad," he said gravely,
"but do not rejoice aloud. It is not right for mortals to rejoice
over the slain. It is not I alone who have killed these men; they
have fallen because the gods willed it. But now give me the names
of those women in the palace who have kept faith with me, and
of those who have been false."

"In the palace," Euryclea replied, "are fifty servants whom we have taught to weave cloth, card wool, and to see to the house. Twelve of these were disloyal to you and refused to obey either Penelope or me. They were never called on to obey young Telemachus, for his mother did not give him authority over the handmaids. But now let me wake my sleeping mistress and tell her the joyful news!"

"Do not wake her just yet," said Odysseus, "but send down to me those twelve faithless women." Euryclea obeyed and brought the twelve before him. They were trembling from head to foot. Then Odysseus called Telemachus and the faithful herdsmen and said: "Carry out the corpses and let these women help you. After that they shall wipe the tables and chairs with sponges and clean the entire hall. When they have done this, take them out to the narrow space between the kitchen and the wall of the court and kill them with the sword to punish them for their arrogance and for doing the will of the suitors." Screaming and weeping the women clung together, but Odysseus drove them to work and kept them at it until tables and chairs were clean, and the blood and filth scraped from the floor with hoes and thrown out of the door. Then the herdsmen crowded them into the space between kitchen and wall where there was no way to escape. And now Telemachus said: "These wretched women, who disgraced my mother and myself, shall not die an honorable death." With these words he knotted a rope from post to post, the whole length of the kitchen, and soon the twelve hung side by side, strangled in the noose like thrushes in the net. They writhed a little while with their feet, but not for long.

Next Melantheus, the goatherd, was dragged into the forecourt and hacked to pieces. When Telemachus and the herdsmen had done this, the work of vengeance was complete, and they washed their hands and feet and returned to Odysseus.

He commanded Euryclea to bring him fire and sulphur to smoke out the stench of death and cleanse the hall. But before she did this, she brought her master a tunic and mantle. "My child," she said, "you must not stand in this hall in your beggar's rags. It does not befit you." But Odysseus let lie the clothing she had fetched and told her to go about her work. When he had purified the hall, the house and the forecourt, Euryclea called the faithful servants. They clustered about their king with tears of joy and kissed his head and his hands. And Odysseus wept too, for now he saw how many had remained loyal to him.

ODYSSEUS AND PENELOPE

Euryclea hastened to Penelope's chamber, her knees almost failing her. Tremblingly but happily she woke her sleeping mistress and said: "Penelope, now with your own eyes you shall see what you have been waiting for these many years! Odysseus has come! And he has killed the suitors who have harassed you and your son and who have laid waste your stores."

Penelope shook the sleep from her eyes and said: "Euryclea, the gods must have stricken you with madness. Why do you wake me with false news from the sweetest slumber I have ever had? I have not slept so well since Odysseus left for Troy. Had anyone but you come to tell me such a story, I should have sent her off with worse than angry words. And even you I spare only because of your great age. But now leave me, and go down to the hall again."

"There is no need for you to be angry," said Euryclea. "The stranger, the beggar whom they all scoffed at—it is he who is your husband! Your son Telemachus has known it for a long time, but he was told to keep it secret until vengeance had been taken on the suitors."

Then Penelope started up from her couch and clung to the old woman tearfully. "If this is really the truth," she cried, "if Odysseus is really here in the palace, how could he alone cope with that mob of hostile men?"

"I myself neither heard nor saw," Euryclea replied. "We women were herded into our quarters and locked in. But we caught the sound of groans, and when Telemachus finally called me, I saw your husband standing upright over a mass of corpses, a sight which, I think, would have gladdened your heart. But now all the bodies have been dragged out and are lying beyond the gates of the court, and the house has been purified with sulphur. You may go down without fear."

"I cannot believe it," Penelope repeated. "It must have been a god who slew the suitors. As for Odysseus—no, he is far from here, and he will never return."

"You have a doubting heart," said Euryclea, shaking her head. "Well then, I shall tell you of a sure sign. Do you recall that time you told me to wash the beggar's feet? It was then I touched the scar you know of, and I wanted to cry out to you, but he caught me by the throat and would not let me speak."

"Let us go down," said Penelope, tremulous with hope and fear. And together they descended and crossed the threshold of the hall. Penelope uttered no word. Silently she seated herself opposite Odysseus, in the full light of the hearthfire. He sat near a tall pillar and fixed his eyes on the ground, waiting for her to speak. But wonder and doubt closed her lips. One moment she thought she recognized him, the next he seemed a stranger, and all she saw was a beggar clothed in rags. At last Telemachus went up to his mother and said almost angrily, yet with a smile: "How can you sit there so coldly, mother? Go to my father, question him! What other woman whose husband returned after twenty years of hardship would act as you do? Have you a stone in your breast instead of a heart?"

"Dear son," said Penelope, "I am lost in wonder. I cannot speak, I cannot question him, I cannot even look into his eyes. And yet if it is really Odysseus come back to his house, we shall recognize each other beyond all doubt, for we have secret signs which no one else knows of."

Then Odysseus smiled gently and turned to his son: "Let your mother try me in her own fashion," he said. "She now scorns me because she sees me in these ugly rags, but I believe she can be convinced! But first we must think of other matters. If a man kills another man of his people, he flees from his house and country, even if his victim has only one or two avengers. But we have slain the noblest young men of Ithaca and of the islands nearby—what shall we do?"

"Father," said Telemachus, "you must decide this alone, for all the world regards you as wisest in counsel."

"Then I shall tell you what I consider best," said Odysseus. "You and the herdsmen and everyone in the house shall bathe and put on your finest garments. The handmaids too shall adorn themselves. Then let Phemius pluck the lyre and play a tune for the dance. Whoever passes our house will think that feasting is still going on, and news of the suitors' death will not spread through the city until we have reached our farms in the country. Then a god will tell us what to do next."

Soon after the palace rang with music, singing, and merriment. The citizens gathered in the street and said to one another: "Penelope must have made her choice, and the wedding celebration is taking place. Fickle woman! Why did she not wait a little longer? Perhaps her husband Odysseus would have returned." Toward evening the crowd dispersed. In the meantime Odysseus had bathed and anointed himself, and now again Athene shed beauty about him, and he rose from his bath like an immortal. When he had returned to the hall, he seated himself opposite his wife. "Strange woman!" he said. "The gods must have given you an unfeeling heart. No other wife would so obstinately refuse to recognize her husband who came back to her after twenty years of suffering. I must turn to you, Euryclea, to prepare a couch for me, for this woman has a heart of iron."

"It is neither pride nor scorn that keep me from you," said Penelope. "I know quite well how Odysseus looked when he left Ithaca on a swift ship. Very well, Euryclea, carry the couch from the bedchamber and heap it well with fleeces, cloaks, and coverlets."

But this Penelope only said to try her husband. He, however, frowned and said: "Woman, these are bitter words that you have spoken. Who has set my bed elsewhere? No one in the world could move it, not if he were in the full strength of youth. I myself built it, and there is a secret connected with it. In the middle of the place where we planned to build the palace grew a tall olive tree, straight and strong as a pillar. I let it stand, and had the rooms so arranged that it was inside our bedchamber. When the stone walls were up, I cut away the leafy branches of the tree, set in a ceiling of wood, and smoothed and carved the trunk. It formed one post of the couch, and the others were made to match it. Then the frame was inlaid with gold, silver, and ivory, and thongs of oxhide were stretched from end to end to hold fleeces and coverlets. This was our couch, Penelope. I do not know whether it still stands, but whoever moved it had to hew the trunk of the olive tree from its root."

When the queen heard these words her knees shook. Weeping she rose from her chair, ran to her husband, opened her arms to clasp him, and kissed his head many times. "Odysseus!" she cried, "you have always been the wisest of men! Do not be angry with me for this! The deathless gods sent us suffering because it would have been too much bliss for mortals to spend their youth in joy, and travel a smooth path to old age. You must not hold it against me that I did not instantly welcome you. My heart was in constant fear that some deceiver might trick me. Now that you have spoken of what no one knows except you and me and old Actoris who came here with me from my father's house, my doubt is dispelled and I am wholly convinced."

Through the night, husband and wife told each other all they had suffered in those twenty years, and Penelope had no rest until she had heard of all the wanderings of Odysseus. But at last they fell silent and went to their couch. Deep peace and quiet reigned throughout the palace.

ODYSSEUS AND LAERTES

The following morning Odysseus prepared for a journey. "We two," he said to Penelope, "have almost drained the cup of sorrow, you with grieving for me, and I with longing to return to my native land. Now that we are together again and masters of what is ours, you shall see to what property still remains in our house. What the suitors have wasted will be made good partly by the gifts they presented at the very last, partly by the spoils and the gifts I brought home with me. But I must go to the country, to my old father who has been mourning my death for so long. Now since the rumor of the suitors' death is bound to spread sooner or later, I advise you to withdraw to the women's quarters with your handmaids, and give no one an opportunity to see or question you."

So saying, Odysseus slung his sword over his shoulder and woke Telemachus and the two herdsmen who were to accompany him. All three armed, and at sunrise Odysseus hastened through the city with them. But Pallas Athene shed a heavy mist about them, so that no one could see the four travellers.

They soon reached the farm of old Laertes, one of the first he had acquired to swell the number of acres which were his by inheritance. In the middle was the house, and all around it were stables, sheds, and other outbuildings. An old Sicilian woman saw to the needs of her master in that remote and lonely place. When they stood before the door, Odysseus said to his companions: "Go in, and have a fatted boar slaughtered in honor of my homecoming. I myself will go out to the fields where my father is probably toiling, and see if he recognizes me. Then he and I will return, and we shall feast and rejoice." With that, Odysseus handed his sword and his spear to Telemachus, and the three went into the house.

But he himself took the path to the fields. First he crossed the orchard. In vain he looked for Dolius, the head gardener, for his sons, and for the rest of the fieldworkers. They had all gone to fetch stones to fence in the vineyard. When Odysseus got there, he found his old father alone. He was busy transplanting a vine. The old man looked like a laborer. He was wearing a coarse, soiled smock covered with patches, and had protected his legs from thorns by wrapping around them strips of leather. His hands were gloved with old hide, and on his head was a goatskin cap.

When Odysseus saw his father in this wretched attire he was so shaken with sorrow that he had to support himself against a pear tree while he wept bitterly. Nevertheless he could not resist the temptation to question his father and try him with gentle reproaches. He went up to the old man who was just loosening the earth around a tree, and said to him: "You seem to understand fruit-growing. Vines, olive, fig and pear trees—all are well-tended. And the vegetable garden is excellently cared for too. There is only one thing wrong, and please do not be offended if I tell you frankly what it is. You yourself are not well taken care of, old man. It is not right for your master to let you go around in soiled, patched clothes. To look at you, one would not think that you were a servant at all. Your build is kingly. A man like you deserves a bath and good food and the comforts due to old age. Tell me, whom do you work for? And is this country really Ithaca, as a man I just met told me? He was, I must say, a discourteous fellow. He did not even bother to answer me when I asked him if a friend to whom I am bound by ties of hospitality was still living here. I want to visit him. For you see, long ago I gave lodging to a man in my own country, and no dearer guest ever crossed my threshold. He came from Ithaca and told me he was the son of Laertes. I gave him the best of all I had and honored him with gifts when he left me—seven talents of the finest gold, a silver pitcher embossed with flowers, twelve tapestries, tunics and mantles, and four lovely and skilled handmaids whom I let him choose for himself."

This was the tale Odysseus invented on the spur of the moment. When his father heard it he lifted his head, and his eyes filled with tears as he said: "You have, indeed, come to the land you inquired about, stranger. But base and arrogant people, whom all those gifts you mentioned would not satisfy, live in it now. The man you are looking for is no longer here. Had you found him, Oh, how amply he would have requited you for what you did for him! But now tell me how many years have passed since your guest, since my son visited you. For it was my son, my poor son who now, perhaps, lies at the bottom of the sea, or whose flesh wild beasts and birds of prey have devoured. His parents could not even clothe him in a shroud! Penelope, his faithful wife, could not close his eyes and weep at his bier! But you—where did you come from? Where is your ship? Who is with you? Or were you a passenger on another's ship and landed here alone?"

"I shall tell you," said Odysseus. "I am Eperitus, son of Apheidas from Alybas. A tempest drove my ship from Sicania toward your shores, and it lies at anchor not far from the city. It is five years since Odysseus, your son, left my country. He was light of heart when he went, and birds of good omen accompanied him. We hoped to visit each other often, and each vowed to speed his guest with splendid gifts."

The world grew dark before the eyes of old Laertes. With both hands he took the dark dust and strewed it over his gray head and broke into loud lament. Then the heart of Odysseus was stirred and almost burst in his breast. He rushed to his father, flung his arms around him, and cried: "It is I, it is I myself, father, about whom you asked! After twenty years I have come home! Check your grief and tearful lamenting, for I shall tell you the good news in few words: I have slain all the suitors in my palace!"

Laertes looked at him in amazement and finally said: "If you are really Odysseus, if you are really my son, give me a clear sign so that I may be sure."

"First of all, father," said Odysseus, "look at this scar. It came from the wound a boar dealt me in the chase, the time you and my mother sent me to her old father Autolycus to fetch the gifts he had promised me. But you shall have other proof. I shall show you the trees you once gave me. For when I was a very little boy and went to the orchard with you, we walked between rows of trees and you told me the names of the various kinds. Thirteen pear trees you gave me, ten apple trees, forty fig trees, and fifty vines which bear great clusters of grapes." The old man could doubt no longer. He reeled fainting against his son, who caught him in his sinewy arms. When he had regained consciousness, he cried in a loud voice: "Zeus and all the gods! I know it is my son, if indeed the suitors have been punished!" Then he turned to Odysseus: "Hardly have I got you back when I am tormented with fresh anxiety for you, my son," he said. "Because of you, the noblest families in Ithaca and the surrounding islands have lost their sons. The city, the entire region will rise against you!"

"Do not be afraid, father," Odysseus comforted him. "Let us not brood over these things now, but go to your house where your grandson Telemachus is waiting for us. With him are the two herdsmen who tend the cows and the swine, and they have prepared our meal."

When they reached the house, they found Telemachus and his companions cutting up the meat and filling the cups with wine. But before he sat down to eat, Laertes was bathed and anointed by his faithful old servant. For the first time in years he put on a kingly robe. And while he was fastening it, Pallas Athene approached, straightened his bowed shoulders, and made him tall and majestic, so that when he joined the others Odysseus looked at him in astonishment and said: "Surely one of the immortals must have increased your stature and strength!"

And Laertes replied: "Had I felt as young and strong yesterday as now, I should have fought at your side, and many a suitor would have fallen beneath my blows."

As they sat down to the meal, Dolius and his sons returned from their work in the fields. When they saw Odysseus, they stood still in amazement, as if rooted to the threshold, but Odysseus spoke kindly to them. "We have been waiting for you," he said. "Come and eat with us now, and save your wonder for another time."

Then Dolius ran to him and kissed his hands at the wrist. "You have come home at last, my dear master!" he cried. "Our wish is fulfilled! But tell me, does Penelope know, or shall we send her a message?"

"She knows everything," said Odysseus. "No messenger is needed." Then the sons of Dolius crowded around their king, and together they feasted at the board.

ATHENE CALMS REBELLION IN THE CITY

In the meantime, rumors of the terrible fate which had overtaken the suitors spread through the city of Ithaca. The kinsmen of the slain streamed from all sides and hastened to the palace where they found the corpses heaped in a corner of the court. With

loud laments they carried them off for burial. The bodies of the
suitors who had come from islands nearby were sent home in
fishing boats.

Then the fathers, brothers, and other kinsmen of the dead
gathered in the market place. Eupeithes, father of Antinous,
was first to speak. "Friends," he said in a voice broken with
tears, "the man I accuse here before you has brought misfortune on Ithaca and on her neighbor islands. Twenty years
ago he took many of our brave citizens off in his ships. And he
lost both ships and men! Now that he has returned alone, he has
slain the best of our young men. Come, let us pursue this evildoer
before he has time to escape to Pylos or Elis! We must seize him
or be disgraced for all time. For our sons and grandsons would
be shamed if we did not punish the murderer of our sons and
brothers. I, at any rate, could not live with this blot on my honor.
The soul of my son would drag me down to the underworld. So
let us follow Odysseus and Telemachus before they can leave
this island!"

His listeners kindled at these words, but just as they were prepared to start their pursuit, Phemius, the singer, and Medon,
the herald, appeared in their midst. Their coming evoked surprise, for no one had dreamed they were still among the living.
And Medon addressed the assembly: "Men of Ithaca, hear what
I have to say to you! What Odysseus has done, I can swear to
you, was not done against the will of the gods. I myself saw an
immortal who, in the shape of Mentor, stood beside him, now
quickening his heart with courage, now casting a spell of madness
on the suitors. It was this god who felled them, who littered the
floor with their bodies."

Terror seized the gathering at these words of Medon's. When
they had recovered from the first shock, gray-haired Halitherses,
son of Mastor, who could look before and after, rose and spoke.
"Citizens of Ithaca," he said, "you yourselves are at fault for
all that has happened. Why were you so slack and indifferent?
Why did you not follow Mentor's and my advice and curb your
headstrong sons who went to the palace day after day, squandering the possessions of our king and harassing his wife with their
demands? You alone are to blame for all that took place in the
palace. If you are wise, you will not pursue a man who has done

nothing but slay the foes who intruded on his house. If you do, misfortune will overtake you, and your own actions will be the cause of it."

When Halitherses had ended, tumult broke out among the people. Some sided with the older man, others with Eupeithes. Some, therefore, remained in the market place while the rest girt on their armor and met outside the city to go forth and avenge their kinsmen.

When Pallas Athene, gazing down from Olympus, saw the angry mob, she went to her father Zeus and said: "Ruler of us all, tell me what your wisdom prompts you. Is it your will to punish the peaceful inhabitants of Ithaca with discord and civil war, or to calm the feud between these two factions?"

"Why inquire about decisions long since made?" said Zeus. "Was it not you who resolved, with my full consent, that Odysseus should come home and avenge the wrongs done to his house? Since I accorded you your wish then, do as you like now. But if you ask my advice, it is this. The suitors have been destroyed; Odysseus shall be king for all time, and this shall be sworn to in a sacred covenant. We gods shall see to it that the kinsmen of the slain forget their anger and sorrow. They shall be at peace with their king and one another, and peace and prosperity shall reign in Ithaca."

The goddess was well pleased with these words. She left the craggy heights of Olympus and darted down to the island of Ithaca.

ODYSSEUS THE VICTOR

The meal in the house of Laertes was over. They were still seated at the table and listening to the story of Odysseus. At last he said: "I fear that while we have been talking, our enemies have not wasted their time. It might be wise for one of us to go to see whether they are coming." Instantly one of the sons of Dolius rose and left the room. He had not gone far before he saw a host in full battle array surging toward the farm. In great alarm he raced back and called: "They are coming, Odysseus, and are almost here! Quickly, take to your weapons!" And up jumped the men seated around the table. Odysseus, his son, and the two herdsmen made four. Then came the six sons of Dolius, and finally gray-haired Laertes and Dolius themselves. Odysseus headed the little troop, and they thronged over the threshold.

Hardly were they out in the open when a powerful ally, Pallas Athene in the shape of Mentor, joined them. Odysseus recognized her at once, and his heart beat high with hope. "Telemachus," he said to his son, "now justify my faith in you. Fight in the forefront and do honor to your line which has always been distinguished for courage and staunchness!"

"Can you doubt me after seeing me fight the suitors?" Telemachus replied. "I shall not disgrace you and our house."

"What a day!" cried Laertes jubilantly. "Father, son, and grandson will vie in valor!" As the last word left his lips, Pallas Athene approached him and whispered in his ear: "Son of Arcisius, you who are dearer to me than all other men, pray to Zeus and the daughter of Zeus, and then hurl your lance." So said Athene, and she filled his heart with courage. He made his prayer and cast his spear, and it struck the cheek piece of Eupeithes' helmet and pierced the jaw of his foe. With a loud clatter of arms the father of Antinous sank into the dust. Odysseus and Telemachus, meanwhile, led their companions against their enemies and raged among them with sword and lance. They would have killed all of them and not one would have returned home, had not Pallas Athene raised her voice and stopped the fighting. "Leave off, citizens of Ithaca," she cried. "Leave off and disperse. This strife shall end here and now!"

Her words rang out like thunder, and the weapons dropped from the hands of the warriors and rolled on the ground. As if a storm had scattered them they turned and fled to the city, intent only on saving their lives. But Odysseus and his men were not terrified by the voice of their ally. High they swung their swords and brandished their lances, and they followed their foes like eagles pursuing their prey.

But Zeus wanted peace. He flashed his lightning into the earth before the feet of the goddess. "Son of Laertes," she said, turning back to Odysseus, "curb your lust for battle, so that the Thunderer may not be displeased with you!" Willingly Odysseus

and his men obeyed, and Athene led them to the market
place of Ithaca. Heralds were dispatched to summon the
people to assembly. They came with tranquil hearts, and
Athene, in the shape of Mentor, set a covenant between the
king and his people.

INDEX

Abantes, a powerful family from Euboea, named after the first of the line, Abas, 313

Abderus, son of Hermes, after whom the Thracian city of Abdera was named, 173

Ablerus, a Trojan, killed by Antilochus, 381

Absyrtus, son of Aeetes and Eidyia, brother of Medea, 106, 124, 126f.

Academus, a local Attic hero, who pointed out to the Tyndaridae where Helen was to be found after she had been carried off by Theseus and Pirithous, 227

Acamas, son of Theseus and Phaedra, hero of the Trojan war, 222, 229, 521f.

Acamas, son of Antenor, brother of Archelochus, Trojan leader in the Trojan war, 334, 427, 438

Acamas, a Thracian, killed by Ajax the Great, 376, 381

Acarnan, son of Alcmaeon and Callirrhoë, 275ff.

Acastus, son of Pelias, one of the Argonauts, 138, 338

Achelous, river-god, eldest of the 3000 sons of Oceanus and Tethys; father of the Sirens, according to one branch of tradition, 193f., 277

Achilles, son of Peleus and the Nereid Thetis, greatest Argive hero of the Trojan war, 312ff., 318ff., 330, 332, 335, 337ff., 343ff., 350ff., 371, 400ff., 412f., 435ff., 449ff., 462ff., 467ff., 474ff., 481ff., 488ff., 502, 504ff., 511ff., 515ff., 565ff., 663f.

Acoetes, helmsman of the pirate ship on which Dionysus was abducted, 62ff.

Acrisius, king of Argos, son of Abas and Aglaia; grandfather of Perseus, by whom he was accidentally killed, 66, 72

Actoris, one of Penelope's servingwomen, 735

Adamas, a Trojan, son of Asius, killed by Meriones, 421

Admetus, son of Pheres and Periclymene, husband of Alcestis, father of Eumelus; one of those who took part in the hunt for the Calydonian boar; one of the Argonauts, 89, 183ff.

Adrastus, king of Argos, son of Talaus; one of the Seven against Thebes, 248, 251ff., 261f., 272

Adrastus, Trojan leader, son of Merops, killed by Diomedes, 334

Adrastus, a Trojan, killed by Menelaus, 381f.

Aeetes, son of Helios and Perse, brother of Circe; husband of Eidyia, father of Medea and Absyrtus, 87ff., 104ff.

Aegeus, son of Pandion and Pylia, father of Theseus, 206, 210ff.

Aegialeus, son of Adrastus and Demonassa; one of the Epigoni, killed by Laodamas before Thebes, 272f.

Aegisthus, son of Thyestes; paramour of Clytaemnestra and usurper of Agamemnon's throne, 573ff.

Aegle, one of the Hesperides, 135

Aegyptius, an Ithacan, friend of Odysseus and Telemachus, 613

Aella, one of the Amazons, killed by Heracles, 174

Aeneas, son of Anchises and Aphrodite, husband of Creusa, father of Ascanius; a Trojan hero, 307, 334, 338, 349, 374ff., 382, 420f., 431, 440, 445ff., 463ff., 517, 531, 545, 547ff., 561f.

Aeolus, son of Hippotes, father of Xuthus; friend of the gods and keeper of the winds, 39, 569, 651f.

Aepytidae, the family name of the descendants of Aepytus, one of the descendants of Heracles, 295

Aepytus, son of Cresphontes and Merope, a descendant of Heracles, 293ff.

Aerope, wife of Atreus, mother of Agamemnon and Menelaus, 573

Aesacus, son of Priam and Arisbe, who predicted that Paris would bring about the downfall of Troy, 302

The Pantheon Fairy Tale
and Folklore Library

African Folktales: Traditional Stories of the Black World
selected and retold by Roger D. Abrahams
0-394-72117-9

"A rousing good read....I suspect Mr. Abrahams' book will be
read a generation hence."—*New York Times Book Review*

**Afro-American Folktales: Stories from Black Traditions in the
New World**
selected and edited by Roger D. Abrahams
0-394-72885-8

"Wonderful...very human and often very funny."—*Booklist*

**America in Legend: Folklore from the Colonial Period
to the Present**
by Richard M. Dorson
0-394-70926-8

"A scholarly book and a popular one....It all comes together
joyously, grandly....It will rightly find a large reading audience."
—*Chronicle of Higher Education*

American Indian Myths and Legends
edited by Richard Erdoes and Alfonso Ortiz
0-394-74018-1

"Probably the most comprehensive and diverse collection of
American Indian legends ever compiled. It is a worthy and
welcome addition to the literature of our native
peoples."—Dee Brown

Arab Folktales
translated and edited by Inea Bushnaq
0-394-75186-8

"A marvelous hoard of popular recited tales, witty and earthy,
fanciful and mundane in equal measure. Rarely has a people's
authentic spirit been so close at hand."—Edward W. Said

Gods and Heroes: Myths and Epics of Ancient Greece
by Gustav Schwab
0-394-73402-5

"A superb volume—keystone for the home library—full of the magic that should be part of our young citizens' inheritance."
—*New Yorker*

Irish Folktales
edited by Henry Glassie
0-394-74637-6

"*Irish Folktales* contains plenty of what Joyce called 'laughtears,' a lot of mysteriousness, and even a bit of splendor."—Richard Ellmann

Italian Folktales
selected and retold by Italo Calvino
translated by George Martin
0-394-74909-X

"This book is impossible to recommend too highly."
—John Gardner, *New York Times Book Review*

Japanese Tales
edited and translated by Royall Tyler
0-394-75656-8

"Enchanting...the stories are variously witty, allegorical, mystical, gross, funny, and enigmatic.... Tyler's poised translations are something of a masterpiece."—*Publishers Weekly*

The Norse Myths
introduced and retold by Kevin Crossley-Holland
0-394-74846-8

"Cheers for Kevin Crossley-Holland.... He is a poet as well as a scholar, and it is in the myths themselves that his passions are most eloquent."—*Village Voice*

Norwegian Folk Tales
Peter Christen Asbjørnsen and Jørgen Moe, compilers
translated by Pat Shaw Iversen and Carl Norman
0-394-71054-1

"A distinguished book of lasting value."—*Commonweal*